ONE LAST SCREAM

This Large Print Book carries the
Seal of Approval of N.A.V.H.

ONE LAST SCREAM

KEVIN O'BRIEN

THORNDIKE PRESS
A part of Gale, Cengage Learning

GALE
CENGAGE Learning

Detroit • New York • San Francisco • New Haven, Conn • Waterville, Maine • London

GALE
CENGAGE Learning

Thorndike Press® Large Print Core.
The text of this Large Print edition is unabridged.
Other aspects of the book may vary from the original edition.
Set in 16 pt. Plantin.
Printed on permanent paper.

LIBRARY OF CONGRESS CATALOGING-IN-PUBLICATION DATA

O'Brien, Kevin, 1955–
    One last scream / by Kevin O'Brien.
      p. cm.
    ISBN-13: 978-1-4104-0566-1 (alk. paper)
    ISBN-10: 1-4104-0566-4 (alk. paper)
    1. Serial murders — Fiction. 2. Large type books. I. Title.
PS3565.B7140054 2008
813'.54—dc22   2007052233

Published in 2008 by arrangement with Pinnacle Books, an imprint of Kensington Publishing Corp.

Printed in the United States of America
1 2 3 4 5 6 7 12 11 10 09 08

32000000186447

This book is for my friend Doug Mendini.

ACKNOWLEDGMENTS

My thanks to my editor and good friend, John Scognamiglio, who always knows just when I need a pat on the back or a kick in the butt. I couldn't have written this book — or any of my others — without him. I'm grateful to everyone else at Kensington, especially the wonderful Doug Mendini. About time I dedicated a book to this classy man!

A great big thank-you also goes to my agents extraordinaire, Meg Ruley, Christina Hogrebe, and the terrific people at Jane Rotrosen Agency.

I owe another big thank-you to Tommy Dreiling, for his support, encouragement, and friendship.

As usual, my talented writer-friends were incredibly helpful with their suggestions on how to make early drafts of this book better. Thank you to Cate Goethals and David Massengill; and to my Writers Group pals,

Soyon Im and Garth Stein.

Thanks also to Lori, at Open Adoption & Family Services, for answering so many of my questions about adoption and foster care.

I'd also like to thank the following friends for their support and encouragement: Lloyd Adalist, Dan Annear & Chuck Rank, Marlys Bourm, Terry & Judine Brooks, Kyle Bryan & Dan Monda, George Camper, Jim & Barbara Church, Anna Cottle & Mary Alice Kier, Paul Dwoskin, Tom Goodwin, Cathy Johnson, Ed & Sue Kelly, David Korabik, Jim Munchel, Eva Marie Saint, John Saul & Michael Sack, Bill, JB, Tammy & Fran at The Seattle Mystery Bookshop, Dan, Doug and Ann Stutesman, George & Sheila Stydahar, Mark Von Borstel, Michael Wells, and the gang at Bailey/Coy Books.

Finally, thanks to my wonderful family, Adele, Mary Lou, Cathy, Bill, and Joan.

CHAPTER ONE

Moses Lake, Washington — 1992
She turned the key in the ignition, and nothing happened, just a hollow *click, click, click.*

"Oh, shit," Kristen murmured. She felt a little pang of dread in her stomach.

The battery wasn't dead, because the inside dome light had gone on when she'd climbed into her Ford Probe a minute ago.

Biting her lip, Kristen gave the key another twist. *Click, click, click.* Nothing.

It was 11:20 on a chilly October night. Hers was the only car in the restaurant lot. Kristen had just finished a seven-hour shift waiting tables at The Friendly Fajita. She'd closed up the place with Rafael, the perpetually horny 19-year-old busboy, and he'd just taken off on his rusty old Harley. Kristen could still hear its engine roaring as he sailed down Broadway. It was the only sound she heard.

9

There was a phone in the restaurant, and she had a key. But she and Rafael had already set the alarm. It would go off if she went back inside, and she could never remember the code, especially while that shrill incessant alarm was sounding. She'd have to go look for a phone someplace else, and then call a tow company or a cab. Her boyfriend, Brian, was out of town at a golf tournament down in San Diego.

"Please, please, please," she whispered, trying the ignition once again. The car didn't respond except for that hollow *click, click, click.*

"Damn it to hell," she grumbled. Grabbing her purse and a windbreaker from the passenger seat, Kristen climbed out of the car and shut the door. She didn't bother locking it.

She took a long look down the street. Most of the other businesses along this main drag were closed for the night. There were a couple of taverns farther down Broadway. Kristen loathed the idea of hoofing it several blocks along the roadside. The waist-length windbreaker didn't quite cover her stupid waitress uniform. The Friendly Fajita's owner, Stan Munch, who was about as Mexican as she was, made her wear this señorita getup with a white, off-the-shoulder

10

peasant blouse and a gaudy purple, green, and yellow billowy skirt over a petticoat, for God's sake. With her short, blond hair, green eyes, and pale complexion, she looked like an idiot in the outfit. But, hell, anyone would appear ridiculous in it. The thing looked like a Halloween costume.

The Friendly Fajita had been open for four months, and it was floundering. Moses Lake didn't need another Mexican restaurant. Besides, the food was mediocre and overpriced. And if that wasn't enough to drive customers away, Stan had the same two Herb Alpert CDs on a continuous loop for background *authenticity*. If Kristen never heard "The Lonely Bull" again in her life, it would be too soon.

Maybe she could flag down a cop car, or a good Samaritan. Kristen ducked back into the Probe just long enough to pop the hood and switch on the hazard lights. She figured that would make it easier for passersby to see that she needed help. Of course, she was also making it easier for the wrong person to see that she was stranded.

It suddenly occurred to Kristen that someone might have sabotaged her car. Just a little sugar in the gas tank — that was all it took. She'd read that before he started killing, the young Ted Bundy liked to screw

11

with women's cars, so he could later watch them when they were stranded and vulnerable.

He just watched them. It turned him on.

Kristen wondered if someone was looking at her right now as she stood beside her broken-down car in front of the darkened restaurant. Maybe he was across the street by the flower shop. He could be hiding in the shadows behind those bushes, studying her through a pair of binoculars.

Or maybe he was even closer than that.

She shuddered and rubbed her arms. "Stop it," Kristen muttered to herself. "You're perfectly safe. There aren't any serial killers in Moses Lake."

Still, she reached inside her purse and felt around for the pepper spray. She wondered if it even worked anymore. She'd bought the little canister over two years ago while a junior at Eastern Washington University in Cheney. She'd majored in graphic design, and planned to move to Seattle. But Brian got a job as the golf pro at one of Moses Lake's courses. It was a big resort town. Kristen had decided to put Seattle on hold, and stick with Brian for a while. There wasn't much need for a graphic artist in Moses Lake. So, here she was, dressed up like a Mexican peasant girl and stranded outside The Friendly Fajita at 11:30 on a cold Wednesday night.

Kristen kept the pepper spray clutched in her fist.

One car passed the restaurant, and didn't even slow down. She waited, and then gave a tentative wave to an approaching pickup, but it just whooshed by. Kristen glanced at her wristwatch — only two cars in almost five minutes. Not a good sign.

She noticed a pair of headlights down the road in the distance. Kristen stepped toward the parking lot entrance, and started waving again, more urgently this time. As the vehicle came closer, she noticed it was an old, beat-up station wagon with just one person inside. It looked like a man at the wheel. He got closer, and she could see him now. He was smiling, almost as if he'd been expecting to find her there.

A chill raced through her. Kristen stopped waving and automatically stepped back.

The station wagon turned in to the restaurant parking lot. Warily, Kristen eyed the man in the car. He was in his late thirties and might have been very handsome once, but he'd obviously gone to seed. His face looked a bit bloated and jowly. The thin brown hair was receding. But his eyes sparkled, and she might have found his smile sexy if only she weren't so stranded and vulnerable. Right now, she didn't need anyone leering at her.

He rolled down his window. "Looks like you could use some help." The way he spoke, it was almost a come-on.

Kristen shook her head and backed away from the station wagon. "Um, I already called someone and they should be here any minute, but thanks anyway."

"You sure?" the man asked, his smirk waning.

"Positive, I —" Kristen hesitated as she noticed the beautiful little girl sitting beside him in the passenger seat. She had a book and a doll in her lap. The child smiled at her.

"Wish I knew more about car engines," the man said. "I'd get out and take a look for you, but it wouldn't do any good. Want us to stick around in case this person you called doesn't show up?" He turned to the child. "You don't mind waiting, do you, Annie?"

The little girl shook her head, then started sucking her thumb. She glanced down at her picture book.

The father gently stroked her hair. And when he smiled up at Kristen again, there was nothing flirtatious about it. "Would you like us to wait?" he asked.

Kristen felt silly. She shrugged. "Actually, it's been a while since I called these people. Maybe I should phone them again." She nodded toward the center of town. "I think there's a pay phone at this tavern just down Broadway. Would you mind giving me a lift?"

"Well, if you live around here, we can take you home." He turned to his daughter again. "Should we give the nice lady a ride to her house, honey?"

Breaking into a smile, the girl nodded emphatically. "Yes!" She even bounced in the passenger seat a little.

Kristen let out a tiny laugh. "I don't want to take you out of your way."

"Nonsense," the man said, stepping out of the car. He left the motor running. "We've taken a vote and it's unanimous. We're driving you home."

He touched Kristen's shoulder on his way to the passenger door. He opened it, then helped the girl out of the front seat. "This is my daughter, Annabelle," he said. "And her dolly, Gertrude."

"This isn't Gertrude!" the girl protested. "This is Daisy! Gertrude is home with —"

"Oops, sorry, sorry," her father cut in. He gave Kristen a wink. "I've committed a major faux pas, getting the names of her dollies mixed up." He opened the back door for his daughter. "C'mon, sweetheart, climb in back and buckle up. And hold on to Daisy. Let's hurry up now. This nice lady is tired, and wants to go home."

Kristen hurried back to her car, switched off the blinkers, locked the doors, and shut the hood. Then she returned to the station wagon. "I live on West Peninsula Drive," she said, climbing into the front passenger seat. The man closed the door for her.

The car was warm, and smelled a little bit like French fries. She noticed an empty Coke can and a crumpled-up Arby's bag on the floor by her feet.

The man walked around the front of the car, then got behind the wheel. He pulled out of the parking lot.

Kristen looked back at her broken-down Ford Probe. She'd call the tow company in the morning. Right now, she just wanted to get home and take a shower. She turned to the man and smiled. "I really appreciate this."

Eyes on the road, he just nodded. He seemed very intent on his driving.

Kristen glanced over her shoulder at the little girl. "Thank you for giving me your seat, Annabelle."

"You're welcome," the child said, her nose in the book.

"So, how old are you, Annabelle?"

The girl looked up at her and smiled. She really was beautiful — a little girl with an adult face. Kristin had seen photos of Jackie Kennedy and Elizabeth Taylor when they were around this child's age, and they had that same haunting mature beauty to them.

"I'm four years old," she announced proudly.

"My, you're almost a young lady!" Kristen turned forward again. "She's gorgeous," she said to the man.

But he didn't reply. Another car sped toward them in the oncoming lane. Its headlights swept across his face. He had the same strange, cryptic smile Kristen had noticed when she first spotted him.

She squirmed a bit in the passenger seat. Moses Lake was an oasis. Just three minutes outside of the bright, busy resort town, it became dark desert, with a smattering of homes. Kristen and Brian's town house was in the dark outskirts.

"Um, you need to take a left up here," she said, pointing ahead. But he wasn't slowing down. "It's a left here," she repeated. "Sir . . ."

He sped past the access road. "Oh,

17

brother, I can't believe I missed that," he said, slowing down to about fifteen miles per hour. "I'm sorry. I'll find a place to turn around here. I must be more tired than I thought. My reaction time is off."

Biting her lip, Kristen wondered why he didn't just make a U-turn. There was hardly any traffic.

"Here we go," he announced, turning right onto a street marked DEAD END. They crawled past a few houses along the narrow road. Kristen counted six driveways he could have used to turn his car around. They inched by the last streetlight, and the darkened road became gravelly. Kristen noticed a house under construction on her right.

"I think there's a turnaround coming up," he said, squinting at the road ahead.

Kristen swallowed hard, and didn't say anything. The car was barely moving. Its headlights pierced the unknown darkness ahead of them. "Can't we — can't we just back up and turn around?" she asked.

"I'm beginning to think you're right," he said. He shot a look in the rearview mirror. "How are you doing back there, honey? You tired?"

"Kind of," the child replied with a whimper.

"She's up way past her bedtime," the man said. "But I *needed* her tonight. She's Daddy's little helper."

The car came to a stop. The headlights illuminated the end of the road and a long barricade, painted with black-and-white diagonal stripes. Beyond that, it was just blackness.

Puzzled, Kristen stared at the man. "Why did you need your daughter tonight?"

He smiled at her — that same cryptic smirk. "If she weren't here, you never would have climbed into this car with me."

Daddy's little helper.

All at once, Kristen realized what he was telling her. She quickly reached into her purse for the pepper spray. She didn't see his fist coming toward her face.

She just heard the little girl give out a startled yelp. "Oh!"

That was the last thing Kristen heard before the man knocked her unconscious.

"God, please! Somebody help me!"

An hour had passed and they'd driven thirty-five miles.

The little girl sat alone in the front passenger seat of the old station wagon. With a tiny flashlight that had a picture of Barbie on it, she looked at her picture book.

19

"Please, no! Wait . . . wait . . . no . . ."

The woman's shrieks seemed to echo through the forest, where the car was parked along a crude trail. But the child paid little attention. She turned the page of her book, and tapped at the dashboard with her toes. Cold and tired, she wanted to go home. She wondered when her daddy would be finished with his "work."

When the screaming stops, that's usually when he's almost done.

She told herself it would be soon.

Seattle, Washington — fifteen years later

Someone had a Barenaked Ladies CD blasting. The music drifted out to the backyard — along with all the talking, laughing, and screaming from the party inside the town house. The place was a cheesy, slightly run-down rental down the street from the University of Washington's fraternity row. Amelia wasn't sure who was giving the party. A bunch of guys lived in the town house, sophomores like herself. One of them — a total stranger — had stopped her this morning when she'd been on her way to philosophy class, and he'd invited her. That happened to Amelia all the time. She was constantly getting asked to parties. It had something to do with the way she looked.

Amelia Faraday was tall, with a beautiful face and a gorgeous, buxom figure. She had shoulder-length, wavy black hair, and blue eyes. She also had a drinking problem, and knew it. So she'd declined many invitations to drink-till-you-drop campus bashes. Her boyfriend, Shane, didn't like the idea of strange guys inviting Amelia to parties, anyway. Among their friends, they were nicknamed the Perrier Twins, because they always asked for bottled water at get-togethers.

But tonight, Amelia wanted a beer — several beers, in fact, whatever it took to get drunk.

A few people had staggered out to the small backyard where Amelia stood with a beer in one hand, and the other clutching together the edges of her bulky cardigan sweater. She gazed up at the stars. It was a beautiful, crisp October Friday night.

She had a little buzz. This was only her second beer and, already, results. It happened quickly, because she'd been booze-free for the last seven weeks.

Shane didn't understand why she needed alcohol tonight. "Before you drink that beer," he'd whispered to her a few minutes ago in the corner of the jam-packed living room, "maybe you should call your therapist. Explain to her why you need it so badly."

In response, Amelia had narrowed her eyes at him, and then she'd chugged half the plastic cup full of Coors. She'd refilled the cup from the keg in the kitchen and wandered outside alone.

The truth was she hated herself right now. She was lucky to have a boyfriend like Shane. He was cute, with perpetually messy, light brown hair, blue eyes, and a well-maintained five o'clock shadow. He was sweet, and he cared about her. And his advice, patronizing as it seemed, had been practical. She'd tried to call her therapist this afternoon. But Karen had gone for the day.

So Amelia was left with these awful thoughts, and no one to help her sort them out. That was why she needed to get drunk right now.

Amelia's parents and her aunt were spending the weekend at the family cabin by Lake Wenatchee in central Washington. Ever since this afternoon, she'd been overwhelmed with a sudden, inexplicable contempt for them. She imagined driving to the cabin and killing all three of them. She even started formulating a plan, though she had no intention of carrying it out. Her parents had mentioned there was construction this weekend on their usual route, Highway 2. The cabin would be a three-hour drive from Seattle, if she took Interstate 90 and Route 97, and didn't stop. Her parents and aunt would be asleep when she arrived. She knew how to sneak into the cabin; she'd done it before. She saw herself shooting them at close range. As much as the notion bewildered and horrified her, it also made Amelia's heart race with excitement.

If only Karen were around, Amelia could have asked her therapist about this hideous daydream. How could she have these terrible thoughts? Amelia loved her parents, and Aunt Ina was like her older sister, practically her best friend.

The only way to get these poisonous feelings out of her system was to flush them out with another kind of poison. In this case, it was another cupful of Coors from the keg in the kitchen.

Amelia was heading back in there when a young woman — a pretty Asian American with a red streak in her long black hair — blocked her path through the doorway. "Hey, do you have a cig? A menthol?" she asked, shouting over the noise. "I can't find another person at this stupid party who smokes menthols."

"No, but there's a minimart about six blocks from here." Amelia had to lean close to the girl and practically yell in her ear. "If you want, I can go get some for you. I have my boyfriend's car, and I'm looking for an excuse to bolt out of here for a while." She drained the last few drops of Coors from her plastic cup. "Just let me get the car keys from my boyfriend, and then we can go."

Weaving through the crowd, Amelia made her way to Shane, who was still standing in the corner of the living room. Apparently, he'd decided that if she could fall off the wagon, so could he. He was passing a joint back and forth with some guy she didn't know.

"Are you drunk yet?" he asked, gazing at her with half-closed eyes.

"No," she lied, speaking up over the party noise. "In fact, I want to get out of here for a few minutes. Give me the car keys, will you?" With her thumb, she pointed to the other girl, who was behind her. "I'm driving my friend to the minimart for cigarettes. We'll be right back. Okay?"

But she was lying. She had no intention of going to the minimart. She just needed his car.

Shane dug the keys out of his jeans pocket. He plopped them in her hand. "Do whatever you want to do," he grumbled. "I don't care."

Amelia gave him a quick kiss. "Please, don't be mad at me," she whispered.

Shane started to put his arm around her, but she broke away and fled. She could hear the other girl behind her, saying something about her boyfriend being cute and that he looked like Justin Timberlake. Amelia didn't really hear her. Threading through the mob of partygoers, she made her way back to the kitchen.

"Hey, wait up!" the girl yelled. "Hey, wait a minute!" But Amelia kept moving. She spotted a half-full bottle of tequila on the kitchen counter amid an assortment of empty bottles and beer cans. She swiped it up, and then tucked it inside the flap of her cardigan sweater. Heading out the kitchen door, Amelia found a walkway to the front of the house. As she hurried toward Shane's beat-up VW Golf, she heard the girl screaming at her from the side of the town house. "Hey, don't forget the cigs! I'll pay you back! I need menthols! All right? Did you hear me?"

Amelia waved without looking back at her, and then she ducked inside Shane's car.

Starting up the engine, she stashed the tequila bottle under her seat, and then peeled out of the parking spot. She didn't look in her rearview mirror as she sped down the street.

Four minutes later, she saw Marty's Mini-Mart on the corner. Only a couple of cars were in the lot in front of the tacky little store; there was plenty of available parking.

But Amelia kept going, and headed for the interstate. If she didn't make any stops along the way, she'd reach Lake Wenatchee by about two in the morning. The gas tank was three-quarters full.

Amelia pressed harder on the accelerator, and kept telling herself that she loved her parents and her Aunt Ina. She'd never do anything to harm them.

Never.

Chapter Two

Ina McMillan hated these sinks with separate spouts for the hot and cold water. Washing her face, she had to cup her hands under the cold, and then switch over to the hot water. It was either scalding or freezing when Ina finally splashed her face. Water ran down her arms to her elbows, dampening the sleeves of her robe. What a pain in the ass. It was a major undertaking just to wash her face here.

She didn't like Jenna and Mark's cabin, and she hated the country. Ina was a city girl.

Actually, her sister and brother-in-law's "weekend getaway" spot wasn't a *cabin*. It was a slightly dilapidated little two-story Cape Cod–style house built in the fifties. There was a fallout shelter in the basement, along with a furnace that manufactured more noise than heat. Ina's bedroom, with its cute dormer windows, slanted ceiling, and creaky twin beds, had a space heater that might as well have had FIRE HAZARD stenciled all over it. She'd been instructed not to leave the heater on overnight. Fine. Whatever. Either way, the room still felt damp, cold, and drafty.

The house was just off the lake, and cut off from the rest of civilization by rolling wooded hills that wreaked havoc on cell phone service. There wasn't a landline phone either. For emergencies, they were supposed to run a half mile around the lake to this old lesbian neighbor's house and use her phone. There was also a pay phone at a diner about three miles away at the mountain road junction.

Just what her sister and Mark saw in this godforsaken shack was a mystery to Ina. For a spot that was supposed to be so relaxing, everything was an ordeal. They couldn't even drive up to the place. Mark had had to park the car by a turnaround on a bluff, and then they'd trekked down a steep trail through the forest, lugging their suitcases all the way. And, of course, Ina had overpacked.

She felt like an idiot for bringing along her lacy burgundy nightgown and the matching silk robe. Flannel pajamas would have been more appropriate.

The sexy nightwear had been a Christmas present from George last year, back when he'd thought it possible to rekindle some romance in their marriage. He was home with the kids right now. They'd agreed this weekend away from each other might do them some good — a time-out from all the tension.

She was silly to think it would be any less tense here, with Mark and her sister.

Ina dried off her face and stared at her reflection in the bathroom mirror. Even with her wild, wavy, shoulder-length auburn hair pulled back in a ponytail, and no makeup, she was still pretty. How often did other 38-year-olds get mistaken for college girls? Well, that still happened to her sometimes. She had clear, creamy skin and blue eyes. And right now, the burgundy nightgown showed off her willowy figure to good advantage.

Padding down the hall to her room, Ina glanced over her shoulder at the partially open bedroom door. Mark and Jenna still had the light on. She half expected, half hoped Mark would come to the door and see her.

He was the reason she'd packed the burgundy nightgown ensemble. Ina wanted to look sexy for her sister's husband.

But Mark wasn't looking at her in the hallway. He was where he belonged, in bed with her sister.

Ina retreated into her damp, drafty little bedroom and, once again, wished she'd packed her flannel pj's. With a sigh, she bent down and switched off the space heater. She turned down her bedcovers. She was about to take off her robe, but hesitated. She heard a noise outside, and suddenly stopped moving.

She listened to what sounded like footsteps. A hand over her heart, she crept to one of the dormer windows and looked down. Ina gasped.

Just below her, a dark figure darted between some bushes.

Reeling back from the window, she turned and raced down the hall. "Mark!" she called, but the word barely came out. She couldn't get a breath. Ina burst into their bedroom. "There's someone outside!" she whispered.

Mark and Jenna were sitting up in bed. "Are you sure?" he asked, putting his book aside.

She nodded urgently. "I saw someone — something — in the bushes right below my window."

"Some*one* or some*thing?*" he asked.

Flustered, Ina gave a helpless shrug. "I — I'm not sure —"

"It was probably just a bear," Jenna said, a copy of *Vanity Fair* in her hands. She was wearing her glasses and one of Mark's T-shirts. "They come around all the time looking for food scraps in the garbage. They're harmless."

Ina hated the way her sister was talking to her as if she were a scared little girl. "Well, whatever it is," she replied, still shaking, "this *thing* is right below my window, and it scared the shit out of me. What, do you expect me to go back in there and just fall asleep now? It looked like a *person,* Jenna."

"I better check it out," Mark grumbled, getting to his feet. "Could be our uninvited houseguest is back."

Biting her lip, Ina watched him throw a robe over his T-shirt and boxer shorts. Mark was balding and a bit out of shape, but he still had a certain masculine sexiness. He slipped his bare feet into a pair of slippers. The *uninvited houseguest* was another reason she didn't like this damn cabin.

When they'd arrived there earlier tonight, Mark and Jenna had noticed several things out of place. Someone had tracked mud onto the kitchen and living room floors. A few empty beer bottles, some cigarette

31

butts, and a crumpled-up potato chip bag littered the pathway from the front porch to the lake. The intruder had even built a fire in the fireplace. Jenna wondered out loud if their daughter, Amelia, had stayed there on the sly with her boyfriend. But Mark, trusting soul that he was, insisted Amelia hadn't touched a drop in weeks, and neither had Shane. Both were nonsmokers, too. So the empty beer bottles and cigarette butts couldn't have been theirs.

Rolling her eyes, Jenna said he shouldn't believe everything Amelia told him. Their daughter had a good heart, but she wasn't exactly reliable — or honest. That was why Amelia was seeing a therapist once a week, to the tune of eighty bucks a pop.

Ina had tagged behind Jenna and Mark. They'd continued to bicker while searching the house for further signs of this uninvited guest. "Well, whoever was here, they're long gone," Mark had said, at last. He'd assured Ina that the culprit probably wouldn't be back. "If it'll make you feel any better, I keep a hunting rifle in the bedroom closet. We'll be okay."

Now, Ina watched him reach into the closet for that rifle. Cocking the handle, he checked the chamber to make sure it was loaded.

"Better bag this *prowler* on the first shot, Mark," Jenna said, still sitting up in bed. She tossed her sister a droll look, then went back to her *Vanity Fair.* "The great white hunter only keeps one bullet in that stupid gun. The rest are in the kitchen drawer downstairs. He hasn't fired that thing since —"

"Oh, would you just give it a rest?" Mark hissed. "Can't you see she's scared?"

"All I see is a lot of *drama,*" Jenna remarked, eyes on her magazine.

Mark ignored her, then brushed past Ina and started down the hall.

Frowning at her older sister, Ina lingered in the bedroom doorway for a moment. Finally, she retreated down the corridor and caught up with Mark on the stairs.

Like a soldier going into a sniper zone, Mark held the rifle in front of him, barrel end up. He paused near the bottom step. Ina hovered behind him. She was trembling. She looked at the front door and then the darkened living room. Logs still smouldered in the fireplace, their red embers glowing. The cushy old rocking chair beside the hearth was perfectly still. Ina didn't see any sign of a break-in. Nothing was disturbed.

Mark crept to the front door and twisted the handle. "Locked," he said.

Ina put her hand on his shoulder and sighed with relief.

He squinted at her. "Did you *really* see something outside?"

Ina scowled at him. "Of course. Why would I make that up?"

"All right, all right, take it easy," he murmured.

Heading toward the kitchen, Mark stopped to switch on a lamp. Ina stayed on his heels. He checked the kitchen door. "We're okay here, too," he announced. Then he unlocked the door and opened it. "Stay put. I'll look outside."

"No, don't leave me here alone!" she whispered.

"Relax. I'll be two minutes at the most. Lock up after me if you're so nervous." He ducked outside.

Shivering, Ina stayed at the threshold for a moment, then she closed and locked the door. What was she supposed to do if he didn't come back? She imagined hearing that gun go off, and then nothing. She couldn't call the police; she couldn't call anyone, because they had no phone service in this goddamn place.

Ina gazed out the kitchen window. She didn't see Mark, and didn't hear anything outside. The refrigerator hummed. It was an old thing from the sixties. The avocado color matched the stove. Gingerbread trim adorned the pantry shelves. The framed "Food Is Cooked With Butter and Love" sign — along with the worn, yellow dinette set — had been in Ina and Jenna's kitchen when they were growing up. But these familiar things gave her no comfort right now.

And it wasn't much help knowing Jenna was upstairs — if she should need her. What could Jenna do?

Her sister was being a real pill tonight. Maybe Jenna knew what had happened between Mark and her. Had Mark said something? This was their first weekend together since she and Mark had "slipped." That was how Mark described it, like they'd had an accident, a little catastrophe. "It was a mistake. It never should have happened. It never would have happened if we weren't going through this awful time right now. We just — slipped, Ina."

It had been a rough summer. Mark and Jenna's 17-year-old son, Collin, had drowned in May, and his death had sent the family into a tailspin. Collin's sister, Amelia, became unhinged and almost unmanageable. They had put her on some kind of medication, and that helped. But there weren't any pills Mark and Jenna could take to remedy their confusion, anger, and hurt. In their pain, they lashed out at each other.

One afternoon in early August, Mark came down to Seattle from their home in Bellingham, and he met Ina for a drink at the Alexis Hotel. He'd come to her for consolation. But they ended up talking about her problems with George. They also ended up in a room on the fifth floor — and in bed together.

She couldn't believe it. Mark, her brother-in-law, of all people. She'd known him for eighteen years and, yes, when he'd first started dating Jenna, she'd had a bit of a crush on him. In his late twenties, he'd been a cute guy, but he'd gained a lot of weight and lost a lot of hair since then. Appearances were very important to Ina, and she'd married the right guy for that. She loved hearing her girlfriends describe George as a hunk. He taught history at the University of Washington, and she relished walking in on his classes from time to time. Whenever George introduced her to the class as his wife, Ina could tell which ones had crushes on him. She'd get these dagger looks from several girls (and often a guy or two) sitting in the front row. She knew they wanted what she had. Her husband was six foot two and kept in shape with visits to the gym three times a week. Sure, his thick black hair had started to gray at the temples, and his pale-green eyes now needed glasses for reading, but those specs made him look distinguished — and even sexier. Mark couldn't hold a candle to George in the looks department. Yet her slightly chubby, balding brother-in-law had made her feel incredibly desirable in bed that afternoon at the Alexis. She'd never felt so sexy and attractive, so validated.

Still, as they were leaving the hotel, Mark started saying it had been a horrible mistake. They'd slipped. They were nice people — and married to nice people. This shouldn't have happened. He blamed it on his grief and the number of drinks he'd had. (Only two scotches; she'd counted.) But Ina knew better. He'd always been attracted to her, and what had happened in the Alexis that afternoon had been long overdue.

She, too, regretted "slipping," but a part of Ina still wanted Mark to find her desirable. Even if nothing ever happened again, she wanted to be desired. And for that she deserved her sister's snippy attitude tonight.

She took another look out the window. The trees and bushes swayed slightly in the wind. On a quiet night like this, she thought she should have been able to hear Mark's footsteps. But there wasn't a sound.

A chill raced through her, and Ina rubbed her arms. She glanced at the doorway to the cellar, open just an inch, and beyond that, darkness. They should have checked down there — in the furnace room and the fallout shelter. Mark and Jenna used it for storage. It was a perfect hiding place.

Moving over to the sink, Ina grabbed a steak knife from the drain rack. She checked the cellar door again. The opening seemed wider than before. Or was it just her imagination? She told herself that if someone was on those rickety old basement steps, she'd have heard the boards creaking. Still, she studied the murky shadows past that cellar doorway. With the knife clutched in her hand, Ina hurried to the basement door and shut it.

The clock on the stove read 12:20. Mark had been gone at least five minutes. How long did it take to circle around this little house? Something was wrong. "C'mon, Mark, c'mon," she murmured, looking out the window again.

She thought about calling upstairs to her sister. Why should she be the only one worried? But Jenna was probably asleep already.

Ina unlocked the kitchen door, opened it,

and glanced outside. The cold air swept against her bare legs and her robe fluttered. Shivering, she held on to the knife. "Mark?" she called softly. "Mark? Where are you? Can you hear me?"

She waited for a moment, and listened.

Then she heard it — a rustling sound, and twigs snapping underfoot. "Mark?" she called out again, more shrill this time. "Mark, please, answer me . . ."

"Yeah, I'm here," he replied, emerging from the shadows of an evergreen beside the house. He carried the hunting rifle at his side, and seemed frazzled. "You were right," he said, out of breath. "Something was out there. I don't know if it was two-legged or four-legged, but I chased it half-way up the trail."

Dumbfounded, Ina stepped back as he ducked inside.

"We're okay now," he said, shutting the door and locking it. "Whatever it was, it's not coming back." He set the rifle on the breakfast table, then reached into one of the cupboards. "Jesus, it's cold as a polar bear's pecker out there. I think we could both use a shot of Jack."

Ina set the knife down beside the gun. She watched him pull a bottle of Jack Daniel's from the cupboard. He retrieved two jelly glasses with the Flintstones on them and poured a shot of the bourbon into each one.

"Has this kind of thing ever happened here before?" she asked warily.

Shaking his head, Mark handed her a glass. "Not quite. We've had bears come up to the house, like Jenna was saying. But I don't think this was a bear." He took a swig of bourbon.

Ina sipped hers. "What makes you so sure this . . . *creature* isn't coming back?"

"Because it was running so fast. The damn thing must be in another zip code by now. But to be on the safe side, I'll pull guard duty down here for another hour or so."

"I'll keep you company," she offered.

"I don't think that's such a good idea, Ina."

She let out an awkward, little laugh. "Why? Are you afraid we might 'slip' again?"

Mark sighed. "I told you before. It won't happen a second time. And it sure as hell ain't gonna happen with Jenna sitting in bed upstairs. God, Ina, what's wrong with you?"

Glaring at him, she gulped down the rest of her bourbon, and then firmly set the glass on the kitchen counter. "I was just asking a simple question. That wasn't a come-on, you asshole."

She started to head out of the kitchen,

but he grabbed her arm. "Listen . . ." But he didn't say anything for a moment. Finally, he sighed and let go of her arm. "We're both tired and on edge, saying things we don't mean. Just — just let's call it a night, okay?"

Ina didn't say anything to him, but she nodded.

"I'm going upstairs to say goodnight to Jenna. Then I'll come back down here to keep watch. You should head up and try to get some sleep." He poured some more Jack Daniel's into her Flintstones glass. "Here. Have another blast of this. It'll help you doze off."

"Thanks," Ina said, taking the glass and moving toward the sink. She still wasn't looking at him. But she could see his reflection in the darkened window as he stepped out of the kitchen.

Ina took a gulp of the bourbon. It was warming and took a bit of the edge off.

She listened to the staircase floorboards creaking. She just assumed it was Mark on his way up to the second floor.

Ina didn't consider the possibility that the sound might be coming from the cellar steps.

The toilet flushing woke her.

Ina had nodded off for only a few minutes. She'd come up to bed about an hour ago, leaving Mark down in the living room with his hunting rifle. As Ina had reached the top of the stairs, she'd heard Jenna calling to her. She'd poked her head into the master bedroom.

Her sister was lying in bed with the light on. "Listen, I'm sorry I've been such an unbearable shrew today," Jenna said, not lifting her head from the pillow. "You must want to clobber me."

"Oh, don't be silly," Ina said. "Go to sleep."

Jenna gazed up at the ceiling. Ina noticed, in this light, her sister was looking old and a bit careworn, and it made her sad. Neither one of them was young anymore.

"I think Mark has been with someone," Jenna said.

Ina let out a skittish laugh. "What are you talking about?"

"He's having an affair, or at least, he's *had* one. I can tell. By any chance, did he say something to George? He's close with George."

Ina shook her head.

"You'd tell me if you knew, wouldn't you? If George said something to you about it?"

"Of course, I'd tell you," Ina said. She sat

down on the edge of the bed, on Mark's side. "Jenna, Mark loves you. He's not seeing anyone else. That's just nonsense. You're worrying about nothing."

"Maybe," Jenna allowed, sighing. "Jesus, I'm so messed up. Nothing's been right since Collin died. I feel like a zombie half the time. It's as if I were walking around with a piece of my insides cut out. It hurts, Ina. It's not just emotional either. It's a — a true physical pain."

"Oh Jen, I'm so sorry," Ina whispered. "There now . . . there now . . ." She couldn't think of anything else to say. She hugged her sister.

Jenna rested her head on her shoulder and wept. Ina felt her sister's tears through the silk burgundy robe.

After a while, they'd said goodnight, and Ina had slinked off to her room. Crawling into the creaky twin-size bed, she felt awful. Instead of supporting her sister during this terrible time, she'd slept with Mark. How could she do that to Jenna? And how could she do that to George?

She would be a better sister, a better wife, better mother, better person . . .

Ina had been telling herself that when she'd dozed off.

Now, she was awake again, listening to the

43

toilet tank refilling. The master bedroom door let out a yawn as Mark closed it. He would be asleep soon, and she'd be the only one awake in the house — this creepy little house in the middle of nowhere.

Ina heard a rustling noise outside, and told herself to ignore it. They were practically surrounded by a forest, and it was full of creatures making noises. Or was it that *thing* Mark had chased halfway up the trail? Maybe it had come back. Maybe it had been watching the house, waiting for him to go to bed.

Ina, quit doing this to yourself.

There it was again, the rustling sound.

Ina tossed back the covers and climbed out of bed. Padding over to the dormer window, she peered outside. She didn't see anything. But she heard those strange rustling sounds again. Was it coming from *inside* the house? Downstairs?

Standing very still, Ina listened. Floorboards creaked, more rustling. It wasn't Mark; she would have heard the master bedroom door squeak open again. Way down the hall and farther from the stairs than her, Mark couldn't hear what she was hearing, not even if he was still awake. She was the only one who heard it, the only one who knew something was terribly wrong.

You're blowing this out of proportion. You got spooked earlier by that bear or whatever it was, and now you're imagining the worst.

That much was true. She was thinking about the type of killer who might lurk within these woods, someone resourceful and clever, and yet savagely brutal. Someone deranged.

Stop it! She'd grown up listening to too many urban legends: the killer with the hook for a hand; the babysitter menaced by a maniac in an upstairs bedroom; and now, her own wild imaginings about this woodland killer.

She heard the noise again, and realized how silly she was. It was just the sound of logs in the fireplace popping and settling. That was all.

Ina crawled back into bed, and pulled the covers up to her neck. As much as she tried to convince herself everything was fine, she lay there tense and rigid, listening for the next sound.

She didn't have to wait long. It came from downstairs again, in the living room, and she could tell exactly what it was: the legs of a chair scraping across the floor. Someone must have bumped into it.

The noise was loud enough that Mark must have heard it, too, because the master bedroom door creaked open again. Then there were footsteps in the upstairs hallway.

Ina climbed out of bed and started toward the door. Her heart was racing. At least she wasn't the only one hearing the noises. And Mark was investigating it. She could hear him on the stairs. "Oh, thank God it's you," he murmured. "Jesus, what are you doing here? You scared the hell out of me. . . ."

A hand on the doorknob, Ina pressed her ear to the door. She could hear undecipherable whispering. But one thing she could make out was Mark saying. "Okay, okay, I'm sitting down. . . ." Obviously, he knew the person who was downstairs. There was more murmuring, and then Mark raised his voice. "Hey, no! Wait a minute, no —"

A loud gunshot went off.

Ina reeled back from the door.

She heard her sister's footsteps along the hallway. Someone else was charging up the stairs. "Oh, God, no, no!" Jenna screamed.

Ina's stomach lurched at the sound of a second blast. She heard someone collapse right outside her bedroom door.

God, please. This isn't happening, this isn't happening.

Ducking into her closet, she closed the door and curled up on the floor. She was shaking uncontrollably. She heard footsteps.

She couldn't tell if they were coming toward her bedroom or moving away from it. She felt dizzy, and couldn't breathe. The dark closet seemed to be shrinking in around her. Ina's whole body started to shut down.

She wasn't sure what had happened, if she'd fainted or gone into a kind of shock, but Ina suddenly realized some time had elapsed. The house was still, and a very faint light sliced through the crack under the closet door. Dawn was breaking.

Was it all a nightmare? As she tried to move, every joint inside her ached. She felt as if she'd been beaten up. Her body was reacting to the trauma. This was no nightmare. It was real.

Ina managed to get to her feet and open the closet door. But she was shaking. The bedroom was still dark with only a murky, early dawn light seeping through the dormer windows. Nothing had been disturbed in the room. The door was still closed.

Ina swallowed hard, and then reached for the doorknob. As she opened the door, she saw the blood and bits of brain on the hallway wall. Only a few feet in front of her, Jenna lay dead on the floor facing that blood-splattered wall.

Ina let out a gasp. Tears stung her eyes, but she didn't stare at her dead sister for too long. She staggered back toward the stairs. She shook so violently she could barely make it down the steps. She clutched the banister to keep from falling — or fainting.

In the dim light she could see only certain areas of the living room. Other spots were still shrouded in darkness. She glimpsed Mark in his robe, sitting in the rocker by the fireplace. But his face was swallowed up in the shadows, and he wasn't moving at all. As Ina warily approached him, she saw that his wavy brown hair was matted down with blood on one side. He stared back at her with open dead eyes and a bewildered expression. The top left side of his head had been blown off.

"Oh, no," Ina whispered, a hand over her mouth. "No, no, no . . ."

Someone emerged from the darkness beyond the kitchen door.

Ina gasped again. She saw Mark's hunting rifle — aimed at her.

Tears streamed down Ina's face as she gazed at the person who was about to kill her. "Oh, my God, honey," she whispered, shaking her head. "What have you done?"

The shotgun went off.

CHAPTER THREE

Her aunt was staring at her, and asking, "What have you done?" And that was when Amelia shot her in the chest.

All at once, she bolted up and accidentally banged her knee against the steering wheel of Shane's Volkswagen Golf. Amelia barely noticed the pain. She was just glad to be awake — and out of that nightmare. It seemed so horribly real. She'd even felt the blood splattering on her face as she'd shot her parents and Aunt Ina at close range.

Now Amelia anxiously checked her reflection in the rearview mirror. She touched her hair. Not a drop of blood anywhere. If she'd washed it off, she certainly would remember. It was a dream — vivid and frightening, but still just a dream.

Shivering from the cold, Amelia looked around. It took her a moment to realize she'd fallen asleep in the front seat of the VW. She'd parked in the small, desolate lot of a boarded-up hot dog stand. The unlit, cracked sign had a cartoon of a smiling dachshund. It read: WIENER WORLD! HOT DOG EMPORIUM — WIENERS, FRIES, & COLD DRINKS!

Amelia wasn't sure where she was, but she could hear cars zooming along on the other side of some evergreen trees across the street from Wiener World. She had to be somewhere close to a highway. She squinted at her wristwatch: 11:15 a.m.

Her head was throbbing and she felt so thirsty she could hardly swallow. She hadn't had a hangover in several weeks, and this was a painful reminder of what it had been like during her drinking days. Now Amelia remembered the party last night, and how she'd treated Shane so shabbily. She remembered grabbing that bottle of tequila and driving off toward Wenatchee. She'd had this sudden urge to get to the family cabin, and make certain her parents and her Aunt Ina were all right. She'd been convinced some harm would come to them.

Amelia felt around under the car seat for that bottle of tequila. There was still some left, and she took a swig from the bottle. But even the jolt of alcohol didn't erase the violent images lingering from that nightmare. Something had happened at the Lake

Wenatchee house; she was sure of it.

Amelia wished she could remember, but everything was a blank from the time she'd sped away from that party on fraternity row to when she'd woken up here just moments ago. She suffered from occasional blackouts — lost time. It usually happened when she was drinking, but she'd experienced these memory lapses other times, too. On several occasions, people claimed they'd seen her here or there, and Amelia didn't remember it at all. It was almost as if she were sleepwalking some of the time.

Had she killed her parents and her aunt during one of these sleepwalking episodes? Was it possible?

Amelia put down the tequila bottle, then dug her cell phone from her purse. Squinting at it, she dialed her mother's cell number. But if they were still at the cabin, the call wouldn't get through. Sure enough, just as she thought, no luck. Biting her lip, Amelia dialed her Aunt Ina and Uncle George's house in Seattle. Her Uncle George had stayed home with her cousins this weekend. If something had really happened, he might know about it.

"Could you please make that announcement again?" George McMillan asked the woman at the concierge desk in the Pacific Place Shopping Center.

Nodding, the pretty concierge with curly auburn hair and cocoa-colored skin gave him a pained, sympathetic smile. She picked up her phone and pushed a couple of numbers.

"Stephanie McMillan, attention, Stephanie McMillan." Her voice interrupted the music on the public address system. "Please meet your father by the first-floor escalators." She repeated the announcement.

"Thank you," George said, nervously tapping his fingers on the edge of the desk. He gazed up at the people passing by the railings on all four shopping levels of the vast skylit atrium. No sign of Steffie. He scanned the faces of the shoppers lined up on the escalators. He still didn't see her. His stomach felt as tight as a fist.

His daughter had wandered off about fifteen minutes ago. Already, George had sweated through his shirt. He imagined every horrifying scenario of what might have happened to her. He saw Stephanie's face on milk cartons. He thought about the call from the police, asking him to come identify the corpse of a pretty, freckled-faced, auburn-haired five-year-old. He imagined looking for the little strawberry mark on her arm — just to make sure it wasn't Stephanie's double. As if there was another like her.

His son, Jody, eleven, was supposed to have been keeping an eye on her. George had taken the kids to Old Navy in downtown Seattle this morning. His wife, Ina, had made out a shopping list that included the kids' clothes and some other things she wanted him to get. After Old Navy, he'd stopped by Pottery Barn in the Pacific Place Shopping Center to pick up candles — specifically, "eight-inch pillars in fig." George had had a big bag from Old Navy weighing down one arm and Steffie hanging on the other. He wasn't sure if fig was tan, brown, or green. Or maybe it was purple — no, that was plum. He had unloaded Stephanie on her brother, then went in search of a saleslady.

At the time, he kept wondering why the hell Ina needed these stupid candles *now.* She wasn't entertaining any time soon. Why didn't she just buy them herself when she got back from Lake Wenatchee? Considering the company and their *situation,* George hadn't been up for the trip this weekend. Besides, someone had to look after the kids. Jenna and Mark had volunteered Amelia's services as a babysitter, but George didn't have much confidence his niece could handle the task, at least not for the entire weekend.

The last few months had been pretty rough for everyone. The drowning of his nephew, Collin, had hit George awfully hard. Collin had had a special bond with his Uncle George, and he'd been like a big brother to Jody. His death had devastated *two* families, not just one. George walked around in a dark stupor for weeks afterward. Maybe that explained why he couldn't see what was happening between Ina and his brother-in-law.

Once George discovered the letter Ina had started to Mark, he realized his wife must have *wanted* him to see what was happening.

In fact, it had already happened — in the Hotel Alexis. "Dear Mark," she'd scribbled on the hotel's stationery.

As I write this, you're in the shower. I still feel you all over me, and inside me. I know what we did was wrong. I'm not arguing with you about that. But we're two good people, who are hurting. We've found something with each other, something that made our pain and loneliness go away. I'm not sure if it's love. But I do know I've

always felt a connection with you. You
haven't —

That was as far as she'd gotten before
she'd half crumpled up the note and thrown
it away — *in their master bathroom,* for
God's sake. It lingered there at the top of
the trash in the silver wastebasket from
Restoration Hardware. George noticed the
note while sitting on the toilet. She'd obviously wanted him to see it. Otherwise, she
would have tossed the letter away in the
hotel room, or torn it up and flushed it
down the toilet, or at the very least, *buried*
the damn thing under some used Kleenex
in the trash.

Ina didn't deny her indiscretion.

"You left that *love letter* in plain sight,"
George pointed out. "God, what were you
thinking? What if Jody had found it? Hell, I
know what you were thinking. . . ." He kept
his voice low. They were in their bedroom,
and he didn't want Jody and Stephanie,
downstairs, to hear. "It's pretty obvious you
wanted me to find out about you and
Mark."

"Now, why in the world would I want
that?" she asked, shaking her head.

"I don't know. Why *did* you want it, Ina?"

George wondered if she'd been dropping

any more clues about her infidelity. The note — with its cringe-worthy prose — mentioned Mark was taking a shower. Had she bothered to bathe at the Alexis that evening, or did she want her addle-brained husband to detect the scent of another man on her?

"I can't understand how this happened," he said finally. "You don't love him. Did you think screwing Mark and letting me find out about it would make me want a divorce? Is this your way of trying to end it for us? You haven't said you're sorry."

Flicking back her long, curly auburn hair, she turned and headed for the door. "I have to get dinner started," she murmured.

"Do you love him?" George asked pointedly. The question made Ina stop in her tracks. "Or did you just use him to sabotage us? For chrissakes, he's your sister's husband, Ina. Tell me the truth, do you love him?"

Facing the door, she shrugged awkwardly. "I don't really know," she whispered. She started to cry, but kept her back to him. "I'm so sorry, honey. Do you hear that? I'm apologizing. I've screwed everything up but good. Maybe I *did* want you to know. You're probably right about that. God, I feel so shitty about this. You're a good man,

George, and a good husband. You deserve better . . ."

He stared at her back, and wondered if this was a variation of the It's Not You, It's Me speech. "I'll be honest. Right now, I'm so furious at you, and so hurt, I'm not sure I have it in me to be forgiving. I need to know if it's worth a try. Do you want to stay in this marriage?"

"I — I can't say for sure," she whispered. "I'm not certain about anything right now."

"Hey, Dad!" Jody called from downstairs. "Dad?"

George brushed past her on his way to the bedroom door. "Goddamn you for doing this," he growled. Then he went downstairs to their son.

Ina wasn't the only one feeling uncertain. In the weeks that followed, it got so that George wasn't sure if he wanted to stay married to her, either. They'd been having problems for at least two years. They'd seen a counselor — six counselors, in fact — until she found one she liked: a "feelings physician" (at least that's what it had said on her shingle) with gobs of turquoise jewelry and green-tinted glasses. George hadn't noticed any medical degrees hanging on her wall, but she'd insisted on being called "Doctor." After twenty minutes of stroking a mangy cat in her lap and listening only to Ina, she'd suggested a trial separation. George had walked out on the session. Ina still went to her once every two weeks on her own. All too often Ina quoted her: "Dr. Racine says I should assert myself. Dr. Racine says I need to be more selfish. Dr. Racine says I need to take time to focus on myself."

He really had to hold his tongue when Ina came out with lulus like that. Ina was beautiful, funny, and intelligent, but as Ina's sister, Jenna, often said, "Ina's only really happy when it's all about Ina."

George had already known that about her. But he'd been in love. He used to feel so lucky. He was just a history professor with a modest income and, somehow, he'd landed this gorgeous woman who had so much class and style. Plus, she and her sister were loaded. The money part never really mattered to him. But Ina could have easily paired off with some hot-shot millionaire who played polo and drove a Porsche. George hadn't even owned a car when he'd met her, and his idea of a terrific time was sitting on the beach, gobbling up a new biography of FDR. And yet he was the one she wanted.

Somewhere in the back of his mind, he'd

always been afraid she would get bored with him. And now that she had, it broke his heart.

Just recently, he'd started imagining his life without her. He thought about a divorce — after fourteen years together. She would get the house, of course. They'd bought it with her money — a four-bedroom split-level in West Seattle. She'd gone nuts decorating it. He wouldn't miss it. He'd do just fine in an apartment somewhere near the University District, so he could be close to school. But the place would need at least two bedrooms for when Jody and Steffie visited. *Visits* with his kids, *allotted time* with them; the notion made him sick.

He wanted to keep the marriage going for the kids. Yet Ina wasn't exactly the most nurturing mother around; at least, it seemed that way lately. All of Ina's shortcomings had become glaringly obvious once he knew about her and Mark. He studied the way she treated Jody and Stephanie, and noticed when she ignored them, or was curt with them, or when she had them fetching things because she was too lazy to get off her ass. ("Jody, honey, get me my purse . . .").

Then again, maybe he was just hypercritical of Ina because somewhere along the line, while wrestling with all his hurt, confusion and anger, he'd fallen out of love with her.

He had to be fair. She wasn't a bad mother. And he was in no position to criticize Ina's parenting skills right now. At least Ina had never lost one of the children while shopping.

It had happened so quickly. George had gotten a saleswoman in Pottery Barn to help him, and together they'd found the stupid eight-inch pillars *in fig.* She'd been ringing up his sale when Jody had come up to the counter and squinted at his father. "Where's Steffie?" Jody had asked, scouting out the general vicinity. "Didn't she come back to you, Dad? She said she was gonna . . ."

"But I left her with you," George had murmured.

She'd been missing for almost twenty minutes now. In his jacket pocket, George felt her inhaler. Stephanie had asthma. What if she was having an attack right now?

He couldn't get past the awful feeling that he'd never see his daughter again. *God, please, if I can find Stephanie, I'll work things out with Ina. I'll do whatever she wants. I'll even go see that stupid Dr. Racine with her. Just please bring Steffie back to me.*

Jody had been peeking into different shops on the shopping mall's main level. Now he

60

hurried back to George at the concierge desk. Shaking his head, Jody looked so forlorn. "Dad, I'm sorry," he said, his lip quivering. "It's all my fault —"

George mussed his son's unruly, brown hair. "It's all right, Jody. We'll find her."

He asked the concierge to make the announcement again. Then he put down his shopping bags and turned to Jody. "You stay here and keep your eyes peeled," he said. "I'll start on the top floor and work my way down. Have the woman call my cell if Steffie shows up. Okay, sport?"

Jody nodded. George kissed his forehead, then hurried toward the escalator. "Stephanie! Steffie?" he called, loudly. People stopped to stare at him, several of them scowling. He didn't care. He brushed past shoppers on the escalator, saying, "Excuse me," over and over again. He yelled out Stephanie's name a few more times. He kept looking around as he moved from each shopping level, stepping off one escalator and starting up a new one.

As George reached the top floor, where the restaurants and movie theaters were, he felt his cell phone vibrating. He stopped in his tracks. He quickly snatched the phone out of his jacket pocket, then switched it on. "Yes, hello?" he asked anxiously.

"Uncle George?"

"Amelia?" he asked.

"Yeah, hi, listen," she said. "Has Aunt Ina called you from the cabin today?"

Flustered, he shook his head. "Not yet," he said into the phone. "She's supposed to call from that diner near the cabin when they go to breakfast. I'm sorry, Amelia, but I —"

"Uncle George, it's past noon. She should have called by now —"

"Amelia, honey, I'm sorry, but I'm in the middle of something. I need to call you back."

"No! Don't hang up, please! Uncle George, something happened at the Lake Wenatchee house, something horrible."

He stood by the entrance of a fifties diner with the cell phone to one ear and a finger in the other to block out all the noise. "What are you talking about?" he asked, trying not to sound impatient.

"Remember how when Collin died, I knew before everyone else? Remember that premonition I had? Well, this is the same thing. I *feel* it. I know something happened at the cabin. You probably think I'm crazy. But I'm scared, Uncle George. My gut instinct tells me they're all dead — Mom, Dad, and Ina. I hope to God I'm wrong —"

62

"Amelia, I'm sorry, but I'm in the middle of something right now. It's an emergency. Let me call you back —"

"This is an emergency too, Uncle George! I'm serious —"

"Honey, I'm going to hang up, okay? I — I'll call you back just as soon as I can, all right?" Wincing, George clicked off the line. He felt awful hanging up on her, but he just didn't have time for Amelia's dramatics right now.

He hadn't even gotten the cell phone back into his pocket when it vibrated again. "Oh, Jesus, please, Amelia, leave me alone," he muttered. He clicked on the phone, and sighed. "Yes?"

"Mr. McMillan, this is Jennifer, the concierge. Your daughter's okay. She hadn't wandered too far. She heard the last announcement, and came right to us. She's here at the desk, waiting for you. . . ."

"Oh, thank God," he whispered. "Thank you, Jennifer. Thank you very much."

Fifteen minutes later, he was walking with the children toward the Pine Street lot where he'd parked the car. George gripped Stephanie's little hand. He felt as if he'd just dodged a bullet. He'd thanked the concierge, stopped by Pottery Barn to tell the saleswoman all was well, and he'd assured Jody that he wasn't mad at him for letting Stephanie wander off. But he still had some unfinished business.

He needed to call back Amelia, and he didn't want to. She'd been babbling on about some *premonition* she'd had that her parents and Ina were all dead.

"Okay, watch your fingers and feet, pumpkin," he said, helping Stephanie into the backseat. He shut the car door and made sure she was locked in. While Jody climbed into the front passenger side, George stashed the Old Navy and Pottery Barn bags in the trunk. He closed it, and then glanced at his wristwatch: 12:35.

Ina definitely should have phoned by now.

He checked his cell to see if he might have missed a call. There were no messages. The only call had been the one from Amelia.

Pulling at her leash, the eleven-year-old collie led the way. Abby knew exactly where her owner was headed. She had that sixth sense some dogs had. When they came to a split in the forest's crude path, Abby sniffed at the ground and quickly veered onto the trail that went along the lake's edge — toward the Faradays' house.

"That's a good girl," Helene Sumner said, holding the leash tightly. A chilly autumn wind whipped across the lake, and she turned up the collar to her windbreaker. Helene was sixty-seven and thin, with close-cropped gray hair. She was an artist, working with silk screens. She had a studio in her house, about a half mile down the lake from the Faradays' place.

Helene had hardly gotten any sleep last night. When those shots had gone off at 2:30 this morning, Abby had started barking. She leapt up from her little comforter in the corner of the bedroom and onto Helene's bed. The poor thing was trembling. So was Helene. She wasn't accustomed to being woken up in the middle of the night like that.

Hunting was prohibited in the area, and even if it were allowed, what in God's name were they hunting at that hour? The tall trees surrounding the lake played with the acoustics, and sounds traveled across the water. Those shots rang out so clearly, they could have been fired in Helene's backyard. But she knew where they'd come from.

She'd just started to doze off again when another loud bang went off around five o'clock. Helene dragged herself out of bed and threw on her windbreaker. Grabbing a pair of field glasses, she walked with Abby to the lake's edge, and then peered over at the Faradays' house. No activity, no lights on, nothing.

She retreated to the house, crawled back into bed and nodded off until 10:30 — very unlike her.

An hour ago, while having her breakfast — coffee and the last of her homemade biscuits — Helene had figured out who must have encroached on her sanctuary. Those three loud shots in the early morning hours must have been some kind of fireworks — bottle rockets or firecrackers.

Now, walking with Abby along the lakeside path, Helene gazed at the Faraday place and thought about the daughter, Amelia. She used to be such a polite, considerate girl — and so beautiful. But there was an underlying sadness about her, too. And talk about sad, it was such a tragedy when the Faradays' son drowned. It had been around that time, maybe even before, when Amelia and her lowlife boyfriend had started showing up at the weekend house without her parents. They were so obnoxious. Helene didn't care about the skinny-dipping, but did they have to be so loud? She heard their screaming and laughing until all hours of the night, and sometimes it was punctuated by bottles smashing. They trashed the lake, too. Helene would find food wrappers, cigarette butts, and beer cans washed up on her shore after each one of their clandestine visits. Those kids were making a cesspool out of her lake.

About a month ago, when the Faradays had come for a weekend, Helene stopped by with a Bundt cake and offered her belated condolences about Collin. Then, privately, she talked to Amelia about her secret trips there with her boyfriend. "It's none of my business what you do with him, Amelia," she told her, walking along the trail beside the water. "But I wish you'd be a little less noisy about it. And so help me God, I'm going to say something to your parents if I see one more piece of garbage in that lake. It's my lake, too, and I won't let you and your boyfriend pollute it."

Amelia stopped and gaped at her with those big, beautiful eyes and a put-on innocent expression. "Oh, Ms. Sumner, I — I don't know what you're talking about," she murmured. "I haven't come here with my boyfriend. I swear. Shane's *never* been here. You must be mistaken."

Helene shook her head. "You can deny it all you want. I know what I saw, Amelia. I'm really disappointed in you. . . ."

Now, as she approached the Faradays' front porch, Helene figured she'd get the same Little Miss Innocent routine from Amelia as last time. She would probably wake her up — along with her boyfriend — since they'd been lighting off firecrackers until the wee hours of the morning.

But something suddenly occurred to Helene that made her hesitate at the Faradays' front stoop. Why didn't she hear any laughing or screaming? People always laughed, yelled, or cheered when they let off fireworks. But there hadn't been a human sound — just those shots.

Abby sniffed at the front door to the Faradays' old Cape Cod–style house. She started whining and barking. The collie backed away. She had that sixth sense.

Something was wrong inside that house.

Although Abby tried to pull her in the other direction, Helene stepped up to the door and knocked. Abby wouldn't stop yelping. "Quiet, girl," Helene hissed. She tried to listen for some activity inside the house. Nothing. Helene knocked again, and waited. She wondered if she should take a cue from Abby and get out of there. But she knocked once more, and then tried the doorknob. It wasn't locked.

Abby let out another loud bark, a warning. But it was too late. Helene was already opening the door. From the threshold, she could see up the stairs to the second floor hallway, where a messy brownish-red stain marred the pale blue wall. Baffled, Helene started up the stairs, having to tug at Abby's leash. Only a few steps from the landing, Helene stopped dead. She realized now that the large stain on the wall was dried blood. Beneath it, Jenna Faraday lay on the floor, her face turned to the wall. The oversized T-shirt she wore was soaked crimson. Her bare legs looked so swollen and pale — almost gray.

Helene gasped. She and Abby retreated down the stairs, and then she noticed what was in the living room. Helene stopped in her tracks. A second dead woman lay sprawled on the floor — a few feet from the kitchen door. She had beautiful, curly auburn hair, but her face was frozen in a horrified grimace. Her burgundy-colored robe and nightgown almost matched the puddle of blood on the floor beneath her. The shotgun blast had ripped open the front of that lacy nightgown. Helene could see the fatal, gaping wound in her chest.

Not far from the second woman's body, Mark Faraday's corpse sat upright in a rocker. At least, Helene thought it was him. Blood covered the robe he wore. The butt of the hunting rifle was wedged between

Mark Faraday's lifeless legs, with the long barrel slightly askew and tilted away from his mutilated, swollen face.

One hand remained draped over the gun, his finger caught in the trigger.

CHAPTER FOUR

"What about that woman who lives down the lake from the cabin?" George asked. "Your dad told me they've used her phone in the past for emergencies. Do you know her number?"

"Oh, God, Ms. Sumner," Amelia murmured on the other end of the line. She sounded as if she were in a daze. "I forgot all about her. We have her number written down someplace, but I think it's shoved in a desk at home in Bellingham."

"Do you know her first name?"

"Hold on for a second, Uncle George. I'm about to go through a tunnel."

"I thought you'd pulled over. You shouldn't be on your cell while driving —"

"God, you sound just like Dad. It's okay. I have friends who text-message while driving."

"Well, then they're idiots," George said to dead air. She must have entered the tunnel.

Holding the cordless phone to his ear, he glanced toward the living room windows. From this spot in the kitchen, he could see through the sheer curtains to the front yard. He'd sent Jody and Stephanie outside so he could phone Amelia and talk to her without the kids hearing. They didn't need to know he was worried about their mother.

While driving home from downtown, George had gotten more and more concerned. Ina had *promised* to call and check in with him this morning.

There were no messages on the answering machine when he'd gotten home with the kids, except two from a panic-stricken Amelia, both within the last hour. Her premonition that Ina, Mark, and Jenna had all been killed seemed preposterous, but unnerving, too.

"Remember how when Collin died, I knew before everyone else?" she'd asked. What George remembered was Amelia claiming after the drowning that she'd *seen* it all — in her mind. She didn't think Collin had accidentally fallen off the dock and hit his head on those pilings. She insisted there was more to it than that. She had a feeling.

George remembered when Amelia had made all those wild claims. He and Ina figured their sweet-but-screwed-up niece was looking for some attention. Amelia must have felt like an also-ran alongside her winning younger brother. Back in 1992, Mark and Jenna had been trying to have a child. Finally, after weeks of foster parenting, they adopted beautiful four-year-old Amelia. They didn't think anyone could eclipse her — until two months later, when Jenna learned she was pregnant.

Amelia adored her little brother. But apparently she became a handful. Mark and Jenna lost more sleep on account of Amelia's nightmares than the baby's feedings. And even when Collin was supposed to sleep through the night, Amelia always woke him up when she jumped out of bed shrieking. The nightmares hadn't yet subsided when Amelia started developing phantom pains and faked illnesses. "It feels like someone's twisting my arm off, Uncle George!" he remembered her screaming during a family Thanksgiving at his and Ina's house. It took several minutes for her to stop crying. According to Jenna, two days later, Amelia claimed her arm was still sore, though she didn't have a mark on her. Other times, she said it felt as if someone were hitting her or kicking her. There were several trips to the doctor and the hospital emergency room for absolutely no reason. By early high school, certain phantom aches and ailments prompted Jenna to rush Amelia to a gynecologist. Jenna had confided to Ina that she thought someone might have been molesting Amelia. But the doctors found no physical evidence of this whatsoever.

Amelia started drinking in high school, too. Despite all her problems, she was a near-A student, and extremely sweet. She had a good heart. If someone sneezed in the next aisle at the supermarket, Amelia would call out, "God bless you." George guessed that her eagerness to please, along with peer pressure, must have started her drinking. She'd been to several therapists, but none of them really worked out until she recently started seeing this one, Karen Somebody. Amelia liked her a lot, but George wasn't sure if this Karen person was doing any good.

The one who seemed to get through to Amelia best was Ina. Since Amelia had started school at UW, they'd seen a lot more of her. Ina relished the admiration of this college girl. They had their Girls' Nights Out together at trendy restaurants and college bars. They also teamed up for shopping expeditions and the occasional pedicure/

manicure at Ina's favorite day spa. She got to be Amelia's fun aunt and confidante.

George wondered if Ina was better at being a fun aunt than a serious wife and mother. It was a terrible thought to have. And just an hour ago, he'd made a deal with God that he would try once again to make it work with Ina.

George continued to listen to the dead air on the phone, and he stared out the window. One of the neighbor kids — Jody's friend, Brad Reece — joined the children on the front lawn. And now the boys were tossing around a Frisbee and ignoring Stephanie.

"Uncle George, are you still there?"

"Yes," he said into the phone. "I thought I might have lost you."

"The old lady's name is Helene," she said. "Helene Sumner in Lake Wenatchee. I'll call directory assistance and get the number —"

"No, let me." He grabbed a pen and scribbled down the name. "I don't want you making all these calls while you're driving. By the way, where are you? Where's this tunnel?"

She hesitated.

"Amelia?"

"I just got off the I-90 bridge. I was — I was visiting a friend in Bellevue."

"Well, listen, if you have nothing else going on, you're welcome to come over —"

"Um, I can't right now, Uncle George. I'm going to see my therapist. Maybe later tonight, huh?"

"Okay. I'll call this Helene Sumner and see if she'll check on the house for us. I'll phone you the minute I hear anything."

"My cell's running out of juice. Let me give you Karen's number in case you can't reach me. Karen Carlisle, she's my therapist. Got a pencil?"

"I'm ready." George scribbled down the Seattle phone number as she read it off to him. "I'll call you. And stop worrying. I'm sure everything's fine."

Speeding along I-90 in her boyfriend's car, Amelia clicked off the cell phone and tossed it onto the passenger seat. She clutched the steering wheel with both hands, and started to cry.

Uncle George had said everything would be fine. But he didn't know what she knew. Amelia hadn't told him the whole story. She'd failed to mention that, in all likelihood, she'd killed her parents and Ina.

Amelia had also lied about where she had been. After waking up at the deserted Wiener World parking lot, she'd driven around for ten minutes until she'd found the freeway entrance. Then she finally saw a sign telling her where she was: Easton, Washington — a little city ninety miles east of Seattle. It was also about halfway to Wenatchee — and *from* Wenatchee. Had she been there last night? Had Easton been a stopover so she could sleep a few hours on her way back from murdering her parents and aunt?

Shane had left three messages on her cell, wanting to know where she'd taken his car. Amelia was driving past Snoqualmie when she called him back. She lied and said she'd had a sudden urge to see the Snoqualmie Falls last night. Yes, she'd gotten a *little* drunk, and decided to sleep it off in the car in the Snoqualmie Lodge parking lot. Yes, she was all right. She just felt awful for taking his car and for the way she'd acted at the party last night.

She couldn't tell Shane the truth. The only person she could really talk to was her therapist, Karen.

Funny, the two people in whom she confided the most were both women in their thirties. They weren't alike at all. Karen, with her wavy, shoulder-length chestnut hair and brown eyes, had the kind of natural beauty other women admired, but only the most discerning men noticed. She was very down to earth, but still had a certain class to her. She could look elegant in just a pair of jeans and a black long-sleeved T-shirt. Meanwhile, Amelia's Aunt Ina was very flashy and fun, sometimes even over the top. All eyes went to her whenever she walked into a room. She was Prada to Karen's Banana Republic.

Amelia remembered how lucky she'd felt when her cool Aunt Ina had decided to spend more time with her. They went to art galleries, the theater, and all these terrific, hip restaurants. But then Amelia had started seeing Karen, who was so compassionate and kind. After a while, she stopped confiding in Ina, who wasn't a very good listener, anyway. Amelia realized her favorite aunt could be pretty selfish. Sometimes she felt like Ina's pet — just this silly, admiring college girl who tagged along in her frivolous aunt's shadow.

Selfish, manipulative bitch, Amelia remembered thinking last night as she'd aimed the hunting rifle at her Aunt Ina. *Amelia's not your fucking pet.*

It was as if someone else were speaking for her — and killing for her. Yet Amelia remembered pulling the trigger. She remembered the jolt from the gun — and the loud blast.

God, please, please, don't let me have done that. Make it not be true. Let them be all right.

She pressed harder on the accelerator.

Watching the road ahead, Amelia wiped her eyes, and then reached for the cell phone on the passenger seat.

She had Karen on speed dial.

"Frank, you need to put down the knife," Karen said in a firm, unruffled tone.

Everyone else around her was going berserk, but she tried to remain calm and keep eye contact with the 73-year-old Alzheimer's patient. The unshaven man had greasy, long gray hair and a ruddy complexion. His T-shirt was inside out, with food stains down the front. The pale green pajama bottoms were filthy, too. In his shaky hand he held a butcher's knife. He looked more terrified than anyone else in the nursing home cafeteria. Just moments ago, he'd accidentally knocked over a stack of dirty trays from the bus table. He'd bumped into the table, backing away from an overly aggressive kitchen worker.

"Drop the goddamn knife," growled the short, thirty-something man. He wore a T-shirt and chinos under his apron. Tattoos covered his skinny arms. He kept inching toward the desperately confused patient. "C'mon, drop it! I don't have all day here!" He kicked a chair and it toppled across the floor, just missing the old man. "You hear me, Pops? Drop it!"

"Get away from him!" Karen barked. "For God's sake, can't you see he's scared?"

Two orderlies hovered behind her, along with a few elderly residents wanting to see what all the fuss was about. The rest home's manager, a handsome, white-haired woman in her sixties named Roseann, had managed to herd everyone else out of the cafeteria. She stood at Karen's side. "Did you hear her, Earl?" Roseann yelled at the kitchen worker. "Let Karen handle this. She knows what she's doing!"

But Earl wasn't listening. He closed in on the man, looking ready to pounce. "You shouldn't steal knives out of my kitchen, Pops. . . ."

"No — no . . . get!" the Alzheimer's patient cried, waving the knife at him.

Wincing, Karen watched the frightened old man shrink back toward the pile of trays. He was barefoot, and there were shards of broken glass on the floor.

Roseann gasped. "Earl, don't —"

He lunged at the man, who reeled back. But the knife grazed Earl's tattooed arm. A few of the residents behind Karen gasped.

The little man let out a howl, and recoiled. "Son of a bitch!"

One of the orderlies rushed to his aid. Grumbling obscenities, Earl held on to his arm, as the blood oozed between his fingers.

"No . . . get!" the old man repeated.

"It's okay!" the orderly called, checking Earl's wound, and pulling him toward the cafeteria exit. "Doesn't look too deep. . . ."

"Fuck you 'it's okay'," he shot back. "I'm bleeding here."

Shushing him, the orderly quickly led Earl out the door.

Karen was still looking into the old man's eyes. "That was an accident, Frank," she said steadily. "We all saw it. No one's mad at you. But you should put down the knife, okay?"

Wide-eyed, he kept shaking his head at her. He took another step back toward the glass on the floor.

"Frank, how do you think the Cubs are going to do this season?" Karen suddenly asked.

She remembered how during her last visit with him, he'd chatted nonstop about the Chicago Cubs. But he'd talked as if it were 1968, back when he'd been a hotshot, 33-year-old attorney in Arlington Heights, Illinois with a beautiful wife, Elaine, and two children, Frank Junior and Sheila. The old man in the stained T-shirt and pajama bottoms used to dress in Brooks Brothers suits. The family moved to Seattle in 1971, where they added a third child to the brood, a baby girl. Frank started his own law firm, and did quite well in Mariner town. But he'd always remained a Cubs fan.

Though she knew it was typical of Alzheimer's patients, Karen still thought it was kind of funny that Frank often couldn't remember the name of his dead wife or the names of his three children and seven grandchildren. But he still recalled the Cubs' star lineup from 1968.

"How do you think Ernie Banks is going to do, Frank?" she asked.

He stopped, and his milky blue eyes narrowed at her for a moment. "Um . . . you need — you need to keep your eye on Ron Santo. This is — this is going to be his year." He lowered the knife. He suddenly seemed to forget he was holding it.

"I thought you were an Ernie Banks fan, Frank," she said. "You know, there's some glass on the floor behind you. Be careful."

He turned and glanced down at the floor. "Yeah, you got to love Ernie. Who doesn't?"

Karen felt her cell phone vibrate in the

back pocket of her jeans, but she ignored it. She took a few steps toward him. "You know, you ought to put down that knife. Should we get some ice cream?"

He frowned at the knife in his hand, and then set it on one of the cafeteria tables.

"Does ice cream sound good to you, Frank?" Roseann piped in. "I think Karen has a good idea there. You recognize Karen, don't you?"

The second orderly carefully reached for the knife and took it away. A few of the residents behind Karen sighed, and one elderly man clapped.

Karen put her arm around Frank. Between his breath and his body odor, he smelled awful. But she smiled at him. "You recognize me, don't you, Poppy?"

A smile flickered across his face, and for a second he was her dad again. "Of course," he whispered. "You're my little girl."

She gave his shoulder a squeeze. "That's right, Poppy. Let's get you cleaned up, okay?" She led her father toward the cafeteria doors.

Later, while the orderly got Mr. Carlisle changed and back in bed, Karen ducked into the employee lounge to check her phone messages. She'd been volunteering once a week at the Sandpoint View Convalescent Home for half a year now, and knew all the staff. It was one way to ensure her dad got special treatment, one way to keep from feeling so horrible for giving up on him and putting him in there.

In addition to her volunteer day, Karen saw her father at Sandpoint View about twice a week. She'd been driving over to visit him this afternoon when the call had come from Roseann, saying her dad was having an "episode." Frank had slipped out of his room and under their radar a few times in the past; he'd even wandered off the grounds once. But this was the first incident in which he'd posed a threat to anyone.

Karen knew Roseann would have to take some measures after what had just happened in the cafeteria. They'd probably start him on a new medication, which would make him even more dopey and unreachable. Or maybe they'd move him into Ward E with the severe cases.

Karen didn't want to think about that right now.

She nodded hello to a nurse, sitting at the table with her iPod and a sandwich. The small lounge had one window with the blinds lowered, and yellow-painted cinderblock walls that someone had decorated with these sappy, inspirational posters entitled Achievement, Friendship, and Tranquility. The photos of people watching the sunset, goldfish in a bowl, and kites flying against a blue sky were fuzzy and the poetic sentiments were written in script. Someone had scribbled BLOW ME in the top corner of the sunset Tranquility poster. There was also a slightly tattered brown sofa, a mini-refrigerator, and a vending machine, along with a coffee-maker on the counter, not far from the sink.

Karen poured herself a cup of their rotgut coffee. She leaned against the counter and checked her cell phone. Amelia Faraday had called.

She had thirty-one clients, and Amelia was the one she cared about the most. At first, Amelia had reminded Karen of someone else, someone she'd lost. Karen figured that maybe by helping Amelia solve her problems, she could help herself. It wouldn't raise the dead, but maybe she could make some of her own pain go away.

She pushed a couple of buttons on the cell and played the voice mail. Amelia's slightly shrill, panic-filled voice was like an assault: "Karen? Karen, I left you a couple of messages at home . . ." She let out a little gasp, then started to cry. "God, Karen, I'm

85

in trouble. Something terrible has happened. I really need to talk with you. Please . . . please, call me back . . ."

She was about to hit the last call return button when Earl swaggered into the lounge. A gauze bandage was wrapped around his wounded arm.

"You!" the creepy little man growled. He stabbed a finger in the air at her. "You're just lucky I don't need stitches. . . ."

Karen put down the phone. "Earl, I'm sorry about your arm —"

" 'Sorry' doesn't begin to cover it," he said, cutting her off.

The nurse took off her iPod headset, sat forward in her chair, and watched them.

"I'm gonna make sure your old man gets some bed restraints. They ought to keep him tied up twenty-four seven." Earl inched closer to Karen until he was almost screaming in her face. "Better yet, they should stick that crazy old fuck in Ward E with the rest of the lunatics before he kills someone. I don't need this shit. That crazy old fuck, I'm gonna see to it they lock him up —"

"No," Karen said resolutely. "No, Earl. You're going to see to it the kitchen knives are locked up. Over a third of the residents here have Alzheimer's or some other form of dementia, and you're leaving knives out where anyone can get at them. My father isn't responsible for his actions, but *you are.* What's more, you wouldn't have that cut on your arm if you'd let me handle him."

His mouth open, he glared at her and shook his head.

"And one last thing, Earl, if you call my father a 'crazy old fuck' again, I swear, I'll punch your lights out — or I'll pay one of the attendants here to do it for me."

The nurse watching them let out an abrupt laugh.

Earl kept shaking his head. "Listen, don't you threaten me —"

"Earl?"

He swiveled around.

Her arms folded, Roseann stood in the doorway of the employee lounge. "Karen's right about locking up the kitchen utensils. I've talked to you about that before. It better not happen again. Now, don't you have some potatoes to peel or something?"

With a defiant grunt, he turned to glare one more time at Karen, then stomped out of the room.

Roseann raised an eyebrow at the nurse. "Show's over, Michelle. So was your break, as of ten minutes ago."

Nodding, the nurse took one last bite of her sandwich, gathered up her things, and ducked out of the lounge.

"Thanks for running interference," Karen said, giving Roseann a weary smile. "How's my dad?"

"Sedated." Roseann plopped down at the table. "We'll give him a rain check on the ice cream. Listen, you and I need to talk about making some adjustments to Frank's routine."

Karen nodded. "I've seen that coming for a while now." She looked down into her coffee cup. Yes, she'd seen it coming, but hadn't wanted to acknowledge the inevitable. It meant giving up on him a little more.

"Do yourself a favor," she heard Roseann say. "Talk to a counselor or join a family of Alzheimer's support group. In all this time, you haven't gotten any help at all. And it's not just about what's going on with your dad. This last year has been pretty awful for you from what you told me about your breakup and what happened with that poor girl. What was her name again?"

"Haley Lombard," Karen said quietly.

"Such a shame," Roseann sighed. "Anyway, you'd be the first one to recommend counseling to somebody in your shoes."

"I know, I know, 'Physician, heal thyself,' " Karen replied.

Roseann was right, of course. But Karen made her living listening to people's problems all day long. And it seemed like the rest of her time lately was dedicated to her father. She didn't want to spend what little time remained in therapy or talking about Alzheimer's. A DVD of a familiar classic was her therapy; it was like having an old friend over. An evening at home with Cary Grant and Eva Marie Saint, or Gregory Peck and Audrey Hepburn, wasn't a cure for her troubles, but it was a Band-Aid that fit just fine.

"Who knows?" Roseann said. "If you joined one of those Alzheimer's groups, you might meet a nice, single man."

"Oh, yeah, right." Karen took one last gulp of the bad coffee, then poured the rest down the sink and rinsed out the cup. "Like I'd want to hook up with some guy whose life is just as screwed up as mine is, thanks to Alzheimer's. Talk about serious relationship baggage. No, thanks. Besides, I'd probably end up running the stupid meetings. You know I would."

"Probably," Roseann muttered, nodding. "But you'd do a damn good job of it. You're not so terrific at helping yourself, Karen. But you really know how to help other people."

Karen managed to chuckle. "Well, thanks a bunch. I —"

Her cell phone vibrated once more, and she checked the caller ID. Amelia again. Karen sighed. "I'm sorry, Roseann. I need to take this." She clicked on the phone. "Hello? Amelia?"

"Oh, thank God!" the girl began. "I'm sorry to bother you, Karen. But something awful has happened —"

"Where are you?"

"I'm sitting in Shane's car — in your driveway. I don't know anybody else I can talk to about this. You're the only one. I've had another blackout, and I think I did something —"

"It's going to be all right," Karen said calmly. She glanced at her wristwatch. "My housekeeper, Jessie, ought to be there very soon. Get her to let you in, and wait for me. If you want, help yourself to a Diet Coke in the fridge. I'll see you in about a half hour. Does that sound okay, Amelia?"

"Yes, thank you, Karen. Thank you so much."

"See you in a bit." Clicking off the line, Karen shoved the phone back in her pocket, and gave Roseann a pale smile. "Sorry, Ro. About that talk regarding my dad, can it wait until later in the week? I have an emergency with one of my clients."

Roseann nodded. "No sweat. Go help somebody. Like I say, it's what you're good at."

Karen patted Roseann's shoulder as she headed out of the employee lounge.

Before taking off, she stopped to peek in on her father. The orderly had cleaned him up, and now he looked so peaceful in his slumber. She wondered if in his dreams he was his old self again, if he wasn't frightened and confused. She took a long look at him, and remembered back in high school when it had been just her and her dad in their big, four-bedroom white stucco house near Seattle's Volunteer Park. Cancer had killed her mother when Karen was fourteen. Her brother, Frank, was married and living in Atlanta. Her sister, Sheila, was away at college. So Karen and her father looked after each other. They had a housekeeper, but Karen did most of the shopping and cooking. It was a lot of work, and took a bite out of her social life. Some afternoons, after school, all she wanted to do was nap. Her dad always let her sleep. He often snuck into her room while she was napping, and covered her with his plaid flannel robe. Then he'd wait a while and fix their dinner — either hamburgers or bacon and eggs. Those were the only things he knew how to cook. She remembered how she'd wake up to the smell of his cooking — and the feel of his soft flannel robe covering her. Sheila had brought him another robe years ago, a blue terry-cloth which he'd taken to the rest home with him. But the old plaid flannel robe still hung in his closet, and Karen sometimes still used it to cover herself when she took a late-afternoon nap.

She gazed at her father in his hospital-style bed and began to cry. She'd been miserable throughout most of her high school years. But now she missed that time — and she missed her father. Wiping her eyes, Karen bent over and kissed his forehead. "See you tomorrow, Poppy," she whispered, though she knew he couldn't hear her.

Stepping out of the room, she wiped her eyes again and peered down the hallway. She spotted Amelia — at least she thought it was Amelia. The young, pretty brunette at the end of the corridor locked eyes with her for only a second. Then she turned and disappeared around the corner.

As he dialed the number for Helene Sumner in Wenatchee, George felt like a fool. He was overreacting. He'd let Amelia's weird premonition get to him. So Ina had promised to call this morning, and didn't. Big deal. She'd broken promises before. This wasn't the first time. Mark, Jenna, and Ina had probably decided to drive someplace else for breakfast. Or maybe they'd eaten at the house, then went hiking and lost track of the time.

Yet here he was, about to ask this old lady to schlep a half mile down the lake and check on his wife and in-laws. He listened to the first ring tone. Through the living room window's sheer drapes, he could see the kids still playing with Jody's friend.

"Yes, hello?" the woman answered on the other end of the line. She sounded frazzled.

"Hello. Is this Helene?"

"Yes. Is this the police? I thought someone would be here by now."

"No, this isn't the police," George replied, bewildered. "I'm calling from Seattle. Your neighbors down the lake, Mark and Jenna Faraday, they're my in-laws. My name's —"

"They're dead," the woman cried, cutting him off. "He shot the two women, and then himself. . . ."

George felt as if someone had just punched him in the stomach. For a moment, he couldn't breathe. Swallowing hard, he caught another glance of his children playing on the front lawn. Stephanie let out a loud scream and then laughed about something.

"I called the police twenty minutes ago," the woman said in a shaky voice. "They still aren't here yet. God, I still can't believe it. But I was in the house. I saw their bodies — and the blood. They're dead, they're all dead. . . ."

CHAPTER FIVE

Salem, Oregon — 1996

Twenty-six-year-old Lauren Tully felt like the walking dead. The pretty, slightly plump brunette worked as a paralegal, and she'd just helped her boss finish up the Bensinger complaint. They'd toiled over the case all week, right up until 9:15 tonight. Her boss would file it in the morning, and said she could take the day off, thank God.

Now that she was outside, Lauren realized what a gorgeous day she'd missed, buried in her cubicle. It was one of those warm, balmy late-June nights. She hadn't had dinner yet, so she'd swung by Guji's Deli Stop on her way home. The four-aisle store was in a minimall, along with a hair salon, a Radio Shack, some teriyaki joint, and a real estate office, all of which were closed at this hour. Guji's was the only lit storefront. They closed at ten. There weren't many customers, and the parking lot was practically

95

empty. Lauren picked up a frozen pizza, some wine, and — what the hell, she deserved it — a pint of Ben & Jerry's. She was coming out of the store when she noticed something a bit strange.

"Damn it!" the man yelled. "I'm sorry, honey. Daddy didn't mean to swear."

His minivan was parked over by the Dumpsters, near the bushes bordering one side of the lot. A big tree blocked out the streetlight, so Lauren hadn't noticed him and a child moving in and out of the shadows until now. The minivan's inside light was on, and the back door was open.

"No, no, no," the man was saying. "Don't try to lift that, honey. It's too heavy. Maybe someone in the store can help us."

Lauren opened her passenger door, and set the grocery bag on the seat. She glanced toward the minivan again. She could see the man now. He was on crutches. He and his little girl were trying to load groceries into the vehicle. One of the bags was tipped over, and two more stood upright. The man turned in her direction. "Excuse me!" he called softly. "Do you have a minute? I hate to bother you . . ."

Lauren didn't move for a moment. Something wasn't right, but she couldn't quite put her finger on it. Still, her heart broke as she watched the little girl struggling with one of the bags. She was about ten years old, and very pretty.

Lauren stepped toward them. "Do you folks need some help?"

"Oh, yes, thank you," the man said. "You're very kind."

"It's okay!" the little girl said — loudly. "I got it!" She loaded one bag into the back-seat, and then quickly grabbed another. "It's not heavy at all! Thank you anyway!"

This close, she could see the man on crutches shoot a look at the young girl. He had such a hateful, murderous stare, it made Lauren stop in her tracks. Nothing in his malignant glare matched that soft, gentle voice coming out of the shadows just moments before.

But the child ignored him and loaded up the second grocery bag. She glanced at Lauren. "Thank you anyway!" she repeated. "You can go back to your car! Good-bye!"

The man turned to Lauren and tried to laugh, but she could tell it almost hurt him to smile. "Well, thanks for stopping," he said with an awkward wave. "It looks like my daughter has the situation under control. Good night."

Lauren just nodded, then retreated toward her car.

On the way home, she wondered why they'd parked on the other side of the lot from Guji's Deli when there were plenty of spaces right in front of the store. Why walk all that way when he didn't have to? And the man was on crutches, too, though she didn't remember seeing a cast on his leg.

If Lauren Tully had turned her car around and driven back to Guji's Deli ten minutes later, she would have found that man on crutches and his little girl in the exact same spot. She would have seen the three grocery bags once again waiting to be loaded into the minivan.

If she had turned her car around, Lauren might have been able to warn 21-year-old Wendy Keefe that it was all a ploy.

The blond liberal arts major at Willamette University had ridden her bicycle to Guji's for a pack of cigarettes. Never mind that her boyfriend made fun of her for being both a smoker and a bicycle enthusiast. She was emerging from the store with her bike helmet under her arm when she spotted the minivan, along with the man on crutches and his daughter. The little girl was crying. Wendy hadn't been there ten minutes earlier, when the man had slapped the child across her face. And he'd slapped her hard. It was too dark for Wendy to see the red welt on the young girl's cheek.

"Excuse me!" the man called. He had a very gentle tone in his voice. "We're in kind of a bind here. I'm afraid we over-shopped. These bags are too heavy for my daughter. . . ."

Tucking the Salems in the pocket of her windbreaker, Wendy approached the minivan. The little girl had been struggling with one of three bags. But now she stopped to stare at Wendy. The child kept shaking her head over and over. Tears slid down her cheeks. She seemed to be mouthing something to her.

"Yes, it looks like you could use an extra hand," Wendy said.

Propped up on his crutches, the father smiled. "I really appreciate this. If you could just slide those bags into the backseat, we can take it from there."

"No problem." Wendy hoisted one of the bags into the back. The young girl stood by the open door. She whispered something, and Wendy turned to her. "What did you say, honey?"

"Run," the child whispered.

Bewildered, Wendy stopped to stare at her.

The father cleared his throat. "If you could get in there and slide the bag to the driver's side. Just climb right in there."

Wendy hesitated.

"Run," the young girl repeated under her breath.

For a second, Wendy was paralyzed. She squinted at the child, who began to back away from her. Wendy wasn't looking at the man.

She didn't see him coming toward her with one of his crutches in the air.

"Run!" the child screamed at her. "No!"

It was the last thing Wendy heard before the crutch cracked against her skull.

The nine-year-old sat alone in the front passenger seat of the minivan. Her face was swollen and throbbing. He'd parked the vehicle on an old dirt road by some railroad tracks. In all the times she'd sat alone in this minivan, parked in this spot, she'd never seen a train go by. And she'd spent many hours here.

Clouds swept across the dark horizon on this warm June night. She could only see the outlines of the tops of the trees ahead of her. The rest was just blackness. She couldn't tell where he'd taken the bicycle lady. The screams seemed far away, maybe somewhere beyond the trees.

She'd had to endure his wrath all the way there, while the woman lay unconscious and bleeding in the back. Usually, he knocked them out with one quick, bloodless blow while they were inside the minivan. But she'd screwed everything up with that nice chubby lady, and he'd heard her trying to warn the bike woman. He kept saying it was *her* fault he had to hit the woman with his crutch. She'd bled on him while he'd loaded her into the back.

He repeatedly reached over from the driver's side and swatted her on the back of the head. "Think you're really smart trying to trip me up," he growled. "That slap earlier was nothing. I haven't even started with you, yet. Would you look at the blood back there? Shit, I think she's hemorrhaging. I wouldn't be surprised if she dies before we even get to the woods. If you'd done what you were supposed to, I might have had time to load her bike in the car. You might have gotten a new bicycle tonight. But, no, too bad for you."

The young woman was still alive. He'd revived her while dragging her toward the darkened woods. Her screams had started out strong, but now they seemed to be weakening.

It wouldn't be much longer.

The nine-year-old dreaded going home. She wished she were older, and knew how this minivan worked. Then she'd just start up the engine, drive away, and never come back. But she had to stay — and endure his punishment later.

She stared out at the blackness beyond the windshield and listened to the screams fading. She thought about how it didn't pay trying to help some people.

That stupid woman had gotten her into a lot of trouble.

Seattle — eleven years later

She pulled over to the side of the tree-lined street and watched Karen Carlisle's Jetta turn into the driveway. Karen may have spotted her in the hallway at the convalescent center, but obviously didn't realize she'd been followed home. In fact, Frank Carlisle's shrink daughter seemed to have no idea that for almost three weeks now, her comings and goings had been carefully monitored.

She knew Karen's routines: when she ate and slept and walked the dog, and what she wore to bed. She'd figured out the housekeeper's schedule, too. She knew when Karen was usually alone and when she was at her most vulnerable. She even knew where they hid the spare house key for emergencies (under a decorative stone in a garden by the back door).

Of course, Karen would wonder about seeing her in the hallway at the rest home today. She might even ask about it. Karen would get the usual wide-eyed, innocent denial, and a very sincere, "I was never there. I don't know what you're talking about."

Actually, today was her fifth visit to that nursing home, observing Karen at work with the patients — and with her dad. The last time, a few days ago, she'd ducked into a room across the hall and spied on Karen saying good-bye to her senile father as he lay in bed. Only moments after Karen had left, she'd snuck into the old man's room. She couldn't resist. He was clueless, totally out of it. His mouth open, he stared at her and blinked.

Just for fun, she'd bent over and kissed his wrinkly forehead — the same way Karen always did. "I'm going to kill your daughter," she'd whispered to him.

Switching off the ignition, she leaned back in the driver's seat. She watched Karen climb out of her car and head toward the house. Despite some neglect, the white stucco held its own among the stately old mansions on the block. As Karen walked up the stairs to the front porch, there was some barking from inside the house. Jessie, the housekeeper, opened the door and let the dog out. His tail wagging, the black cocker spaniel raced up to Karen and poked her leg with his snout. She patted him on the head and scratched him behind the ears. Then he scurried down the steps to take a leak at the trunk of a big elm tree in the front yard.

Jessie stepped outside and said something to Karen. She was a stout, sturdy, grandmotherly woman in her late sixties with cat's-eye glasses and bright red hair that was probably a wig. Jessie didn't usually work on Saturdays. She must have been making up for the fact that she'd only put in a half day on Wednesday.

Watching from inside the car, she rolled down her window.

Jessie was shaking her head at Karen. "Nope, nobody here but us chickens," she heard Jessie say. "I haven't seen hide nor hair of Amelia, and I've been here about twenty minutes."

Karen paused at the front door, muttered something, and then turned to glance over her shoulder. "C'mon, Rufus, let's get in the house." The dog obediently trotted to her.

"How's your dad doing?" Jessie asked.

"Not so hot," Karen said, leading the cocker spaniel inside the house. Then it sounded like she said, "Today wasn't a good day."

Sitting behind the wheel and staring beyond the dirty windshield, she smiled. "Poor thing," she whispered. "Think today was a bad day? Just wait, Karen. Just wait."

In the foyer, Karen took off her coat while Jessie and Rufus headed past the front stairs to the kitchen. The house's first floor still had the original wainscoting woodwork. A few well-scattered, old, worn Oriental rugs covered most of the hardwood floor.

Karen draped her coat and purse over the banister post at the bottom of the stairs, and then followed them into the kitchen. She opened a cookie jar on the counter, and tossed a dog biscuit at Rufus, who caught it in the air with his mouth. Over by the sink, Jessie was polishing a pair of silver candelabras that had belonged to Karen's parents.

Karen sat down at the breakfast table, which had a glass top and a yellow-painted wrought-iron frame and legs. It really belonged on a patio, but had been in the kitchen for decades. The matching wrought-iron chairs had always been uncomfortable, even with seat cushions. Her dad had bought all new white appliances about six years ago, and it brightened up the kitchen. But the ugly old table with the chairs-from-hell remained.

Rufus came over and put his head in her lap. He was nine years old, and had been her dad's main companion most of that time. They'd taken care of each other. At least once a week, she loaded Rufus into the car and drove him to the rest home to see his old buddy. Then she'd walk or wheel her dad outside, and Rufus would go nuts, pawing and poking at her father's leg, licking his hand. The visits with Rufus always cheered up her dad.

She thought about how much freedom her father would lose if they changed his routine and his medication. She replayed in her mind kissing him good-bye about twenty-five minutes ago. It was strange, seeing that young woman who looked so much like Amelia in the hallway, outside her father's door.

"I can't believe Amelia isn't here," Karen muttered. "She was so anxious to see me. I told her to wait."

"Did she say what it was about?" Jessie asked, toiling away on the candelabra.

"Something horrible happened. That's all I know. And that's all I can say without breaking patient-therapist confidentiality."

"Oh, yeah, like I have a direct line to Tom Brokaw. Who am I going to tell?" Jessie grinned at her. "You worry about her more than all your other patients. That Amelia is a sweet girl. The way she counts on you — and looks up to you. Three guesses who she reminds me of."

Karen just nodded. Amelia and Haley were alike in so many other ways, too: the drinking problems, the low self-esteem, and a penchant for blaming themselves for just about everything.

She remembered a discussion she'd once had with Haley, in which the fifteen-year-old blamed herself for her parents' breakup. "Hey, honey," Karen had told her, with a nudge. "If anyone's getting blamed for your parents' breakup, it's me."

That wasn't quite true. When Karen had first met Haley's father four years ago, he'd already separated from his wife. Karen had come to loathe her go-nowhere counseling job at Group Health. Her dad had just started to show early warning signs of something wrong with little episodes of depression and forgetfulness. Karen had recently fired his housekeeper, who had been robbing him blind for months. She'd moved back home temporarily to look after him and take him to his barrage of doctor appointments. As for Karen's love life, it was nonexistent.

It seemed like the only time she had for herself was the hour between returning home from work and cooking dinner for her dad. He was always glued to the TV and *Law and Order,* so she'd change into her sweats, jog to Volunteer Park, then run laps around the reservoir. That section of the park had a sweeping view of downtown Seattle, the Space Needle, and the Olympic Mountains. At sunset, it was gorgeous, and she could almost convince herself that she wasn't so bad off. There were always a few handsome men doing laps, too. Most of them were probably gay, but she still got an occasional, flirtatious smile from a fellow jogger. Hell, something like that could make her night.

And sometimes it could make her stumble and skin her knee. The jogger whose smile had caught her eye and tangled her feet on that warm September evening was about forty years old. He had brown hair that was receding badly, but the rest of him was awfully nice: dark eyes, a swarthy complexion, sexy smile, and a toned, sinewy body.

As soon as she hit the asphalt, Karen felt the searing pain in her knee. She also felt utterly humiliated. The handsome jogger swiveled around and ran to her aid. He kept saying he was sorry he'd distracted her. It was all his fault.

"Oh, no, it's okay," Karen babbled. "I'm fine. I — it really doesn't hurt."

The hell it didn't. But something left over from her tomboy period was putting up a brave, tearless front.

"Jesus, that's gotta smart," he said. "Look, you've got pebbles embedded in there —"

"Really, it's nothing." But then she took a look at all the blood, and suddenly felt a little woozy.

"I have a first-aid kit in my car," she heard him say. "Stay put. I'll be right back."

When he returned, he helped her to a park bench, sat her down, and went to work on her knee. The blood had trickled down to her ankle. He squatted in front of her and meticulously cleaned it up. He also recommended she put some ice on her knee once she got home. Karen tried not to wince while he picked out a few pebbles and applied the Neosporin.

"So, are you a doctor?" she asked, once she got past the pain. "You're really good at this."

"No, I'm an attorney. But I have a thirteen-year-old daughter who thinks she can outrun, out-throw, and out-dare any boy in her class. So I've tended to a lot of scrapes and cuts."

Karen looked for a wedding ring on his hand. There wasn't one.

"Her mother and I have been separated for seven months," he said, apparently reading her mind. But he seemed focused on her knee as he put a large Band-Aid over the wound. "You know, I should take another look at this knee in a couple of nights and see how it's healing. Are you free Saturday night?"

Karen hesitated. His slick yet corny approach took her totally by surprise.

He looked up at her and grinned.

Yes, she thought, *a very sexy smile.*

His name was Kurt Lombard. They had a great first date: dinner at the Pink Door, and a heavy make-out session afterward. Then he didn't call. After eight days, she finally phoned him. She was so relieved and grateful when he asked her out again that she ignored all the signs. Looking back on it, she could see Kurt had immediately established a pattern in their relationship. She'd fallen hard for a ruggedly handsome commitment-phobic charmer. Every time he showed he cared about her, it was intermittent reinforcement. He was like a bad slot machine that paid off just often enough to keep her hooked.

Karen had dated him off and on for three months before working up the nerve to ask how he felt about her. And was he ever planning to divorce his wife? Kurt couldn't even commit to *un*-commit.

When she had patients in unbalanced relationships like this, Karen always advised them to stand up for themselves or get the hell out. But she stuck with Kurt. Eventually, he did divorce his wife, and Karen was relieved he didn't take his new freedom to the limit by dumping her, too. More positive intermittent reinforcement came when he wanted her to meet his daughter, Haley. By then she was fourteen, and out of her tomboy phase. She'd already been arrested once, and rushed to the hospital twice for alcohol poisoning. On their first meeting — dinner at the 5-Spot Café — Kurt had dropped them off in front of the restaurant, and then went to park the car. Standing on the curb in front of the café, Karen found herself alone for the first time with Haley. The oversized army fatigue jacket limply hung on the girl's slouched, emaciated frame. She had a blue streak in her stringy brown hair. And she might have been pretty if not for her perpetual sneer. "So — you're the girlfriend," Haley said.

Playing along, Karen grinned. "And you're the daughter."

"Y'know, my mother's a lot prettier than you," Haley said.

"Yeah? Well, my mother can beat up your mother." Karen shot back.

Staring at her for a moment, Haley twirled a strand of hair around her finger. Finally, she burst out laughing.

Karen realized she had no problem standing up to the daughter — just the dad. She and Haley weren't exactly bosom buddies, but they got along all right. By the time Haley was fifteen, Karen and Kurt were living together in a two-bedroom house in Seattle's Queen Anne district.

Karen's dad was doing better, thanks partly to his new medication, but even more to his new housekeeper, Jessie. She doted on him, but kept him in line, too.

Kurt was a hit with Karen's dad — and with her siblings, Frank and Sheila, when they came to Seattle on vacation with their families. Her friends liked him, too. But when Karen asked Jessie what she thought of Kurt, the housekeeper just smiled cryptically and said, "He's very charming."

"That's it?" Karen asked.

"He's very charming," Jessie repeated.

"But he should pay more attention to the women in his life, namely you and his daughter, the poor thing."

Three weeks after Jessie had made that comment, a terrified Haley confided in Karen that she thought she had syphilis or gonorrhea. Karen made an appointment for her at Group Health, and went with her to the doctor's office. It turned out Haley had a mild yeast infection.

"I won't say anything to your folks about this," Karen told her as they left the office together. "And I'm not going to tell you how stupid it is for someone your age to be having sex —"

"Oops, I think you just did," Haley interjected.

Karen nodded. "Yeah, well, at least be smart enough to take some precautions, okay?"

"Thanks, Karen."

The following weekend, Haley bought her a coffee mug. It had a cartoon of a Garfield-like smiling cat with sunglasses, and said "KAREN is a Cool Cat!" She and Haley had a good laugh over how tacky it was. At first, Karen only used the mug for her morning coffee as a joke when Haley was staying with them. But then she began using it every morning.

Karen became Haley's confidante and surrogate big sister. Haley started to shape up, too, joining a support group to help kick her drinking problem. She was growing into a lovely young woman. But some things she confided in Karen weren't easy to hear: "My mother feels really threatened by you."

"Well, let her know as far as you're concerned she can't be replaced. And if that doesn't work, remind her that she's a lot prettier than I am."

Haley chuckled. "You'll never let me forget about that, will you?"

"Never."

Other things Haley revealed were damn difficult to take. "I was talking to Dad this morning," she told her while trying on dresses in the changing area at a downtown boutique. Karen was helping her pick out a formal for the junior prom. "I asked him if he was *ever* going to marry you, and he got all pissy with me. He said I should mind my own business. So, I told him, if you end up being my stepmother that certainly would be my business, and I'm all for it. But he just got madder and madder." Haley sighed, and nervously wrapped a strand of her hair around her finger. Karen had long ago noticed whenever Haley got perplexed she started playing with her hair like that. "God, he's my father and I love him," she went on. "But he's such an asshole sometimes. Still, you want to marry him, don't you Karen? I mean, you've discussed it with him, right?"

"You know," Karen managed to say after a moment. "I don't think you should wear a long formal to this thing. You'll just look like everyone else. What about a pair of black slacks and a fancy top? I have this sleeveless copper-sequined top at home — and these very sexy black heels. We'll fix your hair so it's up."

"Omigod, that sounds fantastic!" Haley gushed. "I'll look like I'm going to the friggin' Grammys!"

That was exactly how she looked — sleek, sexy, and sophisticated. Kurt couldn't believe it was his little girl going out the door with that awestruck teenage boy in an ill-fitting tuxedo. "It just floors me how she's grown up so fast," Kurt remarked. "In a little over a year, she'll be going off to college."

"And I don't even have a child of my own yet," Karen heard herself say.

But, obviously, he pretended not to hear it.

Lately she'd been watching families and women with babies, and most of those women were younger than her. Not only was her biological clock ticking, there was a race against time with her dad, too. He'd been slipping again; the Alzheimer's was advancing. Maybe it was selfish of her, but she wanted to have a child he could know and hold while he was still somewhat coherent.

"I want to get married, Kurt," she told him. "Is that ever going to happen? Do you see that in our future at all?"

His back to her, he stood at the living room window, watching the limo back out of the driveway. Haley, her date, and a bunch of their friends had hired the car and a chauffeur for the night.

"No," Kurt finally replied. "I don't see it happening."

Karen felt as if someone had just sucker punched her in the stomach. She'd expected him to waffle a bit, and leave her some room for hope. She sank down in a hardback chair, and gripped the armrests. "It's not even a possibility?" she asked.

Still staring out the window, he let out a long sigh. He wouldn't face her. Karen strained to catch his reflection in the darkened glass. "I've been married once and it didn't work out," he explained. "That was enough for me. I don't want to get married

116

again, Karen."

"Well, *this* isn't enough for *me*," she murmured.

He turned and frowned at her. "Jesus, what's gotten into you all of a sudden?"

It wasn't so sudden. Karen knew she should have had this discussion with him three years ago. She was an idiot to wait this long. He'd never really misled her. She'd been lying to herself all this time.

Karen said nothing. She stood up, wandered into their bedroom, and started packing her overnight bag.

She slept at her father's house that night. Within a month, she'd moved out of the Queen Anne house she shared with Kurt. It was almost insulting the way he didn't put up much of a fight. But Haley was devastated. Karen assured her they'd still be friends. Hell, she *needed* friends. After the breakup, Karen had suffered several Kurt Casualties among her acquaintances — mostly other couples who suddenly seemed uncomfortable around her.

She stayed true to her word, and kept in touch with Haley. She felt good about herself with Haley. She'd helped a troubled little teen punkette develop into a sweet and lovely young woman. Karen wanted to rise above the manner of a vindictive ex. So she often had to remind the 17-year-old that talking about her father was verboten.

"You'll have to hear this whether you like it or not," Haley told her, five months after the breakup. They were jogging around the Volunteer Park reservoir together, where Karen had first met Kurt. "Dad's getting married," she said.

Karen stopped abruptly. "What?" she asked, even though she'd heard what Haley had said. A moment passed, and neither of them uttered a word. Karen got her breath back. Small wonder she hadn't tripped and fallen on her face upon hearing the news. To her amazement, she was still standing.

Kurt's fiancée was a 28-year-old Macy's saleswoman named Jennifer. Big surprise, a younger woman.

Haley expressed utter disgust with her father, and claimed his fiancée was a major dipshit. Karen told her they weren't going to talk about it. "When you're near me, you're in a no-Kurt-bashing zone. We don't need to do that here. Our friendship is based on better things."

It was tough sticking to that noble resolve after she'd received one particular e-mail from Kurt. They'd kept their distance since the breakup, and the only contact they'd had with each other had been infrequent e-mails. This one the son of a bitch copied to someone in his office — obviously to show he meant business:

Karen:
Since you've moved out, I've allowed Haley to continue seeing you, because I know your friendship means a lot to her. I think I've been very tolerant about this. Haley told me that she informed you of my marriage plans. So, I'm sure you will understand that I no longer feel your friendship with my daughter is appropriate. This is a somewhat confusing time for Haley, and she has had a few recent setbacks with the drinking. She has also had other problems at school that I won't go into. Suffice it to say, I believe her association with you is creating some inner conflict. Please respect my wishes and give Haley a chance to adapt to the positive changes in her home life with me. Please stop seeing her.
Sincerely,
Kurt

Karen immediately fired off a two-page, single-spaced tirade that began: "Dear Asshole," and went on to tell Kurt what a lousy father he was. She cited several examples.

119

But at the end of the day, Karen didn't send the e-mail. She didn't have it in her to fight with Kurt at that point. Things were getting worse with her dad. He'd become quite paranoid, and a few times the previous week, he'd been so disoriented he hadn't even recognized her or Jessie. He'd slapped poor Rufus on the snout for barking on two occasions, and that was totally unlike him. Karen's brother and sister kept calling long distance for updates on his condition. They wanted her to start looking for nursing homes, and she almost came to blows with them on the subject.

"I know you don't want to give up on him," her brother argued. "But you're being selfish keeping him at home, Karen. He's better off in a full-care facility. It sounds horrible, but for his sake, you'll have to let go."

Karen knew he was right, but she wasn't ready to let go, yet.

And she wasn't ready to abandon Haley either; though she wondered if maybe — just maybe — Kurt was right, too. Even with all her efforts not to badmouth Kurt, her friendship with Haley still threatened the father-daughter relationship. How couldn't it? Perhaps she was being selfish there, too.

Haley phoned her on the sly a few times

over the next two weeks. In each call, she cried hysterically and cursed her father. "How could he do this? He has no right! I can't believe you're going along with him on this."

Karen tried to explain that until she was eighteen, her father, indeed, had every right to slap a moratorium on their friendship. But it was only temporary and, in the meantime, why didn't she give this Jennifer a chance and cut her some slack? And what was this about her drinking again, and some trouble in school?

"C'mon, honey, you shape up, okay?" Karen told her, with a pang in her gut. "And you really need to stop calling me. You'll get us *both* in trouble."

Haley promised to stop calling if they could meet one more time. Karen reluctantly agreed to a dinner together at the Deluxe Bar and Grill, a cozy, trendy burger joint with an old-fashioned bar and a modern gas fireplace. She and Haley sat in a booth. After all those semi-hysterical phone calls, Haley was surprisingly calm and collected — almost at peace with the situation. She explained she wasn't going to plead or argue with her over her dad's decision. And she wasn't going to Kurt-bash either. No, this was about having a nice last dinner together.

"Now, don't make it sound so *final*," Karen said. "We'll be back in touch after you're eighteen, which is in — what — less than a year? By then you'll be in college and making a whole new batch of friends. You'll be fine, Haley. So don't cry in your Cobb salad about it."

Haley just nodded, and gave her a strange, sad smile.

Karen was mostly concerned about her recent setbacks with the drinking, and her problems at school. "I know you're not happy about this, but I understand why your dad thinks it's for the best. Do me a favor, and don't screw up your own life just because you're mad at him. You were doing so well for a while there, honey. Don't mess it up. If you're pissed at your father and want to get even with him, do it some other way. Short sheet his bed, bust up that awful country-and-western CD collection of his, poop in his favorite shoes, I don't care."

Haley rolled her eyes and laughed.

"Just don't ruin your own life to hurt him," Karen whispered. "Promise me you won't."

"I promise." Haley fiddled with a strand of her hair.

"And stop tugging at your hair."

Obediently, she smiled and glanced down at her plate. She played with her fork instead. "Karen, you're not going to forget me, are you?"

Karen reached across the table and took hold of her hand. "How could I? Every morning I have my coffee out of that tacky 'Karen is a Cool Cat' mug you gave me. I couldn't start my day without it."

They hugged good-bye alongside Haley's father's Toyota. Haley offered her a ride, but Karen decided to walk home. It was only a few blocks. She'd been keeping up a brave, everything-will-be-swell front with Haley, and needed time alone to have herself a good cry.

When she got home, she found her dad asleep in front of the TV. Jessie had fixed him fried chicken. Karen washed his dinner dishes, then woke him and got him into his bed. She was about to take a shower when the phone rang. She snatched up the receiver on the second ring, hoping her dad hadn't awoken. "Hello?"

"This is the Seattle Police calling for Karen Carlisle," said the man on the other end of the line.

"Yes, this is Karen." Her grip tightened on the receiver.

"Your name and phone number are listed

in Haley Lombard's wallet as her emergency contact."

Karen had no idea. For a moment, she almost couldn't breathe.

"I'm afraid there's been an accident," he said.

"Where? Is Haley hurt?"

"She went off the freeway overpass at Lakeview and Belmont."

Karen knew that overpass. It curved above Interstate 5, and had a low guardrail along the edge. At one point, the drop was several stories down to the freeway.

"Is she — is she going to be all right?"

"They're taking her body to Harborview Medical Center," he answered grimly. "I'm sorry. Were you her parent or legal guardian?"

Karen closed her eyes. "No," she heard herself answer. "No, I was her friend."

The rest of the night was a blur. She couldn't get hold of Kurt, and there was no answer at Haley's mother's house, not even a machine. Karen didn't want to leave her dad alone; he'd woken up in the middle of the night before, and not known where he was. But she had no choice. All she could do was quietly hurry out the door, and pray he'd sleep until morning.

In the car, she was so frazzled she passed

Twelfth Avenue, probably the quickest way to the hospital. The next possible route, Broadway, was gridlocked. Flustered, she headed downhill to Belmont and the overpass where Haley had had her accident. That overpass eventually led to the highway on-ramp, and once on the interstate she could be at the hospital within two minutes.

But her thinking was muddled. Of course, they were rerouting traffic at the accident site. Cars lined up bumper to bumper as she approached the overpass. A detour sign had been placed at the last turn before the overpass, and a cop waved at her to make a left, where traffic seemed to move at a crawl. Ahead, Karen could see cones lined up, emergency flares sizzling on the concrete, and swirling red strobes from police cars parked at the start of the overpass. She saw something else, too: Kurt's Toyota.

"My God, they made a mistake," she whispered to herself. The cop had told her on the phone that Haley had gone off the overpass, yet there was Kurt's car, all in one piece. The front door was open, and someone shined a flashlight around inside the car. All she could think was *Maybe Haley's okay after all, maybe they got it wrong. . . .*

"Keep moving!" yelled the cop in front of

the detour sign. He waved at her impatiently.

Karen rolled down her window. "The police called me fifteen minutes ago," she said. "They told me to go to Harborview. I'm a friend of Haley Lombard. But I think they made a mistake —"

"Okay, you can go ahead," he grumbled, motioning her forward.

Karen slowly continued down the hill, where the police kept onlookers at bay. She caught another look at Kurt's Toyota. The man inside with the flashlight was inspecting the glove compartment.

"You need to turn your car back around!" another cop screamed at her.

She shook her head and called out the window to him, repeating what she'd told the first patrolman. "I think there was some kind of mistake about the victim's identity." She nodded toward the Toyota. "That's Haley Lombard's father's car over there."

The cop had her pull over to a small lot by a chain-link fence overlooking the freeway. "Lemme get someone to clear this up with you," he grunted.

Karen parked her car and climbed out. For a moment, her legs were unsteady. She kept looking for a mangled section of the overpass's guardrail, some indication that another vehicle had plowed through it and careened down to the freeway. But she didn't see any damage at all. She wandered toward the railing edge and peered over it. About five stories below, on the interstate, a line of emergency flares cordoned off two lanes, and traffic was at a near standstill. Several squad cars, their flashers going, surrounded a smashed-up SUV. A tow truck was backing up toward it. From the skid marks on the pavement, it looked as if the SUV had swerved to avoid hitting something, and then crashed into the concrete divider. The tire markings on the pavement veered in front of a pool of blood. It almost looked black in the night.

Confused, Karen glanced to her right and tapped a young policewoman on the shoulder. "Excuse me. I'm a friend of Haley Lombard's, and they called me. They said she went off the overpass. But her father's car is right there, and I don't see where anyone could have driven off —"

"Haley Lombard, yes," the policewoman said, nodding. She seemed distracted by a voice crackling over the walkie-talkie on her belt. "Hell of a mess down there. An SUV almost hit the body. Thank God no one in the vehicle was seriously injured. Your friend didn't *drive* off the overpass. She *jumped.* It looks like she was drinking. They found a bottle of bourbon in her car. She was DOA at Harborview ten minutes ago. You need to talk to somebody there." She turned away and started barking a bunch of police code numbers on her radio.

Karen couldn't hear what she was saying. She just stood there by the overpass's guardrail, with the wind whipping at her. She was thinking that it all made sense now. She should have seen the signs. Some people about to commit suicide can appear very calm. After a period of torment, they can suddenly seem at peace, because they have come up with a solution for their problems. That had been Haley only two hours ago. She'd taken control of her situation and made up her mind about what to do.

"Karen, you're not going to forget me, are you?"

A loud *beep, beep, beep* from below made her turn toward the guardrail again and gaze down at the freeway. A cleanup truck had backed up toward the dark puddle. Its hoses went on and started to wash the blood away. Pink swirls formed in the water that rippled across the pavement to the highway's shoulder.

Kurt and his ex-wife both blamed Karen.

Haley had lied to them about where she'd been going that night. Kurt pointed out that he'd asked Karen to stop seeing Haley, but she'd met with her anyway, and just look what had happened. She must have said something to Haley during their secret dinner that helped push their girl over the edge.

Karen didn't have it in her to fight with Haley's grieving parents. She didn't go to the funeral. She knew she wasn't welcome.

Just three weeks after the burial, Karen had her first meeting with Amelia Faraday. For a while, Amelia reminded her so much of Haley, it hurt. But since then, she'd gotten to know Amelia, and really couldn't compare her to anyone.

The telephone rang, and Karen jumped up from the breakfast table. She figured it was Amelia again, and grabbed the phone before Jessie even had a chance to wipe off her hands. "Hello?" she said into the phone.

"Is Karen Carlisle there, please?" The man sounded as if he had asthma or something. His breathing wasn't right.

"This is Karen," she said.

"Um, my name's George McMillan. My niece is one of your patients, Amelia Faraday. . . ."

"Is Amelia all right?"

"She isn't with you?" he asked. "I just

spoke with her five minutes ago, and she said she was at your house."

"Well, I'm sorry, Mr. McMillan, but she isn't," she replied. "Amelia called me, too. She indicated there was some kind of emergency. Is everything okay?"

"No, it's not." He cleared his throat, but it still sounded like something was wrong with his breathing. "She — she had this *premonition.* She phoned saying she thought her parents and my wife — that's her aunt —"

"Yes, Amelia has mentioned her."

"Well, see, they went away for the weekend at the family cabin on Lake Wenatchee, and Amelia was convinced they'd all been killed last night." His voice cracked, and Karen realized he was crying. That was why his breathing sounded so strange. "And she — she was right. I talked to someone who lives near the Lake Wenatchee house, and this neighbor, she found the bodies."

"Oh, my God," Karen whispered. She sank down in one of the chairs at the breakfast table. "I'm so sorry. . . ."

Karen heard him trying to stifle the sobs. He explained how he'd spoken to this neighbor — and then the police in Wenatchee. It appeared as if Amelia's father had shot his wife and sister-in-law with a hunting rifle, and then he'd turned the gun on himself.

"My God, Mr. McMillan — George — I'm so sorry," she repeated. "Poor Amelia. You — you said she had a *premonition* about this?"

"Yes, but she doesn't know yet that it's true. I called and tried to persuade her to come over here. But she said she needed to see you. I — I couldn't tell her over the phone what happened . . ."

Karen's front doorbell rang. Rufus started barking and scurried toward the front of the house.

"I think that's her at my door right now," she said into the phone. She turned to the housekeeper. "Jessie? Could you? If that's Amelia, could you please have her wait in my office?"

Jessie nodded, wiped off her hands and started out of the kitchen. "Rufus, knock it off!"

"Mr. McMillan, are you still there?" Karen said into the phone.

"Yes. Would you — would you mind driving Amelia over here? We live in West Seattle. I don't want her to be alone. And it might help my kids if their cousin was here." His voice cracked again. "They're playing outside. They still don't know. My son's eleven, and my daughter — she's only five years old. God, how am I going to tell them their mother's dead?"

Karen's heart ached for him. "I can drive Amelia over," she said finally. "It's no problem, Mr. McMillan. But if I insist on taking her to your house, she's bound to figure out something's wrong. Would you like me to tell her what happened?"

She could hear him sigh on the other end of the line. "Yes. Thank you, Karen. Thank you very much."

When she clicked off the phone, Karen could hear Jessie talking to Amelia: "You sit tight, hon. She'll be with you in a jiff. Rufus, get down!"

Pulling the dog by his collar, Jessie lumbered back into the kitchen and gave her a wary look. "Whew," she whispered. "That poor girl has the fidgets something fierce. She's practically bouncing off the walls in there. I think she's been crying, too."

Karen took hold of her arm. "Jess, do we still have some of Dad's sedatives?"

"You mean those light blue pills that made him a little dopey?"

Karen nodded. "Yes, the diazepam, for anxiety." It was times like this Karen wished she were a psychiatrist rather than just a therapist. Then she could have the proper medications on hand, instead of making do with some secondhand sedatives that were probably beyond their expiration date. "Amelia's going to need something to calm her down. Do we still have those pills?"

Jessie nodded. "On the crap shelf in the linen closet. I've been bugging you to let me clean that out. Good thing you never listen to a word I say. I'll get them." Jessie headed up the back stairs.

Karen went to the refrigerator and grabbed a bottle of water for Amelia. She gave Rufus a stern look. "Stay," she said. Then she took a deep breath and started toward her office at the front of the house.

The room used to be her father's study, and had always been one of Karen's favorite spots in the house. It was very comfy, with a fireplace and built-in bookshelves. But Amelia didn't appear at all comfortable. Dressed in jeans, a black top, and a bulky cardigan, she nervously paced in front of the sofa. Her wavy black hair was a wind-blown mess. Jessie was right. It looked as if she'd been crying.

She rushed to Karen and threw her arms around her. Karen wasn't in the habit of hugging her patients. But she held onto Amelia and gently patted her on the back.

"Where were you?" Karen asked, finally

pulling away a little. "I thought you were going to wait for me here."

Tugging at a strand of hair, Amelia looked down at the floor and shrugged. "Well, I waited for Jessie, like you said to. But after about ten minutes, I got kind of anxious. So I just drove around for a while."

Karen bit her lip. "You, um, you didn't by any chance track me down at the Sandpoint View Convalescent Home? I thought I saw you there about twenty-five minutes ago."

"I have no idea where that even is," Amelia replied, wide-eyed. "What are you talking about?"

Karen shook her head. "Never mind. It's my mistake. Here, I got you some water. Sit down, try to relax."

"I can't sit down," Amelia said, pacing again. "I have a feeling something's happened to my parents."

"I understand," Karen said. "I just got off the phone with your uncle. He called. He was worried about you. He told me that . . ." She hesitated.

Amelia stopped pacing, and turned to stare at her.

Jessie came to the door with the diazepam and handed the bottle to Karen.

"Thanks, Jessie," Karen said. "Could you close the door, please?"

Jessie slid shut the big, bulky pocket door that came out of the wall. Karen shook two pills into her hand. "Amelia, I want you to take these. They're like Valium. They'll chill you out a little."

But Amelia didn't move. She just kept staring at Karen. Tears welled in her eyes. "You want me to take a sedative? What did Uncle George tell you?"

"Take the pills, Amelia."

"Oh, my God," she said, wincing. A shaky hand went over her mouth. She sank down on the sofa. "Then it's true. Aunt Ina . . . my Mom and Dad . . . they're all dead, aren't they?"

Karen swallowed hard and nodded. "I'm so sorry. . . ."

CHAPTER SIX

No one said anything in the car while Karen drove across the West Seattle Bridge toward Amelia's uncle's house. Amelia sat on the passenger side, pensively gazing out her window. Jessie was in back with a grocery bag full of food from Karen's fridge. She'd insisted on fixing dinner for Amelia's uncle and his family.

A bit taken aback by the idea, Karen had wondered out loud if they'd be intruding on the family's grief.

"Nonsense, they gotta eat, don't they?" Jessie had replied while loading up the grocery bag. "You have all the fixings here for chicken tetrazzini — chicken, noodles, Parmesan cheese, sour cream. I'll whip up the casserole, stick it in the oven, and then you and I can beat a path out of there if it looks like we're wearing out our welcome."

Amelia had been inconsolable, sobbing hysterically for twenty minutes until the diazepam had kicked in. She finally slumped back on Karen's sofa. "I should go see Uncle George," she murmured, wiping her eyes. "Poor Jody and Steph . . ."

Sitting beside her on the couch, Karen handed her another Kleenex. "Your uncle asked me to drive you over. I said I'd be glad to."

Amelia nodded. "Thanks."

Biting her lip, Karen studied her for a moment. "You — you still haven't asked how it happened."

Silent, Amelia stared down at the wadded-up Kleenex in her hand.

"Your Uncle George said you had some kind of premonition."

Amelia shrugged helplessly. "It was just a feeling — an awful, awful feeling that something was wrong."

Karen's heart was breaking for her. "Honey, there's no easy way to tell you this. They haven't confirmed it. But it's possible your dad shot your mom and your aunt, and then he killed himself. They don't know for sure yet."

Amelia said nothing. She merely gave out an exhausted sigh, and closed her eyes.

Karen stroked her arm. "I'm so sorry," she whispered.

While they'd gotten ready to leave, Amelia

had just sat quietly on the sofa. Her voice hadn't even cracked when she'd left Shane a phone message, explaining she was spending the night at her uncle's house. She'd told him he could pick up his car at Karen's. She'd said nothing about her parents' deaths. "I'll call you later tonight," she'd finished up listlessly.

Once they'd climbed inside Karen's Jetta, Amelia had suggested they take Highway 99 to the West Seattle Bridge. But after that, she hadn't said anything else.

Karen took her eyes off the road for a moment to look at her now. She was still staring out at the Seattle waterfront and skyline. There was a tiny, sad smile on her face.

"How are you doing, Amelia?" she asked.

She kept gazing out the window at the view from the bridge. "I was thinking about all the trips we took here to Aunt Ina and Uncle George's house — the Christmases, Thanksgivings, and birthdays. It's a long drive down from Bellingham, almost two hours." She traced a horizontal line on the window with her finger. "This bridge was always the landmark, the sign we were almost there. I remember when we were kids, Collin and I used to get so excited crossing this bridge. We loved going to Ina and George's." She let out a little laugh.

"Last Thanksgiving on our way here, I noticed Collin had way too much product in his hair. He had his window open, but his hair didn't budge an inch. I could have broken off a piece of it. I remember teasing him, and Mom and Dad were laughing. Collin's face got red and he started cracking up too. He had the funniest laugh. You should have heard it. . . ."

Still staring out the window, she said nothing for a moment. Then the smile ran away from her face. "That was the last time I drove here with my family. I can't believe they're all gone now. I can't believe I actually could have . . ." She trailed off and shook her head.

From the backseat, Jessie leaned forward and patted Amelia on the shoulder.

Karen glanced at her on the passenger side. Amelia had her head down. She absently twirled a strand of her hair around her finger — the same nervous tic Haley had had.

Karen remembered Amelia doing that during their very first session.

Someone from Student Health Services at the University of Washington had referred the 19-year-old to Karen. Karen didn't have much information on her potential new client, except that her track record with therapists hadn't been too marvelous. She'd been having problems with alcohol and joined this campus group, Booze Busters. That had worked for a while, but she'd fallen off the wagon when her kid brother had drowned three weeks before.

When Karen answered her door for their first session that warm Friday afternoon, she was surprised at how beautiful Amelia was. The soft-spoken, polite girl had wavy black hair and blue eyes. She wore a pink oxford-cloth shirt, khaki shorts, and sandals. She said, "Yes, thank you," to a bottle of water, and sat at one end of the sofa in Karen's study. "So — what do you know about me?" she asked.

Karen settled in her easy chair with a notebook and pen. "Not very much, just what they told me at the U's Student Health Services. Do you know anything about *me?*"

"Not very much," Amelia echoed her, a tiny smile flickering on her face. "But I Googled you. Under 'Karen Carlisle, Counselor, Seattle,' there were a few links. I found out that you're thirty-six years old. You graduated with honors from UCLA. You have a master's in Social Work from the U, and you were a counselor at Group Health for five years before you started counseling on your own. Your name kept coming up in articles about that girl who got killed last month, Haley Something. Was she a client of yours?"

"She was a friend," Karen answered carefully. "But we're not here to talk about her."

"I guess you're right. This is my hour." Amelia sipped her water. "Well, I suppose you know I've been through a lot of therapists. I'm like a one-session wonder with them."

Karen shifted a bit in her chair. "Why is that?"

Amelia shrugged. "They were all dorks."

"Dorks," Karen repeated.

Amelia nodded. "For example, my Aunt Ina recommended this Dr. Racine, absolutely raved about her. And she turned out to be awful. The whole time I was talking to her, she sat there and stroked this ugly cat in her lap. I don't think she was even listening. Every once in a while, she just said something like, 'You own that,' or 'That's valid.' I mean, spare me."

"Okay, so that's one crummy therapist," Karen said. "What about the others?"

Amelia rolled her eyes. "Well, there was this hippie, who seemed very promising until the end of our first session, when he gave me a homework assignment. He wanted me to go home, get some magazines,

141

and clip out pictures and words that made me feel happy — and pictures and words that made me sad. And then I was supposed to make two posters: a happy collage and a sad collage. So I went home, got some magazines, and found this picture of a little girl waving at someone from a car window. I think it was an auto insurance ad or something. I clipped that out, and cut out the word Good-bye. Then I made a little poster of that and mailed it to him."

Karen nodded. She was trying to figure out this young woman, who had come across as so vulnerable and sweet when they'd met just ten minutes ago. But she had a smartass streak, too. Karen wondered just how much of what Amelia said was true.

"Then there was this Arab guy — not that it makes any difference. I just couldn't understand him half the time because his English was terrible. He tried to hypnotize me, and kept screaming at me in his thick accent that I was *reseesting.* And I wasn't, I swear. Honest to God, I was trying to be a good subject."

"Why was he hypnotizing you?"

Amelia sipped her water. She brushed a piece of lint off the sofa arm. Her focus seemed intent on that. "He was trying to get me to remember stuff about my childhood, before the Faradays adopted me. Didn't Student Health Services tell you that I was adopted when I was four?"

Karen shook her head. She made a quick note: *Adopted @ 4 yrs old.* "Do you know what happened to your biological parents?" she asked.

"Nope. One of my first therapists was all hot on finding out about them. So my dad tried to get in touch with the adoption agency in Spokane. Turned out the place burned down after the Faradays adopted me. All their records went up in smoke. My folks thought about hiring a private detective to look into it further. I'm sure it couldn't be too tough tracking down state or county records. I mean, the information's there, somewhere. Am I right?"

"I suppose," Karen allowed. "So did they hire a private detective?"

"Nope. They dropped the idea when I dropped the therapist." She cocked her head to one side and squinted at Karen. "I have a feeling my folks would rather I not know about my biological parents."

"If that's true, it's certainly understandable," Karen said. "How do you feel? Do you want to know more about your birth parents?"

Amelia started to fiddle with her hair, and

wrapped a strand around her finger. "I guess I'm curious."

Karen stared at her, and remembered Haley. She felt a little pang in her heart. "Well, that's normal enough," she said, smiling. "So, Amelia, what do you hope to get out of these sessions with me?"

"Well, I'd like to have more control in my life. I'm tired of being so screwed up."

"In what way do you feel screwed up?"

"I drink. I have blackouts. I don't remember doing certain things."

"What kind of things?" Karen asked.

"For example, I started seeing this really sweet guy, Shane, about two months ago. Well, one afternoon last week, he saw me at a stoplight in the University District in a beat-up Cadillac with some goony-looking urban-grunge type. He said I was all over this guy." Amelia shook her head. "I swear to God, I didn't remember any of it. But after Shane described the guy and his car to me, I had this vague impression that it really happened. I can't help thinking I might have had sex with this other guy. I went and got tested just to make sure I didn't pick up any STDs from this — this *stranger.*"

"So how did the tests turn out?" Karen asked with concern.

"Negative — all around. I begged Shane

144

to forgive me, and he did, thank God. He knows I didn't do it *consciously*." She gave a pitiful shrug. "Anyway, see what I mean about being screwed up and not having any control?"

With a sigh, Karen leaned back in her chair. "Well, you know, Amelia, I don't mean to preach at you. But blackouts, memory loss, and erratic behavior generally come with the territory when people drink excessively."

"I wasn't drinking that afternoon. I was napping all day at a friend's house — at least I *thought* I was napping."

"Were you sick?"

"No. Hungover," she murmured. Her eyes wrestled with Karen's for a moment. "Listen, I was having blackouts when I was in Booze Busters and totally off the sauce. So it's not just connected to the drinking. I've always had this problem with — with *lost time,* ever since I was a kid. I was pretty screwed up back then, too, having nightmares all the time, along with these pains. My mom used to call them phantom pains. But they were real to me, they hurt like hell. I remember one in particular when I was six. I was playing in the backyard, by our dock, and out of nowhere, I suddenly got this terrible burning sensation on the back of my wrist. I let out such a shriek. I swear to God, it felt like someone was putting out a lit cigar on me. Mom thought a wasp might have stung me or something. But there was no sign of anything wrong. Still, it hurt like hell for days afterward.

"That's why I started drinking on the sly in early high school. It numbed these weird pains. And after a few drinks, I'd drag myself to bed and pass out. And I didn't have to lie there for an eternity with my usual tossing, turning, and worrying about the nightmares. Hell, for a long time, drinking was my *salvation.*"

"So — do you think you're better off with an alcohol dependency?" Karen asked.

Amelia shook her head. "I'm not defending my drinking. I'm just saying that I was having these problems a long time before I tipped back my first shot of Jack Daniel's."

"Do you still get these pains?" Karen asked.

"No, thank God. They stopped around the time I was sixteen." Amelia sighed. "Anyway, that's why some of the other therapists wanted to explore my early childhood. I mean, something must have happened to me early on to make me this screwed up, right?"

Karen smiled. "Do us both a favor and

stop referring to yourself as screwed up, okay?"

Amelia smiled back at her. "Okay."

"Can you remember anything from that time before the Faradays adopted you?"

She started to peel at the label on the water bottle. "Just fragments. I remember one night, sitting alone in a car, in the front seat. I was cold — and tired. The car was parked by this forest. It was dark all around me, and I could hear screams. I remember thinking, 'When the screaming stops, then we can go home.' "

Karen stared at her. She didn't write anything down. "Do you know who was screaming? By any chance, did you recognize the voice?"

Amelia shrugged. "Some woman, I don't know."

"Were you frightened?"

"No, I just remember wanting to go home. That's it. There's nothing else to it. Like I said, it's just fragments of memory."

"Do you recall who took you home?" Karen asked.

Amelia shook her head.

"I'm just trying to piece this together, Amelia," Karen explained. "Earlier you said, 'When the screaming stops, then we can go home.' Who's 'we'?"

"I told you, I don't remember," she replied, a bit edgy.

"Okay," Karen nodded, reading her discomfort. "Let's move on. Is there anything else from your early childhood you'd like to tell me about? Did you have any friends or playmates?"

Amelia took a moment to answer, and Karen quickly jotted in her notes: "Young A in car alone @ nite — screams outside — go home when screaming stops."

"I remember there was a little playhouse in a neighbor's yard. I think it was a toolshed, but he'd fixed it up like a playhouse with a small, red, plastic table and chair inside. I have this vague recollection of eating cookies at that little table."

"Tell me about this neighbor. He sounds nice."

She nodded. "He was Native American. I liked him, but I don't think I was supposed to be around him. He had beautiful, long black hair almost down to his shoulders. I couldn't tell you how old he was. Everyone over twelve at that time seemed like an adult to me. He wore a denim jacket. I wish I could remember his name, but I can't." She sighed. "When that one therapist tried to hypnotize me, that's what I was hoping for most of all — to remember the name of that nice neighbor man."

"Have *any* names from that time stuck with you?" Karen asked.

Amelia frowned. "Unca-dween. I'm not sure if it was a person or a place. It could have been a nickname. I know it wasn't my Native American friend, because when I think about Unca-dween, it doesn't make me happy."

Karen scribbled down the name, not quite sure of the spelling. "Any other fragments you might remember?"

Amelia took a swig from the water bottle. "Well, I have a feeling I might have been attacked or molested somewhere along the line. The other therapists all said I was repressing something. But I have this memory of being in my underpants and standing by a tub — I think it was in the bathroom at home. My mother was shaking me and asking me over and over again, 'Did he touch you down there?' I sort of knew what she meant. But she seemed so angry and upset that I pretended *not* to know. I just cried and said I was sorry. I don't know why I was apologizing. I guess I was just scared."

"But the incident she was questioning you about —"

"I don't remember it at all," Amelia said,

shaking her head. "And I have only this vague impression of what my biological mother looked like. She had long, wavy black hair. I remember this one blouse of hers — white with a pattern of gold pocket watches and chains. I thought it was just gorgeous."

"Do you have any memories of your father?" Karen asked.

"None," Amelia answered quickly.

"You mentioned your mother talking to you in the bathroom. Do you remember any other room in the house?"

"I think there was a bomb shelter in the basement." Amelia fiddled with her hair for a moment. "It could have been someone else's house, maybe when I was older. But I remember standing in the basement just outside this big, thick door. I was talking to someone inside the little room. It could have been part of a dream for all I know. But the memory's there.

"The only other thing that stands out about that time was I used to talk to myself in the mirror a lot. I don't think I had many playmates my age, because all I remember is being alone and talking in the mirror." She let out a little laugh. "So what do you make of that? Early signs of a split personality?"

Karen laughed. "Boy, you *have* been to a lot of therapists, haven't you? But let me do the analysis, okay?"

Amelia had started them down memory lane, so Karen let her continue. She asked if she recalled spending time in any foster homes before the Faradays adopted her. In so many cases with adopted children, there were horror stories involving foster parents. But Amelia had no such memories. "I think they were all pretty nice. I didn't stay with anyone for very long. I have a feeling I was on the market for only a short while before the Faradays picked me up. My poor parents, they probably thought they were getting this great deal, because I was a pretty little girl. What a letdown it must have been to find out I was damaged goods."

"Why do you feel that way, Amelia?" Karen asked.

Amelia shrugged.

"Have your folks ever said or done anything to make you feel that way?"

Amelia smiled and shook her head. "No, from the very start, they made me feel loved. . . ." She described going for a walk with her potential new mother on her first day with the Faradays; her first impressions of a playground and a Baskin-Robbins 31 Flavors ice cream parlor not far from their house. She remembered some time later, after the adoption was official, when she learned she would soon have a baby brother or sister to play with. She had her first sleep-over — at her Aunt Ina's apartment — the night Collin was born.

"Is this — the brother who died recently?" Karen asked hesitantly.

Amelia nodded.

"Do you have any other brothers or sisters?"

"No," she muttered. Then she cleared her throat. "It was just Collin and me."

"I'm sorry," Karen said. "Were you . . . very close to him?"

She nodded again. Amelia had tears brimming in her eyes, yet she was stone-faced. There was a box of Kleenex right beside her on the end table, but she didn't reach for one.

"I was told he died in a drowning accident. Is that right?"

"No, that's not right," she whispered, staring at Karen.

She was almost expressionless, yet a single tear slid down her cheek. "My brother's death wasn't an accident. I know it wasn't."

"How can you be so sure?"

Amelia quickly wiped away that one tear. "Because I killed him."

Karen remembered the silence in her study after Amelia had made that statement. It had lasted only a few seconds, but seemed longer, like the silence in the car now, as they reached the West Seattle side of the bridge.

"Stay on this road for a while," Amelia said tonelessly. "The turnoff for my uncle's house is after we pass California Avenue. I'll tell you when it's coming up."

Karen took her eyes off the road for a moment, and looked at her.

Her head tipped against the window, Amelia stared straight ahead with the same stone-faced expression she'd had after telling Karen that she'd killed her brother. And once again, there were tears locked in her eyes.

CHAPTER SEVEN

Amelia's Uncle George answered the door with his 5-year-old daughter in his arms.

Karen hadn't expected him to be so handsome. He wore jeans and a long-sleeved white T-shirt that showed off his lean, athletic physique. He had a strong jaw with a slight five o'clock shadow, and wavy black hair that was ceding to gray. Though his green eyes were still red from crying, there was a certain quiet strength to him.

Karen watched him set down the little girl so he could hug Amelia. The child then wrapped herself around his leg, and pressed her face against his hip. George held on to Amelia for a few moments, whispering in her ear.

"Thanks, Uncle George," she said, sniffling. She turned and nodded toward Karen and Jessie. "This is my therapist — and she's also my friend —"

"Hi, I'm Karen," she said, stepping in

from the doorway to shake his hand. "I'm so sorry for your loss." She introduced him to Jessie, who was carrying the bag full of food. "Jessie figured you and the children could use a home-cooked dinner tonight —"

"Just point us to the kitchen," Jessie announced. "Oh, never mind, I see it — straight ahead." And she started off in that direction.

Karen took off her coat, but held on to it. "If we're at all in the way, please, just let us know," she told George.

"No, you're not," he said. "You're a lifesaver, Karen."

Amelia bent down and pried Stephanie off George's leg. The child clung to her now. Amelia looked so forlorn as she rocked Stephanie. "I'm sorry," she whispered tearfully. "I'm so sorry, Steffie. . . ."

"Why are you sorry?" the child asked. "You didn't do anything wrong."

Amelia winced, and then she seemed to hug her young cousin even tighter.

Watching them, Karen felt so horrible for Amelia and everyone in this house.

George collected his daughter from her. "Amelia, sweetie, do you think you could talk to Jody?" he asked. "He won't come out of his room. I'm really worried about him. Maybe he'll talk to you."

Wiping her eyes, Amelia nodded, and then started through the living room toward a back hallway.

"Jody's my son," George whispered to Karen. He stroked his daughter's hair. They trailed after Amelia. "Five minutes after I told him the news about his mom, Jody ducked into his room and shut the door."

In the hallway, they stayed back and watched Amelia knock on the bedroom door.

"He did the exact same thing a few months ago when his cousin died," George explained. "Jody just worshiped Collin. He was holed up in his room for two whole days. I thought he'd miss the funeral. My wife had to leave his meals outside the door and even then, he hardly ate a thing. He only came out to go to the bathroom." George's voice cracked a little. "God, I don't know what to do. It's such an awful helpless feeling to know your child's hurting. . . ."

Karen felt the same way watching Amelia. She wished there was something she could do to make the pain go away.

Amelia knocked on Jody's door again and called to her cousin, but he didn't answer. "Jody? Please let me in," she called. "I know how you feel, believe me. . . ."

"I'm sorry!" he replied in a strained, raspy voice. "I gotta be alone right now, Amelia. Could you go away, please?"

Her head down, Amelia slinked away from his door. She looked at her uncle, and shrugged hopelessly. "Sorry, Uncle George," she murmured. "Guess I'm just useless. I — I'm so tired. Would it be okay if I went to lie down for a while?"

He nodded, and kissed her forehead. "Sure, sweetie, your bed's all made down there."

Amelia gently patted Stephanie on the back, then wandered through the living room and foyer to a set of stairs leading to a lower level. Looking over her shoulder, she glanced at Karen, and then started down the steps.

"Do you think maybe you could talk to him?"

Karen turned at George and blinked. "You want *me* to talk to your son?"

He shrugged. "Well, you're a therapist. Maybe you'd have a better idea about the right thing to say. . . ."

"You know, I think we should just respect Jody's need to be alone," she whispered, touching his arm, "For a while, at least. If this is how he grieved for his cousin, then

157

it's what he knows. That's how he got through it last time. Why don't we give him until dinner's ready, and try again? Okay?"

He stared at her for a moment, then nodded. "I think you're a very smart lady," he said. "Thanks, Karen."

She smiled at him. "Well, um, I'll go down and check on Amelia."

"Take a right at the bottom of the stairs. The guest room's the first door on your left."

Downstairs, Karen paused in the large recreation room. It had a linoleum floor and high windows that didn't let in much sunlight. There was a big-screen TV, a sectional sofa, and someone's treadmill. Stashed in one corner were a bunch of toys, including a dollhouse. Karen draped her coat over a chair. She gazed at the collection of framed family photos on the wall. She figured the stylish, attractive redhead in the pictures was George's murdered wife. There were also a few photos of Amelia with her family. Karen had been hearing about the Faradays for months, but this was her first actual look at them. She could see a resemblance between the sisters, Jenna and Ina. Studying the pictures of Mark Faraday, she wondered how that pleasant-looking, slightly dumpy man could have shot those two women and then himself. It was hard to comprehend that they were all dead now. In one night, Amelia had lost nearly all of her family — and in such a violent, heinous way.

There were photos of Collin Faraday, too. From the way Amelia talked about her dead brother, Karen had expected him to have been this stunningly handsome, golden-haired teenager. Instead, he just seemed like a normal, nice-looking kid with a goofy smile.

"My brother's death wasn't an accident. I know it wasn't," Amelia had told her during their first session. "Because I killed him."

Karen remembered staring at her, and wondering exactly what she'd meant.

"I promised myself I wouldn't mention anything about it," Amelia had said, squirming on Karen's sofa. "It's too soon to drop a bombshell like that on you. And now the session's almost over. Jesus. Please, tell me you'll see me again, Karen. I trust you, and I can't keep this to myself any longer. Please, don't send me away —"

"It's okay, I'm listening," Karen had said calmly. "We've got time." She wasn't one of those clock-watching therapists. If a patient was in the middle of something important, she never cut them off because of time. In this instance, she luckily hadn't scheduled any other sessions that afternoon, so Karen could go on for another hour or so if it meant understanding Amelia Faraday better. Already, she wanted to help and protect this girl.

"What do you mean, *you killed him?*" Karen asked as gently as possible. "Can you talk about it?"

Amelia nodded. "I was at a Booze Busters retreat in Port Townsend," she replied, sniffling. "Six of us took an RV there for the weekend and camped out. But I had this *premonition* about Collin the whole weekend, all these feelings of hatred for him that I can't explain. I kept thinking about how I would kill him, and it was crazy. I didn't want that to happen. I couldn't have meant it. I didn't even want to think about it. I loved my brother. He was the sweetest guy. . . ." She started sobbing again. "I'm sorry."

"Take your time."

Amelia wiped her eyes and took a deep breath. "I must have blacked out, because all I have are fragments of what happened."

Fragments again, Karen thought. She scribbled the word down in her notes.

"I was standing on the dock in our backyard with Collin," Amelia explained. "Our house is up in Bellingham — on Lake What-com. I hit him with a board or something — a piece of plank, I think. He just — just looked at me, stunned, and — and an awful gash started to open up on his forehead. He let out this garbled, frail cry. . . ." Wincing, she shook her head. "God, it was this weird, warble-type of sound, almost inhuman. And then he toppled off the dock into the water.

"I don't remember anything else. It's like I lost nearly everything from that afternoon, because the next thing I knew, I was waking up from a nap in the RV in Port Townsend — and it was dinnertime. But I had those images in my head. It's how come I knew about Collin before anyone else. I tried to call my folks and tell them something had happened, but they were spending the weekend at their cabin, and the cell phone service is lousy out there —"

"There was no one else staying with Collin?" Karen asked.

Amelia shook her head. "He was alone in the house for the weekend. Before my folks left, I teased him about how he'd be raiding the booze cabinet, watching porn, and having a big party while they were gone. He had a friend coming over that afternoon. He's the one who found him. When Collin didn't answer the door, his buddy went around to the back and saw him floating by the dock. His sleeve had gotten caught on something. They figured he'd had too much to drink, then fallen off the dock, and hit his head on some pilings. Turned out he had alcohol in his system. And maybe that's true, but he didn't die the way they think."

Karen squinted at her. "Have you talked to anyone about this?"

Amelia sighed. "Just my Aunt Ina. She said I was crazy with grief, and that I shouldn't repeat it to anyone. It would just upset people even more."

"You said you were with people from Booze Busters that weekend," Karen pointed out. "How did you manage to break away from the camp, then drive to Bellingham and back without them noticing? It's at least a hundred miles and a ferry ride each way. You'd have been gone the entire afternoon."

Amelia seemed to shrink into the corner of Karen's sofa. She rubbed her forehead. "I don't know how I got there. But I remember what happened. And a neighbor saw me there, too. The police determined Collin must have died around two or three o'clock that Saturday afternoon. Our neighbor, Mrs. Ormsby, said she saw me hosing down our dock around that time. But because I was supposed to be gone the whole weekend, no one really believed her. She's an old woman. They figured she was senile or just wanted some attention. Mrs. Ormsby later said she might have been mistaken. But I don't think she was."

Karen leaned forward in her seat. "But she must have been wrong, Amelia. Don't you see? Your friends would have noticed if you'd left the campsite —"

"I know, I know," she cried. Her whole body was shaking. "But I have these — these *pieces of memory* that tell me I killed him. When I'm alone in bed at night, I can still hear him making that strange, horrible sound after I hit him with the plank. I still hear Collin dying."

Karen let her cry it out. "There are a lot of explanations for what you were feeling — for these sensory *fragments,*" she said finally. "It doesn't mean you killed your brother, Amelia. Your sudden rage toward him, that's not entirely uncommon. I've heard many stories from people who suddenly, for no good reason, became irritable or distant with a loved one — only to lose them within a few days of this inexplicable anger. Even when the death is unexpected, our extrasensory perception can sometimes kick in and start to protect us from the impending loss."

163

Curled up in the corner of the sofa, Amelia gave her a slightly skeptical look. But at least she'd stopped crying.

"You said that you and Collin were close," Karen went on. "Often with family members and loved ones, we can sense when something is wrong — even if that loved one is over a hundred miles away. We can still pick up a frequency that there's trouble. Maybe you just tapped into Collin's frequency. Maybe you have a bit of ESP."

"Do you really believe that?" Amelia murmured, still eyeing her dubiously.

"Well, it makes a lot more sense than the notion that you traveled over two hundred miles without ever really leaving your campsite in Port Townsend. Doesn't it?"

Amelia sighed and then reached for her bottle of water.

"I've just met you, Amelia," she continued. "But you don't seem like a murderer to me. And what would your motive be, anyway? You loved your brother. As for that neighbor woman who saw you, why do you still believe her even after she recanted what she said? No one else believed her, but *you* did. Why do you want to take the blame?"

Karen remembered going on like that for a few more minutes, until Amelia had started to calm down. She'd made her promise to go back to Booze Busters, and they'd agreed to meet twice a week.

That had been four months ago. Karen didn't need to hear bits of a flashback in which Amelia's biological mother asked if someone had touched her "down there" to presume she'd been abused in some way as a young child. All the classic attributions of child abuse were there in the 19-year-old: her low self-esteem, nightmares, flashbacks, lost time, and her assuming guilt for just about everything.

A perfect example of this was Amelia's episode with her boyfriend, Shane, and how quickly Amelia had assumed she'd done something wrong when he said he'd seen her in that car with another man. Amelia had gone and gotten herself tested, because she'd automatically figured herself guilty of infidelity. It never seemed to have occurred to her that Shane might have been mistaken.

There were a lot of problems they worked on over the next four months. And in that time, Karen felt a special bond forming with this young woman who depended on her so much. She was more like Amelia's big sister than her therapist.

Amelia had kept her promise and went back to Booze Busters. And though things still got a little rocky with Shane from time to time, they continued to see each other. Her grades were improving at school. Mark and Jenna Faraday had both e-mailed Karen to tell her what a wonderful job she'd been doing with Amelia. *Her whole outlook has improved 100 percent since she started seeing you,* Jenna Faraday had written.

Karen e-mailed back and thanked them. She'd been tempted to ask the Faradays to reconsider hiring a private detective to look into what had happened to Amelia's biological parents. But she'd left that up to Amelia instead. Amelia was nineteen, and old enough to discuss it with her parents herself. Unfortunately, for the last two months, Amelia had been procrastinating. She admitted she was afraid. "It's not so much I'm worried about having been abused or anything like that," she'd said. "I'm just scared that I might have done something really, really horrible."

"Well, you were only four, Amelia," Karen had replied. "You couldn't have done anything *that* awful. Except for Damien in *The Omen,* how many totally evil four-year-olds do you know? We need to explore this time period in your life."

Amelia's problems couldn't be completely treated until they knew what had happened to her as a child.

Now Karen stared at a framed photo of Jenna and Mark Faraday. They stood on a dock in sporty summer clothes with their arms around each other. The beautiful lake glistened in the background. Karen wondered if it was the same spot where their son had been killed. If so, the photo certainly must have been taken before that tragedy, at a happier time. How could they have known what would occur there? And just a few months later, they would be dead, too.

With a long sigh, Karen started toward the first door on the left. According to George's directions, it was the guest room. The door was closed. Karen was about to knock, but hesitated. She heard Amelia murmuring something. Karen couldn't tell if she was awake — or talking in her sleep.

"No," Amelia said in a hushed tone. "You really don't want that to happen. You don't mean it. You mustn't even think that."

"Yes, well, thank you," George said into the cordless phone. He sat at the breakfast table with Stephanie in his lap. "I'll be here — waiting. Good-bye."

Dazed, he clicked off the phone. "That was the police," he said to Jessie.

Hovering over the stove with a fork in her

hand, she gave him an expectant look.

"They're coming over to ask me some questions. Could I ask you or Karen to stick around and keep an eye on the kids until the cops leave? They'll probably want to talk to Amelia, too. I figure my study's the best place." He glanced down at Stephanie and resituated her in his lap.

Jessie nodded. "No sweat. I can stay here as long as you need me."

He reached back for his wallet. "I'd like to pay you something for all your —"

"Your money's no good here tonight, no sir," Jessie said. "If you need someone to cook, clean, and babysit after today, I'll gladly take your dough. But tonight, you put that wallet away."

Following her instructions, George worked up a smile. "I don't know you very well, Jessie. But I have a feeling you're a gem."

She grinned at him, and then her gaze shifted to Stephanie. "Hey, sweetheart, could you help me fix dinner?"

Warily staring back at her, Stephanie shifted in his lap.

"Oh, c'mon, what do you say? Help me out. Stir the sauce for me, okay?"

" 'Kay," Stephanie murmured, scooting off her father's lap.

Jessie pulled out one of the chairs from

the breakfast table and put a bowl full of the sauce mixture on it. She gave Stephanie a plastic spoon. George watched his daughter, with a determined look on her face, stirring the concoction.

He felt a tightness in his throat. George told himself he wasn't going to break down in front of her, not when she'd just stopped crying herself.

He thought about the police, now on their way. They'd have all sorts of questions about the Faradays' personal problems, their deep, dirty secrets. They'd want to know what had driven Mark Faraday to snap and do such violent, horrific things.

George would have to tell them how Mark and Jenna's marriage had suffered in the wake of Collin's death. Still, he'd never imagined his brother-in-law as the type of man who could harm anyone intentionally. Then again, not too long ago, he'd never imagined Mark as the type of man who would sleep with his wife's sister, either.

Should he admit that to the police? God, he didn't want to go into that with them. Still, he wondered if Ina and Mark's indiscretion had anything to do with what had happened last night. George couldn't begin to guess what had been going through Mark's head when he'd picked up that gun and started shooting.

The three of them were dead. Couldn't people just leave them alone?

No. The media coverage would be crazy. What a scoop: the *love triangle* behind the bloody murders. The scandal might blow over by the time Stephanie was old enough to understand what people were gossiping about. But poor Jody — all his friends would know his mother had screwed his uncle just two months before the guy shot her, his wife, and then himself.

Part of him was so mad at Ina right now for doing this to her family and herself. The irony was she'd always been so concerned with keeping up appearances and impressing people. How would Ina have felt if she knew her sad little affair would become public knowledge?

Maybe he could strike a deal with the police to leave the more delicate matters out of the newspapers. It was worth a try. He really didn't have much of a choice.

He thought about Amelia, napping downstairs. Telling the police about Ina and Mark meant telling Amelia, too. And God only knew how that already fragile girl would take it.

"Am I doing good, Daddy?" Stephanie asked, looking up from her work.

"Oh, you're doing great, sweetie," he said.

She went back to stirring the cream of chicken soup and sour cream concoction. With tears in his eyes, George leaned over and kissed the top of her head.

"Amelia, are you awake?" Karen whispered. Opening the door, she peeked into the dimly lit guest room.

Amelia was lying on one of the twin beds. The pale-green paisley quilts matched the material for the drapes, which were closed. The place looked like something out of a Pottery Barn catalogue. The décor — with all the carefully chosen accents — had that pleasant, slightly generic ambiance. There were two framed Robert Capra posters on the walls — black-and-white Paris scenes.

Stirring, Amelia sat up and squinted at Karen. "Oh, hi."

"Were you on your cell just now?" she asked. "I heard you whispering to someone."

"I — um, must have been talking in my sleep," she said, shrugging.

Karen closed the door behind her, then sat down on the bed across from Amelia. She reached for the lamp on the nightstand between them.

"No, don't, please," Amelia said.

So they sat in the darkness for a few moments. Karen heard muffled sobbing, and looked up toward a vent in the ceiling.

"That's coming from Jody's room," Amelia explained.

Karen listened for another moment, and then sighed. "You're not feeling in any way responsible for what happened at the cabin last night, are you?"

She quickly shook her head. "God, no."

"Honey, it'll help you to talk about it."

Amelia glanced up toward the vent. Jody's muted sobbing seemed to devastate her. She wiped a tear from her cheek.

"You're not responsible for that," Karen whispered.

"Yes, I am," she murmured. Grabbing her pillow, she reclined on the bed and curled up on her side. "It's just how it happened when Collin was killed. All day yesterday, I had these awful feelings that Mom, Dad, and Aunt Ina deserved to die."

"Why did you feel that way?"

"I don't know. It was something evil inside me. I thought about going to the Lake Wenatchee house and shooting them all. It's horrid, I know. It doesn't make any sense. I was so confused. I tried calling you, but you weren't home. I couldn't talk about it with Shane. We went to a party last night, and I just wanted to get drunk. I only had a couple of beers. But it was enough to make me a little crazy. I stole a half-full bottle of tequila, borrowed Shane's car, and just started driving. That's all I remember. I blacked out."

"Oh, Lord," Karen whispered, shaking her head.

"Next thing I knew, I woke up this morning in this empty parking lot in Easton. Do you know where Easton is?" Amelia sat up and stared at her. "It's off I-90, halfway between here and Wenatchee. I must have stopped there to rest on my way back. At first I thought I'd had a nightmare. I kept praying it wasn't real. But I knew it was. I didn't need you to tell me they were dead. I knew how it happened, too, because I'm the one who killed them."

"But you said you had a blackout," Karen argued. "You can't know for sure —"

"It wasn't a dream, Karen. I remember my dad in the rocking chair by the fireplace." Amelia started weeping inconsolably. "I — I shot him in the head. My mom, she must have woken up. God, I can still see her running out of their bedroom. I shot her too — I shot her in the face. . . ." She curled up again, and sobbed into the pillow. "Aunt Ina . . . with her it seemed like later, but I'm not sure. I just remember her standing there in the living room, staring at my dad, and then at me. She said, 'My God, honey, what have you done?' And I didn't say anything. I just shot her in the chest. . . .'"

Horrified, Karen gaped at her. "Amelia, you couldn't have. You're just not capable of that kind of coldhearted —"

"Then how come I know what happened?" she cut her off. "Nobody in this house knows yet except me. I must have been there, don't you see? I'm the one who killed them all."

"It's not true, Amelia," she said, rubbing her shoulder. "It didn't happen like that. Listen to me. Are you listening? If you really did this, what kind of gun did you use?"

Amelia shrugged. "I'm not sure. My dad's hunting rifle, I think. I remember it felt like someone hitting me in the shoulder with a baseball bat every time I fired it."

"Was that the first time you've ever used it — last night?"

"I guess so."

"And you knew how to operate it right away? You knew how to load it and work the safety?" Karen didn't wait for Amelia to answer. She switched on the nightstand lamp. "Are those the same clothes you had on last night? To hear you tell it, you shot them all at close range. Where's the blood on your clothes, Amelia?"

"I must have washed it off," she muttered, glancing down at herself.

"Where? When? During your blackout? Blood doesn't wash off that easily."

Amelia just shrugged and shook her head.

"Honey, you weren't there," Karen said. "I mean, just consider this. How much money did you have on you last night?"

"I don't know, about twelve dollars. Why?"

"It's — what — a hundred and fifty miles to Lake Wenatchee? That's at least three hundred miles round-trip, even longer if you took I-90. You'd have had to stop for gas. Do you remember going to a gas station?"

Biting her lip, Amelia shook her head again.

"Of course not," Karen said. She felt like she was starting to get through to her. "You didn't have enough money for gas, and you couldn't have used your credit card, because you told me during your session on Thursday that you maxed out your Visa. You were talking about how you had to control your spending. Check your purse. I'll bet that twelve bucks is still there." Karen reached for Amelia's purse on the floor between them. "Can I look through this?"

Amelia nodded. "Go ahead."

Karen rummaged through the purse. She

found a loose dollar bill, some change, and then in Amelia's wallet, two fives and a single. "I have exactly twelve dollars and sixty-two cents here, Amelia. You didn't buy any gas."

"Maybe not," Amelia said. "But — well, I've driven to Wenatchee and back on one tank of gas before."

"Then call Shane. Find out when he last filled up the car. Have him look at the fuel gauge now. That'll give us an idea how far you drove. You may have headed off to Wenatchee last night, but I'll bet you never got there." She tucked the money back in Amelia's wallet, and dropped it in her purse. Then she fished out Amelia's cell phone. "It's bad enough this horrible thing even happened. Please, Amelia, don't make it worse by blaming yourself for it. You couldn't have done it. So here — call Shane. Ask him about the gas."

Amelia hesitated, and then took the cell phone from her.

Karen heard something outside. She got up, parted the curtain and peeked out the window. A white sedan and a police car both pulled in to the McMillans' driveway — one after the other. "It's the police," she murmured almost to herself.

"Oh, my God." Amelia switched off the

cell phone. A look of panic swept across her face. "They'll want to talk to me. Karen, please help me. What am I going to say to them?"

Karen turned toward her. "You won't have to say anything." She grabbed her own purse on the bed and found the bottle of diazepam. "You're in no condition. I want you to take another one of these pills. I'll tell the police you're sleeping and can't be disturbed. And you will be asleep, honey, if you just lie back and relax and let the pill take effect. Go ahead and call Shane, just be quiet about it. I'll get you some water."

Karen slipped out of the guest room and found the bathroom next door. She could hear someone in the foyer upstairs. She quickly rinsed out the tumbler, then filled it with cold water. She paused in front of the mirror, then pulled it open to inspect the medicine chest. There it was: a bottle of aspirin in cylindrical tablets, like the diazepam. They weren't light blue, but in the dark bedroom, Amelia probably wouldn't notice. Karen didn't really want her taking another diazepam; she just needed Amelia to think she should be relaxed and sleepy.

As Karen stepped out of the bathroom, she heard them talking upstairs.

"I think she's asleep right now," George

was saying. "Her therapist is looking after her downstairs in the guest room. Could you let her rest for a while longer, and question me first?"

Someone — whoever he was talking to — muttered a response.

"Thanks," George said. "We can talk in here. . . ."

Karen ducked back into the bedroom, then quietly closed the door.

"I've really got to go," Amelia was whispering into her cell phone. "I'll explain everything later, I promise. Love you, too. Bye." She clicked off the line and gazed up at Karen, a tiny look of hope in her eyes. "He just picked up the car at your place. The gas is just under a quarter of a tank. He said it was about three-quarters full when we went to the party last night."

Switching off the light, Karen sat down next to her. She handed her the aspirin and the tumbler of water. "That's about right, isn't it? Approximately a hundred and sixty miles to and from Easton, that's around half a tank. You couldn't have made it to Wenatchee and back without refueling."

Amelia nodded. She swallowed the aspirin with some water, then handed the tumbler back to her. Tears welled in her eyes, and she winced. "It still doesn't make sense. If I didn't do it, how come I have these images in my head?"

"I don't know yet, but we'll find out. I promise." Karen stroked her arm. "Just because you have certain images in your head, it doesn't mean they're true. We don't even know how it happened yet, Amelia."

Pulling away, Amelia laid back and wrapped her arms around her pillow. "Why don't you talk to the police, Karen? Then we'll know whether or not I'm wrong."

CHAPTER EIGHT

Karen sat in the dark while Amelia tossed and turned in the bed across from her. The muffled sobs emitting through the vent from Jody's room upstairs had ceased. Karen guessed the police had been grilling George McMillan for about an hour now, and they were probably getting warmed up for Amelia.

She heard someone coming down the stairs. Karen climbed off the bed just as a knock came on the door.

Amelia sat up, suddenly awake.

Karen opened the door to find Jessie, her face in the shadows. "They sent me down here to fetch Amelia," she whispered. "They'd like a statement, which means they'll be asking her all sorts of rude, tactless, personal questions for the next two hours."

"Well, that's just too much for her right now," Karen said under her breath.

"It's the treatment they've been giving her uncle."

Karen glanced over her shoulder at Amelia, who stared back at them, visibly trembling. Karen couldn't let the police interrogate her, not when Amelia was so distraught and disoriented. "Go back to sleep, honey," she whispered to her. "And if you can't nod off, just lie there quietly until they go."

She stepped out of the guest room and gently closed the door.

"They want her uncle to go to Wenatchee tonight to identify the bodies," Jessie whispered. "He might not be back until very late. I promised him we'd stick around and hold down the fort."

"Yes, of course," Karen said.

"I told you we wouldn't be in the way, but you never listen to me." Jessie tapped her shoulder. "And if we hadn't come here, you wouldn't have met George. Talk about a sweetheart. Oh, and the way he is with his little girl. He's just the kind of man I've always wanted to see you with."

Karen frowned at her. "For God's sake, Jessie, his wife was just murdered last night."

"Well, I know that," she whispered. "Doesn't mean you can't call him in a couple of months and find out how he's doing." Jessie sighed. "I put the little one down for a nap. The poor lamb cried herself to sleep."

They headed up the stairs. Karen could hear George talking as she approached the study.

She knocked, and then opened the door. A handsome, mustached, gray-haired man in his fifties was pacing in front of George, who sat in an easy chair. The man wore a blue suit that looked slept in, and he stopped to glance at her.

George got to his feet as Karen stepped inside the room. He was wearing glasses, the Clark Kent type, which made him look even more handsome — and gentle.

A young, beefy, uniformed cop was also in the room. He sat in a swivel chair by the computer desk. He also stood up long enough to lean over and switch off a small recording device on the coffee table. The three men seemed slightly cramped in the close quarters. There was a small window above the desk, and two walls of shelves packed with books and framed photos of the McMillan clan.

"Detective Goodwin," George said. "This is Amelia's therapist, Karen Carlisle."

"Hello." She shook the detective's hand. "I understand you wanted to meet with

Amelia. But I'm afraid I kind of threw a wrench in that. You won't be able to get a statement from her this afternoon — or even tonight. She's heavily sedated right now."

The detective frowned. "But we need to talk to her."

Karen shrugged. "Well, I'm sorry. She's asleep. It's my fault. She was hysterical earlier, and I had to give her some tranquilizers to calm her down — the maximum dosage."

"The poor thing, it would have broken your heart to see her," Jessie chimed in from the doorway. "All the crying and carrying on, she was just beside herself. Thank God Dr. Carlisle was here."

Karen shot her a look over her shoulder. She knew Jessie was trying to help. But did she have to pour it on so thick — especially with the *doctor* bit? Jessie quietly retreated toward the kitchen.

Turning, Karen locked eyes with George. He hadn't witnessed Amelia in hysterics. He hadn't seen his niece *crying and carrying on* to a level that required her to be sedated. Yet he seemed to know she was protecting Amelia right now. Karen could see he understood.

His gaze shifted to the detective. "Haven't

you gotten enough for the time being? Do you really need to question Amelia *now?*"

The gray-haired detective rubbed his chin and stared at Karen. "How long have you been treating Amelia?"

"Since the beginning of the summer," she replied.

"In any of her therapy sessions, do you recall her mentioning anything about her father that would shed more light on what happened at the Lake Wenatchee house last night?"

She shook her head. "I can't think of anything significant — at least, nothing that would help your investigation."

"Sure you're not holding out on me?" he pressed. "This isn't one of those doctor-patient confidentiality things you're pulling on me, is it?"

"No, sir. If you were infringing on that, I'd tell you."

Frowning, he let out a little huff. "I still want to talk to her."

Karen shrugged helplessly. "Well, I'm sorry."

"Listen," George interjected. "If you're after more information about her dad's state of mind, you won't get much. Amelia has been away at school these last two months. I don't think she knows about her dad and

Ina." He turned to Karen. "My wife and Amelia's dad, they had an affair in August. It was very short-lived. Has Amelia mentioned anything to you?"

Karen bit her lip. "No. This is the first I've heard about it."

He turned to the detective. "See what I mean? You won't get much from Amelia. So leave the poor girl alone — at least for tonight."

"Fine," Goodwin grumbled. Then he glanced at Karen. "But I'd like her in my office at the West Seattle precinct tomorrow morning at nine o'clock — sharp."

Karen nodded. "I'll drive her myself. I'm sorry I couldn't be more help. If that's all, can I go now?"

He sighed. "Fine."

But Karen couldn't leave it at that. She was thinking about Amelia's fantastic *confession* to last night's shootings. She hesitated in the doorway. "May I ask you a question, Detective?"

"Go ahead," he muttered.

"I had to tell Amelia about what happened last night — based on an early report from Mr. McMillan. I really didn't have a very clear idea." She stole a glance at George, hoping this wouldn't bother him too much. "I told Amelia it appeared her father had shot her mother and aunt — and then himself. Amelia asked me what kind of gun he'd used — and where the police had found the bodies. She — um, she wanted details I couldn't give."

The detective stared back at her, unyielding.

"Mark had a hunting rifle, he used that," George answered — almost bitterly, as if he were just so sick and depleted from discussing it. Still, there was a tremor in his voice as he spoke. "My sister-in-law, she was shot in the face. They found her in the upstairs hallway. Ina — my wife — she — um, she was shot in the chest. She was in the living room with Mark. And Mark, he sat down in his rocking chair by the fireplace and shot himself in the head." Over the rims of his glasses, George looked at the older cop. "Did I get everything right, Detective?"

The plainclothesman said nothing.

Neither did Karen. She was thinking about Amelia's version of how it had happened last night. Amelia's story wasn't part of a nightmare or some delusion. The details she'd recalled were horribly real.

In the darkened guest room, Amelia lay in bed staring up at the ceiling. She listened to the voices upstairs in Uncle George's study, distant undecipherable murmuring. But she recognized Karen's voice. Maybe Karen could keep the police from talking to her for a while. But eventually they'd figure out who had killed her parents and her aunt. Karen couldn't keep that from happening.

In fact, Karen couldn't do much to help her at all.

Amelia wondered if she was even that good a therapist. Probably not.

"Stop it," she whispered to herself. "Don't even think it."

Amelia clung to her pillow and curled up into a fetal position. She suddenly felt sick, because along with her doubts, another thought raced through her head — an ugly thought that Karen Carlisle deserved to die.

Around five o'clock, after George and the two policemen had left, Karen went down to the guest room to check on Amelia again. But she wasn't there. Karen felt a little wave of panic in her gut. She glanced toward the bathroom, and saw the door was closed. But she still felt wary, thanks to memories of Haley. While checking the medicine chest earlier, she hadn't been looking for razor blades or sleeping pills.

She gently tapped on the bathroom door. "Amelia?"

"Karen?" she replied in a lazy voice. "If it's just you, come on in."

A warm waft of steam engulfed her as she stepped into the bathroom. The shower curtain had a pattern of fish and seahorses. It was halfway open to reveal Amelia sitting in the tub. Her hair was pinned up, but some wet black strands cascaded over her pale shoulders. Her head was tipped back, and her eyes half closed. "Did the police leave?" she asked.

"Yes, they're gone," Karen replied. She was glad no one had heard the water running down here. They would have known Amelia was awake after all. She wondered if Amelia, on some subconscious level, was trying to give herself away.

"Sit down," Amelia said, with a nod toward the toilet.

Karen lowered the lid and sat down. The tub faucet dripped steadily, and the sound echoed off the blue and white tiles. Amelia didn't seem a bit shy. She had a beautiful body, and Karen was reminded of high school, and her own teenage envy toward bigger-breasted girls. She felt a resurgence of that now.

"So you talked to them," Amelia said. She took a deep breath. "Was I right about how it happened?"

Karen nodded. "You might be close," she allowed.

She didn't know what else to say. How could Amelia have known — without being told — exactly where the bodies were found and how each one had been slain?

The only possible explanation was that perhaps Amelia had some kind of extrasensory perception or clairvoyance. But that was a stretch, and it still didn't account for why Amelia had assumed she'd committed the murders.

With a vague, forlorn look in the direction of the faucet, Amelia soaped up her arms. She wouldn't even glance at Karen. "Do the police still think my dad did it?" she asked.

"Yes," Karen replied. "There's no reason to doubt them, Amelia. It's a terrible thing to comprehend. But your father did this — not you. We'll never know why he did it. But there are things about your dad that will come out now, because of what happened, some things you might not be aware of."

Amelia slowly shook her head. "He would never do anything to hurt my mom — or Aunt Ina. I knew him. He was a good man."

"Well, he was human, too. But you're right. He wouldn't *intentionally* hurt any-

189

body. Amelia, you'll have to brace yourself for certain . . . revelations about him."

"Like what? If you know something, tell me."

Karen hesitated.

"Is it something the cops are going to tell me?" Amelia asked. "I'd rather hear it from you, Karen. Tell me."

Karen wondered: Did she really need to know? At the same time, for Amelia to start believing her own innocence in the shootings, she needed to start accepting the fact that her father was guilty. "Okay," she said, finally. "Your uncle just told this to the police. I'm not sure if you know. But it sounds like your dad and your Aunt Ina had a — an affair. I guess it was very brief and happened about two months ago."

Amelia said nothing. She absently rinsed the soap suds from her arms and shoulders. "I thought Ina was acting a little weird back in August," she mumbled, closing her eyes. "I should have guessed it was something like that."

"I'm sorry," Karen muttered.

"I'm glad to hear it from you instead of the police — or Uncle George."

Karen didn't say anything for a minute. Finally, she sighed. "The police want to see you tomorrow morning," she said. "I think they're mostly interested in what you can tell them about your parents — especially your dad. But if they ask what you were doing last night, you need to be very careful how you answer them. I don't want you wrongly incriminating yourself, because you've had these disturbing . . . visions."

"Don't worry, Karen. I won't say anything to the police." Amelia slid further below the surface, and water sluiced around in the tub. It was up to her chin now. "I was a closet drinker for three years, and no one knew. I became pretty good at covering up and lying. I'll be okay tomorrow."

"Well, I don't want you *lying* to the police. Just — just don't incriminate yourself."

All she could think about was what would happen if Amelia *confessed* to the shootings. Guilty or innocent, they'd book her immediately. And if Amelia didn't end up in jail, she'd end up in an institution. She'd be destroyed.

"Listen," Karen said, "why don't you call Shane back? Invite him to dinner. I'm sure there's plenty. Knowing Jessie, she's made enough to feed an army."

Amelia nodded. "Yeah, I think I'd feel better if Shane was here. But you're not leaving, are you?"

"Not unless you want me to," she said.

"No, I'd really like it if you stuck around, Karen."

She smiled and got to her feet. "Okay, then. I'll go tell Jessie to expect one more for dinner."

Forty-five minutes later, Karen met Shane as he was parking his car in front of the McMillans' house. She knew him from all the times he'd picked up Amelia after her sessions. With his messy, light brown hair, scruffy beard, and perfect white teeth, he looked like a surfer dude, and talked like one half the time. But he had a good heart and was totally devoted to Amelia.

As Shane climbed out of his VW Golf, Karen saw he'd forgone his usual semi-grunge attire and was dressed up in a blue oxford-cloth shirt and khakis. The unruly hair was slicked back with some product. And she saw something else very out of character for Shane: he was crying.

He gave her a forceful hug, and dropped his head on her shoulder. "Shit, I can't believe they're dead," he cried. "How is she? How's Amelia doing?"

"She's okay. She just had a bath." Karen patted his back, then gently pulled away. "Listen, Amelia can't remember exactly where she took the car last night. She talked to you earlier about the gas."

He wiped his nose with the back of his hand and nodded. "Yeah, looks like she used up about half a tank, but I don't care. Screw the car. I just feel so bad —"

"How many miles can you get on half a tank in that car?" she asked.

He glanced back at the VW and shrugged. "About a hundred and fifty. What's the big deal with the car?"

She didn't go to Wenatchee, Karen assured herself. That was at least 150 miles *one way.* "Listen, have you cleaned or swept out your car at all since picking it up at my place?"

Mystified, Shane shook his head.

"Amelia thinks she might have left something in it. Do you mind if I take a look?"

He shrugged. "Knock yourself out."

Karen checked the seat and floor on the driver's side. There wasn't a drop of blood or a bloody rag anywhere; there was nothing unusual except an empty tequila bottle. Karen checked the glove compartment, then popped the trunk and checked in there. Nothing.

"Busted," Shane said, nodding at the tequila bottle. "Did she tell you she fell off the wagon last night?"

"Yes, but we'll worry about that later." Karen tossed the empty bottle in a recycling bin at the end of the McMillans' driveway. Then she gave Shane a nudge. "C'mon, I'm counting on you to make sure Amelia puts away some dinner. She hasn't eaten a thing all day."

Amelia ate, thank God. Shane sat next to her at the kitchen table. Jessie had set all six places in hopes that Jody might come out of his bedroom and join them. She'd used her charms, along with a root beer and a plateful of chicken tetrazzini and garlic bread, to gain temporary access to his room.

To Karen's amazement, fifteen minutes into their dinner, Jody shuffled in with a near-empty plate in his hand. He was a good-looking kid, lean with brown eyes and wavy brown hair. "Is there any more of this stuff?" he asked quietly.

Jessie sprung up from the table and grabbed his plate. She got him a second helping — and got him to sit with them at the table. Shane asked Jody if he could crash in his room for the night. Whichever bunk was free, he didn't care. He just didn't want to be far from Amelia. If Jody still needed to be alone, he didn't show it. In fact, he seemed honored to have his cousin's boyfriend, a college guy, asking to bunk with him for the night.

Karen sat at the head of the crowded table

in Ina McMillan's breakfast nook. She remembered how she'd eaten dinner alone in front of the TV the night after Haley had died, and she'd done the same thing the night she'd put her father in Sandpoint View Convalescent Home. She wasn't feeling sorry for herself; she just wished she had family.

She looked at Amelia on the other side of the table. Shane had his arm around her. But Amelia stared back at her with a sad little smile. She nodded, and silently mouthed the words, *Thank you, Karen.*

Karen smiled and nodded back. And she felt as if she had family after all.

When George trudged through the front door at 12:40 a.m., Jessie began heating up his dinner. He made the rounds, checking in on his kids, kissing them goodnight, and then briefly chatting with Amelia and Shane, who were down in the basement, watching TV.

When he came back up upstairs, Karen asked to talk to him alone. He looked so tired and depleted, but said, "Of course." They stopped by the kitchen, where he poured them each a glass of wine — and another for Jessie. Then Karen followed him into the study. He closed the door after her, then nodded toward the easy chair. "Please, have a seat."

Karen sat down. "Thanks. And thank you for getting the police off Amelia's case today. She was very confused and distraught this afternoon, understandably so. But — well, it wouldn't have been good for her to talk to anyone, especially the police."

"Did she tell you about her premonition?" he asked.

Karen nodded. "Yes, sort of."

George sipped his wine. "Does Amelia think she's responsible for what happened? Is that why you wanted to talk to me?"

Dumbfounded, Karen just stared up him. "How did you know?"

"She had a *premonition* about Collin's death too. At one point, she even told Ina she thought she'd murdered him. Didn't make any sense. She was a hundred miles away when he drowned." George sighed, and ran a hand through his salt-and-pepper-colored hair. "When Amelia called me today with her premonition about trouble at the lake house, I could tell she felt somehow responsible for it. And then her premonition turned out to be true. Anyway, this afternoon, when you wouldn't let the cops talk to her, that cinched it. I figured you were covering for her."

He had another hit of wine, and frowned. "It's crazy. Thank God she didn't say anything about it in front of the kids. You're her therapist. Why would she blame herself for this? I mean, is it some guilt thing left over from her childhood or what?"

"I'm really not sure what it is in Amelia's case," Karen admitted. "But you're right, a childhood trauma could explain a lot. Amelia doesn't have much recollection from the time before the Faradays adopted her. I understand they had problems trying to track down information about the biological parents."

He nodded. "There was a fire at the adoption agency."

"Do you know the name of the place?"

"No, but it was in Spokane. I'm sure the adoption papers are somewhere at Mark and Jenna's house. Amelia and I need to drive up there this week to go over whatever legal documents need going over. I'll keep an eye open for those adoption papers, if you think they might help."

Karen nodded. "Yes, thank you. They might end up helping Amelia — a lot."

He plopped down in the desk chair. "God, I don't want her knowing about this. . . . *thing* that happened between her dad and her aunt." He slowly shook his head. "I'm pretty sure it was just one time, one little episode. Still, for a while there, I didn't think I could ever forgive Ina. Then I saw her tonight, lying on that gurney. Suddenly, her stupid little sin didn't matter anymore." His tired eyes filled with tears. He sat up, and cleared his throat. "Sorry, I hardly know you. I didn't mean to —"

"Oh, no, it's okay," Karen said, waving away the apology. "I'm a therapist. People get emotional around me all the time. It's a hazard of my occupation. I'm used to it."

He just rubbed his forehead.

Karen winced a little at what she'd just said. It sounded stupid. She shifted around in her chair. "Listen, George, if it's any help, I already talked to Amelia about what happened between your wife and . . . and Mark."

He took his hand away from his forehead and stared at her. "You told her . . . about my wife's indiscretions?"

"Yes, I — I needed to convince Amelia that her father was responsible for last night — and not her. She didn't have any idea about how difficult things were at home for her parents."

"But she didn't have to know," he argued. "I discussed it with the cops. They weren't going to put it in the official report. Don't you see? Amelia didn't need to know."

"Oh, God, I'm sorry," Karen said, wincing. "I was worried the police were going to tell her. I didn't want her to hear it from them. If it — if it's any consolation, Amelia seemed to take the news in her stride. And she even thanked me for telling her."

"Well, please don't expect me to thank you," he muttered.

"I think I should probably go," Karen said. "After everything you've been through today, the last thing I wanted to do was upset you. I'm sorry."

"No, don't go. Forget it. I'm just very, very tired," he grumbled. Then he swilled down the rest of his wine.

Karen didn't say anything. She felt awful. At the same time, she tried not to take his abrupt sullenness too personally. The poor man was exhausted, and emotionally devastated.

George pulled himself up from the chair. "Then we're done?"

Karen stood up, too. "Actually, I wanted to ask if you recall Amelia ever having any other premonitions, before the one she had about Collin's death. When she was growing up, did she show signs of being clairvoyant?"

"You mean like ESP?" He shook his head.

"No. I didn't hear about any special gifts along those lines. I heard a lot about the nightmares when she was a kid. She had these weird phantom pains, too."

Karen nodded. "Yes, I heard about those. That's why in junior high school she started sneaking into her parents' liquor cabinet. She was scared to go to sleep, because of the nightmares. The alcohol made her not worry so much, and she'd pass out. It helped numb the pain, too."

He brandished his empty wine glass. "Well, right now, that sounds like an excellent idea."

Karen kept a distance as she followed him from the study back to the kitchen. He refilled his glass with wine, then topped off Karen's and Jessie's glasses. He thanked Jessie profusely as she served him a plateful of chicken tetrazzini. Then he sat down at the head of the breakfast table. He took two bites, and said, "Wow, this is good." But he suddenly seemed to have difficulty swallowing.

Karen stood back near the stove, but she could see tears in his eyes.

George McMillan started to sob over his dinner. "I'm sorry, I can't eat," he cried. "I'm sorry — after you went to all that trouble. . . ."

Jessie patted his shoulder. She pulled a chair over, and then plopped down beside George. Her chubby arms went around him while he wept on her shoulder. "It's okay, honey," she whispered. "Don't you worry about it."

Karen remained by the stove, watching them. She knew, from eating alone so often and on certain nights, that it was hard to swallow while crying.

CHAPTER NINE

Springfield, Oregon — October 2001
Tracy Atkinson felt silly for having reservations about shopping at Gateway Mall that beautiful October night. But there were all sorts of alerts on the news about the spread of anthrax and another possible terrorist attack. Big shopping malls were supposed to be a prime target. She'd been avoiding crowded places for over a month now. The 26-year-old blond dental technician wished she were more like her fiancé, Zach, who kept telling her: "Hey, when your number's up, it's up, and there's nothing you can do about it."

He'd had no qualms about getting on a plane yesterday and flying to Boston for a sales conference. She had to admire him for it.

After a half hour inside the shopping mall, with visits to Target and Kohl's, she started to relax. On her way into Fantastic Footwear, she noticed a backpack left unattended beside a bench. It made her nervous, and she didn't linger in the shoe store for long before coming out and checking if the backpack was still there. Tracy let out a grateful sigh as she watched a teenage boy grab the backpack and strap it on. Sipping from Taco Time containers, he and his buddies wandered toward the cinemas at the other end of the mall.

"Excuse me, do you own a green SUV with an American flag decal on the rear passenger window?"

Tracy swiveled around and blinked at the middle-aged man. He held a teenage girl by the arm. She was pretty, with gorgeous blue eyes, but her black hair was unwashed. She wore the usual punk attire: black jeans and a black sweatshirt, also unwashed. She sneered at Tracy, and then tried to jerk her arm away from the man. But he didn't let go, not even when he pulled a wallet from his windbreaker pocket and flashed his badge at Tracy. "I'm Officer Simms," he said with a polite smile.

He was balding and slightly paunchy, but his eyes had a certain intensity that made him oddly attractive. His smile was nice, too. "I'm sorry to bother you, but I think this young lady keyed the driver's side of your SUV."

"It's just a little scratch," the girl grumbled, rolling her eyes. "Shit . . ."

"It's destruction of private property and vandalism," the man said.

Tracy gaped at them both. She and Zach had bought the green SUV only two months ago. They planned to start having kids right after they got married, and the SUV, though a bit premature, was part of that plan. Zach called it their *babymobile.* He'd put the U.S. flag in the window a few days after 9/11. Tracy couldn't believe this little urchin had keyed their brand-new babymobile. Zach would have a cow.

"Why would you do that?" she asked the girl. Tracy guessed she was about thirteen. "What did I ever do to you? I don't even know you, for God's sake."

The bratty girl merely rolled her eyes again.

"Pointless, just pointless," the man said, frowning. "Listen, ma'am. Why don't you walk out to the parking lot with us? You can review the damage to your vehicle, and decide whether or not you want to press charges."

"Of course," Tracy muttered, still bewildered. "I'm parked outside the furniture store."

But then, he was already aware of that, Tracy reminded herself. In order to know who she was, the man must have seen her parking the SUV in front of the furniture store. Obviously, the kid had keyed the babymobile just moments later, the little bitch.

The funny thing was, Tracy hadn't seen anyone else in the area when she'd left the car forty-five minutes ago. That section of the mall was usually the least crowded. She'd figured the new SUV would be safe there.

She imagined the cop looking for her, and dragging this punk girl around the mall for the last forty-five minutes. Why hadn't he just asked them to make an announcement over the mall's PA system? *Would the owner of a green SUV, license plate number COL216, report to the information desk?* That certainly would have been easier.

"Are you with mall security?" Tracy asked the man. They were walking through the furniture store, the dining room section. He still had the girl by her arm. She seemed to be resisting a little as they neared the exit.

"No, I'm a cop, off duty right now," he replied. "At least, I *was* off duty. If you'd like to press charges — and I think you should — I can radio it in to the station and they'll start filling out the paperwork right away. I'll drive you to the station. I promise it won't take that long."

He held the door open for Tracy, and they stepped outside. It had grown dark out, and chilly. But the lot was illuminated by halogen lights, which gave the area a stark, eerie, bluish glow. There weren't many cars left in this section. Tracy could see the SUV ahead, and on the driver's side, one long uninterrupted scratch. It started above the front tire and continued across the driver's door, then along the back door to the rear bumper. "Oh, damn it," Tracy muttered.

"That's my minivan over there," the man said, nodding at a blue Dodge Caravan parked nearby. "Come with me, and I'll radio this in."

Tracy stared at the girl, who didn't seem to have an ounce of remorse in her. She just looked annoyed, as if they were bothering her. "What the hell is wrong with you?" Tracy asked.

"Don't even try," the man said, dragging the girl toward his minivan. "C'mon . . ."

The girl didn't put up much of a fight as the man slid open the back door, put a hand on top of her head and guided her into the backseat. "Buckle up!" he barked.

He shut the door, then opened the front

passenger door for Tracy. "I promise this won't take long."

Tracy climbed into the front. She watched him walk around the front of the vehicle toward the driver's side. The minivan was a bit stuffy, and smelled like a dirty ashtray. Tracy immediately rolled down her window a little. She glanced at the girl in the rear-view mirror. The teenager was very sullen and quiet. But she stared back at Tracy in the mirror and shook her head. "Stupid," she grumbled.

"What?" Tracy asked. "What did you just say to me?"

The man opened the driver's door and climbed behind the wheel. "You should buckle up, too," he said. "This shouldn't take long. The station isn't far from here."

Tracy automatically started to reach back for her seat belt, but then she glanced out the window at her and Zach's SUV. It didn't make sense to leave the SUV behind. Wouldn't they want to take pictures of the damage? And doing it this way, he'd have to drive her back to the mall later. Following him to the station in the SUV would be easier. She let the seat belt slide back to its original position.

"Say, you know . . ." Tracy trailed off as she gazed at the dashboard.

He'd said he would radio in a report to the police station. But there was no radio in the car. Then it dawned on her: He's not a cop.

"Stupid," the girl repeated.

"Oh, no," Tracy murmured. "God, no! Wait —"

In one quick motion, the man had her by the throat.

All at once, she couldn't breathe. Tracy tried to fight him off, pounding away at him and, at the same time, frantically groping at the door. But she couldn't find the handle. And she couldn't stop him. He was too strong.

With one hand taut around her neck, he practically lifted her off the seat. He was crushing her windpipe. Tracy thought he'd snap her head off. He held a blackjack in his other hand.

For a second, everything froze, and Tracy caught a glimpse in the rearview mirror.

Nibbling at a fingernail, the girl stared at her. There was something in her eyes, something Tracy hadn't seen earlier. It was remorse.

Then everything went out of focus. Tracy desperately clawed at the hand around her throat. She felt something hard hit her on the side of her head.

She didn't feel anything after that.

In the kitchen, it sounded as if the faint, distant moaning might be something in the water pipes, maybe a plumbing problem. The girl had to listen very carefully to hear it. The drip in the kitchen sink, where she'd just washed the dinner dishes, made a more pronounced sound.

She scooped up Neely, the tabby who had been rubbing against the side of her leg for the last few moments. Cradling the cat in her arms, she opened the basement door. She could hear it better: a murmuring that might have been mistaken for one of the other cats meowing. As she started down the cellar stairs, the creaking steps temporarily drowned out that other faint sound.

The 13-year-old stopped at the bottom of the stairs. She stroked Neely's head. She could hear the woman's voice from here, muffled and undecipherable, but sounding human now, a woman crying out.

The girl flicked on the light switch as she stepped into the laundry room. The basement was unfinished, with a concrete floor and muddy-looking walls. Above the washer and dryer, there was a small window and a shelf full of houseplants her mother had collected and nurtured in old coffee cans and cheesy planters. One was a pink ceramic pot with WORLD'S GREATEST MOM in faded swirling gold script on it. That held the philodendron with the vines that draped down across the top of the washing machine operation panel.

Exposed pipes and support beams ran across the ceiling throughout the basement. It was from the far right support beam here in the laundry room where her mother had hanged herself nine years before. The girl had found her there at the end of a rope, dressed in a black skirt and her favorite blouse — white with pictures of gold pocket watches and chains on it. One of her slippers had come off, probably when she'd kicked the stool out from under her. It would have been a horrific discovery for almost any child. But by that time, the four-year-old girl had become quite accustomed to death and suffering.

The girl still watered her mother's plants when she did the laundry twice a week, like some people tended to flowers on a grave.

She continued on to the furnace room, where the muffled cries didn't seem so far away anymore. She could make out parts of what Tracy was screaming: "Please, please . . . can somebody hear me? Help me! My parents have money! They'll pay you . . . please! God, somebody . . ."

She knew the woman's name, because she'd looked at her driver's license: Tracy Eileen Atkinson. Born: 2-20-1975; Ht: 5-06; Wt: 119; Eyes: Brn.

She reached up and pulled the string attached to the furnace room light that dangled from the ceiling. She stared at the big, heavy metal door to the bomb shelter. He'd lodged a crowbar in the door handle, so no matter how hard Tracy pulled and tugged at the door, it wouldn't budge.

"Can anyone hear me? Please! Help me!"

If Tracy was like the others before her, she'd grow tired and stop screaming for help in a day or two. And a day or two after that, he'd grow tired of Tracy and slit her throat.

But until then, Tracy would learn that if she cooperated with him, he would give her some food scraps, maybe even an orange or an apple. If she put up a fight, she wouldn't get anything, except maybe cat food.

Neely meowed, and the girl continued to pet her head as she approached the bomb shelter door. "There now, Neely," she said.

"Is someone out there? Hello?"

She leaned close to the thick metal door. "I can hear you," she called softly. "Can you hear me?"

"Yes, yes. Oh, thank God! You have to help me . . ."

"Listen," she said. "I just want you to know. I didn't touch your car. He's the one who scratched it up."

"What? I don't care . . . you've got to let me out of here. . . . Are you still there?"

Tracy started screaming and pounding on the metal door. But the sound was so muffled outside the bomb shelter, it was quite easy to ignore.

Stroking Neely and pressing her cheek against the tabby's fur, she turned away from the door. She pulled the string to the single overhead light, and the furnace room went dark once again. She switched off the light in the laundry room, then ascended the basement stairs.

She could hardly hear Tracy anymore — unless she tried. And even then, it was just a faint, distant moaning.

Seattle — six years later
"Your father always loved my fried chicken."

Jessie seemed so flattered by the way Frank gorged on her chicken, Karen didn't have the heart to tell her that he'd attacked his serving of shepherd's pie with the same relish last week — and that was the most revolting dish the rest home cafeteria served.

212

"Well, Dad obviously misses your cooking," she said.

Frank sat in a hardback chair with Jessie's home-cooked dinner on a hospital table in front of him. He was dressed in a plaid shirt, yellow pants, a white belt, and slippers. He had a towel in his lap in lieu of a napkin. He'd turned into a very messy eater in the last few years.

Sitting with Jessie on the foot of his hospital bed, Karen was dressed in a black skirt and a dark blue tailored shirt. Sometimes, watching her father gnaw away at a meal — especially finger foods — was pure torture for her. Corn on the cob and spareribs were the worst, but fried chicken ranked high up there, too. Forcing a smile, she could only glance at her father momentarily before turning away.

Karen looked out his window, and the smile vanished from her face.

There it was again — the old black Cadillac with the bent antenna. She'd seen the car several times the last few days. She'd started noticing it after that Saturday Amelia had come to her about the deaths of her parents and aunt. Twice the banged-up Cadillac was parked on her block; another time it cruised along the drive at Volunteer Park while she'd been running laps around the reservoir. She'd spotted the same vehicle in her rearview mirror on her way to pick up Jessie this afternoon. And now it was in the parking lot at the convalescent home.

Karen got to her feet and moved to the window. From this distance, she couldn't tell if anyone was in the car.

"Frank, slow down," Jessie was saying. "The chicken's all yours. It's not going anywhere. Take your sweet time."

"Jessie, come here and look at this," Karen said, gazing out the window. Jessie waddled up beside her. "See that Cadillac out there, the one with the broken antenna? Does it look familiar? I think someone in that car has been following me."

Rubbing her chin, Jessie squinted out the window. "You know, I'm not sure. These old peepers aren't what they used to be. I —"

Karen heard the chair legs scrape against the tiled floor. She swiveled around to see her father with his mouth open and eyes bulging. He pounded at his chest. "Oh, my God, he's choking!" she cried.

"I got him!" Jessie pushed her aside and rushed behind the chair where Karen's father sat, writhing. Within a moment, the big woman scooped him up out of the chair and locked her chubby arms around his stomach. Jessie jerked her forearms under his ribs — lifting him off his feet with every squeeze. Once, twice, three times, four times. Then a piece of food shot out of his mouth.

Karen's father let out a cry, and then he gasped for air. He seemed to sag in Jessie's arms. She lowered him back into the chair, and patted his shoulder. Karen hovered over him. "Just sit there and get your breath back, Poppy," she said. He seemed okay, just a bit shaken.

But Jessie wasn't so well off. Karen gazed at her. She staggered toward the bed and plopped down on the edge. Wincing, she put a hand over her heart. The color had drained from her face, and she started wheezing.

Karen hurried to her side. "Jessie, are you okay?"

She didn't respond. She just sat there, struggling for her breath.

Karen snatched up the phone and called for the doctor on staff. "There's a woman here with breathing problems. Could you come to room 204, quickly please?"

As she hung up the phone, she heard Jessie say, "Aren't you — aren't you supposed to say 'stat'?"

Karen sat down on the bed, and gently

patted her back. "I'd feel like an idiot saying 'stat;' that's for the nurses and doctors. How are you?"

Jessie nodded. "I just overdid it a bit. I'll be peachy in another minute or two." She glanced over at Karen's father and started to chuckle. "Well, I'm glad he didn't let my having a coronary slow him down."

Frank was sitting up and gorging on his fried chicken once again.

Karen managed to laugh, but she noticed Jessie wincing again. She stayed at her side until the doctor arrived with a nurse. Dr. Chang felt Jessie's throat, then put a stethoscope to her chest. He asked if she could walk with him to his office down the hall. Jessie nodded. But she seemed a bit unsteady on her feet as Dr. Chang and the nurse led her out of the room.

Karen hated to see her looking so feeble. Jessie was her rock. She couldn't have managed without her these last four years.

Now that she'd moved her dad into Sandpoint View, Karen was getting pressured by her older brother and sister to sell the house. But she didn't want to sell it yet. She kept Jessie on three days a week. They often took these trips to the convalescent home together.

Her father's face and hands were a greasy

mess. Karen got him cleaned up. Then she washed off the plate and utensils in his bathroom sink, along with Jessie's Tupperware containers. All the while, she thought about Jessie, down the hall, being examined by Dr. Chang. The reality of it was, Jessie wasn't much younger than Dr. Chang's regular patients here.

One good thing, at least she hadn't heard an ambulance yet. Whenever there was a severe medical emergency, they sent for an ambulance and rushed the patient to University Hospital. Many of the ones from this place died on the way.

Karen finished drying off Jessie's Tupperware, and then checked on her father again. He'd moved into the cushioned easy chair, and was dozing peacefully. She decided to give Dr. Chang another five minutes with Jessie before going to his office and finding out how she was doing.

She glanced outside her father's window, and once again focused on that beat-up, old black Cadillac. Was someone really following her? Maybe one of her patients? Most of her clients weren't a threat to anyone, except maybe themselves. Every once in a while she got a truly disturbed new patient. But Karen sent those to a more qualified specialist.

Some of them didn't like being sent away.

Karen looked at her dad again. He was snoring now. He wouldn't be going anywhere for a while.

Grabbing her purse, she retreated down the hallway to the side door, and then out to the parking lot. The cold wind hit her, and Karen shivered as she headed toward the old, black Cadillac. She wanted to get the license plate number. She still had a few connections with the police department from when she'd worked at Group Health Hospital, counseling the occasional crime victim or criminal. She could pull a few strings and maybe get a trace on the plates through the Department of Motor Vehicles.

Approaching the car, she didn't see anyone inside. She wasn't close enough to read the license plate, but started to reach into her purse for a pen and paper. Then she heard a faint, distant wail, and Karen stopped in her tracks. The siren's high-pitched cry grew louder and louder.

The ambulance sped up the street, its red flashers swirling on the roof. It turned into Sandpoint View's parking lot. "Oh, my God, Jessie," she murmured to herself.

Running back to the side door, she ducked inside and raced down the hallway toward B wing, where Dr. Chang had his office.

But as she turned the corner, Karen came upon about a dozen elderly residents hovering outside the TV room. Roseann was trying to get them to disperse. "C'mon now, clear the door, folks," she was saying. "The paramedics need to get to Peggy, and you're blocking the way."

Karen approached her. "What happened?"

"Peggy Henderson fell and hit her head," Roseann whispered. "There's blood everywhere. I think she might have had a minor stroke, too, poor thing. Dr. Pollard is in there with her now. Help me get these people out of here."

Karen glanced in the TV room, and saw the frail old woman lying on the sofa, with the other doctor on staff and a nurse hovering over her. Two bloodstained hand towels were wadded up in a ball by their feet. Pollard was checking her vital signs. Karen didn't have much time for more than a glance. Two paramedics were barreling down the hallway with a collapsible gurney.

Karen turned to Dwight, a tall, spry 85-year-old who was a bit of a know-it-all. Except for his slippers, he dressed as if ready for a round of golf, in a green cardigan sweater and plaid pants. Among those gawking at poor Peggy, he was the least likely to budge. "Dwight, we need you," she said urgently. "Could you help me get these people to clear the way?"

The old man relished being an authority figure. "All right, let's give them some room here!" He kept clapping his hands and poking at his fellow residents' shoulders and backs until they shuffled aside. Of the dozen or so spectators, two had walkers and one was in a wheelchair. Karen helped corral them down the hallway while the paramedics rushed into the TV room.

In the middle of all the commotion, she saw a young brunette in a windbreaker emerging from a nurse's station alcove down the corridor. Karen froze. "Amelia?" she called.

The young woman glanced at her for a second, then hurried farther down the hallway. Karen started after her. "Amelia? Wait a minute!" She wondered why she was running away. Up ahead, the young woman ducked into a stairwell. The door was on a hydraulic spring, and still hadn't closed all the way by the time Karen swung it open again. She heard footsteps echoing in the dim gray stairwell. The walls were cinder block, and the unpainted concrete steps went down to a lower level and then to the basement. Karen paused at the top of the stairs and peered over the banister. She could see a shadow moving on the steps below. "Amelia? Is that you?" she called.

Karen rushed down the stairs, pausing only for a moment when she heard a door squeak open on the basement level. A mechanical, grinding noise suddenly resounded through the stairwell, probably from the boiler. She continued down the steps to the landing and pushed open the door. Karen found herself in a long, dim corridor. Two tall metal oxygen cylinders stood against the wall, along with a broken-down metal tray table on wheels. Someone had left an old rusty crowbar on top of it. Straight ahead, Karen saw the open door to the boiler room. She poked her head in. The room was huge, with a grated floor, a big old-fashioned boiler, a furnace, and a labyrinth of pipes and ducts. She didn't see anyone. Most of the maintenance people went home at 2:00 p.m. on Saturdays.

"Amelia?" she called, over the din from the boiler.

Turning, she glanced back at the corridor. A set of double doors farther down the hall was gently swinging in and out. She would have noticed if they'd been moving before. Had someone just ducked into that room?

Karen hadn't been down here since Rose-ann had given her an employee tour of the place months ago. If memory served her right, there was a storage room beyond those swinging doors. Approaching them, she cautiously glanced over her shoulder at the passageway to another part of the basement. She didn't see anyone, just two large bins full of dirty laundry.

Karen pushed open the swinging doors, and stepped into the dark, cavernous room. The spotlights overhead seemed spaced too far apart, leaving several large, shadowy pockets amid the clutter. To Karen's right was a graveyard of broken gurneys, metal tray tables and other hospital equipment. There were also about a dozen more tall oxygen cylinders.

"Is someone in here?" she called. "Amelia? Can you hear me? It's Karen."

She studied the rows of boxes to her left, some neatly stacked as high as five feet. But others had been torn open, revealing their contents: toilet paper rolls, lightbulbs, paper towels, soap bars, and cleaning supplies. One huge, open carton held bedpans that gleamed in the dim light. Still more boxes were opened and emptied, lying discarded on the floor.

As Karen ventured deeper into the room, she wondered what the hell Amelia would be doing down here. And if it had indeed been Amelia she'd seen upstairs, why had she run away?

Something crunched under her shoe. Karen stopped and gazed down at the thin shards of glass on the floor. Then she looked up toward the ceiling. The hanging spotlight above her was broken. She studied the line of spotlights; most of them had been shattered. No wonder there were so many dark areas in this cellar room. Someone had made it that way.

"Who's down here?" she called.

Karen didn't move for a moment. Her eyes scanned the rows upon rows of boxes, some sections engulfed in the shadows. About twenty feet away, she detected some movement amid the maze of cartons. Suddenly, a dark figure darted between the stacks.

Karen gasped. It looked like a man in black clothes, with a stocking cap on his head. She hadn't seen his face; he'd moved too quickly.

Her heart was racing, and she started to back up toward the double doors. She thought she heard something — a faint murmuring.

"Do it now!" a woman whispered urgently. "Get her!"

Karen turned around and ran for the exit

as fast as she could. Flinging open the double doors, she retreated down the basement hallway. As she reached the metal table by the stairwell, she paused and glanced over her shoulder. The storage room doors were still swinging in and out. But no one had come out after her.

She noticed once again the rusty crowbar on top of the table and snatched it up. She took a minute to catch her breath. With her gaze riveted on the swinging doors, Karen reached into her purse for her cell phone.

She had Roseann's number on speed dial. Her friend answered after two rings: "Sandpoint View, this is Roseann."

"Ro, it's Karen," she said, still trying to get her breath.

"Where did you disappear to? One minute, you're with me working crowd control, and the next —"

"I'm in the basement," Karen cut in. "I followed someone down here. I can't explain right now. But could you send Lamar down?" Lamar was an orderly around thirty years old, one of the sweetest guys Karen knew. But he also had a linebacker's build, a shaved head, and an ugly scar on his handsome face. With his formidable looks, Lamar would have made a good bodyguard. And that was what Karen needed right now, because she'd made up her mind to go back into that storage room.

"Tell Lamar I'm by the door to stairwell C, right across from the boiler room. And could you tell him to hurry, please?"

Karen clicked off the line, and stashed the phone back in her purse. She kept her eyes on the double doors, now motionless. She clutched the crowbar tightly in her fist, and waited.

"Are you going to call the police?" Lamar asked.

He'd given Karen his white orderly jacket to keep her warm, and she felt so small wrapped in it. They stood by a set of concrete steps leading down to a fire door to the convalescent home's basement. The old door, with chicken wire crisscrossed in the fogged window, had had a fire alarm attached to the inside lever. But someone had managed to dislodge the mechanism. Karen and Lamar had found the door half open during their search of the storage room. Five overhead lights had been broken — and recently, too. Using Karen's cell, Lamar had phoned Marco, the head of maintenance. Marco had been in the storage area shortly before going home at 2:00 p.m. According to him, all the lights down there had been working fine three hours ago.

The outside stairwell to the basement was nearly hidden behind a row of bushes on the side of the long, two-story, beige brick building. But from where Karen stood, she had a clear view of the parking lot. The black Cadillac wasn't there anymore.

Lamar nudged her. "So, are you going to call the police, Karen?" He spoke with a very crisp Jamaican accent.

Frowning, she shook her head. Even with her old connections on the force, she'd sound pretty stupid trying to explain what had happened. She'd followed someone down to the basement, to the storage room. She'd seen a man, but couldn't really describe him. She'd heard a woman whispering to him. It had sounded like they'd planned to attack her or kill her — she couldn't be sure. And oh, yes, one more thing: the young woman she'd followed down to the basement was a client, and a friend of hers.

"So, do you think you might have a stalker?" Lamar asked.

"I — I'm not sure," she said, shrugging. She was thinking about last Saturday, when she'd spotted someone who looked like Amelia in the corridor outside her dad's room.

"It's almost dinnertime," Lamar said, gently taking her arm. He led the way through a break in the bushes to the parking lot. "They'll need me back inside. Will you be okay?"

She gave him his jacket back. "Yes. Thank you, Lamar. I'm sorry to drag you down to the basement for nothing."

He shook his head. "It wasn't for nothing, Karen, not after what they did to the lights and the door. I think you were being set up. You watch out for yourself, okay? I don't want anything bad to happen to you. You're one of the nicest people here."

"Well, thank you, Lamar," she said. "Thanks very much."

Biting her lip, Karen watched him lumber away toward the side door. She thought she'd been set up, too. But why?

It was getting dark out, and colder. Shivering, Karen glanced at her watch: 5:05. Poor Jessie had been waiting for her for fifteen minutes. While in the basement with Lamar, Karen had phoned Dr. Chang's office. Apparently, Jessie was all right.

She pulled out her cell phone again, and dialed Amelia's cell number. After two rings, she got a recording.

"Amelia, this is Karen," she said, after the beep. "It's a little after five, and I'm wondering where you are right now. Can you call me as soon as you get this? We need to talk. Thanks."

She clicked off the line, and then shoved the phone back inside her purse. She wondered if she'd called that number twenty-five minutes ago while down in that gloomy basement storage room alone, would she have heard a cell phone ringing?

She remembered something Amelia had told her during their first session. She'd said, as a child, she used to talk to herself in the mirror a lot. She'd tried to make a joke of it. "So what do you make of that? Early signs of a split personality?"

Karen wondered if Amelia would claim to have had one of her *blackouts* this afternoon. Would she only remember *fragments* of this incident, too?

She thought she knew Amelia. She'd believed her incapable of killing anyone. She'd been certain about that.

But now Karen wasn't sure of anything.

"I was sitting there with my blouse off in your Dr. Chang's examining room for twenty-five minutes and for absolutely no reason, except maybe because I'm the *youngest* female patient he's had since he started working there. If that isn't pathetic, I don't know what is."

Karen kept checking the rearview mirror while Jessie, in the passenger seat, explained how her emergency checkup had been a total waste of time. Karen needed convincing that Jessie was all right. She also needed to make sure an old black Cadillac with a bent antenna wasn't following them. But she couldn't make out much in the rearview mirror beyond a string of glaring headlights behind her on Twenty-fourth Avenue.

She'd decided not to tell Jessie about the incident in the basement. No need to put any more stress or strain on her. At the same time, she hated to think she might be leading a pair of potential killers to Jessie's home in the Beacon Hill district.

"You know, I don't like leaving you alone," Karen said, eyes on the road. "I mean, what if you have another spell in the middle of the night?"

"I highly doubt I'll be wrapping my arms around another 170-pound man and repeatedly lifting him off his feet tonight. But if I end up doing that, the fella and I would like a little privacy, please." She chuckled and waved away Karen's concern. "Quit worrying. There's nothing wrong with me except I'm old as the hills and big as a house."

"Sure you haven't been overworking your-self at the McMillans'?" Karen asked. Jessie had babysat, cooked, and cleaned at George's house three days during the past week.

"Oh, it's been a breeze. Those kids are so sweet. And Amelia's been there practically every day, and she helps out a lot. By the way, I've been putting in a good word for you now and then with Gorgeous George. Just planting the seed for when he's ready to start dating again."

"You're wasting your time, Jess. George doesn't like me much. He thinks I'm a busybody."

"Oh, phooey, where did you get that idea?"

Karen said nothing. She briefly checked the rearview mirror again.

She hadn't seen George since the funeral three days ago, where she'd given him a brief, polite hello. Before that, he'd distract-edly nodded and waved at her — while on the phone — when she'd stopped by his house on Sunday morning to drive Amelia to the West Seattle Precinct. Amelia's much-dreaded interview with the police had turned out to be rather benign.

They'd talked with her for only forty-five minutes. They hadn't asked about her premonition, and hadn't seemed very interested in where she was at the time of the shootings. The questioning had focused mostly on her family, especially her father, and his behavior during the last few months.

Since then, Amelia had phoned Karen every day, sometimes even twice a day. Karen always took the calls, and tried to reassure her that she'd survive this. Amelia never mentioned whether or not she still felt responsible for the deaths of her parents and her aunt. But Karen knew it was an issue. They would work on it during their next scheduled session on Monday.

In the meantime, Karen reviewed her notes from several of Amelia's past sessions. She wondered about the origins of her nightmares and those memory fragments, some of which were eerily real. Amelia herself had joked she might have a split personality. But genuine cases of multiple personality disorder were very rare, and all the textbooks pointed out the dangers of misdiagnosing a patient as having MPD. Just the suggestion of it could make certain susceptible patients splinter off into several versions of themselves, worsening their problems, and delaying any kind of real treatment.

Still, multiple personality disorder could

have caused Amelia's blackouts, her *lost time.* Maybe it could also explain why Amelia had been at the rest home today, luring her down to that basement storage room. Lamar had said she was being set up, but for what? Her murder? Was Amelia the host to another personality that was killing everyone close to her?

It started to drizzle, and Karen switched on the windshield wipers. "Jessie, I need your opinion," she said, eyes on the road. "I have a client who says she's seeing and feeling things that are happening miles and miles away to people in her family —"

"Are you talking about Amelia?"

"A client," Karen said, knowing she wasn't fooling Jessie for a second. "Anyway, what do you think of that? Do you believe in ESP or telepathy?"

She was waiting for Jessie to respond with one of those alternative words for *bullshit* only people over sixty used nowadays: *hogwash, balderdash,* or *bunk.*

"I believe in it," Jessie said, after a moment. "If we're talking about picking up signals and pain from other people, then I say, yes, definitely, especially if you're close to that other person. I'm a believer now. When my Andy was so sick, I felt every pain he had. Sometimes I'd even wake up in the middle of the night with the pain. And I knew it was Andy, suffering."

Karen glanced over at Jessie. The headlights, raindrops, and windshield wipers cast shadows across her careworn face. Andy was her son, who had died at age twenty-nine back in 1993.

"He was in Chicago and I was in Seattle. Yet, I felt what he was feeling. If I was sick to my stomach one evening, sure enough, I'd hear the next day that he'd been throwing up half the night. If I had a headache or a dizzy spell, that's what he was having. I've never felt so physically sick and horrible as I did his last week, when he was in the hospice. I was there with him, and for a while, I thought I was going to die there, too."

Jessie let out a sad, little laugh. "You're going to think I'm crazy, but did I ever tell you that Andy still visits me every Christmas? It was his favorite time of year, you know. When he was younger, he used to go crazy decorating the house for Christmas. If it were up to him, he would have put a Christmas tree in every room. That Christmas after he died, my daughter, Megan, and my granddaughter, Josie, were staying with me. Josie was five at the time. I was about to go to bed when I heard her talking to someone. So I stepped into Andy's bed-room, where she was sleeping and almost walked into . . . something that fluttered away, like a bird. It was the weirdest thing. I can't describe it; it was like a ball of air that whirled around and disappeared. For a minute there, I thought I was going nuts. I asked Josie what was happening. And she said, 'I was just dreaming about Uncle Andy, Grandma.'

"Something like that has happened every Christmas since," Jessie continued. "It can be a weird little coincidence, or just this overwhelming feeling, and I know Andy's there. It's funny. Even though I know he's going to show up somehow, he still man-ages to sneak up on me when I'm not expecting him. So, anyway, I'm no expert on telepathy and ESP and that sort of stuff. But I do know for a fact there are forces out there that keep us connected to the people we love, even after we've lost them."

Karen nodded pensively. She could see Jessie's block up ahead.

"So tell Amelia if she's feeling a connec-tion to someone who has died recently, and she's seeing things, well, she's not really all that crazy, at least, no crazier than yours truly."

"I didn't say it was Amelia, remember?"

Karen felt obliged to say.

"Oh, yes, that's right," Jessie replied, deadpan.

She turned down Jessie's block, and checked the rearview mirror again. No one seemed to be following them. Despite Jessie's protests that she was double-parked and getting wet in the rain, Karen walked her to her front door. She made Jessie promise to call if she felt dizzy or short of breath. Jessie assured her that she'd be fine.

But Karen was worried about leaving Jessie alone, and it wasn't just because of her little spell earlier, scary as that had been. No, it was because of the other scare Karen had experienced, in the rest home's basement. Whoever had come after her might decide to go after Jessie.

"Listen," she said. "I don't want to worry you, but I read in the *Post-Intelligencer* there have been some robberies in this neighborhood. So lock your doors tonight, and set the alarm." It was a fib about the robberies, but she wanted Jessie to take precautions.

"Well, there isn't a thing in here worth stealing," Jessie replied, unlocking her door. "I hardly ever set the alarm."

"Well, set it tonight, for me, okay? Humor me."

"Okay, okay, I'll batten down the hatches. Worrywart."

Karen hugged Jessie in the doorway, then scurried back into her car. She started up the engine, but sat in the idle car for a moment. The windshield wipers squeaked back and forth, and raindrops pattered on the roof.

She thought about how Jessie had felt her son's pain, though two thousand miles away from him. Had Amelia made the same kind of connection with her family members when they were killed? Were her nightmare-like visions of their murders a form of telepathy?

Until this afternoon, Karen would have never considered it a possibility. But perhaps Amelia hadn't really felt a telepathic connection with her loved ones at the time of their deaths.

Maybe she was connected to the person who had killed all of them.

In the shadows of a tall evergreen at the edge of the lot next to Jessie's house, she stood in the rain. The hood to her windbreaker was up, covering the top of her head. The old Cadillac was parked around the corner. She already knew where Karen's housekeeper lived; it hadn't been necessary to follow Jessie down the block. But she'd wanted to hear what Karen and Jessie were saying to each other. So she'd climbed out of the Cadillac and skulked into the neighbor's yard. She'd only caught snippets of the conversation through the sounds of the wind and rain. It was sweet how Karen had been so worried about Jessie, and even kind of funny, because they'd both be dead before the week was through.

Karen probably had only a slight inkling of how close she'd come to having her throat slit in the basement at the rest home an hour before. Now there was no mistaking it; Karen had seen her. It wasn't the same as last week's brush with her in the corridor outside the old man's room. This time, Karen wouldn't just *ask* if she'd been at the rest home. She'd *accuse.* And this time, the innocent routine or the blackout excuse wouldn't work. Karen would keep pounding away at her for an explanation.

So she'd have to move fast and kill her, before the bitch started talking about her to other shrinks or maybe even to the police. Karen slept every night alone in the big relic of a house. The dog was a slight obstacle. But she'd killed plenty of animals in her time. This one wouldn't be a problem. And there were plenty of ways to break into that old house, plenty of opportunities.

She watched Karen duck back inside her car, then she just sat idle in the driver's seat for a few minutes. What was Karen Carlisle thinking about right now?

She had a thought of her own, and it made her smile. She was wondering what they'd tell that senile old man at the rest home next week when he asked why the visits from his daughter had suddenly stopped.

CHAPTER TEN

"Hi, this is Amelia. Sorry I can't take your call. Leave a message, and I'll get back to you as soon as I can. Bye."

Beep.

"Amelia, it's Karen again at about 6:15," she said into her cell. She'd just pulled into her driveway and switched off the ignition. The rain had subsided to a light drizzle. "Listen, I'm home now. So call me, either at home or on my cell. It's important. Talk to you soon, I hope." She clicked off the line, shoved her cell phone in her purse, and reached for the car door handle. But she noticed something in her rearview mirror, and suddenly froze. She saw the silhouette of a man as he came up her driveway, toward the car. He was tall and slender with short hair so blond it was almost white. The streetlight was at his back, so she still couldn't see his face. He wore gray slacks and a dark suit jacket with the lapels turned up to protect him from the drizzle. As he reached the back of the car, Karen quickly locked her door.

He knocked on her window. "Karen?" he called. "Karen Carlisle?"

She stared at him through the rain-beaded glass. He was very handsome, with chiseled cheekbones and pale-blue eyes. She guessed he was in his early thirties. "Yes? What do you want?" she called back.

He grinned, and made a little whirling motion with his hand like he wanted her to roll down the window.

Karen started up the car engine again. She pressed the control switch, and with a hum, the window lowered only an inch before she stopped it. "I said, *'What do you want?'*" she repeated loudly.

As he reached into his suit jacket, Karen tensed up, until she realized he was pulling out his wallet. He opened it, and showed her a Seattle Police Department identification card. *Det. Russell Koehler* it said, under a very macho-somber photo of him. "I'd like to ask you a few questions about Amelia Faraday," he said, almost too loudly, as if he wanted to get across to her that he was becoming annoyed by the window between them. "You're her therapist, aren't you?"

Karen flicked the switch, lowering the

window some more. "Yes, I'm her thera-pist," she said. "What's this about?"

"I'm investigating the deaths of her par-ents and her aunt."

"I thought the police had already deter-mined that Mr. Faraday shot his wife and sister-in-law and then himself," Karen replied warily. "Besides, the shootings hap-pened in Wenatchee. Isn't that out of your jurisdiction?"

"Let's just say I have a special interest in the case."

Despite what had happened in the rest home basement and all her new uncertainty about Amelia, Karen still felt very protec-tive of her. She shrugged. "Well, I can't tell you much, at least nothing Amelia has shared with me during our sessions. That's strictly confidential; I'm sure you under-stand."

He chuckled. "I wouldn't dream of tread-ing on your doctor-patient confidentiality. But the fact of the matter is, Karen, I've read the police reports. Amelia came to your house on Saturday afternoon, saying she had a premonition about something bad happening at the family getaway at Lake Wenatchee. That doesn't quite count as a doctor-patient session, does it?"

She stared back at him. "I treat any client

emergency as a professional session."

"Really? So are you going to charge her for Saturday?" he asked pointedly.

"That's none of your business," Karen replied.

He smirked — that same cocky grin again. "You know, Karen, it looks like I've started off on the wrong foot with you. The thing is, I don't believe Mark Faraday shot anyone. I think someone else killed Mark, along with his wife and sister-in-law. Maybe you'd be more willing to cooperate if we sat down together over a cup of coffee and you let me explain where I'm coming from." He glanced over her shoulder at the house as if it were her cue to invite him in, and then he smirked at her. " 'Where I'm coming from,' that's one of those therapy terms, isn't it?"

Karen eyed him warily. She wasn't about to invite this guy into her home. She still wasn't a hundred percent sure he was really a cop. "There's a coffee place on Fifteenth called Victrola. It's about a five-minute walk from here. I'll meet you there in ten. I just need to make a call."

"Who are you calling? Amelia? Or your lawyer?"

Karen flicked the switch and started to raise the window up on him. "Neither."

He grabbed the top of the window to

delay its ascent. "You aren't *hiding* Amelia, are you?"

She released the switch for a moment. "No. Why do you ask that?"

"Because I've been trying to get in touch with her since one o'clock this afternoon, and she's MIA. No one knows where she is — not her uncle, her roommate, or her boyfriend." He glanced back at the house again. "Are you sure Amelia's not in there? That's an awfully big place for just one person. Do you live there alone?"

"It's my father's house. He's in a rest home with Alzheimer's. So, yes, I'm living here alone. And yes, I'm sure Amelia's not in there."

"And you don't have any idea where she might be?"

Karen shook her head. "No, I don't." She flicked the switch, raising the window again. "I'll see you at Victrola in ten minutes," she said over the humming noise. She watched him in the rearview mirror as he turned and strutted down the driveway toward the street. Then she looked at her house, and couldn't help wondering, *Are you sure Amelia's not in there?*

Climbing out of the car, Karen kept her eyes riveted on the house, watching for any movement within the dark windows. She should have turned on a light before running out the front door this afternoon. At least she'd remembered to set the alarm. She glanced at her wristwatch: 6:25. It was strange to feel so nervous about walking into a dark house by herself at this early hour. But then, it had been a very strange day.

Karen approached the front stoop, then tested the doorknob. Still locked; that was a good sign. She unlocked the door and opened it. Flicking on the light, she headed for the alarm box and quickly punched in the code.

She paused for a moment, and felt a pang of dread in the pit of her stomach. Something was wrong. Why wasn't Rufus barking? She anxiously glanced around, then ventured down the hallway to the kitchen. Switching on the light, she hurried to the backdoor. Still locked. Good. She noticed the basement door was ajar. She turned on the light at the top of the stairs and peered down at the steps. "Rufus?" she said. "Here, boy!"

Nothing. Karen shut and locked the basement door in practically one swift motion. She headed toward the front of the house again. "Rufus?" she called out. "Where are you?"

Poking her head in the living room, she stopped dead. The dog was trying to sneak down from the lounge chair her father had had re-covered to the tune of $850 only ten months ago. Naturally, it had become Rufus's favorite spot to nap, when no one was around. "You stinker!" she yelled. "No wonder you didn't bark when I came in. You know you're not supposed to be on that chair. Some watchdog. I could have been strangled, and you wouldn't care, as long as it didn't interrupt your nap."

His head down, the dog slinked toward the kitchen.

"Don't even *think* you're getting a cookie," Karen growled, retreating into her office. She checked her address book. Her contact with the Seattle Police from her days at Group Health was Cal Hinshaw, a smart, dependable, good old boy. She found his number, then grabbed the phone, and dialed. She kept glancing over her shoulder to make sure no one was sneaking up behind her. She could hear Rufus's paws clicking on the kitchen floor, but nothing else.

"Lieutenant Hinshaw," he answered after three rings.

"Cal? It's Karen Carlisle calling, you know, from Group —"

"Karen? How the hell are you? It's been an age. Listen, I'm running late for something and just about to head out. Can I call you back?"

"Actually, I just wanted to hit you up for some quick information."

"Lay it on me. What can I do you for?"

"I'm wondering if you know anything about a Detective Russell Koehler. He just came by asking a lot of questions about one of my clients, and I'm stalling him. Is he on the level?"

"Koehler? Yeah, I know the guy. He thinks his shit is cake. He's been on *paternity leave* the last two weeks. He found something in the employee regs that allowed him to take a month off with pay while his wife pops out a kid, not that I'd think for one minute he'd be any help to her. He's kind of a sleaze. But I hear he knows somebody in the mayor's office, and gets away with a lot of crap at work. You say he's flashing his police credentials and asking questions?"

"Yes, about those shootings in Wenatchee last week, the Faraday murder-suicide case. My client is their daughter. I'm wondering why this cop — on leave — is investigating a practically closed case out of his jurisdiction."

"You got me, Karen. He's always working some angle."

She shot a cautious glance toward the front hallway. "Maybe this man isn't really Koehler. Is he in his midthirties with pale blond hair and blue eyes? Good looking?"

"Not half as good looking as he thinks he is. That's Koehler, all right. Watch your back with him, Karen." Cal let out a sigh. "Listen, I need to scram. Let's get together for coffee sometime and catch up. And keep me posted if you find out why Koehler's sniffing around this Wenatchee case. You've got me curious now."

"Will do. Thanks, Cal," Karen replied, and then she hung up the phone.

Grabbing her umbrella, she set the alarm again, and ran out of the house.

"Do you know how much Ina and Jenna were worth?" Russell Koehler asked in a hushed voice. "The Basner sisters had a little over three mil between them."

Karen leaned over the small table, so she could hear him better in the crowded coffeehouse. They sat by the window. An eclectic art collection hung on the walls with price tags next to each work. About two thirds of the customers sat with their laptops in front of them. Chet Baker's horn and velvet vocals purred over the sound system.

"Guess who now stands to inherit those millions?" Koehler continued. "Nineteen-year-old Amelia Faraday and her favorite uncle, George McMillan."

Karen leaned back and shrugged. "So?"

"According to the Faradays' neighbors up in Bellingham, Amelia was a real hell-raiser. And from *Uncle George's* own testimony, we know his wife was banging his brother-in-law. A close friend of Ina McMillan's confirmed it. So you've got a rebel daughter pissed off at her parents, and this cuckolded history professor, both due to inherit a shit-load of money. You do the math. One, or both, of them could have done the job on Ina, Mark, and Jenna last Friday night — or they hired someone to do it."

Karen frowned over her latte. "Well, you're wrong. Without breaching any therapist-client confidentiality, I can tell you this. Amelia never once complained to me about her parents. If anything, it was the other way around. Amelia said she'd caused her folks some heartache over the years, and wanted to make it up to them."

"She *told* you that. She probably figured you'd be repeating it to some cop, like you are right now. How do you know Amelia wasn't just setting you up?"

"Amelia genuinely loved her parents, Lieutenant. Also, I was with George McMillan hours after he learned of his wife's death, and he was devastated. It wasn't an act. If you're trying to pin the Wenatchee shootings on either one of them simply because they're in line for some money, then you don't have a leg to stand on. Besides, three million split between two people isn't a huge fortune nowadays."

"Maybe not to you," Koehler replied, drumming his fingers on the tabletop. "Not everybody lives in a *castle,* like you do. The police based their conclusion that Mark Faraday was unstable mostly on the testimony of Amelia and her Uncle George, the beneficiaries of this little windfall. I mean, isn't that pretty damn convenient? Maybe three mil isn't such a gold mine nowadays, but it's still a damn fine nest egg. Two people could live very comfortably on that. Not everyone is as lucky as you, inheriting a mansion. Some people have to make their own luck."

Karen glared at him. "I don't think it's lucky that my father lost his mind. And I'm sure Amelia Faraday and George McMillan don't feel lucky about what happened to their loved ones."

"All right, all right, take it easy," he said, rolling his eyes. "You'd be thinking along the same lines as me if you'd seen the house by Lake Wenatchee. I walked through it the day after. I didn't go in there suspecting your client and her uncle. But that's how I felt when I walked out of the place. For starters, there are footprints all around the outside of the house. But there were other partial footprints in the mud they weren't so sure about. The cops figured that most of the prints belonged to Mark, after examining his slippers. And I'm wondering, what the hell was Mark doing out there in his slippers? He must have gone to check on something, maybe a noise, or maybe one of the women saw someone lurking outside the house."

Karen shrugged. "He could have been chasing away a raccoon for all we know." She shook her head. "You're jumping to conclusions —"

"I saw the bloodstains, Karen. I saw them in the upstairs hallway where Jenna got shot in the face. There was a big stain on the living room floor, where Ina got it . . ."

Karen remembered Amelia's description of the scene. It was so dead on.

"But the bloodstain on the living room wall, behind the rocking chair where they found Mark Faraday with his hunting rifle still in his hands, that's what really stopped me. The bullet entered above his left eye and shot out the back of his head about two inches above the hairline on the back of his neck. The stain on the wall was almost parallel to the top of the rocking chair. He couldn't have held a hunting rifle to his face that way, not parallel. He'd need arms like an orangutan to manage that. If Mark Faraday really killed himself with that rifle, the barrel would have been at a diagonal slant, blowing off the top-back of his head. The only way the exit wound and the bloodstain on the wall could be like that was if someone else held the rifle parallel to his face."

Karen automatically shook her head. "But he was in a rocking chair. It might have tipped back —"

"Yeah, yeah, one of the Wenatchee cops gave me the same song and dance about the rocking chair. That might account for Faraday's blood and brains being where they were on the wall. But there's still the exit wound. You can't explain that away. And I'll tell you something else there's no explanation for: the whereabouts of both Amelia and her Uncle George on the night of the shootings. Their alibis aren't worth shit. Uncle George says he was home with the kiddies at the time of the murders. But he could have easily driven to Lake Wenatchee, pulled off the killings, and driven back while the kids were in bed. It's about 150 miles from Seattle to Lake Wenatchee and, driving at night, he could have cinched the round-trip in less than five hours. The guy had the motive and the opportunity.

"As for your client, she ditched her boyfriend at a party around eleven, and then went for a 'drive.' No one saw her or talked to her for the next twelve hours. The coroner estimates her parents expired sometime between two and three in the morning. The aunt died a little later, closer to dawn. They think she must have lingered for a while, after being shot. Either way, that's three or four hours after Amelia left the party, plenty of time for her to get to Lake Wenatchee. She told the police she'd driven as far as Snoqualmie Falls, then fell asleep in a parking lot. Hell, you'd think she'd try to be a little more creative with her alibi."

"She couldn't have driven to Lake Wenatchee," Karen argued. "There wasn't enough gas in her boyfriend's car to get her there and back. And Amelia didn't have the money or credit cards to buy gas."

"So, she could have siphoned some gas. Or maybe she just drove to some designated spot and met her uncle. Then he could have driven the rest of the way so they could pull off the job together."

"That's crazy," Karen whispered. "I saw Amelia on Saturday afternoon, and I got a good look at the clothes she had on, the same clothes she'd worn to the party the night before. Everyone was shot at close range. There would have been bloodstains."

"Yeah, so? She could have easily changed into something else before she started shooting, and then discarded the bloody clothes later. Or maybe she let *Uncle George* do the shooting."

Karen just shook her head at him.

"Obviously, you've considered the possibility that Amelia killed them," he pointed out. "Otherwise, you wouldn't be so fast with your counterarguments about her clothes and the gas in her boyfriend's car. You must have discussed this with her. What did she say to convince you she was innocent? I'd like to hear it, Karen. You convince *me*."

"I didn't need convincing," Karen replied. "I *know* Amelia. I know she couldn't kill anyone."

He cracked a tiny smile. "I'm pretty good

at reading people, Karen. And I could tell just now you really weren't sure you believed what you were saying. I'm certainly not buying it."

It was all she could do to keep from squirming in her chair. "You grossly overestimate your powers of perception, Lieutenant," Karen managed to say. "And it's got you jumping to a lot of wrong conclusions. You've already made up your mind about Amelia and her uncle, haven't you? Anything I tell you that doesn't fit into your preconceived scenario, you simply disregard. Why bother even talking to me? Have you talked to Amelia yet, or her uncle?"

Koehler nodded. "The uncle, yes. But he clammed up pretty tight after a few questions. As for your client, she keeps giving me the slip."

"Then your investigation isn't official police business, is it?" Karen said.

Grinning, he shrugged, "Well, I . . ."

"Before coming here, I called a friend of mine on the police force," she went on. "He said you're on paternity leave right now. What's your angle, lieutenant? Why is this so important to you that you'd take time away from your wife and newborn baby to investigate a case that isn't even in your jurisdiction?"

"Because I care about the truth," he said, with a straight face.

"I'm pretty good at reading people, too, Lieutenant. And you're full of shit." Karen got to her feet. "I've talked to you all I want to right now. If you come around my place again asking me a lot of questions, you better bring your checkbook, because I'm charging you for my time."

She started for the exit, and he called to her, his voice rising above the noise inside the café. "I'll just have to chase down your client and talk to her," he said ominously.

Karen headed out the door, and pretended not to hear him.

"You have — no — messages," said the prerecorded voice on her answering machine.

"Damn," Karen muttered, hanging up the cordless phone in the study.

Amelia still hadn't called her back. Karen felt so torn. She'd just returned from the coffeehouse, where she'd argued Amelia's innocence to that cocky cop. Yet, while walking home in the light drizzle, she'd repeatedly looked over her shoulder for that broken-down black Cadillac.

How could Amelia be so innocent, and at the same time be a potential threat to her?

Could she really have multiple personality disorder?

This *other* Amelia had never emerged during any of their sessions. Sandpoint View was the only place Karen had seen her. Why there of all places?

Biting her lip, Karen picked up the cordless phone again and dialed the rest home. One of the night nurses answered: "Good evening, Sandpoint View Convalescent Home."

Karen recognized her voice. "Hi, this is Karen Carlisle. Is this Rita?"

"Sure is. What's going on, Karen? I heard someone was stalking you this afternoon down in the laundry room or something. What's up with that?"

"Beats the hell out of me, Rita. But it's got me a little nervous about my dad. Would you mind checking on him for me?"

"Don't have to. I just saw him five minutes ago in the lounge, watching TV with a bunch of them. Frank's just fine."

"Could you check on something else for me, Rita? Could you take a look out at the parking lot and tell me if you see a . . . an old black Cadillac with a broken antenna?"

"Sure, no sweat. I'll just go look out the side door. Hold on a minute."

With the cordless phone to her ear, Karen

wandered to the front hallway. She glanced up the stairs to the darkened second floor. She hadn't been up there since leaving the house early this afternoon. She kept staring up at the second floor hallway. Suddenly a shadow swept across the wall.

She gasped and started backing away from the stairs. Then she saw the shadow race across the wall again and realized it was just a car passing outside, the headlights shining through the upstairs windows. She let out a sigh. "You idiot, Karen," she muttered to herself.

"Karen, are you still there?" Rita asked, getting back on the line.

"Yes, Rita?"

"I didn't see a Cadillac in the lot, or parked on the street, either. Does this have anything to do with the whacko who was stalking you?"

"It might. Listen, how late are you working tonight?"

"Until midnight, lucky me."

"Could you give my dad an extra check now and then for me, Rita?"

"Of course I will, Karen. Don't you worry about Frank. I'll make sure he's okay. You look after yourself, girl. Do you have pepper spray? I don't leave home without mine. If you don't have pepper spray or mace, you should keep a knitting needle in your purse."

"Well, I've had a minicanister of mace in the bottom of my purse for years, but I've never had a reason to use it."

"Better make sure it still works. Test it, girl."

"I will. Thanks, Rita. Thanks a million. And if you happen to notice a black Cadillac in the parking lot, would you call me?"

"No sweat. Your cell number's right here at the nurse's station."

After she hung up, Karen was still worried about her father, so feeble and helpless. Visitors wandered in and out of that rest home all day. And there were plenty of temps on the nursing staff. Amelia could have easily passed as one of them.

If there was a photo of Amelia by the nurses' station, the staff could keep a lookout for her, and Karen would feel a lot better. But she didn't have a picture of Amelia. They'd done a pretty good job of keeping her photo out of the newspapers last week.

George McMillan certainly had a picture of his niece among the family snapshots. Karen needed to call him anyway. Even if he didn't like her, she had a good reason to phone him right now. Maybe he had an idea where Amelia was.

Jessie had left the McMillans' number by the phone in the kitchen. Karen went in there, and called him.

George picked up on the second ring. "Hi, Jessie."

Karen balked. "Um, this isn't Jessie. It's Karen Carlisle."

"Oh, I'm sorry. Your name came up on the caller ID, but I just figured it was Jessie."

"No, it's — it's me, Karen," she said, feeling awkward. "I hope I'm not interrupting your dinner."

"No, we just finished. It was spaghetti, the only thing I know how to cook that my kids like. What can I do for you, Karen?"

"I'm wondering if you know where Amelia is. I've been trying to get ahold of her."

"She's incommunicado right now," George replied. "Shane phoned earlier today, all worried about her. He just called back an hour ago. Amelia's roommate said she mentioned something this morning about needing to get away. It looks like she just took off someplace for the weekend. She used to pull this on her parents every once in a while, and it drove them crazy. I hope she's not drinking again. She was doing so well this week, considering everything she's been through."

"Listen, would you mind if I came by tonight? I need to talk with you, and I don't want to discuss this over the phone."

"No problem, Karen," he said. "When can I expect you?"

"I'm leaving the house right now."

"I had a bellyful of Koehler myself," George said. He stood at the kitchen sink, scrubbing a saucepan. Karen stood beside him with a dishtowel in her hand. Despite George's protests, she'd insisted on helping him clean up. His daughter, Stephanie, was in bed, playing with her stuffed animals. Jody and a neighbor friend were watching TV downstairs.

"When he came by yesterday, I thought it was official police business," George continued. "So I let him in, and talked to him for a while. But then Koehler started in about Amelia, saying she could have killed her parents and my wife. He even insinuated that Amelia and I could have been having an affair. He pointed out that, after all, she isn't a blood relative, and niece or no niece, a hot-looking 19-year-old is hard to pass up. That's when I threw him out on his ass."

He handed Karen the saucepan. "Then I called Dennis," he said. "Dennis Goodwin, he was that detective who was here last

Saturday. We drove to Wenatchee together. He turned out to be a pretty nice guy. I could tell he liked me, or at least felt sorry for me. He told me Koehler's on leave —"

"*Paternity* leave," Karen interjected. "His wife just had a baby."

"Mazel tov," George grunted. "Anyway, apparently Koehler thinks he'll make a big name for himself if he cracks this case wide open. He was talking to another cop about the potential for a book deal and movie rights. Anyway, he's not afraid of treading on anyone's toes on the force, because he's very well connected with the powers that be. I guess I didn't do myself any good by pissing him off, but I really don't care."

"Do you mean that?" Karen asked, studying him.

He let out a little laugh. "Well, actually I am a bit worried about what he might do. I'm thinking about Amelia, mostly."

Karen nodded. "So am I. Remember what we talked about last week? It took a lot of persuading on my part to assure Amelia she didn't kill her parents, and your wife. I'm not sure exactly how much I succeeded in convincing her. She's probably still pretty confused. If Koehler goes to work on her, God knows what she'll end up telling him."

"Then he'll go to the media, and make

Amelia out to be a deranged killer." George reached over and turned off the water. "God, I don't want my kids to read that."

Karen said nothing for a moment. Gnawing away at her was the idea that it could be true about Amelia. She dried off her hands, then folded up the dishtowel. "Listen, something happened to me when I went to visit my father in the rest home today. It involves Amelia . . ."

They sat down at the kitchen table, and she told George about her bizarre, scary experience in the basement storage room. She explained her reluctance to diagnose Amelia as having a split personality, and asked if he'd ever noticed any abrupt behavioral changes in his niece. "Not just mood swings," Karen clarified. "But a total shift in her persona, when she might have sounded or even looked different to you."

He shrugged. "I don't remember ever seeing Amelia act like anybody except Amelia. Ina never said anything to me about personality shifts, and she and Amelia were pretty close this last year. Mark and Jenna never mentioned anything either. I . . ." He hesitated. "Wait a sec. You know, Collin said something to me about a month before he died. He and some friends were eating lunch on the bleachers at his school in Bellingham, when he spotted Amelia watching them from across the street. He called to her, and she started to walk away. It struck him as weird, because Amelia was supposed to be in Seattle, and he usually knew when she was coming home to visit. Anyway, when he caught up with her, Amelia acted like a total stranger, he said."

"You mean she didn't recognize him?" Karen asked.

"No, she knew who he was, all right. They talked for a minute or two, then Amelia said she had to go and asked Collin not to tell their parents that she'd been there. I remember Collin saying to me, 'I felt like Amelia was a different person.' He said she didn't seem drunk or anything. She just didn't seem like his sister. Collin was spending the weekend here when he told me this story." George let out a sad sigh. "Huh. You know, that weekend was the last time I saw him."

Karen was about to reach over and put her hand over his, but she hesitated. She cleared her throat. "Um, I don't know much about multiple personality disorder. We'd have to get Amelia to a specialist. We also have to prepare ourselves for the awful possibility that Koehler is right about Amelia."

George frowned. "Do you really think she could have killed her own parents — and my wife? I know my niece, and she could never —"

"Yes, I agree with you," Karen cut in. "The Amelia *we know* isn't capable of murder. I'm saying there could be another person inside Amelia we don't know. Maybe this *other* Amelia was in the rest home earlier today. Maybe she's the one Collin spotted outside his high school that time. Collin said she was like a stranger. We don't know this other Amelia either. We don't know what she's capable of."

George slowly shook his head. "I can't believe it. I mean, Jesus, I've had her here alone with the kids this week. Are you sure?"

"I'm just saying it's a possibility we have to consider. In fact, one reason I wanted to stop by tonight was to borrow a photo of Amelia, any recent photo of her that you might have. I want to post it at the nurses' station in my dad's rest home so they'll keep a lookout for her. You probably think I'm overreacting."

"No, not at all," he said. "We have plenty of family pictures. I'll make sure you get a current one of Amelia before you leave tonight."

"Thank you, George," she said, sitting back in the kitchen chair. "About Amelia, I'd like to get her to someone more qualified in multiple personality disorder. I've never had a true MPD case. There are theories it can be caused by an early childhood trauma. But that's just a theory. And Amelia's early childhood is still a mystery to us. I really —"

"God, I forgot to call and tell you," he interrupted. "I was up at Mark and Jenna's house in Bellingham the day before yesterday with Amelia, and I found the adoption papers." He got to his feet. "They're in my study. I'm not sure how much help they'll be."

Karen eagerly followed him into the study. She remembered some of those fragmented memories Amelia had shared with her about her early childhood: a woman screaming in the woods while young Amelia sat alone in a car; the Native American neighbor she liked; a person or place called Unca-dween; and her mother standing over her in the bathroom, asking, "Did he touch you down there?"

If they could track down more information about Amelia's biological parents, they might discover what those fragments meant. Maybe they'd find the key to Amelia's problems.

George put on his glasses and sifted through a stack of papers on his computer desk. "Here's the file," he said, handing her a folder. "I'm afraid there isn't a lot of information here — no mention of the biological parents or even where Amelia was born, just her first name and the birthday, May 21, 1988."

Karen glanced at the records: sixteen pages of legal documents, most of it boiler-plate stuff. But the adoption date was there: April 5, 1993; and so was the name of the agency: Jamison Group Adoption Services, Spokane, Washington.

Karen nodded at his computer screen. "Could I get online for a minute?"

"Sure, I'll start it up for you." Sitting down, he switched on the monitor, then worked the keyboards for a minute until he connected to the Internet. He quickly vacated the chair for her. "What are you looking up?"

"This adoption agency. I want to read about the fire. Maybe they'll say something about where all their records went, besides up in smoke." She sat down, and did a Google search for Jamison Group Adoption Services, Spokane, WA.

The first four listings were for other adoption agencies in Spokane, and three more, picking up the key words, were for *Jamison* Auto *Services* in *Spokane.* And there was a

Jim *Jamison* offering *group* rates for his limousine *services* in *Spokane.*

Frowning, Karen went to the next page, and then she found something halfway down the list:

<u>FOUR DIE IN SHOOTING . . . Gunman Sets Adoption Agency on Fire . . .</u>
Duane Lee Savitt, 33, walked into the **Jamison Group Adoption Agency** on East Sprague Street at 1:35 p.m. Within minutes, he had shot and killed office manager Donna . . .
www.spokesmanreview.com/news/
shooting/042993 - 14k.

"My God," George murmured, peering over her shoulder. "All this time, I thought the fire was accidental."

Karen clicked on the link, and pulled up an article in the *Spokesman Review* archives, dated April 28, 1993:

FOUR DIE IN SHOOTING RAMPAGE

Gunman Sets Adoption Agency on Fire After Shooting Spree

SPOKANE: Police investigators are still

trying to determine the motive for a Pasco man's shooting spree at an adoption agency, which left three employees dead on Monday afternoon. Before it was over, the gunman set ablaze the small, two-story Tudor house which served as the adoption agency's office. He was shot and killed as he opened fire on police and firefighters arriving at the scene.

Armed with two handguns, several clips of ammunition, and an incendiary device, Duane Lee Savitt, 33, walked into the Jamison Group Adoption Agency on East Sprague Street at 1:35 p.m. Within minutes, he had shot and killed office manager Donna Houston, 51, and Scott Larabee, 40, an attorney for the agency. Anita Jamison, 44, vice president and part owner, was also shot.

"I heard screams, and several loud pops next door," said Margarita Brady, a receptionist at a neighboring architecture firm, D. Renner & Company. Brady immediately called 911. "There were still screams coming from inside the house when I saw the smoke start to pour out the windows . . ."

Karen glanced at the adoption documents

again. Both Scott Larabee and Anita Jamison had signed the contracts.

According to the article, Anita Jamison was still alive when the police finally gunned down Duane Lee Savitt. But she'd been badly burned in the fire and died in the ambulance on the way to Sacred Heart Medical Center.

The article also mentioned that the fire had destroyed volumes of records on file at the agency.

"It probably doesn't have anything to do with my niece," George said, still standing behind her. "But we should Google this Duane Savitt."

"Duane," Karen repeated, staring at the killer's name in the news article. She could almost hear a four-year-old girl trying to pronounce it. "Dween."

"What?" George asked. "What is it?"

"My God," Karen whispered, her eyes still riveted to that name on the screen. "I think we might have just found Amelia's other uncle."

CHAPTER ELEVEN

"None of the women I met last week through that Internet service were worth a second date. Four women, and not one could hold a candle to you."

Karen managed a patient, placid smile for the man seated across from her on the sofa in her study. He was a skinny 42-year-old divorcé with receding strawberry-blond hair, fishlike eyes, and a huge Adam's apple.

"Now, Laird, we've been over this before," she said. "It's called transference, and it's perfectly normal to get a little crush on your therapist. But you need to move on from that. Now, tell me about these women, and why they didn't measure up to your standards."

"Well, for starters, none of them liked *Star Trek.*"

"That's not a good reason. Your ex-wife was a huge *Star Trek* fan, and the two of you fought like cats. You'll have to do better than that."

Laird started listing the faults of date number one. She just wasn't pretty enough for him — this from a guy who looked like a blond Don Knotts. Of course, she was in no position to criticize people for their fickle romantic notions, not when she had feelings for a man whose wife had just been murdered a week ago.

She and George McMillan had spent over an hour last night in front of his computer screen, checking search engine listings for Duane Lee Savitt. George had pulled up a chair and sat beside her. They hadn't found much about the man who might have been Amelia's Unca Dween. Apparently, the police never determined a motive behind his killing spree. There were no records of him ever working at Jamison Group, and as far as anyone could tell, he hadn't known any of his victims. One article suggested Savitt might have been the birth father to a child adopted through the agency. But it was difficult to determine that, since he'd destroyed all their files. A thorough search of county and state records yielded nothing for investigators.

Karen was getting frustrated by what looked more and more like a dead end. But she had George at her side, occasionally touching her arm or shoulder as they found each new potential lead, even if it didn't pan out. She wasn't alone in her concern about Amelia; she had an ally.

She understood why he was a history professor. He seemed obsessed over getting every single fact about this tragedy from nearly fifteen years ago. He was doing it for Amelia, of course. But Karen liked to think he was doing it partly for her, too.

Before she left his house, he gave her a photo of Amelia, so she could post it at the nurses' station at the convalescent home. He walked her to her car, and assured her that he'd keep digging for more information about Duane Lee Savitt.

Karen hesitated before climbing into the car. She couldn't leave there without resolving something, though a sixth sense told her to leave it the hell alone. "Listen, I still feel bad about upsetting you last week. If I was out of line, I'm sorry —"

"What are you talking about?" George asked.

"When I told Amelia about her father and — and your wife," Karen explained. "I meant well. But you're right, it wasn't my place to —"

"Karen, please," he said, shaking his head. "It was a misunderstanding. You don't have to apologize for anything. If I got curt with you, I'm sorry. I was half out of my mind that night. If it weren't for you and Jessie, I don't think I could have gotten through it."

She shrugged. "Well, I didn't do much."

"Are you kidding? You broke the news to Amelia for me that her parents and Ina were dead. That was the last thing in the world I wanted to do. You drove her over here, and made sure she didn't get herself in trouble with the police. Even after what happened to you today — at your dad's rest home, and with Koehler — you're still in Amelia's corner. My niece is very lucky to have you for a friend. You're selling yourself short, Karen. I think you're terrific."

"Well, thank you, George," she said. She felt herself blushing. "I'll talk to you tomorrow, okay?"

George shook her hand, then lingered as she backed out of the driveway. He threw her a little wave. Karen blinked her headlights, and then started down the street.

She thought about him while driving to Sandpoint View and, for a few minutes, she actually wasn't scared. It didn't even occur to her to check the rearview mirror for the old black Cadillac.

All it took to jolt Karen back to scary reality was a long walk down that cold, dark, stale-smelling corridor at the rest home. She posted the snapshot of Amelia on the bulletin board at the nurses' station, along with a note: "If you see this young woman anywhere in or around here, please call me immediately. Many thanks, Karen Carlisle." She wrote her home and cell phone numbers at the bottom of the note.

She checked in on her dad, who was asleep. "G'night, Poppy," she whispered, kissing him on the forehead.

She chatted briefly with Rita, thanking her again for helping her earlier in the evening. Then she walked back out toward her car. The lot wasn't very well lit, and her eyes scanned the bushes bordering the rest home for anyone who might be lurking there. She had her key out, and picked up her pace the last few steps to the car. She made sure to check the backseat before climbing behind the wheel. Then she quickly shut the door and locked it.

All the way home, she kept glancing in the rearview mirror. No one seemed to be following her. Once she stepped inside the house, Karen switched on several lights. She took Rufus on a room-to-room check. While in Sheila's old room (now the guest room) she went into the closet. Her dad used to keep a gun under his bed, but when he'd started showing signs of depression and early Alzheimer's, Jessie and Karen had decided to hide the gun and bullets in another part of the house. They were inside a shoebox on the guest room closet shelf. If her dad had noticed the gun was missing, he hadn't said anything about it.

Karen dug the gun out of its hiding place. As far as she knew, her father had never fired the thing. The same clip had probably been inside the gun since 1987. She didn't know much about guns, but after so many years without use or maintenance, this one probably didn't work. Still, Karen felt better having it, especially when she crept down the basement stairs for the last round of her house check. She kept the gun pointed away from her toward the floor. The main part of the cellar had once been a recreation room for Karen's older brother and sister, but now it was just a storage area. The cheaply paneled walls used to be covered with posters that had come down decades ago. It was impossible to see the top of the Ping-Pong table, now loaded down with her old dollhouse, her brother's ancient 8-track tape player, and boxes of junk. Jessie kept the laundry room neat. But the latch was broken on the window above the big sink, and everyone at one time or another had used it to climb inside the house when they'd forgotten their keys. The furnace room was like something out of a horror movie. Even with a strong light, there were still dark areas behind the furnace, and a maze of pipes that cast shadows on the paint-chipped walls. Spiderwebs stretched across those old pipes. Jessie admitted she never cleaned that room. "You have to be a contortionist to make your way around that furnace. God knows what's back there; I don't even want to think about it. That's the creepiest room in this house." Karen agreed with her. And once she'd checked it, she hurried back up the stairs, shut the basement door, and locked it.

She let Rufus do his business in the backyard, while she stood, shivering at the back door. Then Karen heated up a Healthy Choice pizza for her late-night dinner in front of the TV and a mediocre *Saturday Night Live.* Of course, it was hard to laugh when she felt the need to keep a handgun tucked under the sofa cushion — *just in case.*

She'd fallen asleep on that sofa, with her dad's old robe over her and the gun beneath her. Rufus was curled up on the floor beside her. The TV and several lights remained on. The last thing she'd thought about was the gun. Did she really expect to use it, and on whom? Amelia?

Karen spent most of the morning on the phone with old contacts from Group Health, trying to track down psychiatrists who had experience with multiple personality disorder cases. *You can't be serious* was the most frequent response, and several people just laughed. But Karen did come up with a few names, and left some messages. She figured if Amelia was indeed suffering from MPD, then someone more qualified than herself had to be brought in — and soon. Karen felt out of her league here.

She had two client sessions scheduled that Sunday afternoon, and the second one was with Laird, who always complained about his love life.

"She ordered a Cosmopolitan with some fancy-schmancy-brand vodka, and all I had was a lousy Bud Light," Laird was saying of his most recent Internet date. "And afterward, she tells me we should split the tab fifty-fifty, and I'm like, the hell with that. She wasn't even pretty —"

The doorbell rang, and Rufus started barking. Karen got to her feet. "I'm sorry, Laird. I'll be right back. In the meantime, think about why this woman's prettiness, or lack of it, comes up as an issue here."

She stepped out to the foyer and shut the study door behind her. "Quiet, Rufus!" she called. She always kept him locked up in the kitchen when she had clients over. She wasn't expecting anyone. Amelia still hadn't called back. But it wouldn't have been like her to come over unannounced, anyway. Even with her emergency last week, Amelia had tried to call first.

Karen checked the peephole. "Damn it," she muttered, and then she opened the door.

Detective Russ Koehler stood on her front stoop, wearing a leather aviator jacket, khakis, and a smug expression. He had a tall beverage cup from Starbucks in his hand. "You told me to bring my checkbook next time I came by," he announced. "But I decided to bring a peace offering instead — a tall latte."

He tried to hand it to her, but Karen didn't move a muscle. She just stared at him.

"Listen, I admire the way you stuck up for your client yesterday. But if you really want to help Amelia, you'll cooperate with me. And you know something? I think you'll feel better once we've talked. We're going to connect, Karen. I'm feeling lucky about it.

In fact, I have my lucky shirt on today."

Eyes narrowed, Karen glanced down at his shirt for a second: a white button-down oxford with wide stripes of blue that matched his eyes. She might have been attracted to him, if only he weren't such a snake. He held out the Starbucks cup again.

"C'mon, aren't you at least going to take my peace offering?"

"I'm in the middle of a session with a client right now," she said finally. "And you're interrupting."

"I can wait," he said with a crooked grin.

Karen started to shake her head. "Well, I'm afraid you . . ."

She fell silent at the sight of someone coming up the driveway toward them. She wore jeans, a red blouse, and a black cardigan, and nervously clutched a big leather purse to her side. Her hair was swept back and up from her neck with a barrette. "Amelia?" Karen whispered. She could see she was wearing makeup, a rarity for her. The crimson lipstick and dark mascara looked startling against her creamy complexion.

Koehler turned and glanced at the 19-year-old. Obviously he liked what he saw. Karen noticed the shift in his posture, and even with only a quarter of his face in view she saw a smirk on his face that was almost predatory. "Well, well, Amelia Faraday, at last we meet," he said.

Stopping a few steps from him, she seemed bewildered.

"This is Detective Russ Koehler, with the Seattle Police," Karen piped up.

Wide-eyed, she politely nodded at him.

He grabbed her hand and shook it. "Sorry for your loss. Listen, I'd really like to chat with you —"

"Amelia, I need to see you inside for a minute," Karen said loudly, cutting him off.

"Oh, okay," she murmured, still looking baffled. She turned away from Koehler and started toward the doorway.

But he took hold of her arm. "Now, wait a minute —"

From the doorway, Karen shot him a look. "What do you think you're doing?"

He froze for a moment, then let go of the 19-year-old. "Okay, fine," he grumbled. "Everything's cool."

"Wait here, please." Karen shut the door on Koehler, and ushered her into the house. "Come on, Amelia." Passing the study, she called out, "Laird? I'll be with you in a minute!"

They hurried into the kitchen. Rufus backed away, and barked at them. He even growled a little. "Stop that," Karen hissed. "You know Amelia, for God's sake."

"What's wrong with him?"

"I don't know," Karen said, reaching into the cookie jar. "Too much excitement around here, I guess." She fished out a dog biscuit, opened the basement door, and tossed it down the stairs. Rufus let out a final bark, then eagerly chased after the treat. Karen shut the basement door after him.

"Amelia, where have you been?" she whispered, taking hold of her arm. "I left you four messages yesterday."

"Oh, Karen, I'm so sorry," she said. "I needed to get away. So I rented a car and just started driving. I didn't check my messages. Please, don't be mad —"

"I'm not mad. I'm just confused, and worried about you." Karen patted her shoulder. "Listen, I need you to be honest with me about something. It's important. What were you doing yesterday around five o'clock?"

She shrugged. "I'm really not sure. I've been driving all over. I think I was up near Deception Pass, but that might have been earlier in the day. Why are you asking?"

"You didn't stop by the Sandpoint View Convalescent Home yesterday?"

She shook her head. "I don't even know

where that is, Karen."

"Do you recall running down a gray stairwell to a basement area with a boiler room, and another room that was a storage area?"

She shook her head again. "No —"

"Think hard, Amelia. You don't remember a storage area full of boxes and hospital equipment? There were broken lights on the ceiling, and it was dark. There was a fire door —"

"I don't know what you're talking about." She backed into the hallway.

"You don't have any memory of it at all? Not even fragments?"

"Goddamn it, no!" she cried angrily. "Why are you asking me all these fucking questions? Why are you picking on me?"

Dumbstruck, Karen stared at her. Amelia had never snapped at her like that before. And for a moment, Karen wondered if she was talking to the *other* Amelia right now. Between the makeup and her manner, she almost seemed like a different person. Then again, maybe Karen was looking too hard for a *different* Amelia right now.

She took a deep breath, and tried to smile. "I thought I saw you yesterday at the rest home where my father's staying," she said calmly. She took a small step toward her. "I

— I must have been mistaken. I didn't mean to jump on your case."

"Well, you're scaring me, Karen," she said with a shaky voice. "I don't understand why you're acting like this. What happened?" She glanced toward the front door. "What's that police detective doing here?"

"If I seem on edge, he's one reason why," Karen explained. "He's *unofficially* investigating the deaths of your parents and aunt. By *unofficially,* I mean he's snooping around on his own without any backing from the police department. At least, he doesn't have any backing, yet. He's got a bunch of crazy theories and notions about what might have happened last weekend. This guy's bad news, Amelia. You shouldn't talk to him. And you don't have to —"

The doorbell rang. Rufus started barking and scratching on the other side of the basement door. The doorbell rang again and again until the chiming was continuous. The study door slid open, and Laird stuck his head out. "Is anyone going to answer that?" he asked, over the incessant ringing and the dog's yelping.

Karen moved down the hallway, and gave her client a gentle push back into the study. "Laird, I'll be with you in just one more minute. Sorry about the interruption." She shut the door to the study. "Rufus, can it!" she yelled. Then she swiveled around and yanked open the front door to find Russ Koehler, with his finger on the bell. "Do you mind?" she growled.

"As a matter of fact, I do mind," he replied, finally taking his finger off the doorbell. "I'm going to talk with your client whether you like it or not. And the more trouble you give me, the more trouble I'll make for you — and believe me, I can deliver on that."

Not backing down, Karen shook her head at him. "Amelia doesn't have to talk to you —"

"Oh, Karen, never mind, really, please," she interrupted. She touched Karen's shoulder as she edged past her toward Koehler. "I don't want you getting in trouble on my account. I'll talk to him. It'll be okay. Don't worry."

"No, Amelia, wait —"

But she hurried out the door.

Koehler took hold of her arm, and he grinned back at Karen. "You heard what Amelia said. *Don't worry.*" Then he led her toward the driveway. "My car's parked just down the block. We can go for a drive." He handed her the Starbucks container. "Could you use a tall latte? I bought it for Karen, but she didn't want it."

She took the drink, then glanced over her shoulder at Karen. "I'll call you later, okay?"

From her front door, Karen watched them start down the sidewalk together. "Damn it," she muttered.

They disappeared behind some tall hedges bordering the neighbor's yard. But she could still hear Russ Koehler talking. "You know, Amelia, I had no idea you were such a lovely girl. . . ."

Then his voice faded in the distance, and Karen couldn't hear him anymore.

"I swear, I don't remember much about that night at all," she said, quietly sobbing in the passenger seat.

She'd finished the latte he'd given her about ten minutes ago when they'd taken the Issaquah exit off Interstate 90, about a half hour east of Seattle. The empty container was in the cup holder between them. Russ had been a little worried about potential spilling on the plush interior of his new Audi TT Coupe (one of the benefits of marrying into money). He reminded her a few times to be careful with the coffee. Now he could relax a little, and he focused on getting a confession out of this tasty-looking young thing. He figured her Uncle George probably couldn't keep his hands off her. He couldn't really blame the guy, either. He was convinced the uncle had manipulated her into helping him kill his wife and her parents.

He'd asked that she show him where she'd gone on the night her parents and aunt had died. According to police reports, she'd driven to Snoqualmie Falls. But this Issaquah route was sure a screwy way of getting there. Following her instructions, he'd almost gotten lost on all these winding forest roads around Cougar Mountain Wildland Park. He'd finally pulled into a little alcove at the start of a hiking trail, and shut off the engine to his Audi. By the hiking path, there was a little sign with a cartoon of Dennis the Menace wearing a backpack, and the caption "Don't Be a Litterbug!" Only somebody had crossed out the *Don't.* No one else was parked in the area. The sun was just starting to set behind the tall evergreens to the west.

"Listen, Amelia, I'm going to make sure you get a break for talking candidly with me," he said, letting his hand slide down from the gear shift to her seat. His pinky brushed against her thigh. "I'm very well connected. So you can tell me the truth, and we'll work something out. I don't really blame you. It was your uncle's idea, wasn't it?"

Her head down, she kept crying. She held her purse in her lap. "I haven't been able to talk to anyone about it, not even Karen."

"Is he screwing you?" Koehler asked.

Wincing, she nodded. "I'm so ashamed. My boyfriend, Shane, he's so sweet. I can't believe I've been doing this behind his back. But it's been going on for — for years now."

Koehler couldn't believe his luck. Incest and pedophilia now factored into the story. "How old were you when your uncle started in on you?"

She wept quietly, and set her purse down between the seat and her door. She wouldn't look him in the eye. She leaned forward, and didn't seem to realize it made her blouse open in front. Koehler could see one white, round breast, and the rose-colored nipple grazing at the fabric of her blouse.

He moved his hand to her thigh and stroked it. He was starting to get hard. "It's okay, Amelia. Take your time answering. I'm here for you."

Koehler couldn't stop staring at her breasts. He wanted so much to undo the rest of those buttons on her blouse. His head was swimming.

He didn't notice that she was reaching

inside her purse.

All at once, she swung her arm out and hit him in the forehead with something hard. A searing pain shot through his head, and for a moment, all he could see was white. "Fuck!" he howled.

He touched his forehead and felt blood. It was trickling down into his left eye. Blinking, he tried to focus on her.

Then he noticed the gun in her hand.

"They left here together over two hours ago," Karen said into the phone. She was at her desk, behind stacks of work files. She'd been meaning to straighten them out for months. It was just the busywork she needed while waiting around for Amelia to call. So far, she'd reorganized the *A* through *D* patient records, had two cups of coffee, and given herself a paper cut.

"I tried calling Amelia an hour ago, and nothing," she continued. "I even called Koehler's cell phone, and there was no answer there either."

"I can't believe she went off with him," George muttered on the other end of the line.

"And voluntarily," Karen added. "I tried to stop her. Now all I can think about is Amelia making some sort of confession to that creep. I wasn't going to call you until I heard back from her. I didn't want to worry you for nothing. But now I . . ." She sighed. "Well, I thought you should know. Maybe you want to contact a lawyer or something."

"I appreciate it, Karen," he replied. She could hear the TV on and Stephanie laughing in the distant background. "Let's just wait it out for now. You're the only one Amelia has confessed to, for lack of a better word. She's a very smart young woman. She kept her mouth shut with the police and everyone else about her *visions.* Let's just hope she does the same thing with Koehler."

"You're right. I probably shouldn't have called you this soon."

"Nonsense, I'm glad you told me, Karen," he said. "Why should you be the only one who's worried? Besides, Amelia's my niece. Jody, Steph, and I are her only living relatives. Or maybe I should qualify that — only *known* living relatives. Listen, I've checked the Spokane and Pasco newspaper archives and still haven't come up with very much on Duane Lee Savitt. All I know is that he was an auto mechanic and, according to the people who worked with him at this garage in Pasco, he pretty much kept to himself. No one seemed to really know him. He had a sister, Joy, who died a few weeks before his rampage at the adoption agency. I kept hoping to find the name of another surviving family member in one of the articles, but no dice. But there was something in his obituary in the Pasco *Tri-City Herald.* They mentioned he was buried at Arbor Heights Memorial Park in Salem, Oregon."

"Uh-huh," Karen said. "And — that's a lead?"

"Someone had to pay for the burial, and his headstone, if there is one. It's a pretty safe bet that person knew Duane, too. But so far, that party is nameless. I checked the office hours for Arbor Heights Memorial Park, and they're closed right now. But I'll get in touch with them tomorrow morning. Keep your fingers crossed they still have billing records from 1993."

"I will," Karen replied tentatively. "That — that's great, George."

She didn't want to remind him it was a long shot that Duane Lee Savitt had been Amelia's uncle. If he had been, and they discovered something in Amelia's childhood to explain her condition today, then George might be gathering evidence to exonerate his niece for murdering her parents, and his wife.

She wondered if George was aware of that.

Or was he still so convinced of Amelia's innocence that such a notion hadn't even occurred to him?

Until yesterday, Karen had felt exactly the same way. It helped that George knew about Amelia going off with Koehler. And it helped that he was doing extensive research into what had happened at the adoption agency.

But Karen still felt as if she were the only one worried about Amelia — and what that young woman was capable of.

Russ Koehler was shivering. He wore a T-shirt, and nothing else. She'd made him strip off his shoes, socks, trousers, and underpants after they'd veered off the main hiking trial. Then she'd told him to remove his shirt and start tearing it into small, thin strips. Every forty or fifty feet that they stomped through those woods, branches from shrubs scraping at his naked legs, rocks and sticks chewing away at his cold, bare feet, she made him tie a strip from his shirt to a branch. He'd been marking a trail for her return trip.

"Once I feel we've walked far enough, I'm going to leave you here — alone," she explained coolly. "I'll take down these trail markings, so it's not going to be easy for you to find your way out. Even then, you won't have any money. You won't have your clothes or your precious car. And I'll be far, far away, where you won't ever find me."

Russ was ordinarily quite proud of his body, but now he clutched what was left of his shirt over his genitals. They were shrunken up from the cold. He felt so vulnerable with her walking behind him, staring at his naked ass. She didn't tease him, giggle, or make any lewd comments as they continued through the forest. She seemed so passionless, almost detached from everything. And that scared the shit out of him.

"Listen, Amelia," he said, glancing over his shoulder for a second. "Your plan isn't going to work. If you're on the run, you won't be able to collect your inheritance. Your uncle will get it all. Everyone will think you did it alone."

"Then do you think I might be better off if I just killed you here?" she asked, without a hint of irony or sarcasm in her voice.

"Jesus, no," he gasped. "No, no. I'm saying we can make a deal, and pin the brunt of it on your uncle. He manipulated you, didn't he? And I told you, I know people who have a lot of clout. . . ."

"Tie another strip to that evergreen

branch, will you?" she said.

His hands shook violently as he tried to make a knot around the branch with the shirt strip. Russ glanced up at the darkening sky. Within a few minutes, the forest would be swallowed up in blackness, and he'd be lucky to see his hand in front of his face.

He turned to her, and clutched the torn shirt in front of his crotch. "I — I'm never getting out of here, am I?" he asked.

"Well, you have a lot of challenges," she said, the gun pointed at him. "You'll have bears, coyotes, and maybe even a cougar or two to contend with. Most of the real interesting creatures in these woods come out at night. Did you ever hear that story about the woman who went camping in the woods while she was having her period, and she got mauled to death by a bear? Apparently, the bear smelled the blood, and he tracked her down. So, I'd watch that cut on your forehead, Russ. It could be your death sentence out here. Now, turn around and keep walking. Just a little farther, we're almost there."

He stared at her for a moment. She was screwing around with him. He could tell. She planned to kill him in these woods. Turning, he continued to stagger through the brush. His feet were cold and bleeding. "Listen, Amelia," he said, starting to cry. "My wife just had a baby, for God's sake. You can't kill me . . . please. My son's only a week old."

"If your baby son's so important, why weren't you with him today? Why didn't you buy a station wagon instead of your flashy sports car?"

"Please . . ." he repeated. Just a few feet ahead, there was a small clearing in the forest. He noticed a large, oblong rock on the ground. It was about the size of his fist. He imagined bashing her brains in with that rock, once he had her down.

He weaved forward and continued to make sobbing noises for her benefit. He was banking on the element of surprise. She wouldn't expect a weeping, sniveling man to suddenly attack her. The rock was just in front of him now. He stumbled, then hurled himself to the ground. He even let out a defeated cry. Then he grabbed the rock.

A loud shot rang out.

The rock flew from his grasp. A spray of blood hit him in the face. It felt as if his hand had exploded. He howled in pain. Grabbing his wrist, he brought his hand up to his face so he could focus on it.

To his horror, Russ Koehler saw a bloody,

bone-exposed stub where his index finger used to be.

"You fucking bitch!" he yelled, real tears streaming down his face. Curled up on the ground, he held onto his mangled hand, and glared at her.

Expressionless, she stood over him with the gun.

"Goddamn you!" he hissed. "You've been jerking me around for the last hour, and I've known it. You have no intention of leaving me alive in these woods."

She nodded. "You're right about that."

"You're stupid," he said, gasping for air. "Everyone on the police force knows I'm checking on you. When I disappear, they'll figure out it was you. And when they find my body —"

"Oh, they won't find you, not right away," she cut in. "What I was telling you earlier about all the wild animals in these woods, that wasn't bullshit. They'll take care of you, the hungry ones. They're always hungry. Some of them will even bury your bones. I learned that from *him*. He didn't bury every one of them, you know. Sometimes, he just let nature take its course. If there's enough exposed flesh and enough blood — and enough carnivorous creatures around to smell it — then, it isn't always that necessary to bury a dead body."

"Jesus, you're insane," he murmured, still curled up on the ground. "Did you hear what I said, Amelia? You're in-fucking-sane, you stupid —"

"I'm not Amelia," she said. "I'm Annabelle. And you're the one who's stupid — for not seeing that earlier."

Wide eyed, he stared at her as she aimed the gun at him again. "NO! NO, WAIT! GOD, PLEASE. . . ." He screamed and screamed. But there was no one around to hear him.

And no one heard the gun go off . . . three times.

"Hello?"

Karen heard a baby crying in the background on the other end of the line. "Yes, hello," she said. "Is Russ Koehler there, please?"

"Who is this?" Mrs. Koehler asked, sounding haggard.

"My name is Karen Carlisle." She glanced at her wristwatch: 10:35. "Um, I'm sorry to call so late, but I've been trying to get ahold of your husband, and he's not answering his cell phone."

"I know, I've been trying to reach him too," she replied. "What's this about? How do you know Russ?"

"He came by my office today regarding an investigation," Karen explained. She figured the less she said about it, the better. She decided not to mention Amelia, who still hadn't gotten in touch with her. "Um, Detective Koehler was supposed to call me back, and never did. I was just checking in."

"Well, he isn't here," Mrs. Koehler said abruptly. "If you happen to hear from him, Miss —"

"Carlisle," Karen finished for her.

"Yes. Well, tell him his wife and son are waiting up for him."

Karen heard a click on the other end of the line, and then — nothing.

CHAPTER TWELVE

"Your homework assignment this week is to be good to yourself," Karen said, walking out of her office with her last patient of the day. Cecilia was a divorced forty-something woman with curly gray-brown hair and low self-esteem. Karen opened the front door for her. "List ten things you consider life's little pleasures and do three of them for yourself this week. Treat yourself, okay?"

Nodding, Cecilia smiled at her. "Okay, Karen. Thanks. See you next Monday."

Ordinarily, Karen would have gone back into her study and jotted down some notes about the session, but she still hadn't heard back from Amelia. Twenty-four hours, and still no word. No one had heard from her — not George, Shane, or Amelia's roommate.

Karen always switched off her cellular and set the home phone answering machine for immediate pickup during client sessions.

Between each of her three sessions today, she'd anxiously checked her messages.

With Cecilia out the door, Karen made a beeline to her purse, which was on the chair in the front hallway. She dug out her cell phone and clicked on the messages display. There was one. She recognized Amelia's cell phone number. She knew it by heart, now. Karen pressed the playback code. "Hi, Karen. You're not answering at home, either. You must be with a client. Um, looks like you called me a bunch of times. Sorry, but I've been out of town, and I switched off my phone. I just had to get away from everything and everyone. Shane and my Uncle George left a ton of messages too. I didn't mean to worry you guys. Anyway, I'm back. Call me, and I'll answer this time, I promise! Bye."

Baffled, Karen played the message again. It didn't make sense. Amelia was acting as if yesterday with Koehler had never even happened.

She hit the last caller return, and Amelia answered after two rings. "Karen, is that you?"

"Hi, Amelia. I just got your message."

"And I just got all of yours. Sorry if I gave you a scare. I should have told you —"

"You were out of town?" Karen asked, cutting her off.

"Yes. I rented a car and drove up and down the coast. Now that my credit card's working again, I —"

"And you just got back *today?*"

"Yes, about an hour ago. I blew off a morning class. Why? What's going on, Karen?"

"Did you happen to have a blackout over the weekend? Any lost time?"

"Why do you ask that?" Amelia replied, a sudden edge in her voice.

"Well, I . . ." Karen trailed off at the sound of someone on the front stoop. Rufus started barking in the kitchen. Then the doorbell rang. "Amelia, just a minute," she said, moving to the door. She glanced through the peephole to see a petite, very pretty black woman and a stocky, Caucasian man in his late forties with a bad comb-over. From their somber expressions, office clothes, and the odd pairing, Karen figured they were police detectives.

She backed away from the door. "Listen, Amelia," she whispered into the phone. Rufus's barking competed with her. "I have to call you back."

"Karen, for God's sake, you can't just ask me if I've had a blackout, then say you'll call me back. What's going on? Did something happen over the weekend that I should know about?"

"I can't talk right now," Karen whispered urgently. "There are people at my front door. I'll call you back as soon as I can." She clicked off the line. "Rufus, calm down!" she yelled. Then she opened the door, and put on her best cordial smile for the two of them. "Can I help you?" She still clutched the cell phone in her hand.

The woman flashed her police badge. "Karen Carlisle?"

She nodded. "Yes?"

"Good afternoon, I'm Jacqueline Peyton and this is Warren Rooney." Behind her, the man gave a little nod. Neither one of them cracked a smile. "We're with the Seattle Police," she continued. "We're hoping you might help us locate a missing person. I understand Detective Russ Koehler was here yesterday afternoon."

Karen stared at them and blinked. "He's *missing?*"

"Was he here yesterday afternoon?" the woman pressed.

Karen nodded more times than necessary. "Um, yes, he showed up around this time yesterday — two o'clock. He was here for about ten minutes."

"Mrs. Koehler said you telephoned her

last night."

"Yes, I thought I'd be hearing back from him, and never did." Karen opened the door wider. "I'm sorry. Would you like to come in?"

The two detectives stepped inside the foyer. Karen closed the door after them. The cell phone went off in her hand, and she glanced at the caller ID: Amelia again.

She switched off the phone and stashed it in her purse. "I always thought a certain amount of time had to go by — like forty-eight or seventy-two hours — before the police considered anyone officially missing."

The man shook his head. "In Washington State, there's no waiting period. He's been missing since yesterday afternoon. And at three o'clock this morning, we picked up a DUI driving Koehler's car, a brand-new Audi. He claims he found it — abandoned, unlocked with the keys inside — on Aurora Boulevard."

"What was the nature of Detective Koehler's visit here?" the woman asked.

Karen hesitated. She remembered Koehler walking off with Amelia yesterday. "My car's parked just down the block," he'd told her. "We can go for a drive."

"Ms. Carlisle?" the policewoman said.

Karen folded her arms in front of her.

"Um, I'm a therapist, and Detective Koehler was asking about one of my clients, Amelia Faraday. I believe he was conducting some sort of follow-up investigation into the deaths of her parents and aunt in Wenatchee last week." She figured this wasn't any news to them. George had already told her that other cops on the force knew about Koehler's interest in the case. But they didn't know Koehler had driven off yesterday afternoon with Amelia.

She needed to talk to Amelia before the police did.

"I'm afraid I wasn't much help," Karen added. "I told Detective Koehler it would be unethical to repeat anything a patient shared with me during a session. Not that there's anything to conceal. I've read the newspaper reports, and I don't think Amelia held back on anything when she spoke to the police."

The policewoman cocked her head to one side. Her eyes narrowed at her. "When Detective Koehler left here yesterday, did he indicate where he was going?"

Karen shrugged. "I have no idea where he was headed." All the while, she thought, *God, I'm lying to the police now.*

"But he said he'd call you," the man interjected. "What about?"

Karen shrugged again. "I'm not sure, actually. He didn't specify the reason."

"And when you didn't hear from him, you tried calling him."

She nodded. "That's right."

"You told Mrs. Koehler you'd been trying his cell before phoning his home." The cop finally cracked a tiny smile. "Sounds like you felt his calling back was pretty darn important."

Karen swallowed hard. "I just didn't like the idea of having unfinished police business hanging over my head at the end of the day," she answered carefully.

Neither one of the detectives seemed to be buying her story. The woman cleared her throat. "Ms. Carlisle — Karen, you don't have to answer this. But it would be a big help to us. Do you have a — a *personal* relationship with Russ Koehler?"

"With Detective Koehler?" She let out a little laugh. "God, no, I only just met him the day before yesterday. What, did his wife think that I —"

"Do you suppose Koehler went to see Amelia Faraday after leaving here?" the man asked, cutting her off.

"Um, I really can't say," Karen replied, shrugging.

"Do you have a contact address and

phone number for Ms. Faraday?" he asked.

"Yes, I have that on file. I'll write it down for you." She retreated into her office, took a deep breath, then looked up Amelia's campus address and phone number. She scribbled down the information, then returned to the foyer and gave the piece of paper to the policewoman. "That's her room number in Terry Hall, along with the phone there."

The woman took it. "You don't happen to have her cell phone number, do you?"

Karen hesitated. "Um, I . . ."

"Never mind," she said. "This is good enough. Thank you for your time, Ms. Carlisle."

As soon as Karen ushered them out the door, she ducked back inside, and dug her cell phone out of her purse again. Amelia answered on the first ring. Karen asked her if she was in her room at the dorm.

"Yeah," Amelia replied. "Why did you ask me if I had a blackout? What's going on?"

"Listen," Karen said. "Do me a favor. Finish up whatever you're doing there and get out. Some people might be on their way to see you, and it's best you don't talk to them until I meet with you. Don't answer the phone either. I'll meet you in twenty minutes at the U Library, the Graduate Reading Room. Don't tell anyone else where you're going, okay?"

"Well, okay, I guess. But I wish I knew what the hell was going on."

"I'll explain everything when I see you. Take care."

Karen clicked off the line. Then she headed to the closet and grabbed her coat.

"So, the way I understand it, your niece was adopted through the agency when she was four and, within a month, this Duane Lee Savitt character walked into the adoption place, shot three employees, and set their offices on fire. Is that about right?"

George nodded. He stood by Professor Lori Kim's desk and watched her load her briefcase with books and papers. Her Family and Juvenile Law class had just let out, and the classroom was empty except for the two of them. Lori Kim was a stout Asian woman in her late thirties. She had a few gray streaks in her close-cropped hair and wore designer glasses with her dark-blue power suit. Lori's brisk, no-nonsense manner was occasionally punctuated by a sweet, disarming smile. George had called a few friends at the university, and had heard Professor Kim had a background in law enforcement as well as child psychology.

"I'm wondering if there's a connection between this girl and the shootings at the adoption agency," George explained. "I heard you know something about adoption laws. Do you think Savitt might have gone to the agency, trying to track down the child? At the same time, he torched the place, so I'm wondering if he wanted to destroy records that might link him with one particular child."

"That one particular child being your niece?" Lori Kim asked.

"It's a stretch, yes. But she does have vague memories of an Uncle Duane."

Professor Kim zipped up her briefcase. "Do you mind if we walk and talk? I have a dental appointment at two-fifteen, and my car's parked on the other side of the campus."

"Not at all," George replied. "In fact, I'll even carry your briefcase for you. I was hoping to get some information on my niece's biological parents, but —"

"Oh, that won't be easy," she cut in. She unloaded the briefcase on him, and it was damn heavy. "Those records are closed in Washington State."

George had already found that out the hard way. He'd been on the phone for two hours this morning with several government agencies, talking to a lot of apathetic, curt, and often rude clerks who had told him the same thing: the information he wanted was "confidential . . . unavailable . . . restricted." Finally, he'd given up and started phoning people, asking if there was a professor who knew a lot about adoption procedures. He hoped against hope that Lori Kim might know a way for him to get past all the legal stumbling blocks.

Lugging the briefcase, he walked down the corridor with her on the law school's second floor. She moved at a brisk clip. "If your niece remembers an Uncle Duane before she was adopted by your in-laws, it means she had to be at least three or four years old before she lost her parents — or they gave her up. It's unusual that she'd end up adopted through an agency. She should have gone through the foster care system."

"She did spend time in some foster homes before my in-laws took her," George said. They ducked into the stairwell and started down the steps. "I was still dating Amelia's aunt when Amelia's parents were going through the adoption process. They lived in Spokane at the time. But I know they had a lot of visits back and forth, and a trial period."

"That's how they do it in foster care.

Maybe the adoption agency was involved for some other reason." Professor Kim stopped at the bottom of the steps. "You said your niece spent time in other foster homes. Did the child have any problems or disorders?"

He nodded. "She had frequent nightmares, and she got these phantom pains and illnesses. She practically drove her parents nuts. But that didn't start up until after the adoption went through. By then my in-laws had moved to Bellingham and had a baby boy of their own. We figured Amelia was just vying for their attention."

Lori Kim frowned. "Then again, maybe those nightmares and phantom pains were what got the child bounced out of one foster home and into the next. Might even be why her real parents gave up on her. Children learn very quickly. Your niece might have been on her best behavior with your in-laws during that trial period. When she saw her baby brother cried without getting the boot, she might have figured it was safe to let her pain and fear be heard."

They stepped outside into the sun and a cool autumn breeze. This section of the campus was graced with stately old buildings and magnificent trees with their leaves changing. The grounds were bathed in a riot of fall colors. Classes were in session, so there wasn't the usual mob scene. Only a few students and teachers lingered about.

"Of course, I'm just speculating," Professor Kim continued, as they walked along a paved pathway across the leaf-scattered lawn. "Once in a while, if the foster system has problems placing a child, they may turn to an adoption agency for assistance. It's possible that's what happened with your niece."

"I always assumed Amelia's biological parents were dead," George remarked. "But you mentioned they might have just given her up. Do you think they could still be alive?"

"Anything's possible," Lori Kim replied. "If you want me to come up with a potential reason for why this Duane Lee Savitt did what he did, I can give you about a dozen different scenarios."

"Give me your best one."

"Well, since there weren't any state, city, or county records connecting Savitt with the adoption agency, I'd say he wasn't the child's legal father. But there's a chance he was the birth father. The mother could have lied about it on the birth certificate and transfer papers. Savitt may have also been your niece's natural uncle, just as she remembers. But once again, they didn't come across his name in any records, which means he was most likely a family friend or possibly a blood uncle on the mother's side, and she was married. The maiden names aren't always flagged on those records."

George nodded. "Savitt had a sister named Joy who died just a few weeks before he went berserk at the adoption agency."

Lori Kim stopped abruptly. "It's strange that Savitt waited until the mother died before he tried to track down the child."

"Well, maybe he tried to get custody after his sister died —"

"There would be a record of that," she argued. "You said Savitt shot up the adoption place less than a month after your niece was officially adopted. But under the foster care system, it's a gradual process toward the final adoption. And you said your niece had some false starts in other foster homes. So she had to be in foster care for at least three months, which means the mother was still alive, and therefore gave up the child. Maybe she was too sick to take care of her at the time. One thing for sure, she didn't want her brother to have the girl or she would have given him custody. So, obviously, Savitt waited until his sister was dead before he went searching for his niece. And when he came to the agency, looking for her —"

"They couldn't tell him where she'd gone, because those adoption records are closed," George finished for her. "So, Uncle Duane went crazy."

"Well, I don't quite agree with you on that," she said, resuming her quick gait along the path. "I doubt he'd armed himself for his first trip to that agency. He probably went there once to make inquiries, became frustrated, and then returned with his arsenal."

George got winded carrying the heavy briefcase and trying to keep up with her. "You know, it's weird the police couldn't figure this out."

"Well, they couldn't connect him to anyone at that agency. But you have — if you're right about him being this girl's uncle. And so far, we're just hypothesizing."

"Why do you think he burned the place down?"

"Did any of those articles you read say if he used hollow-point bullets to shoot those people?"

"Yeah. How did you know —"

"Hollow-points are the bullets of choice for most mass murderers. Only God knows what other function they serve. Hunters don't use them. Hollow-points inflict the most damage. And that's probably why Duane Savitt set fire to the place, to inflict the most damage."

"You don't think he was trying to destroy some records?"

"It's possible. But if he was really related to your niece, those same records would be in the foster care system, and he should have known that. Then again, you're trying to figure out the logic of some asshole who took it upon himself to shoot three people who never did a single thing to hurt him. I hope I never comprehend the way someone like that thinks."

"If those records exist in the foster care system, how can I get to them?" George pressed. "You must know some way."

"Get your lawyer, get your niece, and file a petition."

"There's no alternate route?"

"Try to track down someone who knew Uncle Duane."

"I'm giving that a shot right now," George replied. "One of the articles I read mentioned he was buried in a cemetery in Salem, Oregon. I'm trying to track down whoever paid for the plot and the tombstone, if there is one. I figure this person must know Duane pretty well."

"That's good thinking," she said. They headed toward a small parking lot.

"I called the cemetery office this morning," George explained. "The guy there said they *might* be able to help me if I come down tomorrow and talk to him in person."

"Sounds like someone wants his palm greased. Bring money." Professor Kim took her key out of her purse and unlocked the driver door to her blue Geo. "Did you think I'd have some connection, a shortcut way of getting the lowdown on your niece's biological parents?"

George gave her the briefcase. "I'd be lying if I said I wasn't hoping for that."

"Sorry, George," Professor Kim said. She tossed her briefcase onto the passenger seat, and then climbed behind the wheel.

"You were still a lot of help. Thanks."

"Have a nice trip to Salem. And if you end up meeting that friend of Duane's, would you find out something for me?"

"What's that?" he asked.

"Find out why Duane waited until his sister was dead to go looking for the girl. Or maybe I should say to go *hunting* for the little girl. I have a feeling that's closer to what he had in mind. Good luck, George." She shut the door, started up the car and backed out of the parking spot.

George watched her drive away until the car disappeared around a curve in the winding road.

"Karen, I swear, I didn't get back to town until this morning," Amelia whispered.

They sat at the end of a beautiful long wood table. There were twenty matching tables in the Graduate Reading Room of UW's Suzzallo Library arranged like pews in a church, ten on each side. The tall stained-glass windows, ornate hanging light fixtures, and cathedral ceiling inspired quiet meditation. Bookcases were pressed against the stone walls. There were at least sixty other students in the library, and only the slightest murmuring could be heard among them.

Amelia looked pretty in a lavender sweater and khakis. She wasn't wearing much makeup today, and she had her hair pulled back in a ponytail. "I was driving around Olympic National Park yesterday afternoon," she told Karen in a hushed voice. "That's as close to Seattle as I got. I ended up spending last night at a B & B in Port Angeles. I can show you the receipt if you don't believe me. It's in my other purse."

"So, you don't remember coming by my place yesterday?" Karen asked.

Amelia adamantly shook her head.

"We talked in the kitchen," Karen said, trying to jog her memory. "Rufus was acting strange, growling at us."

Amelia glanced down at the library table and frowned. "I'm sorry."

"And you never met a Detective Koehler? The name isn't even familiar?"

"No."

"He gave you coffee, and took you for a drive. . . ."

Amelia brought a hand up to her mouth, and stared back at Karen. "He gave me coffee?" she repeated.

Karen nodded. "Koehler's tall and good-looking with pale-blond hair. He's got a very cocky smile. . . ."

"Are his eyes blue?" she asked.

"Yes," Karen whispered, leaning forward.

"His eyes match the blue stripes in his shirt," Amelia murmured, staring down at the tabletop.

"Yes, that's right."

"I make him take it off and tear it into strips," Amelia continued, almost in a trance. "He ties the pieces of his shirt onto branches in the forest. They're markers. I — I'll need to find my way back to the main trail after I kill him."

Karen swallowed hard. She waited a moment before saying anything. "What forest, Amelia?"

She gazed at Karen. Her lip quivered. "This really happened, didn't it? Oh, Jesus!"

A student one desk down loudly cleared his throat and scowled over his textbook at them.

"I need you to remember, Amelia," Karen whispered. She stroked her arm. "It'll be okay. We're going to work this out. Do you remember where you where? What forest?"

"God, Karen, you must be right," Amelia said, under her breath. "I don't remember being at your house at all, but I was with him. We were driving for long time. He was worried about me spilling coffee in his new car. I remember keeping my purse shut and in my lap most of the time. I — I didn't want him to see that I had a gun in there." She shook her head. "It doesn't make sense. Karen, I don't own a gun. . . ."

"You mentioned Olympic National Park," Karen pressed. "Was this forest anywhere around there?"

Tears brimmed in her eyes. "No. Oh, God, Karen, this is so screwed up. How could I think I was in one place and be in another? I didn't have anything to drink at all yesterday, I swear. . . ."

"We'll straighten all that out. Just try to

remember where you went with Koehler."

"Cougar Mountain Park, over in Issaquah," she replied numbly. "It's nowhere near where I thought I was. But I remember the signs for the park. We walked at least a mile before we veered off the trail."

"They have a lot of hiking trails there. Do you recall which one it was? Did it have a name?"

Amelia shook her head. "I'm sorry."

"Do you remember where you parked, or the name of the road you took there? Anything?"

Amelia closed her eyes for a moment. "It was, um, Newcastle-Coal Creek Road," Amelia whispered. "I remember the turnoff. We went to the fourth or fifth little parking area off that road. At the start of the trail, there's a small sign with a cartoon of Dennis the Menace on it. I don't remember what the sign said, but someone wrote on it. We — we were parked there for a while. He started touching me, and I — I hit him!" Her voice cracked. "God, I hit him with that gun."

Several people shushed her. Karen quickly helped Amelia to her feet. "C'mon, let's get out of here."

"And then later, in the forest, I shot him." Amelia cried, clutching Karen's arm. "He was begging for his life and I shot him in the head. . . ."

People were staring as Karen hurried Amelia down the aisle between the rows of tables. By the time they stepped outside together, Amelia was sobbing and recounting — in fragments — what had happened in that forest. She'd left Koehler's semi-naked corpse where she'd shot him four times. She'd found her way back to the main trail, but didn't remember removing any of the homemade markers from the branches and shrubs along the way. She'd taken Koehler's car, and by then it had grown dark. She didn't remember anything until she was back in Seattle, catching a bus in a sketchy neighborhood along Aurora Boulevard.

"I don't understand it," Amelia said, shaking her head over and over. They sat down on a park bench outside the library. "I woke up this morning at a B & B all the way over in Port Angeles. I could have sworn I spent all of yesterday there. Karen, if you saw me with this man yesterday, and I remember all these horrible things, then they must have really happened. Do you see what that means? I killed this guy. And I probably killed my parents and Aunt Ina and my brother —"

"We don't know that yet," Karen said, rubbing her back. "You could be wrong about what happened to Koehler. You can't hold yourself accountable, not until I've looked into this further. Are you listening to me? You're not responsible for killing anyone, Amelia. We'll work this out together, but you'll have to trust me."

Amelia's cell phone went off — a low hum. Wiping her eyes, she reached inside her purse and checked the caller ID. "It's that policewoman again, the one you told me about," she said, her voice raspy. "Same number as last time."

"Don't answer it. I don't want you talking to her or anyone else until we figure out what really happened. Let her leave another message." She patted Amelia's arm. "Listen, I think it's best you lay low and stay at my place tonight. But I need to check out your story first."

"What, are you driving to Port Angeles?"

"No, Cougar Mountain Park." She glanced up at the sky. "And I'd like to get there before dark."

"You can't go alone," Amelia said. "I should go with you."

"No, you shouldn't. If something really did happen in that forest yesterday, you're in no condition to relive it. I'll be back by six if traffic isn't too nuts." Karen got to her feet, and so did Amelia. "You'll probably need some overnight things. Let's swing by the dorm. We'll call Shane and see if he can take you someplace for the next two or three hours. Maybe you guys can take in a movie."

Amelia nodded. She pressed the keypad on her cell phone, and then listened to her voice mail. "Oh, no," she murmured. "That policewoman, she and her partner are at the dorm now, waiting for me."

"What?" Karen asked.

"She said she's calling from the lobby downstairs at Terry Hall, and they want to ask me some questions."

"Damn," she whispered, rubbing her forehead. "Okay, call Shane. Tell him we need him to do something for us right away."

Twenty-five minutes later, Shane emerged from the crowd in Red Square, the campus's redbrick-paved central plaza and hub. He ambled toward them with a backpack slung over his shoulder. His blond hair was covered up with a stocking cap, and he wore a T-shirt over a long-sleeved T, and baggy jeans.

Jumping up from the park bench, Amelia ran to Shane and embraced him. They kissed feverishly. Amelia broke away, nodded toward Karen, and whispered something to him. Then holding hands, they approached her together.

Karen stood up. "Thanks, Shane. Did you have any problems?"

"Pulled it off without a hitch," he said with a crooked grin. "You were right though, Karen. The two of them were sitting in the lobby — a nice-looking black chick, and this older white guy with Donald Trump hair. They looked like total narcs. But they hardly paid any attention to my coming and going."

"Did you remember my robe?" Amelia asked with her arm linked around his. "And my copy of *Washington Square?* I need it for English Lit."

He kissed her forehead and pointed to his backpack. "It's all in there, along with your black jeans, the pink T-shirt you sleep in, and everything else you wanted. I called the Neptune Theater while I was in your room. They're showing a new print of *The 400 Blows* at 4:15. We're all set."

Karen glanced up at the sky, and guessed she only had about an hour of sunlight left. She didn't want to start hiking down that forest trail after dusk. "Um, Shane, can I talk to you for a moment?" she asked.

"Sure, Karen, what's up?" he said, uncoupling with Amelia for a moment, and stepping toward her.

"I need you to be very, very careful," she whispered. "This may sound strange, but —"

"Are you telling him that I'm *dangerous?*" Amelia asked in a loud voice.

Karen looked at her and sighed. "Amelia —"

"You should. He won't believe it if I tell him." Her voice cracked. "So warn him, Karen. Tell him to watch out for me. I don't want to hurt him, okay?"

Karen patted Shane's shoulder. "Amelia's right," she said in a low voice. "You need to keep an eye on her. If you notice a sudden change or a severe mood swing, call me."

He chuckled. "Are you shitting me, Karen?"

"I'm serious, Shane," she whispered. "You have my number, don't you?"

He nodded. The lopsided smile ran away from his face.

"Stay in public places with her," Karen warned. "Make sure there are always other people around. Don't let her out of your sight for a minute. I'll see you in two or three hours."

"Okay, Karen, sure thing," he murmured. He looked like a hurt, confused little boy as he backed away from her. He slung his arm around Amelia again, and gave her another kiss on the forehead.

"Whatever she told you," Amelia said, "it's true. Okay?"

"Sure, it's cool," he muttered. But he wouldn't look at Karen. "C'mon, sweetheart, let's get out of here. We'll be late for the movie."

They started walking away. Amelia glanced over her shoulder. "Karen, be safe, okay?"

She nodded, and then watched them merge into the crowd of people mingling around Red Square. Karen glanced up at the sky again, and saw clouds moving across the slate-colored horizon. She didn't have much time.

All too soon, it would be dark.

CHAPTER THIRTEEN

The other cars on Newcastle-Coal Creek Road had their headlights on. Karen reluctantly switched her lights on, too. It was like admitting defeat. She'd hoped to reach the hiking trail in Cougar Mountain Park before nightfall. But traffic on I-90 had been miserable, and the thirty-mile trip had taken nearly two hours.

Now it grew darker by the minute. Driving along the snaky, wooded road, she'd passed three parking areas for hikers and other visitors entering the wildlife area. Only a few cars occupied those lots, a bad sign, not many hikers left. As much as she didn't need an audience for this gruesome expedition, Karen loathed the thought of being completely alone in those woods. It would have been nice to know someone was at least within screaming distance.

Karen slowed down as she drove past the fourth parking area: only one car, and no signs posted by the trail. Amelia had said they'd pulled into the fourth or fifth bay.

Biting her lip, Karen watched for the next parking area. She almost missed it, and had to slam on the brakes to turn in to the small, unlit alcove. There were only six spaces, and no other cars. She couldn't even see the beginning of a trail. But then it was awfully dark.

She reached into the glove compartment for the flashlight, and then climbed out of the car. She glanced over at the trees and bushes bordering the alcove, and finally noticed a gap in the foliage. She saw a sign with a cartoon of Dennis the Menace, carrying a backpack. From the distance, Karen couldn't read it in the dark. She shined the flashlight on it: "Don't Be a Litterbug!" Someone had crossed out the *Don't.* It was just as Amelia had said.

Karen couldn't help wondering if everything else Amelia had told her would turn out to be true.

She kept the flashlight on, took a deep breath, and started down the trail. She could hear some people talking not very far away, and that made her feel a bit safer, but only for a few minutes. Soon, she saw them heading toward her, a middle-aged couple wearing hiking gear. They gave her a puzzled look, and Karen realized how odd she must have appeared, on a hiking trail, dressed in her black blazer and slacks, and a blue tuxedo blouse. "You aren't just getting started, are you?" the man asked with concern.

"I'm only going for a mile or so," Karen said. "There are still other hikers around, aren't there?"

"I think you have the place to yourself," the man replied. "We're finishing up."

"Be careful," the woman said ominously. "There are bears in these woods at night, and cougars. It's not called Cougar Mountain Park for nothing."

"Thanks," Karen said with a pale smile. "Good night."

They continued on, and Karen could hear the woman clicking her tongue against her teeth. "Stupid girl . . . at this hour . . . Just wait, we'll hear it on the news tomorrow that she's missing or dead."

Karen trudged on through the gloomy woods. She kept the flashlight directed on the path in front of her. She guessed it would be at least another five minutes before she should start looking for the trail markers Amelia had told her about.

She didn't hear anyone else in the forest, just leaves and bushes rustling in the night wind. Karen felt dread in the pit of her stomach. She tried to brace herself for what she might find. Having volunteered at the rest home for the last few months, she'd seen her share of dead bodies, and had cleaned up blood after several messy accidents. She told herself that she could get through this. She simply had to be dispassionate about it. And, if she found Koehler's corpse, she would turn around, go back to her car, and call George. The two of them would figure out what to do from there.

She started shining the light on the bushes and trees that hovered over both sides of the crude, snakelike path. She didn't see any trail markers, just a few squirrels and raccoons. Their eyes looked iridescent in the flashlight's glow as they gazed at her, and then scurried away. Karen checked her wristwatch. Only 6:20, but it felt like midnight. If she didn't find one of Amelia's markers by 6:35, she'd quit and turn back.

She almost tripped on a tangle of tree roots across her path. And then she heard something that made her stop. Twigs snapped underfoot. "Is anyone there?" Karen called. The noise was unmistakably someone — or *something* — prowling through the bushes. They didn't stop, and they didn't answer her, either. "Hello?" Karen called nervously.

She directed the flashlight in the general area where the noise was coming from. But she didn't see anyone. The sound was fading. The trees and bushes seemed to move as the beam of light swept across them. Then Karen saw it — only a few feet away. A piece of white fabric with a blue stripe was tied to the low-hanging branch of a small, bare brittle-looking tree. She made her way through the brush to get a closer look. She remembered the fabric pattern from yesterday. Koehler had said it was his lucky shirt.

Standing very still, she listened for a moment. Whatever she'd heard earlier, it was gone now. Karen shined the light in the trees, searching for the second piece of Koehler's lucky shirt. She found it through the thick overgrowth, about thirty feet away. She seemed headed in the right direction, but there was no real path. It was nearly impossible to navigate her way in the dark. At one point, she walked right into a branch, and just missed scratching her eye. Touching her cheek, she glanced at her fingertip and saw blood. "Good one, Karen," she muttered, pressing on.

Part of her wanted to turn back. Amelia had been right about everything so far. Karen knew she was close to finding Koehler's corpse. Did she really need to see it? Once she set eyes on it, she'd have to call the police. And then how would she be any help to Amelia?

Still, she forged ahead, following one trail marker after another. She'd counted seventeen of them, and guessed by now she was about a quarter of a mile off the trail she'd started on. Karen found another rough trail, and then came upon a clearing, a little bald spot in the woods, no more than ten or twelve square feet. With her flashlight, she scanned the tree branches for the next marking, but there wasn't one. She had no idea which direction to go from there.

Something darted across the ground in front of her. Karen gasped and tried to catch a look at it with her flashlight. But the thing scampered by so quickly all she saw was a shadow before it was gone. "Relax," she said to herself. "Probably just a rabbit."

She still had the flashlight directed on the forest floor when she noticed something else amid the leaves, twigs, and dirt. One part of the ground was darker, as if stained. The leaves were a different color. Karen took a step closer. Something smelled horrible — like death. She knew that putrid odor from the nursing home. It filled the room when a

330

patient had died.

With the light shining on that dark patch, she could see some of the leaves were the burgundy color of dried blood. Part of the ground was covered with a slimy substance that had attracted bugs. Was this where Amelia had left Koehler's corpse? No doubt, some person or thing had been there for a while. It had started to decay before being moved. Karen wondered if a bear, or maybe even a cougar, had dragged off the carcass.

The fetid smell was too much for her, and she backed away. Shaking, she felt sick to her stomach.

Karen took a few deep breaths, then scanned the forest floor with the flashlight's beam. She was looking for a mound of dirt that might indicate a grave, or maybe even a piece of clothing. But there was nothing.

Still, she knew Amelia must have killed Koehler on this spot. It was where the lucky-shirt markers ended.

She heard something — a rustling sound, and twigs snapping again. She made a wide arc around the slimy patch of ground and directed the flashlight into the woods on the other side. The sound seemed to be coming from that direction. Karen could see only the first row of illuminated bushes and trees. Beyond that, it was just blackness. She thought she saw a bush move. Or was it just the shadows playing a trick on her. "Who's there?" she called.

The rustling noise abruptly stopped. Karen realized no forest creature would freeze up like that. This was a person.

She was paralyzed for a moment, waiting for the next sound.

All at once, there was a shuffling noise, footsteps.

Karen turned and ran, but suddenly the ground seemed to slip out from under her. She fell backward into that oily patch of leaves and dirt. She let out a sharp cry. The flashlight had rolled out of her hands, and she desperately scurried along the ground to retrieve it. Then she struggled to her feet. Leaves stuck to her clothes. As she frantically brushed them away, she felt that slimy, jelly-like substance that had come from Russ Koehler's decaying corpse.

Karen could hear the footsteps coming closer. She spotted the last marker, tied to the bough of a bush by the crude pathway. She ran toward it, and anxiously searched for the next marker. All the while, she could hear that rustling behind her, pursuing her. The trail suddenly disappeared, and so did the markers. Panic stricken, Karen waved the flashlight around, hoping to find a piece of Koehler's shirt on a nearby tree or shrub. Without them, she couldn't hope to find her way back to the main trail.

Had she taken a wrong turn? She noticed a short path amid the foliage, and hurried along until her flashlight illuminated something on the ground in front of her. Karen froze. "Oh, God, no," she murmured. For a moment she couldn't breathe.

At least a dozen strips of Koehler's shirt littered the pathway.

All this time, someone had been behind her, removing Amelia's markers. That someone didn't want her finding her way back to the main trail.

She heard the footsteps again, coming closer. Karen blindly ran through the brush, zigzagging around trees and shrubs, staggering over rocks on the ground. She didn't know where she was headed. She could have been totally turned around and forging even deeper into the woods. Branches lashed at her face, arms, and legs. At every turn, she expected a hand to grab out at her. She prayed for some sign ahead, a light through the trees, some signal that she was near the edge of the forest. She didn't want to die in these woods, as Koehler so obviously had.

All the while, she heard the footsteps thumping behind her, the bushes rustling.

But she could hear something else, too. It sounded like a car approaching. Up ahead in the distance, she saw the beam from a pair of headlights sweep across the bushes and trees. After a few moments, another car sailed by. Karen raced toward the road, and civilization. Her lungs burning, she pressed on. She could actually see the edge of the forest now, and cars whooshing past. By the time she emerged from the woods and felt the pavement beneath her, Karen was almost delirious. She didn't know if she had stumbled back onto Newcastle-Coal Creek Road, or if it was another street. She didn't have any idea how to get to her car from this spot.

She tried to wave down an SUV, but it passed her by, its horn blaring. Karen swiveled around and shined her flashlight into the woods.

She saw him for only a second — a tall figure ducking behind a tree. He had a small shovel in his hand. He couldn't have been more than a hundred feet away.

Karen swiveled around. "Help! Help me, please!" she screamed, waving at another approaching car, a beat-up Taurus.

The car pulled over to the side of the road.

Karen caught her breath. "Thank you, God," she whispered.

■ ■ ■ ■

"This teenager in the Taurus was so sweet. The poor kid, I had him driving one way and then the other before we finally found where I'd left my car."

The cell phone to her ear, Karen stood outside a RiteAid in a Bellevue strip mall. Under the glaring halogen lights, she could see her reflection in the storefront window. With her brown hair a mess, dirt on her clothes, and scratch marks on her face, she looked as if she'd been beaten up.

"Are you sure you're all right?" George asked for the second time.

"Somewhat traumatized, but okay," Karen replied with a shaky laugh.

"And you don't want to call the police?"

"Well, at this point, we don't have a body," she said. "And I'm sure all of those trail markings will be gone by the time anyone goes back into those woods, searching for one. I don't think calling the police would do any good right now. Besides, I'd like to get Amelia some help before the cops and the press start going to town on her. And you'll think I'm crazy, but there's still a part of me that believes she's innocent."

"I feel the same way, Karen," he said.

335

"Still, she could be dangerous, you said so yourself. There's every indication that she killed Koehler."

"I know," Karen sighed. "But that man chasing me through the woods tonight, I think he's the same one who was in the basement at my father's rest home yesterday. I'm more worried about him than I am about Amelia. Shane spotted her being very intimate with some strange man in a car a few months ago. It could be this same guy. Maybe he has some kind of weird power over Amelia. Maybe he's hypnotizing her or something, I don't know."

"I was planning to go to Salem tomorrow," George said. "Jessie's supposed to look after the kids. It was just a day trip, but maybe now, I ought to stay put. You shouldn't have to take care of Amelia all by yourself. She's my responsibility —"

"You're going to Salem?"

"Yeah, I want to find out who paid for Duane Lee Savitt's cemetery plot. They wouldn't tell me over the phone and suggested I come down there."

"You should go," Karen urged him. "If we can find out more about her early childhood, it could end up helping Amelia quite a lot. Go. I'll watch over Amelia. We'll be fine. I don't think the police will be looking for her at my place tonight. They've already been by today. In the morning, I'll get her to a specialist. I have some names."

"Well, your faith in Amelia's innocence is a lot stronger than mine," he said. "She's my niece, and I love her. But I wouldn't trust her around my kids right now. And I don't think I'd sleep very well under the same roof as her."

Karen peered through the RiteAid window. She noticed an aisle marker that said Sleep Aids. "I know what you mean," she said. "I probably won't sleep too well, myself. But I'll make sure Amelia does. Will you call me from Salem tomorrow as soon as you find out anything?"

"Of course, Karen," he replied. "And phone me tonight if anything happens. Even if it's just that you're scared and can't sleep. I want you to call me, okay?"

She smiled. "Okay, George. Thank you."

Karen stirred the ingredients from four sleeping capsules into the chocolate sauce as she heated it over the stove. The diazepam she'd given Amelia last week had calmed her a bit, but hadn't made her sleep. And Karen needed to make sure Amelia was conked out tonight.

Rufus sat at her feet, watching her every

move. He always did that while she was cooking in case she accidentally dropped a piece of food.

Amelia was upstairs, changing into her pajamas. She and Shane had watched *The 400 Blows* and then eaten dinner at My Brother's Pizza. Before calling them, Karen had left a message with Dr. Danielle Richards, the most qualified psychologist on her contact list. Dr. Richards had called back, and agreed to meet with Amelia in the morning.

Shane had dropped Amelia off at 9:20. By then, Karen had already showered, changed the sheets in the guest room, and taken Rufus for a quick walk. After what had happened in Cougar Mountain Park, she'd decided to tuck her father's gun in her coat pocket for the short trip down the block and back. She wished she'd had it with her during that hike in the forest.

Amelia let out a gasp when she saw the scratch marks on Karen's face and hands. Karen reassured her that she was all right. She told her what had happened in the woods, focusing on the fact that there was no actual corpse, and no reason to go to the police just yet.

At the same time, she wondered out loud about the man who had chased her through the forest. Did Amelia know someone who could have done that? It couldn't have been Shane. Did she have any other male friends, maybe someone Shane didn't know about?

Amelia couldn't think of anyone. She became more upset the more Karen pressed the issue, and finally Karen just dropped it. She suggested Amelia change into her pajamas, and they could watch a movie on TV.

That had been about fifteen minutes ago.

She could hear Amelia coming down the stairs now. The crystals from the sleeping pill capsules still showed up in the chocolate sauce. Karen turned up the burner, and rapidly stirred the concoction. Then she went to the refrigerator freezer for the ice cream.

Amelia stepped into the kitchen. Her hair was pinned up; and she wore an oversized pink T-shirt, flannel pajama bottoms, and thick gray socks. She sat down at the kitchen table. Rufus strolled over to her and put his head in her lap.

"I'm making sundaes," Karen announced.

Scratching Rufus behind the ears, Amelia sighed. "Oh, I think I'll pass. I've had a nervous stomach ever since this afternoon. Thanks, anyway."

Standing by the stove, Karen turned to

gaze at her. "But I heated up the chocolate sauce just for you," she said. She tested the sauce with a little dab from her spoon. It didn't have any detectable foreign taste. "Hmm, it's good stuff too. And I know you like chocolate. C'mon, one scoop won't kill you." She prepared Amelia's dish, dousing the ice cream with chocolate sauce. Then she set it on the table in front of Amelia.

Perking up, Rufus showed more interest in the dessert than Amelia did. Karen dished out a scoop of ice cream for herself, and brought it over to the table. She sat down. "Go ahead, dig in," she urged her.

Amelia gazed at Karen's bowl and frowned. "Why aren't you having any chocolate on yours?"

"Because chocolate goes right from my lips to my hips. It's bad enough I'm having this ice cream." With her spoon, she pointed to the bowl in front of Amelia. "C'mon, don't let me be the only one pigging out here. Have some."

Amelia sighed. "I'm sorry, Karen. I don't want it."

"Well, can I — can I fix you something else?" She put down her spoon. "I have the sauce right there. How about some hot chocolate?"

"No, thanks." Amelia stared down at Rufus, and patted his head. "God, I'm so screwed up. You know, for a while, you had me convinced I couldn't have hurt my parents and Ina. And for the last few months, I actually thought I didn't have anything to do with Collin's death. But now, with this Koehler business, it brings everything back again. And the weirdest part about it is, I still don't really *remember* him. It's more like I *dreamt* about him or something. And I still feel like I was in Port Angeles yesterday. Talk about fouled up."

"Remember our first session?" Karen asked. "You told me about your blackouts and that time Shane saw you in a car with some other man. Shane confronted you pretty much the same way I asked you about Koehler. I started to describe him, and then you remembered."

Amelia nodded.

"Do you recall who Shane saw you with? Can you describe him to me now?"

She grimaced. "God, I've been trying to forget him. I don't like thinking about that time."

"Please, it's important," Karen said.

"His name's Blade," Amelia muttered, absently gazing down at the glass tabletop. "At least that's what he calls himself. He's twenty-five. His hair's cut short with little bangs and he's dyed it jet-black. He wears sunglasses a lot, even at night, sometimes."

"Then you still know him?" Karen asked.

Amelia looked up at her. "Still know who?"

"Blade." Karen let out an exasperated little laugh. "The man Shane saw you with in the car that time. You were talking like you still know him."

"Well, I don't —"

"Is he a friend of a friend's?"

Biting her lip, Amelia nodded. "I think so. He must be. I guess that's how I know about him."

Karen reached over and patted her arm. "Amelia, do you remember running down a gray stairwell to a basement? This happened recently. There's a boiler, and it's making all sorts of racket. Down the hall is a large storage room full of boxes and old hospital equipment. Blade is waiting there for you. The lights on the ceiling are broken, and the place is dark. You're down there with Blade . . ."

Amelia yanked her arm away. "Karen, please . . ."

Startled, Karen recoiled a bit. Even Rufus backed away from her.

"I'm sorry," Amelia murmured, her voice cracking. "Could you just — *chill* for a few

342

minutes? I'm so worn out and frazzled and tired. I really don't want to talk about this now. I'm sorry. Please don't be mad."

"No, it's — it's fine," Karen said. She nodded at the bowl in front of Amelia. Most of the ice cream had melted. "You sure you don't want any of that?"

Amelia just shook her head.

Getting to her feet, Karen collected both bowls and took them to the sink. She rinsed them out, and watched the chocolate sauce swirl down the drain.

"I just want to go to sleep and not think about anything for a while," Amelia said. "This is one of those nights when I used to drink until I'd passed out so I didn't have to worry or think about anything. Karen, you don't have any sleeping pills, do you?"

Karen switched off the water. She turned, and gave Amelia a patient, understanding smile. "You know, I think I might."

Ina McMillan was the name on the address label on the old *Vanity Fair* he'd fished out of the recycling bin in front of the house. That was the aunt, the one she'd shot in the chest. Aunt Ina.

He'd been to the house in Bellingham twice, and to their weekend retreat on Lake Wenatchee several times. But Blade hadn't been to this place in West Seattle until tonight. It was a Craftsman-style house at the end of a cul-de-sac. He'd parked the Cadillac a little further up the block. Through the open curtains in the living room, he could see all the way back to the kitchen. Now that he knew whose place it was, he could attach a name to the tall guy he'd seen going in and out of the kitchen. That was Uncle George. And the two brats were her cousins.

She hadn't told him whose place it was. She'd just given him the address, and told him to go check it out. He was supposed to give the place the once-over, because he had to do a job for her there tomorrow. Blade figured it would be a robbery, but he never knew with her.

She hadn't told him exactly what kind of job yet. She would call him on his cell at eleven o'clock, and then let him know. She was kind of a tease that way. She made a game of everything. He liked that about her, but it could also drive him nuts at times. Sex with her was always a game, and it was fantastic. Blade always felt the crazier a woman was, the better the sex. And this one was *crazy.*

He'd checked the windows around the McMillan house. They were about seven feet above ground level, but he could use one of the trash cans or recycling bins to boost himself up and break in. Besides the front door, there was another door off the kitchen in back. In the bushes by the front stoop, there was a little sign for some home security service — no surprise. But he knew how to dismantle those stupid security alarms.

He glanced at his wristwatch: 10:50. Even though the cul-de-sac wasn't well lit, Blade put his sunglasses back on. She said they made him look cool. She also liked the shiny black suit he wore practically everywhere. He sometimes enjoyed posing in front of the mirror wearing his sunglasses and his trademark black suit, brandishing his guns. She took a bunch of pictures of him posing like that.

Tucking the *Vanity Fair* under his arm, Blade strolled back to his car. He sat in the front seat. He could still see the McMillan house from here, but his eyes grew tired and he closed them for a spell.

Funny about that corpse in the woods. He was supposed to have buried the guy last night. She'd even left trail markers for him. But after driving to the park, he just didn't fucking feel like doing all that work. Plus those woods were full of wild animals.

So this morning, she was all over his ass for slacking off. And so he drove back to the park late this afternoon. He'd brought along a small shovel she'd gotten at some army-navy surplus store. He hadn't exactly been looking forward to burying a decayed stiff. But the notion of possibly encountering — and shooting — some forest creatures suddenly intrigued him.

Well, he didn't find any forest creatures, but the stiff sure did. What was left of the guy was covered with crows when he'd found him. Blade puked twice as he dragged the stinking, picked-over corpse to a ditch off the marked trail. He didn't have to dig much to make the shallow oblong hole. With the shovel, he quickly covered him with a layer of dirt, then scattered some leaves and branches over that.

He was headed back to the car when he spotted Amelia's shrink making her way along the trail. There was no mistaking it. She was looking for the dead guy.

It had been kind of fun, chasing her, and scaring the crap out of her. Of course, killing her would have been even more fun, and so easy. He'd had his heart set on killing *something* in that forest.

But he'd had his instructions not to touch her. She wasn't supposed to die in those

346

woods. No, that was happening later.

His cell phone rang, startling him. Blade reached inside his suit-jacket pocket, pulled out the cell and switched it on. "Yeah?"

"It's me," she whispered. "Are you at the address I gave you?"

"Yeah, and I'm sitting in the car, parked down the street. But I can see the place from here. I even figured out who lives there. Uncle George, right?"

"Very good, baby."

"What kind of job do you want me to pull here tomorrow? Can you at least give me a hint?"

"Not over the phone. But I've written it down for you somewhere."

"You and your fucking games," he muttered.

"You love it," she whispered. "I'm at Karen's house. Why don't you come over?"

"Now?"

"Yeah. I'll be watching for you. You said you're in the car?"

"Uh-huh." He put the keys in the ignition. "I'll be right over."

"First, reach under the driver's seat."

Blade bent forward and felt around until his fingers brushed against something.

"I left a note for you," she said. "Take another long look at the house, then read my note. Okay? I'll see you soon."

She clicked off.

Grinning, Blade switched off his phone. He pulled an envelope from under the car seat. Following her advice, he took off his sunglasses and stared at the McMillan house for a few moments. Then he tore open the envelope and read her note:

"Tomorrow, after 4 p.m.: Kill everyone in the house, and take whatever you want."

CHAPTER FOURTEEN

"Karen!" she screamed. "Karen, where are you?"

At her desk with a glass of chardonnay, Karen was studying notes from earlier sessions with Amelia. She sprang to her feet and hurried for the stairs. Rufus followed her.

She'd talked Amelia into taking three sleeping pills, just to ensure they did the trick. Amelia had gone to bed in the guest room about fifteen minutes ago. There hadn't been a peep out of her, and now this screaming.

Karen raced up the second floor hallway and flung open the guest room door. Between the two quilt-covered twin beds, the table lamp was on. Trembling, Amelia sat up in the bed that was farther from the door, her hands covering her face.

"What is it? What's going on?" Karen asked. Rufus followed her into the bedroom.

"I'm sorry," Amelia cried, still covering her face. "I'm so sorry. I didn't mean to scream out like that. I feel like such a baby." She lowered her hands, then slumped back against her pillow. "It's just — I'm used to the dorm and all the noise. It's so damn quiet here, I was going crazy. I started hearing things, and got scared."

Karen sat on the other bed. "Why don't you come downstairs and watch TV for a while?"

She shook her head. "No, I just want to sleep. More than anything, I wish I could have a couple of shots of Jack Daniel's right now, just to relax."

"Not after those sleeping pills," Karen said. "You've been so good lately. I wouldn't let you slide back now anyway. I can bring a radio in here. Or what about a sound machine? My sister gave one to my dad a few years ago. I think it has ocean waves or something."

Amelia let out a weak laugh. "Sure, might be worth a shot. Anything but this awful silence. I'm sorry to be so much trouble."

Karen got up and started out of the room. "No sweat. I think it's just down the hall in the closet. Be right back."

She retrieved the sound machine from the closet's bottom shelf. Karen prayed it would do the trick.

She returned to the bedroom with the sound machine, set it on the nightstand, and plugged it in. The sound came on: waves rolling onto the shore, and the occasional, distant cry of a seagull. "Tranquil enough for you?" Karen asked, with a tiny smile.

Amelia sighed. "As long as I don't have to listen to the sounds inside my head. Do you know what I was hearing when I finally screamed for you?"

"What were you hearing?" Karen asked.

"It was that weird, frail warble Collin made after I hit him in the head with the plank." Tears came to her eyes, and she covered her face again. "I kept hearing my brother dying. . . ."

"You didn't do it," Karen whispered, stroking Amelia's hair. "You're not responsible for it, Amelia. Now, lie down and listen to the waves. Don't think about anything else. Rufus and I can stick around until you fall asleep. Would that help?"

"Thanks, I'm sorry to be so —"

"Oh, hush, it's no bother," Karen said, tucking her in. Then she switched off the nightstand lamp, and made her way to the rocking chair by the window. She settled back in it, and Rufus curled up near her feet.

"You're sweet, Karen," Amelia murmured, over the sound of the fake distant waves. "I often wonder why you don't have a boyfriend. Doesn't make sense, you're so nice, and pretty." Karen heard her yawn. "I — I sometimes think about how lonely you must be."

"Oh, I'm doing all right," Karen answered almost automatically.

"Always helping people, taking care of people, and no one to take care of you, it's not right. Karen, you . . . you deserve to be happy."

Karen said nothing. She felt a horrible ache in the pit of her stomach, and tears welled up in her eyes. But she remained silent. She just kept rocking in the chair, and listened to Amelia surrender to sleep.

Amelia felt herself drifting off as she spoke to Karen. The sleeping pills must have worked after all. In the darkness, she could see Karen sitting over in the corner of the room, by the window. Amelia heard herself slurring her words, and Karen's silhouette seemed to blur.

For a second, just as she started to fall asleep, Amelia no longer saw Karen Carlisle across the bedroom. Instead, she had a fleeting image of her father in that rocking chair, the moment before she shot him through the head.

Bellingham, Washington — six months before
A notice came up on the 36-inch flat-screen TV in the Faradays' den: ALL MODELS ARE EIGHTEEN YEARS OR OVER.

Collin had been looking forward to this moment. His parents had left for Lake Wenatchee that Saturday morning. This was the 16-year-old's first weekend home alone ever, and to get the debauchery rolling, he'd borrowed three DVDs from his friend, Matt Leonard, whose brother had smuggled them home from college: *Whore of the Worlds, Booty Call 9-1-1,* and *Missionary Impossible.*

He was having some of the guys over for poker tonight; at least, that was the plan, if one of them could get his hands on a case of beer and some cigars. Matt would be coming over in about two hours, which gave Collin plenty of time to watch one of the movies and whack off. He'd drawn all the shades and peeled down to his underpants. His hand was already inching past the elastic waistband of his briefs as he watched the opening photo credits for *Whore of the Worlds.* A pretty brunette with perky breasts was shown from the waist up, gyrating on something that seemed to have the kick of a mechanical bull. The credits ran: Amber Anniston as Tami Cruz. Next, a long-haired blonde with a huge rack stared seductively at the camera with her finger in her mouth: Sheridan Madrid as Sheri Savoy.

And then the front doorbell rang.

"Damn it!" Collin hissed, switching off the DVD player. Springing up from the sofa, he frantically dressed and hid the DVD covers behind a sofa pillow. The doorbell rang again and again. "Matt, if that's you, I'm gonna kill you," Collin muttered. He hurried to the front door, and checked the peephole. "What the hell?" he whispered. Then he unlocked the door and opened it. "Amelia, what are you doing here?"

"Oh, nice way to greet your sister," she said with an abrupt laugh. She brushed past him and sauntered into the house. "Mom and Dad are in Lake Wenatchee, and little brother is home alone, which means I caught you in the middle of getting drunk or bopping the bologna. Which is it?"

Collin ignored the question. "Aren't you supposed to be at some Booze Busters retreat in Port Townsend?"

She headed into the kitchen and started hunting through the cupboards. "Don't remind me. They just dropped me off. I told them I needed to get my allergy medication."

"Allergy medication?" Collin repeated.

"Yeah. Good one, huh? Anyway, they're coming back to pick me up in a half hour." She started checking the lower cabinets. "Where the fuck are they hiding the booze nowadays?"

"To the left of the sink, where they've always kept it," Collin replied, squinting at her. "Why are you acting so weird?"

She pulled a bottle of bourbon out of the cabinet. "Well, I'm not drunk, if that's what you mean, little brother." She took two highball glasses from the upper cupboard. "At least, I'm not drunk, *yet.*"

Collin stared at her as she filled both glasses about halfway. He didn't think his sister was drunk. She just wasn't acting much like herself. Since when did she ever refer to him as little brother? He'd never seen Amelia wearing so much makeup in the middle of the day. She was acting like she did that time a few weeks back when she'd unexpectedly shown up at his school. He wondered if it was being away at college that had changed her. "What's going on?" he asked. "What's with the hotshot act?"

She handed him a glass. "You're the hotshot, all alone for the weekend. If you plan to get shitfaced, I want to see it." She clinked her glass against his. "C'mon, chug it."

"Are you nuts? I'm not getting drunk with you."

"Oh, c'mon, don't be such a pussy. Have some fun."

Collin shook his head and put down the half-full glass. "I'm not sure this is such a great idea, Amelia. You know you shouldn't . . ."

She frowned at him. "You know, you can be a real asshole sometimes."

He looked at her, incredulous. *"What?"*

"You heard me," she muttered, plopping down at the breakfast table. "When's the last time we saw each other?"

"Three weeks ago, when you came home for the weekend," he replied, folding his arms. "And before that it was the time you dropped by my school in the middle of the day. Of course, later, you didn't remember that, so maybe it doesn't count."

Apparently, it had been one of her episodes with *lost time*. He wondered if later she'd have any memory of this afternoon. She sure was acting bizarre.

"Three weeks we haven't seen each other," she said. "I come by to say hello, and what do I get?" She made a face and dropped her voice an octave to sound like a surly Neanderthal. " 'What are you doing here?' Real sweet, Collin. Thanks a lot. How do you think that makes me feel?"

Collin sighed. "I didn't mean it that way."

"It's bad enough everyone considers me the family fuckup, and you — you pee perfume. Of course, I'm not even really part of this family, being adopted and all."

"Oh, c'mon, Amelia," he said, sitting down at the table with her. "That's bullshit. Why do you even say stuff like that?"

"You're always so disgustingly good," she sneered. "With Mom and Dad gone for the weekend, I figured you'd finally let loose a little, maybe get drunk or high or something. And I just wanted to be here to see it. Plus to be perfectly honest, I could really use a drink. Sorry if that offends you. But you're making me feel like shit. Are you too fucking good to have a couple of shots with me?"

"All right, okay, fine. I'll have a drink. Jeesh!" He got up from the table and retrieved the highball glass. He quickly tipped it back and took a swallow. It burned. Unlike most of his friends, he really wasn't much of a drinker. Since his sister had a problem with alcohol, he'd purposely avoided it.

She broke into applause. "Way to go! Finish it!"

His throat was still on fire, but Collin forced down the rest of the glass. He gasped for air. The strong, medicine-like taste was still in his mouth. "Okay?" he asked. "God, Amelia, I don't know how you can stand to drink this stuff."

"I'm so proud of you," she said, laughing. "You're gonna feel fantastic in a few minutes."

Collin numbly stared at her. When she laughed, she didn't sound like herself. Or maybe he was drunk already? It couldn't happen that fast, could it?

"I'll make a deal with you." With a sly grin, she nodded at her glass. "I won't have this if you drink it for me."

"No way!" he protested. "Give me a break."

"Why not? C'mon, it'll be fun. You can be the drunken screwup for a change, and I'll be the perfect child and stay on the wagon. It's role reversal. You're not driving anyplace. Go for it. You'll be doing us both some good."

Collin was shaking his head.

"What can happen? At the very worst, you'll get hammered. You were gonna do that later tonight, anyway. Right?"

"Okay, okay," he said, feeling a little funny as he walked to the breakfast table. Collin picked up her glass, and guzzled down the bourbon in two gulps. He coughed and his eyes watered up.

She applauded again. "That's just like you — rescuing me from myself. You took a bullet for me, little brother."

He sank down on the chair beside her and caught his breath. There she went again with that *little brother* bit. Maybe it was something she'd picked up at school. Why was it so important that she see him get drunk?

He started to laugh. "You're acting so completely weird today," he said, grinning wildly. "I swear to God, it's like I don't even know you, *big sister*. I mean, you've *always* been weird, and I've always loved you for it, Amelia. But this — today — is a whole different type of weird. Ha! Or maybe it's me. Am I shitfaced already?" He snickered again, and realized he must indeed be drunk, because he couldn't stop babbling.

Collin reminisced out loud about the times Amelia had raised hell growing up, all the trouble she'd gotten into. He talked about how she'd driven their parents crazy, and he imitated their dad when he went ballistic over something she'd done: " 'Ye Gods, what's wrong with her?' Ha! When

Dad starts in with the Ye Gods, then watch out, we're all in trouble!" Collin couldn't stop laughing.

But then he took a moment to look at her, and Collin realized she hadn't laughed once. She just sat there with a cryptic smile on her face.

"I'm sorry, Amelia," he muttered. "You — you know I love you. I do. It's just that, *Ye Gods,* I think I'm drunk!" He chuckled again.

"We need to get you some fresh air." She stood, and then helped him to his feet. "This might not have been such a terrific idea. I don't want you sick. C'mon, little brother. . . ."

Collin felt a bit woozy, but he could certainly walk on his own. He didn't need her helping him. As they moved into the den, he stole a look at the sofa, where, for the moment, the throw pillow covered up those porn DVDs.

She went to the sliding glass door, and opened the curtain. She struggled to move the door until she finally seemed to notice the stubby, thick beam of wood braced on the floor, tracking for extra insurance against break-ins. Funny, she seemed to have completely forgotten it was there. She moved the beam aside, then slid open the door.

"There now," she said. "Why don't we sit down on the couch, watch some TV —"

"No, no, no," he protested, shaking his head. All Collin could think about was his sister switching on the TV and discovering *Whore of the Worlds* there. "Let's go outside, down to the dock. You're right, I need some air. C'mon . . ."

Leading the way, Collin staggered down the slight slope in their backyard toward the dock, and he realized he was truly drunk.

It was a cool, crisp May afternoon. The sun glistened off Lake Whatcom, and across the calm water he could see the mountains in the distance. The wooden dock was slightly neglected, because they didn't have a boat. But it was still sturdy, with an upper deck that had a railing, and a lower platform that had nothing between it and the water directly below. Ever since they were kids, he and Amelia and their friends often used the dock to sun themselves, and Lake Whatcom was quite swimmable.

Collin glanced over his shoulder. She was following him with the stubby wood beam in her hand. One moment, she had it slung over her shoulder like a baseball bat, the next, she used it like a walking stick as she made her way down the grassy slope. Her black hair fluttered in the wind, and she grinned at him. She seemed to enjoy seeing him inebriated.

Though he might have felt more secure up on the dock's upper platform — with the railing — Collin ventured down three steps to the lower, open tier. The water lapped up almost to the edge of its wooden planks. He could hear her stepping down behind him. "Boy, the lake is beautiful today," he murmured, squinting out at its glimmering surface.

"You're slurring your words," she said. "You got drunk a lot faster than I expected you would."

He wasn't sure exactly what she meant. She'd been *expecting* him to get drunk? But Collin nodded anyway, and kept gazing at the lake and mountains. "Yeah, I am pretty hammered. Do me a favor, okay?"

"What's that?" she asked.

"Please make sure I don't do anything stupid. I hear all these stories about dumbass teenagers getting drunk and they somehow end up getting themselves killed. I don't want that to happen to me."

"Oh, I'm afraid it's too late," she replied.

Collin froze. That wasn't his sister's voice.

"You're not Amelia," he murmured.

He swiveled around to see her raising the wooden beam over her head. Collin didn't even have time to react, or ward off the blow. All of a sudden, that thing came crashing down on him, and Collin Faraday heard his own skull crack.

While hosing the blood off the dock, she thought about the funny, garbled cry Collin had made before falling into the lake. He'd sounded like a feeble old woman. And that strange, gurgling noise, it must have been the blood in his throat when he'd tried to scream out. Whatever it had been, she snickered as she remembered it now.

Her brother's foot had caught on some of the pilings under the dock, and he was floating facedown in the water just below her.

He was their favorite, the child they'd been hoping and trying for until deciding to adopt, and she'd been a mere compromise.

They would mourn him. But they wouldn't have to grieve for very long. Soon enough, they would be dead, too. Soon enough, she would have no family — or friends. She would be the only one left.

And that was exactly the way she wanted it.

Seattle — six months later
Karen woke up, and suddenly she knew someone else was in her bedroom.

Lying in bed with the covers up to her neck, she'd been lightly dozing for the last three hours. She hadn't heard a peep from Amelia down the hall, just that machine churning out the sounds of waves and seagulls. Rufus had fallen asleep at the foot of Karen's bed, but now she heard him sitting up. His dog tags jingled. He started to growl.

She heard a floorboard creak. For a moment, she couldn't move.

Finally, and very slowly, Karen reached under the extra pillow beside her and found her father's revolver.

She could almost feel someone hovering over her.

She quickly sat up in bed. "I've got a gun!" she said.

Rufus started barking furiously.

"God, Karen, no, wait!"

Blindly reaching for the nightstand lamp, she fanned at the air for a moment before she found the light and switched it on. "Amelia," she murmured, catching her breath. "Rufus, hush! That's enough."

"Oh, Karen, I'm so sorry," she whispered, a hand clutching at the lapels of her robe. "I got turned around. I thought this was the bathroom. . . ."

Rufus kept growling at her, punctuating it

with an occasional bark.

"Rufus, cease and desist," Karen said. Her heart was still racing. She tried to smile at her. "It's the next door down, Amelia."

"Thanks. Sorry I woke you." She hesitated in the doorway, and frowned at her. "Do you always sleep with a gun? Or do you think I'm dangerous?"

Karen shook her head. "No, I don't usually sleep with a gun. And no, I don't think you're dangerous. This is about something else, Amelia." She was thinking of the young man who called himself Blade. That was why she had the gun at her side tonight; and why Rufus was sleeping in her bedroom instead of his own little bed in the corner of the kitchen. But part of her still couldn't trust Amelia — not if she was sick.

"Think you'll be able to get back to sleep?" Karen asked.

Yawning, she nodded and turned toward the hall. "G'night, Karen. Sorry I scared you." She gently closed the door behind her.

Rufus let out one last growl, and then settled back down at the foot of her bed. Karen listened for a few moments until she heard the toilet flushing. It was strange. Earlier tonight, Amelia had come down to the kitchen in her T-shirt and pajama bottoms. But she'd put on a robe in the middle of the night, just to go to the bathroom?

Karen checked the digital clock on her nightstand: 4:11 a.m. She switched off the light, slipped the gun back under the pillow beside her, and lay there for several minutes. She thought she heard murmuring. She peeled back the covers, quietly crept out of bed, and then listened at the door. "She's got a gun, for chrissake . . . I can't . . . god-damn mutt . . ."

It was a woman's voice, but it didn't sound like Amelia.

Karen crept back to the bed and retrieved her father's revolver again. Rufus scurried to his feet and looked at her. "Stay!" Karen whispered to him. Then she opened the door and gazed down the darkened hallway. She held the gun tightly. The guest room door was open, but the light was off. Past the waves and seagulls from the sound machine, she could hear the woman whis-pering again: "We'll just have to take care of it tomorrow . . ."

Karen tiptoed down the corridor, but the floorboards creaked and she froze. Rufus poked his head past her bedroom doorway and let out an abrupt bark. The murmuring down the hallway suddenly stopped. Karen heard a rustling sound. "Amelia?" she said. She had the gun poised.

She skulked toward the guest room. She could hear whispering again, only this time, it sounded more like Amelia: "I want two baskets of flowers. Yes, you can . . . But I'm taking my dog . . ."

Karen peeked into the doorway. In the darkness, she saw the silhouette of someone in the far twin bed, nestled beneath the covers. "But I have a ticket . . ." she said in a sleepy voice — Amelia's voice. "That train doesn't leave for a while . . ."

With a sigh, Karen retreated back to her own room, and crawled back into bed once again. She shouldn't have been surprised Amelia talked in her sleep, in addition to everything else. Karen tried to go to sleep, but merely tossed and turned. She told herself everything was okay. She'd be taking Amelia to a specialist in just a few hours.

She kept checking the clock on her nightstand. The last time she looked it was 5:17. She could hear birds chirping. An unsettling thought occurred to her: *What if that wasn't Amelia under the covers? What if it was someone else?*

But Karen told herself she was being silly. And she finally drifted off to sleep.

The clock on Shane's nightstand read: 6:02 a.m. Barely lifting his head from his pillow, he squinted at it. He wondered what the hell that tapping noise was. He and four other guys shared a dilapidated house on Forty-third Street, just a few blocks from the campus. His bedroom was on the first floor, right off the kitchen. It took him a moment to realize the tapping was on his window. Against the faint light of dawn, he could see the silhouette of someone on the other side of the old venetian blinds.

"What the . . ." he muttered, crawling out of bed. He staggered across the cluttered room in his underpants. The tapping continued.

Some of the venetian blind slats were bent and broken and, through the gaps, he could see who was out there. He immediately raised the blinds, and then tugged the window open. He had to crouch so that he could talk to her face-to-face. "Amelia, sweetheart, what's going on?" he asked, in a groggy voice.

She wore a rain slicker and stood on her tiptoes. "Sorry to wake you," she whispered. "I just had to see you, baby."

He started to straighten up. "Well, go around to the kitchen door, and I'll let you in."

"No, no, I can't stay. Karen's practically holding me prisoner at her place. She doesn't know I'm gone. I need to get back there and sneak in before she wakes up."

He crouched down again and hovered by the open window. "Shit, you shouldn't have to stay there if you don't want to. . . ."

She smiled. "It's okay. But I need to meet you later, someplace where we can be alone, with no one else around. You know that boat place by Husky Stadium?"

"You mean where they rent canoes?"

She nodded. "I want you to rent one and take it out on Lake Washington to Foster Island, near the Arboretum. It's over past the Museum of History and Industry —"

"I remember where it is," he interrupted. "We've been there before." Foster Island was a secluded little patch of land accessible by a long, winding, nature path that included a few footbridges. They'd had a picnic there during the summer.

"Good. I'll meet you out there at eleven-thirty."

"Oh, shit," he murmured. "I'm sorry, sweetheart, but I've got my psychology class at eleven."

She frowned. "Can't you skip it for *me?* This is important."

He hesitated. "Sure, I guess."

"I knew I could count on you. Don't tell anyone you're meeting me or mention where you're going. And that includes Karen. I don't trust her anymore."

"What?" He let out a dazed laugh. "But you *love* Karen. You were just bending my ear last night over pizza about how goddamn wonderful she is."

She shook her head. "Not anymore. If Karen calls you, don't even pick up."

"Well, why go back there if you don't trust her? Why all the secrecy? I don't get this, Amelia. . . ."

"I'll explain everything to you on Foster Island at eleven-thirty, and take a canoe out there. It's very important. Will you just do it for me, please?"

"Of course," he murmured. He didn't understand any of this. Most of all, he couldn't understand her. She wasn't acting like herself. "Of course, I'll be there," he reiterated.

"Thanks, baby," she said. Reaching up, she ran her fingers through his messy, light brown hair, then pulled his head down to her. She gave him a long kiss, and slipped her tongue into his mouth. He wanted more, but she pulled away.

"Sorry, I've got morning breath," he whispered with a little laugh.

"It's okay," she grinned and licked her lips. "Do you have morning wood, too?"

Indeed he did. He'd woken up — as usual — with a morning hard-on, which had been revived by that arousing kiss. Shane blushed.

She giggled. "Stand up straight, so I can see it."

He was obedient. "Little Shane's standing up straight, too, babe."

She reached inside the window, and fondled his erection through his underpants. She made this moaning sound he'd never heard her make before. He was embarrassed, but very turned on at the same time.

"I want more of that later," she purred, giving him one final, gentle tug.

Then she suddenly turned around and hurried toward the alley off the backyard. In a stupor, Shane watched her duck inside a black Jetta. It looked like her therapist's car. The engine started up, and the car drove away.

Shane's erection quickly subsided as he stood there in the window. He remembered something Karen had told him the previous afternoon. "You need to keep an eye on her. If you notice a sudden change in her or a severe mood swing, call me."

For a few moments, Shane thought about calling Karen, maybe waking her up, and telling her what had just happened.

But he went back to sleep, instead.

CHAPTER FIFTEEN

The phone woke her up.

Blurry eyed, Karen glanced at the clock on her nightstand: 8:32 a.m. She hadn't meant to sleep this late. But after almost shooting her own houseguest in the predawn hours, she'd been so shaken up, she'd just tossed and turned. She must have nodded off at some point, because Rufus had awoken her with some sudden and inexplicable barking at around 5:45. Then, just as suddenly, he'd gone back to sleep. But Karen hadn't been quite as lucky. The last time she'd looked at the clock, it was 6:41.

At least she'd gotten nearly two uninterrupted hours. Still, she'd overslept — and the damn phone was ringing.

Propping herself up on one elbow, Karen reached for the cell phone on her nightstand. She didn't recognize the caller number. She cleared her throat, then switched it on. "Hello?"

"Karen Carlisle?"

"Yes. Who's calling?"

"This is Jacqueline Peyton with the Seattle Police. I spoke with you yesterday."

Karen quickly sat up. She felt a pang of dread in her gut. They must have found Koehler's body. Despite everything that had happened in those woods last night, Karen still clung to some hope that Koehler was still alive. As of 7:00 last night, there had been no body, and only speculation. She wondered if that was all about to change.

"Ms. Carlisle?" the policewoman asked.

"Yes, I'm here," she said, rubbing her forehead. "How can I help you?"

"We've been trying to locate Amelia Faraday ever since we spoke with you yesterday afternoon. She hasn't been to her dorm. She isn't answering her phone. We've talked with her roommate, her boyfriend, and her uncle, and none of them have any idea where she is. I was wondering if you might have heard from her."

Karen hesitated. "Um, is this about Detective Koehler? Is he still missing?"

"I'm afraid so, yes. We think Amelia Faraday might have been one of the last people to see him, after you, that is."

"I see," was all Karen could think to say.

"Has Amelia contacted you? Do you have

any idea where we might be able to reach her?

"Um, you know, I — I might be able to help you," Karen stammered. "But I just woke up, and I'm a little out of it right now. I was up late last night. Could I get back to you in about twenty minutes, Jacqueline? I have your number here on my cell. Could I phone you back?"

"That would be fine. I'll be waiting to hear from you," she replied.

"Talk to you soon," Karen said, and then she clicked off. "God help me."

She threw back the covers and jumped out of bed. Rufus barked once and got to his feet. He scurried after Karen, down the hallway toward the guest room. All the while, Karen thought about how much she hated lying to the police. And yet here she was, doing just that. If she could hold them off for just two hours, she'd get Amelia to Dr. Richards. She'd have an expert opinion on Amelia's condition. It could help their case. Despite everything, Karen still believed Amelia was innocent on some level.

"Amelia?" she called. "Amelia, are you up?"

No response. The bathroom door was open. No one was in there. She didn't hear anyone downstairs.

Karen got to the guest room doorway and stopped dead. The bed was unmade and empty. Amelia's clothes and her knapsack were gone.

But the sleep machine was still churning out the sounds of ocean waves and seagulls in flight.

"Let me double-check on that," said the thin young man in a swivel chair. Seated across the desk from him, George guessed he was about twenty-four and gay, or metrosexual. He probably hated wearing that cheap-looking blue suit. His blond hair looked painstakingly mussed, and was loaded with product. The young man smiled at George, then turned toward his computer keyboard, and started typing.

He was the only person on duty in the small, modern ranch-style office across the street from Arbor Heights Memorial Park. The hedges bordering the cemetery were neatly trimmed, and the tall wrought-iron gates stood open.

But across the street, George had had to ring the doorbell before being buzzed in by the young man, who introduced himself as Todd. The office had a large picture window, which offered a view of the cemetery. There were three potted palms and two desks, both with computers. One wall was all file drawers, while another had a huge map of the cemetery with color-coded decals over certain areas.

George sat on the edge of his chair while Todd frowned at the computer screen. "No, I'm sorry," he said at last. "We don't have any billing records for Savitt, Duane Lee. I show he passed away in 1993, and he's in plot E-22 on the east hill. But there's nothing else here."

"Are you sure?" George asked. "I called yesterday, and someone here told me they might be able to help me if I came by in person."

Todd sighed. "Well, we don't have any billing information in the computers for burials prior to 1996. There's no paperwork, either. Everything over ten years old gets shredded. Who did you talk to?"

George started fuming. He shook his head. "I don't know. But he told me to come by today. I live in Seattle. I flew down to Portland, rented a car, and drove an hour here to Salem because this guy told me he could help me." George decided not to mention that he'd also paid for a cab to schlep Jessie over to his house at 5:30 in the morning, and then take him to the airport. She'd phoned an hour ago. She'd gotten

Jody off to school and Steffie to the daycare center.

"You must have talked to Murray," Todd surmised. "He has the day off. He's been here since the late eighties. But I don't know how he could possibly remember a transaction from 1993 —"

"Could you call him?" George asked.

Reaching for the phone, Todd winced a bit. "Um, he said he was going hunting today. But I can try."

George said nothing. He knew why Murray remembered that transaction from 1993. It was because the man buried in plot E-22 had murdered three people.

"Hi, Murray, this is Todd," the young man was saying into his phone. "If you get this message, call me at work. You talked to a man in Seattle yesterday, and told him if he came here, you could give him some billing information on the burial of a —" he glanced at his computer — "Savitt, Duane Lee, from 1993. Well, the gentleman is here, and waiting. So call me as soon as you get this." He hung up, then rolled his eyes at George. "I don't know if he'll call back. Like I said, I think he's out shooting Bambi's mother."

The remark was probably meant to elicit a chuckle, but George just glared at him.

"Could you give me directions to this plot E-22?" he growled. "As long as I came all this way, I might as well take a look at the grave."

Todd nodded, then reached for a pre-printed diagram of the cemetery. He circled a tiny square near the lower corner of the map. "Um, just go along the main drive, veer to your right. You'll see a big oak tree and, down the hill from there, a statue of a soldier from World War I. At least, I think it's the First World War. He's wearing one of those weird pith helmets, almost like a hubcap."

George just nodded.

"Anyway, after the soldier, take a left, and E-22 is there." He handed George the diagram.

"Thank you," he muttered. "Listen, I'm sorry to be short with you, because it's not your fault. But I'm just very frustrated and furious right now."

"I understand," Todd whispered meekly.

George stomped out of the office, then crossed the street, almost hoping some driver would honk at him at the pedestrian crosswalk so he'd have an excuse to scream at someone. But there were no cars around. He passed through the cemetery gates, and checked the diagram as he followed the main, two-lane road. It was a cool, overcast morning. The sky was the same light gray color as some of the tombstones. George noticed a few of the markers had photographs of the deceased on them. Printed on laminated oval metal discs, they looked like large, faded campaign buttons. He found the oak tree, then spotted a weathered old statue of the WWI infantryman, which stood out among the other headstones. Walking on the grass, he tried to avoid tramping over the graves. His shoes became wet with the morning dew. He finally found the headstone, a simple, squat slab of dark gray marble: Duane Lee Savitt, 1960–1993.

Beside it was the exact same type of headstone. But this one had a crucifix engraved above the inscription: Joy Savitt Schlessinger, 1963–1993, Beloved Wife & Mother.

"Yes, there are other Schlessingers buried here," Todd told him, ten minutes later. His fingers poised over the keyboard, he studied his computer screen. "Two more, Lon Rudyard and Annabelle Faye Schlessinger." He grabbed another diagram of the cemetery and circled two tiny squares right beside each other. "They're in the same general neighborhood, only you take a right when you get to the soldier statue," he explained.

"Thank you very much," George said.

George retraced his steps from before. He didn't know exactly what he expected to find — perhaps the graves of Joy Savitt's in-laws, or maybe her husband and a second wife. These Schlessingers might not have been at all related to Duane's sister. He turned right at the statue of the infantry-man, then started checking the headstones lined up in front of a long, neatly manicured shrub.

George found them, two rose-colored headstones.

LON RUDYARD SCHLESSINGER
Husband and Father
22 October 1958–13 July 2004

And beside him:

ANNABELLE FAYE SCHLESSINGER
Beloved Daughter, Rest with the Angels
21 May 1988–13 July 2004

"They died the same day," George mur-mured to himself. He wondered if they'd been killed together in an accident. The girl was only sixteen years old. Were Lon and Annabelle Schlessinger the husband and child of Joy Savitt?

Biting his lip, George took another look at Annabelle's date of birth. She was born on the exact same day as Amelia.

"My God," George whispered. "Amelia and Annabelle, they were twins."

"She took the car. I had about sixty dollars in my purse. She took that, too."

With the cell phone to her ear, Karen held Rufus on a leash in the backyard. He hadn't been out yet this morning and needed to go. She kept the kitchen door open so she could hear the home phone if it rang.

"My dog started barking at around a quarter to six this morning," Karen explained. "I'm guessing that's when Amelia snuck out of the house. I called Jessie at your place, and she hasn't seen her. But she'll keep a lookout for my car. Amelia's roommate, Rachel, hasn't seen or heard from Amelia this morning either. Neither has Shane. I also called the rest home where my dad is, and they didn't see Amelia over there, either. I'm grateful for that. I didn't want to bother you, George. I know you're in Salem. But has Amelia called you?"

"No, she hasn't." He let out a long sigh. "This isn't like Amelia at all. I mean, she's disappeared for a day or two before, like she did this weekend. But she's never stolen a car, or money. This is nuts."

"Do you think she might have driven up to the house in Bellingham?" Karen asked.

"Well, I have the phone number for Mark and Jenna's neighbors up there," George said. "Nice couple, Jim and Barb Church. I'll give them a call, and find out if there's any activity next door. You drive a black Jetta, right?"

"That's right." She heard a beep on the line. *God, please, let it be Amelia,* she thought.

"I'll ask the Churches to keep their eyes peeled for your car," he was saying.

"Just a second, George. I have another call." She checked the caller ID, and then quickly got back on the line with George. "Oh, God, it's this policewoman phoning, the third time. I've been dodging her all morning. They've been looking for Amelia since yesterday."

"Listen, I think you better come clean and tell them what's happening, Karen. You don't want to get yourself into any more hot water with the police. Plus, at this stage, you aren't doing Amelia any favors by not reporting this. I hate to even think it, but she could hurt somebody else."

"I suppose you're right," she said, feeling a pang in her already knotted-up stomach.

Rufus tugged at the leash, and Karen let him drag her toward the edge of the garden. She wondered who would walk her dog if she ended up in jail for aiding and abetting a fugitive.

"I may try Shane one more time," she said into the phone. "I had to call him three times before he finally picked up. And when I talked to him, I had a feeling he might have been holding back on something. Once you hear back from Amelia's neighbors up in Bellingham, will you give me a call?"

"Will do," he said. "By the way, I've been to the cemetery, and now I'm parked down the block from the public library in Salem. I need to look up some information. Has Amelia ever mentioned someone named Annabelle to you?"

"*Annabelle?* No, I don't think so. Why?"

"Because I'm pretty sure that's her twin sister."

"Amelia has a twin?" Karen murmured.

"Had," he said, correcting her. "Annabelle died three years ago, the same day as her father. That's why I'm here at the library. Maybe there's something in the local newspaper archives about it."

"She never mentioned a twin," Karen muttered, almost to herself. Amelia had recalled sometimes talking to herself in the mirror as a child. Was that as close as she could come to remembering her twin sister?

While George explained about Joy Savitt and the Schlessinger graves, it suddenly seemed to make sense why Amelia had all these issues — the guilt, the low self-esteem, and the nightmares. At age four, her parents had discarded her, and kept her twin. But why?

"Listen, George, call me as soon as you find out anything," she said, pulling Rufus on his leash as she headed toward the house. "I'll see what I can dig up on the Internet. What was that date the father and daughter died again?"

July 13, 2004 . . .
Lon Schlessinger . . .
Annabelle Schlessinger . . .
Joy Savitt Schlessinger

None of those keywords yielded a result on the search engines Karen had tried. There wasn't anything in the *Oregonian* either. And nothing came up in the *Salem Statesman Journal* archives index. She hoped George might have better luck following a paper trail at the Salem library.

Karen glanced at her wristwatch: 11:20. She tried phoning Shane once more. He didn't answer his cell. She left another message: "Hi, Shane, it's Karen again. I still haven't heard from Amelia, and I'm very worried. I've just talked with her uncle, and we both agree it's time to call the police and tell them what's happened. If you have any idea where Amelia is, please, please, call me back."

Shane stopped rowing for a minute so he could listen to Karen's message.

It was cool and overcast, with a breeze that made the lake slightly choppy, not exactly a great day to be out on the water. Nevertheless Shane had forked over his driver's license and five bucks for the canoe rental. And now his was the only boat in this area of Lake Washington. He'd already crept by the Montlake Bridge, and was edging along the shore near the nature path. He saw two people fishing off one of the footbridges, but no one else.

He couldn't believe Karen was ready to call the cops just because Amelia had borrowed her car. But it was more than that, he knew. Last night, Amelia had been singing Karen's praises and, this morning, she'd told him not to trust her. It didn't make sense.

Shane slipped the cell phone back in his

jacket pocket, and recommenced rowing. He saw a little piece of land with grass and trees jutting out from the wild overgrowth along the shore. He started looking for Amelia. She'd told him she would be there, and she would explain what all this was about. But he didn't see any sign of her, yet.

The water became a bit rough, and his canoe rocked back and forth as he rowed closer to Foster Island. The spot looked deserted. Shane pulled past some reeds and around a bend, where he found a clear spot to maneuver the boat into the shore. He felt the tip of the canoe hit the muddy bottom, then reluctantly he stepped into the water and tied up the boat to a tree trunk.

"Shit," he muttered.

Even though he'd moved quickly from the muddy bank to the grass, his feet had been totally immersed in the frigid lake. His shoes were soaked, along with his socks and his jeans, from the knees down. "Damn it to hell," he growled.

He heard her laughing in the distance.

Then he saw her, emerging from behind a tree. She was wearing the same lavender sweater she'd had on yesterday, and the black jeans he'd packed for her. She had her knapsack slung over her shoulder. She looked very pretty, laughing, with her wavy black hair loose and windblown around her shoulders.

He snarled at her, but couldn't help chuckling, too. "Well, Amelia, my feet are wet, my fucking toes are frozen, and I hope you're happy."

In response, she hoisted up her sweater to flash him her bare breasts. "Does that warm you up a little, baby?"

"Jesus," he murmured with a startled grin. "What the hell has gotten into you today?"

She kissed him. "Right now, I think we both should be getting into this canoe before it floats away." She grabbed him by the hand and started to lead him to the shore.

But Shane balked. "Hold on. Don't you think you ought to tell me what's happening? I mean, this is pretty bizarre. Karen's called me four times this morning. She's freaking out because you took her car, along with some money from her purse."

"Karen's a fucking liar." She scowled at him. "Did you talk to her?"

He sighed. "Yeah, I took one of the calls. She's really worried. The cops have been calling her about you. And she's not a liar. You did take her car. I saw you drive away in it this morning from my place."

"Well, I brought it right back to her house. And if she says I still have it, she's lying. I can't believe you talked to her after I asked you not to. You can't trust her. I told you that."

"Well, what the hell happened? Last night, you were all gaga for Karen, and today, she's a lying skanky bitch. What did she do to you?"

"Can't you guess?" she asked. "Isn't it obvious? She couldn't keep her goddamn hands off me all last night. And then she got really angry with me, because I didn't want to have sex with her. To think, I trusted her and bared my soul to her and, all the while, she just wanted to get into my pants."

"My God, you're kidding," he muttered.

"I'll tell you all about it in the boat," she said, stroking his cheek. "You're the only one I can talk to about this. C'mon, baby, I just need to be with *you* right now, nobody else. Could you pick me up and carry me into the canoe? I promise to warm your feet for you later."

"Sure, sweetheart," he said, obediently hoisting her in his arms. He kissed her forehead and carried her down the grassy slope toward the canoe.

Once he'd pushed the boat away from the

shore and hopped inside, she untied his wet shoes and pried them off. Then she rolled down his soggy white socks and wrung them out over the lake. She rubbed his feet, and took turns tucking each one between her legs. Pressing her pelvis against his cold, wiggly toes, she gyrated and purred. Shane grinned at her. She could see the erection growing inside his jeans. She giggled at how much more feverishly he rowed in response to her foot-warming tactics.

"Thanks for rescuing me from her, baby," she said. "You can slow down now. We're not in any hurry. I brought along something else to keep us both warm." She unzipped her knapsack and pulled out a pint of Wild Turkey.

Shane stopped rowing, and gave her a disapproving look. "Oh, I'm not sure if that's such a great idea, Amelia. You know you shouldn't."

She just smiled at him. She thought it was funny, because her brother had said the exact same thing shortly before she'd bashed his skull in.

She saw the caller ID and quickly answered the cell phone. "George?"

"Yeah, hi," he said. "I just talked to Barb Church up in Bellingham. There's nothing going on next door at Mark and Jenna's house. No sign of your car, either."

Karen was still seated in front of her computer trying to get information on the Schlessingers, but to no avail. She rubbed her forehead. "Well, Shane didn't answer when I called. I left another message."

"I know you don't want to, Karen, but it's time to let the police in on this. Amelia took your car and stole some money. That's not like her. She's not herself. I don't want anyone else hurt because we procrastinated on this. I'm being selfish here, too. Amelia knows where I live. And my kids will be home from school in a few hours."

"I understand," Karen said. "I'll call them." But she hated the idea. All she could think about was how scared, confused, and desperate Amelia must have been to run away like that. She imagined the police hunting her down, maybe even a high-speed chase that would end with Amelia dying in a car crash.

Maybe Karen didn't know that *other* Amelia. But the young woman she knew wouldn't hurt anyone. In fact, Amelia would have wanted to get as far away as possible from her family and friends if she believed herself a danger to them. But where would she go?

"The Lake Wenatchee house," she murmured. No one else was at the lake house, except ghosts.

"What?" George asked.

"Do you think she could have driven to the Lake Wenatchee house?"

"It's possible."

"Didn't you tell me last week you'd phoned a neighbor, some woman who lived down the lake from them? Do you still have her number?"

"It might be in my study someplace. But I don't have it on me."

"Do you remember her name?"

"Helene Something . . . Summers . . . no, Sumner. Helene Sumner."

"Helene Sumner in the Lake Wenatchee area," Karen said, scribbling it down. "I'll call information. Maybe this Helene has noticed some activity over there today."

"And if she *has* seen something over at the house, then what?" George asked.

"Then I'll warn her to stay away. And I'll need you to give me directions to the cabin."

"What, are you nuts? If Amelia's in that house, I'm not letting you go there. That's insane. Besides, you don't even have a car."

"I could rent one."

"Karen —"

"Listen, George, let's not argue about it

just yet. For all we know, Amelia might not even be at Lake Wenatchee." Karen sighed. "Have you come up with anything about the Schlessingers at the Salem Library? I'm not having any luck on the Internet."

"I had the same problem on the computers here. But I went to the periodicals desk, and they're digging up some newspaper microfiche files for me right now. I just stepped outside to take the call from Barb in Bellingham. I'm heading back in there now." He paused. "So — you'll talk to this policewoman, right? Report your car stolen, and Amelia missing. . . ."

"Yes, George, I will," she replied. But she knew it wouldn't be easy. The police would have a lot of questions for her, and maybe a few charges, starting with obstruction of justice.

"Okay. Talk to you soon," he said.

"Bye, George."

She quickly clicked off the line, and then dialed directory assistance for Wenatchee, Washington.

At the periodicals desk, George gave the librarian his driver's license as a deposit for a microfiche file for the *Salem Statesman Journal* for the week of July 11–18, 2004. The two microfiche-viewing machines were at a desk near a bookcase full of reference books and in front of a window looking into the lobby and the Friends of the Library Bookstore.

He switched on the machine, and it made a soft, hair-dryer-like humming noise. George quickly scanned the file until he came to the front page for July 14, 2004, the day after Lon and Annabelle Schlessinger had died. He wasn't sure what he hoped to find — perhaps a story about a car crash or a local boating accident. Maybe the story wasn't even in the local paper. Like Uncle Duane, they may not have even died in Salem.

He didn't see anything on page one, but noticed the newspaper's index in the bottom left corner said the obituaries were on page A 19. George fast-forwarded to it, but didn't see any Schlessingers among the dead. He went back to the first page. These were a.m. Editions. If Lon and Annabelle had died late in the evening on July 13, it might not have made the morning paper.

He scanned forward to July 15, and searched the front page. His eyes were drawn to a headline near the bottom right of the page, taking up three columns. He anxiously read the article:

LOCAL RANCHER AND DAUGHTER PERISH IN BLAZE

Widower & Teen were Salem Residents for 11 years

MARION COUNTY: The two-story house of a secluded ranch outside Salem became the site of a fiery inferno Wednesday night, claiming the lives of widower, Lon Schlessinger, 45, and his daughter, Annabelle Faye Schlessinger, 16. Marion County investigators believe the fire started in the upstairs master bedroom . . .

"Another fire," George murmured to himself. He was thinking about Duane Lee Savitt burning down the adoption agency.

The article didn't exactly say Lon Schlessinger had fallen asleep while smoking in bed, but they sure hinted at it. Annabelle's charred remains were discovered in the hallway by her bedroom door. The Schlessingers had moved to the area in 1993. Mrs. Schlessinger died that same year, "an apparent suicide," according to the article. There was no mention of her dead brother, and his murder rampage, at least, not on page one.

George anxiously scanned down to page two, where there were side-by-side photos of Lon and Annabelle Schlessinger. He was a slightly paunchy, balding man who looked like an ex-jock gone to seed. The high school portrait of Annabelle was startling. George might as well have been staring at a three-year-old photo of his niece.

Biting his lip, George went back to the article, which talked about Lon's membership in two civic organizations, and his love for hunting and fishing. George was more interested in what they reported about Amelia's twin:

"Annabelle was an extremely bright student," said Caroline Cadwell, her sophomore homeroom teacher at East Marion High School. "She was very driven. With her intelligence, beauty, and determination, we were all expecting great things in her future. It's a tragic loss. . . ."

The article ended with a quote from Annabelle's friend and classmate, Erin Gottlieb:

"Annabelle was like a force of nature. She was so strong and determined. She never let anyone get in her way when she made her mind up to go after something, and you have to admire that. I guess it took another force of nature, like fire, to stop her."

It struck George as a slightly cryptic epitaph, almost unflattering.

There was a coin slot at the side of the microfiche viewer and, for two quarters, George made a copy of each page. Then he returned the microfiche file to the reference desk, and asked for a local phone book.

He hoped Caroline Cadwell and Erin Gottlieb still lived in the area. Maybe Annabelle's teacher and her friend could tell him something about Mrs. Schlessinger's apparent suicide and Uncle Duane's killing rampage. Maybe one of them knew about Annabelle's twin sister.

She got Helene Sumner's machine.

Karen waited for the beep, then started in: "Hello, Ms. Sumner. I'm Karen Carlisle, a friend of Amelia Faraday. I'm sorry to bother you, but —"

There was a click on the other end of the line. "Yes, hello," the woman said. "This isn't a reporter, is it?"

"No," Karen said, suddenly sitting erect

in her desk chair. "I'm a friend of Amelia Faraday. I'm calling from Seattle. She drove off early this morning in my car, a black Volkswagen Jetta. I've been trying to locate her. I was wondering —"

"Well, I can tell you where she was as of nine o'clock today," Helene interrupted. "She was at their house, just down the lake from here. It's got the police tape on the front door, but that didn't stop her from going inside, though I suppose she has a right to go in there."

"Then you saw her?"

"I heard screams," Helene said. "That's what got my attention. The sound travels across the water. I've been keeping an eye on the place. The police told me to report any trespassers. Well, I almost phoned them this morning when I heard the screaming and laughing over there. But then I got out the binoculars, and saw it was Amelia."

"Just Amelia, and no one else?"

"I only saw her, though it sure sounded like someone else was there, maybe that boyfriend of hers."

"Boyfriend?" Karen said. "You mean Shane?"

"I don't know his name. I'm sorry. I know you're Amelia's friend, but . . ." Helene paused for a moment. "Are you in college with Amelia?"

"I'm Amelia's therapist, Ms. Sumner," Karen admitted.

"Well, then you must know, for someone so sweet and pretty, she has terrible taste in boyfriends."

"Does he have black hair and wear sunglasses?" Karen asked.

"Yeah, that's him. I'm sorry, I hate to say the word, but he looks like a *pimp,* what with his cheap suit and those sunglasses. But I didn't see him today, just Amelia."

"You said she was at the house around nine o'clock. Have you seen or heard anything over there since then?"

"No. She may have left. She may have gone back inside the house. I'm not sure."

"Is there a black Jetta or an old Cadillac in the driveway?"

"They don't have a driveway. There's a short trail through the woods to the top of a hill, where the road is. The Faradays always parked their car in this inlet up there. Do you want me to go over to the house, and check if she's —"

"No," Karen cut her off. "No, please, don't do that. It could be dangerous, especially if her boyfriend is there. I agree with you, Ms. Sumner. He's a bad influence on Amelia. I don't want you going over there.

If you see him or Amelia anywhere on your property, you should call the police. I don't mean to frighten you —"

"I'm sixty-seven years old, miss," Helene said. "Not many things scare me anymore. I've lived alone in this house by the lake for the last nine years. I have a good watchdog and a loaded rifle. I'll be all right."

"I'm glad to hear it," Karen replied.

This was the only lead she had. And from what Amelia had told her, there was no way to get in touch with anyone at the lake house, except through Helene's landline next door. Karen would have to drive three hours to Lake Wenatchee and hope Amelia was still there. She wondered if Blade was indeed with her this morning. Or was Amelia's multiple personality disorder so severe that she was *screaming and laughing over there* by herself?

"Miss? Are you still there?"

"Um, yes, Ms. Sumner," she said. "Can I ask you for one more favor? Could you give me directions to the Faradays' house?"

"Have another hit," she said, handing him the Wild Turkey bottle.

His hands on the oars, Shane grinned at her. "I think I've had enough. They say booze and boating is a bad mix."

"This is a stupid little canoe," she said, still offering him the half-drained pint bottle. "I don't think it counts. C'mon, have another blast. It'll warm you up."

Shane shook his head. He already had a little buzz, and unlike Amelia, he knew his limits. Though so far, she'd downed surprisingly little for someone who had seemed bent on getting drunk less than an hour ago.

She was acting awfully strange, a total turnaround from last night. She'd been nervous and on edge throughout the movie and pizza, needy, but in a good way that made him feel like the most important person in the world. But then, since her bizarre visit with him this morning, she didn't seem stressed out at all. She wasn't making him feel needed, just manipulated and jerked around. That wasn't like Amelia at all. Her flirting — the foot rubs, flashing him, the kisses, and her dirty talk — had all been a turn-on, yeah, but it all seemed like an act.

Last night, she hadn't been able to tell him why the cops were waiting for her in her dorm lobby. She'd promised to explain later, and begged him to be patient with her. But when he'd pressed her about it again just a few minutes ago, she'd dismissed it, and said they were bugging her with more personal questions about her father. "I just didn't feel like discussing my dad's hang-ups with them again, that's all," she'd explained. "So screw them."

She didn't want to talk about Karen coming on to her last night either. At first she'd acted like Karen had attacked her or something. But now, in the boat, she didn't seem too traumatized about it. Shane began to wonder if anything really did happen with Karen.

He glanced up at the darkening sky, the clouds almost obscuring Mount Rainier in the distance. "Looks like rain. We should head back," he said, working the oars again.

"Party pooper," she muttered. She put the cap back on the Wild Turkey bottle, then slipped it into her knapsack. She kept the knapsack in her lap. "What's wrong with you today anyway?" she asked. "You're acting totally weird."

"*I'm* acting weird?" Shane shot back.

She nodded. "You know, I should be really sore at you. This morning, I specifically asked you not to talk to Karen, and you talked to her anyway. Did you tell her about meeting me here today?"

"No. I didn't tell her shit. I didn't tell anyone." He rowed more fervently. "I'm sorry, but this whole thing is totally schizoid.

You show up at my window at dawn, dragging me out of bed. You've got me ditching psych class and renting a canoe, so we can schlep out here in the middle of the goddamn lake for this secret meeting. My favorite shoes are all wet, and we're about to get rained on. And you're telling me I'm acting weird, because I'm not exactly thrilled to be jumping through all these hoops for you. . . ."

Her head bowed, she hugged her knapsack in her lap and quietly cried.

Shane sighed. "Okay, okay, I'll shut up. I'm sorry. Let's just go back to my place and talk, okay? Nobody's there right now."

"Well, nobody's out here right now, either," she said, pouting. "That's why I wanted to come here — so we could be alone. But you're acting like you don't want to be alone with me."

"That's not true, sweetheart." He stopped rowing, and they drifted for a few moments.

"You're treating me like I'm a stranger," she said, wiping a tear from her cheek. "I've felt it ever since we met on the island. You've been pulling away from me. We're out here alone in this beautiful, romantic spot, and all you want to do is go home."

"I'm sorry, Amelia." He shrugged and shook his head. "I didn't mean to pull away.

I just can't figure out what you're up to today. I —"

"What I'm *up to* today?" she repeated, giving him a wounded look. "What does that mean? You sound like you don't trust me."

"Of course, I trust you."

"Prove it," she said, reaching into the knapsack again.

"What?"

"I said, prove it. Prove to me that I have your trust." She pulled a revolver out of the knapsack.

Shane recoiled, and the boat rocked a bit. "What the hell? Amelia . . ."

Tears in her eyes, she pointed the gun at him.

"Sweetheart, what are you doing?" he whispered. If he'd had a little buzz from the Wild Turkey, he was very sober now. He stayed perfectly still.

"I want to see if you really trust me, if you love me," she said.

Gaping at the gun, he shook his head. "I — I didn't know you had that. Where did you even get that?"

He shrunk back as she got to her feet. The boat swayed back and forth, but she kept the gun trained on him. "Oh, Jesus, be careful," he murmured, wincing.

She sat down close to him. Their legs

pressed against each other, knees bumping. Shane tried not to make any sudden moves.

She stared into his eyes. "A minute ago, you said you didn't mean to pull away from me. If I put this gun in your mouth, would you pull away?"

"Sweetheart, please stop. . . ."

"Then you don't trust me," she cried. "You don't love me. I might as well use this gun on myself. Don't you see? You're all I have left, Shane."

"Don't, please, Amelia. Just — just — just put that thing down."

She held the revolver a few inches from his face. He was so terrified, he could hardly breathe.

"Prove to me that you love me," she whispered. "Let me put this in your mouth. Can't you trust me that much? Just for a couple of seconds? If you won't let me, I swear to God, I'll shoot myself right here. I mean it."

He shook his head.

"Fine," she muttered, then she suddenly turned the gun on herself.

"No!" he screamed. The sound seemed to echo over the lake.

She froze. Her eyes wrestled with his.

"You can put it in my mouth," he said. "If it's that important to you, go ahead."

Shane told himself that she'd had the chance to shoot him ever since they'd gotten out on the lake, if that was what she wanted to do. In some totally screwed-up way, maybe she was right; he'd have to trust her, and this was one way of showing it.

But as she turned the gun toward him, he felt his stomach lurch. Shane thought he might be sick. His hands shook on the oars. "Why?" he whispered. "Amelia, why are you doing this?"

Her forehead was wrinkled in concentration, but there was a strange coolness about her, too, a determined gaze past the tears in her eyes.

She brushed the end of the gun against his lips.

Shane opened his mouth wider, and tasted the dirty metal on his tongue.

"I'm doing this to make certain you love Amelia," she said.

He sat there, trying not to shake, and counting the seconds while she kept the gun in his mouth. It struck him as bizarre, the way she'd said *Amelia* instead of *me,* as if Amelia were someone else entirely: "I'm doing this to make certain you love Amelia."

The notion that she might not be Amelia didn't occur to him at all. Shane didn't have a chance. Before the thought even entered his head a bullet already had.

She dipped her hand in the cold lake water to rinse it off. Blood had sprayed on her face and hair, too. She licked her lips and tasted it: salty and warm. Then she bent over the side of the canoe and washed off her face.

Shane had flopped back so violently that the boat had almost tipped over. Water had sluiced in, and one of the oars had gotten knocked into the lake. Now he lay there on the floor of the canoe in an awkward contortion. The small puddle of water lapping around him was almost completely red now.

She checked his wallet. There were only seventeen dollars in there. She kept ten. She'd noticed the ring on his right hand earlier. It was gold with a beautiful black onyx stone. She twisted it off his finger and dropped it into her purse. Wiping off the gun, she carefully placed it beside his lifeless hand. Then with the one oar they had left, she paddled toward the little island. The small patch of land was still unoccupied. She let the canoe hit the muddy bank. Climbing out of the canoe, she stepped knee-deep into the icy lake. She hoisted the knapsack over her shoulder. She had a change of clothes in there, among other things.

Giving the boat a shove, she watched it drift away from the shore.

Then she turned and headed for dry land.

CHAPTER SIXTEEN

"Sorry I didn't call back sooner," Karen said into her cell. She walked along Boylston Avenue at a brisk clip. She wore a trench coat over her black jeans and her dark green V-neck sweater.

She'd cancelled all her afternoon appointments before running out of the house. It was eleven blocks to her destination, and Karen was in a hurry. She might have taken a cab, but this wasn't a phone conversation she wanted to conduct in the back of a taxi. She'd turned down Boylston to avoid the crowds and the traffic noise along the main drag, Broadway. This street was more residential, with an eclectic mix of brand-new and very old apartment buildings. Trees lined the parkways, and their fallen leaves covered the sidewalk. Karen hadn't encountered too many other pedestrians taking this route.

"I wasn't ignoring you, Detective," she

explained on the phone. "The last couple of hours, I've been busy making calls, hoping to find out where Amelia might have gone. You see, I probably should have told you this morning, but, well, Amelia stayed over at my place last night."

"Is that so?" Jacqueline Peyton said on the other end of the line. "You knew we wanted to get in touch with Amelia. And yet you deliberately kept her from talking to us. Why?"

Karen hesitated. She didn't want to say anything to incriminate Amelia or herself. Hell, she didn't even want to be talking to the police right now. But if there was *another* Amelia out there endangering people's lives, then the police had to be told. At the same time, the Amelia she knew was probably scared, confused, and hiding somewhere, like at the lake house in Wenatchee. And Karen didn't want to see her hurt.

Yet, she'd slipped her dad's revolver into her purse before leaving the house a few minutes ago. Exactly who she intended to use it on she didn't know.

"I'm sorry," she said at last. "But I'm Amelia's therapist, and my first duty is to my client. She's a very sweet, very confused young woman —"

"Did she meet with Koehler on Sunday?"

Jacqueline Peyton pressed.

"I can't say," Karen replied, picking up her pace. "I can't tell you anything we discussed in confidence —"

"You know, Karen, that won't hold up in court."

"Maybe not, but I'm sticking to it. So, here's what I can tell you right now. Okay?"

"Go ahead. I'm listening."

"Amelia stayed at my house last night. After you called me this morning, I went to check on her, and she was gone. So was my car, and about sixty dollars from my purse. My car is a 1999 black Volkswagen Jetta, license plate number EMK903. Are you taking this down?"

"Yes, black VW Jetta, Washington plates EMK903."

"Amelia's uncle, her boyfriend, and her roommate don't have any idea where she is," Karen continued. "Her uncle and I checked, and she's not up at her parents' house in Bellingham. Amelia would never intentionally hurt anybody. But there's someone who could be with her, and I think he's trouble. His name's Blade and he's in his midtwenties. He has dyed black hair, and wears sunglasses a lot. I believe he drives an old black Cadillac with a bent antenna. I don't have any other information about him."

"All right," the policewoman said. "Where are you right now? Are you at home?"

"No, I'm not," Karen said. Just half a block ahead, she could see a green sandwich-board sign on the sidewalk. It had ENTERPRISE RENTAL CAR written on it.

"We'll need to talk to you in person, Karen. And you might want to have your lawyer present."

"Yes, I was afraid of that," she murmured into the phone. And then she clicked off.

While they got her compact economy car ready for her, Karen asked to use the restroom. It was a small, gray-tiled unisex bathroom off the garage. She stood by the dirty white sink, and pulled out her cell phone again. She counted three ring tones.

"Sandpoint View Convalescent Home," Roseann answered.

"Hi, Ro, it's Karen again, just checking in. How's my dad?"

"He's up and around, and having a good day. Still no sign of that girl you asked about."

"Well, good," Karen said, relieved. "You might not be able to get ahold of me later this afternoon. If you do see her, call this number right away. Do you have a pen?"

"Just a sec. Okay, shoot."

"555-9225, that's a Detective Jacqueline Peyton. Tell her you're a friend of mine, and you've found Amelia Faraday."

"555-9225," Roseann repeated. "I'm a friend of yours and I found Amelia Faraday. Got it."

"Detective Peyton will know what to do from there."

"Are you going to tell me what this is all about?"

"I can't right now. But later, Ro, I promise."

"Sounds like you're in a hurry to get someplace."

"Yes, I need to take off soon," Karen said.

"Well, you caught me in the lounge, and Frank's right here. Do you have time to talk with him? Like I said, he's having a good day."

"Oh, yes, thank you, Ro. Please, put him on." She waited, and heard some faint murmuring on the other end.

"Hello, Karen?" he said, at last.

"Hi, Poppy, how are you?"

"Fine. How's my girl doing?"

"I'm okay," she lied. Her voice even cracked a little, because this was one of those rare moments when she felt like she was talking to her father again. Part of her just wanted to say, *Poppy, I'm in trouble.* Instead, she cleared her throat. "Um, I hope to come by to visit you tomorrow."

"Well, I'll be here. Could you bring Rufus?"

"Sure, I will. You sound great, Poppy."

"We're having ham for dinner tonight," he said. "They serve a good ham here."

"Well, enjoy. And I'll see you tomorrow, okay?"

"Okay, sweetie. Take care of yourself."

Then she heard him talking to Roseann: "That was my daughter, Karen. How do you hang up this thing? Oh . . . I see . . ." There was a click on the line.

"Bye, Poppy," she said to no one.

"Why do you want to talk to Erin?" asked the woman on the telephone.

There were five Gottliebs in the Salem phone book, and this was the third one George had called. It was Erin's mother, M. Gottlieb.

"I'm trying to track down some information on Annabelle Schlessinger," George said. He was sitting inside his car, still parked down the street from the Salem Library. "I understand Erin and Annabelle were friends."

There was a silence on the other end of

the line. "Mrs. Gottlieb?"

"Um, how did you know Annabelle?" she asked finally.

"I didn't," he admitted. "That's why I wanted to talk to Erin. You see, I'm doing some research on my family tree — a master's thesis on genealogy, actually. There's a chance I could be related to Annabelle. I was hoping Erin might be able to give me some information about the Schlessingers."

"I don't think she could tell you much. Erin and Annabelle really weren't friends for very long."

"Anything would be helpful, Mrs. Gottlieb."

"Well, I suppose you could phone her at work. You can reach her at the Pampered Pup."

It was a doggie daycare and grooming place located in a strip mall near Willamette University. George had decided he'd get more information out of Erin if they talked face-to-face.

Apparently Erin had been expecting him, one way or another. When he told the Pampered Pup receptionist he was looking for Erin, the heavyset, terminally bored-looking young woman came around the lobby desk, then escorted him to the back. She opened a door that must have been soundproof, because the sudden din of yelps and barking startled him. She led him to an alcove, where about two dozen small- and medium-sized dogs were in cages, stacked one on top of the other.

"Hey, Erin," the receptionist yelled over the racket. "You've got a visitor." Then she wandered back toward the front office.

Erin was thin with straight, dark-blond hair, glasses, and a pierced nostril. She stood at a long steel sink, washing a slightly hyper Jack Russell terrier. She wore a dark-blue work apron over her black sweater and jeans. She nodded instead of shaking his hand. She had on yellow rubber gloves, and worked a portable shower nozzle over the soapy dog.

"Hi, I'm George," he said. "Sorry to bother you here at work."

"It's okay. My mom called to tell me you might be calling or coming by." Erin gave him a wry grin. She had to talk loudly over the continuous barking. "All these alarms probably went off when you told her you were related to Annabelle Schlessinger. Mom always thought Annabelle was a terrible influence on me. So, what did you want to know?"

"Well, I read that story in the *Statesman Journal* about the fire, and what you said

415

about Annabelle." George leaned against the dry end of the long sink. "It was an interesting quote, very poetic . . ."

"Oh, that *force of nature* speech," she said, chuckling. "I got so much shit from my other friends about that. But I honestly couldn't think of anything *nice* to say. Annabelle and I were officially avoiding each other weeks before the fire. But I guess I knew her better than anyone else, so I had to come up with something for that stupid reporter."

"Your mom indicated that you and Annabelle weren't friends for very long," George said.

Washing under the dog's tail, she nodded. "Yeah, she was just a little too clingy and possessive. Can I be totally honest with you? I mean, you didn't know her, right? You don't want me blowing smoke up your ass, right?"

"No, I'd appreciate your honesty. Really, it won't offend me at all."

"Well, it's funny. All the guys were hot for Annabelle, because she was pretty and had big boobs. But she just used them. It didn't take long for me to realize she was a manipulative bitch, and you can throw *crazy* into that soup, too."

"Crazy, how?"

"Well, I guess this goes with the clingy, possessive part of her character. But she wanted us to work out our own secret language, so we could write and talk to each other, and no one else would understand. She even wanted us to dress alike at school. I mean, how queer is that? Oh, and she claimed she could read my thoughts. That was another thing. Annabelle said she was telepathic. I remember laughing at her and saying she was tele-*pathetic,* and she got really pissed off at me. I think that was the beginning of the end for us."

She picked up the terrier and moved it farther down the steel sink. "Better back up," she said.

But George didn't hear her past all the barking and yelping. He was thinking about the matching clothes, a secret language, and some telepathic connection. Was Annabelle hoping Erin would take the place of the twin she'd lost?

"Hey," Erin said loudly. "Unless you want to get doused, better stand back. He's gonna shake it off."

George backed up toward the cages, and watched the dog shake off the excess water. Erin started working a towel over him.

"Did Annabelle ever mention to you that she had a twin sister?" he asked.

"Oh, yeah, *Andrea.*" Erin said, nodding. "She told me *Andrea* was abducted by some pervert neighbor when the kid was four, and he raped and killed her. I mean, talk about creepy and tragic, right? And then I talked to another girl in my class, Deborah Wothers. Annabelle tried to be Deborah's friend for a while, because Deborah's so nice and everybody loves her. But Deborah was smart enough to keep her distance. Anyway, she told Deborah that her twin sister, *Alicia,* slipped and fell in the tub and drowned or some bullshit like that. So, you're telling me she really did have a twin?"

George just nodded. He knew both stories were fabrications, of course. But he wondered if there was a sliver of truth to the abduction incident.

Erin had stopped drying the dog. She stared at George. "So, this twin, how did she really die?"

"She didn't. She's alive, and her name's Amelia," he explained. "The Schlessingers put her up for adoption when she was four. I'm trying to find out why. Amelia doesn't know anything about her birth family. I was hoping you could fill in a lot of blanks for me, Erin. Did Annabelle ever talk about her mother?"

With a dumbfounded look, Erin shook her head.

"Nothing?" he pressed.

"Well, I heard she offed herself when Annabelle was just a kid. She hanged herself in the basement or something. Annabelle was supposed to have found her. I never had the guts to ask her for details."

"What about the father?"

She shrugged. "I used to see him at church, that's it."

"Didn't you ever see him at Annabelle's house?"

"I never went there. I don't think anyone in the class did, either." Erin wrapped the dog in the towel, then carried him to a cage, and set him inside. With a sigh, she pulled off her gloves. "Anyway, I never set foot in the place," she said. "Annabelle always came over to my house. She pretty much hated living out there at that ranch in the middle of nowhere."

"Did Annabelle ever talk about her Uncle Duane?" George asked.

Erin pried a stick of Juicy Fruit out of her pants pocket, then unwrapped it and put it in her mouth. "Nope, sorry."

She put her work gloves back on, opened another cage, and pulled out a miniature schnauzer. "C'mon, bath time, you mangy son of a bitch," she muttered. She set the dog in the steel tub, then stopped and turned to George. "You know who you should talk to? Mrs. Cadwell, our home-room teacher sophomore year. Caroline Cadwell, she was practically a friend of the family. I think she even knew Mrs. Schlessinger. She could tell you a lot."

"Caroline Cadwell," George repeated. Along with Erin, she'd been quoted in the newspaper account about the fire.

Stroking the dog's head, Erin paused to glance at George. "As far as the Schlessingers go, Mrs. Cadwell knows more than anybody else, and she's *seen* more than anybody else. She can tell you all about the fire, too."

"Really?" George asked.

"Oh, yeah," she replied, nodding. "Mrs. Cadwell's the one who identified the bodies."

Salem, Oregon — July 2004
It was 8:50 p.m., and still light out — still pretty hot, too. But she felt a soft, cool evening wind against her bare legs.

Eighteen-year-old Sandra Hartman cut across the deserted baseball field. Her shoulder-length black hair was freshly washed, and she wore a blue blouse, khaki shorts, and sandals. She warily eyed the empty bleachers. The place kind of gave her the creeps at night, even with the late sunset.

She was on her way to meet some friends at Lancaster Mall. They planned to see *Dodgeball,* of all things. The only reason for going was because a bunch of guys she knew were supposed to show up.

Sandra lived eight blocks from the mall. It wasn't very pedestrian-friendly right around there. Ordinarily, she would have driven over. But her parents had taken the car for some business dinner her dad had. When she'd mentioned she might go to the movies, he'd insisted she grab a ride from a friend or stay home.

Everyone was still in a panic over the disappearance of Gina Fernetti just ten days before. The story was on TV and in the newspapers. Regina Marie Fernetti was twenty, a journalism major at the University of Colorado, and home for summer break. She and two girlfriends had gone to the Walker Pool on a busy Saturday afternoon. Gina had driven. They'd just claimed a spot on the grass, and laid out their blankets when Gina announced she wanted to get a certain tape cassette out of the car for her Walkman. She left her purse and blanket behind, and went off toward the parking lot with her car keys. When she didn't return fifteen minutes later, her friends checked the lot. Gina's car was still there, still locked. They searched the pool area, and had her paged over the public address system. The lifeguards even made everyone get out of the pool for ten minutes just to make sure Gina hadn't missed the announcement. Gina's girlfriends finally called Mr. and Mrs. Fernetti who, in turn, called the police.

No one had seen Gina Fernetti since. She'd just vanished.

So Sandra's father was being a bit crazy-overprotective. To appease him, Sandra had tried to get one of her friends to pick her up at the last minute, but with no luck. They were carpooling over to the mall, and it was already crammed. Sandra figured she could get a ride home later from one of the guys, and her dad would be none the wiser about her walking to the mall alone.

She had about twenty minutes until the movie started, and figured she'd be at the mall in ten. Sandra noticed the streetlights go on as she made her way across the baseball field. She slipped through an opening in the fence, and started down a residential street. She didn't see anyone else around. It was a bit eerie and unsettling.

On a warm night like this, more people should have been out. Was what had happened to Gina keeping people inside with their doors locked?

Sandra picked up her pace, but then suddenly balked when a shadow swept in front of her. She realized a car was pulling up behind her with its headlights on. She glanced over her shoulder: a silver SUV.

Strange, five minutes ago, she'd noticed a silver SUV coming up the road toward her before she'd cut through the baseball field. Was this the same one?

The vehicle slowed down and pulled over to the curb in front of her.

"Shit," Sandra murmured. A little alarm went off inside her. She quickly crossed the street, and watched the SUV slowly creep over toward her. She walked as fast as she could without breaking into a sprint. She told herself not to run. As long as she pretended not to notice them, they wouldn't know she was scared and they wouldn't start chasing her — not just yet. Somehow, maybe it would buy her time. She could be overreacting too. Would someone really try anything in a residential neighborhood, where people could hear her screaming? Plus, it was still kind of light out, for God's sake.

Then again, the light hadn't protected Gina Fernetti. She'd vanished in the middle of a sunny afternoon, and no one had heard her scream.

The silver SUV crawled down the street, keeping pace with her. Sandra's stomach was in knots. Could it be some friend of hers, playing a joke? Well, it wasn't funny, damn it. On her left, Sandra saw a two-story white stucco house with a car in the driveway and lights on in the front windows. She thought about running up the walkway and pounding on the door.

She casually glanced to her right at that silver SUV. The driver's window went down. "Hey, Sandra! Are you going to the mall? Do you need a ride?"

It took Sandra a few moments to recognize the driver, and when she did, she let out a weak chuckle. "Oh, my God, you scared the shit out of me."

"Sorry," said the girl behind the wheel, smiling. "I wasn't really sure if it was you or not. I'm headed to the mall. Do you need a lift?"

Sandra hesitated. If she accepted the ride, she'd feel obligated to invite her along to the movie. It was the polite thing to do. But she really didn't like this girl very much. In fact she hardly knew her. She was a sophomore, two years behind her. It was weird how the girl had called out to her from the car window like they were good friends. The only other time they'd ever talked was in the school cafeteria two months before. The sophomore had approached Sandra while she'd been eating lunch with her friends.

"You must be Sandra Hartman," she'd said. "You wouldn't believe how many times people mistake me for you."

"Oh, really?" Sandra had said, with a baffled smile.

"Yeah, I can totally see the resemblance now. We're almost like twins."

"Well, huh, maybe. Anyway, nice meeting you," Sandra had said. Then she'd turned away. Her friends at the table had started teasing her. "Who the hell was that?" Sandra had whispered. And then one of her friends had told her.

That had been the only other time she'd talked to Annabelle Schlessinger.

"Sandra? Are you headed to the mall?" Annabelle asked from the driver's seat of the SUV.

She worked up a smile and nodded. She figured her dad was probably right. In the wake of Gina Fernetti's disappearance, it wasn't smart to walk around alone at night. And it was starting to get dark. She'd be better off riding the rest of the way. So what if Annabelle ended up tagging along to the movie with her? There was no reason to be snobby toward her. In fact, Sandra realized as she stepped closer to the SUV and locked eyes with Annabelle that there was indeed a resemblance between them. "I'm meeting some friends to see *Dodgeball*. Do you want to join us?"

Her mouth open, Annabelle stared back at her and blinked. Stopping, Sandra saw tears well up in Annabelle's eyes. "What's wrong?" she asked.

"I — I really wish I could go to the movie with you guys, more than anything," Annabelle murmured. Then she cleared her throat, and straightened up behind the wheel. "Thanks anyway, but I can't," she said, more control in her tone. She gazed at the road in front of her. "I'm headed to the mall to run an errand for my father. Hurry up, get in."

Sandra walked around the front of the car, a bit puzzled by Annabelle's strange reaction to such a casual invitation. At the same time, everything was coming out all right for her. She had a ride to the mall with no strings attached. She didn't have to spend the rest of the night with Annabelle clinging to her.

"Oh, you've got the air-conditioning on in here," Sandra said, sliding into the front seat. "Feels like heaven."

Annabelle said nothing. She stared straight ahead.

Once Sandra shut the passenger door and buckled her seat belt, the SUV started to inch forward. After a few moments, Sandra glanced at the speedometer: 10 mph. "What, are you afraid of getting a ticket?" she asked. "Why are you going so slowly?"

Annabelle didn't answer. The SUV crawled past the end of the block toward a turnaround area by some woods. The headlights and interior lights went off, and suddenly they were swallowed up in darkness. "What the hell's going on?" Sandra asked.

The car stopped. Hands on the wheel, Annabelle wouldn't look at her. Instead, she glanced up at the rearview mirror. "I'm sorry, Sandra," she muttered listlessly. "I guess you haven't met my father."

"What?" Sandra checked the rearview mirror, and saw a shadowy figure suddenly spring up from the floor. She gasped.

All at once, he grabbed her hair and yanked her head back. It happened so fast, she couldn't fight him off. He slapped a wet cloth over her mouth. It must have been soaked with some chemical, because it burned her face. Sandra's eyes watered up. She tried not to breathe in, and desperately clawed at his hand.

But he wouldn't let go. Almost unwillingly, she gasped for air, and then realized it was too late. Sandra had never experienced this sensation before. She wasn't passing out, or falling asleep, or even fainting. No, this was something different.

Sandra Hartman felt herself surrendering to something very close to death.

Seattle — three years later
"Nope, sorry, I still haven't seen hide nor hair of Amelia," Jessie said into the phone. In front of her on the McMillans' kitchen table, was a pile of laundry, still warm from the dryer. "No calls either, except from Karen, checking up on me about a half hour ago."

"Okay, Jessie, thanks," George said on the other end of the line. "Jody should be home from school in about an hour. Could you take him with you when you go to pick up Steffie at Rainbow Junction Daycare?"

"You asked me that this morning, and I will," Jessie said. "Now, can I tell you something? That cleaning woman of yours isn't worth the powder to blow her to hell. There are dust balls behind your sofa and under the cushions, I found three old French fries, a plastic barrette, some popcorn and forty-seven cents in change."

"Well, you can keep the barrette, but I want the forty-seven cents," George said. "You sure everything's okay there?"

"Peachy," Jessie assured him. "I'm folding laundry, and after this I'm taking out your recycling. Pretty exciting, huh?"

"Well, take a break, for God's sake," George replied. "I'll talk to you later, Jess."

She hung up the phone, and finished folding the clothes. Then Jessie got the recycling bin out of the pantry, and carried it out the kitchen door. She lumbered up to the edge of the driveway and let out a groan as she set the bin on the front curb.

Jessie paused to take a look down the block. She spotted a black car parked about four houses down on the other side of the street. But it wasn't Karen's Jetta, and that was the one she was supposed to be on the lookout for.

This car was just a beat-up old Cadillac.

With a sigh, Jessie turned and headed back for the house.

CHAPTER SEVENTEEN

Karen took the turnoff at Coles Corner to Lake Wenatchee Highway. The scenery along Stevens Pass had been gorgeous: the mountains and rivers, the trees so vibrant with their fall colors, and even a few small waterfalls. But she'd barely noticed any of it. She couldn't stop thinking about what George had discovered, that Amelia had a twin sister.

No wonder Amelia had developed so many neuroses, having been torn apart from her twin at such a young age. With the sudden absence of her sister, Amelia might have taken on her twin's persona. Perhaps she assumed her sister felt abandoned, angry and bitter, even destructive. And maybe Amelia was adopting those traits during her blackouts while the twin sister part of her took over. That *lost time* Amelia experienced kept her from knowing about this sister-half and her activities.

"Or maybe they're just alcohol-related blackouts," Karen muttered to herself. "And you're making way too much of this twin thing."

She passed a sign for Lake Wenatchee State Park, and knew she was on the right track, at least as far as her driving was concerned. According to Helene's directions, she would be at the Faradays' lake house in another fifteen minutes.

Amelia's separation from her twin certainly explained other things: the nightmares and those phantom pains and "faked" illnesses that had plagued her all the way through adolescence. Karen had read accounts of twin telepathy when she was in graduate school. Some were rather dull, dry studies. "Though separated, both twins picked the red ball for the first two experiments, and the green ball for the third, and the red ball again for the fourth. The choice patterns of the separated twins matched in 96 percent of the test cases."

Other accounts were a bit more like a *Twilight Zone* episode. Karen recalled one story about a 55-year-old businessman who woke up in the middle of the night in his Zurich hotel room with severe abdominal pains and a high fever. The doctors in the emergency room at the hospital couldn't find anything actually wrong with him, and his fever went away by the next morning. He got back to the hotel to find a message from his sister-in-law in Columbus, Ohio. His twin brother had been rushed to the hospital the night before with a ruptured appendix.

Karen remembered one of her professors dismissing such stories, though apparently dozens of similar cases were on record.

Had young Amelia, with her unexplained maladies, been feeling the pains and illnesses of her twin sister? Karen remembered some of Amelia's descriptions. *It felt like someone was kicking me. . . . Like my arm was being twisted off . . . It felt like someone was putting out a lit cigar on me. . . .*

She wondered about the awful things being done to Annabelle Schlessinger when her estranged twin sister — miles and miles away — had felt those horrible sensations. What kind of violence had that child endured? Amelia had said she'd stopped experiencing the phantom pains and illnesses about three years ago, when she was sixteen. And Annabelle Schlessinger had died at age sixteen.

Perhaps Amelia's violent nightmares while growing up had been the result of some kind of telepathy. Maybe she was picking up real incidents as they happened to her twin.

Karen could almost imagine her professor laughing at her for such far-fetched speculation. It might not hold up with an American Psychological Association review panel, but there were all sorts of phenomena that couldn't be easily explained. And twin telepathy was one of them.

Karen kept a lookout for the street signs. Along the forest road, she could see the placid lake peeking through the trees. She finally spotted a sign, with a red and white checkered border:

DANNY'S DINER
Breakfast, Lunch, or Dinner
You'll Come Up a Winner!

1 MILE AHEAD ↑

That was the restaurant both Amelia and Helene had described to her — the one near the gravel road that led to the Faradays' lake house.

Karen still didn't know what she expected to find when she got to the cabin. She might have driven all this way for nothing. If Amelia was hiding out there, Karen would calm her down and talk to her. They certainly couldn't put off going to the police any longer. Hell, they were both probably *persons of interest* in Koehler's disappearance, and about a notch away from *fugitive* status, if not there already. But Karen was still determined to protect Amelia, and make sure she got the help she needed.

Up the road a piece, she saw Danny's Diner, a small chalet-style restaurant with flower boxes in the windows and four picnic tables in front. The parking lot was big enough for a dozen cars, and at the moment, half full. As Karen drove by, she noticed the phone booth by the front door.

Eyes on the road, she reached over for her cell phone, and tried to dial her home number. A mechanical voice told her, "We're sorry. Your call cannot be completed. Please hang up and try again."

Helene was right, cell phones didn't work around here. That would make things extremely difficult if she ran into trouble at the cabin. She had to prepare herself for the possibility that Amelia was indeed at the cabin, but not at all herself right now. She might even have Blade with her.

Karen noticed the turn off to Holden Trail, a gravel road that sloped down and wound through the forest. The tiny stones made a hail-like racket under her rental car, and the occasional divot gave her a jolt. Karen had an awful foreboding feeling in the pit of her stomach, along with nerves and hunger, too. She hadn't eaten all day.

She spotted a turnaround on her left. Helene had told her to ignore that one. The inlet the Faradays used was up ahead. Karen slowed down. She could see a little plateau off the bay with enough room for two small cars. As she inched into the spot, Karen could see other tire marks in the gravel and dirt.

After the two-and-a-half-hour drive, Karen's legs cramped a bit as she climbed out of the rental. Grabbing her purse, she took another look at the gun inside. Along with the tire tracks, she noticed a cigarette butt and footprints, too. It looked like more than one person.

So Amelia hadn't come here alone this morning. She must have been with Blade.

Karen saw the footprints again as she made her way down the trail, which was mostly dirt, but some patches were covered in gravel. There were a few stone steps, too, and an old wooden railing at a few precarious spots. She caught a glimpse of the lake between the trees. Finally, the terrain started to flatten out. Karen could see a clearing and the Faradays' house ahead.

A crude flagstone path led to the front stoop of the weathered, two-story Cape Cod home. Karen tried to peek inside the windows as she passed. But it was dark in the house, and she couldn't see anything beyond her own timid reflection.

Strips of yellow police tape with CRIME SCENE — DO NOT CROSS written on them had been taped across the front door. But someone had torn past them, and the loose tape strips now fluttered in the wind. There was also a notice taped to the front door — a green sheet of paper with a police shield logo and CITY OF WENATCHEE POLICE DEPARTMENT along the top. Karen glanced at it. There were two paragraphs of legal jargon, but the last words were in bold print: NO TRESPASSING — VIOLATORS WILL BE PROSECTUED.

Obviously, someone else had already ignored those warnings. Karen was about to knock on the front door, but hesitated. If Blade and Amelia were in there, did she really want to announce her arrival?

Biting her lip, Karen tried the doorknob. To her amazement, the door wasn't locked. Slowly, she opened it. Reaching into her purse, she took out her father's revolver, and then stepped over the threshold. All the blinds were half drawn, and the windows closed. It was dark and stuffy inside the house. Nearly every stick of furniture had been dusted for fingerprints. A dirt trail covered the carpet and floors, obviously from all the police traipsing in and out of the crime scene. By the fireplace, Karen noticed the rocking chair where Amelia's father was found. Behind it, she saw the large splotch on the wall, now a rust color. There were bloodstains on the beige carpet, too, beneath the rocker, and also a few feet away, where George's wife must have been shot. Everything was just as Amelia — and Koehler — had described it.

Karen followed the investigators' trail toward the kitchen, but abruptly stopped at the sound of something creaking. It seemed to have come from upstairs, but she wasn't sure. With the gun in her trembling hand, Karen listened and waited for the next little noise. She counted to ten, and didn't hear anything. She told herself it was just the house settling. She crept into the kitchen. It had gingerbread trim on the shelves and a yellow, fifties-style dinette set. Through the window in the kitchen door, she noticed the yellow police tape again, only this time, it was intact and crisscrossed over the entry.

There was another door in the kitchen,

open about two inches. Beyond that, all Karen could see was darkness. She moved the door, and it creaked on the hinges. She froze. Was that the same sound she'd heard earlier?

She gazed at the wood-plank stairs leading down to the pitch-black basement. Turning to look for a light switch by the door, she saw something dart past the kitchen window. Karen gasped. For a moment, she was paralyzed. She didn't know what to do. It had looked like a person, but she'd only caught a glimpse of her — or him. Whoever it was, they must have been outside, peeking in at her. And they'd moved away from that window so quickly, all Karen had seen was a human-shaped blur.

Clutching the revolver, Karen made her way toward the front door again. She kept checking the windows for whoever was outside the house, but didn't see anybody. "Amelia?" she called. Karen edged toward the door, which she'd left open. She still had the gun poised. "Amelia, is that you? It's Karen. Amelia?"

A dog started barking. "Who's in there?" someone called from outside.

Karen looked out, and saw an older woman with close-cropped gray hair, glasses, and a bulky gray sweater. She had a collie on a leash. "Hush, Abby," she whispered.

Karen quickly stashed the gun in her purse. "Are you Helene?"

Scowling at her, the old woman nodded. "Are you the one I talked to on the phone earlier?"

"Yes," she said, catching her breath. "I'm Karen Carlisle, Amelia's therapist."

"Well, Amelia must have skedaddled," Helene said. "No one's in there. I checked a little while ago."

Karen closed the door behind her. "You went in there after I warned you not to?"

Helene shrugged. "Why should I listen to you? I don't even know you. Anyway, the place is empty." She bent down and scratched her dog behind the ears. "I have no idea when she left. Like I told you on the phone, I saw only Amelia earlier, though it sure sounded like two people were here."

Karen nodded. She was thinking about the double footprints on the dirt trail that led to the house. "Ms. Sumner, before today, when was the last time you noticed Amelia here?"

"Well, she and that boyfriend of hers were carrying on out by the lake a week ago Monday," Helene answered, still hovering over her dog.

"The Monday before the shootings?" Karen asked. She was almost certain she'd had a therapy session with Amelia that Monday. "The fifteenth?"

Helene nodded.

"Are you sure?"

Helene nodded again emphatically. "Monday is my shopping day. When you get to be my age, and you live alone, different rituals become like your companion. . . ."

Karen nodded. She knew exactly what the old woman meant, and it scared her a little that she was already becoming so set in her ways.

"So Monday afternoon, before I headed out to the store, I took Abby for a walk, and I saw Amelia and that creepy young man by the lake. The way they were carrying on, I think they might have been doing drugs."

"What time was this?" Karen asked.

"Smack dab in the middle of the day, around one o'clock."

Karen shook her head. It didn't make sense. If she remembered correctly, her appointment with Amelia that Monday had been in the early afternoon. "Are you sure of the time?" she pressed. "Are you sure it was Amelia?"

Frowning, Helene stopped petting her dog and straightened up. "Miss, I may be old.

But I'm not senile — not yet, at least."

"I'm sorry, but I'm almost positive I was with Amelia, in Seattle, around that exact same time."

Helene scowled at her. "Well, if you were with Amelia on that Monday afternoon, then who was that girl I saw by the lake?"

"Jessie, could you do me a huge favor?" Karen asked. She was in the phone booth by the entrance to Danny's Diner. "Could you drive over to my place and check something out for me?"

"Now?"

"I know my timing stinks with rush hour about to start, but this is important."

"Oh, I guess it's no problem," Jessie said. "Jody just got home from school. I'm supposed to pick up Steffie from daycare at four anyway. We'll just keep driving. The kids can meet Rufus. So what do you want me to do over there?"

"I need you to take a look at my appointment book on my desk, and find out if I had a session with Amelia on Monday afternoon, October fifteenth."

"That's all? I don't get to snoop through anything else of yours?"

"Sorry. I just need to confirm that I saw Amelia on that particular day."

"Monday, the fifteenth," Jessie repeated. "I'll check it out, and give you a ring on your cell in about a half hour."

"Um, cell phones don't work around here for some reason. I'm in a phone booth. I'll call you back."

"Try me at your place in about a half hour. We ought to be there by then."

"Okay. Thanks, Jessie. You're the best."

Karen hung up the phone for only a moment before picking up the receiver again. She punched in her American Express account, and then George's cell phone number.

She caught him waiting for Annabelle Schlessinger's high school teacher, who was busy coaching the cheerleading squad. Her name was Caroline Cadwell, and apparently she'd known the Schlessingers better than anyone else in Salem. "I was going to call you after I talked with her," George told Karen. "So, where are you?"

Through the phone booth's glass wall, Karen glanced at some patrons leaving the diner. "Oh, I'm out and about, running some errands."

"In Central Washington?" he asked pointedly. "Karen, the area code on my caller ID shows 509. Are you anywhere near Lake Wenatchee?"

"I'm in the phone booth at Danny's Diner," Karen admitted. "And before you start in, I've already been to the lake house. Helene Sumner spotted Amelia there this morning. But the place is empty now. The important thing is —"

"I can't believe you went there when you knew I didn't want you to," he interrupted. "Damn it, Karen. You could have gotten yourself killed."

"Well, I didn't," she murmured. The fact that he actually cared touched her. "Anyway, I'm sorry, George."

"Did you even call the police, like we discussed?" he asked. "And please, don't lie again, because I can check."

"Yes, I spoke to them. They still want to talk with Amelia about Koehler's disappearance. I avoided the subject, but told them about her taking my car and the money. I also gave them a description of the car, the plate number, the whole shebang. So, Amelia is officially a fugitive, which scares the hell out of me." She sighed. "Then again, I'm not doing so hot either. That's one more reason I decided to get the hell out of town and come here. The police want to talk to me and advised I have my lawyer present. Anyway, next time you see me, it may be through a Plexiglas window on visiting day."

"I'm not going to let that happen," George said soberly.

Karen let out a grateful little laugh. "You know something? I believe you. Thank you, George." She glanced down at the mud on her shoes from climbing up and down the trail to the lake house. "So, have you found out anything more about Annabelle Schlessinger? How she died?"

"Funny you should ask," George replied. He filled her in on what he'd learned from the newspaper account of the fire, and from Erin Gottlieb.

Karen listened intently. "So Annabelle supposedly died in a fire," she said, almost to herself.

"What do you mean *supposedly?*" George asked.

"I'm just wondering. If Annabelle isn't really dead, it would explain a lot."

"I still don't understand," he said.

"George, do me a favor. Find out as much as you can from Annabelle's teacher about this fire, and how they identified the bodies. Find out if there's any chance Annabelle could still be alive."

George figured he must have looked suspect, a 38-year-old man sitting all alone on the bleachers. His hands in the pockets of his sports jacket, he tried not to stare at the high school cheerleaders on the field. They worked on their routines while a boom box blasted music with an incessant drumbeat. George had noticed a few of the girls looking at him, whispering among themselves, and giggling. He'd also gotten a few strange glances from the guys on the football team as they'd hurtled past him, running their laps around the track.

He didn't feel vindicated until Caroline Cadwell backed away from the cheerleading squad and sat beside him on the bleachers. "Who's the hunk, Ms. C?" one of the girls called. "Your boyfriend?" Another cheerleader let out a wolf whistle.

"Okay, girls, you want to impress this guy?" she shot back. "Let's see a routine in sync for a change! Rachel Porter, you can kick higher than that!"

Caroline Cadwell was a skinny, fortysomething woman with short tawny hair and big hazel eyes. Though pretty, she also had a certain gangly quality that reminded George of an ostrich.

When he'd approached Caroline after her last class had let out at 3:00, George had explained he was a relative of Joy Savitt Schlessinger. He'd used the same family

tree thesis cover story he'd given Erin Gottlieb's mother. Caroline had seemed a bit
dubious at first, but said she could talk with
him later while she monitored cheerleading
practice. After waiting on the bleachers for
the last twenty minutes, George hoped this
Schlessinger family friend would open up to
him.

"So, George, you're studying your genealogy," Caroline said, smoothing back her hair
from the wind. The pulsating music from
the boom box droned on, and the girls went
through their routine, but Caroline seemed
oblivious to it all. "Tell me, how are you
related to Joy? Are you a long-lost cousin,
or what?"

The way she looked him in the eye and
smiled, Caroline had the teacher stare down
pat. Despite all his years in front of a class,
George hadn't quite perfected that Don't-
Give-Me-Any-Nonsense look.

"I'm not doing a thesis, Caroline," he
admitted.

She nodded. "Yeah, the more I thought
about that, the more I wasn't really buying
it. What do you want, Mr. McMillan?"

"I'm trying to find out some information
about my 19-year-old niece's birth parents.
She was adopted when she was four. Her
name is Amelia Faraday, but I believe it was

Schlessinger before that."

Caroline's eyes wrestled with his for a moment. Then she sighed, shifted around on the bleacher bench, and glanced toward the cheerleaders again. "What kind of information are you after?" she asked.

"Anything that might help," George replied. "Amelia is a sweet, intelligent, pretty young woman. But she also has a lot of problems. She's had problems ever since she was a child. I'm hoping you could help us understand why that is."

"By *us*, do you mean Amelia's parents and yourself? Why aren't *they* here?"

"They were killed, along with my wife, a little over a week ago," George explained. "My two children and I are Amelia's only living relatives, at least, the only ones I'm aware of."

"I — I'm sorry for your loss," she murmured, visibly flustered. Then she covered her mouth and slowly shook her head. "My Lord, both families gone. It's as if that poor girl were cursed."

"I hear you were friends with Joy Schlessinger," George said.

She sighed. "Well, I probably knew her better than anyone else around here. I met her and Lon when they first moved to Salem in 1993. I was part of the Salem

447

Cares Committee, and one of our functions was to roll out the welcome wagon to new residents. Depending how sociable people were, we could be a blessing or a major pain in the ass. Anyway, the Schlessingers seemed to appreciate our efforts. They were from Moses Lake, Washington."

"And that's where the twins were born, in Moses Lake?" George asked.

Nodding, she scrutinized the cheerleading squad again as they took a break between routines. "Not bad, ladies!" she called. "Let's see the next routine. Nancy Abbe, do me a favor and turn down the music a notch."

She turned to George again. "Anyway, I felt sorry for Joy. The poor thing was in a new city, and didn't know a soul. Plus she was stuck on this ranch on the outskirts of town. Lon was very, I don't know, remote, always off hunting and fishing. I got the feeling in the course of a normal day at that ranch he probably said a total of eleven words to her. He and Joy's brother, Duane, used to go camping and hunting together. Duane lived in Pasco. He's the one who introduced Lon to Joy. I only met Duane once, which was quite enough for me, thank you very much."

"You didn't care for him?" George asked.

"No, sir," she replied, frowning. "He was one of those short, wiry, overly macho types — very high strung, like a little pit bull."

"Sounds as if you had him pegged pretty quickly, and early, considering what he went on to achieve."

"Then you know about it," she said, rubbing her arms. "Yes, he struck me as a time bomb ready to go off. He wasn't very social. I don't think anyone in Salem ever met him. He just showed up to go hunting with Lon — that's it. No stops in town, no dinners out, nothing. The only reason I met him is because I used to drive out to the ranch to visit Joy, and he happened to be there that day. He and Joy were both odd ducks. She was a bit overzealous on the Bible thumping for me. I mean, I'm a Christian and very spiritual. It's why I stayed friends with Joy, even though I never really felt close to her. Being a friend in need seemed the Christian thing to do, y'know? I think, deep down, she had a good soul. But Joy was one of those fire-and-brimstone fundamentalists. She used religion the way some people use alcohol, as an escape from reality. I don't think she had a handle on what was going on around her." Caroline shrugged. "Then again, considering what life had to offer poor Joy, it's no wonder she needed some escape."

"What about her daughters?" George asked. "How was she with them?"

"There was only Annabelle when they moved here from Moses Lake," she explained.

George nodded. It made sense, because Amelia had been adopted through an agency in Spokane, Washington — about a ninety-minute drive from Moses Lake. Obviously, the Schlessingers had transplanted to Salem without her.

"Did Joy ever tell you what happened to Amelia?" he asked.

Caroline winced a bit, then sighed. "Amelia's the main reason they moved away. When the girl was four years old, she was abducted and molested by a neighbor man. Later, they found out this same man had raped and murdered a young woman who worked in a restaurant in Moses Lake."

George just stared at her. This was what Karen had been looking for, the *incident* in Amelia's early childhood.

"Lon shot the man dead," Caroline continued, "just as the police were closing in on him. They rescued Amelia, but the little girl wasn't the same after that. Joy and Lon had the worst time with her. They took her to several doctors, but I guess she was

450

beyond help. She kept trying to run away. She even tried to kill herself — a four-year-old, for God's sake. Joy caught her with one of Lon's guns. They finally had to put her into foster care. It just broke Joy's heart, but they couldn't handle her anymore. Apparently, Lon didn't want to, but Joy totally relinquished custody. She had no idea where her child was. They told all their acquaintances in Moses Lake that Amelia had been sent to live with relatives up in Winnipeg.

"Anyway, not long after they moved here, Joy's mental health started to deteriorate. I don't think she ever recovered from what happened to Annabelle's twin. They weren't here very long, just a few months when, one day, little Annabelle discovered her mother dead in the basement. She'd hanged herself. She left a note, apologizing to God and her family, and asking *me* to look after Annabelle."

"And a few weeks later," George interjected. "Duane Savitt went on a killing rampage at the adoption agency in Spokane. Do you know why? Do you have any idea what that was about?"

A pained look passed over Caroline's face for a moment. She turned to glance at the cheerleaders, and then stood up. "Okay, ladies! That looked great. You can wrap it

451

up a little early today. Nancy, can you drop off the boom box in my office? Thanks!"

Hands in the pockets of her sweater, she stood on the bleachers and watched the cheerleaders disperse. She waited until the last girl left the field, and then she glanced down at George. "No one else in town knew about Amelia," she said quietly. "Joy had asked me to keep it a secret. I believe Annabelle got similar instructions. Growing up, she didn't talk about her twin — not until high school. Then I hear she told a few friends different stories about a twin who had died. But I believe Annabelle, her father, and I were the only ones who knew the truth."

She sat down beside George again. "When I read about Duane Savitt shooting those people and setting that adoption agency on fire, I knew what it was about, at least, remotely."

"But you didn't go to the police," George said.

Caroline sighed and shook her head. She stared out at the empty spot on the field, where the cheerleading squad had been practicing minutes before. "No. I heard they spoke to Lon. The story he gave them was that his brother-in-law had been estranged from the family for years. I was the only one in town who knew differently. I suppose Duane was as elusive with the good people of Moses Lake as he was with Salem folk. Because no one from Moses Lake stepped forward, claiming to know Duane. I know, because I read a lot of articles about that Spokane massacre."

"I read them too," George said. "You, um, you could have given the police some idea as to Duane's motive. They never did come up with one."

She nodded. "I know. But Lon asked me not to say anything — for Annabelle's sake. She'd been through a lot, and was still trying to get over her mother's suicide. This awful news about her Uncle Duane was devastating." Caroline slowly shook her head. "I felt a certain responsibility to Annabelle. After all, Joy had asked me to look after her. So, I didn't say anything. The police never approached me about it. I was never forced to lie, thank God. I just didn't say anything to anybody." She turned and gave George a sad smile. "You're the first one I've told."

"I understand," George murmured, nodding.

Caroline glanced out at the playing field again. "You know, years later, when Annabelle was fourteen, she asked me to explain what her uncle had done. I told her what I could. And then Annabelle said something very strange. She remembered her Uncle Duane asking her several times if she knew where Amelia was. Isn't that peculiar?"

Caroline pushed back her windblown hair and sighed. "How did he expect that little girl to know where her sister was living when her own father didn't even know?"

"Yep, I have the appointment book right in front of me," Jessie said on the other end of the line. "I'm in your office. It's here in the book: Amelia Faraday, Monday, October fifteenth, two p.m. And there's a red check-mark beside it."

That was Karen's way of indicating the client had shown up for the appointment and needed to be billed.

"Then her twin must be alive," Karen whispered. She slouched back against the phone booth's door.

"What are you talking about? Whose twin?"

"Um, I'll explain later, Jessie."

The lights went on outside Danny's Diner, and Karen realized it was getting dark. "Listen," she said into the phone. "Is everything okay there?"

"Terrific. The kids are playing with Rufus

in the kitchen, and he's lapping up the attention. We'll take him out to the backyard so he can do his business. Is there anything else you need done here before we head back to George's?"

"No, thanks. You're great, Jessie. Remember everything I told you this morning? Well, it still stands. If you happen to see my car or if Amelia shows up at George's —"

"I know," Jessie cut in. "Be careful . . . she could be dangerous . . . call the police . . . do not pass Go, do not collect $200 . . ."

"I'm serious," Karen said, "doubly serious now."

"We'll be careful, hon. You drive safe. Talk to you soon."

"Thank you again, Jess."

She hung up, then immediately called George again. She was charging all these calls. Her American Express bill would be nuts, but right now she didn't care.

George answered on the second ring. "Karen?"

"Yes, hi —"

"Looks like you're still in that phone booth by the diner," he said. "I have the number on my cell. Let me call you back there in fifteen minutes, okay?"

She hesitated. "All right. But have you talked with Annabelle's teacher yet?"

"I'm doing that right now. Sorry to make you stick around there. Go inside the diner and grab a Coke or something. I'll call you in fifteen."

"Okay, but you should know —" Karen heard a click.

"Annabelle's alive," she said to no one.

"Can we take Rufus home with us?" Stephanie asked. She wouldn't stop petting him, even while the dog lifted a leg and peed on the hydrangea bushes near Karen's back door.

"Well, I don't think Karen would like coming home to an empty house tonight," Jessie said, standing on the back steps. The kitchen door was open behind her.

Jody held Rufus by his leash. He pulled his kid sister away from the dog. "Leave him alone for a minute so he can take a dump. Jeez!"

Stephanie resisted for a few moments, and finally turned toward Jessie. "Why don't Karen and Rufus come live with us?"

"I'm working on that one, honey," she replied. "Now, Jody's right, you have to leave Rufus be for just a minute or two. And you need to calm down, too."

Stephanie had asthma, and she'd left her inhaler at Rainbow Junction Daycare this afternoon. They'd be on pins and needles until they got back home, where she had two more inhalers. In the meantime, Steffie wasn't supposed to exert herself or get over-excited.

"Just take it easy, sweetheart," she called to her. "Why don't you . . ." Jessie trailed off as she heard a noise behind her in the kitchen.

She turned around, and gasped.

Standing by the breakfast table, she wore a rain slicker and clutched her purse to her side. She had a tiny, cryptic smile on her face.

"Oh, my God, you scared me," Jessie said, a hand on her heart. "What are you doing here, Amelia?"

CHAPTER EIGHTEEN

"Sorry about the interruption," George said, tucking the cell phone in his sports coat pocket. He'd stepped down to the playing field to take Karen's call. Now he made his way back up the bleachers. "Where was I?"

"You asked me about the fire," Caroline Cadwell said.

Nodding, he sat down beside her. "So the police called you late one night in July. . . ."

"Yes, I had no idea Lon put me down on his insurance policy as his emergency contact. There was no next of kin, so they called me to identify the remains."

"Did you drive out to the ranch that night?"

"Oh, no. They didn't get the bodies out of there until about two in the morning. Because the ranch was so remote, it took a while for the fire trucks to arrive and even longer to get water in the hoses. In the meantime, the whole upstairs was burnt, along with most of the first floor. You can still see what's left of the place if you drive a couple of miles outside town. They haven't leveled it yet."

Shuddering, Caroline rubbed her arms. "Do you mind if we head inside? I'm starting to feel a chill."

"Not at all," George murmured.

"Can you imagine?" she said, heading down the bleacher steps with him. "All that destruction, a house left in cinders, because someone was smoking in bed. But that's how it happened, just like the old cliché. Lon had a Camel going, and he dozed off. What a stupid waste. Anyway, they asked me to come to the morgue the following morning at 9:30. I don't know why they put me through it. I mean, the fire was at the Schlessinger ranch. Lon was forty-six and Annabelle was sixteen. The two bodies were a male in his late forties and a female in her late teens. It wasn't too tough to figure out who they were."

George walked with her along the playing field toward a side door into the school. It was an ugly, three-story granite building from the Reagan era. Eyes downcast, Caroline kept rubbing her arms. "It was pretty awful," she muttered. "I had to go into this cold, little room that smelled rancid. I'm sorry, but the stench was horrible. That was one of the worst parts. The bodies were covered with white sheets, and they had them on metal slabs. First, I identified Lon. There was nothing left of his hair. His face was just blood, blisters, and burn marks, but I still recognized him. However, Annabelle — well, she was a skull with blackened skin stretched over it. Her mouth was wide open like she was screaming. . . ."

George noticed tears in Caroline's eyes. He gently rested his hand on her shoulder.

"I'd known her since she was a little girl," she said, her voice quivering. "I'd watched her grow up into a beautiful young lady. I had a hard time believing that — *thing* was Annabelle. The height and body type were Annabelle's, but I couldn't say for sure it was her. Then I remembered the bracelet."

"What bracelet?" George stopped with Caroline as she pulled out a handkerchief and blew her nose.

"Annabelle had a favorite bracelet, silver with these pretty roses engraved on it," Caroline explained. "She wore it all the time. It used to be her mother's. The bracelet was about two inches wide, and covered up an ugly scar. Annabelle had burned the back of her wrist rather badly when she was a child.

"Anyway, I asked the attendant in the morgue if I could see her left arm. He lifted the sheet and showed me. And there was the wide silver bracelet, almost melded to her burnt skin and bones. Then I knew it was her."

"That's how you identified Annabelle's body?" George asked. He wondered if the local police and coroner realized Ms. Cadwell had based her positive ID on a piece of jewelry around the wrist of a charred corpse.

"Well, what other proof do you want?" she shot back.

"Maybe dental records," he muttered. "Did they check their dental records?"

"I don't think so. Why should they?"

Because I know someone who thinks Annabelle could still be alive, George wanted to answer. But he didn't want to argue with Caroline Cadwell over something that had happened three years ago. She had no reason to be suspicious about the fire. And she'd been very forthright with him.

George held open the door for her, and Caroline strode into the school, murmuring a thank-you under her breath. She stopped and leaned against a trophy case in the school hallway. Wiping her eyes again, she gave him a tired smile. "I always get emotional when I think about Annabelle. I was sort of her honorary godmother. It's no wonder I had a hard time identifying her remains. If only you knew how pretty she was. . . ."

"But I do know," George reminded her. "My niece is her twin. I know exactly what you mean. Amelia's very beautiful."

Caroline nodded pensively. "You know, it's ironic. I used to worry about Annabelle spending so much time alone on that ranch in the middle of nowhere. Lon continued to go off fishing and hunting for days at a time." Frowning, she shook her head. "I just didn't understand his nonchalance. You see, for several years, we had a — a series of disappearances. Several young women in the area vanished without a trace. A few were even former students of mine. So, maybe I was more sensitive and worried about it than some people. But I couldn't help thinking about Annabelle, alone on that ranch, a perfect target for whoever was out there preying on young women." She shrugged. "And after all my concern, Annabelle ended up dying in a fire, started by her father's cigarette."

George stared at her. "How many girls

disappeared? Did they ever find any of them?"

"At least a dozen or so in a period of about ten years," she said. "A while back, they discovered the partial remains of a young woman in a forest about twenty miles from here. They never found any of the others. And they never found the killer either."

"So he's still out there somewhere?" George asked.

"I think he's moved on to a different area," Caroline said, shuddering again. "Like a predator finding a new kill zone. Anyway, it's been about three years since the last girl disappeared. Her name was Sandra Hartman. She graduated from here just two months before her disappearance. I taught Sandra her sophomore year. She was supposed to meet some friends for a movie, but never showed up."

"You said this was three years ago?" George asked.

She nodded.

"Was this before or after the Schlessinger ranch burned down?"

"About a week before," she answered. "Why do you ask?"

"I'm not sure," George replied truthfully. It just seemed strange that the girls stopped disappearing once Lon Schlessinger had smoked his last cigarette.

Karen glanced at her watch again. It had been almost twenty minutes now. She sat near the phone booth at one of the picnic tables in front of the diner. While waiting for George to call back, she'd gone into the restaurant and ordered a Diet Coke and a serving of fries to go. She'd come back out, sat down, and tried to eat. But she'd been too nervous; and after only a few fries, she'd tossed the bag out. Her soft-drink container was still on the table in front of her.

She couldn't stop thinking about Amelia's twin. If Annabelle was alive, it would explain so much.

Months ago, Shane had thought he'd spotted Amelia inside a strange car with a strange man at a stoplight in the University District. Amelia had had only the vaguest memory of it, after Shane had prompted her with a description of what he'd seen. Had he actually spotted Annabelle?

Karen remembered Amelia coming by her place the day before yesterday. She'd been acting so peculiar, and even looked a bit different. Hell, even Rufus had detected something wrong with her, and kept growling at her. Then she'd walked off with Koehler. Karen had figured the *other* Amelia had walked into her house that afternoon. She'd thought the *other* Amelia might have killed Koehler.

But there was no *other* Amelia. It was another person entirely.

How could Amelia — even with multiple personalities — be in two different places at one time?

She'd been in Port Angeles when Koehler had disappeared a hundred miles away in Cougar Mountain Park. And she'd been on a Booze Busters retreat in Port Townsend when her brother had died in Bellingham. The Faradays' next-door neighbor hadn't seen *Amelia* hosing down the dock around the time of Collin's death. No, she'd spotted *Annabelle,* washing away his blood after she'd bashed his skull in.

Karen shifted restlessly on the picnic table bench. She gazed at the darkening horizon, and then over the treetops in the direction of the Faradays' lake house.

Helene Sumner had seen Annabelle, and her boyfriend, Blade, at the house just days before Amelia's parents and aunt were brutally killed there. The Faradays would have opened the door to Annabelle, believing her to be their daughter. They may not have even lived long enough after that to realize their mistake. In Amelia's all-too-accurate dream, she remembered her Aunt Ina's last words before a bullet ripped through her chest: "Oh my God, honey, what have you done?"

Everything started to make sense, if Annabelle was indeed alive. She was the killer. But what was her motive? And what accounted for Amelia having these fragmented memories of her sister's violent actions?

An SUV pulled into the lot by Danny's Diner. Karen glanced at her watch again. She got to her feet and checked the phone inside the booth. Had she hung up the receiver improperly after her last conversation with George?

No, there was nothing wrong with the phone, except George's call hadn't come through on it yet.

"God, you're right!" a girl shrieked. "My cell phone isn't working. Shit! And I told Tiffany I was going to call her."

Karen saw three young teenage girls, and the haggard-looking mother of one of them, coming around the corner from the Danny's parking lot. All the girls were talking at once, and loudly, too. But Karen heard one of them over the others: "Look, there's a pay phone!"

Karen quickly ducked into the booth and closed the folding door. She picked up the receiver, but kept a hand over the cradle lever, pressing it down. "Oh, yeah? Really?" she said into the phone. "Well, I'm not surprised. . . ."

A gum-snapping girl with long brown hair stopped in front of the booth while her friends and their chaperone filed into the diner. She fished a credit card out of her little purse. What a 14-year-old was doing with a credit card was beyond Karen. She turned her back to the girl, and kept up her pretend conversation on the phone: "I had no idea. Well, she should take care of that right away."

After a few moments, Karen heard a clicking noise behind her. She glanced over her shoulder. The girl was tapping her credit card against the phone booth window. She glared at Karen, and then rolled her eyes.

Karen opened the door. "Hey, I have another important call to make after this," she said. "So, you may as well just buzz off, okay?"

"Bitch," the girl muttered. Then she swiveled around and flounced into the restaurant.

Suddenly, the phone rang. Karen's hand jerked away from the receiver cradle. "Yes? George?"

"Yeah, hi," he said. "Listen, I think you're

right about Amelia's twin. There's every chance Annabelle is still alive. . . ."

She stood in Karen's kitchen, gazing at the housekeeper.

Outside, in the backyard, George McMillan's children played with Karen's dog. They hadn't noticed her yet.

"Amelia, everyone's been searching high and low for you, honey," the housekeeper said. She furtively glanced over her shoulder at the children, then took another step inside and closed the kitchen door behind her.

"Where's Karen?" she asked.

"She drove to the house in Lake Wenatchee, looking for you," Jessie said. "She rented a car. Her own car's missing. Did you borrow her car, honey?"

"No, I didn't." Her eyes narrowed at Jessie. "Do you know if Karen has been to the lake house yet?"

Jessie nodded, and moved over to the cupboard. "She called about fifteen minutes ago from some diner up the road from there. You just missed her." Jessie pulled a container of lemonade mix from the cabinet. "I promised the kids I'd make them some lemonade. Would you like some, honey? Or maybe a nice cup of tea?"

"Don't bother yourself," she muttered.

"Sit down and take a load off, for goodness sake." She moved over to the refrigerator and took the ice tray out of the freezer. "I'll make enough lemonade for you, too. You have something cool to drink, and then we'll call your Uncle George. He's been worried about you, too."

She sat down at the breakfast table. "Where is Uncle George?"

"He had to go down to Oregon for some research thingy," Jessie said, retrieving four tall glasses and a pitcher from another cabinet. "He'll be back tonight, though. Karen, too. I guess we have to wait before we can reach her on her cell — something about bad phone reception around there."

Past Jessie's chatter, she heard the children outside, laughing. The dog let out a bark now and then. She glanced down at the purse in her lap. Inside, something caught the overhead kitchen light, and glistened.

The serrated-edged, brown-leather-handled hunting knife in her purse was a souvenir from the ranch. It had belonged to her father. He'd skinned his kill with it on hunting trips. He'd also used it on some of his women once he'd finished with them.

She remembered back when she was just a little girl, those furtive trips at night had seemed like such long ordeals. But in reality he'd done a quick job on the women they'd picked up together. The longest he'd gone on with one of them had been close to two hours. He'd dug their graves ahead of time, and driven them out to the preselected spot. She remembered those nights alone in the car, listening to the screams, waiting. He'd come back, covered with sweat, and often blood. He'd pull a piece of candy out of his pocket, and toss it to her. "That's a good girl," he'd say. "You're daddy's little helper." Then he'd pop open the trunk, get out the shovel, and promise to be back soon.

And he'd kept his promise. He'd always return within a half hour.

A few times, Uncle Duane came with them. Those nights always took longer. And he smelled bad in the car on the way home.

Her father always called it his *work.*

It wasn't until a few years after her mother died that her father began to take his work home with him. The longest he ever kept one of them in that fallout-shelter-turned-dungeon was eleven days and nights and that was Tracy Eileen Atkinson. There was something about her that he liked more than the others. For a while, she'd thought he'd never grow tired and bored with Tracy. But he did.

She'd snuck down into the basement and peeked in on her father as he finished Tracy off with his hunting knife. One quick stroke across the neck. She still remembered the startled look in Tracy's eyes, the thin crimson line across her throat that suddenly unleashed a torrent of blood.

That was when she first coveted her father's hunting knife. She was thirteen years old at the time.

She still hadn't tried it out on anyone, yet. Karen was going to be her very first kill with the old knife. She'd had it in her robe pocket when she'd *accidentally* stumbled into Karen's bedroom late last night. But the joke had been on her. She'd had no idea Karen had been sleeping with a gun beside her.

Two days before, she'd thought she had Karen cornered in the basement of that rest home. But Blade had botched it.

Returning to Karen's house this afternoon, she'd figured the third attempt would be the charm. But she hadn't figured on finding Karen gone, and the housekeeper with those two brats here in her place.

She stared at Jessie, hovering over the counter, her back to her. Outside, the children were howling, trying to get the dog to bark. She glanced inside her purse again.

No reason she still couldn't break in her father's old hunting knife, no reason at all.

"So honey, where have you been all day, for Pete's sake?" Jessie asked, pulling something else out of the cupboard. "Karen and your uncle have been calling just about everyone and asking if they've seen you. They didn't leave one turn unstoned as my Aunt Agnes used to say. . . ."

"I borrowed Shane's car and went for a long drive," she replied coolly. She studied the way the chubby housekeeper was bent over the counter, and how she had the glasses lined up. She couldn't see what Jessie was doing. Something was wrong.

Getting to her feet, she stepped up behind Jessie, and purposely bumped her in the arm, hard.

Jessie let out a little gasp, and a prescription bottle flew out of her hand. It rolled across the kitchen counter, and about a dozen light blue cylindrical tablets spilled out.

"Oops!" Jessie said, with a jittery laugh. "Look what you went and did. My arthritis medicine, I forgot to take it this morning."

She swiped the prescription bottle off the counter, and glanced at the label. "This is diazepam," she said, locking eyes with Jessie. "It's a sedative. And they're not yours. They're for the old man in the rest home, Karen's father. That was a silly mistake."

Jessie nodded and laughed again. "I'll say. I must be getting senile." She stirred the lemonade in the pitcher, and the ice cubes clinked against the glass.

She put the prescription bottle down. "The lemonade's ready, Jessie." She reached inside her purse again. "Why don't you call the kids in? And leave the dog outside, okay?"

"They have old yearbooks there at the high school library, right?"

"Yeah, I guess," George allowed.

Her back pressed against the phone booth's glass wall, Karen nervously tugged at the metal phone cord. "Could you get Annabelle's teacher to show you pictures of those girls who disappeared, and then make photocopies? You said she taught some of them. . . ."

"Yes," he answered tentatively. "But why do you want their pictures?"

Karen hesitated. She was thinking about one of Amelia's earliest memories: waiting alone in a car by a forest trail at night and hearing a woman scream. *When the screaming stops, then we can go home.*

"It might sound a little crazy," she said at last. "But I think if we showed pictures of those young women to Amelia, she might remember some of them."

"Karen, these girls were all abducted between Salem and Eugene," he pointed out. "I told you, the Schlessingers put Amelia up for adoption while they were still in Moses Lake. How do you expect her to remember things that happened in Salem when she's never even been here? It doesn't make sense."

"Maybe not," she said. "But I think Amelia has some sort of window into what's happening in her sister's world. She might even believe it's happening to her. I'm not sure I even understand it myself. But I have a feeling Mr. Schlessinger was somehow involved in the disappearance of these young women. If Annabelle knew about it, then Amelia might recognize one of those yearbook portraits. It might even trigger a memory. It could be the key that unlocks a lot of doors."

George sighed on the other end of the line. "I think I understood about ten percent of what you just said. But I have every confidence in you, Karen. I'll make the photocopies for you."

"Thanks, George," she said.

She didn't know how to explain it to him.

She didn't understand it herself. How could Amelia have these premonitions, recollections, and sensations when all the while these things were happening to her sister, Annabelle? If Annabelle had indeed killed Amelia's family and Koehler, why did Amelia blame herself for those murders?

She'd told Karen that she'd felt the blood splatter on her face while shooting her parents and aunt. She said she'd used her dad's hunting rifle. "It felt like someone hitting me in the shoulder with a baseball bat every time I fired it."

Karen wondered how Amelia could feel those sensations.

Yet, it made sense somehow. During their first therapy session together, Amelia had described one of her early phantom pains — a severe burning sensation on the back of her wrist. She'd said it felt like someone was putting out a lit cigar on her. And just minutes ago, George had told her about Annabelle's bracelet. She'd worn it to hide an ugly burn mark on the back of her wrist from a childhood accident.

George obviously thought she was crazy to imagine Amelia might *recollect* those missing young women, because of her special connection with Annabelle. There was no easy way to explain. It was a phenomenon that had mystified Karen years before she'd even met Amelia, back when she'd been in graduate school. Trying to explain it was almost like solving an old riddle: *Why did the twin in Zurich have a fever and feel abdominal pains?*

"Karen, are you still there?" George asked.

"Um, yes, I'm here."

"So, you think Amelia and Annabelle's father was somehow involved in these disappearances," he said. "Well, I'm with you on that. Sure seems like an awfully weird coincidence to me. The first girl vanished about a year after Lon and his family moved here. And the last one disappeared a week before the fire that killed him. Plus, if what you say is true, and Annabelle is still alive out there killing people, well, it would explain some of her behavior, wouldn't it? The fruit doesn't fall far from the tree."

"Like father, like daughter," Karen said. "Another thing, if young women started to disappear after Lon moved to the Salem area, they must have *stopped* disappearing somewhere else."

"Moses Lake," George murmured.

"Caroline mentioned that in Moses Lake a neighbor man had molested Amelia."

"That's right," George said. "The cops later found out he was also responsible for abducting and murdering a waitress. Do you think Lon was somehow involved in that, too?"

"Maybe," Karen said into the phone. "It's worth checking out."

She thought about those memory fragments from Amelia's childhood. In one of them, Amelia's mother had her in the bathroom and she was asking the child, stripped to her underwear, "Did he touch you down there?" But Amelia had no memory of ever being molested.

"Can you ask Caroline if she knows whether or not this neighbor man was a Native American?" Her hand tight around the receiver, she listened to George murmuring to Annabelle's teacher.

After a moment, he got back on the line. "No, Caroline says Joy didn't mention anything about race, just that he was a neighbor."

"Then Caroline probably wouldn't know the name of the Moses Lake waitress who was murdered," Karen concluded.

She heard George talking to Annabelle's teacher again. Then he came back on the line. "Sorry. Joy didn't go into that much detail when she told Caroline the story."

But Karen wanted the details. The incident with the neighbor in Moses Lake had traumatized Amelia to the point that she had to be separated from her family. And yet, she had no clear memory of it or of the family she'd lost.

Lon Schlessinger had shot the neighbor dead. And this neighbor had apparently abducted and killed a local woman. Such a story would have been in the newspapers, at least, the local newspapers.

"Listen, George, I'm heading to the Wenatchee library," she said. "I want to find out more about this incident with the neighbor. Maybe there's something about it in the old Wenatchee papers."

"If it's any help," he said, "Amelia was officially adopted in April of '93, and she spent a few weeks in foster homes before that. So the incident with the neighbor couldn't have happened any time after February."

"Thanks. I'll start in February '93, and work backward until I find something. I'll keep my eyes peeled for young women missing-person cases in the area, too. I'll call you the minute I find something. I should be able to reach you on my cell once I'm out of these woods."

"Okay. Be careful," he said.

"Don't worry about me, I'm fine," Karen said.

"Be careful anyway. I keep thinking about Helene Sumner, and how she spotted Amelia at the lake house this morning. It could have been Annabelle, you know. And she could still be around there." George paused. "Watch out for yourself, Karen."

Karen had been right about Amelia. There was something wrong with her.

She stood too close, still clutching her purse and occasionally peeking inside it as if she were hiding some secret treasure in there. And then that strange smirk on her face, it was so unlike the Amelia she knew.

"Oh, let's give the kids a few more minutes outside with Rufus," Jessie said, forcing a chuckle. She wiped her hands on a dish towel. "They're having a blast, and that pooch hasn't seen this much attention since God knows when." She nervously gathered up the light blue pills from the kitchen counter. *Nice try, old girl,* she thought.

Karen had cautioned Jessie that Amelia might be dangerous, and said to call her immediately if she should happen to run into the 19-year-old. Jessie hadn't taken the warning too seriously. *Amelia, dangerous? That sweet thing?*

But then, suddenly, the young lady showed up in Karen's kitchen. No doorbell, no knocking, she just waltzed right into the house, bold as you please. Brazen as the guts of Jesse James, as her Aunt Agnes used to say. That was the first sign that something wasn't right.

So Jessie closed the kitchen door, to discourage Jody and little Steffie from coming inside, and to keep them out of harm's way.

The young woman in Karen's kitchen seemed too hard-edged and cold. Though unable to put her finger on it, Jessie detected something *off* about her, the strange way she acted, looked, and talked. Then Jessie caught a glimpse of something glistening in her purse. It was a knife.

She remembered Karen's warning. She also remembered where she'd last seen those light-blue pills that had made old Frank so dopey and tired. They were in the spice cabinet, beside the aspirin and Karen's vitamins. She thought she was being so clever with the lemonade routine. If Amelia was indeed dangerous, sedating her was one way to nip the situation in the bud and not do anyone harm. Jessie figured that once Amelia was down for the count, she could call Karen, and the police, if necessary.

But she'd been foiled even before slipping the stuff in her surprise guest's glass.

Well, it seemed like a good idea at the time.

Trying not to shake, Jessie dropped the diazepam tablets back inside the prescription bottle. She could hear Jody and Stephanie in the backyard, laughing, and barking along with Rufus.

Leaning against the counter, the young woman picked up one pill Jessie had missed. "Why were you trying to drug me, Jessie?" she asked. She handed her the tablet. "Did Karen warn you that I might be unstable?"

"What in the world are you talking about?" Jessie put the prescription bottle away, and then moved to the refrigerator. "That's just silly," she added, plucking a lemon from the shelf. She closed the refrigerator door, and reached for the knife rack.

"What do you think you're doing?" Suddenly the girl grabbed her by the wrist. She hit Jessie in the chest with her elbow. Whether or not it was an accident, it hurt like hell.

Jessie staggered back, and the lemon rolled across the floor. "Good Lord! I was just going to cut up a lemon for the lemonade!" She rubbed her chest and winced.

"It's a mix. You don't need to do that," she shot back. With a quick jerk, she released Jessie's wrist. "Now, go call the kids in,

Jessie. They've been out there with that mutt long enough. I'd like to see my little cousins."

Trying to catch her breath, Jessie glanced toward the backyard.

Rufus started barking furiously. A second later, the front doorbell rang.

Jessie turned toward her. "Well, I — I better answer that before Rufus has the whole neighborhood over here," she said loudly, competing with all the yelps and barks. Jessie didn't wait for a response. She swiveled around and quickly headed for the front door, almost expecting the young woman to grab her.

Rufus was going crazy outside. Jessie could hear Jody talking to him. "What is it, boy? What's going on?" His voice, along with Rufus's barking, seemed to come from the side of the house now.

Jessie flung open the front door, and recognized Chad, a tall, stocky, soft-spoken man in his early thirties. He was one of Amelia's patients, and he looked like he was sorry he'd rung the bell. "Is Karen here?" he asked, over the dog's yelping.

Jessie could only guess how frazzled she appeared, and Rufus, straining at his leash, was leading the two children around from the side of the house toward the front stoop.

Poor Chad looked as if he just wanted to flee. "Um, I have a five o'clock appointment with her," he explained, with an apprehensive look over his shoulder.

"Down, boy! Take it easy!" Jody chided Rufus.

"Down, boy!" Stephanie echoed.

A hand over her heart, Jessie stared at him. "Karen — she had to cancel her appointments today." She glanced back toward the kitchen. "Um, didn't you get her message, Chad?"

"Oh, nuts, I probably should have checked my answering machine," he replied. He bowed down toward Rufus. "Hey, there, pooch."

"Don't go away, okay?" Jessie said, distractedly. "Stay there. You too, kids. I'll be right back."

With trepidation, she headed down the hall toward the back of the house. She edged past the kitchen entryway and gazed into the empty room. The back door was wide open.

Jessie hurried to the door, and then looked out at the backyard: no one.

Biting her lip, she closed the kitchen door and locked the deadbolt. Then she tried the door to the basement. It was already locked. No one could have gone down there.

Right beside her on the kitchen wall, just inches from her head, the telephone rang. Jessie almost jumped out of her skin. She quickly snatched up the receiver. "Yes, hello?"

"Is this Karen?" a woman asked.

"No, this is her housekeeper," Jessie replied, again, her hand on her heart. She stepped out to the hallway as far as the phone cord would allow. She saw Chad, Rufus, and the children still at the front stoop. Chad was crouched down, petting the dog and talking to the kids.

Jessie sighed. "Karen isn't in," she said into the phone. "Can I help you?"

"I'm looking for Amelia Faraday. I'm her roommate, Rachel."

"Amelia isn't here right now. She — um, well, she just left."

"Do you know if she's coming back?"

I hope not, Jessie thought. But she merely cleared her throat and said. "I'm not really sure, hon. Is there something I can do for you?"

"Well, this is kind of an emergency," Rachel explained. "If you see her, please, tell her to call me *immediately.* I've got the police ringing the phone off the hook here. They're looking for her."

"Really?" Jessie murmured.

"It's pretty awful news," Rachel said. "It's about her boyfriend . . ."

"You mean Shane?" Jessie asked.

"Yeah, you know Shane Mitchell?"

"Yes, I do. Is he okay? What's happened?"

"He, um, well, he's dead," the girl explained, a little crack in her voice. "They found Shane in a canoe, drifting in Lake Washington by the 520 Bridge. It looks like he shot himself."

Meredith Marie Sterns was a pretty brunette who had disappeared the summer after graduating from East Marion High School in 1999. She had a dimpled smile and "Rachel" hair copied from Jennifer Aniston's hairstyle in *Friends.*

"Meredith spent most of that June backpacking around Europe with a friend," Caroline explained.

George stood over the Xerox machine, making a photocopy of Meredith's graduation portrait. They were the only ones in the high school's administration office; everybody else had gone home already. They had several old yearbooks piled on the secretary's desk beside the copier.

"I remember the Sterns were so worried that something might happen to Meredith while she was wandering around Europe,"

Caroline continued. "But it was less than a week after she'd returned home that it happened. She went with some girlfriends to see the Fourth of July fireworks at the park. I guess it was about twenty minutes before the fireworks were supposed to start when Meredith excused herself to go use the restroom. And she never came back. . . ."

George once again studied the photo of the girl with the Rachel hair. "She was so excited about going to Chicago in the fall," he heard Caroline say. "She'd been accepted into Northwestern. She was going to be a drama major."

Caroline had a story like that for every one of the missing young women. Part of George wanted to hurry up and just get the photocopies made. The sooner he hit the road, the sooner he'd be home with his kids. He was worried about them.

But he didn't rush through the task at hand, and he respectfully listened to Caroline's reminiscences for each missing girl. The stories broke his heart. Each one was somebody's daughter, sister, or fiancée. Each one had dreams and plans for her future. Each one had disappeared without a trace.

Twenty-two-year-old Nancy Rae Keller was an accomplished pianist who had performed in several concerts. She'd been earning some extra money as a waitress at a fancy restaurant called The Tides in Corvallis. The last person to see her alive was the restaurant manager. Nancy Rae had finished up her shift one Thursday night in March 2002 and headed out to her car. Nancy Rae's car had still been in the restaurant's parking lot on Friday morning. George couldn't see it in the black-and-white photo, but according to Caroline, "Nancy Rae had the most beautiful red hair."

The youngest to disappear was Leandra Bryant, nicknamed Leelee. The 15-year-old had been babysitting for two toddlers until 10:30 on a Saturday night in April, 2001. The children's father had offered to drive her home, but Leelee lived only two blocks away and insisted on walking. She should have been safe. But somewhere along those two blocks in a quiet, residential area of Salem, Leelee Bryant vanished.

The last among the missing young women was Sandra Hartman, the 18-year-old who had disappeared on her way to the mall to meet some friends for a movie.

George looked at the slightly grainy photocopy of Sandra's graduation portrait, and he saw a resemblance between the beautiful dark-haired senior and Amelia. It was the last photocopy he'd made. The Xerox machine still hummed for a moment before it wheezed and then switched off.

"Were any of these girls friends of Annabelle's?" he asked.

Caroline arranged the yearbooks by year. "No, only two of the girls were in school at the same time as Annabelle. And I don't think either one of them ever had Annabelle over to their homes or anything. And, of course, I'm sure they never went out to the Schlessinger ranch."

George remembered Erin Gottlieb telling him that she hadn't set foot in the place. "That ranch in the middle of nowhere," she'd called it.

"You said the ranch house is still there?" he asked.

"Yes, but it's just a burnt-out shell now," Caroline replied. "There's hardly anything left of it. I don't think anyone's been out there in years."

George studied the photocopies again — all those pretty young women who had disappeared. "Could I ask you for one more favor, Caroline?"

She nodded. "Sure."

"Could you tell me how to get to the Schlessinger ranch?"

CHAPTER NINETEEN

WENATCHEE - 23 MILES said the sign just past Leavenworth.

With a breathtaking view of the Cascade Mountains, the quaint Bavarian village was a big tourist attraction in central Washington, and one of the Route 2 landmarks Karen was supposed to look for on her way to the Wenatchee Public Library. The waitress at Danny's Diner had given her directions. Just to be sure, Karen telephoned the library on Douglas Street, and found out that, yes, they were open until 8:00 tonight; and yes, they had available both the *Wenatchee World* and the *Columbia Basin Herald,* which served Moses Lake. The microfiche files for both newspapers went back thirty years.

White-knuckled, Karen gripped the steering wheel and studied the winding, hilly highway ahead.

She realized now it was Amelia's twin in the hallway and basement of the convalescent home the day before yesterday. "Do it now," she'd heard Annabelle whisper. "Get her!"

Karen had heard the same hushed voice last night: "She's got a gun, for chris-sakes . . . I can't . . . goddamn mutt . . ." At the time, Karen had figured Amelia must have been talking in her sleep. But now, she knew it had been Annabelle, probably whispering to Blade.

If Annabelle had *accidentally* stumbled into her room last night to kill her, where had Amelia gone? Karen was positive *Amelia* had fallen asleep in the guest room last night. Some time later, perhaps before that predawn intrusion, a switch had been made. Karen wondered if Amelia had left on her own accord. Or had Annabelle — after so many years with her father — also become an expert at making young women vanish without a trace?

Her cell phone went off, and Karen realized she was finally out of that call-restricted area. Eyes on the road, she blindly reached inside her purse. She checked the caller ID: her home phone number. "Hello?" she said into the phone, a bit wary.

"Karen, it's me, Jessie. Thank God I didn't get that stupid 'Your call cannot be com-pleted as dialed' recording again."

"You're still at the house," Karen said. "Is everything okay?"

"Hardly. I have terrible news." Her voice dropped to a whisper. "I still haven't told the kids. They're in the kitchen with Rufus. Shane is dead. That poor dear boy, can you imagine? It looks like he shot himself. . . ."

"Oh, my God," Karen murmured, the cell phone to her ear. "Are you sure? How did you find out?"

"Amelia's roommate told me. She called looking for Amelia. That's the other thing, Amelia showed up here quite unexpectedly, acting very strange. . . ."

A car horn blared. Karen suddenly realized she'd been drifting into the oncoming lane. A pickup truck barreled toward her. She jerked the wheel to one side. Tires screeched as she swerved back into her lane, and beyond, onto the shoulder off the highway. For a few, fleeting, gut-wrenching seconds, she thought the car would flip over.

"Good Lord, what's happening?" she heard Jessie ask.

Karen caught her breath, and veered back into her lane. "Nothing, I just need to get off this road, that's all." She saw a turnoff to an apple orchard ahead, and took it. Slowing down, she crawled over to a gravelly turnaround area for the one-lane road. Then she put the car in park. She listened while Jessie told her about the disturbing episode with Amelia, who "just wasn't acting like her sweet self."

Yes, Jessie said, she'd called the police after Amelia had made her hasty exit, and a patrolman had stopped by. He'd checked around the premises, and that was it. "He seemed to think I was a major kook," Jessie said. "I mean, Amelia never really threatened me or anything. But she had that knife in her purse, and it gave me the heebie-jeebies. Still, the worst thing she actually did was hit me in the chest when she grabbed my arm, and that might have been an accident. And here I was, trying to slip her some of those knockout pills, because you told me she was dangerous."

"Jessie, she is," Karen said. "She's very dangerous."

"I know, I believe you," Jessie replied. "But when I told this patrolman that the police were looking for her, he didn't know a thing about it."

Apparently, Amelia Faraday had not yet officially become a person of interest in Detective Koehler's disappearance.

"Anyway, we're still at your house," Jessie said, her voice a little shaky. "The cop said they'd call back here if he found out anything more. But I want to get these kids home."

"Have you talked to George, yet?" Karen asked.

"I thought I'd wait until we were safely at home before giving him the latest developments. I didn't want to worry him."

"Yeah, you're right," Karen sighed.

She stared out past the windshield at the starter trees in the orchard, lined up in a row. Their leaves fluttered in the breeze, and dusk loomed on the horizon. Her heart ached, and she wanted to cry for Shane, but there was no time.

She didn't for a minute believe he'd shot himself.

"Listen, Jess, please, be careful driving home," she said at last. "Make sure you aren't being followed. Keep an eye out for my car — and that black Cadillac."

"What black Cadillac?" Jessie repeated.

"The old black Cadillac with a broken antenna. It was following me around over the weekend. I told you —"

"Oh, Lord, honey, how do you expect me to keep track of all this stuff?" Jessie said, exasperated.

"Well, just watch out for it *now,* okay?"

"*I've seen it,* for Pete's sakes. A car matching that description was parked just down the block from George's house earlier today. It was still there when Jody and I left to pick up Steffie."

"Oh, my God," Karen murmured. "Listen, Jess, don't go back to George's. Better not stick around my place, either. Take the kids to a hotel, and make sure you're not being followed. Just hide out there for a while, order room service, and watch pay-per-view movies. I'll handle the bill. Call me once you get settled in, okay?"

"Well, all right," Jessie said. She sounded a bit perplexed. "I'm just not sure what hotel —"

Karen heard a beep, and checked the caller ID. She recognized the number: Amelia's cell phone.

"Jessie, I have another call," she said hurriedly. "Can you just get yourself and the children to a hotel? Any hotel, it doesn't matter: the Westin, the Marriott off Lake Union, anyplace. . . ."

"I hear you," Jessie replied.

"Thanks, Jess. Just make sure no one's following —"

"Yeah, I know," she cut in. "*Make sure no one's following us.* Will do. Take your call. I'll phone you in a bit." There was a click on the line.

Karen switched over to the other call.

"Amelia? Is that you?"

"Hi, Karen," she murmured. "You must be so mad at me right now. I just listened to all the messages from you and Uncle George and Shane. I'm sorry. I didn't mean to worry you. It was awful of me to run away this morning."

Karen wasn't certain she was really talking to Amelia. It certainly sounded like her; and the call was coming from her cell phone. "Well, you, um, you couldn't have run very far," she said. "I just got off the phone with Jessie, and she said you paid her an unexpected visit at my house about a half hour ago."

"What?" she shot back, sounding stunned. "Karen, that's impossible. Why would Jessie say that? I'm nowhere near your house — or Seattle, even. I'm calling from Grand Coulee Dam."

The car engine was still running. Karen turned off the ignition, and listened to the motor die. "Grand Coulee Dam?" she repeated numbly.

"Yeah, I know, it's pretty crazy, huh? But I woke up from this horrible nightmare last night. In the dream, I was — I was attacking you with a knife, and you were screaming. . . ." She trailed off. "Anyway, I suddenly woke up, all sweaty. I was so scared

495

that it might have really happened. I listened at your door, and heard you snoring. Did you know you snore?"

"No, I didn't," Karen said.

"Anyway, I figured you were okay. But I realized I had to get out of there before I hurt you, or somebody else. So I packed my things and snuck out of your house at around four o'clock this morning. I walked up to Fifteenth, and called a cab."

"You didn't take my car?" Karen asked.

"God, no. I'd never do that without asking you," she replied. "I had the taxi drive me to Shane's place. I borrowed *his* car, then drove to the house in Lake Wenatchee. I know it sounds nuts, but I just wanted to get as far away from everyone as I could. But when I went down to the house, I just couldn't make myself go in. So I climbed back inside Shane's car, and kept driving east."

"What time was this?" Karen asked.

"Oh, around eight-thirty or nine," she replied.

According to Helene Sumner, Amelia had been at the lake house at around just that same time. But she'd heard Amelia talking to someone, and laughing.

"Were you with anyone?" Karen asked.

"No, why?"

"Nothing, go ahead. You couldn't step inside the house, so you went on driving."

"That's right, so I ended up here at the Grand Coulee Dam. I've been here for the last few hours, Karen."

"What have you been doing there?" she asked.

"Well, I ate, I napped a little in the car, and I looked at the damn dam." She let out a skittish laugh, but then her tone suddenly turned serious. "Anyway, I've been here. I swear to God. This can't be another one of my blackouts. There's no way Jessie could have seen me in Seattle this afternoon. I'm at least four hours away. . . ."

Karen still couldn't help wondering if she had Amelia on the line or her twin, being very clever. "Amelia, do you remember our session the week before last, when you accidentally broke that cheap vase on the coffee table in my office?"

She listened to the dead silence on the other end of the line. There hadn't been a vase on her office coffee table. There had been no such occurrence. But Annabelle Schlessinger wouldn't have known that.

"Remember that session, Amelia?" she pressed. "Do you recall what we were discussing at the time?"

More silence.

"Amelia, are you still there?"

"Karen, I don't know what you're talking about," she replied, at last. "Did I break a vase of yours? Oh, my God, is this something I blacked out?"

Closing her eyes, Karen smiled. "You know what? My mistake. That was someone else entirely. Never mind. Listen, I'm in Wenatchee right now —"

"What?"

"I'll explain when I see you," Karen said. "I can probably get to Grand Coulee Dam in about ninety minutes."

"Let me meet you there in Wenatchee instead, okay?" she asked. "I've kind of been-there-and-done-that here today, and I'd like to hit the road. I was about to head that way, anyway."

Karen hesitated. It made sense. They'd save at least an hour and a half traveling time back to Seattle if Amelia came to her. "Okay," she said finally. "Could you meet me at the Wenatchee Public Library on Douglas Street?"

"Sure, I know where that is," she said. "See you there in about two hours. I'm leaving right now. Oh, and if it's okay with you, I don't want to hang around Wenatchee too long, Karen. I'd like to be back in Seattle before nine tonight, and get the car back to

Shane. I think he's kind of mad at me. He wasn't answering his cell phone earlier. Anyway, you don't mind if we meet up and then get a move on, do you?"

"No, that's fine, Amelia," she replied.

She couldn't tell her anything more, not right now.

"Then I'll see you soon, Karen."

"Drive safe," she said.

Before she headed out on the road again, Karen phoned Detective Jacqueline Peyton. After all the times she'd refused to pick up the policewoman's calls, Karen figured it probably served her right that she got Detective Peyton's voice mail. Karen waited for the beep.

"Hello, Detective, this is Karen Carlisle again," she said into the phone. "My housekeeper called the police about forty minutes ago. Amelia Faraday — or rather, someone pretending to be Amelia — was just at my house. I'm sure she's driving my Jetta. You have the plate number. I'm pretty sure she had something to do with Shane Mitchell's death, too. I hear the police found Shane in a canoe on Lake Washington, and they believe he shot himself. But it was this woman who looks like Amelia. She's dangerous. In fact, I think she killed Detective

Koehler. I'm sorry I haven't been very co-operative in your investigation up to this point, but I can explain later. If you —"

The answering machine let out another beep, cutting her off. The connection went dead.

Karen realized she'd used up all her time.

Rural Route 17 outside Salem wound around a slightly scrawny forest area with several well-spaced dirt road turnoffs to farms and ranches. Old-fashioned mailboxes with the addresses on them stood at the edge of the long driveways. George couldn't see most of the farms and ranch houses from the car. They were too far down those winding private drives. The last vestige of daylight was fading. George switched on his headlights.

About three miles back, he'd passed a town of sorts. Sherry's Corner Food & Deli had a gas pump over to one side — along with a sign: RING FOR SERVICE! The store also advertised DVD rentals, fresh coffee, beer, and live bait. Across the street from them was a squat, beige brick storefront that had UPPER MARION COUNTY POLICE stenciled on the window. There was a patrol car parked in front of the place, along with an army recruiting sandwich-board poster by the entrance.

George imagined what it must have been like for Annabelle Schlessinger, living out here, alone a good deal of the time, according to her teacher. Small wonder Annabelle hadn't had any friends over to her father's ranch. There was nothing out here. Sherry's Corner was about as exciting as it got; even that was miles away.

George was beginning to think he'd passed the Schlessingers' place; the last driveway had been at least a mile back. But then the car's headlights swept across a driveway with a rusty, old, dented mailbox beside it. The address numbers and name on the mailbox were barely legible anymore: RR #17–14 — SCHLESSINGER.

He turned down the bumpy, one-lane dirt road, which ceded to patches of crab grass and tree roots. There were also some fallen branches to navigate, along with old beer cans and other garbage. George figured the ranch must have attracted curious and bored high school kids who wanted to see where those two people had burned to death. So, maybe some of Annabelle's classmates had been to her home after all.

Taking a curve in the road, George saw the ranch house ahead, just as Caroline Cadwell had described it: a two-story, burnt-out shell. Wood planks boarded up the front door and windows. He noticed even more garbage littered around the blackened edifice — faded fast-food bags and more rusty beer cans. Over to one side stood a dilapidated barn, its door boarded up. Between it and what remained of the house were a stone well, covered with graffiti, and a tall wind pump creaking in the breeze.

George parked the car and switched the motor off. That squeaky wind pump was the only sound he heard now. He walked around the charred structure, kicking at the occasional pop bottle or beer can in his path. He tugged at a plank that was nailed over one of the windows. It didn't budge. In the backyard, he noticed sporadic patches of wildflowers between one side of the barn and a wooded area. They were the only bit of beauty and color on this drab, desolate place.

He wondered if the Schlessingers had buried some of their dead ranch animals there. Wildflowers were supposed to indicate a grave.

Or was something else buried out there?

The photocopies of the missing young women were folded up and tucked inside George's sports jacket pocket. He automatically touched the square bulge over his breast to make sure they were still there.

Glancing toward the burnt house again, he saw the wood panel over the back door was askew. George stepped up to the door, and pulled at the plank. It moved easily. The lock and handle on the soot-stained back door had been broken off. He opened the door. From the threshold, he studied the kitchen. It took a few moments for his eyes to adjust to the darkness. But he could see the room had survived the fire. The green linoleum floor was filthy and littered with garbage from intruders. The only piece of furniture left was a broken chair, lying on its side. The old stove still stood against the grimy walls, but it had been stripped of the oven door and a few of the dials. All the windows — covered up by the planks outside — were broken. The curtains were in tatters. The place was cold, with a stale, stuffy, acrid odor.

George wondered what the hell he expected to find here. He touched that square bump in his sports jacket pocket again.

The local fire and police departments had already been through the place, along with a few scavengers. If they hadn't uncovered anything, how did he expect to fare any better?

But those people had been looking for a cause of the fire, while others had been scrounging for a piece of furniture or a knickknack worth stealing. Still others had been seeking a cheap, morbid thrill, or a remote spot to get drunk.

George was pretty certain no one else had searched this place for evidence of the missing young women. He kept thinking about how it was just too much of a coincidence that they'd started to disappear when Lon Schlessinger had moved into this house, and that the last one had vanished a week before this place had turned to cinders.

George walked through the kitchen, and listened to the old, weakened floorboards groaning beneath him. The front hallway and living room hadn't fared as well as the kitchen. The walls were blistered and blackened. A huge section of the charred floor had collapsed. George could tell there was a basement to the house, but it was too dark to see anything. The stairway to the second floor had been destroyed. Only the black skeleton of a newel post and two steps remained. He had no way of going up to the second floor, where they'd found Annabelle's and Lon's remains.

Every time George breathed in, he smelled the soot and grime. He could even taste it now. He retreated back to the kitchen, and he found the door to the Schlessingers' basement. Opening it, he carefully started down the stairs. Halfway down, he heard a rustling noise that made him stop. A faint light seeped in from an uncovered small window that was broken. Below it was a shelf full of cheap planters holding brittle-looking vines of long-dead plants. Below that, there was a hose connection where a washer machine must have been. George listened again to the light rustling. He figured some rodents had made their home down there. He stopped and tucked his trouser cuffs inside his socks, and then continued down the stairs. Wire hangers dangled from an exposed pipe along the ceiling in what must have been the laundry room.

The next room was nearly pitch black, and had caught all the debris from the living room floor collapsing above it. George took out his cell phone and switched it on. He used the little blue light to navigate through the cobwebs and the rubble. He saw an old-fashioned furnace over to one side, and directly ahead, a big, heavy-looking door. It looked like one of those old bomb shelters. He gave the door a tug, but it barely moved. Putting the phone back in his pocket, he yanked at the door again, this time with both hands. It squeaked open just a few more inches. He tried one more time, but the door didn't budge.

Switching on his cell phone again, he slipped it through the narrow opening and then glanced into the room. The blue light was just strong enough so he could see, past a haze of dust in the air, a cot and a bare metal bookcase against the wall. An old army blanket lay in a heap on the dirty floor. But he couldn't see anything else from where he stood at the doorway. The light wasn't strong enough. He couldn't even tell how big the room was.

Turning around, George made his way back through the darkness and debris until he reached the basement stairs. He hurried up to the kitchen, and then out the door. It felt good to breathe fresh air again. But he still had that awful sooty taste in his mouth. He ran to the car, popped open the hood, and took out the jack.

He needed to get a better look inside that little room in the basement. As much as he didn't want to think like someone who abducted and murdered young women, George could see that little room as a perfect dungeon. Maybe Lon liked to hold on to his toys for a while before he grew tired of them. What better place than that fallout shelter with the cot and a blanket?

Inside the house again, he headed back down the basement stairs with the jack. George switched on his cell phone once more as he weaved around the wreckage and maneuvered his way to the bomb shelter door. He had a tough time bracing the jack in a horizontal position, but finally got it to stick. He worked the lever, and listened to the heavy door creak open wider and wider. But then the lever started to resist and buckle, and no matter how hard George pushed, the door didn't move another inch.

The gap was a little over a foot wide. Stepping over the jack, George squeezed through the narrow opening. He prayed the jack wouldn't collapse on him. He imagined himself trapped in this tiny room, in this desolate house in the middle of nowhere.

He brushed against something with his foot, and heard a tinny, clanking noise. George directed the cell phone light toward the floor, and saw at least a dozen empty tin cans. He checked out the labels: most of them were for a cat food called Purrfect Kitty. There were a few empty cans of Del Monte brand sliced peaches, too. George also noticed a plastic bucket in the corner, tipped over on its side. There was nothing

else in the tiny room, just the cot, the bar-
ren metal bookcase, and a discarded blanket. The only new discoveries he'd made
were these lousy tin cans and a bucket,
hardly worth all his painstaking effort to get
inside the place for a better look.

He seemed to be chasing after nothing.
Hell, maybe it was indeed just a lousy coincidence those girls had started disappearing once the Schlessingers had moved here.

George poked at the blanket with his foot.
Suddenly a rat scurried out from under the
folds.

"Shit!" he hissed, dropping his cell phone.
The light stayed on just long enough for
him to see the rodent crawl out the gap in
the doorway. Then everything went black.

George tried to catch his breath, but he
couldn't. A panic swept through him. He
thought he'd be able to see a very faint light
through the doorway opening, but no. He
couldn't see a damn thing, not even his
hand in front of his face.

Standing there, paralyzed by the dark, he
heard a strange buckling noise. It sounded
like the jack ready to give out. The big,
heavy door made another creaking sound.

"Oh, Jesus," George whispered. He knew
the phone had dropped somewhere near the
bookcase. Blindly, he waved his hand

around until he touched the metal shelf. He crouched down and started patting the floor. "Shit, where is it?" he muttered. "God, please . . ."

His hand brushed against the phone, and it slid across the floor. "Damn it," he growled. He anxiously felt around under the bookcase. Then something stung his finger. George snapped his hand back. "What the hell. . . ."

He wondered if it was another rat. But this was more like a pinprick.

Behind him, he heard the door giving out another yawn.

Shifting around, his knee touched something on the floor. George reached down and found the cell phone. He switched it off, and then on again. The light came on once more. "Thank God," he murmured.

He looked at his wounded index finger. It was bleeding.

Crouching down close to the floor, he used the cell phone light to check under the metal bookcase. He saw the pin sticking out on the back of something that looked like a name tag. He reached for it, carefully, so he wouldn't stab himself again. But he must have knocked it farther back against the wall. He had to squeeze most of his arm under the bookcase until his fingertips finally brushed against the badge, or whatever it was. Clasping it between his fingers, he slid his hand out from under the case.

He shined the light on it. "Oh, Jesus . . ."

It was the kind of name tag waitresses wear. This one was green with white indented lettering that said YOUR SERVER IS NANCY RAE.

George didn't need to look at the photocopies he'd made. He remembered Nancy Rae Keller, the talented pianist and part-time waitress, who had disappeared one Thursday night in March 2002 after finishing work at a Corvallis restaurant.

According to her former teacher, Nancy Rae had had beautiful red hair.

A loud groan emitted from the fallout shelter door. The jack buckled under the pressure.

George lunged toward the opening, slamming into the door just as the jack gave way. The device snapped out of place and flew into the pile of debris in the outside room. George was halfway through the opening when he felt the door move. It scraped against his leg, and he winced at the pain. But he didn't stop until he'd made it out on the other side of the big, heavy door. And all the while, he'd kept his cell phone and Nancy Rae's name tag firmly in his grasp.

He knew he'd hurt himself. No doubt his leg was bleeding. But that didn't matter right now. He'd gotten out.

And in a way, after five long years, so had Nancy Rae.

CHAPTER TWENTY

The Schlessinger ranch — July 2004

She sat on her bed, painting her toenails — Sassy Scarlet. Her tabby, Neely, was curled up beside her. It was still pretty hot out, so she had the box fan in the window. A U2 song played softly on her boom box. Annabelle wore cutoffs and a sleeveless T-shirt. Her black hair was pulled back in a ponytail.

She had a friend from school staying over tonight.

Annabelle hoped to chat a bit with Sandra. But she had to wait first, until her father finished with Sandra down in the basement. He'd been at her now for about a half hour.

At last, Annabelle heard him clearing the phlegm from his throat and lumbering up the stairs to the second floor. He passed her room without looking in, and continued on to his bedroom.

Annabelle shoved Neely off her bed, then got to her feet. From her bedroom, she peered into her parents' room. Her father couldn't see her, but in a darkened window across from her parents' double bed, she caught his reflection. He was wearing a T-shirt and work pants. He plopped down on the bed, then lit a cigarette. In a few minutes, he'd go take a shower and wash Sandra off.

Slipping on a pair of flip-flops, she snuck out of her room, and down the stairs. As she passed through the kitchen, she got a waft of her father's body odor, still lingering from when he'd passed through just minutes ago. He must have really worked up a sweat down in the basement. Annabelle paused for a moment, as she heard the pipes squeaking and the shower starting in the upstairs bathroom.

She got another dose of that musky stench as she started down the basement stairs. But at least it was cooler down in the cellar. In the laundry room, she grabbed a bath towel from on top of the dryer. Carrying it into the furnace room, she pulled on the string for the overhead light.

Annabelle listened to Sandra crying in the fallout shelter, but the sound was muffled. She laid the towel by the big, heavy door, then sat down on it. "Sandra? Can you hear me okay?"

There was a gasp, and then she cried out, "Who's there? Is somebody there?"

"It's me, Annabelle," she called to her. "Listen, I can't talk long —"

"Get me out of here! Please, please, you have to help me. . . ."

Why do they always say the same thing? she wondered, fanning at her toes and blowing on them so her nail polish dried faster. *Just like Gina, and all the others.* She let Sandra scream and beg for another minute, and then finally interrupted her. "Listen, I can't spring you out of there right now. It's just too dangerous. But I'll help you. I promise, you won't have to stay in there long —"

"No! You have to get me out of here *now!* Please, Annabelle, I want to go home, please!"

It was nice, the way Sandra called her by name. Annabelle leaned against the door. "Hey, Sandra? Please don't be mad at me for this, okay? He forced me to do it. But I'll make it up to you, I swear."

"I'm not mad at you," she said, her voice still full of panic. "In fact, my parents will give you money if you help me. I'm sure of it. They're rich. . . ."

Annabelle frowned. The offer of money was nice, sure. But an offer of friendship would have been better. She had this notion about killing her father and helping Sandra escape. Of course, then she'd have to go on the run. But she'd already planned for that. For several months now, she'd drawn money out of her father's account with forged checks and the occasional trip with one of his credit cards to the ATM at Sherry's Corner. So far, she'd stashed away over three thousand dollars. There was also her mother's jewelry, and a silver service that belonged to her grandparents. Annabelle figured she had about six or seven grand worth of crap around the house that she could hock.

She imagined, after several days in captivity, Sandra would bond with her. And if she helped Sandra escape, Sandra would do the same for her. Like in *Thelma and Louise,* life on the lam with her new best friend would be an adventure. She and Sandra already looked alike. People would probably mistake them for sisters, or even twins. That would be nice.

"Sandra, I left you something in there," she said. "That stuff he used to knock you out, it's chloroform, and sometimes it burns your face. I knew he'd be using it tonight, so I left you a little jar of Noxzema under that old rag in the corner. It'll help soothe

the irritation. I left some chewing gum there, too."

He always starved them for the first twenty-four hours. The promise of food and water always made them more cooperative, especially after an initial bout with true hunger. Some of them were probably even grateful to get the cat food.

"Annabelle, I really, really want to go home. He hurt me. I'm in pain. . . ." She started crying again. "I miss my mom and dad. Please, please, help me. . . ."

Annabelle let her cry for a few moments. "I'll help you escape, Sandra," she said, finally. "But it's impossible tonight. Just hang in there, okay? And listen, if I get you out, I can't possibly stay here. You'll have to help me get away. Can you do that? Do you promise to help me make a clean break and go start somewhere else?"

"Yes, of course!" Sandra answered, almost too quickly. "I promise. I'll do anything you want. Just get me out of here! Please . . ."

"Sandra?" she said, her face pressed against the crack in the big door.

"Yes?"

"Earlier tonight, you asked me to go to the movie with you," Annabelle said. "Were you just inviting me out of politeness, because I was giving you a ride? Or did you really want to hang out with me? Because I'm not sure if I fit in with your friends —"

"Oh, no, I — I wanted you to come with us," Sandra replied. "I wasn't just being polite. I like you, Annabelle. You seem very nice." But the tone of her voice smacked of desperation, as if her life depended on giving the right answer.

And, of course, it did.

With a sigh, Annabelle got to her feet and gathered up the bath towel. "I need to go now," she said. "I don't want him to know we're in cahoots —"

"No, God, please, don't go. Annabelle, don't leave me here . . . please. . . ." Sandra started pounding on the other side of the door.

Annabelle turned away. She reached up and pulled the string to the overhead light in the furnace room. Standing in the darkness, she listened to Sandra Hartman begging her to stay and talk just a little longer.

It felt kind of nice.

Wenatchee, Washington — three years later SEARCH CONTINUES FOR MISSING MOSES LAKE WOMAN said the headline near the bottom of page 3 of the *Columbia Basin Herald* for October 21, 1992.

Karen had found it almost by accident.

517

She'd been at the Wenatchee library for forty-five minutes now, scanning microfiche files, moving backward from February 1993. She was searching for a news story, but didn't quite know what kind of headline to expect, maybe something like *Child Snatcher Shot Dead* or *Dramatic Rescue Reveals Waitress-Killer.*

So far, she hadn't come up with anything, except a slight crick in her neck from all the tension. She tried not to rush through the files, but after scanning the headlines on the first five pages of every edition for two months, she started skipping days. Karen kept reminding herself that she wasn't in any hurry. Amelia was supposed to meet her here in an hour.

She hadn't heard back from Jessie, yet. Nor had George phoned with an update. Most surprising of all, Detective Peyton hadn't returned her call. And so far, she hadn't found a damn thing in the Moses Lake newspaper files, until now.

There was a photograph of the missing woman: a thin, pale-looking blonde with big eyes and short, curly hair. Karen read the caption: "Kristen Marquart, 22, was last seen leaving work at The Friendly Fajita on Broadway in Moses Lake last Wednesday night."

According to the article, Kristen's car was still in the restaurant parking lot the following day. Investigators determined the car had been tampered with, but they didn't say exactly how. Kristen, a graduate of Eastern Washington University, had been missing for a week when the article was written.

Karen saw the second-to-last paragraph, and grimaced. "Oh, God, here it is," she murmured to herself.

Kristen Marquart's disappearance is the most recent in a rash of missing person cases in the Columbia Basin area, all young women. In August, Juliet Iverson, 20, vanished while picnicking with friends at Soap Lake. In March, Othello resident Lizbeth Strouss, 24, disappeared after finishing her night shift at a convenience store. Earlier in March, Eileen Sessions, 27, of Moses Lake vanished after dropping off her two children at day care. After 17 days, her remains were discovered near a hiking trail in Potholes State Park forest near the Potholes Reservation.

Four women had vanished in eight months, and the authorities didn't have any suspects. Karen had been hoping to find a story like this, and now that she'd found it, she felt horrible. These women weren't just part of some puzzle. They were real.

And it seemed even more likely now that Amelia's birth father was a monster.

Karen wondered if he'd abducted and killed any more young women before moving to Salem. Or had Kristen Marquart been the last?

Staring at the screen in front of her, Karen realized she must have scanned past the news story about Lon Schlessinger shooting the neighbor who had allegedly molested Amelia. That neighbor was also blamed for the murder of a waitress. Was the murdered waitress Kristen?

With a heavy sigh, Karen started to scan over the newspaper records again. This time, she wouldn't skip over any days. Her eyes were getting blurry from too much reading, too much driving, and too little sleep. But she kept searching for the story she'd missed.

Hunched in front of the warm, wheezing microfiche-viewing machine, she read every headline on the first few pages of every edition of the *Columbia Basin Herald* until she found a front-page headline on Monday, November 16:

CHILD ABDUCTION SPARKS SHOOTING DEATH

Dead Man Linked to Disappearance of Moses Lake Woman, Possibly Others

MOSES LAKE: The apparent abduction of a 4-year-old girl on Sunday led to a police standoff and the shooting death of a man, now linked to the disappearance of a Moses Lake woman in October.

Six hours after Lon Schlessinger, 34, reported his young daughter as missing, he led police to the house of a Gardenia Drive neighbor, Clay Spalding, 26. Police arrived at the scene at 5:45 p.m. to see the child escaping from a bedroom window in Spalding's ranch house. The girl was dressed in only her underwear. When Spalding began to chase after the terrified child, Schlessinger shot him with a Winchester hunting rifle. Spalding, an unemployed artist, was pronounced dead on arrival at Samaritan Hospital at 6:20.

Police found the child's clothes inside Spalding's home. They also made another startling discovery in the unkempt residence: a wallet full of identification and a locket, both belonging to Kristen Marquart, 22, a waitress and Moses Lake resident who has been missing since October 14.

Marquart was last seen leaving her place of employment, The Friendly Fajita, on Broadway in Moses Lake. Authorities are now reexamining the disappearance of three other young women in the Columbia Basin area for a possible connection to Spalding.

According to Miriam Getz, 70, who lived next door to Spalding for two years, her neighbor was "quiet and considerate, but very strange, something of a loner." She added: "He made people uncomfortable, and I think he enjoyed doing that."

Getz reported that the Schlessingers had asked if she'd seen their missing daughter at 11 a.m. on Sunday. She later spotted the child in Spalding's backyard, and immediately telephoned the Schlessinger house. In a 911 call to Moses Lake Police, Lon Schlessenger said he intended to confront his Gardenia Drive neighbor.

Lon Schlessinger shot Clay Spalding in front of four Moses Lake policemen, and apparently, seconds later, the panic-stricken little girl ran into her father's arms. If Lon was in any kind of trouble for taking the law into his own hands, there was no indication of it in the article. They tactfully avoided calling Amelia by name, but did mention: *"Lon Schlessinger is a ranch foreman at G. L. Durlock, Inc. in Grant Country. The Schlessingers have been Moses Lake residents for five years. They have two children."*

There was a photograph of Clay Spalding on page two. Karen remembered Amelia's description of her neighbor, the nice Native American man with beautiful, long black hair. He'd converted a backyard toolshed into a playhouse for her. She'd eaten cookies in there at a little red plastic table.

The driver's license photo of Clay Spalding showed a swarthy, handsome man with straight, near-shoulder-length black hair and a slightly defiant look in his dark eyes. According to the article, two years before, Spalding had inherited the ranch house on Gardenia Drive, along with a large sum of money, from the home's previous owner. Prior to moving to the Schlessingers' neighborhood, Spalding had lived on the Potholes reservation.

Two paragraphs later, the article pointed

out that of the four recently reported missing women from the area, Eileen Sessions was the only one confirmed dead. Her remains had been discovered in a forest at Potholes State Park, not far from the reservation.

Still, perhaps not to show too much bias against the alleged child snatcher, the article quoted Naomi Rankin, a friend of Clay Spalding's, as well as a longtime Moses Lake resident: "I've been very close to Clay for several years. He was a brilliant artist and a lovely person. I don't think he was capable of hurting another human being, especially a child."

Karen wondered how Amelia could have only a vague, pleasant memory of this neighbor man, and not recall any of those nightmarish events from that October afternoon. "I liked him," Amelia had said, "but I don't think I was supposed to be around him."

"I don't get why we're supposed to stay in a hotel tonight," Jody said.

He sat in the front passenger seat with one foot up on the dashboard. Stephanie was in back, sorting through an old Bon Marché bag of kids' books, puzzles, and toys that had been on the Ping-Pong table in Karen's basement. The junk had originally belonged to Karen when she was a child. Jessie used to break out the bag of toys whenever Frank Junior or Sheila came to town and brought their kids to visit old Frank — anything to keep the children entertained for a while. She figured Stephanie would need something to while away the next few hours at the hotel.

There was a sci-fi convention in town, as well as an endodontists' convention, just her luck. All the hotels were full. But the clerk at the Edgewater Hotel had taken pity on her and found her a room at the Doubletree over by Southcenter Mall. Her timing was doubly awful, because of rush hour. They sat in bumper-to-bumper traffic on southbound I-5.

"I'd rather be in hell with my back broken," Jessie muttered, one hand on the steering wheel of George's car. She glanced in the rearview mirror again: no sign of Karen's Jetta or a black Cadillac. That was one consolation. If Karen was worried about them, they weren't in any danger right now. Nothing was going to happen to them in the middle of this traffic jam. Nobody was moving.

"Jessie, why do we gotta stay at a hotel?" Jody asked again.

"Oh, um, your dad thought it would be a good idea," she lied. "They — they're doing some work on the power on your block for the next few hours. We won't have any electricity, and rather than rough it, we're gonna live high on the hog at a nice hotel for the next few hours."

"They're waiting until *night* to screw around with the electricity?" Jody said. "That's kind of dumb. You'd think they'd do it during the day — when we don't need the electricity so much."

"So write to your city councilman," Jessie said. "There's stationery at the hotel, and there's also pay-per-view TV with new movies, *and* room service. You'll love it, Jody, I promise. With the room-service dinner, they give you these little bottles of ketchup and mustard. It's really neat. The best part of all is you don't have to do your homework while you're there."

She figured he wouldn't argue or ask questions about that.

"I hate mustard!" Stephanie announced from the backseat.

"Well, you can just keep it for a souvenir, sweetie," Jessie replied. "They also have little bars of soap and little bottles of shampoo. And here's hoping they have an honor bar for dear old Jessie."

Once the kids were settled, she would treat herself to a glass of wine, or rather, *Karen* would treat her. That bizarre episode with Amelia had really shaken her up. She'd never seen Amelia act that way before, so creepy and smug, like a totally different person. And it was pretty darn unnerving to hear she was supposed to have been on the lookout for a black Cadillac today. That big, old beat-up car had been parked down the block from George's house since before Jody even got back from school. She wondered if anyone was sitting inside it, and if they were still there, waiting for her and the kids to come back.

"Are we gonna be at the hotel soon?" Stephanie asked.

"Well, unless I can shift this car into *leap,* we aren't going anywhere," Jessie muttered, eyeing the gridlock ahead. They weren't even past Safeco Field yet. "Hang in there, Steffie. We should be checking in to the hotel in about a half hour, tops."

"Y'know, we gotta go home first before we go anywhere else," Jody said quietly. "Steffie needs her inhaler."

"Oh, shhhh—" Jessie stifled herself. "Do you know the brand, honey? Can we pick another one up for her at a drugstore?"

"Can't," Jody said. "It's a subscription."

"Prescription, honey." She sighed. "Oh, Lord. . . ."

"She really needs it, too," Jody pointed out. "Mom used to say it was like asking for trouble if Steffie went anywhere without her inhaler. That's kind of a weird expression. Do you know what that means exactly? *Asking for trouble?*"

Jessie saw the sign for the West Seattle Bridge ahead, the exit for George's house. "Yes, I know exactly what it means," she said.

Biting her lip, she put on her turn signal, and started merging toward the West Seattle turnoff.

Sitting in the crummy little office across the street from Sherry's Corner Food & Deli, the sheriff had I Don't Have Time for This Shit written across her face.

She stared at George from behind a computer and a pile of paperwork on her big metal desk. Decked out in her brown sheriff's uniform, she was about forty-five, with short, dishwater-blond hair and a long, narrow, horselike face. Her lipstick was on crooked. "Let me get this straight," she said. "You want me to go over to the old Schlessinger ranch and start digging up their backyard? And this is based on the fact that you were snooping down in their basement and found a name tag with 'Nancy Rae' printed on it?"

"Yes," George said, showing her the waitress badge again. "Nancy Rae Keller; she worked at a restaurant in Corvallis."

The cut on his leg from the fallout shelter door scraping him wasn't too serious. But it still stung like hell, and he'd torn his pants leg. He'd cleaned it up in the restroom in the sheriff's office.

George now sat in a metal chair with a green Naugahyde-covered cushioned seat and sturdy armrests. He imagined those armrests were used to keep a felon cuffed to the chair. But he couldn't see that happening around here much. One look at the place seemed to confirm that it wasn't exactly a hub of activity. A map of Marion County decorated the off-white wall, along with scores of police bulletins, many sun-faded, dusty, and starting to curl at the edges.

Yet, the sheriff acted as if she was in the middle of a major crime bust, and he was taking up her time.

"Nancy Rae has been missing for five years now," George pointed out. "She's one of several missing-person cases in the area, all young women."

"I'm well acquainted with those old missing-person cases," the sheriff said. She waved at the four ugly metal file cabinets behind her. "I have all of the files there . . . somewhere. I also have all this *here,*" she said, slapping at a pile of papers on her desk. "And it needs to be processed and filed. Now, I can't just drop everything and go on an archaeological dig with you in the Schlessingers' backyard. First of all, you're lucky I don't charge you with trespassing, Mr. McMillan. That ranch is private property."

"Well, I don't think I'd be the first one to trespass there," George replied, at the risk of incurring her wrath. "The place is pretty trashed. I saw a lot of beer cans and garbage."

"Yes," the sheriff nodded. "For a while there, certain morbid teenagers hung out there to get drunk, but we put a stop to it. That waitress tag probably belonged to one of them."

"I doubt it. If you knew where I found it —"

"All right, so you want to go out there now and start digging?" she cut in. "Based on what — a *hunch?* And some tidbit you read in a book of amazing facts about wildflowers indicating grave sites? We can't do that,

Mr. McMillan. First, we'd have to call a judge for a search warrant, which we'd be damn lucky to get by noon tomorrow. We'd also have to notify the current property owner. The ranch was bought by some chemical company in Boise eighteen months ago. A fence was supposed to go up around the place last year, but it didn't happen . . ."

She stopped to look at her deputy, who ambled through the doorway. The skinny, dark-haired young man wore a brown uniform and had a goofy-looking buzz cut. Walking around the counter, he carried a small bag and a can of Diet Coke.

"Twenty minutes for a lousy roast beef sandwich?" the sheriff asked him. "What did Sherry have to do? Kill the cow?"

The beleaguered deputy set the bag and soda on her desktop. "They were out of potato salad, so I got you chips," he muttered.

"Fine, fine, thanks, Tyler," she grumbled. The sheriff tapped a pile of folders on the corner of her desk. "File these, and then clock out. I don't want the county paying you overtime tonight. That's just more paperwork for me. I get more done without you here, anyway."

Sighing, he collected the files and stepped toward the metal cabinets behind her.

The sheriff opened up the can of Diet Coke. "If you're serious about this, Mr. Mc-Millan, we can't just start digging over at the Schlessinger ranch. We need to go through the proper procedures. That'll take time. Now, I see you there, tapping your foot, and if you're anxious to get going on this, you have a long wait ahead."

George squirmed in the chair. What had made him think he could get back to his kids tonight? If the cops actually followed his tip and found some bodies at the Schlessinger ranch, they'd want him to stick around. Hell, it might take days before they even uncovered anything.

"I'll tell you what," the sheriff said, reaching into the carry-out bag. "You leave Nancy Rae's name tag with me, along with a number where I can get ahold of you. I won't charge you with trespassing. And I'll pass your tip onto the state police in the morning."

George sighed. At least that freed him up to go home. But it meant waiting for confirmation that Lon Schlessinger was responsible for the disappearance of all those women. George also wondered if the sheriff even took him seriously enough to bother contacting the state police.

"Listen," she said, obviously reading his

hesitation. "The last of those missing-person cases was over three years ago. . . ."

Behind her, the deputy stopped filing and glanced over his shoulder. "I went to school with Sandra Hartman," he said. "She was the last one —"

"Yes, Tyler, I know," the sheriff said, dismissing him. She unwrapped her sand-wich. "You've already told me all about it. I'm not talking to you right now."

The deputy sneered at her back. Shaking his head, he resumed his menial task.

The sheriff rolled her eyes, then turned to George. "Anyway, my point is, it's an old case. If the late Lon Schlessinger is some-how involved, and there are indeed bodies buried on his property, nothing about that will change between now and tomorrow morning. I can assure you, Lon will still be dead. And on the off-off-off chance some bodies are buried on his ranch, they won't be going anywhere, either."

Frowning, she peeled the wheat bread back and inspected her sandwich. "It can wait until morning, Mr. McMillan," she said distractedly. "So please, quit tapping your foot. Leave the name tag and your phone number. And let me eat my lousy dinner in peace."

Ten minutes later, George was parked across the street at Sherry's Corner Food & Deli. He'd left his rental on the far side of the lot, behind a Winnebago so the car couldn't be seen from the precinct office. He was surprised the Food & Deli had shovels for sale, but then it made sense, considering the neighborhood. George bought some Neosporin for his leg, as well as a shovel and pick. He felt like a smuggler carrying them out of the store in full view of the sheriff's office across the street. He quickly loaded the tools into the trunk of his car.

Shutting the trunk, he peeked around the back of the Winnebago. George saw the deputy come out of the police station. He headed across the road again for another trip into Sherry's Corner.

"Tyler?" George said, moving toward the store entrance. "Deputy?"

The young man stopped to stare at him. "Hey, you're still around," he said, half smiling. "So the bitch didn't scare you away?"

"No, she didn't," George said. "Listen, deputy, how would you like to help solve Sandra Hartman's disappearance, and maybe make your boss look like an idiot in the process?"

"Well, last I heard, dear," the old woman said. "They sent Amelia to live with Joy's relatives up in Canada someplace."

Miriam Getz was petite with thick, cat's-eye glasses and short curled hair that was light brown with a pinkish hue, obviously from a bad dye job. She wore a string of pearls and pearl earrings with her lavender sweat suit.

After making a few calls, Karen had found out Clay Spalding's former next-door neighbor was still alive. But the 84-year-old Miriam was no longer living in Moses Lake. She now resided in New Horizons, a rest home in East Wenatchee, just a fifteen-minute drive from the library.

New Horizons wasn't on a par with Sandpoint View, but it was pleasant and certainly clean enough. Karen had caught Miriam in the corner of the TV lounge, working on her crossword puzzle. There were about a dozen other residents in the room, watching *The Russians Are Coming, the Russians Are Coming* with the volume a bit too loud. Over where Miriam sat, it was a bit quieter, but her cronies still burst into laughter every few moments.

Sitting down beside her, Karen had explained that she was Amelia Schlessinger's therapist, and she needed to find out more about Amelia's childhood. Miriam had heard about Joy Schlessinger's suicide shortly after the family had moved to Salem. But she hadn't known Lon had died, too, more recently.

"What about Annabelle?" Miriam asked, putting aside her crossword puzzle.

"I'm pretty sure she's still alive," Karen told her. "But I don't know her like I know Amelia. I'm trying to help Amelia remember certain things from her childhood, especially that incident with Clay Spalding fourteen years ago."

Miriam shook her head. "Gracious, I'd think she'd be better off not recalling any of it."

Karen gave her a sad look. "Well, she isn't, Mrs. Getz — Miriam," she said quietly. "I think she might need to know. I've read some of the newspaper accounts of what happened. It sounds like you know more about it than anyone."

The old woman nodded. "I suppose I do."

"I was counting on that, Miriam," she said. "So, can you tell me about Clay?"

She frowned a bit, then shrugged. "Well, he was this Indian who, excuse me, *Native*

American, who used to work for my neighbor, Isadora Ferris. She was elderly. . . ." Miriam let out a sad laugh. "Listen to me, I'm probably older now than she was then. But she was a frail thing with Parkinson's. Anyway when Izzy passed away, she left the house to Clay, along with several thousand dollars. And believe you me, that didn't go over well with the neighborhood. It didn't help matters either that Clay let the place go to pot, and after he'd kept it so beautiful while he was working for Izzy, too. It was a sweet, little one-level ranch house. I never could figure out why he didn't take better care of it. Sometimes, he even put these odd *art* pieces of his on the front lawn, usually some weird concoction made out of tin cans and wire hangers and Lord knows what else. It could look really junky out there."

She sighed. "But to be fair, he was a nice, quiet neighbor. He even shoveled my walk for me one winter. And he was very sweet to those twins, too, especially Amelia. He didn't get along with Lon or Joy. But for some reason, that one little girl liked him."

Karen nodded. "That's the impression I got, too. Amelia told me about a little playhouse he had in his backyard. It's one of the only things she remembers about him."

Miriam sighed, and fidgeted with her pearl necklace. "Yes, well, he *seemed* harmless enough, at least I thought so, until that day."

"Can you tell me what happened?" Karen asked. "Do you remember?"

"As if it was yesterday," Miriam said. "Around eleven o'clock that Sunday morning, Joy phoned me, asking if I'd seen Amelia. Well, Amelia or Annabelle, I couldn't tell the difference, but I hadn't seen either one. I guess Lon had gone searching for her over at Clay's house earlier, and Clay even let him look through the place. Apparently, Amelia wasn't there. But wouldn't you know? Around five o'clock, I looked out my kitchen window and spotted that little girl in Clay's backyard. She was all by herself, bundled up in a jacket. I saw her come out of that playhouse and duck in Clay's kitchen door. So I immediately called Joy. Then Lon got on the line. He asked me to come over and tell him *exactly* what I saw. Well, once I told him, Lon announced he was driving to the police station. He said he'd bring an armed police officer back to Clay's house. Then off he went, and he took Annabelle with him."

Miriam removed her glasses and rubbed the bridge of her nose. "Well, about twenty minutes later, Lon was back, with Annabelle. The child was hysterical, squirming and shrieking to raise the dead. Lon had his hand over her mouth most of the time. He said he didn't even make it to the police station, because Annabelle started pitching such a fit. None of us could figure out what was wrong with her." Miriam put her glasses back on. "But do you know what I think it was?"

Karen just shook her head.

"It didn't occur to me at the time, but I think Annabelle must have somehow known her twin sister was in distress. You know how some twins have a certain — *thing* between them?"

"Twin telepathy," Karen said, nodding.

Miriam nodded, and patted Karen's knee. "That's what I think it was. Anyway, poor Annabelle was carrying on so badly, they locked her in her room."

Karen squinted at her. "The child was upset, and their way of handling it was to lock her in her room?"

"My sentiments exactly," Miriam whispered. "But Lon ruled the roost in that household, and he's the one who locked Annabelle in the twins' bedroom. Then he fetched his hunting rifle and called up the police. He told them he was headed over to Clay's house to confront him and get his little girl back. All the while, Annabelle was screaming and crying behind that locked door. My heart just broke for her."

Miriam clicked her tongue, and shook her head. "I told Lon I didn't think the gun was necessary. I kept saying, 'Let the police handle it, for goodness sake!' I was so worried Amelia would get hurt. But Lon couldn't be stopped, and out the door he went. I followed him down the block. Joy stayed behind. Lon was almost at Clay's house when I heard the sirens. Two police cars came speeding up the block. Then, over all that noise, I heard screams.

"I turned toward Clay's house and saw that pitiful little girl climbing out a side window and crying for help." Miriam closed her eyes and put a liver-spotted hand over her mouth. "All she had on was her *underwear.* I just get sick when I think about it. After that, everything happened so fast: the sirens, tires screeching, all the policemen shouting, and that poor, sweet child running across the yard, practically naked. And this was November, mind you. Clay came out the front door, and he started to run after Amelia. That's when Lon shot him. I remember how in midstride, Clay suddenly flopped back and fell on the ground."

Miriam let out a long sigh. "Then Lon

threw his rifle down, and Amelia ran into his arms. She was hysterical, crying, but Lon kept rocking her and telling her, 'You're safe now, baby.' "

"And Clay Spalding was dead," Karen murmured.

Miriam nodded. "I think he died in the ambulance on the way to Samaritan Hospital."

"What about Amelia?" Karen asked. "I understand she was never really the same after that day. I hear her parents had a very hard time with her."

"Well, it might have been more gradual than that," Miriam said. "I know she was giving Lon and Joy some problems even before that Sunday. So Lord knows how long Clay had been — *pawing* at that poor little girl. I heard stories later that he had Polaroid snapshots of Amelia, *undressed.*" She shook her head. "Anyway, if she had problems before that day, well, you're right, they just got worse and worse after that. She tried to run away several times. I remember once, talking in the front yard to Joy and the twins, and a pickup truck came speeding up the block, like a bat out of you-know-where. I said to Joy something about how they could kill somebody, driving that fast. And before we knew it, Amelia broke away and ran into the street smack dab in front of that pickup — *on purpose.* The driver almost had an accident, swerving to avoid her. Four years old, and she was trying to kill herself. Can you imagine? Lon and Joy kept her home most of the time after that, and they didn't take visitors. I hardly saw her. Then I heard they sent her to stay with Joy's relatives, a cousin, I think."

Karen imagined Lon's solution to Amelia's problems was to lock the tormented girl in her room most of the time.

"What about the sister?" she asked.

"Annabelle? Oh, she was very well behaved. I don't think they had any problem with her." Miriam rubbed her chin. "No, the only time I ever saw her kick up a fuss was that afternoon before the shooting. And then later, I remember noticing her in her bedroom window, looking out and crying. I guess she'd seen the whole awful thing. But she didn't act up or anything after that, not like her sister."

Karen reached over and put her hand on Miriam's bony arm. "Did Lon run into any legal trouble for the shooting?" She winced a little. "I mean, even if it seemed justified, some people might say he took the law into his own hands."

Miriam frowned. "Well, I know there were

some concerns. But Lon cooperated with the police a hundred percent."

"Did a doctor ever examine Amelia to determine whether or not she'd actually been molested?"

With a pained look on her careworn face, Miriam shrugged. "I really don't know. But they found her clothes in Clay's bedroom. And in the kitchen drawer, they found a wallet and a necklace belonging to a woman who had been missing for nearly a month, a waitress."

"Kristen Marquart," Karen interjected. "I read about her."

Miriam nodded, then shuddered a bit. "You can just imagine what it was like for me to realize I'd been living next door to a serial killer for two years."

"Did they ever find Kristen's body?"

Miriam fiddled with her necklace again. "No, I don't think so."

"And did they ever really connect Clay with any of the other disappearances?"

"Well, they found whatever was left of one poor woman near the reservation where he used to live. That was enough for me. Oh, this girlfriend of Clay's raised a big fuss. . . ."

Karen nodded. She'd already left a voice mail for Clay's friend, Naomi Rankin, who still lived in Moses Lake. But Naomi hadn't phoned back yet.

"She insisted he was totally innocent, and incapable of hurting anyone. But she didn't see what I saw that day. No, she certainly did not."

"Then you believe Clay murdered those young women," Karen murmured.

Miriam glanced at Karen over the rims of her cat's-eye glasses. "Well, dear, the girls stopped disappearing after Clay was shot dead. So what do you think?"

"I have to go to the bathroom," Stephanie announced. "Real bad."

"Well, hold on a little longer, honey," Jessie said, with a glance in the rearview mirror. "We're almost there. The last few blocks are always the worst."

Driving up the cul-de-sac toward George's house, Jessie kept looking for that beat-up black Cadillac with the broken antenna. She didn't see it. She didn't spot Karen's Jetta either. Nothing looked unusual or out of place as she pulled into the driveway: no strange cars, no smashed windows, no one lurking around the house.

Approaching the front door with the children, Jessie didn't notice anything wrong with the door handle. To be on the safe side, she would have left the kids in the car while she ducked into the house for the damn inhaler. But Steffie had to go to the bathroom. She was all fidgety and squirming as Jessie unlocked the door. At least the door was still locked. That was a good sign.

"Now, let me go in first," Jessie announced, reaching for the light switch.

But Stephanie darted past her through the doorway, and made a beeline for the bathroom off the kitchen. Jessie had left the light on in there.

"I gotta go, too," Jody said, heading toward the facilities by his bedroom.

Rolling her eyes, Jessie turned and saw the door open to the front closet, with the light on. Had she left it like that?

She remembered setting the alarm code before hurrying out of the house earlier. It should have started beeping when they came through the front door. Something was wrong. "Steffie? Jody?" she called.

Starting toward the kitchen, Jessie glanced around the living room, and stopped dead. "Oh, no," she murmured. She felt this awful sensation in the pit of her stomach. For a few seconds, she couldn't move.

The drawers to the antique cabinet were left open. One drawer was taken out completely and dumped on the floor.

She heard a toilet flush. Continuing toward the kitchen, Jessie saw that someone had been through the dining room break-front, too. More open drawers, a few of them dumped out and scattered on the floor. The silver candlesticks on the dining room table were missing. All Jessie could think about was getting the children out of there, and then calling the police from a neighbor's house.

"Kids, we need to leave!" she called nervously.

"What?" Jody called back. "What's going on?"

Jessie turned and saw him coming from the bedroom hallway. But Jody suddenly stopped in his tracks. His mouth open, he gaped at Jessie and shook his head.

She realized he was looking at something behind her. She heard a whimpering sound, and recognized Steffie's cry. Jessie swiveled around, and for a moment, her heart stopped.

Stephanie stood trembling in the kitchen doorway. Tears streamed down her face. She'd wet herself.

Standing behind her was a young man with black hair and sunglasses. He wore a shiny black suit, and held a gun to Stephanie's head.

CHAPTER
TWENTY-ONE

"Holy crap, I think I found something," the deputy said. He stopped digging for a moment and gaped down into the hole.

George hadn't had much difficulty persuading Tyler to follow him out to the Schlessinger ranch. The deputy had had a little crush on Sandra Hartman back in high school, and for a while, he'd obsessed over her sudden disappearance. And George had been right about Tyler's hatred for his boss. He'd suggested that if they found a body buried on the ranch, Tyler could say he'd gotten suspicious and followed George out there while off duty. And yes, wouldn't the sheriff look stupid after that?

Tyler had a flashlight in his car, and they'd set it on a tree stump so it shined in the general direction of the wildflowers. They'd chosen a patch, and started in. George had worked the pick, and Tyler had manned the shovel. While they'd worked, the deputy had gone on and on about how much he couldn't stand that ballbuster boss of his. They hadn't even dug two feet down when Tyler had noticed the bones.

George grabbed the flashlight from the stump, and directed it into the pit. He figured Lon must have been lazy and careless about disposing of his victims' bodies, because the grave was way too shallow.

And the bones were way too small.

"It's a fucking cat," Tyler grumbled. He leaned on the shovel, and glanced at the other wildflower patches. "You were right about these pretty little buds indicating a grave. But I bet this is a boneyard for fucking cats. Ranchers and farmers often have a mess of cats to keep mice and rats away."

"Well, let's try one more," George said, putting the flashlight back on the tree stump. He grabbed the pick again. "Just to be sure, okay? I mean, if it's another cat, it won't take us long to find it."

"I think we're wasting our time here," the deputy said. "And I don't want to miss *American Idol* tonight."

"Just another fifteen minutes," George said, swinging the pick into a new section of wildflowers. "Just think, you might help solve Sandra Hartman's disappearance. What was she like, anyway?"

They dug for twenty minutes, while Tyler talked about what a knockout Sandra had been. Then George got a call on his cell phone. He checked the caller ID. It was home. He dropped the pick, and clicked on the phone. "Jessie, is that you?" he asked.

"Yes. Hello, George," she said.

He could tell immediately that something was wrong. "What's going on?" he asked warily.

"Oh, we have a situation here," she said. "Y'see, my sister's sick, very sick, and I need to go see her. She lives in Denver. Anyway, how soon can you come home?"

"Um, it'll take at least two and a half hours," he said. "Jessie, I'm so sorry about your sister —"

"Well, we had a family emergency here, too, George," she said stiffly. "Steffie had a bad asthma attack. I called the doctor. She's fine now. She's resting. But she's asking for her daddy."

He could tell from Jessie's tone, it was more serious than she let on.

"If it's worse than that, Jessie, please, tell me," he said. "I'd rather know now."

"No. But I need you to hurry home."

"Well, could you put Steffie on the phone? I'd like to talk to her."

"Um, I can't, George. Like I said, she's

resting. Just come home as soon as you can, okay?"

"I will, Jessie, thanks. I'm leaving now."

"Be careful," she said. Then there was a click and the line went dead.

He hit the disconnect button. "I've got to go," he murmured. "A family emergency up in Seattle, my daughter needs me."

Tyler leaned on his shovel. "How are you getting back there?"

Wringing his dirty hands, George shrugged. "On the way down here, I flew to Portland and then rented a car."

"It would be faster for you if you took a charter from McNary Field here in Salem," Tyler suggested. "You'd zip home in no time at all. The airport's not too far from here. Want to follow me out there?"

George hesitated. "Thanks, but could you give me directions instead?" He glanced down at the new crater they'd dug. It was at least three feet deep

The deputy gave him a wary look and chuckled. "Holy crap, you want me to keep digging?"

"Just ten more minutes, please," George said. "If it was a cat, we would have found it by now. Something else is down there."

Tyler took a moment, then nodded. "Okay, I'll keep at it," he sighed. "So, let me tell you how to get to McNary Field from here."

The man with the sunglasses took the receiver away from Jessie's face and hung up the phone.

"Good job," he said, with a tiny smirk.

While holding the phone for her, he'd kept the other extension — George's cordless — to his own ear. He clicked that off, and then set it on the kitchen counter.

Jessie was tied to a kitchen chair, her wrists bound together behind her with duct tape.

She'd been tied up like that for the last twenty minutes now. Their intruder had forced Jody to strap her into the chair. He'd used Jody's little sister as a negotiating tool, and the 11-year-old boy had been very cooperative.

"That's right," he'd told Jody, one hand over Steffie's mouth. The other held the gun to her head. "Now, wind the tape around fatso's stomach and the chair back. Strap her in real tight. Huh, you might need a few yards to get around all that blubber. . . ."

Shooting him a look, Jody hesitated.

"Just do what he says, honey," Jessie whispered. She was worried Steffie would have an asthma attack right there. The little girl trembled and quietly wept while the intruder tickled her earlobe with the revolver barrel.

Jessie sat there helpless as he made Jody wrap the tape around her ankles, fixing them to the chair's front legs. He tested Jody's work, pulling at each adhesion.

Then he took the children into their bedrooms. Cringing, Jessie listened to him barking instructions to Jody on how to tie up his sister. She heard Steffie whimpering the whole time, and Jody telling her to be brave. Jessie prayed and prayed that the next sound she heard wouldn't be a gunshot.

"That's right, put the tape over her mouth," the man said at one point.

Jessie listened to Steffie's muffled whining.

"C'mon, your turn," the man growled to Jody. "Take me to your room."

For the next few minutes, it was deathly quiet. Then suddenly, Jody let out a loud cry. It sent a jolt through Jessie's heart. "What are you doing to him?" she cried.

She waited anxiously for the next sound. Finally, she heard Jody's stifled moaning. At least he was still alive.

"There's no reason to hurt the children!" she called. "We're not stopping you. Please, just take whatever you want and leave!"

A few long moments passed before the young man ambled back into the kitchen with the cordless phone from George's study. "Oh, I'm not leaving for a while," he announced. "In fact, we're all going to wait here for their daddy to come home."

Then he'd forced her to make the call to George.

Jessie couldn't figure out why he wanted George to rush home. But she realized this wasn't an ordinary robbery. This was something much worse.

She stared up at that pale, young man with the jet-black hair and those tiny bangs over his forehead. Jessie wished she could see his eyes behind those dark glasses. "Listen, what's your name, anyway?"

He didn't respond. But he seemed to be studying her behind the sunglasses.

"Well, you heard George tell me that he won't be here for another two and a half hours," Jessie continued. "Since we're stuck here together that long, I should at least know you by name, *any* name. What should I call you?"

"Call me Your Majesty," he replied, deadpan.

"Well, Your Majesty, I want to compliment you on the way you dress," Jessie said. "That's a very snappy suit. It shows you're serious and have a lot of self-respect. I think you're also smart enough, and compassionate enough, to care about those kids. You must know they're scared, and very uncomfortable."

"They're fine, hog-tied on their beds."

Jessie sighed. "The little one has asthma. If she has an attack, we won't be able to hear her. You've taped up her mouth. She could suffocate." Jessie's voice started to shake. "And she's wet herself. I'm sure you saw that. You have a heart. I know you do. If you'd just let me change her clothes and wash her up. Then the two children and I, we'd sit quietly on the sofa together. You could still keep our wrists and ankles tied. . . ."

"You talk too fucking much," he said coolly. "Would it help shut you up if I tied a plastic bag over your head?"

Jessie stared at him, and didn't say another thing.

George was driving down Rural Route 17 about a mile away from Sherry's Corner Food & Deli when he saw the patrol car in the distance. The red strobe lights on the roof flashed and glowed in the darkness ahead. He heard the siren's wail.

"Oh, no," he muttered. If that was the

sheriff on her way to the Schlessinger ranch, he didn't have time to talk with her or answer questions. He couldn't stop for anything. He needed to get back to Seattle. He could tell from talking with Jessie earlier that he hadn't gotten the full story about the situation at home. Something was terribly wrong.

He watched the cop car, speeding toward him. The flashers were getting brighter.

Tyler must have found a body. Why else would the sheriff be speeding toward the ranch? Well, they could carry on without him.

George saw a mailbox and the driveway to a farm on his right. Switching off his headlights, he made the turn. He navigated down the dark, narrow, gravel road that wound behind some trees. Then he slowly turned the car around. The sound of the police siren grew louder, closer. Hands on the steering wheel, George watched the police car speed by.

His cell phone rang. The deputy had given him his cell number earlier. George recognized it. "Tyler?" he said.

"I found another skeleton," the deputy said. "It wasn't a cat this time. You were right. There are human remains out here." He let out a sigh. "Jesus, I still can't believe it. This could be what's left of Sandra Hart-man right here in front of me."

"Did you call the sheriff and tell her?" George asked, though he already knew the answer.

"Yeah, she's on her way," Tyler answered. "She wants you to come back and show us exactly where you found the waitress's name tag. The state police are on their way, too. This place is going to be like Grand Central Station in about an hour."

George winced. "Listen, Tyler, do me a favor. Pretend you couldn't get ahold of me. I can't stick around. I need to get home to my kids. It's an emergency."

There was no response on the other end.

"Tyler?"

"Okay, but I don't think she'll believe me."

"Thanks." George switched his headlights on again, and started back onto Rural Route 17. He didn't see the police flashers in his rearview mirror. The sheriff's car had sped down the road, out of sight.

"Could you do me another favor?" George asked. "Don't tell them where I'm going, okay?"

"Well, I can't guarantee they won't figure it out, but I'll try to stall them."

"Good. Thanks. And hey, don't let that creep of a sheriff grab any credit for finding those bodies. You're the one who did it."

"Okay," he said, with a dazed laugh. "Jesus. I'm really blown away. I still can't believe it. I'm standing here, looking down at this skeleton, and it could be Sandra."

His eyes on the dark road ahead, George didn't say anything for a moment. He was thinking that Sandra had been the last young woman to vanish. And Annabelle was still alive.

"I wouldn't expect to find Sandra Hartman's corpse out there on the ranch," George said finally. "You're more likely to find her buried in Arbor Heights Cemetery — beside Lon Schlessinger."

The Schlessinger ranch — July 2004
"Sandra, can you hear me?"

She leapt up from the cot. Hobbling toward the big, bulky door, she accidentally kicked a few empty tin cans. She'd been living on Purrfect Kitty cat food, canned sliced peaches, and water for the last several days and nights. As long as she'd cooperated with him, she'd gotten food.

"Annabelle?" she cried, leaning against the door. "Is that you?"

"I'm getting you out of here *now*," Annabelle called. There was a knocking sound, and then a loud clank, as if something metal had dropped to the concrete floor.

It was the same noise Sandra had become accustomed to hearing before *he* came in to beat her or screw her, or whatever he had an itch to do to her that particular night. "Assume the position!" he'd call, before opening that big door. She had to kneel by the cot, her back to him, and her arms at her sides. Then he'd start in on her.

But this was Annabelle. For several days now, Annabelle Schlessinger had promised to help her escape. Each time, she'd said the same thing. "If I spring you out of here, you have to help me get away and start someplace new, okay?" Annabelle had kept telling her to be patient and hang in there. It would only be another day or two.

They'd always talked through the closed, bolted door. But now that thick, cumbersome door squeaked open. Sandra felt her whole body trembling. She couldn't wait to get out of there. She didn't even think to grab her shoes. She just started pushing at the door.

Annabelle stood and blocked the door opening for a moment. Her hair was cut short and dyed blonde. "Do I look different?" she asked with a hopeful smile.

Sandra balked.

"I told you, I'm getting out, too," Annabelle said.

"Well, you — you look great!" Sandra gasped, not sure what to say. "Let's go, okay? All right?"

Annabelle grabbed her hand and led her toward the basement stairs. "C'mon, we just need to get some stuff out of my room. . . ."

Sandra's legs buckled as she raced up the stairs with Annabelle. She hadn't run for days; she hadn't even been able to walk more than a few steps without turning around in that cramped, filthy cell. She stumbled on the stairs, but quickly got up again and kept moving.

At the top step, she noticed the kitchen door directly ahead. It had a window in it. She could see outside. It was night.

Annabelle started to run past the door. Sandra stopped abruptly. "Wait!" she whispered. "I thought we were getting out of here."

"I told you," Annabelle said, tugging at her arm. "I need to get some stuff in my room first."

"But he might come back. Please, for God's sake. . . ."

"He might come back?" Annabelle repeated, laughing. "He's upstairs, out cold. He had too much to drink, as usual. He passed out on the bed."

Sandra tried to pull away, but Annabelle wouldn't let her go. "What if he wakes up?" she asked, tears in her eyes. "Please, Annabelle, I just want to get the hell out of here!"

"Would you relax?" Annabelle said, dragging her into the kitchen. "I know what I'm doing. I gave him the same stuff he used on you the other night, chloroform. Believe me, he won't wake up. I told you I'd do this right, Sandra. We're *walking* out of here in ten minutes."

As Annabelle led her through the kitchen, Sandra noticed the telephone on the wall. "Why don't we just call the police? Everyone must be looking for me."

Annabelle swiveled around. "We can't involve the police, stupid!" she hissed. "Goddammit, don't you remember? I'm the one who set you up, the same way I set up Gina and all the others. I'm as guilty as he is." She grabbed a lock of her recently dyed blond hair. "Why do you think I went to all this trouble to look different? I need to get away and start new someplace else. You promised you'd help me. . . ."

"I will," Sandra said, flustered.

"I stole a car yesterday, and stashed it behind some bushes near the end of the driveway," Annabelle said, leading her to the front hallway. "The thing's an ugly piece

560

of crap, an old Tempo. I just moved it a few minutes ago — our *getaway car.* It's parked outside the front door right now."

They started up the stairs to the second floor. "I've secretly been taking money out of my father's account for months," Annabelle explained. "Plus I've got some of my mother's jewelry. I can hock that." She paused at the top of the stairs. "Oh, speaking of jewelry . . ." She took off her bracelet.

Catching her breath, Sandra gazed at the ugly mark it had covered on the back of Annabelle's wrist.

"I want you to have this," Annabelle said, slipping the wide, silver bracelet onto Sandra's wrist. She did it in an almost ceremonial way. "It means we're one and the same."

Baffled, Sandra stared down at the bracelet.

Annabelle was pulling her down the hallway. "C'mon, take a look at him," she said. "He's totally unconscious."

"Can't we just *go?*" Sandra pleaded. "Please, I want to get out of here."

"No, I need to say good-bye to him," Annabelle insisted. She dragged her into the master bedroom.

Her father lay on the bed, his jeans unfastened in front and a T-shirt riding high on his exposed, hairy beer gut. It rose up and down as he breathed heavily in his sleep. Sandra could see the red marks on his face from the chloroform.

Annabelle stared at him, and her grip on Sandra's arm tightened. "I hope you wake up in time to feel the flames," she whispered to her unconscious father. She shook with rage. "I hope you'll be in terrible, terrible pain, you fucking scumbag."

Then she spit in his face.

Sandra winced. "Annabelle, please, you're hurting me. . . ."

The talon-like grip on her arm loosened, and then Annabelle released her. She wiped the tears from her eyes and took a few deep breaths. "I better give him one more dose of this stuff," she said, reaching for a bottle and rag on the bureau.

"What did you just say about *flames?*" Sandra asked numbly.

But Annabelle didn't answer. Her face pinched up and turned away from her work, she soaked the rag with chloroform.

Sandra rubbed her arm and, once again, frowned at the silver bracelet on her wrist.

When she looked up, she saw Annabelle coming at her. Before Sandra knew what was happening, Annabelle shoved her against the wall and stuffed the rag in her face.

Sandra's head slammed back against the wall. Dazed, she fought and struggled to push Annabelle away, but the other girl was stronger. The fumes were too much. She tried not to breathe in, but it was no good. She couldn't move. She felt paralyzed.

"You promised," she heard Annabelle say. "You're going to help me get away and start new someplace else."

After that, Sandra didn't hear anything.

Sandra Hartman didn't feel anything either, not even later when the flames burned her body beyond recognition. She never regained consciousness during the fire. She never felt the horrible, excruciating pain.

But Lon did.

CHAPTER
TWENTY-TWO

Amelia still hadn't shown up yet. And she wasn't answering her cell phone.

Standing on the steps outside the Wenatchee Public Library, Karen felt the cold night wind cut through her. She glanced at her wristwatch: 7:00.

She couldn't have missed Amelia. She'd been at the rest home for no more than a half hour. The trip had been worthwhile, too. Miriam Getz had given her a better idea about the incident that had traumatized Amelia as a child. Still, it didn't make sense that Amelia clung to such sweet memories of this neighbor man who had obviously been trying to molest her. The only people who didn't believe that Clay Spalding was pure evil were Amelia and Clay's friend Naomi Rankin.

Karen had left Naomi a second voice mail, but still no response.

However, the person she was most concerned about right now was Jessie. It had been at least ninety minutes since she'd spoken with her. How long did it take to find a stupid hotel room, anyway? Jessie certainly should have called her by now to say that she and George's kids were all right. Something must have happened. And Karen had no way of getting in touch with her, because Jessie didn't own a cell phone.

She took out her phone and punched in George's number. Maybe Jessie had gotten in touch with him instead.

She caught George in his car on his way to the Salem airport. He told her about the graves at the Schlessinger ranch.

The wind kicked up, and Karen shuddered on the library steps. "Well, there were four missing-person cases in Moses Lake in 1992," she said into the phone. "The last one was a few months before the Schlessingers moved to Salem. I'm still trying to dig up more information about that incident with the neighbor molesting Amelia. So far, it seems pretty much the way Annabelle's teacher described it to you. In the meantime, I'm standing in front of the library here, freezing my butt off, waiting for Amelia."

"Are you *sure* it's Amelia?" George asked.

"Almost positive," Karen said. "She borrowed Shane's car and drove out to Grand Coulee Dam early this morning. God knows why Grand Coulee Dam. But she's on her way here now. If all goes well, we should be back in Seattle before ten." She sighed. "Anyway, I'm worried about Jessie and the kids. Have you heard from her?"

"Yeah, that's why I'm trying to get home. Jessie called a little while ago. I think something's wrong at the house."

"What do you mean?"

"Steffie had an asthma attack. She's supposed to be okay now. But I'm not sure Jessie's telling me the whole story."

"She called from your house?" Karen asked.

"Yeah —"

"And Jessie didn't say anything to you about running into Amelia at my place this afternoon?"

"But I thought you said Amelia's been at Grand Coulee Dam all day."

"She has been." Karen told him about Jessie's brush with *Annabelle* that afternoon, and how Jessie had noticed Blade's Cadillac parked outside George's house earlier in the day. "Jessie didn't tell you any of this?" Karen asked.

"No, she didn't say anything —"

"Did she mention that Shane is dead?"

566

"Oh, no," George murmured. "God, no, she didn't. . . ."

"The police think he shot himself," she said sadly.

"Jesus, Karen, what's going on?"

"I told Jessie to take the kids and check in at a hotel," she explained. "It doesn't make any sense that she'd go back to your house. George, something's wrong."

"Well, maybe she just got a little mixed up with everything that's happening," he said. "Plus, Jessie has a family emergency of her own, too. She has to take off for Denver tonight. Her sister's very sick. It sounds serious."

For a moment, Karen couldn't say anything.

"George," she whispered, at last, "I'm sorry, but Jessie doesn't have a sister."

"I've called ahead and chartered a plane," George said. "I should be at the Salem airport in about five minutes. I'll call you when I land in Seattle. That should be at around eight-thirty. Can you stick around until then, Jessie?"

"Yes, that's fine," she said into the phone the young man held to her ear. He listened in on George's cordless. Jessie was still strapped to the chair, with her hands taped behind her. She'd lost some of the feeling in her arms.

"Any updates on your sister?" George asked.

"No. I was just about to call them," she replied.

"Is it your sister Estelle, the one with Alzheimer's?"

Jessie hesitated. He somehow knew this was a setup. "Yes, it's Estelle," she said, going along with the fake name George had picked. "I'm really worried the old girl won't last the night," she said carefully.

"I'm sorry to hear that, Jessie," he replied. "Well, I'll be there soon, unless you want me to send someone else over there to take over."

His Majesty shook his head at her.

"No, I — I can hold down the fort until you get here."

"Could I talk to Steffie? Or is she still asleep?"

"Sorry, George, she's still napping." Jessie glanced up at the young man. Behind him, through the living room window's sheer drapes, she could see someone walking up the McMillans' driveway. Jessie couldn't tell who it was. The person was too far away. With his back to the living room, the man in the dark glasses hadn't noticed yet.

"What about Jody?" George was saying on the other end of the line. "Could you put him on the phone for a second?"

Jessie's throat went dry. "Um, I — I'm sorry, George, he's in the bathroom. He just stepped in the shower." She watched the woman approaching the front door now. It was George's neighbor from across the street, a sixty-something divorcée named Sally Bidwell. She was thin with short silver hair and wore a black pantsuit. She'd been out of town at the time of George's wife's death, but had been over twice this week to see if they needed anything. George had told Jessie that Mrs. Bidwell had an extra key to the house in case Jessie ever got locked out.

As she came closer to the house, Mrs. Bidwell stopped and stood on her tiptoes so she could peek into the living room window.

Jessie tried not to stare at her. She didn't want His Majesty to see they had a visitor.

"Well, it looks like I struck out again," George said. "But they're both doing okay, Jess?"

"Yes, George," she said. "For now, they're okay."

"Thank you, Jessie. I'll get there as soon as I can."

The man started pushing the phone

harder against her face. "Hurry up," he mouthed.

"Okay, George," she said. "Good-bye."

The man in the sunglasses quickly hung up the phone, then clicked off the cordless. " 'For now, they're okay?' What's that shit? Was that your way of telling him something's wrong?"

Jessie just helplessly shook her head at him. She glanced toward the living room window again, but didn't see Mrs. Bidwell.

Suddenly, the doorbell rang.

The young man quickly snatched his revolver from the kitchen counter and crept over toward the front door. The doorbell rang again.

Jessie heard a muffled cry coming from Jody's room.

His back pressed against the wall, the man waited. He had the gun drawn. He seemed very calm and cool, or maybe it was just because Jessie couldn't read his expression behind those sunglasses.

Outside, Mrs. Bidwell backed away from the door. Craning her neck, she stood on her tiptoes again and tried to get another look into the living room window. Squirming in the chair, Jessie wondered if Mrs. Bidwell could see her though the sheer drapes. She held her breath and watched the young man reach over for the door handle.

Mrs. Bidwell lingered on the front stoop, trying to peek inside the house.

Because the Lake Wenatchee shootings had been such big news, the McMillans had endured their share of snoops this week. Jessie had seen a few driving down the cul-de-sac to catch a glimpse of the house, and others actually came right up to the house and tried to peek into the windows. In contrast, there were also several nice neighbors who had stopped by with flowers, casseroles, and condolences, Mrs. Bidwell among them. But she'd always struck Jessie as a bit oversolicitous and meddling.

At this point, Jessie wasn't sure if she wanted Mrs. Bidwell to see anything or not. She figured George would know how to handle this. But she didn't trust Mrs. Bidwell.

Finally, the woman shrugged her shoulders and turned around.

Jessie let out a sigh.

The man in the sunglasses moved over to the edge of the living room window, and he peered outside.

Through the sheer curtains, Jessie watched Mrs. Bidwell walk back up the driveway. But then she stopped and glanced inside the car for a moment. She turned toward the house again.

The man ducked back, and the sheer curtain fluttered.

Mrs. Bidwell stared at the window for a few moments. Then she took another few steps toward the house again. Pausing for a moment, she reached into her purse. Then she continued down the driveway past the front walkway, toward the back door. Jessie couldn't see her through the living room window anymore.

The man darted back into the kitchen. Swiping a dishtowel off the counter, he turned toward Jessie and grabbed her by the hair. Jessie struggled as he stuffed the dishtowel in her mouth. Helplessly, she watched him scurry over to the back door.

The neighbor knocked a few times. And then Jessie heard the door lock being manipulated. Mrs. Bidwell was using the spare key. Jessie wanted to scream out a warning, but she couldn't.

The kitchen door opened. "Hello?" Mrs. Bidwell called, stepping into the kitchen. "George? Anyone home?"

The young man waited on the other side of the door with his gun ready. Mrs. Bidwell couldn't see him, but she spotted Jessie, bound and gagged in the chair. All Jessie could do was shake her head at the woman.

For a moment, Mrs. Bidwell stood there, paralyzed, gaping at Jessie.

The man with sunglasses tucked his gun in the waist of his pants. Mrs. Bidwell swiveled around. She let out a gasp, then bolted toward the door. But he slammed it shut in front of her. He grabbed her and slapped his hand over her mouth. Arms flailing, the thin woman tried to fight him off, but he was too big for her. She struggled and kicked, but he didn't let go. All the while he held onto her, he hardly changed his expression. There was just the hint of a smirk on his face as he carried out his task — like a robot, not a trace of emotion.

He took his hand away from Mrs. Bidwell's mouth for only a few seconds as he reached for his revolver again. She screamed, until he clubbed her over the head with his gun.

The woman let out a feeble cry. She was stunned, but still conscious. She started to squirm as the man with the dark glasses dragged her into the living room. He threw her on the couch. Mrs. Bidwell let out another gasp, as if she'd gotten the wind knocked out of her.

The young man grabbed a sofa pillow and put it over her face.

Then he fired his gun into the pillow.

Jessie watched in horror as the woman's body twitched and convulsed with spasms. Then she slumped across the couch, suddenly still. Feathers from the pillow floated in the air around her. Jessie caught a glimpse of Mrs. Bidwell's face — her open eyes and the huge, gaping hole in her left cheek. Then the young man gave the corpse a forceful shove. The woman rolled over on her face. A bloodstain started to bloom beneath her on the beige sofa.

The young man seemed annoyed as he moved away from the body. Frowning, he brushed the pillow feathers off his shiny black suit. He straightened his tie, readjusted his sunglasses, and then headed for the kitchen sink. Turning on the cold water, he ran his hand under the stream.

"Fucking bitch bit me," he grumbled.

Tears in her eyes, Jessie stared at Mrs. Bidwell's corpse. For the last forty minutes, Jessie had been hoping against hope the young man would just take whatever else he wanted and then leave. But now she knew that wasn't going to happen.

Now she knew he wasn't going to leave this house until he'd killed her and the children.

■ ■ ■ ■

"Oh God, George, you're walking into a trap."

"I know," he said.

It was one of the only things George was sure about.

At this point, he figured either Annabelle or Blade, or both of them, were holding Jessie and his children hostage at his home. And they wanted him there, too.

"Karen, I really have no choice," he said into the phone. He kept his eyes on the road. He'd just passed a sign indicating McNary Field was straight ahead. He knew he was close to the airport because he saw a Best Western and a Holiday Inn Express just up the road. "I have a feeling they're keeping the kids alive so Jessie will cooperate with them," he said. "And obviously they're using Jessie to talk me into coming home. I'm hoping no one will get hurt as long as they're still trying to lure me there. I have about ninety minutes to figure out a strategy. I'm not calling the police, at least not yet. Maybe when I get to Seattle. We'll see."

He let out a nervous sigh. "Karen, if you could keep digging into Annabelle's past, maybe you can figure out what the hell she wants, why she's doing this. You know psychology. Why is she killing everyone close to Amelia? If I could figure out what Annabelle's after, that would help me when I walk into the house ninety minutes from now."

Tears stung his eyes, and George felt his throat closing up. "I might be able to bargain with her, give her what she wants, or at least figure out where she's most vulnerable. Maybe I can get my kids and Jessie out of there alive."

"I'll do what I can, George," she said. "Amelia should be here any minute now. Maybe we can get her to intervene and talk to her sister. Maybe that's all we'll need. Whatever this is, it's between the sisters."

"I think you're right," George murmured.

He suddenly realized he'd just passed a turn sign for the airport. "Karen, listen, thank you. I've got to go."

"Okay, call me when you get to Seattle. Take care, George."

He clicked off the cell phone, and turned the car around in an Arby's parking lot. He backtracked and found another sign for the airport. In the distance, he heard police sirens, which seemed to become louder as he got closer to the airport. George saw an intersection ahead, where traffic was at a standstill. Two cop cars with their flashers on sailed through the junction and turned onto the airport drive.

As traffic started up again, George made a left through the intersection, and then took a right to the airport on Aviation Loop. He had a bad feeling in his gut. He could see the two patrol cars, parked in front of the terminal's main entrance, their flashers still swirling.

He wondered if Tyler had caved and told the sheriff where he was headed.

George pulled into the lot and parked. Overhead, a plane was landing. George's ears got a blast of the engine's roar as he climbed out of the car. The night air had a chill to it. He clutched the lapels of his sports jacket up under his chin, and spied the two police vehicles in the distance.

A maroon minivan with RESIDENCE INN written on the side door had pulled up behind the squad cars. The driver, wearing a blazer the same color as the minivan, had gotten out of the car to talk to one of the cops. After a few moments, he stepped away from the cop car, waved, then ducked back into his minivan. He drove through the parking lot toward the main road.

George waved him down. "Are you with the Residence Inn?" he called. It was a stupid question, but still, the guy stopped.

The driver rolled down his window. He was in his early twenties with wavy black hair and a touch of acne. He nodded at George. "Yes, sir, are you headed there?"

"No, I'm meeting someone who needs a room for the night," George lied. "Do you know if they have any vacancies?"

The driver reached into his maroon blazer and pulled out a card for the Residence Inn. "Call that number, and they'll take care of you."

"Much obliged," George said. Then he nodded toward the police cars. "What's the hubbub about, do you know?"

The young man nodded. "They got a tip from some guy about a bunch of dead bodies buried at a farm outside of town."

"A bunch of dead bodies?" George repeated.

He nodded. "Yeah, they've dug up three so far, and they think there are a lot more." With his thumb, he pointed to the patrol cars. "One of those cops is a buddy of mine. He said this is going to be big. So, better book your pal's room with us pretty quick. Once all the news people get here — and that'll be soon — all the hotels will fill up."

"Thanks, I'll get on that." George nodded toward the cop cars again. "So what are they doing here? Are they the welcoming committee for the news people?"

The driver shook his head. "No, they're looking for the dude who tipped off the county police about the stiffs, some Seattle guy. They want to hold him for questioning. They think he's trying to blow town."

"Imagine that," George murmured. He tucked the Residence Inn business card in his pocket. "Well, thanks for the help. Have a nice night."

The minivan drove off, and George ducked back into his car. He thought he was going to be sick. What the hell was he going to do now? He had to get home to his kids. He didn't even want to think about how scared Jody and Steffie probably were right now, and what was being done to them.

He couldn't afford to stick around the airport any longer. No doubt, those cops had a description of his car, maybe even the license plate number.

George backed out of the parking space. He watched the two squad cars in his rearview mirror as he merged onto the airport drive. They didn't move, thank God.

He started driving, not even sure where he was headed. He just needed to get away from this airport and the police. It would take him an hour to make it to Portland by freeway. But he'd probably be detained at the Portland airport if he tried to book a flight or a charter. He couldn't *drive* all the way back to Seattle. That would take at least four hours, and he ran the risk of some cop spotting his car. They'd be looking for him all along I-5.

"Do you even know where the hell you're going?" he cried out loud. His hands, white-knuckled, gripped the wheel.

He took a few deep, calming breaths. George caught a glimpse of the street name as he went through an intersection: Waverly Drive. He realized he was close to Willamette University. The traffic became heavier as he headed into a commercial area full of bars, restaurants, and coffee shops.

George saw a sign: ATOMIC CYBER CAFÉ. He also noticed a parking space, and immediately pulled into it.

The Internet café was dimly lit and about half full of college kids slouched in front of the computer screens. "Can I get Internet access here?" George asked the barista behind the counter.

The young man had a small square of beard hair under his lower lip, and glasses. He wore a red apron. "You bet," he nodded. "The first half hour is free with a beverage. All I need is a driver's license for a deposit."

"Thanks." George slapped a five-dollar bill and his license on the counter. "Just a regular coffee, please, or whatever you've got that's quick."

A few moments later, George tried not to spill his coffee as he hurried over toward the free terminals. There were a few by a nicely dressed, uptight-looking man in his fifties, who gave George a narrow glance. Sitting down near him, George realized the guy was looking at porn. George ignored him. He switched on the terminal, and connected to the Internet. He brought up Google, and then typed in Salem, Oregon, Charter Helicopter.

He got two results: both businesses in Jefferson, Oregon. He pulled out his cell and called the first place, Coupland Aeronautic, Inc. He wasn't sure if anyone would be answering at 7:20 on a Monday night. His chances of actually chartering a helicopter at the last minute like this were probably nil.

A woman picked up: "Coupland, this is Kate."

"Hi. I'm in Salem, and I need to get to Seattle as soon as possible. Could I charter a helicopter for tonight?" he asked.

"You're in Salem, that's about a half hour away," the woman said. George could hear her fingers clicking on a keyboard. "If you can get here by eight o'clock, we'll have you in Seattle at eight-fifty tonight. Does that sound good to you?"

"That sounds great to me," George replied.

"Hello, Naomi, this is Karen Carlisle calling again. . . ."

Karen sat in her rental, parked across from the Wenatchee library. Though she got clearer phone reception outside, Karen had ducked inside the car to avoid the cold. It had also started drizzling. From the driver's seat, she had an ideal view of everyone coming and going at the library. She was still waiting for Amelia. It had been well over two hours since they'd last talked, and still no answer on her cell.

Naomi Rankin wasn't picking up either. This was Karen's third message in ninety minutes for Clay Spalding's friend. She now understood how telemarketers felt pestering a total stranger. In the last two messages Karen had tried to sound friendly and professional. She hadn't mentioned Clay or the Schlessingers. She'd just left her name and phone number, and said it was extremely urgent that Naomi call her back.

Though she didn't want to say too much on the answering machine, Karen decided to start explaining herself for message number three. "I'm sorry to keep calling," she said. "But I'm a friend of Amelia Schlessinger's. I'm hoping that name is familiar to you. I understand, years ago, you and Amelia had a mutual friend. If I could talk with you for just a few minutes, I —"

There was an abrupt click on the line. "Listen, if you call here one more time, I'll get the cops on your ass."

"Naomi?" Karen asked meekly.

"I don't have to talk to you," the woman growled. "Shit, I thought I'd heard the last from you assholes fifteen years ago. Get a life, okay?"

"Please, don't hang up," Karen said. "I'm not calling to harass you —"

"Yeah, I'll bet you aren't," she muttered. "I've heard it all. There's nothing new you can tell me. So piss off."

"Naomi, wait! You want to hear something *new*?" Karen had a hunch this would get her to listen. "Right now, the police are digging up corpses at the old Schlessinger ranch outside Salem. Young women started disappearing in the Salem area back in 1993, when Lon Schlessinger moved there

583

from Moses Lake. Isn't that about the same time women *stopped* disappearing around Moses Lake?"

There was a silence on the other end of the line.

"Naomi?"

"Who are you?" she murmured.

"I'm a friend of Amelia's, and she doesn't recall much about her childhood in Moses Lake. But she does remember a Native American man — a neighbor who was very kind to her. You and Amelia seem to be the only ones from around there who don't think Clay was a monster."

"So, I'm not totally alone. Amelia, of all people. . . ."

"I read about what happened, Naomi. And from the way you reacted to my call, I get the impression people must have harassed you for defending Clay in the newspapers."

"And on local TV, too," Naomi said. "For a while there, I averaged about eight threatening calls a night. I also got my share of hateful stares at work and around town. If you really want people to hate you, just speak up for someone who's been labeled a serial killer and a child molester. For years, I still received those creepy calls, even after I changed my number. I didn't let them list

584

me in the phone book until about three years ago." She sighed. "I'm sorry about earlier. I wasn't sure who you were when you left those first two messages. I thought it was some sort of scam or a telemarketer. But then you mentioned the name Schlessinger, and I just got sick to my stomach. It was a real blast from the past." She paused. "So, they found bodies on the Schlessingers' property."

"That's right," Karen said. "Lon's been dead for three years. His ranch house burned down with him in it."

"You know, I always knew Clay was framed for that woman's disappearance," Naomi said. "Now it all starts to make sense. Lon killed those women. You've read the newspaper account of it, so you know the story. He was in Clay's house earlier that day, hours before he shot Clay. He could have planted that waitress's wallet and necklace while he was there looking for his runaway kid. God, all this time I thought the cops had planted that stuff. I knew for a fact Clay couldn't have abducted that waitress. He and I were together the night Kristen Marquart went missing."

"Did you tell that to the police?"

"Of course. I practically screamed it from the rooftops. But no one believed me. I was in love with Clay for several months. So no one really took me seriously and, after a while, I just made them angry. A lot of people in that neighborhood already had a negative opinion of Clay, anyway. He didn't quite fit in on Gardenia Drive."

"Because he wasn't white?" Karen asked.

"Oh, I guess that might have had a little something to do with it," she admitted. "But Clay carried around a chip on his shoulder after inheriting that house. He felt everyone still regarded him as Izzy's yardman. I think he did things to piss people off. He stopped mowing the lawn, and let the place go just to prove he wasn't a yardman any more."

"I heard from his neighbor that he used to display some of his art on the front lawn, too," Karen said.

"Who did you talk to?" Naomi asked. "The old lady?"

"Miriam Getz."

"Yeah, she had it out for him. She and two of Lon's cop friends were the main *witnesses* who said Clay was trying to molest Amelia that day."

"Well, I don't think she was lying to me, Naomi," Karen said delicately. "Outside of the art displays and letting his lawn 'going to pot,' as she put it, Miriam didn't seem to have any problem with Clay as a neighbor.

But her mind changed when she saw what happened that day."

"She might not have been *lying* about what she saw," Naomi pointed out. "But she sure jumped to the wrong conclusion."

"Well, she saw a little girl in her underwear, crawling out of Clay's window, screaming for help," Karen said. "I've tried to figure out how *not* to jump to the same conclusion Miriam did. I'm thinking along the same lines as you, Naomi. Lon Schlessinger was pure evil. He must have set Clay up. I think you're right about him planting the wallet and the locket. But this incident with Amelia . . ."

"Lon used to beat her and her twin," Naomi said. "Did you know that?"

"No, but I'm not very surprised."

"He hated Clay from the word go. I don't know if it was because Clay was Native American, or because of his long hair, or the artwork on the front lawn. But Lon despised Clay. Maybe that's why the little girls turned to Clay when their dad started abusing them. They knew they had an ally with Clay. God knows, they couldn't go to their mother. She was totally clueless. Amelia ran away to Clay's house several times, more than her twin. I remember Clay saying Lon had Annabelle on a tighter leash, and she was afraid of him. She was a lot more obedient and likely to give in to her father's demands. Clay used to teach art to the kids on the reservation, and he knew about children. He said Amelia was a little rebel. That's why she and Clay got along so well. They both had that defiant streak."

"And as the more rebellious of the twins, Amelia probably got more severe and frequent beatings," Karen said.

"Right," Naomi said. "I saw some of the bruises on that little girl. It was revolting."

"Why didn't you report it to the police?"

"Clay tried. One time, when Amelia was over there, he touched her back and noticed her cringing. He asked her if anything was wrong, and she said, 'I think I was a bad girl again.' Then she showed him her back, and it was all black and blue and purple. Clay could hardly keep from going over to the Schlessingers' and kicking the shit out of that son of a bitch. I talked to him on the phone, and got him to calm down. I told him to take a few Polaroids of the bruises and then we could go to the police. Well, he did that, only he reported it to some cop who was a fishing buddy of Lon's. Clay didn't know. This cop didn't do a damn thing except ask Clay how he'd gotten the little girl to take off her blouse. They twisted it around. After Clay was shot, these stories circulated that he had photos of the little Schlessinger girl naked. But those were pictures of her bruised back, which he'd tried to give to the cops."

"Oh, my God," Karen murmured.

"So, weeks later, that Sunday morning Amelia went missing, Lon came over to Clay's looking for her. Clay let him come in and look around. But he also took that opportunity to tell Lon that if he found one more mark on Amelia, he'd kill him. Anyway, after Lon left, Clay called me. He said it was obvious Amelia had run away again, and he thought she might show up at his house eventually. He wanted me to come over. He also figured if Amelia had any new bruises, *I* should take the Polaroids, and then we'd call the state police, a lawyer, or child protective services."

Naomi let out a long sigh. "I was at work when he called me that Sunday. They needed me there to work the register at the goddamn Safeway. I remember Clay asking me, 'You mean, you can't take a few hours off to help a child who might be in trouble?' Then he hung up. That was the last thing he ever said to me."

Naomi started to cry. "I was still at work when someone at the store told me Clay

589

had been shot because they'd caught him trying to molest a neighbor's little girl. I couldn't believe it, and I still don't. Clay never would have hurt Amelia. I might not have been there to see how it happened. But I know they have it wrong. There's a difference between what people saw that day and what's true. I'm certain of that."

"I agree with you," Karen said. "Do you think it's possible Amelia was in her underwear because she wanted to show Clay some new bruises?"

"I wondered that, too," Naomi said. "But they'd have said in the newspaper that she'd recently been beaten and then, no doubt, used it as more evidence against Clay. Besides, I don't think Clay would have let her take off a stitch of clothing after that cop made those innuendos about the Polaroids."

"Well, maybe Amelia was napping —" Karen started to say. But a click on the line interrupted her.

"I'm sorry. Just a sec," Naomi said. "Let me see who this is."

She clicked off, and while Karen waited, she figured even if they came up with a reason why Amelia had been in her underwear, they still couldn't explain why she'd run screaming from Clay's house and into her abusive, sadistic father's arms.

Naomi clicked back on the line. "Are you still there?"

"Yes."

"Listen, there's a crisis at work, and I need to go over there, to the same Safeway. I'm a manager there now. How's that for progress?"

"Well, congratulations," Karen said, with a weak laugh. "Thank you for talking to me, Naomi."

"If you're ever able to figure out what really happened that day, let me know, okay? You have my number. Sorry I wasn't more help."

"But you have been, believe me," Karen said. "Amelia's still in trouble. And you have helped her, Naomi. You have."

"Well, thanks. Take care."

Karen clicked off the line. She sat in the front seat of the car and watched the raindrops sliding down her windshield. Across the street, a woman stepped out of the library, put up her umbrella, then headed down the sidewalk. She disappeared around a corner.

Karen glanced at the library doors again and then at her watch: 7:50.

"Damn it," Karen murmured. "She should have been here at least an hour ago."

Amelia was once again missing.

The car window was open. Amelia felt the cold wind whipping through her hair and an occasional raindrop on her face. She was driving Karen's Jetta, on her way to Wenatchee. She felt tense, but excited, too. She thought about how she'd finally get to use her father's hunting knife slitting that bitch, Karen Carlisle's, throat.

Amelia woke up with start, and in total blackness. She'd been having these horrible dreams all night. This was the latest, her gleefully planning Karen's murder.

Earlier, she'd had a nightmare in which she'd put a gun in Shane's mouth and pulled the trigger. They'd been in a rowboat on a lake somewhere. She'd washed Shane's blood off her face and hands with lake water. It had seemed so real. But Amelia kept telling herself these were just nightmares. She was still asleep in the spare bedroom at Karen's house.

But why was it so dark? And what had happened to the sound machine? She didn't hear the waves and those seagulls. In fact, she couldn't hear anything.

A panic swept through her. She didn't remember the bed feeling this hard, or the scratchy blanket. It smelled musty, like a basement.

Something had happened in the middle of the night.

Amelia had thought she'd dreamt that, too. She'd seen herself at night in Karen's backyard with a strange-looking, pale man with jet-black hair. They'd lifted a decorative stone from the garden, uncovering where Karen hid the house key. Then they'd snuck into the house. The next part, Amelia figured *must* have been a dream, because she and the man had been in Karen's spare bedroom, standing over *herself* in the bed. She'd watched herself sleeping. Bending over the bed, the man had put a damp cloth over her face. It had burned. For a moment, she'd felt as if she were suffocating.

Had it all really happened? It must have, because she was no longer in Karen's guest room. This dark, dank room was in a totally different place far away from all sounds and light.

Amelia sat up and blindly groped around for a light. Her hand brushed against a lamp beside her, and she switched it on. Someone had taken away the lampshade, and the bare lightbulb was blinding. It took Amelia a moment to recognize the secondhand lamp from the guest room in the lake house. Sitting up on a cot with an army blanket over her, she glanced around the gray little room. There were a few boxes shoved against the wall, a stack of old records and board games, some old paint cans, and a broken hard-back chair.

Amelia ran a hand through her hair, and realized most of it had been chopped off. They must have cut her hair, very short, while she'd been asleep, but why? She touched her nose and lips. They still burned from whatever was on that cloth the man put over her mouth. She had no idea how long ago that was. She looked around for a clock or a mirror. But there wasn't one on the makeshift nightstand beside her. Someone had turned over a box to hold the lamp without a shade.

But they'd left her an opened can of Del Monte sliced peaches, a pack of chewing gum, and a small jar of Noxzema.

Amelia stared across the room at the big, bulky door. It was closed.

She knew where she was. This place had always given her the creeps. For years, she'd been afraid of somehow getting trapped here.

She was in the family cabin by Lake Wenatchee in the basement fallout shelter.

And yet, somehow, at this very moment, she could still feel the motion of Karen's car, and a cold breeze through the open window kissing her face.

And she knew Karen was going to die.

CHAPTER
TWENTY-THREE

She wandered up and down the aisles at the Wenatchee library, searching for Amelia. Karen figured she might have missed her somehow. But she'd already walked around outside the building in the cold rain searching for Shane's car. She'd seen plenty of vacant parking spots, and no sign of the VW Golf. She'd already explored the reference, periodicals, and nonfiction sections with no luck. Now, as she zigzagged around the shelves of books in the fiction section, Karen heard an announcement over the PA system saying that the library was closing in five minutes. Above her, every other row of overhead lights went off.

Karen was filled with a lost, hopeless feeling. She kept thinking about how Amelia was the only one who could get through to her sister, Annabelle. She might even know Annabelle's next move.

After four months with Amelia in therapy,

Karen still didn't have a handle on her. What kind of therapist was she anyway? Even with all she'd uncovered about Amelia's childhood, Karen still felt as if she didn't really know her. It baffled her that little Amelia had fled from Clay's house the way she had that day. Besides her twin, he'd been her only friend, and she'd run away from him, screaming.

"The Wenatchee Public Library is now closing," a woman announced over the public address system. "We will be open again tomorrow at 10 a.m. Please exit through the front doors. Thank you and have a nice evening."

Slump-shouldered, Karen wandered toward the front of the library. She wasn't sure about what to do, except maybe call the state police. She could give them a description of Amelia, and Shane's car, and then ask them to look for a motorist in trouble on Highway 2, somewhere between Grand Coulee Dam and Wenatchee.

A little blond girl, who apparently didn't want to leave the library, was screaming and crying as her father dragged her toward the exit. Karen held the door open for him. He nodded at her, muttered "Thank you," then finally scooped the screaming, squirming kid into his arms. Karen watched them walk down the library steps. She thought about how Lon Schlessinger had handled that same situation by throwing the hysterical child in her room and locking the door.

She remembered what Miriam had told her about Lon taking Annabelle with him on his aborted trip to the police station that Sunday afternoon fifteen years ago: "He said he didn't even make it to the police station, because Annabelle started pitching a fit. None of us could figure out what was wrong with her."

Karen hiked up the collar to her trench coat and started down the library steps. She could still hear that little girl screaming as her father carried her to their car, halfway down the block. Karen suddenly stopped dead. The rain was stronger now, but she didn't move. "Oh, my God," she whispered. "He never went to the police station. He went and switched the twins."

It was exactly as Naomi Rankin had said: "There's a difference between what people saw that day and what's true. I'm certain of that."

Annabelle had been the cooperative twin, the one their father had had on a tight leash. She'd pretended to be her sister that afternoon.

It was a skill she would hone later as a

young adult.

Ignoring the rain, Karen stood on the sidewalk. Behind her, the lights inside the library went off. All she could think about was Amelia, struggling in her father's arms as she'd been smuggled out of Clay's house, dressed in her sister's clothes. Karen could almost hear her screams, until her father had clasped his hand over her mouth and locked her in her room. And from her bedroom window, Amelia might have seen everything that had happened down the block at her friend Clay's house. She might have even seen her father gun him down.

No wonder they'd found it necessary to get rid of the child after that. She'd been too rebellious. She'd seen too much.

No wonder Amelia had blocked out all memory of her family — a demented, violent, serial-killer father, an ineffectual mother, and the twin sister who had betrayed her.

Karen suddenly realized her cell phone was ringing. She grabbed it and checked the caller ID. She didn't recognize the number, but the area code was local: 509. "Hello?" she said into the phone.

"Karen, it's Amelia. . . ."

"Oh, thank God," Karen said. "Where have you been?"

"I'm sorry. Are you still waiting for me at the library in Wenatchee?"

"Yes. Didn't you get any of my calls?"

"No. Something must be wrong with the frequency, because I tried to phone you several times, but it didn't answer. It didn't even go to voice mail."

"Where are you, honey?" Karen asked.

"Well, I feel like such a lamebrain. I decided to try a different way back, and ended up getting lost. I totally overshot Wenatchee, and then Shane's car broke down. It's been a nightmare. . . ."

"Where are you now? I'll come pick you up."

"Well, I ended up getting a tow from this garage my dad used to go to near Lake Wenatchee. They were about to close, so I asked one of the guys there to give me a lift to this little restaurant near our lake house."

"You mean Danny's Diner?" Karen asked.

"Yeah. How do you know about Danny's Diner?"

"I was there earlier today," Karen said. She started walking toward her car. "I'll explain when I see you. Listen, this is important, okay? Have you had a — premonition about something happening at George's house?"

There was silence on the other end.

Karen stopped in her tracks. "Amelia?"

"Um, I'm not sure what you mean."

"Have you had any feeling that something's wrong at George's house, something with Jessie or the children?"

"No. Why are you asking?" There was a little panic in her voice. "Karen, are they okay?"

"Um, for now, I think they're all right." Karen hurried toward her car. "I'll be at the diner in about thirty minutes. And please, please, don't go anywhere, Amelia. I need your help with something, and it's very important. We have a lot to talk about, too."

"Does it have anything to do with why you're in Wenatchee?"

"Sort of," Karen said, climbing inside her car. She shut the door and started up the ignition. "I'll explain when I get there. I promise."

She switched on the wipers and headlights. She didn't hear anything on the other end of the line. "Amelia?"

"If you were at Danny's Diner, you must have gone to the lake house," she said. "Were you looking for evidence that I was there the night everyone was killed?"

"Amelia, I *know* you weren't at the lake house that night." Karen pulled out of the parking spot, and started down the road.

The highway on-ramp was two blocks ahead. "Stop blaming yourself for that, and for a lot of other things," she said, "even things dating back to your early childhood."

"My God, you found out about my real parents, didn't you? Are they still alive?"

Karen didn't answer. It wasn't something she wanted to tell her over the phone.

"Karen, please. For God's sake, don't make me wait. Alive or dead, I'm not going to fall apart if you tell me now. I don't even remember them. I'd just like to know. Are they alive?"

"No, honey, I'm sorry. They're both dead."

"Were they dead when the Faradays adopted me?"

"No, they were alive at the time. Amelia, I'll explain it all when I get there."

"Do you know why they gave me up?"

"I have a pretty good idea, now," Karen admitted. "But I'd rather not talk about it over the phone. Besides, I'm just about to get on the freeway. I need to hang up. Just stay there and wait for me. We have a long drive back to Seattle. I'll tell you everything then."

"Karen?" she said, a sudden urgency in her tone.

"What is it?"

"Earlier just now, you asked if I had any

premonitions about something happening at Uncle George's house. . . ."

"Yes?" Karen said, her grip tightening on the steering wheel.

"Well, I've had this awful feeling most of the night that someone's in danger. But it's not Uncle George, or my cousins, or Jessie. I keep thinking something bad is going to happen to *you,* Karen. Please, be careful. Okay?"

"Well, I — I will be. Thanks," Karen managed to say. She swallowed hard, and then started onto the highway on-ramp. "Just stay put and I'll see you soon."

"All right," she said. "Good-bye, Karen."

Standing in the booth outside Danny's Diner, Annabelle hung up the phone and started laughing. She loved screwing with Karen's head like that, warning her of the danger ahead. And yet Karen was rushing here, probably speeding all the way to her demise.

It was unfolding perfectly, even better than she'd planned. Looking back now, if she'd killed Karen in the basement of that rest home — or in her bed last night — her death just wouldn't have had the proper impact. It was important for Amelia to see Karen, her therapist, her confidante, her last remaining friend, dead. It was important for Amelia to realize that she had no one left but the twin sister she'd forgotten she had.

Amelia had run away by herself that Sunday morning in November nearly fifteen years ago. She hadn't said a thing to her about it. Amelia had just disappeared, leaving her alone to deal with their angry father. And when he was riled, it never mattered who had misbehaved, he lashed out at whoever happened to be around at the time. The only way she and Amelia had survived up to that point had been by sticking together and being there for each other. They had their own secret language. They could read each other's thoughts. They protected each other. And it wasn't just because they loved each other. No, it was more than that. Whenever Amelia got a beating, Annabelle felt it, too, and vice versa. Amelia only made things worse for *both* of them when she incurred their father's wrath, which she frequently did. Their father may have beaten Amelia more often and more brutally, but Annabelle still felt every punch, slap, and kick.

One of the worst sessions had been after their dad had gone out to punish a bad woman. It had been one of those nights

Uncle Duane had come along to help their father with his "work." They'd brought Amelia. Apparently, she'd done everything they'd told her to do. But as soon as they'd put the bad woman to sleep in the car, Amelia had started screaming and crying. She'd even tried to jump out of the car. Their father and Uncle Duane had been furious with her. She'd almost ruined everything. It had been a night of agony for both twins. Amelia had bruises all up and down her back. But Annabelle had felt every blow, too. The next day, Annabelle couldn't get out of bed, she ached so much. But even with all her pain, Amelia had snuck off to that Indian's house. She didn't tell Clay *why* she'd been beaten. She only showed him the marks on her back. "Clay took pitchers of me," Amelia later told her. Annabelle never got to see the "pitchers," but after that, they weren't allowed to go anywhere near Clay's house.

Weeks later, on that chilly Sunday morning in November when Amelia ran away, Annabelle knew where she'd gone. So did their father. But he didn't find Amelia hiding over at Clay's. However, Annabelle knew her sister was there, hiding from both Clay and their father. Even though Amelia hadn't told her about her plans to run away, and even though they would both get in trouble for it, Annabelle kept silent. She didn't want to betray her sister.

Sure enough, a few hours later, Mrs. Getz called from down the block, saying she'd spotted Amelia in Clay's backyard. Their father asked the old woman to come over, and tell him exactly what she'd seen. Annabelle got scared when her father announced he was taking her with him to the police station. She thought she and her sister might end up in jail or something.

But once Annabelle climbed into the car with her father, he told her, "You'll have to be your sister for a while. It's pretend."

She'd been only four years old at the time, but Annabelle remembered everything about that day. She recalled feeling relieved the police weren't going to arrest her or Amelia. Her father drove around the block, and parked in back of old Mrs. Getz's house. They cut through her yard. He kept telling Annabelle if she said one word, cried, or even coughed, he'd smack her.

They crept through the bushes and into Clay's backyard, past the little playhouse that Amelia loved. The windows at Clay's house were too high for her to see, but her father got a look inside. At the risk of making him mad, Annabelle kept tugging at his shirtsleeve. "Is she in there?" Annabelle whispered.

With a sigh, her father finally lifted her up to the edge of the window so she could see. Inside, Amelia sat at Clay's kitchen table, eating a cookie and drinking orange juice. Clay was on the telephone. He hung up the receiver, then moved over to the table. "C'mon, pumpkin," she heard him say, his voice a bit muffled through the glass. "I want you to lie down and take a nap. I need to talk to some people. They're going to help you. They'll make sure he won't ever hurt you again."

Annabelle kept waiting for Amelia to say, "What about my sister? Can you make sure my sister doesn't get hurt, too?"

But Amelia didn't say anything. She just finished her cookie.

Annabelle's father set her back down on the ground. Crouching along the side of the house, they moved over to another window that Clay had just opened a bit.

Annabelle tugged at her father's sleeve again. She wanted to know what was happening. "Stop that," he hissed. "Want me to crack your face?"

She kept very still and said nothing for several minutes.

"Goddamn redskin, he doesn't know who

he's dealing with," her father muttered, almost to himself. "Well, I've already planted something in there for you, Cochise, and it'll fix you, but good. Smug, uppity son of a bitch."

He turned to Annabelle. "Take off your clothes," he whispered.

Aghast, she just shook her head. It was cold out. And besides, she didn't want anyone to see her naked.

"Do it!" her father hissed. "You can leave your underpants on if you want. I need to put your clothes on Amelia, so Mrs. Getz thinks she's you. I told you, you're going to be Amelia for a little while."

Her father explained how she would have to sit and wait on the bed in Clay's house until she heard a police siren getting close. That was her cue to climb out this window and start screaming.

Trembling, Annabelle nodded obediently and started to undress.

Her father pushed the window up, then gave her a boost to the ledge. She crawled into the bedroom. Gasping, Amelia sat up in Clay's bed. Annabelle put her fingers over her lips and shushed her. She could hear Clay on the phone in the kitchen: "Yes . . . I've been on hold for five minutes now. Is there anyone in that office? Yes . . . yes . . . I know it's Sunday, but I have a situation here . . ."

When their father climbed through the window, Amelia recoiled. She looked like she was about to scream. Within seconds, he was on her, stuffing a handkerchief in her mouth. She struggled as he started to undress her. "C'mon, help me put your clothes on her," he whispered to Annabelle.

"Well, all I'm getting are these damn recordings," Clay was telling someone on the phone in his kitchen. He sounded so frustrated. "But I don't want to leave a message, damn it. . . . No, I need to talk with a person. . . ."

Annabelle wanted so much to put on Amelia's clothes, but her father had insisted she run outside in her *underwear.* Humiliating as that might be, it was better than a beating. She helped her father smuggle Amelia out the bedroom window. Then she crawled into Clay's bed and waited. It seemed like forever.

"Fine. Screw you," she heard Clay say in the kitchen. "I'll get someone else to help me."

Finally, she heard the sirens in the distance. Clay called to her, thinking she was Amelia. "Are you okay in there, pumpkin? You asleep?"

She didn't answer. She listened to the sirens getting louder and louder. Shaking, Annabelle moved to the window. She hadn't even gone outside yet, and already she was cold. Peering over the ledge, she thought she might hurt herself crawling out there.

Clay came to the bedroom doorway. "Amelia?"

Wincing, Annabelle jumped out the window and hit the ground. She could hardly breathe, and yet, somehow, she forced out a scream. She saw the police cars with their lights flashing. They pulled up in front of Clay's house. Then she saw her father marching toward the front door with his hunting rifle.

Annabelle let out another shriek and started running toward the police cars, until she heard the loud bang.

She swiveled around at the edge of the front yard. Clay must have come out the front door to chase after her. But now he lay sprawled on the ground, with blood all over his shirt and his long black hair in his face.

At first, Annabelle was horrified. But then she thought about how her twin sister had abandoned her, and run to this man for protection. He was going to help Amelia, and didn't even mention helping *her*.

Suddenly, she liked that he was dead. It felt good.

After that, things between her and Amelia were never quite the same. Amelia was different, withdrawn, and acting crazy most of the time. Her parents finally sent her away to live with another family.

Then they moved to the ranch in Salem, without Amelia.

While Annabelle endured her father's abuse and those awful nights she was forced to help him with his *work,* she still picked up snippets of her twin sister's experiences in a series of foster homes. Amelia wasn't very happy, but her life was easy in comparison to Annabelle's plight. Then something happened to Annabelle that was worse than her father's most severe beating, worse than those long, lonely nights in the car, listening to those women scream and beg.

What happened was Amelia had decided to forget about her.

Annabelle never really forgave her for that.

She knew her sister was adopted by the Faradays. She still had a glimpse into Amelia's sweet, privileged life with them, but she didn't get to be a part of it. As far as her lucky sister was concerned, she didn't exist, and never had.

After her mother had killed herself, her

father and Uncle Duane kept grilling Anna-belle about where Amelia was. They knew she'd had a special connection with her twin. Though Annabelle knew her sister's last name was now Faraday, she didn't tell them a thing. She somehow sensed they wanted Amelia dead. And Annabelle was still very protective of her sister, even though she didn't deserve it.

Later, Annabelle figured it out. Her father and Uncle Duane had planned to do away with Amelia shortly after Clay had been killed. In a rare moment of clarity, Anna-belle's mother intervened. She persuaded her husband to put the problem child into foster care.

When she was a teenager, Annabelle found some documents tucked away in her father's desk drawer. Shortly before the move to Salem, her mother and father had signed papers completely relinquishing parenthood of Amelia.

But once her mother was dead, Anna-belle's father and her uncle were desperate to track down Amelia. They wanted to kill her, because of what she knew and what she might tell. They had no idea Amelia had forgotten all about them.

Stupid Duane had killed those people at the adoption place and gotten himself killed for nothing.

She didn't talk about Amelia with anyone until later in high school. Annabelle thought it might make her more interesting to people if she'd had a twin who died. But it didn't make her popular. And all the while, she had a window into her sister's life. Annabelle had her nose pressed up against that window. She knew Amelia Faraday had a kid brother and parents who loved her. She lived in a beautiful house with a dock and a lake in the backyard. They had a weekend home, not far from another lake.

The closest Amelia Faraday ever came to true misery and pain was when Annabelle experienced it firsthand. Even then, Amelia had no idea where the sensations and visions came from.

It hurt Annabelle to be disregarded like that. It hurt more than all the physical pain and horror she'd endured growing up on that ranch with her awful father.

Now Amelia was beginning to feel some of that pain firsthand. First her brother, then her parents and her aunt, her boyfriend. One by one, the people Amelia loved weren't there anymore. Within an hour, her therapist — along with her uncle and her cousins — would all be dead, too.

Amelia would have nobody, except the

sister she'd chosen to forget.

Huddled inside the phone booth in front of Danny's Diner, Annabelle listened to the rain beating on the roof. She made another call. It rang twice before he picked up. "Yeah?"

"Hi, babe. How's everything there?"

"Fine," he said, "except we got one down."

Annabelle frowned a bit. "Already? Was it one of the kids?"

"No, a snoopy old bitch of a neighbor. But I have it under control. I asked the housekeeper, and she said the lady lived alone. So nobody's going to come looking for her. In fact, I'm tempted to check across the street and see if she has anything in the house worth taking. Bet she has a shitload of jewelry."

"Now, don't get greedy," Annabelle said. "Stay put. I don't want any of the other neighbors to see you going over there. They might call the cops. You could screw this whole thing up. You've collected a car full of crap from Uncle George's. That's enough. What's the latest on Uncle George, anyway?"

"The last time he talked to fatso, he said to expect him around nine o'clock."

"Good. Well, be careful, babe. I got these vibes from Karen that they suspect something. So, if you get nervous, or things don't seem right to you, then just abort. Shoot the maid and the kids, and get the hell out of there. We'll worry about the uncle later."

"I won't get nervous," he said.

"Well, once you've finished them all off, hurry here, baby. I need you."

"Huh," he grunted. "You just want me to help you escape."

"Well, you promised," she said. "You're going to help me get away, and we'll start new someplace else. See you at the lake house around midnight."

Annabelle hung up the phone, and stepped out of the booth. She walked through the cool night rain back to Karen's car in the parking lot of Danny's Diner. She glanced over the swaying treetops in the general direction of the lake house.

Once she'd killed Karen, she'd wait for Blade. He was in love with her — at least he thought he was. He would be easy to kill.

She had a two-gallon tote container of gasoline in the trunk of Karen's car. That would be enough to set the lake house on fire. The cops would find two burnt bodies in there, Karen and Blade. She knew what she was doing. She'd pulled it off without a hitch three years ago. Funny, she'd pretty much told Sandra the same thing she'd told

Blade moments ago: "You're going to help me get away, and we'll start new someplace else."

When she'd said *we,* Blade had probably thought she'd meant her and him.

But she wasn't thinking of him at all.

His hands taut on the steering wheel, George studied the road ahead. He'd made it to the city of Jefferson in less than twenty minutes. Speeding along I-5, he'd kept his eyes peeled for patrol cars.

While in the cybercafé, he'd checked MapQuest for directions to Coupland Aeronautics, so he knew the helicopter place was only about a mile ahead in this industrial area. George passed several warehouses, a railroad and container yard, and a chemical plant.

He'd just talked with Karen, who was on her way to meet Amelia at the restaurant near the Lake Wenatchee house. Apparently, Amelia didn't have any premonitions about the kids or Jessie being in trouble — not yet, at least. Karen said she'd call again from the pay phone when she got to the restaurant. George couldn't help remembering the last time someone had promised to call him from that place. It had been Ina, the day of her murder.

Although he wanted to phone Jessie again, he decided to wait until he was ready to board the helicopter. The more he thought about how scared Jody and Steffie had to be, the harder he pressed on the accelerator. George started to pass a truck in front of him, but as he veered into the oncoming lane, he saw an SUV barreling toward him. Its horn blared. George swerved back into his own lane behind the truck, again. He got ready to try once more, but noticed the truck's right turn signal blinking. It slowed down to a crawl to pull into a Chevron plant. George tried to go around it again, but another truck nearly ran into him. Its horn continued to wail, even after George swung back into his lane.

Catching his breath, he waited for the trucker in front of him to make the damn turn. Then he saw a clear road ahead, and he pushed harder on the gas.

George passed Donahue Drive, one of the last major intersections before the helicopter pad, at least, according to MapQuest. And then he noticed the flashing light in his rear-view mirror. "Oh, shit," he murmured, releasing his foot from the accelerator. "God, no, please. . . ."

The cop car was descending on him. He could hear the siren now.

"Please, God."

George's stomach was in knots as he slowly pulled over to the road's shoulder. The lights in his rearview mirror were blinding now. For a moment, the bright strobes illuminated the inside of his car. And then the policeman passed him.

George sagged forward against the wheel. He took a deep breath, and pressed on. But he couldn't stop trembling. He watched the squad car take a right turn ahead. He hoped the cop wasn't headed to Coupland Aeronautics.

For the next few blocks, he drove at the 35-miles-per-hour speed limit. Then he noticed the airfield ahead to his left. Two helicopters were parked on the airstrip. George didn't see a cop car anywhere near the place. Yet his hands still shook on the wheel as he went beyond the tall chain-link fence and followed the signs to customer parking. He didn't think he'd breathe right or stop shaking until he saw his kids and knew they were safe.

He was just pulling into one of the parking spots when someone trotted out of the trailer office. George rolled down his window and saw that it was a woman in her midthirties, wearing a gray jumpsuit. She was pretty with dark brown hair, pulled back in a ponytail. "Mr. McMillan?" she said, approaching his car.

George nodded a few more times than necessary. He was waiting for her to say something like, "I'm afraid the Salem Police are looking for you. . . ."

Instead, she leaned toward his car window and smiled. "Hi, I'm Kate. You spoke with me earlier. If you need to park for more than twenty-four hours, go ahead and take a spot where that green sign is."

George glanced over his shoulder and saw a green sign on a light post: LONG-TERM PARKING. He looked back up at the woman and nodded again. He was still shaking, and he could tell she'd noticed.

"They charge twelve bucks a day for long-term parking," she said. "It'll be added to your bill. And speaking of paperwork, it's all ready for you. Just come on into the office. We'll get it signed, and we'll be on our way to Seattle. I'll be your pilot tonight, Mr. McMillan. Do you have any luggage for your trip?"

He shook his head. "No, I don't. But thanks."

"Okeydoke," she said. "Then I'll see you in the office." She turned and trotted back toward the trailer.

George tried to take a few calming breaths

as he maneuvered over to the long-term parking area. It just dawned on him that this was a rental, and he'd have to somehow get it back to the rent-a-car company. But that didn't matter right now. He was just relieved he'd be on his way to Seattle soon, with no one detaining him. No delays.

Still, he couldn't stop trembling, even after he'd parked the rental and locked it. Standing beside the car, he took out his cell phone and dialed home once more. He just needed to hear Jessie assure him again that Steffie and Jody were all right.

George listened to the ring tones, four of them so far. Something was wrong. Why wasn't Jessie picking up? He'd figured they were checking his caller ID. They must have known his cell phone number by now. If they were trying to lure him there using Jessie and the kids, they would have had her pick up by now.

The machine clicked on. Hi, you've reached the McMillans. Sorry we're not here to take your call. But if you'd like to leave a message for George, Ina, Jody or Stephanie, just talk to us after the beep!

It was Ina's voice on the recording. He still hadn't changed it.

The beep sounded. George kept wondering why no one was picking up. "Hello,

Jessie?" he said into the machine. "Um, it's George. I'm on my way. I should be there around nine o'clock. I just wanted to touch base with you. Are you there, Jessie? Jody? Steffie? Well, I guess you're not there. I'll see you guys soon, okay?"

He clicked off the line. Then he punched his home phone number again. Another four ring tones went by while George gazed out at the two helicopters on the airstrip. One of them was waiting for him. Ina's recorded message came back on.

George quickly clicked off the cell phone. He had a horrible feeling in his gut. No one was picking up at his house — just the voice of someone already dead.

CHAPTER
TWENTY-FOUR

At Danny's Diner, the burgers and sandwiches were served in red plastic baskets, lined with paper. Desserts came from a rotating display case near the cash register. The walls were decorated with neon beer signs, mounted fish plaques, and another sign by the counter that said:

Our Credit Manager is HELEN WAITE. *If you want to pay on credit . . .*
GO TO HELEN WAITE!

The dinner crowd was dwindling in the cozy, homey little restaurant. Karen noticed a family of four in a booth, an older couple at one of the tables, and two trucker types, both at the counter with a few stools between them.

And Amelia was nowhere to be seen.

The waitress, a chubby blonde with a Farrah Fawcett hairdo left over from the seventies, told Karen she could sit anywhere. So

Karen plopped down at a window table and prayed that Amelia just happened to be in the restroom.

She waited three minutes, then got up and checked the ladies' room. No one.

This was crazy. Amelia had called from here thirty minutes ago. She'd been stranded, without a car. Karen had practically begged her to stay put, too. And now she was gone. How could someone just vanish like that?

But then, that sort of thing had happened a lot, back when Amelia and Annabelle's father had been alive.

With a nervous sigh, Karen sat back down at the table. She decided to give Amelia three more minutes. Then she'd call her from the phone booth outside. Of course, if Amelia was anywhere in the vicinity, her cell phone wouldn't work. So it was probably pointless.

Karen glanced at her wristwatch. George would touch down in Seattle in less than an hour. They were counting on Amelia to somehow intercede with her sister.

Had she somehow already met up with Annabelle?

Karen looked out the rain-beaded window. Against the darkness, she saw only her own reflection. She looked haggard and worried.

The blond waitress came by for Karen's drink order. Karen noticed her name tag: YOUR SERVER IS CONNIE.

"Could I have a Diet Coke, please?" Karen said. "Also, Connie, I was supposed to meet someone here. Have you seen a very pretty, 19-year-old girl with shoulder-length black hair? She should have been here about a half hour ago."

Connie shook her head. "Nope, sorry, I haven't noticed anyone like that tonight, hon — been here since four. I'll get your Diet Coke in a jiff." She sauntered toward the kitchen.

Digging out her cell phone, Karen checked the last caller. She left her trench coat on her chair, then hurried outside. Ducking into the phone booth, she checked the number over the receiver. It was a match. Amelia had been here.

As she stepped out of the booth, Karen saw someone walking along the roadside. Coming from the direction of the lake house, she seemed to emerge from the darkness.

"Amelia?" Karen called to her.

Although it was still drizzling lightly, she dawdled. Her black hair was in wet tangles, and the navy-blue rain jacket was too big on her. The sleeves came down to her fingers. She seemed lost in thought. It was another few moments before she appeared to notice Karen, and then she waved and ran toward her.

"Amelia, what are you doing out here?" Karen asked. "You'll catch your death."

She gave Karen a hug. Her cheek felt cold. "I'm sorry. Were you waiting long?"

"Not very," Karen said. Pulling away, she held her at arm's length and looked at her. Karen noticed she wasn't wearing any makeup. "What were you doing, honey? Why didn't you wait in the diner?"

She let out a long sigh, and tugged at a strand of her hair. "Oh, I decided to walk down to the cabin. But I only got halfway there before I chickened out and turned back. I keep thinking it would be good therapy for me to go there and see it."

"I don't think that's such a great idea," Karen replied. "You'd only get upset if you went there now. It would be pointless." She put an arm around her. "C'mon, let's get you some coffee, something to warm you up."

As she ushered her into the restaurant and back toward the window table, Karen heard the blond waitress call out to someone: "Well, hi there, Frenchie!"

The two of them sat down. "We should

make our orders to go," Karen said. "I'd like to get on the road soon. . . ."

"Frenchie?" the waitress chirped again.

Karen looked up and realized she was approaching their table. "Well, Frenchie, aren't you going to say hi?" the waitress asked.

Karen stared across the table. "Amelia?"

Still tugging at a wet strand of hair, she looked up at the waitress. "Oh, hi . . . Connie," she said, obviously reading the name tag.

"When you walked in just now, you acted like you didn't know me," the waitress said.

She smiled up at her. "Oh, I'm sorry. I'm kind of spacey today. How are you?"

"I can't complain," the waitress replied. "Who'll listen?"

"Did you just call her 'Frenchie'?" Karen asked.

The waitress nodded. "I don't even have to give this one a menu. She always orders the same thing, the French dip. Every time she comes in here with her folks, she . . ." The waitress trailed off, and a pained look passed across her face. She shook her head. "Oh, hon, I'm so sorry. All of us here felt terrible when we heard about it. . . ."

"Thanks, Connie," she murmured, her head down.

"I'll get your drink order, hon," Connie said. "The usual? Sprite?"

She nodded. "Thanks very much." She waited until the waitress retreated toward the kitchen, then she leaned across the table to Karen. "I can tell she's embarrassed. Could you excuse me for a minute, Karen?"

Getting to her feet, she walked over to the counter. She murmured something to the waitress, who was at the soda machine. Connie put down the glass of soda, then came around the counter and gave her a hug. After a moment, the tall, white-haired cook ambled out from the kitchen and quietly spoke to her, too. He shook her hand, but she leaned in and kissed him on the cheek. He blushed a bit.

Finally, she came back to the table. "They're so sweet," she whispered. "They're getting our drinks to go, and are refusing to take any money, not even a tip. Listen, I need to use the bathroom, and then we can get going, okay?"

Karen watched her walk toward the restrooms.

Five minutes later, they stepped out of Danny's Diner, carrying their drinks, along with two pieces of pie that the waitress insisted they have for free.

"God, Karen," she said, stopping to look

627

back at the tacky, little chalet-style restaurant. She had tears in her eyes. "Aren't those people nice? It makes me sad to think I'm probably never coming back here."

Karen just patted her arm, and said nothing.

They headed to the rental car, and Karen unlocked the door for her.

She hesitated before climbing inside. "Karen, I know you're in a hurry to get to Seattle, and we have a lot to talk about," she said. "But could we go by the lake house first?"

She grimaced. "Oh, Amelia, like I said, I don't think you should go in there —"

"Please, Karen, I feel I need to do it for closure. On top of that, there are some things of mine in that house, and I don't want to have to come back here." She sighed. "I really don't think I could go in there on my own, or with anyone else for that matter. You're the only one. C'mon, it's just a five-minute drive. Can't we just do this, and get it over with?"

Karen stared at her for a moment, then she took a deep breath and nodded. "All right, Amelia. We'll swing by, if that's what you really want. Hurry up, get in."

She climbed into the passenger seat, and set their drinks in the cup holders.

Karen got behind the wheel, then handed her the carryout bag. Starting up the car, she backed out of the parking space. Karen paused before shifting gears, and turned toward her. "Are you sure you want to go?" she asked. "Honey, you should know, there are still bloodstains. And everything's covered with dusting powder for finger-prints. It's not going to be pleasant."

She nodded glumly. "I figured as much. But I still want to go, Karen. And I want you there with me. Like I said, I need to have closure."

"Okay," Karen murmured.

Then she pulled onto the dark, winding road toward the beach house.

The big monster of a door wouldn't budge.

Amelia had tugged and tugged at the handle, but it was no use. Someone must have jammed the lock on the outside.

Panic-stricken, she couldn't get a normal breath. And she was shivering in the cold, windowless little room. Amelia kept the itchy blanket wrapped around her. Under that, she still had on her T-shirt and flannel pajama bottoms from last night. Her bare feet were freezing and filthy from walking on the dirty concrete floor.

She'd already searched every inch of the

place, looking for a wrench, a crowbar, or *anything* to pry the door open. At the same time, she realized it would probably take a jackhammer to penetrate the damn thing.

During her search, she uncovered a watercolor she'd painted of the lake house back when she was ten. It was pretty godawful. No wonder the thing had ended up in the fallout shelter behind some boxes. Her parents had framed it, but the glass in the frame was now cracked. Amelia slipped the watercolor out of the frame, and saw a sheet of black cardboard backing it. With that behind the glass, it was almost like a mirror — a cracked mirror.

Amelia looked at her reflection, and the close-shorn haircut someone had given her while she'd slept. She could see the skin irritation around her nose and mouth.

"Why is this happening?" she whispered, tears welling in her eyes. "Who's doing this to me?"

Whoever it was, they were probably coming back for her. They'd left her food, a light, and a blanket. They wouldn't have done that if they weren't coming back. They wouldn't have left her anything if they expected her to die in this gloomy little crypt.

Her hands shaking, Amelia slipped a piece

of broken glass out of the frame. It was about eight inches long, and very sharp along the edge. If someone did come down here, she would be ready for them.

For some reason, she thought of Karen Carlisle. The last thing Amelia remembered was falling asleep in Karen's spare bedroom, while Karen sat in that rocker in the corner. Had Karen decided that she was so dangerous she had to be locked up? Had Karen shorn her hair like a convict and then stuck her in this makeshift little prison?

Amelia couldn't think of any other explanation. Maybe that was why she had this sudden, inexplicable contempt for her therapist and friend. She was as close to Karen as she'd been to the family she'd just lost. Amelia remembered having had this same loathing for her brother, Collin, before his *accident,* and for her parents and Aunt Ina the night they'd died in this house.

All she could think about was slitting Karen's throat.

Wrapped up in the blanket, she sat down on the edge of the cot and stared at the jagged piece of glass. She told herself that she could never hurt Karen. Amelia started to cry.

But she didn't let go of the glass.

She stared at Karen and shook her head. "How could I feel things from this twin I didn't even know I had?" she asked. "How could I have forgotten all about her?"

Karen took her eyes off the road for a second. "Well, you have to consider, you were four years old when you last saw her." She searched for the little inlet off Holden Trail, but she couldn't see much beyond the headlight beams in front of her. It was a treacherous drive at night with no guardrail along the side of the road, nothing to stop the car from tumbling downhill if she overshot her lane.

They were both silent for a moment. The windshield wipers squeaked, and rain tapped on the roof. Karen wasn't sure what to tell her. There was so much to explain. She'd decided Amelia didn't need to know about her father just yet. That could wait. But she had to understand what was happening now. It was very likely they'd need her to talk to her twin sister, and reason with her.

"A lot of bad things happened to you, Amelia," she went on. "I think you made yourself forget most of it. That's how you were able to survive. But your twin didn't forget you. She still has you on her frequency. I think she's had a very hard life, too. You must have experienced some of it secondhand with those phantom pains and the nightmares."

"So you're saying this twin sister killed my parents, and Aunt Ina and Collin?" she asked, incredulous. "And I was on her *frequency?*"

Karen nodded. "Yes, I'm sorry, Amelia. But I think you were picking up those violent sensations and images from her. That's why you blamed yourself for everything she was doing."

She shook her head. "I'm still blown away. Why is she doing this?"

Karen sighed. "I don't know for sure. Obviously, she has a grudge against you or something. Maybe she resents that you've ended up having a better life."

"Or maybe she feels I abandoned her."

"Well, whatever her reasons are, Amelia, you need to remember it's not your fault."

"So her name's Annabelle," she murmured. "My God, all this time I thought I had a split personality or something."

"No, you've just been picking up on the things she was doing. You didn't know it, but you have a window into her world." Karen saw a turnaround on the left. "Isn't this it?" she asked.

"Um, yeah," she said distractedly.

Karen pulled into a small alcove, but she didn't switch off the ignition. "Listen, before we go down there, I need to ask you again, Amelia. Are you picking up any kind of *feeling* that something's wrong at your Uncle George's house? Do you sense that George, your cousins, or Jessie are in any kind of trouble?"

She looked back at Karen and shook her head. "Why do you keep asking that? *Are* they in trouble?"

"Your Uncle George is worried, and so am I." Karen glanced at her wristwatch. George would be landing in Seattle within a half hour.

She turned off the ignition. "Listen, Amelia, on our way back, I want to stop by Danny's again and phone your uncle. Then I might have you call his house. If Annabelle is there, we'll need you to talk to her."

She let out a stunned little laugh. "Karen, I don't understand any of this. Are you saying my sister's at Uncle George's house?"

Karen nodded. "We think it's possible. Are you sure you're not sensing something? You've always known ahead of time what your sister's planning. You're not feeling anything?"

She shook her head. "Nothing about Jody or Steffie. Right now, I just feel this very strong need to go to the lake house. Please, Karen." She opened the car door. "Don't worry about the trail at night. Just hold on to my hand. I know it by heart by now."

Karen got out of the car and paused at the top of the trail. In the darkness, she could barely see the path through the trees and shrubs. But she was thinking about something else that didn't seem right. She'd figured Amelia would have been far more concerned right now about the safety of her only surviving family members. Instead, she was bent on visiting the lake house one more time for *closure.* Karen was waiting for George's plane to land before calling and consulting him on their next move. But Amelia didn't know any of that. It didn't make sense that a final trip to the lake house was such a priority.

There had been a moment back at the diner, when she hadn't recognized the waitress. A tiny alarm had gone off in Karen's gut, then.

She thought about all the other people Annabelle must have duped before killing them. Did the Faradays, George's wife, or Shane ever realize before their violent deaths that they were staring at Amelia's twin?

"C'mon, Karen." She smiled and held out her hand. "I'll lead the way."

Karen hesitated, but then grabbed her hand. Engulfed in darkness, she started to follow her down the trail. She took cautious little steps in the direction she was being pulled. Around her, she heard raindrops pattering on leaves, and branches rustling in the gentle wind.

She thought about her dad's old revolver in her purse. "Amelia, remember what we were talking about in your last session?" she said, hating the nervous little wiggle that crept into her voice. She cleared her throat. "Um, you were telling me how you really resented Shane sometimes, and for no apparent reason. Remember that?"

She paused. "No, Karen, I don't. I don't recall saying anything like that."

In the dark, Karen couldn't see her face, or her expression. Did *Annabelle* know she was being tested again? Or was this *Amelia,* quite understandably, not remembering a conversation that had never happened?

"Actually, it's weird you should mention Shane, right after you asked about those premonitions," she went on. "I can't help thinking something might have happened to him. And I — I feel I've caused it somehow. What do you make of that? Do you suppose I just feel guilty, because I borrowed his car without asking him?" She started moving again, pulling Karen's hand. "Anyway, I'm worried about him, Karen. He's not answering his cell, and he hasn't returned any of my calls."

Karen could hear the vulnerability in her voice, and it sounded so much like Amelia. She wondered how she was going to tell her that Shane was dead. There was so much Amelia still didn't know.

Karen continued down the slope with her, blindly following her lead. She could only make out shapes in the murky blackness around her, and every step seemed precarious. She had to put all her trust in her guide.

"Careful, Karen," she heard her say. Her grip tightened. "It's a little slippery here. And there's a big ditch on your right."

Karen felt the wet ground and gravel under her shoes. She told herself: If this is Annabelle, she could have so easily killed you by now.

"We're almost there, Karen. Thank you for doing this." She steered her around a curve in the trail. "So, about Shane, do you think he's okay? You don't suppose this — *Annabelle* — has gotten to him, do you?"

"I — I can't say for sure," Karen replied, feeling horrible. She couldn't tell her the truth right now. It was too much.

"There's a railing and some flagstones coming up, and then we're out of the woods."

With her foot, Karen tapped around the dirt and gravel until she felt the flat flagstones beneath her. She held on to the wooden railing with her free hand. She could now see Amelia's silhouette and, in front of them, a clearing, and the Faradays' lake house.

They started up the stone pathway to the house.

The terrain had flattened out, but she still held onto Karen's hand. "Y'know, when we go back to Danny's Diner, I'm calling Shane again." Her voice had a little tremor to it. "And then let's try to track down this twin sister I didn't know I had. We need to stop her before she hurts someone else."

"We will, Amelia," Karen said.

"My God, look at this," she muttered, stopping to stare at the front door. The strips of yellow police tape fluttered in the wind.

"Are you sure you want to go in?" Karen asked gently.

"Yes, it's something I've got to do," she

said. Letting go of Karen's hand, she stepped toward the door. "We keep a key hidden up here."

Karen watched her reach up and pat along the top of the doorway frame. The sleeve of her oversized rain jacket slipped down her bare arm. Karen saw an ugly scar on the back of her wrist. She stifled a gasp.

Amelia had remembered the pain. But Annabelle still carried the scar.

"Here it is," she announced, the key in her hand. "I was afraid the police might have found it and taken it." She brushed aside some of the loose yellow tape, and put the key in the lock. "My, God, it's not even locked. . . ."

Karen couldn't move. She just stared at her, and tried to get a breath.

Annabelle opened the door, then turned toward Karen. "Do you want to lead the way this time?"

Karen shook her head. She waited until Annabelle stepped inside the house, then she reached inside her purse for the revolver. She came to the doorway, and saw the 19-year-old standing in the middle of the living room.

"Oh, my God, Karen, look at the blood," she cried. Annabelle was a very good actress. She recoiled, then opened her bag and frantically dug into it. "God, I think I'm going to be sick."

Karen already had the revolver out — and pointed at her. "Stop it, Annabelle," she said.

But Annabelle pulled something out of her purse.

"Hold it right there!" Karen yelled.

Annabelle froze. Karen still couldn't see what was in her hand.

For a moment, there was dead silence, and then a faint murmuring sound. It came from the basement, and yet seemed so far away, too. "Karen? Is someone there? Karen! Help me!"

Karen recognized Amelia's voice.

She didn't see the blackjack in Annabelle's hand, the same deadly little leather-covered club her father had used on Tracy Atkinson and several others when he'd knocked them unconscious.

All at once, Annabelle swiveled around.

Karen didn't even realize what was happening. She was still thinking about Amelia, downstairs somewhere. She saw Annabelle swinging her arm toward her. Then she felt the awful pain on the side of her head. She didn't even have time to raise the gun.

Karen crumpled onto the floor just inches away from the bloodstains left by Ina McMillan.

"Hi, you've reached the McMillans," Ina said on the recording. "Sorry we're not here to take your call. But if you'd like to leave a message for George, Ina, Jody, or Stephanie, just talk to us after the beep!"

The beep sounded, and then George's voice came over the answering machine. "Jessie?" he said anxiously. There was a lot of noise in the background — car horns honking, a whistle blowing, and people talking. "Is anyone there? Hello . . ."

"Let's keep Daddy in the dark a little longer," said the young man in the sunglasses. "It just means he'll be all that more anxious to get here."

Jessie didn't say anything. She stared at him with dread. She couldn't feel her arms anymore, and it was hard to get a normal breath. But she was more worried about the children. She hadn't heard a peep from Stephanie's room in almost an hour. Jody had let out a few muffled coughs about ten minutes ago, but not another sound. She wondered if they could hear their father's voice right now.

"I can't figure out why you're not picking up," George said on the machine. "I'm thinking maybe Steffie had another asthma attack, and you had to go to the hospital. Um, Jessie or Jody, if you get this, call me on my cell as soon as you can. Let me know what's happening. It's 9:15, and I'm at the airport. The line for taxicabs is nuts. I'll try to get there soon. It might take another half hour. Jessie, thanks for waiting around. I know you need to fly out to Denver tonight. You might need some money. I don't think you know about the safe in the house, but I certainly have more than enough in there to pay for your ticket. When I get home, I'll make sure you're covered. . . ."

The young man chuckled. "Jackpot," he whispered. He snatched the cordless from the counter. "Make him tell you where this safe is, and then get the combination." He reached for the kitchen phone.

"I think this machine's about to cut me off," George was saying. "See you soon — I hope." He clicked off, and the recording beep sounded.

"Shit," the young man muttered. He put down the cordless, and hung up the kitchen phone. "Well, we'll have to call Daddy back in a little while." He smirked at Jessie. "So, it sounds like you don't know anything about this safe, huh?"

Wide-eyed, she just shook her head at him.

George clicked off his cell phone. He nodded to the eleven-year-old. "Thanks, Brad," he said, over all the noise from the cop show on TV. "You can turn that down now."

He stood in the Reeces' family room, an open area with a vaulted ceiling right off the kitchen and breakfast nook. He looked out the sliding glass door at the Reeces' back lawn. Amid the trees and tall hedges at the far end of the yard was a little pathway Brad and Jody used to go back and forth to each other's houses. George couldn't see his house from here. The bushes were too tall.

Jody's best friend since first grade, Brad was a slightly beefy red-haired boy with thick glasses. He wore jeans and a T-shirt advertising *My Name Is Earl,* his and Jody's favorite TV show. He had the tough, surly look of a wrestler, but he was very sweet. Lucky, too, it turned out.

George's helicopter pilot had radioed ahead for a taxi, and a cab had been waiting for him when they'd touched down at Boeing Field. George had tried to phone his neighbor across the street, Sally Bidwell. He'd thought about using her house as a

sort of command post and holding area —
a safe haven for the kids and Jessie, if he
could get them out of the house. But Mrs.
Bidwell hadn't picked up her phone. So
George had tried the Reeces, and gotten
Brad. His parents had gone out for the
night, and he was home alone. In fact, he'd
tried calling Jody earlier in the evening to
invite him over for pizza, but no one had
picked up. He'd thought about cutting
through the backyards, knocking on the Mc-
Millans' back door, and inviting Jody in
person. But at the very last minute, he'd
decided against it. Lucky.

Jody's friend had certainly come through
in a pinch, too. Brad had already scurried
around the house and come up with everything George had figured he might need: a
crowbar, a screwdriver, and a sharp
serrated-edge kitchen knife. The items were
laid out on the Reeces' breakfast table.

George put his cell phone back in the
pocket of his sports jacket.

Brad aimed the remote control at the TV
and hit mute. "Do you think you ought to
put some of that black stuff on your face,
too, Mr. M?" he asked.

"That's not a bad idea, Brad," he said.
"But I think I'm okay without it."

He glanced over at the mute TV. George

wasn't sure if, over the phone, the cop show had sounded like an airport taxi stand. He wasn't even sure if his message had gotten through to anyone. He could only hope it had. He hoped his fabrication about a safe full of money in the house would keep whoever was there preoccupied. They'd wait for him now. He'd made it clear that no one else had the combination. And they'd need to keep his children alive if they wanted his cooperation. It might even prompt them to have Jessie phone him back.

He knew Annabelle Schlessinger — or her friend — hadn't broken into his home for money. But he also knew that a 19-year-old on the lam wasn't about to pass up the chance for a safeload of cash.

If they thought he was still at the airport, they wouldn't be expecting him within the next five minutes.

His hand shaking, George slid open the glass door.

"You sure you don't want me to come with?" Brad asked anxiously.

"No, thanks, I really need you here," George said. His stomach was full of knots as he collected the crowbar, screwdriver, and knife from the kitchen table. He slipped the knife and screwdriver into the side pocket of his sports jacket. "If I can get

Jody, Steffie, and Jessie out of there, I'll send them over to you, Brad. Then you can call the cops." He'd already told Brad this, but it merited repeating. "And if in twenty minutes, you don't see any of us —"

"Then I call the cops, and get them to haul ass over to your place — 9203 Larkdale," Brad interjected.

George nodded, then he mussed Brad's red hair. "You know, Jody's very lucky to have you for a friend," he said. "You and he will be talking about this night for a long time."

He stepped outside.

"Good luck, Mr. M," Brad whispered, standing in the doorway.

George gave him a nod, then ran to the hedges bordering the Reeces' backyard. Weaving through the bushes and trees, he saw the back of his house. It had been nearly twenty hours since he'd left home to catch a flight to Portland and drive to Salem. Now, that seemed like days ago. He was beyond tired, running on his wits and pure adrenaline. And he still couldn't stop shaking.

He noticed lights were on in the kitchen and living room and master bedroom. The kids' rooms were dark. George couldn't see anyone, or anything else. From the edge of the yard, he crept up toward the house, to Jody's bedroom window. But it was too high to see inside.

Grabbing a plastic patio chair, George pushed it against the side of the house, then he stepped onto the seat. It was a little wobbly, and he clung to the window ledge as he peered into the bedroom. He saw his son in the darkness, curled up on the bed, hogtied with his hands and feet behind him. Duct tape covered his mouth. His eyes were closed. George was overwhelmed with rage and frustration. But at least Jody was breathing.

Two windows down, he looked in on Stephanie, tied up on her bed in the same fashion, like a little animal. She was trembling. He could see the tears on her cheeks. The piece of duct tape over her mouth seemed too big for her little face.

He kept telling himself, *at least they're alive.*

Their backyard sloped a bit, and the kitchen was closer to ground level. George didn't need the patio chair to look inside the window. He heard the TV going, a small portable they kept at the end of the kitchen counter. Suddenly, someone walked right past the window, and George quickly ducked down. He waited a moment, then straightened up and peeked over the window ledge.

The intruder in his kitchen was a young man with pale skin and very black hair. He wore sunglasses and a black suit. He'd probably seen *Reservoir Dogs* one too many times. He looked like a cocky son of a bitch. He turned down the TV and said something to Jessie.

George could see her, tied to a kitchen chair. At least she didn't have any tape over her mouth.

The creep in the sunglasses grabbed the cordless phone from the kitchen counter. It looked like there was a gun on the counter, too, but George wasn't sure. Beyond the kitchen, he had a glimpse into the living room, where someone was sprawled face-down on the blood-soaked sofa. It looked like his neighbor, Mrs. Bidwell.

"Oh, my God," George murmured, horrified.

The young man picked up the receiver from the kitchen wall phone, and started dialing. He held the phone to Jessie's face, and then he switched on the cordless from the study so he could listen in.

All at once, George's cell phone went off.

"Shit!" he muttered, ducking down again. He quickly dug the cell phone out of his jacket pocket and switched it off. Crouched down against the house, he gazed at a patch of lawn illuminated by the light pouring out the kitchen window. He watched a shadow looming in that silhouette. He knew the young man was standing at the window directly above him, looking out. For a few seconds, George didn't move. Finally, the shadow moved away. "Couldn't have been anything," he heard the young man say. "You sure you don't know where this safe is? I've just about turned the master bedroom upside down."

George dared to peek over the window ledge again. Jessie was shaking her head. "You heard him on the phone earlier. I don't know a thing about it."

"It's screwy he's not answering his cell," the guy muttered. Then he said something else, but he moved too far away from the window for George to hear.

George glanced at the patio chair that he'd left beneath Stephanie's bedroom window. He decided to try getting Jody out first. Jody would be faster, and less panicked than Steffie.

Crouched against the house, George caught his breath. He'd expected to see someone looking exactly like Amelia in there. But it appeared as if the man in the sunglasses was running the show by himself.

George wondered where Annabelle Schlessinger was.

Her head throbbing, Karen regained consciousness. She lay facedown on the dirty living room floor of the Faradays' beach house. Her hands were tied behind her with some kind of cord. She could still hear Amelia's muffled cries for help coming from the basement. But she didn't hear the rain anymore. Karen wondered how much time had gone by.

A shadow passed over her, and she squinted up at Annabelle. Karen almost didn't recognize her. Her hair was cut in a short shag style. She'd also changed into a black sweater and jeans. In her hand she held the revolver that had belonged to Karen's father.

Karen realized she must have been unconscious for at least a half hour. Annabelle couldn't have cut her hair and changed clothes in much less time than that. Thirty minutes. George was already at his house by now.

"Is Blade here?" Karen asked warily.

A tiny smile flickered across Annabelle's face. "You know about Blade? Well, I'm impressed." She shook her head. "No,

Blade's in Seattle, running an errand for me. In fact, I'm pretty sure he's finished and on his way here now."

Karen was thinking of George, Jessie, and the children. They could already be dead right now. Tears welled up in her eyes. Then she heard Amelia's muted cries again.

"Where have you got her?" she asked. "In the basement? Do they — do they have a storage room down there?"

"They have a fallout shelter," Annabelle replied, still standing over her.

Karen shuddered. George had told her about his discovery in the fallout shelter at the Schlessinger ranch. "I'd have thought you wouldn't want to be anything like your father," Karen muttered, her face still against the carpet. "And here you are, Annabelle, following in his footsteps."

"Not exactly," she replied. "I have no intention of killing Amelia. I don't want that at all. But my sister will learn what it's like to be abandoned and totally alone. She has that coming to her."

Karen suddenly felt Annabelle's foot on her neck. Some dirt from Annabelle's shoe trickled into her ear. Annabelle started to apply a bit of pressure on her neck and the side of her face. "In just a little while, Amelia will have no friends or family left," she said. "You see, Blade's been at *Uncle George's* house. So Amelia's uncle, her little cousins, and your maid too, I'm afraid, they're all — poof, gone. You're going to be on the casualty list, too, Karen, very soon. Then Amelia will have no one, except me — the sister she forgot she had. But you know something, Karen? I'll forgive her for deserting me. I'll stick by her, the way she should have stuck by me."

"For God's sake, how could Amelia have *stuck by* you?" Karen countered. She felt even more weight pressing against her neck. "Your parents gave her up. They sent her away."

"Yes, but she didn't have to fucking *forget* me," Annabelle shot back.

Karen felt more weight pressing against her neck. She could hardly breathe.

"We could have still been there for each other," Annabelle said. "We were for a little while, after they put her in foster care. I could still sense what she was going through, and I knew she picked up on my feelings, too. We might not have talked, or seen each other. But we still *shared.* I didn't feel so alone — until her life got better. Then she turned her back on me, Karen. It was like screaming in one end of a phone, with no one listening. I knew she was there, but she cut me out of her life. All I could offer Amelia was pain, so she decided to forget about me."

"What would you have done if you were her?" Karen asked, barely able to get the words out. "Can you really blame her?"

To her amazement, the pressure on the side of her neck and face eased up. Annabelle stepped back. "Go ahead, I'm listening," she said.

Karen swallowed hard and caught her breath. "Amelia was four years old at the time," she said. "She didn't make a conscious decision to forget you, Annabelle. She was just trying to survive. Didn't you do some pretty awful things to survive, yourself?"

Annabelle stared down at her for a moment. "Well, thank you, Karen," she said finally, with a trace of condescension. "Knowing that makes it easier for me to forgive Amelia. After tonight, the police will be looking for her. Me, too, I guess, since I have her face. I've already cut her hair." She patted her own new, short hairstyle. "Like it? I bought us some coloring, too, Auburn Sunset, it's called. Blade got Amelia and me fake ID's, too. I posed for both of us in a wig. Blade thinks he's running away with us, but I'm leaving him behind. It's going to be just Amelia and me, the way it always should have been." She let out a sigh. "You know, my parents used to tell people they'd sent Amelia to live with relatives in Winnipeg. Isn't that funny? Because I think Amelia and I will end up in Canada someplace."

Karen rolled over on her side, and stared up at her. "Your plan is flawed, Annabelle," she said carefully. "You know that, don't you? Amelia will never get over this . . . *genocide* of her adopted family and friends. She won't forgive you for it. She'll never understand."

"That's why I need you to talk to her for me, Karen. You'll make her understand."

Annabelle grabbed her arm, almost breaking it as she pulled her up to a standing position. Karen tried to keep from stumbling. She was dizzy, and her head ached.

"One last counseling session," Annabelle said. "You've done family counseling before, I'm sure. It's all about understanding, forgiveness, and moving on."

Pressing the gun to Karen's back, Annabelle prodded her into the kitchen, and then to the basement door.

With the screwdriver, George pried off the bedroom window screen. He stepped down from the patio seat, and carefully set the screen against the house. Then he grabbed the crowbar, and boosted himself back up again. The window wasn't locked, but he still had to prod the crowbar along the sill to get the damn thing to move. It resisted, making a loud creaking sound.

Jody suddenly squirmed on the bed and rolled over on his side. His eyes lit up when he saw his father. But George couldn't help worrying. That little bit of noise could have given him away. Any minute now, he expected Annabelle's friend to appear in Jody's doorway with a gun in his hand. He'd just seen what that lowlife had done to Mrs. Bidwell.

His heart racing, George worked quickly. He pulled the window open, stopping only for a moment as it squeaked again. The patio chair beneath him moved, and he almost lost his balance. Grabbing hold of the ledge, George pulled himself up. He climbed through the opening, then into Jody's bedroom. He could hear the TV more clearly now. And he could hear Jessie, too.

"Would it kill you to go in there and take the tape off their mouths for just a few minutes?" she was saying. "Lord, it's been over two hours. . . ."

"Get off my fucking back," the man retorted. "Want to join your friend over there on the couch? Now, you need to give their daddy another call, and find out where this safe is . . ."

George crept to Jody's bed. He leaned over and whispered in his ear. "Don't make a sound, okay?" He carefully peeled the tape off his son's mouth. Jody gasped, then took several deep breaths.

Taking the kitchen knife, George cut at the tape around his wrists and ankles. With his shaky hands, he was so afraid he might nick him, but he didn't. Once free, Jody threw his arms around him. George could feel that he'd sweated through his shirt.

He whispered in Jody's ear again. "I want you to jump out the window and run to Brad's house. He's waiting for you."

Jody shook his head. "I'm not leaving you guys. . . ." He climbed off the bed. But his legs must have fallen asleep, because they suddenly buckled underneath him. George caught him before he tripped, and then he helped his son to the window. "I'll be okay, Dad," Jody whispered. But he still leaned on him. "Don't ask me to run out on you guys. I want to help. . . ."

George hesitated. "All right, you wait outside here. I'll lower Steffie down to you in a few minutes. Then take her to Brad's. I'll get Jessie out, and we'll meet you there. Understand?"

Jody nodded. "I love you, Dad."

Giving him a kiss on the forehead, George helped him out the window, and then down to the patio chair. From there, Jody hopped to the ground. But his legs gave out on him again, and he stumbled, like a paratrooper landing. Jody seemed to roll with it. He quickly pulled himself up and nodded at his father again.

Moving to the bedroom door, George peeked toward the kitchen. The young man stood in front of Jessie, holding both phones again, one to his own ear, one to Jessie's. "George, this is Jessie," she was saying into the kitchen extension. "Are you there? Pick up . . ."

George darted down the hall to Stephanie's room. He saw that she'd wet herself, and it incensed him. He just wanted to kill that smug bastard for doing this to his children. He took a few breaths, then moved toward Steffie's bed. She seemed to be sleeping.

As George started to bend over her, Stephanie suddenly gaped up at him and tried to cry out. "Quiet, sweetie," he whispered in her ear. "Please, hush. I'm going to cut you loose and take you into Jody's room. But you mustn't make a sound."

George paused for a moment. Jessie had stopped talking. He heard footsteps. The young man was coming toward the children's bedrooms.

Creeping back to Stephanie's door, George stood with his back to the wall. He had the knife ready.

It sounded like the man had stepped into Jody's room, but George wasn't sure. He glanced over at Stephanie and put his finger over his lips.

Wide-eyed, she stared at him and suddenly became very still. Then a shadow swept over her. She knew enough to look away from her father — and at the man standing in her doorway.

George remained perfectly still.

The shadow moved away, and the footsteps retreated. The young man was headed toward the living room now. George heard a click, like a door opening or closing.

He hurried back to Stephanie. He gingerly cut the tape around her little wrists and ankles, and then lifted her off the bed. It seemed cruel, but he kept the tape over her mouth for now. He couldn't risk her crying out again as he smuggled her into Jody's room. Carrying her out to the hallway, he stroked her hair.

He didn't hear anyone talking in the kitchen. Peering around the corner, he saw only Jessie. Tied to the kitchen chair, she struggled with the tape binding her wrists in back of her, but to no avail. George wondered where the hell the man with the sunglasses had gone.

Ducking into Jody's room, he carried Steffie to the window. He looked outside, and his heart sank. Jody wasn't there.

Whimpering, Stephanie clung to him. He couldn't drop her out the window. It was too high for her, and she was terrified.

Suddenly, the kitchen door slammed.

George swiveled around. He skulked back to Jody's bedroom doorway and glanced toward the kitchen again. For a moment, he couldn't breathe. It was as if someone had just punched him in the gut.

He saw the young man holding Jody up by his back collar. Blood trickled from a gash on the corner of Jody's forehead. He seemed dazed, barely able to stand. The young man pressed a gun to his ear.

George was paralyzed.

Even with those dark glasses on, it was obvious the man was staring right at him. "Hi, Daddy," he said. "Look who was trying to run away. I think I heard his skull crack when I hit the little bastard." He smirked. "So, do I get a reward for finding him?"

A flat-edged shovel was wedged under the handle of the fallout shelter door.

That big, heavy door muffled Amelia's voice. "Who's out there? Karen? Please, somebody . . ."

With her hands tied behind her, Karen stood in the Faradays' cold, clammy cellar. Among the clutter, there was a washer and dryer pushed against the wall, a bicycle, and some boating equipment. Karen noticed a drain in the middle of the concrete floor, and cobwebs on the exposed pipes running along the low ceiling.

Annabelle kicked the shovel aside, and it hit the floor with a loud clang. On the other side of the door, Amelia suddenly fell silent.

Karen felt woozy from the blow to her head earlier, but she fought the nausea and dizziness. She furtively pulled at the cord around her wrists while Annabelle was busy with the door. The hinges groaned as she opened it.

Amelia stood by a cot in the grimy little room. Her hair had been cut in a short shag style identical to her sister's. Despite the blanket wrapped around her, she was trembling. She wore the same T-shirt and flannel pajama bottoms she'd had on last night. In her hand, she held a jagged piece of glass. Dumbstruck, she stared at Annabelle.

For a moment, neither one said a thing.

"Are you going to pretend you don't know me?" Annabelle asked finally.

Amelia slowly shook her head. Clearly, she couldn't comprehend what she was seeing. She didn't move.

Karen kept tugging at the cord around her wrists. The skin there started to chafe and burn.

"Tell her who I am, Karen!" Annabelle barked. She suddenly grabbed Karen's arm and jerked her forward.

"Amelia. . . . honey, this is your twin sister, Annabelle," she said carefully. "You haven't seen her since you were four, not since before the Faradays adopted you. Do you — do you recall telling me that you often talked into the mirror when you were a little girl? You —"

"You have to remember me," Annabelle cut in, her voice choked with emotion. "Just look at me, Amelia. I'm your sister, your *real* sister. Those others, they weren't your real family."

Amelia stared at her. "My God, *you* killed them, didn't you?" she whispered.

661

Annabelle let go of Karen's arm. "I did it to bring us closer together," she said. "You needed to feel what it's like to have absolutely no one. That's what happened to me after you left, after you forgot about me. You need to feel that *firsthand,* so we can be the same again."

Karen edged back from her again. She kept pulling at the binding around her wrists. She felt it loosening.

"You killed my parents," Amelia whispered, squinting at her twin, "and Collin and Aunt Ina. . . ." She still had the piece of glass in her shaky grasp, as if ready to strike. "I *felt* it when you killed them. I thought it was me. . . ."

"I'm closer to you than any of them ever were," Annabelle said. "And we can be sisters again, Amelia. We'll be there for each other. You really don't have a choice. There's no one left."

"My God," Amelia whispered, tears in her eyes. "You shot Shane, too. In a boat. I saw it. I thought it was a nightmare. Oh, Jesus, he's dead, isn't he?"

Annabelle nodded. "I had to. It makes us closer. My boyfriend will die tonight, too. It's one more thing we'll share. We don't need them if we have each other. Don't you see?"

Suddenly, she grabbed Karen again, and yanked her toward the fallout shelter doorway. Karen stumbled onto the dirty, concrete floor. Annabelle pulled her up by her hair.

"Stop that!" Amelia cried. "Stop hurting her!"

"Karen, make her understand!"

Trembling, she knelt in the doorway. She frantically tugged at the cord around her wrist. She could almost squeeze her hand past the knot. "Your sister wants you to start someplace new with her. She killed that police detective. The police think you did it. They'll probably blame you for my death, too. Annabelle's making it so you have no one else to turn to except her."

Annabelle rolled back her sleeve and pressed the revolver to Karen's head. "And I'll look after you, Amelia, I promise," she said. "I've forgiven you for turning your back on me. You'll forgive me, too. You'll have to. I'm the only family or friend you have left."

Tears streaming down her face, Amelia stared at her twin sister. "That mark on the back of your wrist," she murmured. "I felt it when that happened. Someone burned you. . . ."

"Our father put a lit cigar out on me. You

663

felt it, too?"

Amelia nodded.

"See?" Annabelle said, with a tiny smile. "We feel each other's pain."

Karen tried not to squirm as the cord scraped a layer of skin off her knuckles. Still, at last her hands were free. But she kept both hands clasped in back of her. The cord dangled off one wrist.

"Please, Annabelle, put the gun down," Amelia said, finally. "You don't have to do this. Let her go. Karen's my friend."

"I know she's your friend," Annabelle whispered, nodding. "That's exactly why she has to die."

"Wait. Look at me," Amelia said, imploring her. "Do you *really* feel what I'm feeling right now?"

Annabelle nodded.

"Okay," she said. Then she slashed the piece of glass across her own hand.

Annabelle let out a shriek. The gun flew out of her grasp.

It happened so fast, Karen wasn't sure if Annabelle had dropped the gun in a moment of panic or if she had actually felt the glass, too. Karen only knew that the revolver dropped on the floor right in front of her. She dove on it.

All at once, Annabelle was on top of her,

frantically clawing at her, struggling to retrieve the weapon. Karen fought back. She wouldn't let go of the revolver. With her elbow, she smacked Annabelle on the side of her head, but the young woman was relentless. She tugged at the revolver and scratched at Karen's hands. Suddenly the gun went off.

An earsplitting shot echoed in the tiny gray room.

Jody went limp and fell to the kitchen floor at the man's feet.

George quickly put Stephanie down and started toward his son.

"No way!" the man said in a loud voice, glaring at him from behind the dark glasses. He had his .45 trained on Jody's crumpled body. "First you show me the safe, then you can tend to the kiddies."

Crouching down, George carefully pried the duct tape from Stephanie's mouth. He watched her eyes tear up with the pain. Once he pulled the tape off, she gasped for air, and then started crying. She threw her arms around his neck. "Daddy, Daddy . . ." was all she could say.

The young man grabbed Jody by the collar, then dragged him across the kitchen floor as if he were a bag of laundry. Then he dumped him at Jessie's feet. George could see Jody was still breathing. But he was afraid his son might have a concussion.

"We need to get him to a doctor," Jessie said.

"Shut the fuck up!" the man snapped. He turned to George, and pointed the gun at him. "I want to see where this safe is," he said. "C'mon, show me, and bring the little brat with you."

"It's in the living room," George lied. He took one more look at Jody, still breathing, but not moving a muscle. The blood from the gash on his forehead had trickled down to his jaw.

"*Where* in the living room?" the man pressed. "I've been all over this dump."

"Around this corner," George said, shielding Stephanie's eyes from the sight of Mrs. Bidwell's corpse on the sofa. Steffie cried softly. Her whole body was trembling. George patted her on the back. "When I say *go,* run as fast as you can out the front door," he whispered. "When I say *go.* Okay, honey?"

She sniffed, then nodded her head.

"Good girl," George said under his breath.

"So where is it, man?"

George nodded to an antique oval mirror on the living room wall. It was 24 by 18 inches, with a very ornate, pounded-tin frame.

"The mirror?" the young man said. "Shit, I already looked behind there, asshole."

"Well, then you weren't looking very carefully," George replied.

"Show me."

George patted Steffie on the back again. "I need to put you down for a minute, sweetie," he said, setting her on her feet. "Be a good girl, and remember what I told you."

Stephanie clung to his leg.

Swallowing hard, George reached for the mirror on the wall. "The money's not in the wall, it's in the back of the mirror," he lied. He glanced back at the man with the sunglasses, and then lifted the mirror off the wall. It was lighter than it looked, only a few pounds. "There's about six thousand dollars back here, sort of an emergency fund. It's yours. Just take it and *go*. Do you hear me? Just *go!*"

All at once, Stephanie scurried toward the front door.

The young man turned his gun on her.

He didn't see that behind the mirror frame, there was nothing. He didn't see George swinging the mirror at him with all his might.

A shot rang out. The young man howled in pain as George hit him in the face with the mirror. There was an explosion of glass.

Squeezing his eyes shut, George turned his head away for a second.

When he opened his eyes again, Stephanie was gone, and the front door was open. The .45 lay on the carpet amid shards of reflective glass.

In a stupor, the young man stared at George. His sunglasses had been knocked off his face. His eyes were listless. Blood dripped from several little bits of broken mirrored glass embedded in his face. One large piece was stuck in his neck. In a daze, he pried it out. Blood gushed from the fatal wound, cascading down the front of his white shirt, tie, and the shiny black jacket.

He remained standing, looking stunned.

George heard the sirens from police cars coming up the street. He realized Jody's friend, Brad, must have called the police. The searchlights and beams from the red strobes poured through the windows. For a few seconds, the same light danced off the mirrored fragments in the young man's face.

Then he collapsed dead on the floor.

Through the sheer window curtains, George could see four police cars pulling in front of the house. One policeman ran across the yard and scooped up Stephanie.

George started toward the kitchen, and stopped dead.

His forehead still bleeding, Jody stood near the kitchen counter with a tired smile on his face. He staggered toward his father, and threw his arms around him.

Dazed, George embraced his son. He glanced over at Jessie, a bit unsteady on her feet, slowly making her way into the living room. George realized Jody must have untied her. He kissed the top of Jody's head. "God, you — you sure had me fooled," he murmured. "I thought you were practically dead."

"Me, too," Jody said, with a weak laugh.

"We still need to get you to a doctor," George said. With an arm around his son, George dug the cell phone out of his pocket. He checked for messages. There were two Jessie had left on the home phone and two more from that sheriff in Salem. No one else.

"Are you calling Karen?" Jessie asked.

He nodded. "It's been nearly two hours."

It rang and rang. No one picked up. It didn't even go to her voice mail.

Jessie gave him an apprehensive look. He just shook his head at her.

When he'd last talked to Karen, she'd

been on her way to meet Amelia at the restaurant near the lake house.

George stayed on the line. He didn't want to hang up just yet, not even as the three of them started toward the front door.

Jessie paused for a moment and looked down at something on the carpet amid the mirrored fragments. Frowning, she kicked it out of her way and then moved on.

The bent, broken sunglasses skittered across the floor.

CHAPTER
TWENTY-FIVE

Breathless, Karen ran along the water's edge.

Her head was still throbbing, and her lungs burned, but she pressed on toward Helene Sumner's house. She could see the lights on inside her cottage farther up the beach.

She'd left Annabelle Schlessinger in that grimy, little fallout shelter with a bullet in her stomach. Annabelle's black knit top had been soaked with blood by the time Amelia had staggered back down to the cellar with several dishtowels from the kitchen. They'd managed to move Annabelle to the cot, and pulled off her blood-sodden sweater. Karen had told her to lie still and keep the towels pressed against the wound.

But Annabelle wouldn't stop screaming and squirming. Her shrill cries echoed off the walls of the little gray chamber. Her legs were curled up toward her stomach as if some shifting in her organs had locked them there. Pale and trembling, she seemed very afraid. "Don't let me die in here!" she cried several times. She'd lost a lot of blood, and Karen noticed her breathing was shallow. She wasn't sure about her chances. At the same time, she couldn't help wondering if Annabelle was stronger than she let on. Was it an act to throw them off guard?

Karen remembered something Naomi Rankin had told her about Annabelle always being the weaker twin. Amelia was the stronger one.

The cut across the palm of Amelia's hand wasn't too deep. Karen wrapped a wet dishtowel around her hand to slow the bleeding. Amelia admitted the searing pain in her stomach — exactly where her sister had been shot — was far more severe.

She promised to look after her twin sister. "Helene Sumner's house is closer than Danny's Diner," she told Karen, catching her breath as they paused in the fallout shelter's doorway. "You're better off calling the paramedics from there."

Furtively, Karen tried to pass the revolver to her, but Amelia shook her head. "I won't need it," Amelia whispered. "She won't try anything."

"How can you be so sure?"

"Because," she said with a pale smile, "I can *feel* it, Karen."

"Just the same," Karen murmured. "I'll leave this upstairs on the kitchen counter. You haven't been through the living room yet, have you?"

Amelia shook her head. "No, why?"

"Don't go in there if you can help it," Karen said. "I'll explain later."

Coiled up on the bed, Annabelle let out another shriek. "Hurry, goddamn it! I'm bleeding to death!"

"Watch her like a hawk," Karen whispered, giving Amelia's shoulder a pat. She raced up the basement stairs. She left the revolver on the kitchen counter, and then ran out of the lake house.

That had been only five minutes ago, and yet it seemed like forever.

Helene's dog started barking as Karen banged on the front door of her cottage. "Ms. Sumner!" Karen cried. "Ms. Sumner, I need to use your phone! Please! It's an emergency!"

The old woman answered the door with a robe on and a rifle in her hand. It took her a moment before she seemed to recognize Karen from that afternoon. She held her collie by the collar while Karen, frazzled and out of breath, asked if she could use her phone to call the police. "There's been a shooting at the Faradays' cabin," she explained. "Somebody's hurt."

"My goodness," Helene murmured. She pulled her dog aside and cleared the doorway. "C'mon, Abby, move it. Come in, come in. I thought I heard a shot about fifteen minutes ago. The phone's right there in the kitchen. . . ."

Helene's kitchen had a huge old-fashioned stove, a blue Formica-top breakfast table with three mismatched chairs, and the only working telephone in about a mile. It was a yellow, wall-mounted phone with a dial instead of a touch-tone pad. Karen called the police on it.

The 911 operator said they'd be at the Faradays' house with the paramedics in fifteen minutes.

"Is it Amelia who was hurt?" Helene asked, once Karen hung up.

With a hand still on the receiver, Karen shook her head. "No, it's — a relative of Amelia's. Could I make another call? It's long distance, but I'll pay you back."

Helene nodded. "Go ahead."

Karen dialed George's cell phone number. She nervously tugged at the phone cord and counted the ring tones. On the fourth ring, he picked up: "Hello?"

"George, it's Karen," she said, the words rushing out. "Is everyone okay there?"

"Yes, yes, we're all fine," he said, sounding just as anxious as she was. "Thank God you called. I've been so worried. How are you? How's Amelia?"

Relieved, Karen just wanted to sink down in one of the chairs at Helene's breakfast table. But there was no time. She quickly explained to George what had happened. "I'm not sure if Annabelle's going to pull through," she said.

"Well, her boyfriend didn't make it," George remarked. "Just a second . . ."

Karen heard him talking with someone on the other end. Then he got back on the line. "We're here at the West Seattle police station," he said. "My house is a mess. We can't go back there tonight, and Jessie says all the hotels in town are booked. She thought you wouldn't mind putting up Jody, Steffie, and me for the night."

"Not at all," she said. "There's plenty of room. Please, make yourselves comfortable. Jessie has a key."

"Thanks. Think you and Amelia will make it home tonight?"

"It might be a few hours, yet," Karen said, still catching her breath. "We'll have a lot to explain to the police here."

"I'm probably in for the long haul myself," George said. "Salem's finest have quite a few questions for me. If I make it to your house before you and Amelia, I'll wait up for you."

"That would be really nice, George," she said with a little smile. "Listen, I should get back to Amelia and her sister."

"Please, be careful, Karen," he said.

"See you later — at my house."

She hung up, and then started to dig into her purse. "Thank you, Ms. Sumner. Do you think five dollars will cover it?"

Frowning, Helene shook her head. "Put your money away, for goodness sakes. Do you need any medical supplies? I have some bandages and hydrogen peroxide. . . ."

"I think we're okay," Karen replied, heading for the door.

"What exactly happened?" she asked. "Did I just hear you say something about Amelia's *sister?*"

"I'll explain it to you later, okay?" Karen said, still frazzled. She opened the door. "I really need to get back. Thank you again, Ms. Sumner."

But Karen stopped abruptly. In the distance, she heard a strange pop — like a firecracker going off. Helene's dog let out a yelp. The old woman put a hand over her heart. "My goodness, there it is again."

Karen gazed at her and blinked.

"That's the same sound as before," Helene explained.

"Oh, no," Karen whispered. She turned and started in the direction of the Faradays' house. At first, she just took a few cautious steps, but then she started moving faster.

"I wouldn't go back there!" Helene called. She held on to her dog's collar to keep her from chasing after Karen. "Miss, I wouldn't go there! That was a gunshot! Wait for the police!"

But Karen didn't stop. She didn't hear her. She was thinking about Amelia.

And she was running for her life.

Ten minutes before Frank Carlisle's old revolver was fired for a second time that night, Amelia had been standing in the doorway of the fallout shelter. She'd watched over her twin sister, curled up on the cot with a bloody dishtowel on her stomach. Shivering in just her bra and jeans, Annabelle looked so vulnerable. There were patches of blood smeared on her exposed pale, creamy skin. Her every breath seemed like a struggle. "I'm cold," she whispered, her teeth chattering.

"I know, I'm cold too," Amelia replied,

wincing as she clutched her own stomach. The cut on her hand was starting to sting, too. She wondered if her sister also felt it.

Amelia had bled all over that itchy old blanket when she'd slashed the palm of her own hand. She knew there were extra blankets up in the bedrooms. She'd told Karen earlier she didn't think Annabelle would try anything. But she wasn't so sure anymore. She noticed the large piece of glass still on the floor beside Annabelle's shoes. Amelia and Karen had removed her brown suede flats in an effort to make her more comfortable.

Amelia quickly retrieved the shard of glass. "I'll get you a clean blanket," she said, finally.

"Thanks," Annabelle whispered. It seemed like an effort as she lifted her head to look at her.

Amelia backed away from the fallout shelter, but then she hesitated. She had a bad feeling about leaving Annabelle unguarded. She didn't know if it was her own intuition or if she'd read her sister's thoughts. But suddenly she didn't trust her.

"I'm sorry," Amelia murmured, with one hand on the thick, heavy door. She pushed it shut.

"Amelia, no!" her sister cried, her voice

muffled.

Amelia set down the piece of glass. Then she grabbed a square-edged, short-handled shovel from the floor, and propped it under the door handle. "I'll be right back," she called to her sister. She had a déjà vu sense about this moment, about talking to someone locked in a bomb shelter. Amelia didn't remember ever experiencing this before — certainly not here in the basement of the lake house. She wondered if something similar had ever happened to Annabelle.

Ascending the basement stairs, she felt slightly winded and dizzy. Between the pain in her gut, the slash across her hand, and everything else, it was a wonder she hadn't fainted yet. In the kitchen, Amelia went to the sink, and slurped some cold water from the faucet. She splashed her face, and felt a little better. Then she grabbed the revolver off the counter.

Annabelle's purse, a large leather satchel, sat on the kitchen table. Amelia peeked inside it to make sure her sister didn't keep a gun of her own in there.

Annabelle didn't have a revolver, but she had a blackjack and a hunting knife. Amelia glanced around the kitchen for a place to hide them. She finally stashed them in the refrigerator inside the crisper drawer. She dumped the purse's remaining contents onto the tabletop to make sure she hadn't missed anything. Amid the junk, she noticed Annabelle's wallet: her lipstick and compact; several loose bills, some twenties among them; chewing gum; and a beautiful black onyx ring.

It was Shane's ring. He'd loved it. That ring had belonged to his grandfather.

Amelia felt a pang in her gut, and she started to cry. Clutching the ring in her wounded hand, she wandered toward the living room. She'd forgotten Karen's warning not to go beyond the kitchen. She hadn't been prepared to see all the dried blood on the wall behind the rocking chair. Another large bloodstain marred the carpet. In both cases, she knew whose blood she was looking at, because she'd seen it happen through her sister's eyes. She'd seen Annabelle murder her mom and dad, and Ina, as well as Collin, and Shane.

Amelia tearfully gazed at Shane's ring again, then she kissed it and tucked it inside the pocket of her flannel pajama bottoms.

Now the only thing she held was the revolver.

Her sister knew about guns. But Amelia didn't. She'd never really fired a gun before.

She'd only experienced it secondhand.

Amelia forced herself to go halfway up the stairs, until she saw the bloodstains on the wall by where Annabelle had shot her mother. Almost in a trance, she walked back down the steps and out the front door.

She needed a practice shot. She didn't want to screw it up when she did it for real. Though barefoot, and dressed in only her pink T-shirt and flannel pajama bottoms, Amelia barely felt the cool night air whipping at her. She didn't even notice that the ground was wet and cold, and hundreds of stars were out tonight. All she thought about was showing Annabelle that she could kill, too. She picked out a target — a pine tree about thirty feet from the house. Aiming the revolver at a branch, she squeezed the trigger. On the branch, there was a small explosion of bark, wood, and pine needles. She felt a jolt in her hand, and the sound made her jump.

But she hadn't dropped the gun.

The shot still echoed across the lake.

She could do this, Amelia told herself. It was easy.

She turned around and headed back inside the house. She would tell Karen and the police that Annabelle had suddenly attacked her. They'd believe her, too. Amelia couldn't help smiling a tiny bit. She was already thinking like her sister.

With the gun in her hand, she passed through the living room, and then into the kitchen. Once again, she glanced over at Annabelle's purse and its contents strewn on the kitchen table. She wondered if she'd missed anything, perhaps some jewelry belonging to her mother or Ina.

All at once, she started to feel faint again. She couldn't get a decent breath, and she was deathly cold. The only thing keeping her going was her anger. Amelia tried to ignore the signals, the strange feeling that her sister was already slipping away.

She didn't notice anything familiar amid the debris from Annabelle's purse. She opened up the wallet, and saw some fake ID's and credit cards that were obviously not hers. Amelia didn't recognize any of the names on the cards.

She found a photograph in the wallet, creased and worn as if it had been carried around for a long, long time. It was a picture of two identical, dark-haired little girls in overalls, holding hands and smiling at the camera. The color was so faded, and the images nearly washed out. But Amelia remembered those overalls were a very pretty shade of green.

She remembered, and she started to cry again.

Karen ran as fast as she could.

Somewhere along the way, she'd stumbled over a tree root and hit the ground hard. She'd banged her knee, but dragged herself up and relentlessly pressed on toward the sound of that gunshot. Her throat had gone dry, and it hurt every time she tried to breathe. Still, she didn't slow down.

She kept hoping to hear the police sirens. But there was nothing except Helene's dog barking in the distance. She couldn't even see the Faradays' house yet.

Karen kept wondering who had fired the gun. At this point, it could have been either Amelia or Annabelle. And at this point, she was probably already too late.

All of a sudden, she stumbled again and hit the damp sand. It knocked the wind out of her. Pulling herself up once more, her hand brushed against a piece of weathered driftwood. It was almost the size of a baseball ball — with a few rounded-off knobs where branches had once been. Karen picked it up off the ground, and then caught her breath for a moment. She wondered if this piece of wood was anything like the plank Annabelle had used to bash in Collin Faraday's skull.

Clutching the makeshift club tightly in her fist, Karen hurried toward the Faradays' house. She could see it in the distance now. The lights were on in the living room and the front hall. As she came closer, Karen could see the open front door and the silhouette of someone sitting on the front step. "Amelia?" she called.

Shivering and pale, she'd thrown a blanket over her shoulders. Even closer, Karen recognized the flannel pajama bottoms. She noticed the bloodstained dishtowel wrapped around her hand.

But Karen abruptly stopped when she saw the revolver in her other hand. "Amelia, did you — did you fire the gun?"

Tears in her eyes, she nodded.

"Did Annabelle attack you?" Karen asked.

"No. I didn't fire it at anybody," she replied with a tremor in her voice. "Annabelle — she's dead. I left her alone for a few minutes, and when I went back down there, she was dead." She let out a little cry. "I never had a chance to talk with her — to understand. . . ."

Karen sat down beside her on the front stoop. She didn't know what to say. She just gently patted her back and let her cry.

Hearing a noise behind them, Karen

glanced over her shoulder. She didn't see anyone in the doorway, but she noticed some drops of blood on the floor. There was a trail leading out to the front stoop, and it wasn't old, dried blood, either. It was fresh.

Earlier, they'd managed to suppress the bleeding from the cut across Amelia's palm. Mystified, Karen glanced at the dishtowel around her hand. Then she glanced down toward the stoop at the small puddle of blood. Another drop hit the puddle. And it wasn't coming from Amelia's hand.

It wasn't coming from Amelia at all.

Karen gasped. She noticed that nearly all the color had drained from the 19-year-old's face, and sweat beaded on her forehead. But she was smirking. And she had the gun aimed at Karen. Even with a bullet in her gut, and sitting in a puddle of her own blood, Annabelle was still smiling.

At that moment, Karen figured she was as good as dead.

A shadow suddenly passed over them both. Karen glanced back in time to see Amelia in the doorway. Amelia raised the square-edged, short-handled shovel, and brought the flat end of it crashing down on her sister's head. It made a hollow ping as it cracked against her skull. Annabelle let out a cry, and the gun went off. A spray of dirt exploded from the ground near Karen's feet.

Annabelle lurched forward and toppled onto the ground. The revolver flew out of her grasp. Stunned, she rolled over on her back. The blanket fell aside, exposing the gaping wound in her stomach, and two blood-soaked dishtowels.

Amelia warily stood over Annabelle, as if her sister were a wounded rabid dog. She kept the shovel in her hands, ready to strike her again if necessary. She was shivering in just her oversized T-shirt and nothing else.

Karen gaped up at her. In the distance, she heard the police sirens.

"I left her alone for a few minutes," Amelia said, catching her breath. "I thought about killing her, and then suddenly, I started to remember everything. I felt sorry for her. So I went down there again, bringing her a blanket, and she clubbed me in the head with her shoe."

Sprawled out on the ground in front of them, Annabelle laughed. But then she started to cough, and blood sprayed out of her mouth. She coughed again, and more blood spewed out. Suddenly, she couldn't seem to get a breath. A look of panic swept over her ashen face. She seemed to be choking on her own blood.

Karen started to get to her feet. But

Amelia moved more quickly. She tossed aside the shovel, and hurried to her sister's side. She held Annabelle's head in her lap.

Annabelle reached up and touched Amelia's cheek. Her every gasp was a death rattle.

Amelia gently smoothed back her sister's hair. "It's okay, Annie," she whispered.

Karen watched, and didn't say a word as Annabelle Schlessinger struggled for her last few breaths. Amelia's twin listlessly stared up at the starry sky. Then her jaw slowly dropped and one last breath escaped from her mouth.

Amelia kept stroking her hair for another minute. "There now, Annie," she whispered. "There now. . . ."

The wail of the sirens became louder and louder. The headlights and red strobes illuminated the forest behind the lake house.

Amelia didn't have any tears in her eyes when she covered her twin sister's face with the blanket. She finally stood up, and then wandered over to Karen. She wrapped her arms around her and dropped her head on Karen's shoulder.

"I don't feel the pain anymore," she whispered.

Epilogue

Karen opened her eyes as the squad car turned down her street. To her amazement, there were no TV news vans or police cars parked in front of her house, no reporters or onlookers. All was quiet on her block at 6:40 that morning.

Both she and Amelia had nodded off intermittently in the back seat of the patrol car for the last forty-five minutes. This was their fourth ride in the back of a police car since leaving the Lake Wenatchee house so many hours ago.

It had been during that first trip — to the Wenatchee Police Station — that Karen told Amelia about her biological father and mother, and about something Amelia had wanted to know for a long, long time. The cops and the ambulance only used their sirens when other vehicles or pedestrians were around, but their red flashers remained on for the whole trip. "Back when we had our very first session, you mentioned some-thing to me," Karen said during one of those quiet periods. Amelia clutched her hand. The ambulance, carrying Amelia's dead twin was in front of them, and the red strobe illuminated the back of the police car. "You mentioned that when some of those other therapists tried to hypnotize you for information about your childhood, what you wanted most of all was to remember the name of that nice neighbor, the one with the playhouse."

Amelia nodded. "Yes, I still feel that way."

"His name was Clay Spalding," Karen said, smiling. "And he was a good man."

Two policemen from Moses Lake came to the downtown Wenatchee station at around midnight. Karen made certain to set the record straight with them about Clay. She knew Naomi Rankin had always held her head high at work and around town. She'd never been ashamed of her friendship with Clay. And now, people in town would understand why.

A doctor was called in to patch up both Amelia and Karen. Amelia didn't need stitches in her hand, but the doctor ban-daged it up. Karen received an ice pack for the bump forming on her head, where Annabelle had hit her with the blackjack.

They both got a dose of Tylenol, too.

Between the two of them, they drank about a gallon of bad coffee in the police station while answering scores of questions over and over again. The Wenatchee station was surrounded by reporters, TV news crews, and spectators. The precinct had become a hub of activity with e-mails, faxes and phone calls coming in and going out to Moses Lake, Salem, Seattle, and Issaquah.

There was a TV on in the officers' lounge. It was tuned to CNN. They'd made the national news. Karen and Amelia caught a brief clip of George being interviewed. He stood by the West Seattle Police Station's main entrance. He looked tired and haggard, but still handsome. Off-camera reporters held microphones in front of him. "No, I don't think I'm a hero or anything," he said, shaking his head. "My friend, Jessie Shriver, my son, Jody, and my daughter, Stephanie — they're the real heroes. And I want to thank Jody's friend Brad Reece for all his help. He was really there for us. And most of all," George went on, "I want to thank Karen Carlisle. She's a friend of my dear niece, Amelia Faraday. More than anyone, Karen helped save my family."

By dawn, Karen heard that Salem police and local FBI, working through the night at the old Schlessinger ranch, had so far excavated seven bodies from shallow graves on the property. They planned to continue digging through the day. They were also reexamining missing-person cases, all young women in the Salem and Moses Lake areas, as well as in Pasco, where Duane Lee Savitt lived until his death in 1993.

Exhausted, yet wired from so much coffee, Karen and Amelia were taken by helicopter to Issaquah. Once they landed, they had another trip in the back of a cop car to Cougar Mountain Wildland Park, where Karen pointed out for the police the path she'd used in her fruitless search for Detective Russ Koehler's body.

With Karen's assistance, and in the light of dawn, the local police had better luck than she'd had two nights before. They found Koehler's picked-over, half-buried corpse in less than an hour.

Karen suggested they check to determine if he'd been shot with the same gun used to kill Shane. She had no doubt that Annabelle had pulled the trigger each time.

Someone had tipped off the press about the Cougar Mountain Park expedition; so the place was swarmed with TV cameras and news vans by the time Karen and Amelia were whisked out of there.

That had been forty-five minutes ago, and Karen had expected more of the same as they approached her house.

"I shouldn't jinx it by saying this," she murmured, waking up from her nap in the back seat of the police car. "But I can't believe there aren't any reporters here."

"Well, the newspeople got to sleep sometime, I guess," replied the cop behind the wheel. "Enjoy the peace and quiet while you can."

Amelia was practically sleepwalking as they started up the front walkway together. Karen kept an arm around her, almost holding her up. Before they even reached the front stoop, Jessie opened the door and Rufus scurried out. Whining, he excitedly nudged Karen's leg with his snout over and over. She petted him and scratched him behind the ears. Amelia petted him, too. His tail wagging, Rufus seemed to lap it up. Only twenty-four hours before, he'd growled and bared his teeth at her twin. Somehow he knew the difference. He let out a happy yelp.

"Hush, Rufus!" Jessie whispered. She wore a blue sweat suit, part of the limited wardrobe she still kept at the house from the days when she'd looked after Karen's father. Considering what she'd been through the night before, Jessie looked surprisingly rested and fresh.

"Well, you two are a sight for these sore ones," she whispered, waving them in. Then she put her finger to her lips. "The kids are asleep in the second guest room. George got in at three this morning. He tried to wait up for you, but conked out on the living room sofa."

She gave Karen a long hug. "Oh, sweetie, thank God you're okay," she said, patting her back. "Did you girls get anything to eat?"

"Doughnuts," Karen murmured. "I think we need sleep more than anything."

"Your dad caught you on the Channel Five Sunrise News in the lounge at the rest home," Jessie said. "He phoned here just a few minutes ago. You might want to call him before you hit the sheets, let him know you're all right."

Jessie broke away and led Amelia inside the house. "Poor thing, you're asleep on your feet, just like a horse. I changed the sheets in the guest room for you. There's even a sound machine in there. You can sleep as long as you want. I'll try to keep the kids quiet."

From the doorway, Karen watched Jessie and Amelia go up the stairs. With a sigh, she sat down on the front stoop, and pulled her cell phone out of her purse. She had Sandpoint View Convalescent Home on her speed dial. When they answered at the front desk, Karen asked to be connected to the lounge. She recognized the voice of the nurse on duty there.

"Hi, Lugene, it's Karen," she said quietly. "Is my dad there in the TV room?"

"He sure is, Karen. We've been seeing you on the news. You'll have to give out autographs next time you're here. How are you doing? Are you okay?"

"Yeah, but I'm pooped."

"Well, I'll get Frank. I know he's eager to talk to you. By the way, it looks like it's one of his good days, Karen."

While Karen waited for her father to get on the line, Rufus wandered over and set his head on her knee.

"Is this my girl?" her father said on the other end. "My famous daughter?"

"Hi, Poppy," she replied, patting Rufus's head. "I understand you saw me on the news."

"Are you all right? Are you home yet?"

"I'm sitting on the front step right now with Rufus. I'm pretty tuckered out."

"Jessie said that good-looking fellow who was on the news is staying there with his kids. Sounds like you have a full house there. It's been a while since that's happened."

Karen smiled wistfully. "You're right, Poppy. It's been a long time."

"Must feel good," he said. "Well, I should skedaddle. I have to get dressed. I don't like going to breakfast in my bathrobe like some of these folks here. We're having blueberry pancakes this morning. They make very tasty blueberry pancakes here. Get some sleep now, honey. Okay?"

"Okay, Poppy. Have a good breakfast, and I'll see you soon."

"My angel," he said, before hanging up.

Karen waited until Rufus trotted inside, then she quietly closed and locked the front door after him. She heard the shower running upstairs, and knew it was Amelia. Though she felt grimy, Karen wasn't certain which she needed more, a bed or a bath.

Peeking into the darkened living room, she saw George curled up on her sofa. His shoes were off, and the sports coat he must have used to cover himself had slid down past his hip. Karen went to the hall closet and retrieved her dad's old robe, the one she still used to cover herself when napping on that same couch. She tiptoed into the living room and gently draped the robe over

George. With his slight beard-stubble and that sweet, peaceful expression, he looked so handsome while he slept.

Then his eyes opened, and he took hold of her hand. "I tried to wait up," he said with a sleepy smile. "Are you okay, Karen?"

Hovering over him, she nodded. "Fine, just tired."

He squinted at her. "Jody has a bump on his forehead in the exact same place as you do. Sure you're okay?" He squeezed her hand.

She nodded again.

"Jessie says you and I need to go out to dinner soon and discuss how much overtime we owe her for yesterday and today. I think we should, don't you?"

Karen smiled and nodded once more.

He brought her hand to his face, and then kissed it. "Thank you for my family, Karen."

"Karen?" Amelia called from the guest room.

She was just emerging from the bathroom. A waft of steam drifted out the doorway after her. Karen wore her terrycloth robe and had a towel wrapped around her head. She'd decided to shower before turning in, and was glad now that she had. It felt as if she'd washed away everything from the last twenty-four grueling hours.

Jessie had ducked into Karen's dad's bedroom for a catnap. She planned to go shopping in an hour so she could fix breakfast for everybody — bacon, eggs and waffles, the works.

Karen had thought she was the only one still awake in the house.

"Karen, is that you?" Amelia called softly.

The guest room door was ajar. Karen pushed it open and looked in on Amelia.

The shades were drawn, and the sound machine was on. Amelia sat up in bed, wearing one of Karen's T-shirts. Her dark hair was in tangles from her shower twenty minutes before.

"Can't you sleep?" Karen asked, padding into the room. She sat down on the edge of the bed.

"I was just lying here, thinking," Amelia whispered over the sounds of waves and seagulls. "It'll be nice to spend some time later today with Uncle George, and Jody and Steffie. Ever since Collin died, I haven't been able to really look them in the eyes. As much as I tried and you tried, I couldn't quite get over the feeling that I'd killed him. Now I know the truth. After so many months, it'll be good to look my uncle and cousins in the eyes again."

Karen reached over and smoothed back Amelia's tangled hair.

Amelia glanced at a black onyx ring on the night table. Beside it was a worn, faded photo of two identical, dark-haired little girls in overalls. They were smiling and holding hands in the picture.

Amelia sighed. "I realize now what Annabelle went through, and how much she must have suffered." She shrugged and shook her head. "But I — I can't cry for her. . . ."

Amelia wrapped her arms around Karen, then rested her head on her shoulder.

"It's okay," Karen said, holding her. She knew the tears would come later.

And she would be there to help her through it.

The employees of Thorndike Press hope you have enjoyed this Large Print book. All our Thorndike and Wheeler Large Print titles are designed for easy reading, and all our books are made to last. Other Thorndike Press Large Print books are available at your library, through selected bookstores, or directly from us.

For information about titles, please call:
(800) 223-1244

or visit our Web site at:
http://gale.cengage.com/thorndike

To share your comments, please write:
Publisher
Thorndike Press
295 Kennedy Memorial Drive
Waterville, ME 04901

IN THE PIT WITH PIPER

IN THE PIT WITH PIPER

"Rowdy" Roddy Piper

with Robert Picarello

BERKLEY BOULEVARD BOOKS, NEW YORK

A Berkley Boulevard Book
Published by The Berkley Publishing Group
A division of Penguin Putnam Inc.
375 Hudson Street
New York, New York 10014

This book is not authorized by or affiliated with the WWE. The WWF is now the WWE.

Copyright © 2002 by Flying Noodles, Inc.
Book design by Tiffany Kukec
Cover design by Rita Frangie
Cover photograph by Colin Bowman

PRINTING HISTORY
Berkley Boulevard trade paperback edition / November 2002

Visit our website at www.penguinputnam.com

Library of Congress Cataloging-in-Publication Data

Piper, Rowdy Roddy, 1954–
In the pit with Piper / by Rowdy Roddy Piper with Robert Picarello.
p.   cm.
ISBN 0-425-18721-7
1. Piper, Rowdy Roddy, 1954– 2. Wrestlers—Canada—Biography. I. Picarello, Robert.
II. Title.
GV1196.P56 A3 2002
796.812'092—dc21
2002026004

PRINTED IN THE UNITED STATES OF AMERICA

10 9 8 7 6 5 4 3 2 1

I would like to dedicate this book to all of my deceased
Frat Brothers, including:

Owen Hart
Adrian Adonis
Ravishing Ric Rude
Dino Bravo
Brian Pillman
Jay "The Alaskan" York
Kerry Von Erich
David Von Erich
Mike Von Erich
Chris Von Erich
Andre the Giant
Art Barr
Johnny Valentine
Rick McGraw
Gorilla Monsoon
Wahoo McDaniel
Davey "Boy" Smith
Lou Thesz

Contents

Foreword

Bret Hart

IN this business, there aren't too many real people. Roddy Piper is definitely one of the real ones.

A stand-up guy, Roddy always shook everyone's hand in the dressing room—big, small, old, and young. He was polite and different from all the big names I ever met.

When I got to the WWF in '84, Roddy was already on top of the card as their number one heel. He didn't have to give me the time of day—but he did.

Long before cliques in wrestling had become a major angle, the big clique was Don Muraco, Bob Orton, Adrian Adonis, Mr. Fuji, and Roddy. They didn't hang out together for "political" reasons but for comradeship. One night, after a Hart Foundation tag match, Roddy invited Jim "The Anvil" Neidhart and me up to a hotel room for a beer with the boys, and they let us into the fold. It was a privilege to sit with these top stars, soaking up their advice on wrestlers, wrestling, psychology, angles, and territories. The camaraderie in those lonely hotel rooms provided some of the most insightful and significant lessons a young apprentice like me would ever get.

One day I mentioned to Roddy that my dad had some relatives on his side by the name of Toombs, Roddy's real last name. As it turned out, Roddy is from Saskatoon, as is my father, Stu, and we found it curious that in North Dakota the Harts and the Toombs were indeed blood-related. To what extent nobody knew. Ever since this discovery, Roddy and I have referred to each other as "Cuz."

One of the greatest moments of my career was when I challenged Roddy for the WWF Intercontinental title at *WrestleMania VIII* in Indianapolis. We'd never really had any matches together, and to have one this big, in the sold-out Hoosierdome, plus millions more watching live around the world on Pay-Per-View, was going to be a challenge. Roddy had an indifference to pain, working as hard as anyone I ever knew, and at *WrestleMania VIII* I knew he bore the brunt of it for me. To win the Intercontinental title from my mentor was an amazing accomplishment for me.

As the years went by, I found myself in numerous situations where I desperately needed some good advice, and I often joked about shining a spotlight in the sky like Batman and Roddy would always be there. I could always trust Roddy, knowing that his advice wasn't just good, it was the best. I was able to work my way up in the business, forever grateful for his counsel.

Being a wrestler was like being in a tribe. The best thing that any of us had going was the feeling of brotherhood we shared. Too many wrestlers end up as wrestling tragedies. For me, I followed Roddy like a Sioux brave followed Crazy Horse. He was a real warrior, who could truly lay claim to being a chief.

In the world of professional wrestling, the true giants don't always face one another, sometimes they stand side by side facing the world.

Thanks, Roddy, for being a true friend and hero.

And that's a shoot.

—Bret "The Hitman" Hart

Preface

Piper on Larry King

MICK Foley once said to me on the Larry King show, "Piper, it's usually the guys that didn't make it that are bitter. Why are you so bitter?"

Mick brought up the point that I couldn't see the trees for the forest, and for this I'm forever grateful. As you read you might get the same idea, but I'm going to try and take you back with me on what's been a wild, wacky, and glorious journey as a professional wrestler.

I love the sport of professional wrestling and all that it has given me. It's allowed me to see the world, earn a decent living, raise a beautiful family, and meet lots of great and interesting people. It has also taught me to have the utmost respect for anyone who has ever stepped foot in a professional wrestling ring. I know firsthand that it ain't easy. The athlete in you takes a physical pounding seven days a week from all the wrestling you're doing all over the world, while your brain takes a mental beating from all the time you spend alone on the road away from your family and home.

Lonely on Road

As you'll find out in my book, there were many times in my life when I didn't see the green of the trees that Mick was talking about because I was always on the run—and it's very hard to notice anything in life when you're running with your head down. But my forefathers took me in and not only taught me how to wrestle, but also how to walk through life with my head up and become somebody. I am forever grateful to them for passing this knowledge on to me, so that's one of the reasons I decided to sit down and pen this book. *In the Pit with Piper* allows me to get my story out there for everyone to read and enjoy, and it also allows me to pass some knowledge down to people who are interested in getting into the business. They can read and learn about the hard road that I traveled to break into the rough and tough sport.

I started to write this book two years ago, and boy, let me tell you, it's been a learning experience. I went through six people before I found the crew to help me get everything right. I have tried to get all the people, places, names, and facts correct, as I did the entire book from memory, and I was as honest as I can be.

But I have to tell you, the deeper and further I went back in my life and career, the harder the task became. To be honest, I almost gave up three times, but one night I got a call from a good friend, Bob Friedman, who is the vice president of Celebrity Placement in Detroit. After screening a hundred literary agencies for me, he came up with Warwick Associates, operated by a wonderful team of people headed by Simon Warwick-Smith and Patty Vadinsky, who took me on as a client. Not only did they dive into the project headfirst with me, but they baby-sat me through the entire process. Eventually, Simon and Patty got me a deal with Penguin Putnam books to publish my work, and here I am 100,000 words later. Thank you to a fine editor, Kelly Sinanis. We may never have gotten this book published if she hadn't battled for us. I must also give thanks and gratitude to writer Rob Picarello for his countless hours of hard work and sleepless nights in helping me write this book. Without him, this project would never have gotten done, and he is truly one of the finest in his field and one of the most devoted workers I have ever met. Thank you, Rob.

These people are responsible for helping me get the book out of my head and onto the shelf, and for this I am truly grateful.

Also, this book would not be possible if not for people like Leo Garibaldi, Gene LeBell, and Red Bastien (the best man at my wedding), who took me under their wings as a young misfit. These men, along with so many other greats from their generation, allowed me to learn the art of wrestling well enough so I could earn a living from it. My forefathers had me in school 24/7 teaching me the ropes in both my life and my sport. *[handwritten: Teachers]*

Then there are my Frat Brothers who stood toe-to-toe with me through the good times and the bad. Rick Martel, Greg Valentine, Sergeant Slaughter, Don Muraco, Bob Orton, Bret Hart, Mr. Fuji, Andre the Giant, Ric Flair, and even my old nemesis, Hulk Hogan. Once you have done battle with someone long enough, there grows a strong, silent bond and a mutual respect.

There are two people who do not get enough credit for their contributions who also need to be acknowledged. Cyndi Lauper and her tireless manager, Dave Wolff, were so instrumental in bringing wrestling into the mainstream. I am a big fan of both of these people and I know how important their roles were in getting the wrestling boom started. I was there to witness what these two wonderful people did, and I thank them. *[handwritten: Rock + Wrestling - huge]*

I also must give credit where credit is due. Although I rag on him and we disagree *a lot,* Vince McMahon deserves some praise. If he had not seen and seized the opportunity, putting everything on the line for wrestling, I would not have the notoriety that I do today. Vince McMahon Jr., I thank you.

However, the person who not only helped me through the toughest parts of my career but also taught me how to become a decent human being is my beautiful wife, Kitty, whom I have been with for twenty-four years. If God were to line up all the girls in the world for me and ask me to pick a wife, I would still pick Kitty. She is my life. While I was lucky enough to marry Kitty, she also blessed me with my support group, my beautiful children: Anastasia, Ariel, Colton, and Falon, whom I have always lovingly called my "Corn Muffin." They all have exceeded my highest expectations and they all have my undying and unconditional love.

Kids

Last but not least, my friend and business associate Lewis Rach for his relentless patience, and for putting up with my bullshit and never wavering. On January 31, 2002, Lewis became the only man I don't know how I'm ever going to be able to pay back, literally saving my life by getting me to Cedars-Sinai Hospital when I was clinically dead after a terrible car accident.

saved Roddy's life Lewis Rach

From one true friend to another, thank you, Lewis.

Finally, this book goes out to my fans who have watched me grow up before their very eyes every night. From the bottom of my heart I thank you all. May you all be in heaven a half hour before the devil even knows you're dead.

Ever Forward,
Roddy Piper

Roddy Piper Is Born

MOST normal people come into the world on a specific day of a specific month during a specific year. Not me. While I was born Roderick George Toombs on April 17, 1954, in Saskatoon, Saskatchewan, I didn't truly come to life until fifteen years later when I found my true calling—pro wrestling—which would eventually give me my real identity of "Rowdy" Roddy Piper.

I took up the rough and tough sport in 1969, but before that I was an outcast in society who was going nowhere fast. The only thing I was good at was playing the bagpipes. To tell you the truth, I don't know why I started playing the instrument. Though my father was Scottish and my mother was from Ireland, I didn't learn from them how to play the bagpipes. I was really young—about five or six—and living on an Indian reservation called The Pas in Manitoba when I started playing the pipes, and I don't even recall who introduced me to them. I don't think it was one of my neighbors because I was the only white kid living on the reservation and I can't imagine myself playing the bagpipes and dancing around a fire with

Chose an instrument w/a Kilt!

fourteen Apaches. Why didn't I pick the guitar and become the next Eric Clapton or choose the drums and become a great drummer like Ringo Starr? No. God gave me the bagpipes, so that made me an underdog from the beginning, because you know what comes with the bagpipes—a kilt—not a dress, but a kilt! But while there is nobody alive who can help me solve the mystery of when and how I started playing, no one can dispute that I'm good on the pipes.

leaves home @ 13

At thirteen, I left home and decided to give it a go on my own. I hitchhiked from place to place and I played my bagpipes, leaving my case open, hoping to make a quarter, which would allow me to get into a youth hostel. But I was never in one place for a very long time. I was constantly on the move, and wherever I went, my bagpipes followed. One year the two of us teamed up with a band called Keber Fe and took part in a competition in Toronto at the C&E Gardens. We were up against the best pipe bands from around the globe, and believe it or not, we came in fifth—in the world. Pretty impressive for someone who isn't sure why he started playing the instrument in the first place, don't you think?

5th in the world

JD

But the rest of my early memories aren't as special. As a matter of fact, they're kind of shitty. To put it plainly, I was a delinquent who had a knack for finding trouble, and even when I wasn't trying, trouble found me. Now, even though I don't agree with most of Canada's rules, I do have a lot of respect for the country, especially since the powers that be kept me out of reform school. You see, Canada had a couple of experimental programs that tried to put juvenile delinquents on the straight and narrow, and I became the country's white mouse for quite a few of them.

One of the first years I was in school, I was enrolled in a program in which the teachers were teaching us math and spelling through some new methods. Well, unfortunately for me, none of them worked. To this day I still can't spell a word and the only time I can add is when a promoter is paying me. So, you see, I didn't have a very good crack at school from the beginning. I would have loved to stay in and get an education and become a psychologist—that's what I really wanted to be. But years later the only Yale degree I would get would be ADD.

Another program I got involved in was one in which the Canadian government actually put me in boot camp with the Canadian Armed Forces. I had to put in six weeks of basic training and then show up once a month for a year until I was finished with the program, which would give me an honorable discharge. I never imagined myself wearing a uniform and serving my country, but this training turned out to be a good thing for me. It kept me off the streets and out of trouble for a while and instilled a powerful belief in discipline in me that has stayed with me until this very day. The army also taught me to be an expert marksman. I became good with a machine gun and even better with a knife—all things a juvenile delinquent should learn. It was organized fighting—and I liked it!

After I received my honorable discharge, I was once again back to my nomadic life, living in hostels or on the streets. Like I said, in my travels as a teen, I tried as best as I could to stay in school and get an education. Also in my travels, I got involved in school athletics. I started playing sports like football, basketball, and hockey, but even though I was a natural athlete, I could never have made a dime off any one of those sports. But one sport I tried and liked was wrestling. I picked up on it quickly, maybe because my father and uncle were both amateur boxers and it was in the blood. As a matter of fact, when I was living at home, they used to take me down to the basement and try to teach me about boxing and also how to protect myself. Wrestling also came naturally to me because I'd been fighting all my life.

One of the youth hostels that I got into had a Police Athletic League and an amateur wrestling coach. From the very first time I locked up with someone, I excelled on the mat. At the age of fifteen, I won the 167-pound Amateur Wrestling Championship of Manitoba. This was quite an accomplishment and confidence booster for me because, believe it or not, I was a shy reserved kid who didn't look for any attention. When I entered this tournament I had no idea what to expect, especially after I got my ass kicked in my very first match against an opponent who was not only two weight classes above me, but who also had a build that resembled Chris Benoit's.

But surprisingly enough, I won all my remaining matches, and as luck would have it, I met up with the Benoit-like wrestler again in the finals. Not expecting to win the match, I wrestled defensively against my opponent in the first round because I felt I lacked the size, experience, and mostly the confidence that was needed to pull off a victory. But something happened in the second round that not only turned the finals around, but also my wrestling career. I hip-tossed my ripped foe and heard him grunt and groan as he landed. This gave me the boost I needed, as I now realized that I had a chance. In the third round, I had confidence to go on the attack and even got the grappler in a half nelson. But just as the ref was counting the guy out, the bell rang, ending the round and match. I was pissed because I thought I had the pin when the bell rang and I also thought I had lost the match. But to my surprise the ref came over and raised my arm in victory, and this gave me all the confidence in the world to go after what I wanted for the rest of my life.

One of my friends was enrolled in a professional wrestling school run by a guy named Tony Candello, who was a barber by trade. My friend said, "Why don't you come on by and see what's going on?" So I went and was introduced to Candello. My friend told his teacher that I was an amateur wrestling champion and dollar signs must have flashed before this guy's eyes. You see, Candello not only ran this pro wrestling school, he was also a renegade, outlaw promoter who was looking to make a buck. He started making me all kinds of promises, and told me to sign a contract and he would turn me into a professional wrestler. At first I went along with this guy, but after talking to him some more, I realized he was just trying to get money out of me, which was like trying to get blood out of a stone because I certainly didn't have any money. By this time I had been on the streets for two years and I wasn't about to be anybody's fool. When he left the room, I stole the signed contract out of his briefcase, but still got booked on a wrestling card because they thought I went to the school.

The first professional event that I took part in was way up in the tundra for a local promoter named Al Tomko in Churchill, Manitoba. Tomko packed into his van his lineup for the evening—which included me and five other scary-looking wrestlers, who could all rival the local Sasquatch in looks and size, and two lady midget wrestlers, who had nice long hair on their legs, which I guess kept them warm during the harsh winters. We took the van to the airport, where a twin-engine pontoon airplane was waiting for us and was going to drop us off at the pond nearest our destination in Churchill. As the plane was going up, one of the midgets nudged me and pointed out that there was oil coming out of the left engine. Not wanting to alarm anyone and also being the new kid on the block, I gracefully went up to the pilot and informed him that the left engine was leaking oil. Without missing a beat, the calm, cool, and collected plane flier answered me: "Yeah, I know. She leaks a bit. I've been meaning to get that fixed."

Needless to say, we made it to our destination, which was a lumber camp that was filled with the loneliest, nastiest-looking bunch of lumberjacks that I had ever seen in my life. These guys, who Tomko informed me loved the sight of blood, made our group look like a bunch of raving beauties.

The setup was even worse looking than the lumberjacks. There was no wrestling ring, just some mats on the cold, hard floor, and no chairs, just some broken-down wooden stools in the kitchen area where the lumberjacks ate. But we still managed to put on a good card for the jacks, who left the place smiling from ear to ear, as they got to see some good matches and some bloodshed. Unfortunately for me, the blood being lost was mine. But I didn't care. As long as Tomko gave me my fifteen bucks for the night, I was happy.

We made our way back to the plane, and there was our pilot with a big can of oil, filling up that engine again so he could fly us

First Fight at a Lumber Jack Camp

back. When we landed, we all piled back into the van and made our way to find a place to sleep for the night. I was so sore and achy that I couldn't wait to take a shower and crawl into bed. After driving for some time, Tomko pulled up and stopped in a state park and said: "All right. Here we are." Now I was wondering what was going on. Did someone have to go to the bathroom? Nope. Turns out the park was going to be our home for the night. The ladies had the luxury of sleeping in the van, while us guys had to find a comfortable spot outside among the stars and nature.

after First Math had to to sleep out side

Al, being the caring promoter that he was, took it upon himself to build us a campfire to keep us warm while we searched for our beds for the evening. I chose the most comfortable picnic table that I could find and tried to catch some sleep after my first long night as a pro wrestler in the "big leagues." I thought the adventure was going to be put to rest right there on the picnic table, but it was only beginning.

I got up in the middle of the night to use the Porta Potti, and just as I was sitting down to do my business, I heard lots of commotion and what sounded like a roar coming from outside the stall. I pulled open the door a little, only to see a huge creature running around our camp. At first I thought nothing of it, thinking it was just one of our wrestlers taking a piss and having some laughs. But the joke would be on me. A few moments later I found my world turned upside down when the Porta Potti was sent flying, launching shit and me into the air.

Bear attack

When I got up off the ground, I heard everybody yelling at me to get into the van because there was a wild bear running loose in our camp. With my pants down to my ankles, I ran as fast as I could to catch up with the group and jumped, bare-assed, into the moving van, narrowly escaping the claws of the wild beast. But just when I thought I was safe, Tomko and the group tossed me back out of the van because I stank—not to mention the shit that was now all over the seats in Al's van. Ah yes, I was already enjoying life as a pro wrestler.

Tomko then allowed me to live in his gym, and the only thing
I had to do in order to stay there was help keep the place nice and
clean. My time spent in the gym was memorable, because not only
did I have the pleasure of working out with some of the biggest and
best wrestlers on the circuit, I also had quite a few laughs.

For instance, one time Al wanted me to repaint some of the
equipment that had become worn and old looking from all the use
and abuse over the years. So I took some paint and proceeded to
give the dumbbells and plates a fresh coat of royal blue, using some
white to paint the numbers. But as a joke, I repainted them all the
wrong weights. I painted twenty-five pounds on the forty-pound
dumbbells and eighty pounds on the ninety-five-pound dumbbells.

You can imagine how much I laughed watching five-hundred-
pound bench-pressers like Superstar Billy Graham and Hercules
Cortez trying to figure out, "What's wrong with me today?!" The
confusion on their faces alone was priceless, although short-lived.
You see these forefathers of mine weren't dumb. They made Tomko
weigh the dumbbells. After they figured out what had happened,
they found their own brand of humor, dragging me across the speed
bumps of the mat, again and again and again, and practicing their
best moves on me. Quite honestly, they beat the shit out of me. The
incident not only gave me another lesson in humility, it also left me
out on the street again.

But with all the wrestling I was doing, I was able to rent a room
of my own for twenty-five dollars a month from a lady in Winnipeg
named Melanie. She was always singing that song "I've got a brand
new pair of roller skates, you've got a brand new key . . ." However,
she was over three-hundred pounds and I didn't ever want to know
if the key fit! Anyway, Melanie rented me her front porch. I had a
hot plate, a bed, and two candles on the wall. Now, Winnipeg is a
city where the temperature sometimes drops to sixty below, and I
was sleeping on a porch! But it was better than being on the streets.

I enrolled in a school that wasn't too far away from my place.
Even though I was never really good with books, I wanted to get

School

about him

I know

want anyone

didn't

an education. I tried to stay in school, but it was hard. I was an outcast because with all the moving around I did, I was always the new kid in class. That first day was undoubtedly the toughest. I was always nervous when I had to walk into a room filled with strangers and introduce myself. It became twice as hard when I started wrestling.

So now I walk into the new classroom, and because I'm wrestling every night, I'm pretty marked up. Half of my face is raw, and I walk in and everybody turns to stare at me, and they're wondering "Who is this guy?" And I don't want them to ask any questions. I don't want them to know what I'm doing. I mean, if they ask me what school I came from, what am I going to do, give them a list? And if they ask me where I live, what do I say? On a porch, like a dog? So I just kept to myself, and everyone started thinking I was some tough guy, coming to school with scars and bruises all over my body. No one knew me well enough to know what I did outside of school—hell, I don't even think they knew my name. And even if they did know my name and had the nerve to ask me questions, I didn't give them direct answers because I didn't want anyone to know my business.

I was always hiding behind some kind of mask. But the truth of the matter is that Roddy Piper was always a scared-to-death coward who was extremely introverted and insecure. I had nothing in common with any of these kids and I didn't know what to say to them. There were many times back then when I was scared to death—and there were many times after that when I was scared shitless, too—but I learned over time that it was okay to be afraid. What's not okay is having those emotions stop you from doing what you want to do.

Introvert!

shy

My education came to a screeching halt on the day I was supposed to take part in my first pro match in a big-time league, the American Wrestling Association. I was all excited during the day because not only was I going to take part in an AWA event, I was also going to be making twenty-five bucks for the bout—a ten-dollar

AWA - First big time League
Gets $2500

bump up from my other matches. But I almost didn't make the match in the Winnipeg Arena that night because I had gotten into trouble during the day with four or five other students and we all had to stay after school.

I don't remember what we did to get punished, but I do remember why I walked out on school for good on that day. As I sat at my desk thinking about the night's match, my teacher ordered me up to the front of the classroom to help the other detained students clean the blackboard. When I approached her desk, she handed me a brush and sarcastically asked me if I had somewhere better to be. I answered her by saying, "Yeah, I do. I can see me telling the Crusher tonight why I was late for the match, that I was a bad boy in school and had to stay after and clean the blackboards."

Well, I made it through the afternoon and raced to get ready for the match. This was big-time for me, and I had told all my friends about it. My pipe-band buddies had decided they would help me make a grand entrance. I was going to wear my plaid trunks and these ridiculous high-topped green boots, and my full pipe band, all wearing kilts, would be wailing away as I stepped into the ring. On my way to the arena, I snuck into the Marlboro Hotel, a familiar stomping ground for me. I was always slipping into that hotel at night, hunting down room-service trays that guests had chucked out in the hall—they left a lot of good food on those trays. But on this night, I wasn't looking for a meal. I stole a wicker basket, which I was also going to use on my way into the ring that night. I wanted to fill it with roses, but I couldn't afford them, so I settled for dandelions that I picked out of the grass.

After all the rushing around, I managed to get to the arena an hour before the match and I found out that I was facing Larry Hennig. Hennig was thirty-five years old and weighed about 320 pounds. He looked like a Viking; he had no neck, and there was hair growing out of his ears, nose, and teeth. He had just lost the World Heavyweight Championship, and this was his next fight, and boy was he mad. He growled to the promoter, "Go tell that kid,

'Just be like a Greyhound bus and leave the driving to us.' " I had no idea what was going on. Being the lanky and inexperienced wrestler that I was, I wasn't going to argue with a guy who was twice my age, not to mention twice my size.

Besides, this was big stuff. Not only was the money good, the AWA was the big time, where so many wrestling greats had passed through the promotion. Grapplers like Superstar Billy Graham, Dusty Rhodes, Billy Robinson, Nick Bockwinkle, Verne Gagne, Ric Flair, Sergeant Slaughter, and Hulk Hogan, just to name a few, at one time or another, graced these mats. I went there with the full intention of giving it my best shot, hoping that somehow I would get noticed.

Pipers

My entrance alone that night got me noticed. I came into the arena led by a full wailing pipe band—four pipers, two snares, and a bass drummer wearing a big, fuzzy hat with a pint of scotch stuck in the hole of it, as tradition always dictated. Me, I was 167 pounds soaking wet, in the middle of these guys, with my basket of dandelions, which I was sharing with the crowd, to their complete disbelief.

Gets name

As I approached the ring apron, the announcer, who didn't know me from Adam—all he knew was that my name was Roddy—said: "Ladies and gentlemen, coming to the ring at one-hundred and sixty-seven pounds, Roddy, uh, the, uh, Piper."

Thus the birth of Roddy Piper!

Crowd shocked

They were shocked; they had never seen anything like it. This was all new to the audience and to Hennig and to me. There were no grand entrances in those days. There was no music blaring from the arena speakers or pyrotechnics all around. Wrestlers just used to walk into the ring ready to fight. I'll never forget the look on Hennig's face when I finally stepped through the ropes. If looks could kill, I would have been dead twice over before the bell even rang. As I got into the ring, all I saw was a large human mass with lightning coming out of his eyes and thunder coming out of his ass. The bell rang, and the next thing I knew, Hennig had snatched me as fast as a rattlesnake and hit me so hard I fell backward. I was falling through the ropes and would have hit my head on the concrete if it hadn't been for the kindhearted Hennig. He reached through the ropes and grabbed me by the hair, ripping some of it out as he saved my life, only to pull me back in the ring and give me his finishing hold, called "The Ax," and then cover me. Figure that it takes a three-count in order to beat a guy, and add another seven seconds to that, and you have my first world record in professional wrestling. I have the honor of being beaten in the shortest amount of time in Winnipeg Arena history—ten seconds!

Pinned in 10 sec

I left the ring and went back to the locker room feeling dejected. My pipe band was gone; they had left the arena not too proud of my performance. I wasn't too thrilled about what happened that night either. My nose was broken and I was ashamed of myself because I thought I was a tough guy. As I sat there sulking with my head between my legs, Tomko came up to me, and all I remember seeing were his penny loafers. I didn't look up because I thought he was going to bawl me out or at least duke me out of my two bits, but instead he said, "Kid, you did great! How'd you like to go to Kansas City?" I said, "Is Larry Hennig going to be there?" And he said, "No, no, don't worry. We won't overmatch you again."

broken nose

So he slipped me across the border to wrestle. Tomko had been frequently going across the border to matches in the United States, and he put me in the backseat of his Lincoln Continental and threw a couple of blankets over me. When we got to the border patrol he played me off as his son, saying, "Yeah, I got my son with me. He's always sleeping, the lazy kid," and remarkably they let us through without a problem.

Tomko snuck me into US to wrestle

Our first stop across the border was a very old, old-fashioned hotel called the Calhoun Beach Hotel, where my elders often provided studio wrestling for people as entertainment. I grappled with Superstar Billy Graham and his huge twenty-four-inch arms, and against many other wrestlers, all of whom outweighed me by at least a hundred pounds. If you go back and look at some of the tapes of

Superstar Billy Graham

Jobber
got beat up

these old wrestling broadcasts, you'll see I was the guy that was always being squished! They just beat the shit out of me every chance they had, and seemed to enjoy it more and more each time. One night in the locker room after a match, Superstar joked and said to me, "Sorry we were a little short on TV time. Next time I'll give you more time, kid." I said in reply: "Yeah, right." I knew that Superstar didn't care how quick I lost the match or how much air time I had. Graham caught on that I wasn't buying his bullshit and started laughing. It was my first "ribbing on the square" (which you'll learn more about in chapter 3) experience, and the first time I called anybody on anything. But at this time in my life, I realized that I wasn't the brave young lad that I'd thought I was. I was a coward. I feared everything, therefore I feared nothing, and that's why I showed up.

Besides being a punch dummy in the ring, I was also known as a resourceful fellow who could get anything the guys needed, from the lady at the bar to a room at a sold-out motel. Basically, I was a promoter's dream. Outside of our group, no one knew I existed, or cared. If I died, they'd move on to the next guy, and if I got busted, they'd deny knowing me. The only good thing for me was the experience of dealing with different kinds of people, from saints to serial killers, and I started not to scare too easily.

But what other choice did I have? I was a teenager who had no education, no close friends or family members to help me out, and no driver's license to help me get around. I relied on all these guys to help mold me into someone who was going to be successful. Whatever they wanted or needed me to do I was going to do it, no questions asked. If they needed me to go over the border with them for a match and would say, "Be there at three," I made sure I was there by five to three.

In my early years in the sport, I was shuffled around from one guy to another, and I had to give them one cent per mile for gas in order to pay for a ride. At this time gas was really expensive. There was a gas shortage in effect and you could only buy it according to your license plate—odd numbers on some days, even numbers on others. Well, if we were driving from Winnipeg, Manitoba, to Minneapolis, which is five hundred miles, we certainly couldn't make that trip just on one full tank. So when we ran out of gas, we'd fill up using a "six-foot credit card." What's that, you ask? It's a garden hose. I would sneak out at night and siphon gas from whatever vehicle I could find. The farms were usually the best places to hit. All the farmers had these huge gas cans that they used for their tractors, and I would fill those up and then put the gas in our car.

Steal gas

The only drawback was that farmers also usually had German Shepherds, and unfortunately I don't speak German. You try running with two full five-gallon gas cans with dogs biting at your heels. Those mutts would chase after me, and I'd knock the shit out of them with that garden hose. I knew that if I didn't get back to the car with gas, I'd be the one getting the beating.

Here's another example of how I was treated (or mistreated) at the time: During the wintertime when we were driving from gig to gig, the guys would put the heat on high enough so that the warmth would reach only their feet. I would be alone in the backseat freezing my balls off. One time, it had to be about 30 below outside and I was curled up in the back with my bologna sandwich and my bottle of 7UP, trying to stay warm, and the guys were busting my chops, saying, "Ah, damn, it's so hot up here." About halfway through the drive, my bottle of pop exploded all over me, leaving me colder than I was before—and without a drink for my lunch! Ah, the life of a professional wrestler.

Being the new kid on the block, I had to pay my dues like everyone else had done before me, but I also found the family and support I had never had as a kid. I didn't realize it at the time, especially when certain guys were ribbing me, but I'll never forget what guys like Bulldog Bob Brown, Ken Ramie, Lord Alfred Hayes, the Viking, Ronnie Etchinson, and Maurice Mad Dog Vachon did for me. These guys all took me in like one of their own and made me who I am today.

Guys who raised him

At one time or another, Ramie, Hayes, the Viking, or Etchinson would get on me because I was so young and played the bagpipes and I wore a kilt. They would tease me and pretend to come on to me.

Once I walked into an empty dressing room. All of a sudden the bathroom stall door flies open and there's Ramie sitting on the can playing with his pipe. I looked around and I realized there was nobody there but him and me. Now, to play a joke, there has to be an audience to get a laugh out of it—there has to be at least three to tango, doesn't there? But there was no third party laughing in a corner. It was just me and him. I really thought he was coming on to me.

Hazing ✓

A few days later, Lord Alfred Hayes, who is hung like a horse, comes up to me as I'm getting out of the shower. He's naked and starts running after me, swinging his dick and yelling "Roddy, Roddy." He's twirling that thing around like Roy Rogers trying to lasso Dale Evans.

Another night, I'm standing in the dressing room in Kansas City and Bob Geigel, a great amateur and professional wrestler and promoter, calls me over. "Hey, kid, I want to talk to you." I was very interested to hear what he had to say about wrestling; I was always looking to get advice from guys who'd been around for a while and were top-notch wrestlers.

I was so engrossed in what Mr. Geigel was saying that I tuned out everyone and everything around me. I was so distracted by Geigel that I was leaning against a bench with my hand behind me and somebody put something in it without me even realizing it. Finally Mr. Geigel finishes talking, and I notice that something is in my hand, so I squeeze it a few times, and turn around to see that it's Lord Alfred Hayes's donkey-size penis. My mentors were now rolling around on the floor laughing at me, as this whole thing had been a setup.

Me, I felt humiliated, hurt, embarrassed, and angered all at once. You've got to understand, I had been living on the streets for two years. When you're on the street, you're constantly fighting not to get raped. I thought I was away from all that. I thought I was in a room with a bunch of men I could trust, but now I didn't know what to think. And I couldn't do anything, because there was nobody in this group who I could beat up. So what the hell was I going to do? I got to the point where I wouldn't shower in the same room as them anymore. I would get to the arena, change into my kilt in the car, then wait outside until it was my turn to go on. Then, after I finished, I would go back outside the arena to wait for my ride. If we didn't hit a gym along our bookings route where I could shower, I would stay dirty because I was convinced that these guys were a bunch of queers.

Looking back, I realize this is when I officially became accepted into the world of professional wrestling. You see, after a few months, there was the "stink factor" again for the second time in my life. But unlike the first time, when I stunk up the van, these wrestlers didn't abandon me. My mentors realized how much damage they had done to me and they wanted to make things right. One night Geigel came up to me and told me not to take life so seriously, and that "the boys are just jerking around!" I said, *"That's my* problem." He told me, "If they didn't mess with you, it would mean they didn't like you!" I thought to myself, "Do they have to like me *this* much?"

In my very early years, these men, one at a time or sometimes in a group, had me in school twenty-four hours a day. They taught me everything, starting with the basics, the three W's—wrestling, women, and whiskey. They wanted to make sure that I had a proper education. They also used me to get dates for them. They lovingly called me "bait." We'd go out and all these thirty-five-year-old guys with scars all over their faces would use me to attract women they wanted to meet. They'd see a woman they liked, and would say, "Go get that one for me," and I'd bring her over to the table. Whenever we wrestled in Dallas, Fritz Von Erich would have me take out a fire marshal's daughter so he could pack more people into the arena than the fire laws would allow. These were the types of things

I had to do when I was a young professional wrestler. Ain't life great?!

One wrestler in particular who left a lasting impression on me during this time was a man named Ivan the Terrible. This guy was big and burly and he was always dressed in a nice suit and wore a hat like Frank Sinatra. Just looking at him was enough to set your teeth chattering, knees knocking and bring a tear to a glass eye—I had to take a trip with him from Kansas City to Wichita.

Ivan didn't talk to me for the first 150 miles of the trip—I mean he didn't say two words. The only sounds that were heard in the car—a Cadillac—came out of the radio speakers; Ivan loved to listen to talk radio. After being on the road for about three hours, he finally turned to me and asked, "Are you hungry?" I told him I was and he pulled over to an old-fashioned roadside diner. He parked the car and got out, telling me to go inside five minutes after him. What? I was crushed! I almost cried. Had I done something wrong? Maybe he really didn't like me and didn't even want to be seen with me. But I was going to do whatever he said, so five minutes later, I walked into the diner and found Ivan sitting at the counter.

We spoke a different language called "Carney," which originated in the carnivals where professional wrestling started back in the late 1700s in the U.S. So, as I walk into the restaurant, Ivan tells me in Carney to sit down. You know, when guys sit at a counter, it's common practice to leave an empty stool between between you, so that's what I did. But then Ivan says in Carney to get away from him. "Ah, man," I thought to myself. "This guy must really hate me!" Now I know why they called him Ivan the Terrible. So I moved five or six seats down.

Ivan had already ordered the best meal in the house—a steak, salad, and everything that came with it—and the waiter came up to me and asked what I'd have. Well, I didn't have much money, and to be honest with you, I was a little shaken up. So I said quietly, "I'll just have a Coke, please." At this point Ivan turned to me and bellowed loud enough for the entire place to hear, "What's wrong,

Ivan the Horrible

kid, aren't you hungry?" He then told the waiter to give me the same thing he was having. Now remember, up until this point there had been dead silence between us. I thought this guy hated me. He wouldn't let me come into the restaurant with him. He wouldn't even let me sit near him, and now he was ordering dinner for me? He even started talking to me. So now I thought, maybe he did like me, and I became a little bit more relaxed by the time my food came.

Then all of a sudden Ivan told me to order lemon pie. Okay, fine by me. So when the waiter came by, Ivan ordered a piece of pie and I said that I'd like one, too. But as soon as the words came out of my mouth, Ivan started going crazy. He started yelling at me, telling me he had fought in the war and didn't want some punk kid mocking him. I had no idea what was going on, but Ivan's face was turning all red, and then he grabbed his chest and white foam started coming out of his mouth. Holy shit! This guy was having a heart attack or something.

With foam oozing out of his mouth, he told me in Carney to come over to him, and when I did, he told me to get him the fuck out of there. But instead of listening to him, I panicked and I started yelling for the waiter to call for an ambulance. Ivan now pulled me *Faked* close and called me a stupid shit and ordered me to take him to the *a* car. I wasn't about to argue with this guy, so I said: "Fine, I'll take *heart* you to the car." *attack*

Now, you have to understand, this guy was about 285 pounds, *for* and I was at least a hundred pounds lighter. How the hell was I *a* going to carry him to the car? But somehow I managed to do it. I *free* dragged him along, and the next thing I knew, I was in front of the *meal* diner, trying to stuff him into the passenger-side seat of the Cadillac. I was so worried that he was going to die on me that I couldn't do anything right. I finally got Ivan in the car—at least I thought I did— but when I tried to close the car door, I slammed it on his ankle. Now Ivan got even more pissed and he started screaming for me to get into the car and drive. So I jumped into the driver's seat and started driving, even though I didn't have a license and I had no idea where the hell I was going. As I drove, Ivan remained slumped over in his seat, holding on to his mangled ankle while cursing the shit out of me. And then suddenly, from out of nowhere, he stopped, rose up like The Undertaker, and looked in the visor mirror, wiping the foam from his face and calmly pulled the remainder of an Alka-Seltzer tablet from his mouth. There was nothing wrong with him! This was just how he got a free meal. Then he went into the glove compartment and, as calm as can be, marked on his map where we had just been so he would know to avoid the place the next time he was in town. A little farther down the road, Ivan told me, "Hell, kid. What do you think you're doing? Pull over! You ain't got no license. That's illegal. What are you trying to do, get us arrested?"

That was when I really knew I had found my calling. An "epiphany" I believe they call it. Ivan's antics aside, I suddenly knew that after all the years of being a misfit, I had finally found my "home" in wrestling. I had never felt so sure about anything in my entire life. Little did I, or anyone else for that matter, know at the time that I was about to embark on a successful career during which I would make millions of dollars. *Make millions*

hits Roddy - this is for me!!

Most folks only have one dad; I now had one hundred, all cool in their own way. These gentlemen taught me to defend myself. Obviously physically, but twice as hard and more important, mentally. They not only trained me in all matters of life, they are also responsible for the birth and direction of the beast within me. They taught me that the wrestler, like the mouse, is a survivor. He must be able to fend for himself and also be aware at all times of his natural enemy—in the wrestler's case, it's the P.

One sad day in St. Louis I witnessed just how much power the snakelike P has. Stereotypically, a P is about five feet six inches, a 210-pound organism with a potbelly, wearing the same suit he's worn for the last twenty years, who smokes cheap cigars (that he had probably mooched) and sports a rug that looks like poodle roadkill. The P stands for "Promoter"—the sleazy men who used to run territorial wrestling promotions worldwide.

On this day, the promoter walked up to one of my fathers and said, "You stupid, fucking nigger!" and then continued to rip into him. I don't know if they knew I was there, but I just stepped back outside into the hallway waiting for him to pummel the P like he did his opponents in the ring. As far as I was concerned, he was a dead motherfucker. You have to understand, here was this pint-sized white guy yelling at a 320-pound black guy who could beat him to a pulp in an instant. But instead of pounding the P, my father did nothing. He just sat back and took it. To this day, I'll never forget watching in horror as one of my idols, a guy head and shoulders above other men, melted into the floor, taking all this crap from a promoter. I got very angry at my father, thinking, "Hit him! He just called you a fucking nigger!" I was almost in tears. My mind was racing. "Why are you being such a coward?" Then I became very sad. I realized that he took it because he just wanted to walk away with his day's pay.

I didn't comprehend it at the time, but that was pretty damn honorable, man. Forget about dignity—his family had to eat. He did what he had to do to put a meal on the table, and I respect that. What I saw in St. Louis that day gave me a foundation that will stay with me forever. Part one of this foundation is a love for my brothers, who put their families above all else, including personal pride. And part two is lifelong hatred for promoters and the common housefly.

Most important:
1. Family
2. Hatred for sleazy promoters

2

The Los Angeles Years

1973 — Moves to Cal — L.A.

EVERY person in this world is born with distinct talents and a unique personality, but our true identities don't blossom until we meet certain people or live in certain surroundings. For me, this area was Los Angeles. I remember the first time I set foot in this town of make-believe. I was nineteen and looking to make a name for myself in the sport of wrestling. Red Bastien, who was the booker in Dallas, where I had been wrestling for the last six weeks, suggested that I head to California. He had talked with a good friend of his, Leo Garibaldi, who was looking for young talent. So in 1973, I packed my bags in my Vega, which took me all of fifteen minutes, and I was off to California.

At this stage in my life, every time I entered a new territory, I would roll down my car window and warn the state and its citizens that I was coming to town. In L.A., my yell went something like this: "Look out, California. Roddy Piper is coming to town and I'm gonna kick your fucking ass!"

While the scream never worked in any other place, somehow

The scream

L.A. was different. Los Angeles was the site of the very first big break for Roddy Piper. I made a name for myself at the Olympic Auditorium—the same place where some of the wrestling greats from the past, like Gorgeous George and countless others, used to wrestle. As a matter of fact, their pictures hung on a wall inside the auditorium, and I remember telling Leo that I would love to one day get my picture up on that wall, too. Without thinking anything of it, Leo told me to give him a picture and he would get it put up there. I told him no. I didn't deserve to be in that company.

Not yet anyway!

The first thing I did when I got to L.A. was head over to the arena to find Garibaldi. He looked me up and down and said, "Who the hell are you?" I told him that I was Roddy Piper. "Who?" Roddy Piper, Red Bastien sent me. And he said, "Oh yeah. The locker room is down there."

Once I found Garibaldi, the next thing I had to do was find a place to stay. I asked the other wrestlers where the guys usually stayed, and they told me about a place on Ocean Avenue named the Flamingo Hotel. You couldn't rely on the bookers to do anything for you. There were no frills, they didn't pay for anything. If you got there you got there, if you didn't you didn't. So I booked myself into the hotel the guys recommended. Actually, it's the same hotel used in the movie *White Men Can't Jump,* starring Woody Harrelson and Wesley Snipes. How I managed to survive in this joint for two and a half years is beyond me, as there was a murder in our back alley about once a week. The owners of the place must have known that I was going to be "rowdy" while I stayed there, they gave me the room closest to the alley where all the murders were taking place.

Garibaldi was the booker and Mike LeBell was the promoter for the territory. Mike's half brother, Judo Gene LeBell, one of the toughest guys in the world, took a liking to me—thank God! I'd go down to his dojo to train, and eventually I earned a black belt. Gene gave me, Chuck Norris, and Bruce Lee black belts, and I don't think

Black Belt

Leo Garibaldi booker
Mike Lebell Promoter — bro Gene Lebell trained R.

many more. <u>Gene became like another father to me.</u> I have the greatest respect for him. He trained me physically while Leo trained me psychologically. These two men are responsible for helping me make it in the sport of professional wrestling.

But before I get into my wrestling career in L.A., I would like to just give you a taste of the craziness that went on every day while I was living in California.

This was the time when Joe Gold, the founder of the famous Gold's Gyms, sold his facility in downtown Santa Monica with the understanding that he wouldn't open up another Gold's Gym close by. So what did Joe do? He went down about ten blocks and opened up another gym, calling it World's Gym. Once he opened his new gym, he got back all his old clients—Ken Wahler, Frank Zane, Arnold Schwarzenegger, Lou Ferrigno, and all the wrestlers. I, of course, followed the pack, <u>as did my pal Jay "The Alaskan" York.</u>

Jay and I became tight in L.A., wrestling together, training together, partying together, and getting into trouble together. I remember one time I got into a mess of trouble because of Jay—of course he also saved my ass. See, there was this popular Renaissance fair every year in Los Angeles, and Jay had this booth. It was quite a gimmick. He had this big cross where you could tie up your mate and whip him or her with a cat-o'-nine-tails that was made out of paper. He would attract customers by saying, "Me lords and me ladies, come and give them the punishment they deserve." People would come and pay a dollar or fifty cents, or whatever it was, and then Jay would gently bind them to the rack and let their mates have some fun in the sun. It was a big joke, and everyone seemed to enjoy the attraction and left the booth laughing.

One day I was hanging out at the fair with Jay and this gal comes up to the booth wearing a long black cape with a hood. She was holding on to another girl, and her husband was standing by her side. The girl turned to Jay and me and asked politely if she could put her husband on the rack. Jay, thinking nothing of it, agreed and proceeded to tie him up. Jay went to give her the paper

World Gym

Jay York Good Friend

cat-o'-nine-tails, but she informed him it wasn't necessary, because she'd brought her own. She then whipped out a stick from under her cape and started to beat the shit out of her husband. She was just wailing away on him, until Jay jumped in to stop her, telling her that she can't do this because it's a family place. But Jay, being the old-school type of wrestler and businessman that he was, made her an offer on the sly so that he wouldn't miss out on a payday. Jay asked the lady if she wanted to rent the rack when the fair closed down at 7 P.M. Without hesitation she agreed, and they set up a place and time to meet later that evening. After the deal was cut, Jay told the lady and her Gothic friends to get lost because they were killing his business.

After the fair ended, Jay asked me to take the rack over to the other side of the grounds to meet the couple. So, being the good friend I am, I took the contraption to the other side of the fair, but when I got there it wasn't just the couple waiting for me—there was a whole group of people. Thinking nothing of it—I'd seen weirder people come through the ropes on any given night—I set the rack up for them. Being the kind guy that I am I also showed them where to put their arms, using myself as an example. As I was demonstrating how to use the rack, a woman came up to me and tightened up the leather straps. Now there was nothing I could do to free myself, and the next thing I knew, they had a bonfire going and there were these rocks arranged in different formations and all kinds of weird shit, and they all started chanting. It was almost like something you would see on a movie set downtown. But this was no set or movie—it was very real!

Now I really began to panic. The woman started scratching her nail down the right side of my cheek, down to my throat, as though she were intimidating me with a butcher knife. Then these guys wearing black capes with hoods started walking over to me. They were actually in a circle, closing in on me, getting closer and closer with the chanting getting louder and louder. I now thought, "I'm gonna die."

Thankfully, before the ritual went any further, York came over with his twelve-foot bullwhip and started snapping the thing at the devil worshipers like Indiana Jones. That caused them to back off and allowed him to free me from the rack. To this day, I really don't know what they were going to do to me, but thank goodness Jay and his trusty whip showed up when they did. Jay freed me and I immediately started running for the hills. But not Jay. He went over to the devil worshipers and not only took his cross back, but also had the balls enough to ask the satanic couple who rented the prop for the money they owed him. No one, not even the devil, was going to stop Jay from earning a payday.

I always found myself getting into trouble when I was around Jay. We did a lot of partying together. One night Jay and I, along with his brother Ned, who, like everyone else in L.A., was working as an actor, were hanging out. We were at the Flamingo Hotel, where all the fun and dangerous games took place in the city. To show you how close I lived to danger every day, the Flamingo was located half a block from a place called Tommy's Famous Hamburgers, a place where a famous serial murderer, the Hillside Strangler, had claimed one of his victims. One of the saddest signs I've ever seen in my life hung on a telephone pole outside Tommy's. It said PLEASE HELP ME. It was posted there by the young girl's parents, and I'll never forget it because the words were painted in blood red on the sign right under her beautiful picture.

After getting high, the three of us went our separate ways. Jay went home to his house and Ned followed him out the door to his home in the Hollywood Hills. I had the shortest trip of all three of us. I just got up off my couch and went to my bedroom.

But when Ned got home, he didn't go right to bed. He just kept smoking and getting dusted all night. By the time the sun came up, he was completely out of it. For some reason, he went out into his backyard in his boxers, tank top, and sandals and started playing with a ball. He must have accidentally thrown it over the fence and into his neighbor's yard because when he reached over the fence to get the ball, the neighbor's dog took a hunk out of his hand. Now Ned started freaking out. He was bleeding all over the place; blood was dripping down his arm and got all over his tank top.

This was the day after the Hillside Strangler had killed a young woman whom Ned had recently worked with. Ned was pretty shaken up by the whole thing and had been talking about it all night to us while we were getting high. For some bizarre reason, Ned convinced himself that *he* was the Hillside Strangler, that he killed his friend and all these other women. He was really out of it, hysterical, and called the police to turn himself in. He told the cops where he lived, hung up the phone, walked out front, and sat on the curb with his wrapped, bleeding hand waiting to be taken into custody. When the police came, Ned started babbling about the latest victim, saying things that only somebody who knew the girl would know. At this point the officers were convinced that they had the murderer and it went out on the news wires.

By the time I got up, it was about five o'clock in the evening and I switched on the TV as I was getting ready to go to the arena to wrestle, and every station was reporting that the Hillside Strangler had been caught. To my surprise they were showing Ned York's picture. Then I saw a live shot of Jay entering the police station, wearing his wide-open Pendleton shirt—which revealed his hairy chest—tight jeans, lineman boots, a buck knife hanging by his side, and a twelve-foot bullwhip around his neck, going in to prove his brother's innocence. If you think I was surprised that evening, just think how Ned felt when he woke up in jail! He came out of his stupor and said, "What the hell am I doing in here?" Jay and Ned had a lot of explaining to do, and I'm not quite sure how they managed to convince the police that they had the wrong guy, but they finally did, and the cops let Ned off on some minor charge. This was the type of shit that was going on every day at this time in my life in L.A.

While I was in California, I crossed paths with greats from all walks of life. At one time or another, I hung out with one of the funniest comedians of our time, Andy Kaufman; got in the ring with "The Greatest" boxer ever, Muhammad Ali; had the pleasure of working with one of wrestling's true good guys, Lonnie Mayne; and also met up with the first black heavyweight wrestling champion, Tiger Nelson.

In the early stages of my career, I was taught not to socialize with the fans because it could hurt your career. You didn't want to get too close to them because if they could touch you and talk to you, why would they pay to come and see you or why would they watch you on TV?

But there was this one fan who would come to the back door of the Olympic Auditorium and would always manage to get into the matches for free. He was an impersonator, who did this great impersonation of Elvis, and this act always went over well with the cops, who would then let him in to see the show.

Once he got inside, he always managed to find me and kept telling me how hilarious I was, and he also loved to imitate me. After a while I got used to seeing him around, so I thought nothing of talking to him and I even would hang around with him after the matches. The comedian had a van, and I'd get into the van with him and he'd ask me to say something funny to him. So, thinking that he wanted to hear a joke, I'd say something like: "My first wife died of poison mushrooms, my second wife died of poison mushrooms, and my third wife died of a brain concussion." He then asked, "What happened?" and I answered, "She wouldn't eat the poison mushrooms."

Not amused by my joke, the comedian would just stare at me with a deadpan look on his face and say, "No, say something funny." Well, I asked him what he found funny and he told me that he thought I was funny in the ring. This is where we differed. I didn't find anything funny about what I did in the ring for a living each night.

I asked him what he thought was funny. He recalled one night in the Olympic Auditorium when I was on the microphone and I

had just busted up two or three wrestlers. They were lying on the
floor, I was bleeding, and the crowd was going wild, starting to riot.
I just said, "Is there no justice?" and the comedian thought this was
hilarious. The irony of me bleeding over a couple of wrestlers and
saying is there no justice with a riot coming, well, that wasn't funny
to me. But this guy thought it was; this guy who I am talking about
was Andy Kaufman.

Andy would sometimes take me to a place called the Improv and
he would get up on the stage and do my interviews as part of his
act. After about ten minutes of doing this, the people would yell at
him to get off the stage, telling him he wasn't funny. But he would
still try to get over with the crowd with my material until he'd finally
storm off the stage.

This was a different business, the comedy business. He was supposed to entertain these people by making them laugh, but all he
was doing was pissing them off to the point where they all wanted
their money back. I wasn't understanding what he was trying to do.
He was a great comedian, who had so much great material—especially the skit he used to do with the bongo drums—why was he
using my interview material to try and make his audience hate him?

Andy was quite a character. I remember Andy would have comedy concerts in this little arena in L.A., and after the show he would
take everybody from the audience in a yellow school bus for chocolate mousse pie at one of his favorite restaurants in town. He was
also working on a show called *The New Dick Van Dyke Show*, and
one day Andy took me to meet the star of the show. So he said to
Dick Van Dyke, "This is Roddy Piper," and Van Dyke said, "So
this is the genius you've been talking about?" Apparently he'd told
Dick Van Dyke all about me, about my wrestling at the Olympic
Auditorium and my work on the mic. But I just hate compliments,
I don't want to listen to them. I just retract, hide, go back into my
little shell. I never understood why Andy was so fascinated by me.
He was a master at his craft, but for some reason he was mesmerized
by the world of professional wrestling.

Never saw Andy again

Andy never smoked, drank, or did anything wrong that I knew of, as far as his health was concerned. I remember, just before I left L.A., I went to say good-bye to him. I told him I was moving on and his eyes actually welled up with tears. He said, "I'll make you proud of me, Roddy." That's the last time I ever saw Andy Kaufman.

Lonnie Mayne

Another great guy I had the pleasure of meeting in Los Angeles was a wrestler named Lonnie Mayne. He looked like Santa Claus and drove a Trans Am, and boy, was he a madman! Two of the things that I remember most about this guy were that he loved to drink Southern Comfort out of a Coke can and that he also loved to have fun with the guys.

Once he was driving to Bakersfield with his tag partner Ron Bass, and he bet Ron a "hit in the head with a frying pan" that they would see a deer in their travels. Ron agreed to the wager, sure that he would win the bet because there were no deer on the route they were driving. Well, the two get to Bakersfield, and just as Ron thought, they didn't spot any deer on their journey. When they got to the apartment they were sharing, Ron reminded Lonnie of their little bet and then proceeded to tap Mayne on the head with the frying pan.

At that time wrestling in Bakersfield was every Thursday, so the following week Lonnie wanted a chance to get even, so he made the same bet with Bass. Once again there were no deer on the drive, and Lonnie got bonked a second time. But one day Lonnie finally got even. Bass and he were again taking the drive from L.A. to Bakersfield and Lonnie spotted a deer on the side of the road as they were driving to their match. He was ecstatic, but said nothing until they got back to their apartment. Once they got inside, Lonnie picked up an iron frying pan and called Ron's name. Ron turned around and *pow!*—Lonnie knocked him out cold, and split open his head.

Lonnie was always fooling around. He would do things like set my shirt on fire when I was in front of the camera on live TV, but it was all in good fun. The next day he would buy me a new shirt that was twice as expensive as the one he ruined the night before. That's just the kind of guy he was. He liked to have fun and really was a great guy.

When I met him he was just about to wind up his wrestling career and go into the real estate business with his dad. But unfortunately he found out he had cirrhosis of the liver and was about to die.

He never did get to go into business with his father, and it had nothing to do with his liver disorder either. One night, after a match in San Bernardino, I saw Lonnie holding on to the side of his car and puking. I asked him if he was all right and he told me not to worry, that he was fine, so I went home. The next morning I got a call from Lonnie's wife, telling me that he hadn't come home the night before, and immediately I started to cover up for him, thinking maybe he was jerking around.

Thinking quick, I told his wife that maybe he'd gone to San Francisco a day early. But the following day I got another call from Lonnie's wife, and she still hadn't heard from him. I soon learned the truth behind Lonnie's disappearance. He left San Bernardino in his Trans Am the night I saw him after our match. I was told that he was driving on the freeway in the far right lane, and his car drifted over the other three lanes, went over the grass median and into oncoming traffic, and hit a woman and her child head-on.

The impact of the crash was so bad that it not only killed everybody instantly, it also left Lonnie's body unidentifiable. As a matter of fact, the only way the police were able to identify the body was through his wrestling license, which he had on him. When the news came out that Lonnie had died, immediately everybody was saying that it was a suicide, but I don't believe that. Lonnie Mayne was consumed with what I call "the Sickness," which you'll learn more about in chapter 12. He was too good a man to ever take anyone else's life if he was going to take his own.

Wrestling in Los Angeles also allowed me to meet superstars in

Go to Japan 70's

Ali

other sports. It was through wrestling that I was able meet "The Greatest" boxer of all time.

Muhammad Ali was scheduled to fight Antonio Inoki in Japan on June 25, 1976. The Japanese fans loved watching their top fighters take on American athletes. Mike LeBell had an in with Japan and I started going to the Orient to wrestle as *Stan Hansen's* first tag-team partner. The Japanese promoters loved having Americans come to their country to wrestle because the matches always drew huge crowds and made them lots of money. The people loved wrestling, but their version of the sport was somewhat different from ours. If there was some spectacular move or pin, the people would all just clap. They were so polite. Quite a difference from the matches and the audiences I was used to back in the States.

Ali's match against Japanese wrestler Antonio Inoki took place in Tokyo. Judo Gene LeBell was the referee in this fight and I was on this card via satellite from Los Angeles. Antonio Inoki lay on his back for almost all of the fifteen rounds, and he just kept kicking Ali's legs. You could see the black-and-blue marks appearing on his legs during the match. People couldn't understand what was going on.

*Ali
Inoki
Rackly
on
card*

When Ali was training for this fight, he held a press conference in the Olympic Auditorium. At the time I was the Light Heavyweight Champion of the World (the only world title I have ever held and the only one I ever wanted to hold; all the rest of them are just heavy and they beep when you go through the metal detectors at the airport). At the press conference, a karate champion tried to leg-dive Ali while his entourage and camera crew watched his every move. Ali was able to hold his own against the jerk, who was trying to make the boxing champ look like a fool, while making a name for himself at the same time.

*Press
conference*

I was sitting in the front row taking all this in and Ali looked over and pointed to me. In typical Ali fashion, he started saying to me, "You. I want you. I want you in the ring." I had just wrestled in some matches where the loser had to shave his head—and I lost.

*Shaved
head*

I must admit I have an ugly bean; there are a whole bunch of gashes where things have hit me over the years, so it was not pretty. So there I was, bald, wearing my green corduroy suit, and Ali's taunting me to come into the ring with him. I looked around to make sure he wasn't talking to anyone else, and when I realized that I was the only one sitting there, I said okay and went into the ring.

On my way, Judo Gene LeBell was looking at me like "what the hell are you doing?" and I just shrugged my shoulders as if to say, "I don't know, Gene." Muhammad Ali then locked up with me wrestler style, and nobody believes me to this day, but I heard Ali say, "Hip-toss me." I wasn't about to argue with the champ, so I hip-tossed him. Over he went, his shoe fell off, and all of a sudden all of these Muslims with bulges in their jackets started charging into the ring. Knowing that these guys weren't coming into the ring to shake my hand, I hightailed out of there as fast as I could. But I think the reason Ali called me onto the mat that day was because he was such a great man that he was just looking to give a young kid like me a break and some exposure. He was that kind of an athlete, one who was so secure about who he was that he could afford to be that kind.

I also had the pleasure of meeting another sports legend, although I didn't know it at the time.

When you enter the Olympic Auditorium you come into a hallway that has a huge heavy steel door. It's like you're entering a dungeon. You have to go down these steep stairs. The paint on the wall is peeling and there are these huge pipes overhead that drip with condensation. As you walk down this cement hallway, you can either go to the right or the left, but whichever way you go, there are just these holes in the wall with concrete and benches. Welcome to the Olympic Auditorium locker room. It was always musty down there, and when you picked your cubicle of death and dumped your gear on the bench, the rats would scurry away.

Despite the shitty locker rooms, there was still an allure to wrestling in the Olympic Auditorium. Many greats from the past had graced the halls of this historic landmark. I was to find out by chance that a great from the past was still among us.

When you first entered the locker rooms there was a big massage table, and there was also a black gentleman named Tiger Nelson. Tiger was about 108 years old. He would say hello to everyone who came by and call them "horsecock." He used to wash our backs in the shower after the matches. He was quite a tall man, but all crippled and hunched over. He wore slippers and big baggy pants with an untucked blue shirt, like a gas-station attendant. Tiger was hip, though; he was a rapper before rapping was cool. He was a fine and honorable man. He would hear the showers go on, and then you'd hear him shuffling in his slippers to go get his washcloth and bar of soap, which resembled the kind you'd get from any Days Inn, and he'd be ready so he could scrub your back.

No matter who you were he would always say, "Oh horsecock, you could've heard that heat in Tokyo." He was talking about what a great-quality match you had. The truth of the matter was that he hadn't seen a match for thirty-five years. Tiger stayed in the locker rooms during the matches. Wrestlers would usually tip him a little something. I took a liking to this old man and I'd usually give him thirty or forty bucks or whatever I could. He used to call me "Misser Piper, sir."

I started talking to Tiger on a weekly basis, and he would tell me about the heat he heard in Tokyo, scrub my back, and shuffle on out. One day I finally asked him why he called everybody horsecock. He laughed and said, "Well, sir, everybody likes to be called horsecock, and dat ways I don't have to remember anybody's name."

After a match one night, I was coming out of the arena and I ran into Tiger as he was counting his tips. I said good night and he asked me what time it was. When I told him it was 11:30, he grabbed his head and bent over, let out a groan, and said, "Oooh, I done missed my last bus, Misser Piper." I told Tiger not to worry, that I'd give him a lift home. He was hesitant. "Well, sir, not many white folk live where I do, sir," he said, but I told him that I didn't care. In hindsight, what he was really trying to tell me was, "I don't want some honky son of a bitch like you in my neighborhood." But I didn't get it, and kept insisting. He really didn't want the ride until I told him that I just got a brand-new Cadillac. He started laughing and said to me, "I ain't never had a ride in a Cadillac, sir." Out of pride he insisted that I take two bus transfers in exchange for the ride.

So I drove Tiger home that night into Watts in L.A., and he invited me in. His place was about fourteen feet long and about eight feet wide. It had one of those old hot plates made out of porcelain, a cot, a chair, a sink, and a tiny bathroom. He invited me to sit in his chair and asked, "Misser Piper, sir. Are youse a drinkin' man?" And I told him that I was and he asked me if I had ever tried the Ripple. I said, "Yes, Tiger, I've drunk a lot of Ripple," even though I had never touched the stuff until that night. So he reached under the carpet and pulled out a bottle of Ripple. He was a little embarrassed when he realized that I saw that he had the bottle stashed under the carpet, so to save face, he told me that he liked his Ripple warm, and I said, "Me, too, Tiger," as I took a swig out of the bottle.

I noticed a scrapbook on the table and I started looking through it. There was a picture of two guys. Both of them were wearing black ties and tails with a stovepipe hat, and I said to Tiger, "Gee, that guy looks like Bob Hope." And he responded, "That *is* Misser Hope, sir." I asked Tiger who that other man was, and he told me that it was him and that he used to own a nightclub at that time and that Bob Hope used to work for him. "I's used to wears me a top hat and them there tails and tuxedo, and when I wore that, people used to gives me respect." He also said that when Bob Hope came into the club he would take his cane, kick it around and bounce it off the floor, and Tiger would snatch the cane right away from him. Tiger said, "You know, that's why Misser Hope took up golf."

There was another picture in the album of a beautiful black lady. I asked him who that was and he said it was his Rosie. I asked him what happened to her, and was she still with us. He said, "No, they think that she may have just wandered into the wrong neighborhood." Then he remained silent, and I could see the sadness in his eyes.

I didn't know how to respond, so I just kept looking through the scrapbook. I came across another interesting photo in Tiger's book, a boxing match from an aerial view. I thought I recognized one of the guys in the photo, and I asked Tiger, "Is that Jack Johnson?"

"Yes, sir, Misser Piper. That's Misser Jack Johnson himself," he said.

"I'll be damned. Jack Johnson! Who is he fighting?"

Tiger said, "Why, Misser Piper, he's fighting me."

"Wait a second, Tiger, you fought Jack Johnson?"

He said, "Yes, sir, I did."

I excitedly said, "That's great. That must have been a great career move. That must have put you on top of the world."

"Misser Piper," he said, "I'll tell youse what happened. I was a young, bold stud, and I comes out that first round and there's Misser Johnson, and we's went toe-to-toe hittin' back and forth, and I went back to my corner after the first round. Ins the second round Misser Johnson comes out and he hit me wit a left hook and it done felt like a mule kicked me in the head, and I starts a wobblin' and alls of a sudden these big black arms came around me and Misser Johnson whispered in my ear, 'Just hold on, nigga, just hold on.' Misser Johnson jus' kept holdin' on to me for fifteen rounds fors the rest of that there fight."

I then said, "So, Tiger, that must have made you a contender."

He answered, "No, sir, Misser Piper. It done killed my career."

I asked him what he meant, and he told me that he couldn't ever get another fight. Tiger paused and took another swig of Ripple and then started coughing really bad and holding his side. When he settled down he continued his story, telling me that because he went fifteen rounds with Jack Johnson, nobody wanted him fighting against their boy. It killed his career. He lost his nightclub and he lost everything. He wasn't a businessman. He had been getting by on his reputation as an athlete.

Tiger started coughing really bad again, and he turned to me and said, "Misser Piper, sir, I's starting to get the aches again. Do you mine if I go lay down for a whiles. You'se welcome to stay." I thanked him and said that I was going to go. He asked me to turn the light out for him. As I was closing the door behind me, I heard him cough, and that was the last time I ever heard or saw Tiger Nelson alive. The next time I laid eyes upon Tiger was when he was being buried. He must have been in the service because the Legion buried him. There were four people there including myself. Tiger Nelson's real name was Theodore Roosevelt Reid.

This was a hard reality check for me. How could someone who was once at the top of his profession wind up scrubbing wrestlers' hairy backs for a living and end up dying alone? But I was determined not to let it get to me. I learned how to dismiss things like this from my mind and to block things out, and I had a lot of practice at this over the course of my life. The Sickness of my sport was well embedded in me. It was consuming me. I was living, breathing, and eating what I was doing.

The territory had been pretty much running at rock bottom, not having drawn a lot of people for quite some time. In order to better my performance on the canvas, I used to go to Melnick Hall at UCLA where they had wrestling tapes from 1956 to 1960 that I watched during the day. These tapes showcased the talents of Dick Lane, Gorgeous George, and other famous grapplers from L.A's past. I would watch the reels over and over again, stopping the action and replaying it when I saw something that I wanted to learn.

But I was doing just fine on my own in spite of what Leo had been thinking when he first laid eyes on me. He must have been saying to himself: "This kid is too young. There's nothing I can do

Would watch old Wrestling Films

with this guy. Nobody likes the bagpipes and stuff like that. And on top of all that, he wears a skirt to the ring!" But he took a chance on my nineteen-year-old skinny ass anyway, and it wound up working out for both of us. I would change the face of wrestling before anybody on the West Coast realized what hit them.

Leo booked me against a wrestler named Java Ruuk, whose real name was Johnny Rodz. Just before the match against this mean-looking wrestler, who'd grown up on the tough streets of New York, Garibaldi seemed to be having second thoughts about having me face him. Leo knew Ruuk was very vicious and unorthodox between the ropes; he would just get in the ring and scratch and claw at you until you couldn't take it anymore.

But instead of taking me off the card, Leo came up with what *he* thought was a great plan. He said to me, "Come here, kid. I'm gonna give you a break. This is what I want you to do. I want you to go in there with this Java Ruuk and basically don't touch the guy. I don't want no offense from you. I don't want you to wrestle him, I want you to let him beat you and beat you down and then pin you one, two, three." Then he walked away.

Now I'm thinking to myself: "Break? Some plan. Then what?" But what I failed to realize at this time was that I was in Hollywood, where everything—and everyone—is make-believe. If you wanted to have any success in Hollywood, you had to be able to act no matter what your job was. It wasn't like IBM was calling to make me an executive or that that job as a brain surgeon had finally opened up; it was this or sweep the streets. Java Ruuk then proceeded to beat me to death in the ring and the crowd loved every last minute of it. Me, I was thinking this was dumb, and I was humiliated after I lost because I couldn't fight back, but in retrospect, I have to say that Leo Garibaldi was a total genius in the sport of professional wrestling.

Before the next week's match, Leo had this T-shirt made up for me that said: I'D RATHER SWITCH THAN FIGHT. Leo got the idea for the saying from a popular TV commercial for cigarettes. It was the

Java Ruuk

one with the guy with the black eye who said, "I'd rather fight than switch." Well, Leo, being the genius he was, made me wear the shirt into the ring the next time I had a match with Ruuk. Instead of getting the stuffing beat out of me again, Leo had me on the microphone doing interviews as Java's manager and new tag partner, explaining to the crowd that "I'd rather switch than fight." I told them that it had nothing to do with Java kicking the crap out of me the week before, but rather that I wanted to be the Arab wrestler's spokesperson because I cared so much and I'm such a nice guy!

This got a tremendous amount of heat with the mostly Mexican audience, as there was a large Hispanic population in Los Angeles and most of them had come to see the wrestler kick my ass again and not for me to make an about-face and become his manager and new tag partner. This little incident marked the beginning of a new phase in my wrestling career. I was learning how to become a master on the mike.

Working the mic.

Well, at first I didn't want to talk about myself, so I decided I would talk about Java. This was just laid upon me and I didn't know what to expect, but like FDR once said, "Some people just have greatness thrust upon them." So I looked over at Java Ruuk with that ugly rug on his head, and the words just started flowing naturally.

a natural

All of a sudden I had found a platform where I could become a man and make my mark, instead of having to take the backseat and let things happen to me. I was now front and center, and I liked the feeling of power. I had three cameras on me and six thousand people listening—a lot different from standing on a street corner playing my bagpipes and people just walking right past me. Now I had all of this attention. What was I supposed to do? I just got real comfortable, real quick on the mike, and everyone in attendance was listening and believing what I was saying. They forgot all about the beating that Java once gave me, and with all the anger spewing through the mike, I made these people believe that I was proud and not a coward.

Like to talk

1974 Java Ruuk

Up until this time I had probably done only two or three interviews. But I felt I had a bit of a knack for telling people what was going on. I had nineteen years of venom building up in my belly, and as I started doing these interviews, the edge in me started to come out. There was no preparation here. It was live TV, so it was all ad-lib. I was just put in front of the camera at the Olympic Auditorium, and they would say, "Okay, you've got three minutes. Tell us about yourself, and talk about Java Ruuk."

Here I was, a Canadian kid in Los Angeles in 1974, standing there with a kilt on and bagpipes in my hand, in front of six thousand Hispanics, next to a Puerto Rican acting like an Egyptian madman wearing a towel from the Motel 6 on his head, and they all wanted *me* to do something. So without hesitation, I blew up my bagpipes for them. Now, being a former bagpipe champion, I knew I could play them well, but the audience had no idea what to expect. At that moment all I could think of was Jack Benny and his violin and how bad he had played that instrument over the years. I realized how good he had to have really been in order to play that bad! The bagpipes, like the violin, are a beautiful instrument, but when they are up in your face, they tend to be pretty annoying, especially when you've got a good bagpipe player trying to play really bad!

Jimmy Lennon was the ring announcer that night. He was a fine man and probably the most famous ring announcer in boxing at that time. He also saved my life, later in my career, when he refused to get out of the way as a crazy gunman with a .45 automatic tried to take a shot at me right as I was about to enter the ring. After security subdued the lunatic, and after my match, they emptied the guy's gun, and there was a bullet with my name on it. If it hadn't been for Jimmy Lennon standing in this guy's way, I don't know what would have happened.

But getting back to my story about that night with Java Ruuk . . . I asked Jimmy Lennon to ask the crowd to stand for the Scottish national anthem and he did his best to comply. But they certainly hadn't paid good money to watch me play the pipes. These people

Bag Pipes

Plays Pipes

wanted action, but I wasn't going to let them have their way until I had mine. Even though all six thousand people were booing me, wanting me to put the pipes down and wrestle, I acted like I didn't care. Even Ruuk was going back and forth in the ring like a crazy man, wanting to tussle, but I still wanted to play my bagpipes. It took about two or three minutes and finally the crowd shut up and let me play. I started playing "Isle of Skye" while Lennon held the microphone down by what's called the chanter, which is the part of the bagpipes where the fingering is done, and now the music came blaring over the PA system.

Plays as part of act.

The booing ceased as people must have thought, "Hey, that's sort of a nice tune." But they were in for a big surprise when I started holding and dragging out the B, C, and E notes, sending annoying sounds throughout the Olympic Auditorium. These people now started coming unglued, and they started booing and throwing cups and lit cigarette butts in the ring at me.

That night marked the beginning of my new art—the art of ring psychology. I would play these annoying notes on the bagpipes and the people would boo, but they loved every second of it. I was amazed that I could control the masses. As the people would come to the crescendo of their booing, I would start to play the bagpipes really well, playing a jig like "The Irish Washerwoman." As soon as I noticed the people clapping and starting to get into it, I would play that annoying C note again. It was like torture. It was fucking annoying. They just wanted me out of there. All this emotion, and the match hadn't even begun! So by the time the bell rang, these people were ready to kill me, and the scary part of it all was that most of them probably could have, because remember, I was still a scrawny teenager at the time.

Got Boo'd

Well, after I got this heated crowd reaction the first time, Garibaldi started putting me out there as much as possible. He had me wrestle on the first match, then I'd referee the next bout, then I'd manage someone later on, and would finally wrestle in the last match. This went on for about six months, at a seven-nights-per-

Involved in numerous matches

Henry Winkler story

week clip. Well, it didn't take long for the word on me to start getting out, and soon I was meeting quite a cast of characters.

One of the characters I met at this time was none other than actor Henry Winkler. I was working out at the dojo with LeBell, and there was this movie they were shooting at the Olympic Auditorium with Winkler called *The One and Only*. Winkler was playing the part of an actor who became a wrestler because he was out of work, and LeBell got me a small part in the film.

Right before the scene with Winkler, LeBell grabs me like we were going to fight and slaps me hard three or four times in the face, and says to Henry, "You see this kid, you can't hit him too hard." Well, when it came time for "The Fonz" to hit me, he blasted me with this German helmet, knocking me a little too close to the camera. I then heard the director say, "I got me another Robert Redford here. Look at that. He's already cheating on his close-ups!"

After this experience, the director talked to me and wondered if I was interested in having an acting career. I said no, but in spite of this I was still sent a Screen Actors Guild card in the mail, even though I never asked for it or wanted any part of it! I was in the limelight of wrestling for the first time and I had found a home and a family. I wasn't about to let go of my family to be in the movies. Finally, I had something solid, and a place that would accept me for what and who I was. Little did I know that the director who'd asked me about acting had been Carl Reiner, and I turned him down— another brilliant career move!

Carl Reiner

Garibaldi started boasting that I was "going places that no other man has gone before." Well, Mike LeBell proved that to be true. Mike was a promoter who always came up with these ideas that didn't apply to wrestling. Some were good and some were bad, but this next one was an interesting one, though I found it to be humiliating.

Mike came up with a routine where I would hypnotize people. So, one night, I get to the arena and LeBell hands me this plastic gold watch on a plastic gold chain and I'm on TV hypnotizing Keith

Frankie, who later became known as Adrian Adonis. I'm telling him, "You're going to lose the match. You're going to lose the match," as I'm swinging the fake gold watch in front of his face. Now, you have to imagine the amount of embarrassment I was feeling at this time. Here I was, a kid among giants like Lonnie Mayne, Andre the Giant, and Harley Race, and I'm out there supposedly hypnotizing another wrestler. There was no sports-entertainment back then. They were all just laughing at me off camera and I felt humiliated.

Next thing I know, LeBell and Garibaldi are getting phone calls from the people in town who wanted to have me hypnotize them so that they could try to forget their troubles. Not wanting to pass on an opportunity to "help the public" (and draw a big crowd), Leo and Mike had me start coming to the arena at five o'clock—three hours before matches began—just so I could work "my magic." They had me set up in the balcony at the Olympic Auditorium with a lopsided table and the cheesiest red candle I had ever seen in my life. The line of people who were already there when I got to the arena was amazing. These people actually thought I could do this and were showing up by the boatload. People would come to me with all sorts of problems, and in no time I found myself saying things like: "You will get a hard-on; you will make love with your wife; you will find your dog . . ." Crazy stuff like that.

So now I go along with it for a while thinking it's fun and part of my job. This went on for about two months, and there were sometimes 200 to 250 people waiting for me to put them under my spell. I just couldn't believe these people actually thought I could do this.

But it all came to an end one day when reality checked in. Among the seventy-five or so people on line waiting to see me was this Mexican gentleman who was about forty years old. I asked him what his problem was. Basically, I was being an insensitive shit. He started talking to me about his family in front of all these other people. He starts crying and telling me about his wife who has cancer and his terrible problems with his kids. I'm thinking, "Wait a second, why am I doing this?" It was the first time I realized how much power one holds in one's hands simply by being featured in the media. That's the first time in my life that I applied morality to professional wrestling. I realized that I couldn't do this to these people. There would be no more hypnotizing coming from me. It was the first time I was drawing the line in a sport that's lineless. At the risk of losing my job, I told Leo and Mike that I was through deceiving these people and that the routine would not go any further.

Garibaldi argued with me, but I kept insisting that I couldn't do this anymore. After a while he understood my point and the next week I stopped doing the hypnotizing thing. This was the first time also that I started developing the "wrestling morals" and vowed I would not cheat the wrestling fan like that and jerk their feelings around ever again.

But now I had the added burden placed on me to come up with a promo for my next fight, which was against the very popular Chavo Guerrero. So the next week I showed up on TV sitting on a donkey, which was painted like a zebra, just like they do in Tijuana. I was wearing a sombrero and I had a carrot on the end of a stick, which was dangling in front of the donkey. Of course I was wearing my kilt and saying terrible things about Guerrero, while wearing an antagonizing T-shirt that said CONQUEROR OF THE GUERREROS. I started talking about "wetbacks" and how they were so uneducated and stuff like that.

The television station called Mike LeBell because they got so many complaints about my behavior. They were worried about the ratings, so the next week I had to go on TV and apologize to the Hispanic population. I said I didn't mean any disrespect and I would learn the Mexican national anthem on my bagpipes and play it in honor of their wonderful people. A few weeks went by and I started bragging about how good the anthem sounded on the bagpipes and that I'd soon be ready to play it. So now comes the Wednesday before the Friday-night main event, and I went on TV and said, "I've got it, I've learned the Mexican national anthem on the *gaita*"—

Spanish for "bagpipes." By this time these people believed that I had some sincerity in me, and couldn't wait to hear this new rendition of their country's song.

Well, don't ever let me fool you.

That Friday's house show was sold out and I was the single main event, so it was the first Olympic sold-out show that I was responsible for. In those days you and your opponent were directly accountable for drawing people to the matches, unlike today, when the federations tow the line. This was also the night when I was supposed to belt out my rendition of the Mexican national anthem before belting my opponent in the ring. The event was going to be on Channel 34, which would be broadcast across the nation in Spanish. Chavo wanted no part of my antics. He came from a big, well-known wrestling family (and I think I tackled every one of them except Mama Guerrero during my career) and he was more interested in taking part in the match than in the hype.

When I entered the ring that evening, I asked Jimmy Lennon to ask the crowd to please stand, as I was going to play the Mexican anthem on my bagpipes. The entire crowd stood up—mothers holding their babies, fathers standing at attention with their kids, some with their hands over their hearts and others with their caps off and their heads bowed, waiting to pay homage to their beloved Mexico. Lennon then placed the microphone down by my chanter, and I looked around in awe, knowing that the entire crowd and TV audience was now waiting on me. I blew up the bagpipes and I started playing, only it wasn't the Mexican national anthem . . . it was "La Cucaracha"!

Well, it's safe to say that the night was pretty much over. Up came the chairs, up came the knives . . . the entire place came unglued in a matter of seconds. L.A.'s finest, who were near the ring, now had a full-fledged riot on their hands. They whipped out their nightsticks, but even those didn't deter all these angry people from rushing the ring. I had to learn the art of punting people pretty quick. Pele couldn't have done as much punting as I did that night.

I would let them come up onto the ring apron because you've got to duck between the second and third rope in order to get in, and— boom!—I'd land a swift, quick kick to their chops and send them flying onto the auditorium floor. I learned to be pretty good at keeping the ring clear. Unfortunately, I didn't make it out without getting a few bumps and bruises myself, and I was also stabbed on this night. After Mike LeBell found out I was stabbed, he said, "Well, this is why they pay so much for those seats." Ah, the price of fame . . .

Even though it doesn't sound like it, this night went in my favor. The word started getting around about this guy who was selling out the West Coast, a territory that had been virtually dead. And the next thing I knew, I was flying to San Antonio, courtesy of the Hispanic TV station, to wrestle this young up-and-comer, Tully Blanchard, in his first pro match. He was the son of the area's promoter, Joe Blanchard. I'll never forget the feeling of walking into that arena with all these people knowing who I was. Up until this time I had never had this type of recognition. I drew quite a crowd that night in San Antonio.

I remember there used to be a policeman there named Rosie, whose job was to keep the crowd and the wrestlers under control. He carried a double-sided blackjack. On one side was sawdust, and on the other end was the real blackjack. Many times the promoter would send Rosie into the ring and he would hit the wrestler with the soft side of the blackjack to get control of him. Anytime a fan or somebody undesirable came unglued, Rosie would just switch that blackjack around and whack them until they were back under control.

After my match with Blanchard, I went back to the dressing room, and Terry Funk, the World Champion at the time, who had just completed his match, also came back. Just as I was getting out of the shower, a Hispanic fellow who was about six-foot-four and 270 pounds came backstage looking for some trouble. I remember Terry just charging this guy; he had his world-title belt in his hand

and just nailed this thug right in the face. Seconds later Rosie was on the scene with the blackjack. Rosie pulled the guy's pants down and hog-tied him with his own belt so he couldn't move, cuffed him, and kicked the shit out of him.

This began the violent era of my life, when violence became okay. I had already been stabbed once, and now my wrestling family and I, on one hand, and the wrestling fans, on the other, became two different worlds. At this time in my life I was a loose cannon. Challenge me about wrestling being fake and you wouldn't even have time to get the words out of your mouth. I would already be across the table with my hands around your throat. That's just what you did when someone questioned the morals of your livelihood. I was now in the dojo every day with Judo Gene LeBell, learning how to break bones. Gene LeBell is one of the toughest men I know, and now he was teaching me the ropes and how to hold my own against anyone. I was fighting by day and wrestling by night.

But all the training in the world couldn't have prepared me for one memorable match in Fresno. Whenever I tell this story people think I'm being funny, but to be honest with you, I didn't think it was funny then and I still don't find it funny now.

Roy Scheiers, a promoter on the San Francisco circuit, approached me about wrestling a bear. I can remember thinking to myself on the drive up to Fresno that I had never heard of this guy called "The Bear," but I took the booking anyway.

Well, the night arrives and I'm fashionably late as usual because I'm the star. (Well, in reality I'm not a star; there is no such thing. The only reason they call you a star is so they can butter you up and pay you less money; that's why you always avoid promoters.) When I finally get to the arena in Fresno, I walk in the locker room and there it was . . . standing on its hind legs, this huge, hairy creature with a bottle of Wild Turkey between its paws, and it's just guzzling that whiskey. The monster finishes the pint, smashes the bottle on the floor, and then the trainer gives him a Coke and he dumps that into his mouth in one shot, too, and lets the bottle go crashing to the floor. This is the first thing I see when I enter the dressing room . . . a fucking drunk bear! In the car over to the match, I'm thinking I'm wrestling Bear Man, but now I'm face-to-face with this real live Kodiak bear!

I'm informed that the bear's name is Victor—like I need to know its name; there were fifteen wrestlers in the dressing room and one bear and I need to know its name so I can identify him?—and that he weighs about 650 pounds. The trainer came over to me and explained the rules of wrestling a bear. He told me that you don't want to hit the bear, because he's got those huge paws and he'll swat you in the head and break your neck before you know what hit you. The good man also informed me that the bear's claws had been taken out and his front teeth were missing, but then he told me not to get my finger near the back of his mouth because he'd bite it off. Then the trainer told me how to lock up with the bear. He said that I've got to get up close to the beast, and once I'm close, the trainer will jab him in the ass with this stick. This will make the bear stand on its hind legs, and now it's my job to get up underneath him and get his paws on my shoulders and my hands on his shoulders. See, bears don't like to stand, so I have to move quick in order to keep him up on his hind legs.

So I'm considering my options. Here I have a drunk bear named Victor who weighs more than three times my weight and wants to either bite off all my fingers or break my neck when I get in the ring with him. Just as I'm about to make my decision about whether or not to go through with this, my good friend Jay comes up to me and slaps me in the ass like a football player does and, while laughing, tells me to "Go get 'em kid!" I figure he's laughing because he knows how nervous I am to go wrestle this bear.

So I'm in the ring, the bell rings, and the trainer jabs the drunk bear in the ass with the stick and I get up and I lock up under the bear. To win a wrestling match, you've got to pin the guy's shoulders to the mat for a three-count. When you lock up with a bear, you realize that a bear don't got no shoulders, so how the hell are you gonna beat him? Bears are natural wrestlers. They know how to arm-drag you and go behind you. This is exactly what the bear did to me. The next thing I know I'm down on the mat with about eight inches of bear snout up my ass, and for the life of me I can't figure out why. The people are laughing hysterically, but I fail to see the humor in this situation. All those rules that the trainer told me went right out the window. I clawed, beat, scratched, bit, and everything I could think of to do, and still I had bear up my ass. The people are now laughing so hard they're crying and little do they know that this bear is killing me. I'm getting mauled here and I really think I'm gonna die. I give the high sign to the trainer and yell, "Get this motherfucker off of me!" I was fighting for my life here.

Well, before I go any further, let me tell you why the bear loved my bum so much. It all goes back to the slap on the ass from my "good friend" Jay. He was not showing support, he was actually putting a handful of honey on my tights, giving the bear reason to go after my sweet ass. The bear smelled the honey and he was having a feast on the sticky smorgasbord on my ass. He even got under my trunks and pulled them down. But when he ran out of honey, he wasn't too happy. All that bear wanted to do was kill me.

The trainer finally ended up tranquilizing the beast, but it took a while for the drug to kick in. It takes about two minutes, which feels like two days, and in the meantime the bear continued to kick the shit out of me. I did everything I could to slow him down, but he just kept coming. Every time I turned around I was getting slapped back by the bear. Thankfully, the tranquilizer took effect and the bear passed out. I didn't care that my trunks were down around my ankles, I was just glad to get out of there alive. But the fun didn't end there. As I was trying to pull my trunks up and get out of the ring, my foot caught on the ropes and I took a nosedive, and went down headfirst right on the concrete. I'm now lying there with my shorts down and my ass exposed for all to see. Just another day in wrestling paradise. Now, you might think what Jay did to me that night was mean and evil, but this is how wrestlers play.

Back in Los Angeles, I started to keep a .357 Magnum with me at all times. I was into "fast drawing" the gun. York, an ex-marine, and I were always talking about firearms. One day I was at the gym and I left my pistol in my room at the Flamingo. I came back and the maids had found the gun and were all standing around causing this big commotion.

One of the rules I had been taught was that you should always keep the first chamber of your gun empty; this way, in case you hit the hammer accidentally, a round won't go off and hit somebody. In the next chamber you put a blank because if someone was coming, you can go ahead and shoot at them with the blank without having to worry about killing them. If they're still coming you're going to need the other four rounds! I stuck by this rule religiously.

Anyway, the maids had pulled the trigger and fired the blank, thank the good Lord! They were all looking for the lead and for dead people, I guess, and I tried to calm them all down before the police were called. If the police had come into my apartment that day, I would have been in a world of trouble.

The messed-up thing about my life at this point was that even though I was having more success than I ever imagined, I was also more reckless than I had ever been. I was portrayed as a rebel in the ring and started living up to the role outside of the ring. I became the image, despite the consequences. I couldn't see right from wrong at the time. All I know was that I went from driving a piece-of-shit Vega to a Caprice Classic almost overnight. My world wasn't about morals. No, the world of wrestling had its own code.

The code was powerful and it fucked up most of my life. I gave an oath, my word and my honor, to protect the sport of professional wrestling. As I tell you these things now, I'm having trouble because this code was so instilled in me. These men were and still are my family, my Frat Brothers. I swore to protect them and watch their backs under all circumstances. This has cost me a lot of money and many sleepless nights in my career. But for better or for worse, this code defined my life.

Wrestling has taught me many lessons: You always give 110 percent in your match. When you're finished, never make contact with the promoter, just get away from him. Never back down or take a back step, always hold your ground, no retreat, no surrender.

Wrestling also gave me my identity. I was never a "character." I was Roddy Piper. Nothing about me or my life was a show. Professional wrestling is not phony. The outcome may be predetermined, yes, but how you get there is your business and your pain. It is very real. The truth is, wrestling is very competitive and only the best get to the top. Wrestling took this kid, Roderick George Toombs, and formed him into the man known as "Rowdy" Roddy Piper.

The more aggressive I was, the better I did. The more aggressive I was, the more people backed off, and I felt more comfortable, especially doing television interviews. I know now that this aggression was a mask, a shield. Under my tough-guy exterior, I'm a very *Real* tender guy with feelings, but with my mask on, no one could hurt *Roddy?* me.

Over time I learned to become a one-man survival team. If there is one thing I've learned in life, it's that at the end of the day I am all alone, nobody really gives a damn. It's either do or die. And this philosophy is my biggest nemesis. From what I have been taught, being a coward is so shameful that I would rather die than have people perceive me as one.

No coward!

3

Ribbing on the Square

My becoming a loner with a do-or-die attitude allowed me to pick my game up a notch. Being on the apron every night was becoming routine; either I was kicking an opponent's ass in a match or I was part of a riot. The more aggressive I was on the mat and mike, the more I was getting recognized in the industry. But this aggression wasn't an act; it was honest. I had finally found a way to release all these pent-up emotions that were locked inside of me. My performances in the ring were getting a lot of attention on the West Coast and the word was getting back to promoters across the country. Mike LeBell was like a reporter on the beat, informing wrestling bigwigs like Vince McMahon Sr., one of the top dogs in the East, and other promoters of big networks how popular I was becoming and how much money I was drawing. Even though I was a heel, I was a crowd favorite. My unique personality and fighting style drew fans to the arena in record numbers.

The buzz became so strong that McMahon Sr. wanted me to come to New York to wrestle in Madison Square Garden. Everyone seemed to hear about it before I did. Word spread all over the country that this "boy wonder" was going to New York. It was a big deal because I was just twenty years old; they never had anyone in New York this young that they would consider as a main-eventer. I remember when LeBell told me. He asked, "Kid, what does MSG mean to you?"

20 yrs old invited to the Garden

"It's something they put in Chinese food that's bad for you," I answered.

"No. What does MSG mean to you?"

"Mike, it don't mean nothing to me."

Mike was beginning to turn red. "Madison Square Garden! I got you booked in Madison Square Garden!"

So I was off to the Big Apple.

As it turned out, I would not only get to experience wrestling at the Garden, I would also learn another hard and valuable lesson as I became the victim of a common practice in the industry called "ribbing on the square." Despite not having anything to do with physical contact, ribbing on the square is one of the most lethal weapons in professional wrestling. It is a form of warfare disguised as humor. As you can imagine, these ribs can do serious damage to one's psyche.

Embarresses the wrestler very often

Ribbing is practiced industry-wide. Wrestlers do it, promoters do it, but the intent is always the same: to bring the unsuspecting victim to his knees, and in some cases even to get rid of him.

I remember one time, there was this wrestler in Portland who was constantly getting over, and he felt he was underpaid. He was always riding his promoter, trying to get more money, but the P didn't want to pay him.

At this time the National Wrestling Alliance (NWA) used to hold these annual conferences in Vegas, and all the territory owners would go to these closed sessions where they talked about how to keep the wrestlers' salaries down. They didn't want some wrestler from the West Coast talking to some guy from the East and comparing their salaries; they wanted it to seem like they were all earning the same. It was just organized tyranny.

So at this conference, the promoter from Portland said that a particular wrestler was giving him a hard time about making more money. The promoter from Kansas City agreed to help him and a few weeks later showed up at an event in Portland. After the match, he called over the problem wrestler and said, "Gee, man, you were great. I could really use someone like you. What are you getting paid here?" Now, the wrestler thought this was his opportunity. He told the guy that he was unhappy in Portland, that he didn't feel like he was being treated well. So the promoter said to him, "Look, why don't you do the right thing? Give your notice . . . you don't want to burn any bridges. Then move your wife and kids to Kansas City. We'll find you a nice house, we have great schools, and you'll be set." So that's what the wrestler did. He packed up his family and moved.

They booked him once in Kansas City, but then they never used him again. So now this guy is out of a job, he just bought a new home, uprooted his kids, and all so that the promoters could remind him who was boss. Ribs like this tend to mess up your day a bit.

I had experienced ribbing before in my career, but in New York I would get a lesson that I wouldn't soon forget.

As soon as LeBell booked me in New York, he started burning up the phone lines to let everyone and their mother know that I was going to be wrestling at Madison Square Garden. Promoters were coming in from all over the world . . . Japan . . . Germany . . . Everyone who was anyone was going to be there to see this "boy wonder" who was selling out all over the West Coast.

In preparation for my trip, I started bulking up, trying to put on a little extra weight. I trained real hard. New York was a big man's territory, where there were people like Andre the Giant, who was seven-four and weighed in at 520 pounds, and Superstar Billy Graham. There wasn't anybody there wrestling under 280 pounds, so basically I was a midget going into a giant's world. I was six-

Promoters from all over / Wanted to see Roddy [handwritten marginalia]

Roddy undersized

foot-one and my weight at this time was 210 pounds, so I knew I had to start training in a different way to put a little bulk on.

Another thing I did to get ready for New York was go shopping. I bought this sharp three-quarter-length leather jacket. It cost a couple of hundred dollars, which was a lot of money for me then, but I got it because I wanted to make a good impression on everyone. Actually, I had no clothes except for one green corduroy suit, a pair of jeans, and my moccasins, so I felt I had to splurge a little in order to make myself appear successful.

When the day came for me to pack up and go, I had Killer Brooks drive me to the airport. We got there, he drove me straight to the door, but then I paused for a second and something in my gut told me something was wrong, that I shouldn't go. So I turned to Killer and said, "Take me home." He was like, "What? What are you talking about?" I just told him I wanted to go home. Killer just sat in the driver's seat looking at me like I had grown two heads or something. "Are you fucking crazy? This is Madison Square Garden!"

Got to airport then turned around

I just said, "Killer, I don't know. I'm just going by my gut. Take me home."

He reluctantly took me home, and in order to get myself off the hook with LeBell and McMahon, I lied, telling them there was bad weather for my connecting flight to New York and I couldn't make it. This is the only time in my entire wrestling history when I chickened out. I just had a gut feeling. I just didn't want to go.

Lied to Mike Lebell

I thought that was the end of that, but the next week when I came back into the Olympic Auditorium, Mike LeBell ran up to me and said, "Hey, don't worry. I got you rebooked on the next card in Madison Square Garden." I immediately said to myself, "Motherfucker. Are you kidding me? I don't want to go."

Re booked

The Garden had a wrestling event once every three or four weeks, and Mike had taken it upon himself to get me on the very next card. Now I was even more scared to go to New York. Why? I don't know. You can ask Sigmund and his brother Freud. Maybe they have the answer. All I knew was I had to go to New York to wrestle and I really didn't want to. But now what was I supposed to do? Here was a guy helping me out and getting me my biggest break thus far so I could make a name for myself and I was trying to figure out every way possible to sabotage my journey. Was I fucking crazy? This was a chance of a lifetime. And now that Mike had put his ass on the line and rebooked me, there was no way I could back down on him two times in a row, especially if I wanted to stay in the sport. Finally, I got the nerve to go to Madison Square Garden, where I learned a real rough lesson that toughened me up both as a human being and as a professional wrestler.

I arrived in the city and made my way to the arena. I have to admit I was pretty nervous, but I put a good mask on. Backstage, I was greeted by the nicest people. I remember Captain Lou Albano, Freddie Blassie, the Grand Wizard, Domenic Denucci, and some of the other wrestlers going out of their way, making sure I was comfortable.

Captain Lou, Freddie, and the Grand Wizard even went as far as coming up to me and saying, "Hey, kid, we've been watching you on TV. We don't want you here; you're too good." They were all laughing, and I thought, "Oh, isn't that nice, what a nice compliment." They wished me good luck and patted me on the back. So I'm thinking; "Hey, what was I so afraid of? This isn't too bad."

I went about my business getting ready for my big match. I went into the locker room and looked for the farthest corner I could find. I put on my kilt and boots and then grabbed my bagpipes to get it ready for the evening's performance. The bagpipes are a woodwind instrument, so before you play them you have to get the reeds wet. This process can be quite annoying, especially when you're in the confines of a small dressing room with other wrestlers. But I had been doing this my whole career, and after getting over the initial shock of the sounds, none of the guys ever really seemed to mind.

But what I didn't realize was that this was a different set of wrestlers on a different coast. The guys I was around before when

I got my bagpipes ready were friends, mentors, and father figures. The guys in the New York locker room were strangers. While I initially thought everyone at the event was making an effort to be nice and to make me feel at home, I would find out the hard way that they were really just ribbing me through their smiles.

My time to shine was moments away. I was all dressed and ready to go, and I played my pipes a little in the hallway before I went on. I also wanted to warm up a bit before my match, so about ten minutes before I was slated to wrestle, I left my bagpipes in the dressing room and went off to do some push-ups out in the hall, trying to get a quick pump. I wanted to look as big as I could. After all, folks, as you remember, I'm a midget in a giant's business. After doing a couple hundred push-ups, I was ready to go and went back to the room to pick up my bagpipes and made my way up the runway to the famous ring.

When my opponent and I entered the ring for the second match of the night, the announcer asked the crowd to be quiet. He told them they were about to be treated to a special rendition of the Scottish national anthem on the bagpipes played by Roddy Piper. It took about three or four minutes to get the sold-out crowd settled— it's hard to get twenty-four-thousand New Yorkers to shut up when they've paid thirty-five dollars apiece to scream. Finally they're quiet, and all eyes are on me. The promoters are all fixed on me. I could also see other wrestlers peeking through the curtains into the arena trying to get a look. They all came out wanting to see what was so special about this "boy wonder."

Having all the confidence in the world at that moment, I blew up the bagpipes to start to play. I blew and I squeezed. I blew and I squeezed. I blew and squeezed that bag as hard as I could with my left elbow, but no sound was coming out. I'm thinking to myself, "What the hell is going on? What's wrong with my pipes?" I continued to blow and my face turned red. I looked over at the announcer, who was holding the mike and he was just waiting. My opponent was getting impatient. And I certainly wasn't getting a good reception from the crowd. They were like, "Send the amateur home. We came to see professional wrestling."

Finally, frustration and embarrassment took over and I dropped my bagpipes and charged the guy. I pinned him within two or three minutes and then I left the ring and went back to my dressing room, trying to figure out what had gone wrong. Here I was, a kid from nowhere on the world's biggest stage with some of the world's biggest wrestlers, and I flat out bombed. The crowd was looking for me to play the bagpipes and then give them a good wrestling match, and what did I give them? Nothing. The only thing that blew that day was me in the ring. I went back to the dressing room and sat staring down at the floor, too embarrassed to even look anyone in the eyes.

When all was said and done, Vince McMahon Sr. basically said, via messenger, "Don't call us, we'll call you." It was the first black mark against my talent, and that night I became probably the biggest joke in the industry for at least the next month.

On the plane back to Los Angeles, I examined my bagpipes, trying to figure out what was wrong with them. The raw anger I had felt in the ring came back to me when I stuck my hand in the chanter and pulled out a wad of toilet paper six feet long. Son of a bitch! I found out later that Freddie Blassie was the one who had done the dirty deed. That lousy bastard and all the rest of them were all smiling and laughing in the dressing room with me beforehand, but I found out the hard way that the last laugh was on me.

It took years for the real story of what happened that night to come out. And I realize now that when they joked, "We don't want you here; you're too good. We want to keep our jobs," they really meant it. Those guys were intimidated by me. They were scared I was gonna move in on their territory. Knowing this is a small consolation, though. The damage was done. I had bombed for the first time ever in my career and was the laughingstock of the industry. The incident was humiliating, but what was worse was the realization that I had been manipulated by some of the best in the sport of wrestling, and they had robbed me of a young boy's dream of being on top in the biggest territory in the world. It would be at least ten years before I was invited back to wrestle in New York.

That night in Madison Square Garden was a really tough lesson for me. Many years later I did an episode of *Walker, Texas Ranger,* and became good friends with the star of the show, Chuck Norris. Chuck and I got along really well not only because we were both actors and athletes, but also because we both had mutual feelings about practical jokes. During our friendship, we exchanged industry stories, both good and bad, and I remember he once said to me that he didn't like people making him the brunt of their jokes. I told him that I was the same way, and proceeded to let him in on the humiliating incident in New York.

I let him know that they had really hurt my feelings, and I was even more mad at myself for letting them get past my mask. But I knew that somehow I had to recover because a sensitive wrestler just wouldn't make it. I explained to Chuck that it made me have a rhino skin that just got thicker and thicker. Looking back on the experience, I know the New York gig tainted me, and that it was a hell of a lesson to learn and a tough way to learn it. But it never happened to me again. Fool me once, shame on you. Fool me twice, shame on me.

Another infamous "rib war" happened earlier in my career and almost cost a wrestler his life—twice. The ribbing involved two wrestlers who wound up getting way too carried away with their mischievous deeds, almost leading to disaster. One of the wrestlers who was involved in this rib was Johnny Valentine. He was this big guy who would come to the ring with this long robe, and he would just stare at the fans. They would go nuts! They believed in Johnny and everything he was about in the ring. He would just take a man and push the guy's head back and pound the dog out of him! I remember watching Johnny wrestle when I was a young wrestler in Houston and we'd be on the same card. He was always amazing.

The other player in the incident was Jay "The Alaskan" York, who I'd hung out with in L.A. Jay was about six-foot-six, had a bald head and beard, and wore a big open Pendleton shirt showing off his huge hairy chest. He also had a big-ass belt around him, and wore jeans with lineman boots with a buck knife hanging on his hip. Oh yeah, I almost forgot his most important accessory, his twelve-foot bullwhip, which, if you recall, had saved me from that crazed witch and her cult at the Renaissance fair.

At one time these two were working in the same territory, so they started ribbing each other back and forth—all in fun and games. Valentine, for example, used to love to shit in wrestlers' shoes. He had a very special and unique talent that I have never seen duplicated to this day. When shitting in the unsuspecting victim's shoes, he could top off his masterpiece with the perfect Dairy Queen whip every time. Now try and imagine this scene for a second. You've got this mammoth monster not only doing his dirty business in this poor soul's shoes, he's also wiggling his bum to get that perfect whip on there! Classic stuff! You just can't make up something like that!

As if the shit in the shoes wasn't enough, another time, on the road in Canada, Johnny took a garden hose, ran it from a kitchen to York's brand-new Cadillac convertible, and filled the convertible up with water—in Canada, during the winter! Needless to say, York had a block of ice in his car in the morning.

About a month later Jay retaliated. While Johnny was out drinking in an all-night club, Jay hired a welding truck and had Valentine's car welded with angle iron to the parking meters. I remember Jay telling me that he waited until 4 A.M. for Johnny to stagger out of the bar to find his car. Jay said that Val was so drunk that he didn't even notice what had been done. Then Valentine got in his car and started it up, thinking he was going to pull away. But it wasn't to be. Johnny put the car in drive and hit the gas and tried getting out of his spot, causing sparks to fly everywhere and the smell of burning rubber to pollute the air. Maybe Val was too drunk to notice even this because he still tried to get out of the spot by putting the car in reverse. Again no luck. Johnny then got out of the car to go back into the bar to call a tow truck because he thought something was wrong with his car. As he stepped out, he tripped over the angle iron, causing him to curse and scream.

Now it was Johnny's turn again.

Johnny had a Halliburton, which was a type of locking suitcase that all the wrestlers wanted but couldn't afford. A Rolex and a Halliburton were signs of success, and Johnny had them both. Whenever we wrestled, we would give Valentine whatever valuables we had and he would lock them in his case for safekeeping.

Since Valentine was the main-event draw, he was always on last, and he spent most of the night in the dressing room while everyone else was wrestling in the arena. So one night Johnny was in the locker room, and he noticed that Jay York left his inhaler out. Jay had asthma and after a match he would have to take a few puffs on this breathing device to get his wind back. Valentine took the inhaler—Jay was in the ring wrestling at this point—and dumped out the medicine and filled it with lighter fluid. When Jay came back from the ring looking for a breather, he reached for his inhaler and took a couple of big puffs and immediately fell to the ground convulsing. He couldn't breathe.

By this time Johnny was in the ring wrestling for his usual forty- to fifty-minute match. When Jay finally came to, he figured out what had happened. He was steaming mad and he quickly got dressed, went out to his truck, and grabbed his sawed-off shotgun and put it under his trench coat.

He came back into the dressing room and Valentine was in the shower. When Val stepped out of the shower, Jay opened his trench coat and leveled the sawed-off shotgun at him. Jay was going to kill him. Valentine just stared at Jay, looked into his eyes, and started laughing, like he didn't believe Jay would pull the trigger. Something in Johnny's laugh snapped Jay out of it, and he sort of came to his senses. But he was still pissed as hell, so he pointed the shotgun at Johnny's Halliburton and blasted a fucking hole in it six inches wide, causing everybody's jewelry, wallets, and valuables to be blown away. There were also twelve wrestlers who were deaf for two days after that loud blast! Jay told me later that the thing that saved Val's life was when they made eye contact. If Val hadn't started laughing in disbelief, Jay would have shot him.

While Johnny didn't realize that Jay had been dead serious the night before, he came to that conclusion the next morning when his car wouldn't start. He stepped out of the car and opened the hood—only to find dynamite wired to the distributor. But Jay did him a favor by disconnecting the distributor, saving him from blowing to bits. Also under the hood was a note saying: "See how close you came?!"

The two men finally got together and said enough is enough.

Or so we thought.

A few months go by and Johnny is in the shower after a match. Harley Race and a bunch of the other wrestlers are in the locker room shooting the breeze when Jay York comes storming in as Valentine is just walking out of the shower. York yells, "You son of a bitch, I told you never to fuck with me again! I told you I'd kill your ass!" Then he pulls out a .357 Magnum from under his jacket, points it at Val, and shoots.

Well, it looks like a bullet hit Johnny, as there's blood everywhere in the stall and he's hunched over shaking in the corner of the shower grabbing his chest. York is now slowly looking around like he's flipped. What Jay didn't know was that Harley Race, who was on his far right-hand side, had reached down and gotten on his own piece and hid it under his towel. Harley tells York to put the gun down, but Jay doesn't listen. Unbeknownst to Jay, Harley then reaches under his towel and puts his finger on the trigger of his gun and again orders York to put his weapon down. But Jay just wasn't listening. Just as Harley was about to shoot Jay, Valentine starts laughing, gets up, and walks out of the shower, showing everyone the wrappers from packs of ketchup he got from the concession stand.

The other wrestlers and I were all amazed, not only at how real the incident looked, but also how close Jay came to being blasted by Harley! But I should have known. What did I say the rules of a .357 Magnum were? First chamber empty, second one blank . . . but that bastard York had us all fooled.

Valentine was a master both in and out of the ring. He took a liking to me and I'll never forget a piece of advice he gave me. He said, "I can't make them believe that wrestling is for real, but I sure as hell can make them believe I am." I took those words to heart, and from that moment on based my entire career on them.

After three and a half years, it was time for me to say good-bye to Los Angeles and Leo Garibaldi and Judo Gene LeBell and hello to Portland, Oregon, and my old-time wrestling friend Buddy Rose and local promoter Don Owens. I first met Buddy when he started wrestling in the AWA for Verne Gagne. I hadn't seen him for years, but then he started coming to L.A. to go to the racetrack. Rose had been wrestling in Portland and he was the biggest star they had at the time. He had once made me an offer to come to Portland to wrestle, but I turned him down. But the more I thought about the offer, the more I liked it. I knew that in order to get to the top of my sport, I had to keep on going and get bigger and bigger and bigger.

It was a big step for me. It was one of the hardest things I had to do at that point in my career because L.A. was the first place where I had gotten over as a solid main-eventer. And to leave and go somewhere where I wasn't known and start all over again took a lot of courage. What was I, nuts? I was already king in L.A. Why would I want to leave the biggest entertainment town in the world to go wrestle in front of a bunch of Trailblazers? And how was I going to tell LeBell and Garibaldi? It's easier to give your notice when you're not drawing money and your promoters and bookers haven't built the territory around you. But when they build the cards and matches around you, it sorta makes you feel like you owe them something.

These two top-notch men had helped me so much with my career. Leo, a bona fide wrestling genius, prepared me mentally for the ring, while Judo Gene took over my physical training. Under their guidance, I was able to develop my own style of wrestling—a style that would help me put the "Rowdy" in Roddy Piper. Because of them I formed a kind of wrestling that was like street fighting. It was during this time that I developed a wrestling technique that people were all of a sudden talking about, one that was not technical at all. It had some really unorthodox moves—a lot of kicking, trying to take your foe's eyes out, putting your finger inside your opponent's mouth and trying to rip the skin out, cross-facing, choking, and gurgling—all stuff that wasn't seen nightly in regular professional matches. But despite having mixed emotions about the move to Portland, I decided to go for it. I may not have been blessed with a lot of common sense, but nobody can ever accuse me of not having humongous balls.

After three and a half years together, all Leo told me before I left was, "Thanks for all the blood and guts, kid." He didn't even shake my hand. That's just the nature of the sport. Wrestlers come and go and you try not to get too close. But Leo and Gene gave me the tools I needed to succeed. I left Los Angeles a consummate professional wrestler, ready for any kind of action, baby—as Pedro Morales used to say. I was ready to take on anybody and anything, and I was afraid of nothing.

Leo Garbaldi
and Gene Lebell

very

The Portland Years

THE next challenge in my wrestling career would take place on the Oregon circuit. I hopped into my brand-spanking-new silver Caprice Classic and said good-bye to L.A. and hello to Portland. In keeping with tradition, when I reached the city limits, I opened up my window to alert the new town that Roddy Piper had arrived. But this time something was different. Instead of having to roll my window down, I just had to push a button, because now I was driving with power—both in my car and in my career. Once I felt the cool Oregon breeze, I stuck my head out of my Caprice and yelled, "Look out, Portland, here I come, and I'm going to kick your fucking ass!" Of course no one heard me but God. After all, who else was listening? And moreover, who else cared?

I then made my way into town and hooked up with Buddy Rose. He would introduce me to Don Owens and his brother Elton, who was also a promoter, controlling the Eugene, Medford, and Salem promotions. During my time in Oregon, I would find Don Owens to be one of the fairer promoters in the professional wrestling busi-

promoter
Don Owen

ness. In my eyes, he and Paul Bosch were tops. However, Elton was a character and was down there with the low of the low. He was an oddball. He would always introduce himself to people by saying, "Hello, I'm Don Owens's brother Elton." And everything about this guy was bad. He wore a bad toupee that looked like poodle roadkill, smoked cheap cigars, and was a heavy drinker. He paid the wrestlers off in dollar bills and rolls of quarters and would watch your facial expressions while he forked over the cash. The established guys there—Stan Stasiak, Johnny Eagles, Jonathan Boyd, Killer Brooks, and Jimmy Snuka—all tipped me off about what to do when Elton was paying me. They said to never smile because the reason he would stare at you when he was paying you was that he was waiting for you to crack a smile. And the minute your lips turned upward and you looked happy, Elton would stop the cash flow right there, figuring you were satisfied with your payout. It's safe to say that he wasn't very popular with the guys.

Elton also had one other quirk. In every match he wanted us to shoot for the first minute or so. He would give twenty-five dollars to the winner and fifteen to the loser. The object of this shoot was to pin your opponent for a one-count, which enabled the prick to determine the winner. What that old fuck didn't know was that we got together before the match and agreed to split the forty dollars. The way we determined who was going to be pinned for the one-count was very simple: we flipped a coin just like they do before the kickoff of every NFL game. We really didn't give a shit who won the toss or shoot, we just wanted half the cash.

After every match, Elton would come into the locker room and say, "Oh boys, that was a hell of a shoot." At the end of the day everyone was happy. We got to split the money and Elton got a hard-on. I guess he never heard of Viagra.

Other than Buddy, one of the first wrestlers I came into contact with in Portland was "Killer" Tim Brooks, who was also known as "The Waxahachie Wildman." Besides helping me get started on the

Oregon beat, it was Tim who was to introduce me to the love of my life, Kitty.

Killer was a wonderful man who had hair all over his body—except on his head. And he loved to smoke these little cigars. He was the full wrestling package in more ways than one. The promoters both loved and hated to have him on their cards. Brooks was a hot commodity who could help sell out a territory in an instant, but he was also a time bomb that was waiting to explode. The cigar-loving grappler had a rebel side in him that was great in the ring but dangerous outside of it.

Despite the cigar stench he reeked of, I took an instant liking to him; especially when he and I teamed up to play some nasty tricks on Elton Owens. Killer Brooks was surely one of a kind.

One of the finer memories I have of my time with Killer was when we were wrestling on a card in Salem for Elton. It was in a dirty building that had old dried-up blood on the floors and walls in the cruddy dressing rooms from years of use and abuse by wrestlers. It was definitely one of the worst facilities either of us had ever wrestled in, but we tried to make the best of the situation. Unfortunately Elton had a way of making a bad situation worse. One night, just as we're all getting ready to go out and give the Salem people their money's worth, Elton strolls into the locker room, sucking on one of his cheap cigars, and starts running his mouth. At one point he gets so wrapped up in what he's saying that he takes his cigar out of his mouth and puts it down on one of the tables in the dressing room so he can rant and rave about the night's matches. Elton is so busy yelling at us that he doesn't notice Killer grab the cigar and stick the lip end up his own ass and twist it around a couple of times, and then put it right back where he found it. Now, folks, I swear this is the truth. About five minutes later Elton finishes his rant, turns and picks up his cigar, and puts it in his mouth. We were all holding in our laughter, trying to keep a straight face. Watching Owens suck on that ass-wiped cigar, I was dying inside. Holding in the laughter was so hard that my eyes started watering. Elton looked at me with a puzzled expression and asked me what was the matter. I didn't dare say a word because I was afraid I'd just burst out laughing. So I just shrugged my shoulders. Elton just shook his head and told us to hurry up and get ready for the next match. As he was walking out of the locker room, he took a big puff of his cigar and muttered, "Aaaugh! It smells like shit in here." It's times like that you just don't forget!

Another crappy Elton Owens story came when we were wrestling in Roseburg, Oregon. Again the cheap son of a bitch booked us to wrestle in a dump. This place didn't even have locker rooms, just a big stage that everybody used to change on. To make matters worse, there weren't even any showers. In order to get cleaned up after the match, we had to walk through the crowd, past the hot-dog stand, and take turns using the sinks that they had kept the hot dogs in. Now just imagine the scene after the match: a bunch of sweaty, smelly wrestlers are all trying to share this little ol' sink. Let me tell you, it wasn't a pretty sight.

Another thing that wasn't pretty was that there were no bathrooms close to the stage. In order to reach the toilet, we again had to make our way through the crowd, past the hot-dog guy and past the sink. Well, it just so happens that I had to go to the bathroom right before I was supposed to go on. There was no way I was going to make that trek down through the arena, through all the people who hated me and who I was about to perform in front of. It would have been easier if I had to take a piss; I could have found a corner or bottle anywhere. But number two was going to be tricky. So I found a dark spot on the corner of the stage, took a brown paper bag, pulled my trunks down, and proceeded to take a monstrous shit, hoping to hit the bag. But as I'm squatting, Elton decides to come up onstage. Thinking quickly, I hold the corner of the bag and start doing free squats, with my trunks just far enough up to cover my front. As he comes by, he stops for a second and, thinking I'm doing exercises before I go on, says, "Ah, you're a good kid, always staying in shape. But jeez, it smells like shit in here!" Elton left and

I finished my dump and threw the bag over by the furnace, and then I went on to wrestle.

Killer and I were not only sharing laughs together at this time, we also were living together. Johnny Eagles had helped Killer and me find a lovely place in the same apartment complex where he was living. The two-bedroom place was very nice—at least before *we* started living in it.

The two of us did pretty well for ourselves while we were living together, both in the ring and on the social scene. There was one girl in particular who left a lasting impression on me. Killer Brooks had this girlfriend we called "Wombat." Whenever he wanted to sow his oats, he'd go into his room with Wombat. To tell you the truth, I don't really know what went on behind those closed doors because I was doing my own thing, but in all honesty I didn't want to know. I would wake up early every Saturday morning to go to the gym because there would be all this "funk" in that apartment— tons of empty beer bottles and cans, cigar butts, and what looked like spit on the floor. What these two did nobody knows, but shit was starting to grow in there, man! And to top it off, there was this terrible aroma that filled the apartment that seemed to exude from Killer's room after a night of combat.

Wombat was a nice-looking girl and all, but what she could be doing with Killer and to Killer was beyond me. When I'd come back from the gym she would be gone, so I hardly ever saw her. But one time Wombat came over to the apartment to see Killer and he wasn't there. One thing led to another and I "fiddled" with her. After I did the nasty, I felt bad for making it with my roommate's girl. So I did the honorable thing that a wrestler would do and decided I wouldn't tell him. It would just cause animosity between us and, more importantly, make my life a living hell. I would have to sleep with one eye open each night, afraid that Killer would come into my room and pull a Lorena Bobbitt.

Well, I soon found out that I didn't need Killer for that. I kept my little secret from my big friend for about a week until I noticed this thing starting to grow on the base of my penis. I swear to you, it had lungs of its own and was getting bigger and nastier looking by the day. I know I had a big decision to make: Do I tell Killer about what happened, hoping that he'll not only forgive me, but also provide me with some info on how to get this alien off my dick? Or do I say nothing, let my dick fall off, and live the rest of my life penisless? Hell, I knew the answer right away . . . I'm telling Killer!

So finally I had the balls to tell Brooks. I approached him and said: "Killer, I've got a confession." I pulled my pants down, and he goes, "Ah, you've been with Wombat. That's okay, but we're gonna have to fix that." I was relieved. Killer was not mad at me, and more importantly, he had a remedy for my Wombat-itus. He tells me to sit down and he comes back holding this white-hot needle, that he just heated up on the stove, holding it with a pair of pliers.

As soon as I saw him holding that steaming needle with the pliers, I jumped up out of my seat and said, "Whoa, Killer! What are you going to do with that?" He tells me to "sit down, drop your pants down, and pull your dick out." I then said, "Killer, are you sure about this?" The next thing I know he jabbed that needle into the alien—damn, that hurt!—and squeezed it so hard I thought it was going to burst! But he came through for me in a big way. While I still have the scar from that memorable prick, the disease never showed its ugly ass again, so I owed Killer big-time for helping me out.

As for Killer and me, the only problem we had was during our first meeting. If we were going to be a pair, we had to decide what we were going to do on the wrestling circuit. Both of us had been wrestling as heels throughout our careers, and Buddy Rose was also a heel at the time and was the main draw in the Oregon area. So the three of us had a powwow to try and decide how we were going to solve this problem. There were too many chiefs and not enough Indians. We had a choice to make here: we could try to cut one another's throat for the biggest piece of the pie, or we could come up with an arrangement that we were all comfortable with so each of us could come away with an equal slice. We decided that Buddy Rose and his partner, Ed Wiskowski, would be the main heels and we would become another entity. I started out my career in Portland with everyone hating me, but would make an about-face in almost no time, becoming a well-liked wrestler with the Oregon fans.

The first night I was in Portland I wrestled Johnny Eagles on live TV. People had never seen anything like me before. From the bagpipes to the kilt, they didn't know what the hell to expect from me. They were used to seeing these veterans grapple the old-fashioned way. They weren't used to seeing a young kid go full throttle, looking for more and more action.

First match in Portland

What was also amazing and unique at this time in my career was that I didn't tell the people how to feel about me. I just did my thing on the mat and let the people make up their own mind. This is where the real depth, psychology, and foundation for Roddy Piper was born. I was fearless. This was also the second place where I could free-fall and further develop the interviews I started in L.A., establishing rules such as "nobody tells me what to say in an interview." While living in Los Angeles, I once ran into Ella Fitzgerald and she gave me a great piece of advice: "Give them a good beginning and a great ending, and they will forgive a lot in between!" The lady had it down.

At this point in my career I had ascertained that interviews were 75 percent of professional wrestling. So on any given night my interviews had the power to make people who were sitting home and watching me on TV get so pissed off that they would elbow their wives in disbelief, then get up, get in the car, drive to the arena, pay to park, buy a handful of tickets and some popcorn, and get in their seats to yell at me while I was in the ring for my match. So when the night was over everybody went home happy. I would go back to my hotel room with their money and they would go home smiling because they'd been able to air out their frustrations.

Learned how important the interview was

How did I rile these fans up so bad? you ask. Well, it all stemmed from my unique style of wrestling interviews that was still in development at this time. Yes, I had reached a certain level of skill on the mike while I was in L.A., but now I was given free rein in Portland to try and further develop my unique style, which incorporated current events into my interviews. What was going on around town or in the world always seemed to strike a nerve in people. I also put honesty into my interviews. The technique I started to adapt to professional wrestling was one that was both direct and subliminal. For example, one time after an annual event, the Portland Rose Festival, where they have all these floats similar to the Macy's Thanksgiving Day Parade, I did an interview that was full of double entendres. I took advantage of some poor unfortunate boob who was supposed to measure all the floats before the event began on Saturday morning to make sure they would fit down the blocks of the parade route. But he must have been asleep at the wheel because as the pipe bands were playing and all the normal hoo-hah that goes on in American parades was taking place, a rolling exhibit tried to turn the corner, but found out too late that it couldn't fit.

On TV that night, I started mocking the whole situation of a float getting stuck. I said to the now-attentive crowd: "Let me get this straight. You people got a float in a parade that can't even get around the corner. How stupid are you? Don't you know that the square pegs don't go in the round holes . . . ?" and as I am doing this I'm lifting the sporran of my kilt. I am insinuating some type of sexual meaning by this gesture, but I'm talking about something totally different.

Then I ripped into the guy who was supposed to measure the floats. What kind of brain surgeon was he? I then take the remark a couple of steps further by questioning the local politicians and teachers: "These are the same people I'm paying taxes to, the same people I'm trusting to teach my children in school? You want me to put my children in a school in a town that can't figure out how to

get a float around the corner in the biggest event of the year?" Fact
of the matter was, I was twenty-three years old and didn't even have
any kids. The crowd got so mad. They all took what I was saying
to heart. The people of Portland thought I was calling the whole
town stupid—you bet your ass I was!

While in Portland, I worked on a TV show that was taped in
front of a live audience and aired on Saturday nights. Knowing how
I could really rile up a crowd, Don Owens expected me to do an
interview in the Crow's Nest (an elevated platform above the ring
where the night's host conducted interviews for all to see) each
show; the only restriction I had was a time limit that was due to
the length of the program. In order to get my point across I had to
do some new things. So to better prepare, I started talking out loud
in the car more and also started writing things down. I became an
innovator of the concise and educated wrestling interview, which I
was now treating as a kind of art form.

People were getting into my interviews so much that they were
taking everything I said as gospel. If I said it, they believed it. I was
getting more attention than I could ever have hoped for. The fans
were now watching and imitating my every move. Just to give you
an idea of what was going on at the time, one night after I had
cleared the ring during a televised match, I got up on the second
turnbuckle and I raised both my eyebrows twice in celebration for
what I had just done. Little did I know that the cameraman had a
close-up of my face right at that particular moment. After that, for
about a month, every place that I went, people would come up to
me and raise their eyebrows.

It was just this little thing I did accidentally, and now wrestling
fans everywhere were copying me. It made me realize how intently
people were paying attention to me. But with this awareness came
responsibility. I felt pressure not to let the fans down.

Fans appreciated the seriousness and value of the interviews. The
show became a real moneymaker. It brought the wrestling interview
to new heights. People were actually coming and paying their hard-

earned money more for the interview than for the wrestling. This became more evident later in a show called *Piper's Pit,* but I'm getting ahead of myself. Now, because of the interviews and all of the new things we all were doing on the show, Don Owens received the highest ratings that he had ever gotten in the thirty-year history of the program.

I was always looking for new ways to make my segments better—things that would leave an impression on the audience. One night I remembered a trick I learned while I was wrestling in the Canadian Maritimes. This guy called the Beast taught it to me. This piece of business involved breaking a full bottle of Heineken beer over your head. I had never tried it but I had seen the Beast do it. I just never had any desire or need to smash myself in the head with a green bottle of beer. What a waste of beer! But now I decided to give it a go on live TV. I didn't tell anyone. This was another cardinal rule of mine: never tell anyone what I was planning to do.

Break bottle against head

When the time came for my interview, I broke the full bottle of beer against my forehead to promote an upcoming match. The impact of the blood streaming down my face from glass cuts, and beer everywhere, was such that the audience made very sure they came to the match. And they wouldn't be disappointed because I took that intense aggressive energy into the ring and it guaranteed a good performance. I don't recommend you try this at home because if you don't swing the bottle hard enough, you'll simply knock yourself out.

Bleed

About this time I also made it a rule never to talk about another wrestler's family. In these interviews I was developing, you had to have some serious rules because they could easily get too personal. For instance, I might tell a joke or a one-liner like: Do you know why Ric Flair sleeps with two girls at the same time? So that when he falls asleep they've got someone to talk to. Ric Flair is a married man. I always took the wrestler out of the context with his real family so that he wouldn't personally feel any emotion from the interview. But it didn't always work that way; people got pretty mad at some of the things I said and did. I was the first guy to put any significant premeditated psychology into the interviews. I also brought up anything close to my opponents that was real. I got very much in their faces. As Adrian Adonis once said to Vince McMahon Jr., "Piper shoots his mouth off in the interview, but he always goes and backs it up." This is another good rule of interviewing. Your interview must be in sync with your match. In other words, you must carry through into your match what you said beforehand. Otherwise your interview means nothing.

This was one of the secrets of drawing money; I'd get in the ring and back up what I'd say in interviews. This helped me become a fan favorite. I'd always have some reality base in every interview. Not just saying that I was going to rip a wrestler's lungs out, or that I was going to tear his eyes out; that's illegal, and we all know it's not going to happen in the ring. So I would base my threats on truth, on what I really could do to my opponent between the ropes.

But sometimes the truth isn't as it appears on television. One night in Portland, Buddy Rose stole my kilt after I took it off in the ring, on what was billed as live TV. The event was aired two hours after it was taped. This show had been live for years, this was only its third week of being broadcast on tape delay, and not too many people knew about it. Well, Rose proceeded to take my kilt up to the Crow's Nest for an interview while I was still in the ring. I stopped wrestling and kept looking up at the Crow's Nest, getting the crowd's attention, and together we watched Rose put lighter fluid on my kilt and set it on fire. Upon witnessing this travesty, I ran from the ring and headed up to the Crow's Nest. I attempted to put the fire out with my bare hands, burning myself in the process. When this came on TV, people started calling the fire department because they thought the building was going to burn down. By the time the fire department arrived, there was obviously nobody in the arena because the match had taken place two hours prior. It's safe to say that the fire marshal failed to see the humor of this, but it did hit the papers the next morning!

Another time Buddy Rose came into the ring with a coat hanger. He started choking me and dragging me around the ring, which truly hurt a lot and knocked the wind out of me, but thankfully, he let me live. In the process, I was taken back to the dressing room on a stretcher, and one of the old-timers took a yard of gauze, rolled it up and twisted it around my throat, and put his knee in the back of my head, then "sawed" the ropy gauze back and forth until it left a burn mark on my neck. That took about thirty seconds, and two minutes later I was back in the arena, barely able to speak and bleeding from the coat-hanger incident. The audience saw the blood and burn mark and it left a lasting impression on them. Now the fans were watching wrestling from a different perspective. While they had been viewing other matches and saying "Oh, that's phony," they were now tuning in to my matches and saying "Did you see what Roddy Piper did? It's real!" You see, folks, I was walking on a mighty fine line here, wasn't I?

My performances were now drawing in big money and crowds. My evolving style in the ring kept the audience confused and interested at the same time. It was impossible for anyone not living inside my head, and not being "in the know," to make the distinction between what was real and what was not. That and that alone was good enough to make people buy tickets.

I've often been asked how wrestling helped my acting ability. To be honest, it was probably the worst thing that I could have done. When the movie *They Live* came out in 1988, a critic (I learned over the years that critics can't do anything, they can only talk or write about doing things) for the *New York Post* wrote: "Anybody who thinks wrestlers are actors is wrong." That of course was a direct attack on my acting, but these are the same people who were criticizing my wrestling by writing that it was all acting. When I was on the mat I was considered an actor. When I was on the big screen I was called a wrestler. I don't think it was *me* who was confused. There's a simple explanation for this. Wrestling does *not* help acting.

[handwritten marginal note: Portland developing into a big act]

You could say that acting is implosion, while wrestling is explosion. Basically they are opposite.

My performance in the squared circle caused people to react in different ways when they met me outside the arena. People don't know how to take wrestlers. In no other sport is the athlete on the spectators' TV staring at them and talking to them about their hometown, pissing them off, getting them angry. When people finally meet me in person, there are so many things going through their heads that they don't know how to react. I'm not the guy in the Super Bowl who ran for the winning touchdown. I'm not like the guy on the basketball court who scored a lot of baskets. I'm the guy who's been stabbed three times, who once wrestled a bear and who makes a living challenging people twice my size, so what do they say to me?

Anyway, I didn't only establish myself on the mike and on the camera while I was in Oregon. I also kicked some serious ass in the ring. Within three or four weeks on my new circuit, I had won every title the territory had to offer, including the Tag Team Championship with my partner Killer Brooks. Between the two of us we had so many title belts that we needed a wheelbarrow to carry them into the arena before our matches. As you can imagine, this always went over *real big* with our opponents. Wrestling was again starting to swell in popularity on the West Coast at this time, and I remember how people were talking about me being the tops out west and Ric Flair being the king of the East Coast. In Charlotte, North Carolina, Flair, like me, was kicking ass and gaining a reputation for himself.

The two of us had our promoters calling and bragging about our most recent performance each week. The first thing Don Owens did every Monday morning was brag to other promoters all across the wrestling world how he was selling out the Portland Sports Arena. The first question they would ask him was, "Well, who do you have on top?" And he would tell them: "This kid Piper."

Well, I don't know why they were shocked. Mike LeBell had

Mike Lebell L.A.

Meets
Kitty

Killer
Brooks
Introduces
Them

been doing the same thing down in L.A. for three and a half years while I was there. Now Owens was selling out Portland, Oregon, for twenty-six weeks in a row! The buzz on Piper on the West Coast and Flair on the East Coast was showing that a new art had entered the world.

Around this time Killer Brooks introduced me to my future wife. It was so hard to meet any nice girls in our business. Just the number of miles we put in traveling around Oregon made a real relationship almost impossible. I'm not going to lie; we had women in every city and state we were in, but none of them were the type you'd want to settle down with. None of us had time to court a girl. Our weeks always looked the same. On Monday we'd usually make a trek out to Longview, which was sixty miles each way, then we'd wake up on Tuesday and make the long haul to Roseburg, which was a four-hundred-mile round-trip. Wednesday was even more of a killer, as we had to travel three-hundred miles each way to Medford. But we would catch a break on Thursdays because we only had to travel to Salem, which was about fifty miles away. Friday was Eugene, which was about 110 miles one way, and Saturday we'd be in Portland. Sunday was usually a rest or travel day, depending on our booking. There was no time for dating, just fun and games on the road. And let me tell you, I was definitely living up to the "Rowdy" nickname I had. The animal in me was really feeling the jungle beat. But even though I was partying the night away, something was missing. Even though I was a young, good-looking, popular, and successful wrestler, I still felt I wasn't complete.

One night Killer and I were driving home from a match and we were hungry. But we just couldn't stop anywhere to grab something to eat because number one, we wanted steak or some kind of meat, and number two, it was midnight and not too many places were open. Our only option was this place called Jo-Jo's on Sunset Highway in Portland.

So we pulled up to the joint and went inside to fill our empty stomachs. Little did I know that Jo-Jo's was going to be the place where I'd meet the girl of my dreams. I was sitting there eating my juicy steak when of all a sudden out of the corner of my eye I spotted this vision of loveliness. Around the corner came this little gal—she couldn't have been more than nineteen years old at the time—and I'll never forget that moment or what she was wearing. She had on a little Jo-Jo's uniform with a little brown skirt and her hair was up in a bun, and she was just real wholesome looking. She so impressed me that I blurted out, "You know, Killer, that's the kind of girl a guy would like to marry."

Meets Kitty

I had no intention of trying to meet her, let alone trying to talk to her, but Killer wouldn't hear any of that. He called her over, and he said in his best growling voice, "Hey, you. Beautiful. Come over here for a second." But at first she wouldn't come. As a matter of fact, she went straight over to her manager and asked to change sections so she could get away from us. We finally got her to come over to our table and I got the balls enough to ask her out, but she stone-cold turned me down. As a matter of fact, for six weeks straight I was eating steak at Jo-Jo's trying to get this beautiful girl to go out on a date with me, but I was getting nowhere fast. Finally, as a last resort, I gave her my number because she would never give me hers. I told her if she ever wanted to go out one night to give me a call. A few days later she finally gave me a chance, and I haven't let her out of my heart since. Her name is Kitty.

Didn't want to wait on Rodd

Turned down

Our first date was kind of comical. Because of my life as a pro wrestler, dating was kind of new to me. Like I said before, we were out with a lot of women on the road, but we were just looking to party and have a good time. So on my way over to pick up Kitty, I was wondering, "What do you do on a first date?" So being the natural romantic that I am, we went to the park behind the school nearby and swung on the swings. While it was kind of nice, it was also a little odd. Not only was I not used to being in a park on a date, I had a .380 9mm automatic holstered under my jacket that she didn't know about, and I had smoked a joint on the way over, and then took some quaaludes so I could come down! What was

Had a gun, Pot, Quaaludes on First date

Swung on the swings

this poor pretty girl getting herself into? Here was this sweet little Bambi swinging on the swing next to this big wolf in sheep's clothing.

But to be honest, I wouldn't change a thing. It all turned out perfect in the end because that relationship developed into a twenty-four-year marriage, and although Kitty's love of animals has cost me a fortune, it was worth it for the four beautiful children she's given me. From the first time we met, we both felt an intense familiarity, closeness, and ease with each other. I think that soul-mate comfort came into play here. But I was hot on my career, and Kitty's desires led her away to Walla Walla to be with the show-horse circuit she loved. Over the next two and a half years we kept in touch and dated whenever we were in the same town. I can honestly say that I've never met a greater lady than Kitty. With all the shit I put her through over the years, never once has she said she was leaving me, and believe me, as we go along here you'll see if anybody ever had a reason to leave anybody, it was her! I'm not the easiest guy to be married to. But even through all our problems, she's been right there for me, and that's why I'll always have a special place in my heart for Jo-Jo's and Kitty.

Around this time I also started using catchphrases in my segments. I started saying things like: "Every time you think you've got all the answers, I change the questions." Or another famous one: "I came here to chew bubble gum and kick ass, and I'm all out of bubble gum." These, like so many other things I did as a wrestler, would be duplicated but never equaled. Everywhere I went, people would know these sayings by heart and scream them to me, whether I was wrestling in their home arena or waiting in line to buy a six-pack of Heineken. Another reason people began screaming at me in Portland was that I started hanging around with a wrestler named Rick Martel. He is the brother of a guy I had wrestled ten years earlier who had died, Michel Martel. Rick ended up becoming one of my best friends. He is not only an amazing wrestler, he is also a truly amazing man. The fact that he looked like Sylvester Stallone

2½ years

Famous 2 Lines

Rick Martel

didn't hurt either, as we had girls by the dozens whenever I was with Rick. Because of his looks, Martel had so many options other than wrestling—there was Hollywood, where he almost became Stallone's double in a couple of movies—and there were always modeling agencies knocking on his door. But for some reason, he chose to stay with wrestling and selfishly I was glad because I loved the time we spent together. I can honestly say we shared many laughs over the years. I especially loved when he had to do interviews. You have to understand, Rick was a great wrestler, but interviews were not his forte. His French accent killed whatever he was trying to say. Between the girls screaming for him and that terrible accent, you never knew what was being said.

One of the things I would do during my interviews was read one of my fan letters on the air. It would always say something like, "Dear Roddy, I watch you wrestle all the time and I think you're the greatest wrestler in the world. I love you and I hope to see you soon. Please kick Buddy Rose's ass. I'll love you forever. Love, Beverly. P.S.: Can you get me a date with Rick Martel?" And then I'd crumple the letter and I'd throw it down and pretend to be mad, bolting from the Crow's Nest, saying that I was going to find Martel.

When I'd find him, I'd take my frustration out on him by yelling at him, telling him about all his love letters that I was getting and that I was sick of them. This type of banter went back and forth between us for some time. Rick became another extraordinary tag partner of mine. We did everything together both inside and outside of the ring.

One story I'll never forget happened when we were in Washington during the eruption of Mount St. Helens. Rick had just gotten a brand-new black Firebird that he had shipped over from Hawaii when he was wrestling there. I remember the day I went with him to pick it up. We had to travel two hundred miles, and when we finally get there, he's like a kid on Christmas morning. We get in the shiny vehicle and one of the first things he does is open up the sunroof. He then takes the beautiful piece of machinery on the highway and puts the pedal to the metal and we start joyriding at 100 mph, both of us enjoying every second of the rush. About two weeks later, we again hit the road, but this time it was for business. We jumped in the black beauty with our wrestling gear on a gorgeous sunny day in Portland, ready to make the trek to Tacoma, Washington, for a match. Neither of us had a care in the world on this day. We had the radio going, sunroof down, sunglasses on, as we were speeding down the highway toward Washington. But our fun in the sun would soon come to an end. As we're driving, the whole road becomes covered with this grayish substance and then we see the entire sky go gray on us. The next thing I know there's this loud boom and we slide head-on into a tractor trailer that jackknifes in front of us. The impact of the crash was so hard that the door handle I was holding on to for dear life ripped off right in my hand. We then realized that Mount St. Helens had erupted and the truck had stopped out of panic. A car containing an old couple had also crashed into the truck. The entire place was now covered with ash, and it looked like we just had a snowstorm. You could hardly see your hand in front of your face. We knew that there were going to be cars coming behind us, so we both tried to get out of the car, but weren't having any luck. I tried to kick my door open, but it was jammed shut because the frame of the car had been bent. Then Rick, as calm as 007, taps me on the shoulder and says, "Monsieur, the sunroof is down, we just need to climb up through the sunroof." So we climbed out to safety—at least I thought we were going to be safe! No sooner had we gotten out of the smashed car than Rick and I were busy saving lives. Me, being the honorable man that I was, was busy saving my own life, as I had to jump onto a cement highway divider in order to dodge an out-of-control car that was coming right at me while Rick was trying to help out the elderly couple who had been hurt. Bless his heart. Maybe that's why he got more fan mail than me.

The police finally arrived on the scene. They got there almost as the crashing stopped and started passing out masks, much like you would see a doctor wear during surgery. Just as I noticed that there were highway patrolmen all over the place, I realized that I had left my Haliburton in the car. I told Rick about my dilemma and he told me to go get it before the cops took the smashed car away from the scene. As I went back to the car, Rick was giving out his insurance information to the cops so he could get reimbursed for his totaled car. After I retrieved my case, I went over to Rick and asked the cops to hurry up the paper-filling-out process, as we still had a match to get to. I'd be damned if I was going to let a volcano eruption make me miss a match. When he was done, Martel turned around to get one last look at his dream car and he looked so sad—like the commercial with the Indian holding on to his heart as somebody goes by and litters, and a tear falls out of his eye. The next thing I know we had our thumbs out, and a semi picked us up and we got into Tacoma an hour late. I must admit the ride wasn't the most pleasant, as I sat between Rick and the driver with the gearshift up my ass, but we made it to the match. When we got to the arena, we were greeted by Dutch Savage, the territory's promoter, who was so concerned about our well-being that he said, "Where the fuck have you two been? You're always late. You've got no damn respect." Rick and I just looked at each other and went inside to get changed for our match. We wrestled and got a ride home some other way. Even Mother Nature couldn't keep me from wrestling in the ring.

We were now selling out places like Vancouver, British Columbia, and the promoters had to go to bigger buildings in order to accommodate all the fans. This had never happened before. The wrestling business was really starting to pick up in North America. But with this success came cockiness. We felt as though we were above the law and that the laws of society didn't apply to us. We felt that as long as we weren't hurting anybody else, we did what we had to do to get to the next town to entertain the fans and make our next dollar. We never knew, it might be our last dollar or our last match.

But even though I was wrestling in front of these huge crowds and having success like never before, I wasn't always "Hot Rod." Every night wasn't the perfect wrestling night for me. I had my share of embarrassing moments in the ring. One night in Vancouver, Rick and I were scheduled to wrestle in a cage match against another popular tag team, the Sheepherders (later to be known as the Bushwhackers), and I remember walking out into that arena and the energy in the building just got my blood pumping. It was a full house and the crowd was going crazy, and I remember walking down the aisle and seeing the cage for the first time, and for some strange reason I just tore ass toward it. Strangely enough, I started scaling the thirty-foot cage, making my way to the top. Now, you have to understand why this was so strange—not only did I have no idea what I was going to do when I got to the top, I also happen to be scared to death of heights! So what the fuck was I doing thirty-feet up in the air? And if you think I was crazy, Rick was right behind me. But once I got to the top and I put my foot over, the cage started wobbling. The last thing I saw was the Sheepherders looking up at me like, "What the fuck, is this guy nuts?" and then I lost my balance and I fell down on my back between the cage and the ropes. Once Rick saw me come crashing down, he gingerly started to make his way back down so he could enter the cage the normal way— through the door. Meanwhile, there I was lying under the bottom rope with my legs up like an old whore and my kilt over my face. I must've looked like Heidi Fleiss that night, but the Sheepherders weren't interested. They were content with the sheep that night. Me, I wanted to make it look like I had meant to do what I'd done, so I just jumped up after the fall looking to start the match.

Eventually, Rick and I decided to move in together. We got a place at the infamous Bomber Hotel. This was a place where most of the guys were staying and it became more like a frat house than our home. There would be all sorts of shenanigans going on at all times of the night at the Bomber.

We would come home and there would be girls there making

Rick & Roddy roomies

Here I am at age fifteen, sporting the always attractive plaid tights and lime-green boots. As Don Muraco once told me, "Conan the Barbarian you weren't."

Roddy Piper's Personal Collection

Goofing around with Sgt. Slaughter, we were imitating Ole Anderson, the Charlotte promoter who I lovingly dubbed "Pig-Face." Boy, did it catch on.

Roddy Piper's Personal Collection

A year after the first *WrestleMania*, Mr. T and I went at it again in *WrestleMania 2* on April 7, 1986. This time we were wearing boxing gloves.

From the Archives of George Napolitano

George Napolitano

While I didn't need a championship belt to be on top, the crowd would go wild every time I won one.

Controversial talk-show host Morton Downey Jr. and Brother Love
during a segment of "Piper's Pit" in *WrestleMania V*.

George Napolitano

I twisted Dory Funk's arm and pulled
Wahoo McDaniel's hair as hard as I
could, but both men just kept coming
back for more.

George Napolitano

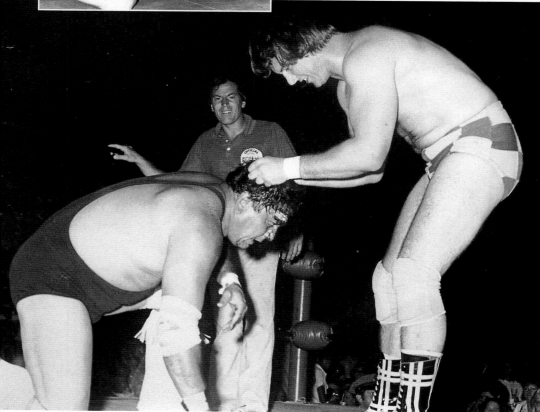

I'm sure this is one skirt Jerry Lawler wishes he had never been
so up close and personal with.

George Napolitano

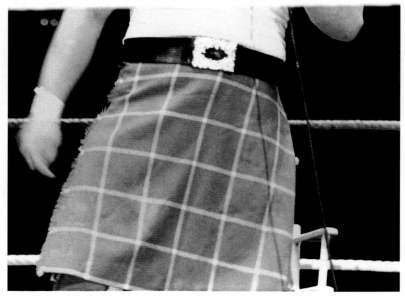

"How much did you say you were going
to pay me for *WrestleMania*?"

George Napolitano

food for us, sleeping in our beds, girls on the porch—anywhere you looked we had girls. Wrestling had reached the height of its popularity in Oregon and we were taking advantage of it. The tag team of Roddy Piper and Rick Martel was so hot in Portland that a local appliance-store owner named Tom Peterson asked us to make an appearance. Four thousand people showed up at this store on a hot and muggy day, and there were just three tables set up against a wall in the back. After a couple of hours of this madness, we were hot and sweaty and told Mr. Peterson that we needed a break. The store owner didn't even offer us anything cold to drink, so when we were in the back of the warehouse we decided that we'd exit through the back door, leaving Peterson to deal with the angry crowd and our promoter.

The industry was becoming so big so fast that even the promoters didn't know what to do. Wrestling had never had this type of attention before, so they were learning on the fly just like us how to deal with it. We now were at the point where we could fill the PR Center in Portland on a regular basis. One of the best draws was always me against Buddy Rose. We built up our rivalry to the point where people couldn't get enough. The rivalry got so intense at one point that Buddy put his prize possession, his yellow Lincoln Mark IV, on the line. The car was even brought into the building for all the fans to see. We also gave the fans an extra-special treat for the bout and decided that it was going to be a cage match. This match was an unbelievable show that lasted for forty long minutes. In the end I came out of the cage not only the winner, but also the proud new owner of a Mark IV. The best part of winning this match was not getting the car or beating Buddy, it was the reaction of the fans when they saw me driving the yellow Lincoln—soon to be known as the Yellow Canary. They would all scratch their heads and wonder: "Wow. Maybe wrestling really is real?"

Within the next three months the fans in Portland all knew that I had really taken Buddy Rose's car away from him. The title was transferred to me and everything, so the line between reality and fiction was very fuzzy. This was exactly what I had played on to draw money. But Buddy would have the last laugh. We had two matches called Loser Leaves Town, where the loser had to literally pack up and leave the territory. Back in those days, there was one rule to follow in a Loser Leaves Town match: never pack your stuff in advance because if you did, there was a possibility that you'd tip off the fans, and then why would they bother to come?

We didn't want to be like the wrestler who, years earlier, had tipped and ticked off the fans when he was scheduled to take part in a Loser Leaves Town match and he showed up at the arena driving a U-Haul that was packed with all his belongings. The wrestler had the intention of wrestling in the match and hitting the highway right after. Well, on this night he got an early start because no one stayed to see his match.

Not Buddy and me. We were ready to give the fans their money's worth.

Our match sold out in record time and Buddy and I decided that we could milk the fans for another Loser Leaves Town match on another night, so we decided to go the full sixty-minute time limit in front of the capacity crowd and end the contest in a draw. The only catch was that we had to find a way to make the audience believe that we were going all out for the win. In this case, our plan was very simple but very effective. You have the good guy (me) and the bad guy (Buddy) battle even almost the entire match, and then at one point both wrestlers get knocked out when the referee does the ten-count at the forty-five-minute mark and the bell rings. The fans now went crazy thinking that there was a double count-out and nobody was going to have to leave town. Just as the fans were ready to riot because they felt like they were ripped off, the ref ordered two pails of water and screamed, "The match will continue!" He took a bucket and dumped one on me and one on Buddy and we both came to. We were now ready to go again and the fans went wild!

The first thing I did was to take a bite out of Buddy, which made him bleed profusely. I followed that up with a series of pin combinations that Rose just made it out of. The fans were now totally back into the match, thinking at any second that I was going to beat Rose, but at the fifty-five minute mark, the psychology came into play. With Buddy lying prone on the ring floor, I climbed up on the ropes and flew off in his direction looking to land a knee drop. But I missed and he rolled over and immediately went to work on my "hurt" leg, trying to make me give up. As this is going on, the ref is letting the crowd know how much time is left in the match. The fans now start thinking: "Roddy, don't give up, you've only got a few minutes left!" But I'm still screaming from the "pain" that Buddy was inflicting on my leg. Just as I'm about to utter "I quit," the bell rings, ending the match in a draw. The fans all jump from their seats screaming and clapping, thankful that I didn't give up!

They hadn't gotten closure for what they paid to see. So a re-match was immediately announced for the next week, which was another sellout. This time I got pummeled, pulverized and pinned by the town heel. I was leaving the promotion back in Buddy Rose's hands. I was now headed to North Carolina to take on new challenges and challengers. I was thankful for the opportunity Buddy had given me to better my career and was grateful for the Yellow Canary, which could do 110 mph all day long and never chirp.

Flair

The Charlotte Years

after Portland–Charlotte

So now my Portland years are behind me and I'm off to North Carolina, where East is about to meet West. If you remember, at one time I was the talk of the entire West Coast and Ric Flair was the talk of the East. But now the two of us were going to be playing for the same team. There was no longer going to be miles of road and different time zones separating us. Flair and I were going to be wrestling on the same circuit and we were about to go head-to-head. Would there be enough room on the same card for two young pioneers with big egos? I was about to find out.

I had been in contact with a wrestling buddy of mine, Ray Stevens, who I had wrestled with on the San Francisco beat, and he put me in touch with his booker in Charlotte, George Scott. After hearing how well I did in Oregon, Scott invited me to come to North Carolina to give the East Coast a try. So I packed up the Yellow Canary and hit the road.

On the way, I stopped at a place called the Silver Dollar Saloon—I think it was in Montana. I checked into the hotel and headed straight for the bar. The saloon had silver dollars every-where—they were laminated on the bar, on the walls, all over the place. There were a few guys in the bar and we got to talking. They mentioned that they played football with Wahoo McDaniels. I had met Wahoo years back when I was in the AWA. So we were talking and drinking. Actually, we got to drinking pretty hard and I don't remember much from that night, but I do recall that someone brought up the age-old question: Is wrestling real or is it phony? I also recollect a bit of a fight taking place, but I couldn't tell you much else because the next thing I remember is waking up in my room. I was lying on top of the bedspread with all my clothes on. My watch, my money, and my wallet were on the bedside table. I looked around and noticed that the door was ripped off the hinges and there was a cowboy hat in the middle of the floor. I don't know what happened, but I do know one thing: there are times when one must decide to "fight or flee" and this was where flee came in. I jumped out of my bed over the cowboy hat, grabbed my belongings and hopped into my car, and took off.

I drove through Oklahoma, and when I got tired again, I stopped in some small town—I don't remember the name of it. Of course the first thing I did was hit the local bar. The next thing I know, I'm again in a fight. Some guy pulled a knife and the police showed up. Like I said, this was a local dive, so who was the only guy the cops didn't know? That's right, me. So they kicked me out and I got back in the Yellow Canary and away I went again.

Finally, I arrived in North Carolina, and I checked into the Tuckasegee Days Inn. While the place was a step above the Bomber Hotel, the craziness I experienced in Portland was nothing compared with what I was about to embark on. Most of the wrestlers who were working the circuit were living at the Days Inn, and over the course of time we developed a camaraderie that was second to none in pro sports. We were more than coworkers or a fraternity—we really were like blood brothers. Sure, don't get me wrong, we had our fun and games, but we also had one another's back in times of trouble. We looked out for one another's safety not only on the mat, but also when we were traveling in the States or abroad.

Some of the awesome talent that was wrestling in the NWA, which was run by Jimmy Crockett (yes, he was related to Davey), was Ray Stevens, Jimmy Snuka, Ricky Steamboat, Ric Flair, Dory Funk, Jack Mulligan, Jack and Jerry Brisco, Dusty Rhodes, Harley Race, Andre the Giant, and Gene and Ole Anderson.

As you can tell by the names, this was a place where the Big Boys in the business were performing. Each and every one of these guys was an established star, so there was no way Crockett could go wrong in whatever card he put together. He knew he was going to give the audience their money's worth every night and we knew we were going to be paid well for our performances. But just because we all were good at what we did and were earning a decent living didn't make our schedules any easier. As a matter of fact, the better we did, the higher the demand was for us.

There was still the long two- to three-hundred-mile trips each way and the long six- to seven-night workweek. So we made the most out of the time we spent together. We tried to have fun both inside the ring and out. But what may have looked like fun to others was really just a way for us to keep our sanity. If all the wear and tear between the ropes and the drugs and alcohol didn't kill us the night before, we had to get up and go to the gym and try to sweat off whatever we did the previous evening. But in order to get the energy to hit the weights the next morning, each of us had his own poison to take in order to get him going.

After hitting the weights, we'd take to the road again. But believe it or not, there was a method to our driving madness. Besides our ring gear, we also had on hand in the car the wrestling "survival" kit. This included some Neosporin to fight infection just in case we got a cut, some Ting for crotch rot, an antibiotic just in case we got sick, some beer in case we got wired, some sleeping pills in case we couldn't sleep, and a pistol in case we needed protection.

We would then get into town and pound on one another's body

for a couple of hours, and when the event was over, we went out in search of a nightspot that had good food, better booze, and "bad" women. The key to not feeling any pain after matches was to drink as much alcohol and take as many downers as humanly possible to try to make you forget you were living in a time capsule. This socializing after matches also gave us a chance to think up new strategies for drawing a big house again the next night.

Tuesdays were always the roughest days out east. No matter where we were wrestling the night before, we had to be in the TV studio the next morning at 10 A.M. so we could cut our promos and do our interviews for the upcoming matches. Nobody was exempt from this chore. It made for a very long day and night because we had to cut about ninety two-minute-and-fifty-four-second interviews and then head out to Raleigh for the night's matches. This would have been a tough schedule for any sober businessman or athlete, but try to keep on doing it after taking a pounding in the ring and at the bar the night before . . . it sure as hell wasn't easy.

Even though I thought I knew the ropes, I wound up learning a thing or two in the studio on those miserable Tuesdays. After winning my first belt, the Mid-Atlantic TV title, from a veteran grappler named Paul Jones on November 1, 1980, I ragged on him about his age in an interview. I said something like: "Yeah, Paul Jones, you're so old that every time you go by a cemetery two guys chase you with a shovel." Well, maybe the joke was funny, but in thirty thousand words or more Jones explained to me why calling him old would not draw any money. He pointed out that I had to be more careful with how far I went with my material because the more trash I talked about a wrestler, the worse I'd make him look. So if I went into the ring and knocked my opponent from here to eternity, who did I really beat? What did I prove by beating up this so-called loser, or old man in Paul's case? I now learned that the more I built up my foe, the more impressive my win would be in the eyes of the fans.

My next big win in Charlotte came over a wrestler who used to

Ric Flair

always say, "If you want to *be* the man, you've got to *beat* the man!" and that man was none other than Ric Flair. George Scott decided to put me up against his top draw for the United States Heavyweight Championship a little over two months after I won my first belt. And I have to admit, it wasn't easy. It wasn't give-and-take like people think. Flair had a reputation in Charlotte and did not want to lose his championship strap. Even though we all knew it was a business, egos and pride were still involved.

Interview Tuesdays were really paying off big-time. I did what I wanted to do in front of the camera, but always had the good of the promotion in mind. I was way ahead of my time with what I was doing with interviews. I did the very first vignette interview with music and a production. I was in a dog-collar match with Buzz Sawyer in Atlanta. For the interview, I brought in a red pickup truck and tied my dog Feather, a miniature pinscher, to the back. I climbed up onto a table with my hands tied behind my back, a hood over my head, and a noose around my neck. All the while the song "Bad to the Bone" was playing. I wanted to show everyone how tough I was, so I hanged myself by the dog collar. They just pulled the table out from under me and I hung for a while, then they put me back on the table and I picked up the puny mutt and said, "Sawyer, you're no mad dog; you're just a miniature pinscher." It was a very hip interview. They made a tape of it and passed it around the office so everyone could watch it. Nothing like this had ever been done before. Like I said, I was ahead of my time.

But when I found out I was going to go head-to-head with Charlotte's hometown favorite, Flair, I decided to spice things up a bit. We were scheduled to square off in January of 1981 for the championship belt, so with the holidays still in the air, I decided to give my opponent a present in the ring that night in front of all his fans. I wrapped up the Mid-Atlantic Championship belt in Christmas paper and went on TV with Flair and gave him the generous gift. When he opened it, I informed him and the audience that I was relinquishing my title to him in order to go after his U.S. Heavyweight Cham-

Did Prom
hurt himself

Jan 1
1981
Charlotte

pionship. This got a lot of heat. Ric had had no idea I was going to come out and do this, but he was a pro and it worked out great. I found out that the element of surprise, as long as it's in the right context, worked out really well, getting an honest reaction. Sometimes it backfired in my face, but not on this night. I went on to win the heavyweight belt from Flair that evening and held on to the title for over six months, which was a rarity in those days when the titles seemed to change hands almost every week.

Although Flair didn't like losing to me—what professional athlete likes losing?—he didn't let it come between us outside the arena, and we quickly became close friends. I really posed no threat to him or his career. Even though we did the same thing for a living, we were both entertainers and two very different people. Ric Flair wore a robe, I wore a kilt. Ric Flair dyed his hair blond, I didn't. I played the bagpipes, Ric Flair didn't. We were cut from completely different molds. Therefore we were never really at each other's throat (unlike Hogan and me). Ric also had a huge nose, I didn't.

I also have to admit that Ric Flair got me into more trouble than I care to remember. But he always made me laugh. I think I went through three lives in the time I spent with that man and I honestly wouldn't change a thing or trade a memory for anything in the world. Despite all the trouble he got me into, I love him deeply.

Speaking of someone I adore deeply, Kitty, the love of my life, was at this time still working the show-horse circuit and I had located her whereabouts in Wilsonville, Oregon. Now that I had established myself and was having some success in Charlotte, I begged her to come live with me. My girl then sold everything, including her beloved horse, and came to North Carolina with her cat and dalmation, Ryiethumnne R., to be with her man. It would have been nice if her man was there to greet her when she arrived, but my baby had no such luck. I had sent her the plane ticket, but on the day she arrived I forgot to pick her up at the airport and she waited there for me for six hours. That right there should show you how great and devoted this woman is. When I realized what I had done,

I apologized and promised I would never let her down like that again. Kitty and I became an instant item, soon to become three items!

I was now living large. With my girl now by my side and a championship belt around my waist, I couldn't have been more happy. My victory over Flair again established me as a bankable star—this time on the East Coast. This was now the fourth territory that I was selling out. Promoters again realized that I was definitely not a flash in the pan, and was someone to be reckoned with. I was wrestling and living with a fear-nothing attitude, and got by on the one basic rule of "no retreat, no surrender." As Terry Funk put it, "I was building the legend." The "Sickness" was so consuming at this point that nothing else mattered.

The shot George Scott was kind enough to give me paid off and I was one of the territory's top draws. Wrestlers on the circuit were not only losing titles to me, they were also following my lead. A short time later I would part ways with Scott. This was through no fault of his. He was a good man; I just saw a better opportunity with Ole Anderson as my booker, and I took it. Ole was great for me because he helped me learn some of the complexities of the business that I was unfamiliar with. Yes, I had sold out other arenas, but there was an incredible amount of up-and-coming young talent in America and Canada and I needed to know the ins and outs of the biz in order to stay on top.

The in-ring feud between Flair and me really ignited a fire in the wrestling industry, so I wanted to learn everything I could in order to keep the flame lit. Having the luxury of working alongside greats like Dusty Rhodes, Andre the Giant, Dory Funk, Terry Funk, Jack Brisco, Jerry Brisco, and countless others taught me a lot. I learned from Jerry Brisco how to keep going even when there was a tough act to follow. Jerry had the unfortunate pleasure of following his big brother Jack Brisco in the territory after he was a champion. I once asked Jerry how he did it and he said, "Just a little have-to, Pipes, just a little have-to." In other words, he had no other choice if he wanted to work in the business. This was another lesson I had to learn before I got my wrestling degree.

Ole Anderson also taught me the lesson of drawing money. At this time I had been in Charlotte for about seven or eight months, and the intensity that I created with some of my interview techniques drew big crowds to our shows. But one night Ole pointed out to me how things could be much better. We were in Richmond, Virginia, for a card and I was wrestling Flair. I remember it like it was yesterday. The place was packed to the rafters and Ric and I went at it real good for about twenty-five minutes and wrestled what we thought was a solid performance. After the match, people were coming up to us and complimenting our effort. But not Ole. I knew I had nicknamed this guy Pig Face for a reason. He was a very good wrestler, but he was a bully. Plus, I knew he had a glass jaw, but that was beside the point. Ole had a great psychology for drawing money, and he told me that the match that night sucked. I called him on his statement and asked him how he could say that when the people were screaming their heads off throughout the match and all the guys were coming up to Ric and me telling us how good we were. He said we looked like two Mexicans out there. Mexican wrestlers are known for their high-flying quick style, so that's why he said that—at least that's what I think he meant. Anyway, the fact of the matter is, he said, that I was flying out there like a lily, just flipping and flopping around like a fish out of water, not really doing anything worthwhile. He said that sure, the people were happy, but what reason did we give them to come back? Ole asked me: "If you were going to have a street fight and you looked at somebody and they jumped on the hood of their car and did a back flip, would that make your day?" I said, "Yeah, I'd spike 'em into the ground." He said, "Well then, why the hell were you doing that shit off the ropes?"

Anderson gave me a half-hour speech about planting my feet on the ground and being a real fighter, and about making those people respect you for the battler that you are. And you know something?

Drawing Fun

Interview Day

Flair watched Piper x for this w/ Dusty

Pig Face was right. As soon as I stopped the flipping and flopping and planted my feet on the ground, I started to draw even more money. This minor adjustment allowed Ole Anderson and me to see firsthand how Roddy Piper could draw huge crowds and make millions and millions of dollars for a promotion.

But while my wrestling performance improved on the mat, my time on the mike was also a big part of my success. The interviews I did with the legendary Dusty Rhodes on Tuesdays in the studio helped turn me into an all-around performer. Interview day would begin and they would call your name and you'd get up off of the bleachers and go in front of the camera. The interview clock would be set at 2:54, and once the time started rolling, so did I.

One Tuesday, all these great wrestlers, including Dusty, were standing around in the room waiting for their turn. Dusty Rhodes was probably the king of the promos at the time and I happened to be wrestling him that particular week. I would cut a promo, then he would cut a promo. I would say things like "a big and great man like Dusty Rhodes—look at the pecs on him. It looks like he had six litters of puppies." He would then come back with something on me. I would go back to him with, "Whenever he goes swimming someone tries to harpoon him." We just went toe-to-toe without giving the other a chance to think or breathe in fear of not being able to keep up with the verbal jabs. After a while I noticed that the whole world seemed to stop in the room, as Flair and all the other wrestlers were now watching our war of words like it was a championship match. That day really put me on the map in terms of being able to keep up with one of the masters on the mike, and it gave me some more confidence and dignity among my Frat Brothers.

These great men really knew how to teach the ropes and they also knew how to shell out praise just as much as punishment. Not too long after that day with Rhodes, Jimmy Crockett called everyone together. I had once again gone word for word with Dusty and was simply just trying to catch my next breath when he called us in. He

said that he had an award to give out, and he asked me to come up
to the front to accept it. I never had this happen to me before or
after this. It was an award from *Pro Wrestling Illustrated* for the
hardest-working wrestler voted by his peers.

I was numb after I heard the announcement. I walked up to the
front of the room to Crockett, and all of the wrestlers, including my
old friend Lord Alfred Hayes, were clapping for me. I graciously
took the award from Jim, but walked away without uttering a word.
I was taught by Lord Alfred Hayes to always keep your composure.

I really couldn't believe I was being presented this award, especially in this very competitive dressing room. The other guys worked
just as hard as I did, and if it wasn't for them, I wouldn't have been
there. We were all part of a team. As much as we were cutthroat to
one another at times, you never said something bad about any of
our guys, otherwise you'd have a handful of monsters ready to kick
the daylights out of you. But the truth of the matter is that we were
a group that was willing to die for one another if the situation arose.

I don't mean any disrespect, but this type of camaraderie doesn't
exist in today's world of pro wrestling, or in any sport, for that
matter. A lot of people today think wrestling began when the WWF
began, but there were so many great men before the WWF. All these
talented guys had all this knowledge that they passed on to us, and
they took care of us like we were their own. That just isn't done
today.

Also at this time in my career, I stopped playing the bagpipes.
But the reason I stopped had nothing to do with advice from any
of my peers; it had all to do with my health. Before I put the pipes
away for good, I would walk down the aisle with the blow stick in
my mouth, and the fans would hit the pipes, driving the blow stick
into my teeth and gums. I would be bleeding even before I got into
the ring. This got old fast for me, and made eating a very painful
affair! I also didn't need a warm-up for me and the crowd anymore.
I was now in tune with the audience. As soon as I made my way
from behind the curtain, I could tell you what the people were think-

ing. I could tell you as I was walking up the aisles in the arenas if I should start fast or I should start slow. I had learned to control the crowd and not let them control me. Over the years you learn to walk into the ring slow so you can get that feel.

But while this style let you get a sense of the night's audience, it also served another purpose. We used to get paid a percentage of the house. Wrestlers would get blackballed if they were caught with a clicker, counting how many people were at the event. So over time you learned to count the house as you walked into the ring. One time a P gave me a count on the house. I had been in this building a few other times and learned what a sellout was, so I could count that venue by sight without a clicker and I would usually be within $5,000. Well, I knew that this promoter was cheating me and my fellow wrestlers, so I asked him what the house was. He didn't really want to answer the question, but all the other wrestlers were looking at me and him from the dressing room. So the snake tells me the house is $15,000. Well, I knew for a fact it was double that. The other guys were looking at me and the promoter, waiting for a confrontation, but instead there was dead silence. All the other wrestlers were bowing their heads because they were wondering, "Now what are we going to do?" Most of these guys were afraid to call the P on anything. They felt that the promoter had complete power. Well, I was taught different.

As a rebel, I was taught that your power was your talent and that you shouldn't be afraid to quit, because your abilities would land you another job. I wasn't afraid to start over again. I wasn't afraid to move. I wasn't afraid of the P or anybody else. I was trying to point out to my coworkers the tyranny that was taking place here. I took off my kilt and trunks and put my street clothes back on just as intermission was ending, and I walked through the crowd to the ring. I caused a stir in the arena because I wasn't in my ring attire; I was just carrying my Halliburton—no Rolex at this time—and sporting my tennis shoes—no alligator boots just yet. I climbed through the ropes and into ring, where I ripped the mike out of the announcer's hand. I then proceeded to tell the crowd: "Ladies and gentlemen, the promoter won't pay me the money that he owes me to wrestle, so I'm going to leave the building and I'd advise you to get your money back, too." Then I laid the mike down and walked out the front door. From what my buddy Jay York told me, it was one of the best riots of the year!

I'm a pretty tough customer all the way around, especially when I think I'm being taken for a fool. I'm not afraid to say no, and I'm not afraid of man or beast. I think my wrestling that bear early in my career and standing toe-to-toe—if you want to call it that—with Andre the Giant proved that! You know, after you have all 550 pounds of Andre the Giant come down on your chest several times in your life, what more is there to fear? I know there is a God— experiences such as these made me see Him several times over! (As far as religion is concerned, I've always been a Christian. Throughout my life and career, I've always seen those bumper stickers that say, I'VE FOUND HIM. Well, to be quite honest, I've never lost Him. I've never been a Bible-thumper, but I think the fact that I'm a Christian has probably saved a lot of people's lives—including my own. During some of my dark times, it's helped me prevail in life and try not to hurt anyone.)

One promoter who always seemed like he was out to hurt all the wrestlers was this man in Atlanta by the name of Jim Barnett. He was one of those Ps who had power and fear working for him against all his wrestlers. They all catered to this guy for some reason and I never understood why. I was introduced to Jim by Ole Anderson during one of my many Tuesday interview sessions. And the first time I saw this guy I knew there was something strange about him; he said to me (in his Southern accent), "Oh my boy, what a lovely smile." He was a weird fellow who used to sit there in his three-piece suit and sniff his tie. Jim was good friends with a lot of the Georgia Bulldog players and you knew right away which ones he was familiar with because they all had Rolexes. Barnett was nuts about these players in more ways than one.

Ole had been talking me up to this Southern promoter for quite some time, telling him how well I had done in the industry, and the two men dreamed of putting together the best promotion in the entire world and were relying on Flair and me to carry them there.

At about the same time Flair had taken me to this place called Franco's in Richmond, Virginia, and had me buy all these suits and these expensive camel-hair jackets. He wanted me to make a good impression on Barnett, but dressing me up in clothes from Franco's was like putting perfume on a pig! Well, neither my clothes nor mike skills impressed Barnett the first time around and he would have fired me if Ole hadn't convinced him to give me a second chance.

The Atlanta promoter had put me on with Gordon Solie, a wonderful announcer, and when my first night on the job was over, Jim called Ole and blasted my work. He told Ole over the phone, "I thought you said he could talk. Fire him—he's terrible." But Anderson stuck up for me. He told Jim that I had bought a new suit jacket for this gig and asked him to give me another shot. Barnett agreed. When I got there next Saturday, the ratings had gone up one and a half points, so now Jim changed his tune; he was all sweetness, saying, "Oh my boy, how are you? Oh, you must come up to my office and see me sometime." Ole just smiled at him and said, "I told you so . . ." So now I was working two territories at the same time—Charlotte and Atlanta. I had to be insane to agree to do this, but the Sickness fueled my fire.

But I still hadn't completely won Barnett over. The next test he threw at me came in the form of a wrestler named Bob Armstrong. The grappler, who was also a fireman by trade, knew Barnett was out to get me, so he decided to help me out. Before the interview that would be going out live on TBS on *Championship Wrestling*, Bob came over to talk to me very quietly. He told me to say on the air that he had skinny legs. This normally would have been a no-no because remember you never go after your opponent's weaknesses (remember the time I knocked Paul Jones in an interview about being old?), but Bob was going above and beyond the call of duty for me here. So I'm doing the live interview with him before the fight and I'm being pretty damn obnoxious, which I'm good at (as my wife says, when I want to, I'm the best asshole in the world) and I used the ammunition Bob gave me beforehand, saying something like: "How do you expect to beat me with skinny legs like that?" In return, Bob said, "Did you ever see big legs on a race-horse?" He turned to walk away, but I saw that I had ten seconds left in our interview, and so I really went on the attack. This is when I started to become pretty good at improvising. I waited until Bob was a few feet away from me, and one of the things I said to him was: "Well, if I'm ever at a horse race, I'll be sure to bet on you." That line in itself got the fans in The Omni going wild, and we went from averaging $20,000 to $60,000 overnight.

I was now a smash success in wrestling in Atlanta and Jim Barnett was beaming. Ole Anderson was now pushing me harder than ever, and I was going as hard as I could in order to please the guys. So now I was wrestling Monday through Friday, once each day, and twice on Saturday and Sunday. Each event was a two- to three-hundred-mile drive away. When we started to do the double shots we got into taking private planes. I was also wrestling in a third territory—Canada. The schedule was crazy. Every night a referee would slip me a jar filled with an assortment of drugs like Placidyl, Tuinal, and Valium and other painkillers. We're talking a shitload of pills. They did this so they could keep pushing and pushing.

We worked hard on our wrestling and even harder to survive. I remember one night with Don Muraco. Don was an important influence on my life. He was a tremendous wrestler. I did a piece of business with him and Gordon Solie that I will never forget. It was a big telecast on Ted Turner's TBS network. Solie had just had a hip replacement and Muraco kind of brushed up against him, but it was kind of rough, and this started a "fight" between me and Muraco. The fight began in the studio and we brought it into the ring. There were a bunch of wrestlers trying to pull us apart, and it just got crazy. I feel it was one of the better "pull-aparts" in wrestling history.

A typical night with Don Muraco would consist of wrestling, driving home, and drinking pretty heavily. One night we were in the car and Muraco was doing 85 mph. The next thing I knew, we hit the Canadian border. I don't know how we got there, but we made great time!

Things get a little murky here. The next morning we woke up in this huge mansion. I didn't know where I was or how I got there. I looked around for Muraco, but he was nowhere to be found, so I yelled out for him. I heard him yell back to me in the distance, and we kept yelling, following the sounds of our voices, until we found each other. He didn't know where we were either, so we thought it best if we just hightailed it out of there. We got into our car, stopped at a gas station, and asked for directions to the nearest airport. The car was a rental, and we just left it at the entrance to the airport and bought tickets to the town where we had to wrestle that night. I remember waiting at the gate to board the plane and hearing an announcement asking the owner of the Hertz rental car that was abandoned at the front door to claim it. We ignored it and got on the plane. We never heard another thing about the car.

I've gotten away with a lot of shit in my life. They say God takes care of fools and babies! This one time we were driving back from Canada to the United States and we had just reached the border. René Goulet was at the driver, Nikolai Volkoff was in the front passenger seat, and me and the Iron Sheik were sitting in the back. What you need to understand at this point is that I was the only illegal alien in the car!

So the border guard comes up to the car and asks to see our ID. René says, "My name is René Goulet and I am from Quebec. I have been coming over here for years and do not need ID. I never have."

The guard asks Nikolai if he has any papers and he says, "My name is Nikolai Volkoff, and I am from the Ukraine. I do not have any papers. I do not need any papers. My papers are in the White House with the president."

So now the guard gets to the Iron Sheik, whose real name is Cosmo Husary. He had been an amateur wrestling champion in Iran and a bodyguard for the shah of Iran. The guard looks at the Sheik and raises an eyebrow. You see, this was at the time when those Americans were being held hostage in Iran. The Sheik says, "My name is Cosmos Husary, the Iron Sheik, the two-time World Champion. I come from Tehran, Iran. I do not need papers."

That's it. The guy makes us all get out of the car. He never even got to me. He orders René to open the trunk, and Nikolai Volkoff says under his breath, "This is just like the gestapo." The guy whirled around and said, "What did you say?" And the next thing I know, we're all in this cement room in the immigration office. Oh, what I failed to tell you is that I had a quarter ounce of hash on me. I quickly put it in my lip, because in Charlotte everyone chewed tobacco. We were in this room for about a half hour, and that hash started kicking in and I'm trying to hold it together. The guard comes back in; he had called Washington to verify these guys' papers. Finally, he gets to me and asks me, "What's your name?"

I said, "My name is Roderick George Toombs."

"Where'd you go to school?"

"St. Mary's," I said.

He turns around and says, "That's the only one I believe!" But since everybody's papers checked out, he had no choice but to let all of us go.

But I wasn't always so lucky. Another tangle with the law happened in Charlotte. I like to refer to this story as "The 2001 Space Odyssey Cadillac Demolition Derby." Everyone was driving brand-new Cadillacs. I had a brand-new Cadillac, Flair had a brand-new Cadillac, the Briscos had a brand-new Caddy, and Byron Scott—who was the son of George Scott, the man responsible for bringing me to Charlotte—had his father's new Cadillac.

Well, we had been in this club all night long, and Byron had been sucking us dry by milking drinks from all the wrestlers. For some reason, Byron and I got into an argument and he went outside and got into his father's car. I followed, and Byron, who had his driver's side window open about an inch, hollers, "My dad made you everything you are today." At which point my left fist went right through his windshield. Now, this kid decides maybe it's time he should move, so he started the car to take off. I rushed to my Cadillac and Jack Brisco limped to get into the passenger side. But Jack had a cast on his leg and didn't get in the car all the way before I hit the gas. Unbeknownst to me, my wheels were turned all the way to the left, so when I hit the gas, the Caddy shot hard to the left and flung Brisco out the door. I tried to grab him and caught ahold of his belt, but we both just went flying out onto the pavement. My car, however, continued moving and went straight toward Byron's car right in the middle of the driver's side. It was as if my car knew exactly where to go.

George Scott wound up taking me to court. He said, "Well, I am responsible for bringing Roddy in." And he was. He is a good man; this incident had nothing to do with George Scott. So I bowed down and paid the fine, and that was the end of it. Kitty, however, was none too happy about how our new Cadillac looked!

Another story that comes to mind is about a fellow named Art Barr. He is no longer with us. Art was a young, bighearted fellow who was full of talent. I had never trained anyone to be a professional wrestler—I mainly kept to myself—but this guy was worth a shot. I had an interview with him and I had some wrestlers hold a sheet in front of him and told him to strip down naked. I threw him some clothes and put baby powder in his hair. We removed the sheet and unveiled Beetlejuice. He was dancing to Harry Belafonte's song "Day-O" and the crowd loved it! Only Art Barr could have pulled that off!

He got to be a real big star in Mexico. I think he was making about $5,000 a week. He would call me for advice and I would treat him like a little brother. One time I was making a movie in Mexico City, and I met up with Art. I put him in one of the final scenes of the movie playing a waiter. After the shot, I took him up to my room and gave him a talk. I've only given three people this particular talk. I told him that he was going too hard and that if he didn't stop he was going to die. It was quite emotional, we were both crying, and I made him promise me that he was going to slow down and take care of himself.

About two months later I got a call from one of his relatives telling me there was big trouble. I was given a phone number to call and it turned out to be Art's mother's house. She told me that Art was dead, that he was lying there with his little son in his arms. He had just died. I don't believe they had even called an ambulance or the police yet. I told her she should probably call an ambulance, but she just said, "He's dead and it's your fault." Then she hung up. I guess they figured that I killed their son, that I had influenced him to live his life the way I lived mine. It makes you realize the power you have to influence others. It still breaks my heart to think of Art. I'm sorry he's gone. I loved him and I miss him. I wasn't even welcome at his funeral.

At this time I was hanging around with a man named "Wildfire" Tommy Rich. Tommy was Southern born and Southern bred. He was a fine guy and a talented wrestler and we got along great. Wrestling was starting to swirl, and it was because of national TV and people like Tommy Rich, Dusty Rhodes, Ric Flair, and the Four Horsemen, just to mention a few.

Tommy Rich was just a good ol' boy. He had a very unique outlook on life. He was really trying to get into shape and guys were telling him that he had to go to the gym and watch his diet. So one day we're at a restaurant and Tommy orders tuna fish and we said, "Tommy, that's great, but you also have to go to the gym."

He says, "Damn man, I'm eatin' tuna fish! I can't do everything!" He then proceeded to guzzle more beers than I would care to count.

We were traveling in West Virginia, where it was lawless. We were going into places where no one else had ever been, but that could be watched on TBS Super Station. One night we were driving along on this eight-lane freeway, and Tommy's cousin says we have to stop the car because he has to pee. Well, we had a cardinal rule that we just didn't stop to take a piss; we'd been abiding by this rule for years. But Tommy's cousin was whining, so I finally pulled over and he jumped out of the car to pee. No sooner did he get out than I just took off and left him out there in the middle of nowhere. I drove about three minutes, but Tommy wanted me to go back and get his cousin. Now, there was this cement divider in the middle of this freeway and no way to get over to the other side and go the other way without driving to the next exit. So I just turned around; I did a one-eighty, put the lights on high beam, honked the horn, and drove 80 mph straight toward oncoming traffic. We never did find the kid; it took him about a day to get home! Poor bastard.

I got into crazy shit with Tommy all the time. Tommy had this speedboat. One time we had been up all night and we had the bright idea to get a paddleboat for our wives. Kitty was pregnant with our first child at the time and we didn't think it would be a good idea for the wives to be in the speedboat; they might get sick from all the waves. So Kitty and Tommy's wife were in the paddleboat and Tommy and I could whip through in the speedboat. We took the boats to the beach, and at about 10 A.M., we were starting to run out of beer, so Tommy said, "I'll go get it." He jumped up and ran like Carl Lewis from the towel to the boat. He hit the throttle as hard as you could, and that boat went right up . . . and right into a log sticking out of the water. That boat sank just like the Minnow, man! By that time, if only for the benefit of our wives, we decided to go home.

Yeah, we were always getting into trouble, but I've always had a guardian angel—how else could I have survived half of the shit I've been through? I've been in quite a few car wrecks. We were always running those highways fast, and a lot of different substances were running through our systems. There was one crash in particular that shook me up, but it didn't stop me. I was in a car in Tennessee with Tommy Rich, Nick Patrick, who was a referee, and Brad Armstrong. I was driving and had been behind the wheel for a while, and I was banging back a few. I was doing about 100 mph, and up ahead the road curves and I see this bridge, and I know I'm just not going to make the turn. But I don't panic under fire. I manage to straighten the car out, but we go off the road into this embankment. By the grace of God, the Lincoln nose-dived in such a way as to just flop us over the embankment. Another five feet and we would have dropped twenty-five feet into the river!

We got out of the car and climbed up the embankment and there was this old Tennessee house; it looked like it came straight out of the movie *Deliverance*. And sitting on the porch in a rocking chair was this old guy with a long beard and a corncob pipe, and he's just rocking and watching us. Finally, he takes his pipe out of his mouth and says in a thick Southern drawl, "I knew you weren't going to make that turn."

The old guy actually helped us tow the Lincoln out of the ditch and we were off again. When we returned the car to Hertz, we just parked it way in the back and got out of the place quickly. But the truth is, after incidents like this, I am the reason why the Hertz office in Newark Airport wouldn't rent cars to wrestlers for five years!

But you take things like that in stride. Actually, when you're on tour you lose it; nothing really matters. You're working real hard, wrestling nonstop, and you just do what you want to do. Time doesn't even matter. I remember once, Tommy, Dusty Rhodes, and I went out to the parking lot of our hotel at two in the morning and we got the ring posts out of the trucks and just decided to set up the ring right there in the parking lot. The ring boys were yelling at us, trying to chase us away, but hell, we wanted to wrestle. But the fun wore off fast. We got halfway through setting up the ring and got tired, so we just went to bed. If you thought the ring boys were angry at us before, you should have seen them when we abandoned all the stuff in the parking lot and left them to clean it up. Boy, were they pissed!

We did stuff like this because we didn't care. We were working so hard we were numb. And we weren't afraid of anything. We did what we wanted to do and what we had to do, and we didn't let anything or anyone stop us.

Hell, even a plane crash couldn't stop me!

I was in Greenville, South Carolina, one afternoon and had to be in Savannah, Georgia, that night. A bunch of us were making the trip in this private plane. It was me, Wahoo McDaniels, Sergeant Slaughter, Jimmy Valiant, and this guy Freddy, who was the pilot. I remember that my left wrist was broken, only I didn't know this at the time. I had wrestled Wahoo and I took that big, old oak leg of his and jumped down on him and caught my wrist the wrong way. It hurt like hell and I was wearing it in a sling. So we're in this plane and Wahoo is giving me shit. "Boy, only sissies wear slings," he said to me. "Take that thing off." I listened to him and that's why I have this big bump on my wrist 'til this day.

But anyway, we were just about to fly into Savannah when the plane hit an air pocket. We dropped about five hundred feet! We were all thrown around. Sergeant Slaughter, all 290 pounds of him, was thrown clear across the plane. I was bounced out of my seat and my head hit the top of the plane so hard that I broke my neck! We were all stunned, but we landed safely. When I got out of the plane I needed two guys on either side of me to hold me up because I didn't have my equilibrium. They got me to the arena, and believe it or not, I wrestled. I don't know how I did it. I don't remember the match. But I didn't miss the shot. If you can walk, you can wrestle. That's the rule.

Ole was pushing me harder and harder, and I was going nonstop. I was at the top of my game, the toast of the town, and Jim Barnett was beaming. But I would soon find out that Barnett wasn't really what he was made out to be. The guy went around bragging about who he knew and how smart and powerful he was, but I would soon learn it was all a charade. Barnett impressed a lot of people in the industry with smoke and mirrors. He told everyone he'd graduated top of his class at Yale and was Phi Beta Kappa, but it came out that he had only attended one seminar at Yale and never was enrolled in the university at all. He had this picture on his wall of former president Jimmy Carter with a headlock around one of his wrestlers. He wanted everyone to believe he had connections and rubbed elbows with bigwigs. I later learned he paid $5,000 for that photo. But to be honest, I never really paid attention to who he said he knew or to any of the objects he owned. All I knew was that I was bringing in a lot for cash for this guy and he rewarded me by giving me one of the first written contracts for $5,000 a week in the industry.

I was told by Ole Anderson that Barnett was set to take on the entire industry and he wanted me to be a big part of it. I was asked if I would be afraid to go in and work against promoters in other territories, and even though I knew there were definite boundary lines in the industry that you didn't cross, I still said yes at the time. At that point in my career I was willing to do anything to succeed, even if it meant breaking the rules. I didn't give a damn. I was willing to wrestle anybody, anyplace, anytime. I didn't care. But this grand plan never got off the ground. Barnett ran into one big problem. Jim had a connected friend in Chicago, and this guy didn't want him crossing into the Illinois territory, so Barnett backed off the idea. The whole concept of Jim and Ole taking over the wrestling world was now off.

But the two men were still able to put together one of the biggest wrestling successes in the sport's history when they collaborated on Starrcade. While Ole and Jim were plotting to take over the industry, Vince McMahon Sr. had just done the first outdoor wrestling show in New York's Shea Stadium, which brought in over $550,000 and featured Larry Zbyszko vs. Bruno Sammartino. Larry was an underling of Bruno, and when McMahon turned Larry against the legendary fan favorite Sammartino, he needed a huge venue to

Starrcade 83

accommodate all the people who wanted to witness the match, so he finally settled on the home of the New York Mets.

The success of this event caused Jimmy Crockett to dial up Barnett, Ole, and Dusty Rhodes because he wanted to one-up McMahon and his New York extravaganza. He wanted to put together something even bigger that wrestling fans would be talking about for years. It was decided that there would be a big show out of Greensboro and it would be broadcast via Pay-Per-View on the cable networks. The four men combined their efforts along with wrestlers like Ric Flair, Harley Race, Greg Valentine, and me, who were all hot. It was decided that there would be a double main event. There would be a cage match with Harley Race vs. Ric Flair for the world title. At this time, in 1983, there was a guy in Oklahoma called the Junkyard Dog, who was gaining popularity. He would fight wearing a dog collar. I told the promoters that Greg Valentine and I would fight a dog-collar match, so I went out and got all the necessary equipment to pull off this unique match. I found a truck chain, which was going to be displayed in the lobby so the people could actually touch it and see what I was going to use. And I had some spiked leather dog collars made up with sheep's wool inside. The reason I put the sheep's wool inside was to protect our necks from the leather, but all it did was give us a nasty rash.

Dusty Rhodes, Ole and Gene Anderson, and I sat down and decided that this had to be a very brutal match from start to finish. We wanted people to be talking about it for years. When we went to different towns, we wanted people to pack the houses just to see one of our dog-collar matches. This is why it had to be very bloody and brutal. It was a good plan . . . unless you were one of the wrestlers involved in the match!

When the night came for us to put on our show, everyone was high-strung. You could feel the tension in the air. Just before the bell rang for the dog-collar match, Greg and I agreed to try not to break each other's nose or teeth, but with this kind of match, well, it was what it was and we both knew what to expect. I knew going

Dog collar. w/ Valentine

Made it Bloody & Mean

in that Valentine had the reputation for hitting his opponents very hard whenever he wrestled, so I was prepared.

The first thing we did when we got in the ring was try not to let each other get the chain because we both knew that if the other guy got the chain he would use it mercilessly. And needless to say, once we each got ahold of that chain, we got carried away. My left eardrum was broken and I lost 50 percent of the hearing. The damage was irreversible. I certainly can say that it was one of the most barbaric matches of my career, but it sure did get over with the people. They loved every second of it! And while Greg and I loved that the audience loved it, the problem was we had to do it another forty-five times over the next 60 days!

Over that span of time the cuts and bruises would heal, but that darn sheep's wool started making us look like we had some sort of disease around our necks. Valentine was really angry at me for putting the wool in the collars because it was itching him like crazy. He would take the chain and wrap it around his fist and hit me in the head, yelling, "Why did you put this stupid fucking wool in these collars!" Yet the original dog-collar match helped the *Starrcade* Pay-Per-View really set the wrestling world on fire, and when all was said and done, the event exceeded the expectations of all the parties involved, making it one of the most successful wrestling events ever held.

And when it was over, Barnett wanted even more control over his territory and his wrestlers. I was one of the hottest wrestlers around and we were selling out every town. Because I had a contract, they expected me to become a corporate man. Well, I got news for you . . . that ain't me.

By this time I was really out of hand. I was crazy-ass nuts! I was packing in the crowds, but I was also breaking all the rules. You would think that with my wife expecting our first child, I would have slowed down a bit, but Tommy and I liked living life on the edge together. We had the Sickness bad and there was no stopping us . . . Until one night when we had to wrestle in Chattanooga.

We were on our way to the match and Tommy was driving. He took a wrong turn, and by the time we realized we were lost, we had gone two hundred miles in the wrong direction. We got directions from a couple of cops in a squad car who offered to help us when they found out we were lost. They told us to put the hammer down and that they would warn all their buddies who were positioned on the highway that we would be flying on through. So taking the kind officers' advice, Tommy just floored it the rest of the way, but we were still three hours late. The matches were scheduled to start at three o'clock and we got there after six. Everyone was mad at us. But the guys stalled the crowd enough that we still got our matches in. Nevertheless, this would be the last match I wrestled in for Barnett and Ole. After the event was over and Tommy and I were getting ready to go to the next town, Ole Anderson stopped us and said: "Tommy, you can take this up with Barnett, and Piper, you're fired. You can talk to Barnett if you want. I don't give a shit."

I said, "I don't need to fuckin' talk to nobody. I'm outta here!"

I went home to Kitty, who was seven months pregnant, and told her I'd been fired. Wonderful person that she is, she just hugged me and said she loved me. The next day they sent over some poor little referee—the guy was scared shitless—and he said I breached my contract because I was late for the match. To make matters worse, they blackballed me and I couldn't wrestle in the States anywhere, and then they turned me over to the IRS.

Who is "they"? you ask. Well, I can only speculate. People were now telling me that they smelled a rat and that all the evidence pointed to Tommy. They kept whispering in my ear that Rich had been in that territory for so long that he set me up to be canned, but to be honest, I still don't believe this.

It was a rough time for me. I really didn't have anyone to talk to about what had just gone down; I didn't trust anyone in the promotion and I didn't talk to my wife about the situation because pro wrestlers are taught not to bring their work home with them.

It was the honorable thing to do. You take care of your kids and your family at all costs and put work second. You never bring your wife to a match, and you never talk business with her. Why bring the stress home? Why even discuss wrestling with your wife? What is she going to tell you? How to take a body slam?

But don't let me fool you. There are other reasons why guys didn't want their wives or girlfriends at the arena. One of them was insurance just in case somebody had a girlfriend on the side. But most of these Frat Brothers were good family men and they just didn't want their wives or kids to see them take a beating. Every one of these men was a great provider and dad. Night after night these men proved that any jerk-off can have a child, but it takes a real man to be a father. So it was a hard-and-fast rule to never, ever involve your family in the sport.

Jerk to be a Dad

So because I didn't really talk about my work situation, I still had all this ugliness going on inside me. I couldn't believe those sons of bitches had blackballed me. And to think I had actually called some of these guys my friends at one time. Just like Sonny King once took a knife to help me when someone tried to stab me, I would have taken a knife to protect any of these guys—little did I know it was going to be one of them stabbing me in the back!

1983

This was when Ric Flair and I became really close. He was—and is—a true friend. I had no job; no wrestling promoter wanted to take the chance of using me and ruining his good name. I couldn't wrestle anywhere, so I decided to move back to Charlotte with Kitty and try to start fresh.

Close w/ Flair

In order to get all our stuff back to Charlotte, Kitty and I had to drive in separate vehicles. I rented a U-Haul truck, which I was going to drive, and my wife was going to take our Cadillac along with our miniature pinscher, Feather. I wasn't looking forward to the drive because, number one, I knew the time alone would just have me thinking about what had just gone down in Georgia, and number two, I had the unfortunate pleasure of riding with our other dog, a giant and retarded dalmatian named Ryiethumnne R. Little

Moves from Georgia to Charlotte

did I know that crazy mutt would keep me "entertained" the entire ride back to North Carolina.

But I really shouldn't have been surprised because both of our dogs, as retarded as they were at times, had given Kitty and me plenty of laughs over the years. For instance, Feather came into our lives one day after I proposed to Kitty in Atlanta. Unbeknownst to me, my wife-to-be had gone to the pet store in town the next day. She fell in love with this pup and asked the shop owner to put the little guy in the window. Then Kitty brought me down and *by accident* we passed the store and she pointed out to me how cute and cuddly the mutt was and how great it would be for her to have a dog like that to keep her company while I was on the road. So okay, I fell for the bit hook, line, and sinker, but a funny thing happened on the way home that night. I noticed when we picked up the little pup and took her home that she was a shaking mess. We couldn't stop Feather from trembling the first few days we had her. But that problem was solved when Kitty and I went out to dinner one night.

I took my lovely bride-to-be out on the town and forgot that I had left my box of Valiums on the floor at home, as we had no furniture. So when we got back from dinner, we found the box on the kitchen floor all torn to pieces and Feather just lounging around without a care in the world. The Valiums calmed that dog right down and smoothed those nerves right out! She went on to live another sixteen calm and cool years with us.

Ryiethumnne R., on the other hand, was anything but calm, especially in cars. The dog hated being on the road for any period of time because she had been in an accident once before in Walla Walla and was not very comfortable riding in a car. So I knew I was going to have my hands full with this dog for the entire 250-mile trip. But I thought if I kept the radio on and her distracted I'd be all right. Boy, was I wrong! No sooner had we pulled away from my old house than that dastardly dog started barking. My first means to try to keep her quiet was just to tell her to shut up, but that didn't work. That would have been too easy. The next thing I did was turn up the radio, but still that bastard wouldn't shut up. We were now going on about an hour and a half and Ryiethumnne was still woofing, so at this point I'd already lost it so I started barking back at the annoying animal. But whatever I was saying in dog language wasn't working either. After about another half hour, I couldn't think of anything else to get this dog to shut up, so I gave her my jacket to chew on, hoping it would occupy her for a while. As soon as she got ahold of my jacket, she took a bite out of it, and with the piece of cloth hanging out of her mouth looked at me and continued barking. That fucking dog barked all the way to Charlotte, not giving me any time to think about why I was leaving Atlanta. Boy, I hated that dog, but I love her for what she did for me that day. Without knowing what she was doing, that dalmatian kept my mind off being blackballed.

Once I got settled in Charlotte, Ric gave me a call and made me an offer I couldn't refuse. Flair and I had always gotten along, and as a matter of fact, he dubbed me the "John Wesley Hardin" of wrestling for the last twenty years. Hardin was supposedly one of the toughest gunfighters of the Wild West, who killed some twenty men—one just for snoring! He got caught, went to jail, and then came out a lawyer. As for me, while I knew I would never become a lawyer, at this time in my career I was full to the brim with talent that I was dying to express. Besides my wrestling skills, I had always watched Flair's back and he knew that I would continue to do so. Flair asked me if I wanted to travel with him overseas to work in some events in places like San Juan or Santo Domingo and I immediately told him yes. While I didn't like being away from my pregnant wife, I had an obligation to her and my unborn child to earn a living so we could have a place to live and food to eat. I almost had work in Dallas for a booker named Gary Hart, but he tried to get me at a bargain-basement price of $1,200 per week. I knew I couldn't accept this money, not when I used to make $5,000 a week, and more importantly, I had a wife and a kid on the way, so I had to take the best offer out there for their sake. I told Hart to have a nice day and I opted to go overseas with Flair to earn my keep and win my reputation back.

Flair

Wrestling Outside the U.S.

Blackballed?

I couldn't wrestle in the States, so I hopped on a plane with Flair and headed overseas. Back in those days traveling on a plane was much different than it is today, especially since there was no in-flight entertainment. If you were in the air for six hours, you didn't have a couple of movies to keep you occupied. You either had to hope for a talkative and interesting passenger sitting next to you or you had to kill the time sleeping or reading a good book. But us wrestlers never had to worry about anything like that with Flair on board. He lived for those long flights. As soon as the FASTEN SEAT BELTS sign was taken off—sometimes sooner—Ric would turn to me and say, "Hey, Pipes, what do you think?" I knew what he was about to do, so I just answered, "Do whatever you want, man." Ric would then grab his $5,000 robe from the overhead compartment and go into the bathroom to change. He would strip out of his Armani suit and into his birthday suit in less than five minutes, and then come back to his seat wearing nothing but his expensive robe. The bright

Ric wore Robe on plane

red velvet garment looked like it had been taken from the honeymoon suite in a seedy Las Vegas hotel, but he wore it well.

After getting comfortable, he would then take the tray from the stewardess and serve the free drinks to everybody on the airplane. The crew always loved the sweet talker and always allowed him to do whatever he wanted. Before you knew it, he'd be walking up and down the aisles hootin' and hollerin' with the passengers, and making his newfound friends his favorite drink in the world, the Kamikaze. At first this would cause me a great deal of embarrassment, but I guess after the 150th or 160th time, you just learn to go with it. Ric loved having fun and being the center of attention. Add these two qualities to his genuine heart of gold (a rare combination), and that is what has made Ric Flair the legend that he is.

But Ric didn't only clown around when we were in the air. He also liked to have fun while we were still on the ground. For instance, whenever we left Santo Domingo we would land in Florida and have to go through customs. One time, around Christmas, Flair and I were in a festive mood. While we waited in line we started singing "Jingle Bells" and Ric began to dance. I had seen Ric dance before, but on this day he was really cutting a rug. After several minutes of holiday cheer, the customs guy had seen about enough, and he came out from behind his desk to tell us to knock it off.

At about the same time we were being told to keep our traps shut, we noticed Jack and Jerry Brisco were also waiting to go through customs. How they didn't see or hear us causing a commotion is beyond me, but it turned out to be a good thing because now we decided to take our party to the other side of the room and mess with the Briscos. After yes-ing the customs officer to death and telling him we would behave, we quietly made our way toward the Brisco brothers, and without them ever seeing us, we went and leg-dived them from behind, knocking the two big lugs on their asses. If you thought we were loud before with our singing, you should have heard it when the four of us were rolling on the floor in the customs area. Here you have two Indians, one platinum blond, and a red-faced (or should I say shit-faced) guy in a kilt. How we didn't get arrested that day I'll never know. It was just another memorable day in wrestling paradise!

At this time we were again wrestling our motherfucking asses off. It wasn't all fun and games; we did have to work when we went on these trips out of the States. As a matter of fact, there was one time in Santo Domingo when I thought we weren't going to make it out alive from that armpit of the world. It was one of my first international trips with Ric and he was scheduled to wrestle the most popular wrestler in that area. I believe the man's name was Jack Benitez. Even though Flair and I had never heard of him, the entire city looked up to this guy like he was some sort of wrestling god.

The people were so in love with him that they would supposedly fill the streets just to see their hero train. Ric and I found out when we got down there that Benitez's entire training regime consisted of him running a half mile across a bridge in town. But Ric and I didn't question this because we didn't want to piss anybody off. After all, this was a country that was run by generals under martial law and the way one got higher in rank was by controlling or killing as many people as possible. Taking us out wouldn't be a problem at all for them. In their eyes, we were just two white guys from the United States. They probably would have seen it as a mercy killing.

There was a huge buzz in the city on the night of Ric's match against the town boy wonder. The arena, which had no windows or air-conditioning and was hotter than a sauna, was packed to the rafters with locals who had come to see Benitez take on the American. It was like nothing I had ever seen before. Ric and I were escorted out of the locker room to the ring by armed guards, who not only had guns in tow, but were also carrying six-inch nightsticks that had a three-inch chain on the end. The son of the country's president was even in attendance that night. I remember the soldiers, who took a liking to us, pointing him out as we made our way to the ring. He was seated in a special area and he was surrounded by a bunch of guys wearing these funny-looking swirly hats.

I have to say, even though the crowd was on us from the moment we stepped into the arena, I wasn't scared or intimidated at all, as the soldiers made us feel very safe and secure from the get-go. I knew that Ric wasn't the least bit scared either, especially when he saw what Benitez looked like when he came into the ring. This Jack guy was so small that we originally thought he was part of the midget wrestling match scheduled before Ric's bout.

So instead of just going out there and kicking the snot out of this guy one, two, three, Flair gets one of his bright ideas. He wants me to keep interfering in the match by constantly pulling Benitez's legs, which would piss off not only Benitez but the crowd as well.

So once the bell rang I did what Ric wanted me to do, which really ticked everybody off. The fans were really going nuts! The president's kid even got into it and started jumping up and down screaming unpleasantries toward Ric and me. His friends with swirly hats also got up and started yelling. At first I thought, "This is great! Look how much these people love their wrestling!" But once I noticed the swirly-hat guys patting their sidearms, I knew we were in trouble. We weren't in Kansas anymore and the guards were no longer on our side.

The soldiers started using the sticks with the chains on the closest person to them—which of course was me! Flair was safe in the beginning because he had the high ground in the ring and also because they didn't look at him as the bad guy; the whole place hated me because of what I was doing to their hero. But after a while they turned on Ric, too, and we both were in the fight of our lives—*for* our lives. The entire army and arena were now after us and we had no place to go. I had my back to the ring and I grabbed a chair for protection while my partner-in-crime was still in the ring. We had no idea how the hell we were going to live to tell about this one. Then all of a sudden a Puerto Rican wrestler, the Masked Invader, came running out of the locker room to try to help us get out of the ring unharmed. Somehow or other he managed to create a path down the aisles and got us back to the dressing room, where we thought we would find safety. But when we got there the place was a mess. All of our stuff was either stolen or trashed, including my wedding ring and a special diamond king ring that Johnny Rodz (Java Ruuk) had given me a while back.

But the chaos didn't end there. There were still people who literally wanted to kill us pounding on our door. The nut jobs managed to get the door open and started throwing pieces of concrete at Ric and me. So now with our backs again up against a wall and nowhere to go, Flair asked me as we were ducking out of the way of the stones: "Dom Pérignon, Pipes?" Here we were with our lives in danger and Flair was still a joker.

This craziness went on until about two o'clock in the morning when finally someone got an ambulance up there, which whisked us away to safety without the huge crowd that had gathered outside knowing. That was one time when I truly thought there was no way out!

Another frequent stop on our international wrestling itinerary was San Juan. The boys loved wrestling there because of the nightlife and the casinos. To be honest, it wasn't my cup of tea because I'm not a gambler. But I do remember one time that me, Ric, the Brisco brothers, and Frenchie Martin were down there and I did reach into my pocket to try my luck. Well, needless to say, I found out that night that not only was I a reckless drunk, I was also a reckless gambler. I think we stayed in a place called the Condado Hotel, and as soon as we checked in, the guys wanted to hit the tables. At first I had no interest, but I tagged along just to pass some time and have a little fun.

As soon as we got to the casino floor, Flair wasted no time as he grabbed a waitress and ordered up ninety-nine Kamikazes to get the night and a buzz rolling. It's been said that Ric used to throw his drinks over his shoulder when he thought no one was looking or that he'd tell the bartender to water his down, but to be honest, I wouldn't know, as I was too busy drinking my share. So after a couple of drinks, I loosened up and was willing to try my luck at

PP,
Ric + Paddy in P.R. @ a Casino

usually not a Gambler but was drunk

the tables. Believe it or not, I had beginner's luck that night and I walked away with a stack of chips in my pocket.

After a couple of hours of drinking and gambling, I left the hotel with Jack and Jerry Brisco and Frenchie Martin to explore the night scene of San Juan. After stopping at a few more watering holes, we decided to return to our hotel and the casino, where I could cash in the winning chips that I still had in my pocket. But to our surprise the casino was closed. I think I was more pissed than anybody else that night because I wanted to get my money, so we decided to bring the party back to my room. On the way upstairs I decided to take my frustrations out on tall tropical plants that were in my path. In typical wrestler fashion, I clotheslined the plants one by one, knocking dirt and leaves all over the pretty hallways.

As soon as we got back to the room, one of the guys broke out some marijuana and the party started all over again. But no sooner had we started to party than there was a knock on the door, and just by the sound we knew it couldn't be good. I asked who it was and the knockers informed me that they were the police. The wrestler who had the pot jumped up to dump the remaining stash in the toilet, but in true wrestling style he didn't dump it right away. Instead, he just went into the bathroom and closed the door, hoping that the cops would go away without searching the room.

When I opened the door to the hallway, I found five police officers and two dogs standing right before me. They informed me that they had seen me on the hotel camera knocking over the plants, and before they went any further, I pulled out my hundred-dollar chips from my pocket—there went my winnings!—and started handing each of them a couple, telling them that I was sorry and that it wouldn't happen again. They told me that I would be leaving in the morning, which I was more than happy to do. They left without asking me any more questions. While I was relieved that I didn't get arrested, the guy in the bathroom was also happy, but not because I didn't have to go to jail. He had saved his supply of pot, and as soon as I shut the door, the partying continued.

But sometimes when I look back on that night, I think I might have been better off spending the night behind bars. After the cops and dogs left, we got so wasted and someone came up with the bright idea of doing shots out of Frenchie Martin's boots. Frenchie had these boots that he'd been wearing since Gandhi took the big walk for salt, and we all put liquor in one of them and started drinking out of it. The next morning we were all sick as dogs. We must have come down with athlete's throat or something from all those shots.

But the antics in San Juan weren't limited to the casino and our rooms. One day Jack and Jerry Brisco took advantage of Ric and me being intoxicated. They challenged us to a friendly game of basketball on the hotel courts, and Flair and I, being the ultracompetitive athletes that we were, decided to take them on, even though we were seeing double and wearing our bathing suits and were barefoot at the time. It was like playing four against two, with us having the disadvantage. But we didn't care. We thought, drunk and all, we could beat them. The Briscos, on the other hand, were sober and were wearing regular clothes with cowboy boots—not exactly uniforms meant for a basketball game either. Thinking back, I realize that we should have known something was up because of the way those two clowns were dressed, but we had just consumed so many Kamikazes that we weren't in any position to pay attention to detail. After running around the court like maniacs for a while, we finally caught on to what the Brisco brothers were doing. Jack and Jerry were just passing the ball back and forth, making Ric and me chase after them like two idiots. They had no intention of ever shooting. They just wanted to tire us out and get a good laugh. We not only left the court that day steaming mad at the Briscos, we also could barely walk because of all the cuts on our feet from playing barefoot on the concrete. To try and relieve the pain in our feet, we raided the local drugstore and bought several tubes of Anbesol and a couple of boxes of gauze. We still had a match to wrestle that night, so we figured that the Ambesol would numb our feet so we could dance

on the mat that night like Fred Astaire and Ginger Rogers—Ric
being Ginger of course! But just like the old saying goes: "You play,
you pay." And boy, did we ever pay that day and night!

Another time I almost paid dearly I was on my own in San Juan.
I somehow had gotten separated in the city from my Frat Brothers
and was in a rush to catch a flight to our next gig. I was in a state
of panic, not only because I had two matches the next night, but
also because there were only two flights a day to Canada, so if I
missed my flight, I was going to miss my matches and that wouldn't
go over well with the promoters, who I was trying to get back in
good graces with. On my way back to my hotel to pick up my
things, I ended up getting into an argument with two local guys,
one of whom just happened to be carrying a gun. Well, the argument
got so heated that the police came to see what was going on, and
before I knew it, these locals were telling the cops that the gun was
mine. The police believed the two locals over me and tossed my ass
in jail. Let me tell you, folks, it was no picnic being tossed behind
bars in San Juan, especially if you wore a kilt and were as Irish
white as I was. I have to admit there were some tough dudes in
those cells, and you definitely had to make people aware of you. I
kept telling the guards that there had been a big mistake and that
it wasn't my gun, but they ignored me until the next morning.

Finally, for whatever reason, they believed me and released me,
but it was too late for me to catch my flight. I called ahead to the
promoter of the event and he got Terry Funk to fill in for me. Aside
from this fiasco, I have never missed a wrestling match because of
my health or any other reason. I made every match that I was ever
booked on, but Funk started a joke that he made a living by taking
the shots that I missed. Whether Funk knew it or not, this did not
help me in my quest to have my name erased from the blackballed
list and gain back the trust of the promoters.

One of the guys I wrestled on the international scene who left a
mark on me to this day is Pedro Morales. When you talk about
Morales, his lethal left hook isn't the only thing that comes to mind.

I remember a funny story regarding him and another monster of the mat, Koko B. Ware.

One evening Morales was out partying after a match until the wee hours of the morning. It was well-known by everyone on the circuit that Pedro loved his cognac, and that particular night he loved it so much that he kept it company until 7 A.M. He finally found his way back to his room, which adjoined Koko's, and closed the drapes to keep the sun that was now coming up out of his eyes when he lay down to sleep. But just as Pedro's head hit the pillow, he heard a greeting from Koko's room: "Good morning." Pedro, who is one of the finest men I ever met, answered back politely in his Spanish accent, "Amigo, good morning. But please, I'm just going to bed." A few minutes went by and Pedro heard another "good morning," and again responded calmly, asking his friend to please let him get some rest. But by the time the third greeting rolled around, Pedro lost his cool. The tired wrestler jumped out of his bed in his boxer shorts, white tank top, and dress-sock suspenders and promptly went out in the hall and smashed in his fellow wrestler's door. But to his surprise, Pedro found an empty room. Koko was nowhere to be found. The only living creature occupying the wrestler's room was his pet parrot, Frankie, who was flying around loose. The parrot was part of Koko's act and he always took it with him when he traveled.

Pedro now felt really bad because he realized that it was the parrot and not Koko who kept saying "good morning." Morales then proceeded to put the door back on its hinges so his friend's pet bird couldn't fly out, and went straight to the front desk to apologize to the owner of the hotel and also to pay for the damages he had just caused.

Even before I got in the ring with Pedro, I felt like I knew him. Ric and the guys had told me all about him so I'd be better prepared when I faced him in the ring. Morales was also curious about me. Ricky Steamboat would tell me later that before our match, as we were getting ready to face each other, Morales went up to Ricky and asked him, "Hey, is this Piper guy any good?" Steamboat said he told him to be careful because Piper would stay on him the whole match. We both tried to get as much info on each other beforehand so there wouldn't be any surprises once the bell rang.

Well, all the inside info the guys gave me on Morales wound up doing me no good because Pedro nailed me with one of the most lethal shots in the history of wrestling. We were wrestling in a baseball stadium that night where the ring was positioned right on the pitcher's mound and I was prepared for a physical match with the very strong firepluglike wrestler, but little did I know he had other ideas. When the ten-minute mark came, I had Morales in a headlock and he worked himself out of the hold and threw me on the ropes. I came back at the guy full speed off the twine and he hit me with a left-hook move that toppled me over. After getting up from the canvas, I put on the afterburners and charged Morales full throttle, and that's when he unleashed his patented blow. *Boom!* He nailed me with this open-hand palmed shot right smack in my liver. The whole stadium reacted to the flesh-on-flesh whack and groaned *"Whoa!"* in unison. They must have been thinking, "That poor son of a bitch!" I still need a transplant to this day from that vicious blow.

I had now become a regular on the international wrestling circuit and was making a good living flying to places like San Juan, Santo Domingo, and Japan. However, after paying my dues, I was finally getting some work again in the U.S., as Jimmy Crockett agreed to book me back in Charlotte. I was once again in familiar territory, like the TV studio on Tuesdays doing the weekly interviews. I have to give Jimmy credit because most promoters would not have done this. He put his ass, neck, and reputation on the line for me and I didn't let him down, as the Charlotte territory started to do great business again, which was my way of paying Jimmy back.

Working in Charlotte gave me the chance to spend more time with Kitty. Unfortunately, I spent most of my time with her in front of the fireplace, as it was winter and the furnace broke in the house that I was renting. So every night for a month I had to stay awake to throw logs on the fire in order to keep my family warm. But I'm glad I was there because I was able to witness when Kitty gave birth to our first child, our beautiful daughter Anastasia. It was one of the happiest days of my life. Anastasia came into the world on a Monday and I was back in the studio on Tuesday to do my interviews and would wrestle that evening in Raleigh, North Carolina. Ric Flair, Harley Race, the Briscos, Dusty Rhodes, the Funks, and Andre the Giant—they were all there hanging around the studio. There were empty coffee cups, chicken bones, and exhausted wrestlers lying like carnage all over the room. You could just feel the pain in the place. Most guys were just coming off a 250- or 300-mile trip from the night before.

One of the guys, I think it was Ray Stevens, said to me, "Hey, I heard you had a kid. Congratulations." All the guys came up and shook my hand. Then someone else said, "Hey, Poppa Piper!" At this point Jerry Brisco mustered all of the strength he had and lifted his head up off the bench he was lying on. "Pop a Piper? Who the hell could live through that?" he muttered. Well, Ric Flair heard this and just started horse-laughing. One thing about Ric is that if you want somebody to know something, you tell Ric Flair and the word will get around. He'll stooge on you, right in front of you. No, he's not really a stooge; he's a helluva man. So he told everyone, "Pop a Piper, get it?" and he laughed hysterically. That joke went around for years, but eventually it went back to Poppa Piper, because later in my career guys would come to me with questions and looked to me as a father figure, and the original way I got the name got lost in the shuffle.

Life was looking up again. I had my wife, my new daughter, and I was riding high in Charlotte. I had put all that shit from Atlanta behind me and was coming back just as strong as ever. I remember one night, Kitty and I were watching television and I was flicking through channels trying to find something interesting for us to watch when I stumbled upon a show on TBS with Deborah Harry

Debbie Harry [handwritten annotation]

from the rock group Blondie. Deborah Harry and Blondie were huge back then. They had hits like "Call Me" racing up the charts, and in this interview they somehow got her on the subject of wrestling and she said on national TV, "The worst thing they ever did was fire Roddy Piper." This showed me that not only was I known outside of my territory, I was known outside of the sport. Hell, one of the hottest rock stars in the world was a fan!

Well, this not only got Kitty's and my attention, it also created quite a buzz on the New York/New Jersey circuit. Jimmy Crockett told me that Vince McMahon Sr. was interested in using me in New York when Crockett was finished with me. This was a very honorable thing to do. Usually promoters would use and abuse the wrestler for the benefit of the territory and *then* throw him a bone telling him another P wanted him in their territory. Me, being the honorable wrestler that I am, I immediately gave my six weeks' notice as soon as I found out.

All of a sudden there was a new call of the wild! This was now the start of the second plot to take over the world. Basically I was again the "chosen one"—or at least that's what I was being told. McMahon, who told me he was going to take over the wrestling world, liked my interview style and said he was going to build the territory around me. What I didn't know was that he had probably told the twenty-five other rebels who were there the very same thing! I'm almost positive that Vince McMahon Sr. used the same line on guys like Paul Orndorff, Dave Schultz, Bob Orton Jr., Jimmy Snuka, Don Muraco, and countless others. But I wasn't too concerned at that time because I was back wrestling in the States and now wanted a shot at making it in New York, which had at one time in my career intimidated and embarrassed the hell out of me.

Vince Sr. wants Roddy in NY [handwritten annotation]

gonna be different this time [handwritten annotation]

F3Q540

Flair 7541 Thumb drive video

Always a crowd favorite even though a heel?

what is story line of Portland –

① Meet in Charlotte – Early 80's
Helps Roddy out? No work for Roddy?

② Cyber Sunday 2006 – Tag Team Champs
Payback to Roddy — England - hurt

③ Hall of Fame speech

7

The New York Years

Kitty being told back to NY.

FTER getting the news from Crockett that McMahon wanted me in New York, I went home to my wife and daughter and said, "Honey, we're going to New York." Kitty gave me one of those "you have to be kidding me" looks, but she never uttered a bad word about having to relocate again. She just rolled with the punches and trusted my judgment. No matter what, Kitty always gave me her full support. I wanted to give my wife and baby everything they deserved and New York had a lot to offer. I was well aware of Frank Sinatra's advice in the song "New York, New York," that if you can make it there, you can make it anywhere, and I was determined to prove that I had what it took. I was also just so in love with my daughter Anastasia, who reminded me of Shirley Temple, that I wanted her to have the best life had to offer. So if it meant packing our bags and going to New York and starting over, I was prepared to do it.

At this point in our lives Kitty was used to the craziness. My wife had been through a lot with me already, so another move

Kitty

wasn't that big a deal. Bob Orton had once told me to drink apple-cider vinegar every day because it was good for my joints. Well, I drank half a bottle of cider vinegar every night for six months straight, and nothing! If Kitty could live with me coming to bed smelling like a salad every night for half a year, I'm sure she could handle New York. Poor Kitty, the crazy shit I put her through.

I'll also never forget the one night in Charlotte when some insane fans found out where we lived and came to our apartment and tried to harass us. It was about midnight. The baby was asleep and Kitty and I were lying on the bed, talking and cuddling. All of a sudden we heard this hootin' and hollerin'. I got up and went to the window; our apartment looked out onto a parking lot, and there I saw two pickup trucks filled with North Carolina rednecks. They were circling the lot with their brights on, honking their horns and shouting, "Hey, Piper, we know you're in there. Come on out. We'll kick your ass!"

I had always been a lone wolf, but now I realized I wasn't on my own anymore. I had a wife and a child. I was now a father, and this was all pretty new to me, so my first reaction as Father of the Year was to overreact.

I happened to be packing two guns in the house at the time, so me, Smith, and Wesson went outside to see what these punks wanted. I ran out the door, without even buttoning up my jeans, my .357s in hand, and I just began shooting. Those rednecks turned white, just like Casper the Ghost, and scrambled to get out of there. But I just kept running and shooting, running and shooting, hoping to nail one of the bastards. Just when I had one of the trucks in my sight, my jeans fell to my ankles, causing me to do a perfect nosedive square onto the concrete. I fell flat on my face, scraping the dog out of my nose and knees. I looked up just in time to see the taillights of those trucks hightailing out of the lot.

Kitty came outside and sauntered up to me ever so calmly. She found me lying facedown on the ground with my pants down and both guns still in my hands and she said very quietly, "Are you finished, Roderick? Do you think we can go back into the apartment now, sweetheart?" I asked her to hold the guns as I pulled my pants up, and we went back inside like nothing happened. This is why I love Kitty so much. She takes me for who I am and allows me to be myself. But the key word is "Roderick" coming out of her mouth. The minute she uses my full name I know she means business. If it comes from anyone else, it won't work, only from Kitty. She has saved my life so many times over the course of our relationship that I've lost count.

Kitty has been putting up with my shit not only from our first date in the park, but also from our first day as man and wife. In 1982, we got married one afternoon in Portland in an old Scottish church, and not only didn't we go on a honeymoon afterward, but I left her alone on our wedding night to go wrestle in a match. To this day we still haven't gone on a honeymoon.

When it was time to leave for New York, we packed up our car and hitched a U-Haul trailer to the back of the Cadillac and said good-bye to Charlotte. After making the straight drive, we finally hit New York, and of course I kept with my tradition of letting a new city know that I was in town. I opened up my window and yelled: "New York City, Roddy Piper is here and I'm gonna kick your ass!" My wife looked at me strangely. This was the first time that anyone had been in a car with me when I did this.

The first thing Kitty, Anastasia, and I did was try to find some-place to live. Instead of living in the heart of all the craziness of New York City, we decided to look around in New Jersey, which is far enough away from the hustle and bustle but close enough that you could still feel the city's pulse. After driving around a bit, we settled for a small hotel right on the ocean in Sea Bright, New Jersey. After what was about to happen to me and my family, you would think I would remember the name of the place, but I guess deep down I'm just trying to forget.

Once we got settled in the room, I called a couple of people to find out when and where I was wrestling and then I was off to work.

I began wrestling all over New York and New Jersey with people like Sergeant Slaughter, Don Muraco, and Mr. Fuji, who also lived in the New Jersey area. Almost immediately I was back to wrestling regularly and keeping crazy hours. One particular night I got home from the matches around 1:30 A.M. and everyone was sound asleep. I was also dead on my feet, so I cuddled in bed with Kitty thinking I was in for a long night's rest. With our room being right on the water, the sound of the ocean waves, plus the fact that I hadn't stopped a lick since we got to town, knocked me right out. About two and a half hours later, Kitty was frantically trying to to wake me up. As soon as I heard her crying, it got my attention and heart racing and I jumped right out of the bed. When my bare feet hit the floor I realized that our entire room was flooded with three to four inches of water, with more coming fast and furious. My heart began racing even more when my thoughts shifted to the whereabouts of my baby girl, who was usually sleeping in her playpen that was now floating across the room. As the freezing seawater awoke me fully, I found Kitty had already rescued Anastasia and placed her safely in her Moses basket on top of the dresser. Thank God she was safe.

I quickly gathered my family and went right for the door, and you wouldn't believe the amount of water that just poured in when I opened it. The force almost knocked me off my feet, so it was a good thing that Kitty was behind me holding the baby. When we got outside, there was probably about a foot and a half of water, so my first priority was to get my family up to higher ground. After doing this, I made my way back to our car, which was parked outside our room, only to find that the front doors of the vehicle were already submerged. Knowing that there was no way for me to move it, I proceeded to unhook the U-Haul trailer so I could get it to safety because it had all of our valuables in it, including a mason jar with all the money we had in the world. (I still did not believe in putting my money in the bank.) So now I had the unfortunate pleasure of pulling this humongous trailer out of harm's way by these two huge chains, by myself, like Hercules. Using every muscle and ounce of strength I had, I managed to get the damn thing to higher ground, away from the shoreline. A couple of our things wound up getting ruined, like one of my wife's favorite collectible horse pictures, that still has the water stains on it to this day, as it hangs on our wall. But all in all, most of our stuff was okay.

As I was pulling the trailer, I could hear the National Guard calling out to the people on the loudspeaker, warning them about the flood and also offering to help take everyone out of the storm and to safety. They picked up my wife and Anastasia and put them in the front of the truck, and later on I caught up to them and jumped in the back. We were then taken to a local school gymnasium for shelter, and as soon as I knew Kitty and the baby were safe and dry, I hit the road to try to find us a new place to live. After searching for a couple of hours, I finally got us a room for the month at the local Hilton, but before I gave them any money, I made sure the room was on the fifteenth floor.

While I was gone, one of the New Jersey newspaper reporters came by the shelter and took a picture of my soaking-wet wife and my baby sitting in a chair. The next morning when we woke up nice and dry in our hotel, we were hit with another shock. I ordered us breakfast from room service and with our order came the morning newspaper. To our surprise, on the front page is a photo of my wife and daughter that said DESTITUTE FAMILY. Well, Kitty was clever enough to give the reporter Sergeant Slaughter's real family name so as to not draw attention to us, but it gave us the good laugh we needed after the ordeal we just had been through. I even teased Kitty that morning, saying, "Who would have guessed that you would be on the front page of a paper in New Jersey before me? Now we have two celebrities in the family."

After breakfast, I went back to our flooded hotel to try to fish out our car, and within a few hours I had dumped all the water from the soaked interior and had it up and running. But the Cadillac was never quite the same after the flood and it eventually blew up a few months later, at which time I left it on the side of the road

Picture in Newspaper

and never saw it again. After our thirty-day stay at the Hilton, we settled into an apartment in Woodbridge, New Jersey, where Don Muraco lived.

Don and I even got to experience one of the most important days in the world of pro wrestling together. We were in Harrisburg, Pennsylvania, for an event that would make history.

Vince McMahon Sr. had decided that he and his son were going to take over the world. He called me personally and told me that I was "The Chosen One." He said he had big hopes for me, but he wanted to make sure that I wasn't afraid to work against any other promoter. I had no problem with this, but like I said before, little did I know that Vince Sr. had this same conversation with every other top renegade in the nation.

So we all were called into Harrisburg. It was like a *Who's Who* of wrestling. There were about twenty-five guys here: Paul Orndorff, Jimmy Snuka, George "The Animal" Steele, Mr. Fuji, Andre the Giant, Adrian Adonis, Jesse Ventura, David Schultz, Ken Patera, Sergeant Slaughter, and all these other rebels. It was first thing in the morning and we had all just come off the road from wherever we were and no one had any idea why they were calling a meeting. We were hungover, tired, road hard, and miserable. All we knew was it was ten o'clock in the morning, and we had to do interviews that day and wrestle three times later that evening. So everyone was doing whatever they had to do to come alive: chugging a pot of coffee; dancing on a mountain in Peru; Andre's got his wine; Mr. Fuji is sitting over there eating his garlic.

All of a sudden Vince McMahon Sr. and Jim Barnett come into the room, and we're all standing around trying to figure out what's going on. They asked us all to find a seat and sit down, like we were in school or something, and that just set some guys off. I really don't think they realized how pissed the guys were. They even took Andre the Giant away from his bottle of wine, which was like flirting with death! What the hell were they thinking? Anyway, after an

Called the top 25 Wrestlers to Harrisburgh. Introd VM

The New York Years   133

hour of their begging and pleading for us to sit down, the twenty-five gorillas all took a seat.

We were now all ears, and wanted to know what the heck they wanted. Then they brought in some puny guy, an announcer, whose name was Vince McMahon Jr. He stood between Vince Sr. and Barnett. What a power play—so they thought! What were they trying to do—fuckin' intimidate us? They sat twenty-five top guys down thinking we'd be eager to hear what they had to say, but they were wrong. We were all established stars who had proven our drawing power over the years and who could get jobs anywhere. The McMahons and Barnett were shitting in their pants as we sat there with "what the fuck do you want?" looks on our faces.

Vince Sr. had a habit of shaking quarters in his hand, and let me tell you those quarters were going a mile a minute that day because I think he realized that we were all onto his "you're the Chosen One" bullshit. And Barnett was no better as he frantically stood in front of us in his Armani suit, smelling his tie and looking around for the nearest exit.

They then proceed to tell us that Vince Jr.—some freakin' announcer—was going to open the orders. Well, we all wanted to know what fuckin' orders they were talking about because if it was for breakfast, we all could have gone for a nice steak with some eggs at that moment.

Vince begins the meeting by saying: "Thank you all for coming, I guess you all know why we are here." And immediately Dr. David Schultz says, "Yeah, we're here to wrestle, what the fuck are you here for?"

McMahon Jr.'s face turned beet red and Senior was shaking his quarters faster and faster. Barnett, that little troll, just kept sniffing the shit out of his tie. We saw the fear in their faces. They were like three deer caught in the headlights. They had twenty-five gorillas in one room, and they had forgotten to bring the bananas!

And at that moment we knew we had them. It was a moment of triumph. For the first time the wrestlers were driving the Greyhound. We knew we had the promoters backed against the wall. There was nothing they could do. What were they going to say? McMahon Jr. cut short his speech and asked if anyone had any questions.

The room was silent. You could feel the tension and we could feel the power that we had. But then Tony Atlas, a big and strong black wrestler, broke the silence when he raised his hand and said: "Excuse me, Mr. McMahon, I got a question. You see, Mr. Mc-Mahon, every night I see Arnie [Arnie Skallard] and I get me an advance. At the end of the week when I get my paycheck, my check ain't that big."

The room was again quiet and Don Muraco slowly turned to Atlas and said: "You stupid asshole!"

At this time—let's give credit where credit is due—McMahon Jr. seized the moment. He said to Atlas: "Well, you see, Tony, I know you guys are wrestlers, but three minus one is two, and two minus one equals one. So you see, as you take it away it gets smaller and smaller." He's talking to us like we were a bunch of fuckin' kindergartners.

For three glorious seconds we had been triumphant. There was a feeling of solidarity in that room and we finally were getting the respect we thought we deserved. We had conquered the promoters . . . until Tony Atlas asked the magic question and McMahon rolled with it. Senior's quarters started shuffling a little slower, Barnett stopped sniffing his tie, and the red left Junior's face. We were now on equal ground again.

We also found out that memorable day that the three men not only wanted us to wrestle only for them in New York, they also wanted to lock us all down by having each of us sign contracts so we would be able to work only for them. Well, after my last contract experience in Atlanta I wasn't about to sign my name on the dotted line for anyone, and I wasn't the only one who felt this way. No one wanted to sign a contract and give away their rights to wrestle elsewhere. But the guys eventually gave in and signed on with Vince.

Vinces wanted everyone to sign exclusive contracts

I was the very last wrestler to sign and that's only because I had no other choice—which you'll learn about later on in this book.

In his conspiracy to take over the world, Vince McMahon Jr. was making a very smart and ruthless move and only a few of us caught on to his real intentions. He wanted to corner the market, and the first thing he needed to do was sign all the best in the biz. What he was really trying to do was establish a brand—a federation that was bigger than the individual stars who wrestled in it.

Normally, when we were in an arena, the billboard outside showcased the talent that was going to wrestle that night, such as Roddy Piper vs. Hulk Hogan, and that would be what attracted the people. But McMahon slowly changed the billing on the marquee to highlight the WWF instead of putting our names there. While our names were still drawing record crowds, McMahon was trying to make it look like it was the WWF name and not the wrestlers that was bringing in the fans.

Eventually, of course, the WWF name had all the power, and with the wrestlers losing the top billing, McMahon could now pay them much less. It was now the WWF coming into town as opposed to whatever the main event was. But let's get something clear folks. McMahon did not make the WWF—the wrestlers did!

The suits didn't realize that it wasn't going to be easy keeping twenty-five stars happy all the time. It was one thing for a promoter to keep the ego of one superstar under control, but when all of a sudden you've got a bunch of wrestling rebels from all over the globe in one room, sharing one pie, you've got problems, especially when each guy was promised that he was going to be the main draw! On any given evening you never knew who was going to explode. At each event, we would sit around in the dressing room waiting for someone to snap. Adrian Adonis, "Macho Man" Randy Savage, the Iron Sheik, Tony Atlas, Mr. Fuji, and countless others—we all took our turns letting off some steam in front of our peers.

Before the WWF and WCW came into existence, wrestling was a sport that was very territorial. Back then there was a definite respect for one another's well-being in the ring and the territory you wrestled in, and if you didn't respect either rule there were consequences. The same held true for the promoters and their promotions. You just didn't invade somebody's region. But McMahon had visions of entering other guys' territories and cornering the market of the wrestling world. That's why he brought in all the best from the different areas around the country. He had a vision of an organization that reached out way beyond the tristate area and he figured if he had the best wrestlers locked up under contract to him, no one in the sport would be able to match his product. But none of us wanted to double-cross any of the promoters we were tight with in other states. Again, we had no idea where this was leading and we wanted to protect our contacts in the wrestling world.

Over the years I've seen wrestlers and promoters get hurt badly when they were caught crossing the lines. There were very strong ethics inside the dressing room. Rules, such as you never went into another guy's bag (his poke) for any reason. Even if you needed a brush and you saw one sticking out of another guy's poke, you never went over and just grabbed it. A guy's personal property was his and his alone, and if a wrestler violated the steadfast rule, he would face a stiff punishment. When it came to our livelihood, we weren't very tolerant or forgiving, especially to our own, who should have known better.

One time, unbeknownst to us, there was a thief in our room who had been stealing money from us for about a month, but no one caught wind of it because he was a smart thief. He would take only a little cash at a time while the guys were out wrestling in the ring. For example, one time a guy was talking out loud to himself, saying: "I thought I had a hundred dollars here and there's only eighty." Another night, some wrestler said: "Jeez, I could've sworn I had four-hundred-dollars?" and he only had three-hundred-dollars. Stealing was probably the worst thing a wrestler could do because we all were already aware that we were being ripped off by the promoters.

But this thief wasn't smart enough to fool everybody. Having been around the sport for so long, the late, great Gorilla Monsoon and the elders in our room suspected something was going on, and without saying a word to any of us, they put out some bait to catch the rat. One night Monsoon put a special invisible solution on some money that he left hanging out of his pocket, hoping the thief would strike.

Even though none of us knew about it, the elders' plan worked to perfection, as the thief did indeed go for the bait, and stole the money from Gorilla's pocket. When he went into the shower to get cleaned up, his dirty deed was uncovered as his hands turned beet red once the water hit them. And after a few seconds, the water wasn't the only thing hitting this prick. The undeniable lie-detector test revealed who the culprit was and the elders immediately pummeled him in the shower and laid him out bare naked in his stall. After they were through giving him the beating of his life, which left him unconscious, the elders turned on all the hot-water heads and left the thief there to bake. Justice is swift and decisive in the wrestling world.

Let's just say that he not only almost lost his life that night in the shower, he also lost his right to wrestle on any pro circuit. We just didn't take too kindly to people who were stopping us from feeding our families. From that moment on, this particular wrestler was blackballed from the sport and, to my knowledge, never wrestled in another city again.

Speaking of other cities, Vince McMahon Jr. thought he had the right to make us wrestle anyplace that he booked us because he was paying us well—not well enough, but it's easier to get fucked big—even if it meant stepping into another promoter's territory.

This would cause problems for both McMahon and the wrestlers. One of the problems that McMahon had was in Charlotte, which was run by the Jimmy Crockett, a territory I was all too familiar with. There had always been a line drawn in Richmond, Virginia, between Virginia and Washington—very Civil War–ish.

This line was very much respected over the years and no one really ever tried to cross it.

Except McMahon, that is.

The New York promoter tried to go and run against Jimmy Crockett in Charlotte, and once I saw this, I told McMahon that I wouldn't work against Crockett or Don Owens. Again, I had no contract or guarantee at that particular time, so I wasn't just going to burn any bridges for Vince McMahon or anybody else. But I also had to be realistic. The business was changing, and if I wanted to earn a living in pro wrestling, I had to change with the times. Sure, it went against who I was and what I stood for to work in a territory of someone who at one time in my career helped me out, but I still had to put food on the table for my wife and kids.

But I have to hand it to him, Vince always finds a way to get things done if he really wants it that bad. One way Vince was able to get around the territory politics was to have a benefit event in the area for a wrestler named Rick McGraw, who had just recently passed away. (I had the pleasure of wrestling against Rick in his very last match.) The benefit took place in Charlotte, with all the proceeds going to McGraw's family, and while it was a nice gesture to help a fallen colleague's family in their time of need, it was really more about breaking the wrestling boundary line. It was a way for McMahon Jr. to move in on Jimmy Crockett, and once he crossed that line, there was no stopping him. He was ready to make the world of wrestling his own and no territory was off-limits.

But even though he wanted to own all the territories in the states, McMahon was still too cheap to pay for all our traveling expenses. We would only be flown to events if they were more than three hundred miles away. For example, if we were wrestling some events in Ohio, he would fly us into the first city—say, Cincinnati—and then we had to drive to the other cities on that tour. He wanted to get the most bang for his buck without having to go into his pocket for anything extra. Speaking of extra, McMahon now also had us doing some promotional work for our upcoming matches in the cities where we were working. While I didn't mind helping promote the sport and our matches and interacting with the fans, I did mind if people were going to try and make us look like buffoons.

There was one time in Cincinnati when I was wrestling in the main event against Hulk Hogan. I was told that I was going to be presented with an award from the mayor of the city before my match. So that night, just before I was ready to go on, I put on my kilt and belt and wet myself down. I draped a bath towel around my neck and made my way to the ring, ready to fight. The arena was packed. Wrestling had really taken off at this point in time and everybody wanted to get in on the action—even the mayor of Cincinnati. When I got into the ring, there was the mayor—supposedly the youngest mayor ever—and he grabbed the mike and said, "Ladies and gentlemen, I have an award for Roddy Piper, the biggest cheater and low-life wrestler in the business . . ." The mayor went on and on, hurling insult after insult at me. I immediately took offense, not only at what he was saying, but also at how he was demeaning my sport. I wasn't about to let anyone diss my sport—not even a mayor. I grabbed the towel from around my neck, folded it in half, and started beating the living shit out of the guy. I kept hitting him over the head so hard that he finally fell out of the ring. This mayor was trying to make me look like some kind of cartoon character. He thought wrestling was phony and wrestlers were just a bunch of buffoons; he didn't realize that he was in the ring with a real-deal pro wrestler who never took a back step from anybody.

At first everyone couldn't believe what I was doing, but as soon as the mayor hit the floor, a group of policemen ran to help him up. They looked like they wanted to arrest me and the fans were irate. But I had a match to wrestle. Out came Hogan and I picked up on him where I left off with the mayor. I thoroughly trounced him. Now the fans were really going wild. They were screaming and throwing things at me. I had just beaten up their mayor and pummeled their favorite hero right before their eyes. However, now I had a problem. It was thirty feet from the ring to the locker room and I had to walk through a horde of furious fanatics to get there. The police certainly weren't going to protect me after what I did to their mayor, and I literally had to fight for my life just to get back to the dressing room. But this just goes to show you that Roddy Piper isn't afraid to show anyone just how real he and his sport are—even if it means beating up some prepubescent mayor in front of ten thousand of his people.

Despite these little run-ins with people who thought they could make us look stupid, our sport at the time was rising in popularity faster than ever. We were in demand all over the country and McMahon had us traveling and working a crazy schedule.

At that time as a testament to Muraco and Snuka's talent, the WWF had the weight of its business on their shoulders. Snuka and Muraco were selling out venues nightly. But, Vince thought that Hulk Hogan was everything a wrestler should be: big and musclebound. Vince fell in love with him as a top draw, and the Hulkster grabbed hold of the opportunity and ran with it. The two started scheming about how they were going to take over the wrestling world by killing off all the other top wrestling talent in New York. The decision to use Hogan as "The Chosen One" was made.

Vince Sr. was riding high with wrestlers such as Bob Backlund, Jimmy Snuka, and Don Muraco, but Junior had made a pact with Hogan. Vince Jr. and Hogan had a plan but there was one obstacle. The problem, folks, was very simple. Jimmy Snuka had put twenty-five years of blood, sweat, and tears into professional wrestling along with an unusual amount of talent and a body God must have chiseled himself. The fans were infatuated with the mystique of Superfly. This was making it impossible for Vince Jr. to carry out his plan of making Hulk Hogan the ultimate fan favorite.

Of course, no one's denying that Hogan played a major role in catapulting wrestling to the height of its popularity in the eighties. But people fail to realize that although Hulkamania was "running wild" at the time, he was usually running from "Rowdy" Roddy Piper.

Vince Falls In Love w/ Hogan

Hulk huge because of Roddy

Yes, Hogan played his "say your prayers and take your vitamins" role perfectly, but it still wasn't enough to gain the number one spot over the SuperFly. Junior still had to achieve his goal. So, this is what Junior did, and I'll let you folks make up your minds. He promoted a cage match to take place in Madison Square Garden in October 1983.

The cage match had such quality to it, that people still talk about Snuka and his cage dive to this day. It was one of the biggest moments in WWF history. McMahon heavily publicized this match, and he even talked SuperFly into this upcoming finish. This is exactly how it went folks. At the fifteen minute mark in the cage match, Snuka bodyslams Muraco. Snuka heads for the turnbuckle corner. As he starts climbing, cameras are flashing in anticipation of Snuka doing his patented dive—the entire garden was standing waiting for this beautifully executed move.

SuperFly, being the pro he was, didn't stop at the turnbuckle, he climbed to the top corner of the thirty-foot cage. With each step he took upward, the fans were in awe. Jimmy continued climbing to the top of the cage and stood barefoot and erect, lovingly panning the crowd in MSG, as they were exploding with excitement. He bends his knees and swan dives thirty-five feet down, directly onto his target, Don Muraco—and hits him perfectly. The ref dives down with a one count. I have never seen MSG so electrified in my life! Then the ref gives a two count, and Muraco kicks out. Snuka ended up losing this match because Muraco got out the cage door. Now, McMahon has made room for Hogan.

Little did everyone know that Hogan was popping vitamins like M&M's in order to try and keep up with me on the mat. Vince Sr. and Junior never expected Roddy Piper to be able to rival their new Chosen Son. I mean out of the twenty-five top dogs, I was the smallest. I didn't have any angles, I didn't have the office behind me. All I had was what my forefathers taught me and what I had learned from my wars in the ring. But that was enough to get me over.

[handwritten margin note: Hogan doing Roids? to keep up w/ Piper]

8

"Piper's Pit": The War to Settle the Score

Became #1 Mic man

Schult vs 1983 Orndorff feud led to pipers pit?

BESIDES being a top wrestler in the ring for the WWF at the time, I also became the Federation's main man behind the mike. I was managing two wrestlers, Paul Orndorff and Dr. David Schultz, and one night in 1983 I participated in an interview with them that led Vince to my own segment, "Piper's Pit," in the WWF.

Schultz was kind of a bully who always tried to push his weight around and Orndorff was wired and tight like the championship racehorse Man O' War. During their two-minute-and-fifty-four-second interview that night, the two burly athletes tried to hog all the mike time, not to mention that these larger-than-life wrestlers were blocking my puny ass from getting any airtime. All the wrestlers who were watching this caught on right away. Schultz and Orndorff went at each other shoulder to shoulder, leaving me lost in the background. Each wrestler had his own share of mike time, with Orndorff going first, then Schultz. They were trying their hardest to get themselves over, while also purposely leaving me in the shadow of their masses.

But at the two-minute fifty-second mark with only four seconds to go, I stole the show. I put one hand on Orndorff's shoulder from behind, and one hand on Schultz's shoulder from behind, pushed myself right in front of them, now blocking them from the camera, and said with all the charisma I could muster: "Roddy Piper—giant killer!" And the interview ended. It was the last thing the viewing audience saw and what they remembered most. My Frat Brothers also saw it and they started horse-laughing because these two guys who had tried to bury Roddy Piper during the almost three-minute interview were themselves buried in four seconds. This ad-lib not only brought the audience and wrestlers to their knees, it also opened a door for me with *Piper's Pit*.

After that successful ad-lib bit, I approached Vince McMahon Jr. in St. Louis about giving me a shot at an interview segment every week. I told him to give me three weeks, a bow tie, and a mike stand, and if I didn't "cut the mustard" I'd be out of there, no questions asked.

What did he have to lose? I tried to show the WWF head honcho that I could better serve him and the company in front of the camera, stirring the pot, than in my then-current role as a rebel manager. Well, Vince not only bought into the concept hook, line, and sinker, he had the stage crew build me my very own set, which added a bit of glitz and glamour to my segments.

One of the main reasons I established "Piper's Pit" was that there was battle among the wrestlers over how much TV time each person had, and the way it was being designated. Again, remember, you now have twenty-five of the top wrestlers in the world working in the same federation, vying for the fans' attention, so at some point egos are going to get in the way. The TV time also became an issue because the guys saw it as their opportunity to bring the spotlight on them rather than on Hulk Hogan, who McMahon was pushing down the wrestling audience's throat. Hogan was capitalizing on Vince's push and his movie fame with Sylvester Stallone in *Rocky III*, and most guys were convinced that he and Vince had cut a

Faust-like deal with the devil. They were partners-in-crime and all the rest of us were just supposed to be window dressing.

But not me. I wasn't going to settle for being second fiddle to anyone. Even when I was managing Orndorff and Schultz, I was still trying to get myself over with the crowd and get recognized. That's when it occurred to me to use my mouth. My big mouth had gotten me noticed earlier in my career in places like L.A., Charlotte, Atlanta, Canada, and Portland, so why should New York and the WWF be any different?

Again, I was going to stay away from the private family matters of my wrestling guests, but almost everything else was fair game. I wanted to keep my visitors on "Piper's Pit" off balance while also keeping the audience entertained. Right from my very first guest— wrestler Frankie Williams—I went for the jugular, rendering my guest teary-eyed and almost speechless.

Although at first it must have seemed odd to see a macho guy in a kilt interviewing another tough guy, they quickly learned that *real men do wear kilts!* The audience fell in love with "Piper's Pit" and labelled me the man they love to hate. They looked forward to me either bringing out the animal in these wrestlers or bringing them to their knees. With Williams, I did the latter.

Frankie Williams was a wrestler from San Juan who had been wrestling a long time but had never won a match. So as soon as he sat down for his interview on "Piper's Pit," I asked him, "Frankie, where are you from?"

And he answered me in his San Juan accent, "I'ma froma Columbis, Ohio."

I turned to him and said, "Oh, youra froma Columbis, Ohio, huh? Well, let me tell you something. You oughta go back to Ohio and get a job as a shoe salesman because you stink as a wrestler! You have never won a match in your life."

Now this kind of thing was unheard of in wrestling. In a wrestling interview, you usually try to put one guy over as you battle back and forth, but to say you've never won a match and that you stink had never been done before. It actually tugged at Frankie Williams's pride and he tried to defend himself, explaining to me and the viewing audience why he had never won.

"Iya maya neva havea won a matcha ina mya life, butta everytimea I goa ina there, Iya givea my wholea hearta," Williams said defensively.

And I said to him, "Well, your whole heart ain't enough," and at this point we stand up and I start hitting Frankie to push him backstage through the curtain so I could finish the segment. But Frankie's pride was so hurt that it really turned into a fight. I now had to turn it on—*boom! boom! boom!*—to get rid of him, and once I finally threw him out, I turned to the camera and said one of the many phrases that became my trademark: "Listen, you don't throw rocks at a guy that's got a machine gun."

The fact that things got so real and so physical on the air was impressive enough, but when I scored at the end with that punch line, it hit the wrestling AP in no time and the ratings started pouring in.

With the great buzz and fan reaction to the first "Piper's Pit" segment, my notoriety was well on its way. Both the fans *and* the wrestlers now looked at "Piper's Pit" as a contest to see who would blink first. But I always kept everyone off balance because "every time they thought they had all the answers, I changed the questions!" This got around the wrestling world very quickly, and before you knew it, kids at university frat houses weren't the only people watching the show—wrestling had now made its way into the homes of doctors, lawyers, kids, and parents alike. It was now hip to be watching the squared-circle sport, especially "Piper's Pit"!

Along with the personality clashes, the beauty of "Piper's Pit" was that nothing was ever written in stone for the segment. We didn't have the same guests each week and it was strictly improv. Every time it was a new experience for the audience and for me. You could always expect the unexpected, and that's what made it so popular. "Piper's Pit" was also a forum that allowed the WWF to cross wrestling over into other entertainment industries by bringing on all kinds of talent as guests. One of the first stars to appear on my show was eighties singing sensation Cyndi Lauper, with her manager, Dave Wolff. Both music-industry giants were friends of Captain Lou Albano and they loved watching me on "Piper's Pit" each week.

Well, once I found out that Cyndi was going to be a guest, I went to work, gathering material on the girl that just wanted to have fun. Besides thinking of some witty things to say to her, I had some visual tricks up my sleeve. À la Lauper, I had a clothespin hanging from my ear and had my hair spiked, which generated tremendous heat from the crowd. This would be a very important development because from that point on, Cyndi and Dave Wolff got very much involved in wrestling, and this really turned the rock-and-roll community on to the sport.

But I didn't limit my nonwrestler guests on "Piper's Pit" to the music industry. One time, at an event in Madison Square Garden, John Stossel from *20/20* came in to do some interviews, and I had him on "Piper's Pit." Once a month we did the show on NBC in place of *Saturday Night Live*: it was called *Saturday Night's Main Event*. And while Stossel was on with me, his crony was trying to get an interview with another wrestler, Dr. David Schultz, asking him if wrestling was real or fake. Schultz was now giving the *20/20* employee the business big-time, and Stossel just cut away from us and said he was going to take care of the situation. Now, I was standing about fifteen feet away from them and I saw the cocky TV personality grab the microphone from his associate and tell his crew to turn the cameras on. As soon as his guys were ready to go, Stossel said to Schultz, "Is wrestling real or is wrestling fake?" Well, no sooner did he get out the words that questioned our sport's integrity than he got a huge whack upside the head. Schultz openhanded the *20/20* reporter and knocked him down, yelling in his face, "Is that fake, asshole?" He then openhanded him again, and Stossel went down and was nearly crying for his mum. While the incident got

Schultz and wrestling a lot of attention from the press, it also ended up costing the WWF and/or Schultz a bundle after Stossel sued.

While the battle between Stossel and the WWF was resolved in the courts, another war was about to take place that brought further attention to pro wrestling. On February 18, 1985, MTV broadcast *The War to Settle the Score* live from New York's Madison Square Garden, with Hulk Hogan and me being the main event. In the months leading up to this event, I had played all my cards right. The combination of me being the Federation's number one heel and the popularity of "Piper's Pit," along with my association with Cyndi Lauper and Dave Wolff made my going head-to-head with Hulk Hogan a no-brainer.

During the negotiations for the big event, Wolff was a liaison between Vince McMahon Jr. and MTV. Lauper, who was the female vocalist of the year at the time, was going to be the rock star who would lure music fans to watch the mat sport, and Hogan and I were going to be responsible for carrying the unique event. This presented no problem for the two of us. There was always a natural chemistry between Hogan and me that was second to none.

One night we were all in Madison Square Garden and Cyndi and Dick Clark were giving an award to Captain Lou Albano, who had been in the video for her smash hit song "Girls Just Want to Have Fun." Well, before Captain Lou could even utter "thank you" to the two presenters, I came and took the award and smashed it over his head. I then almost caused the youthful-looking Clark's hair to go gray when I turned and stared menacingly in his direction and he screamed: "Please don't hurt me!" I decided to give Clark a break, but Cyndi Lauper wasn't so lucky. In typical heel fashion, I went after the poor helpless girl, and without hesitation I ended up kicking her in the head, which drew all sorts of boos and hisses from the crowd.

But believe me, things could have been much worse for the colorful singer if I had wanted them to be. Before this whole scenario unfolded on TV, Dave Wolff had asked me if I would kick Cyndi during the presentation of the award to Albano in order to get the fans buzzing about the rock and wrestling connection. But he wanted to be reassured that I wouldn't hurt her. I told Dave that I was up to the task and that I could make it look like I really kicked and injured her. But about thirty minutes before the "kicking event," a fellow from the WWF's New York office came up to me and planted a vicious seed in my head when he said, "The end of Cyndi Lauper's career could be the beginning of yours." This sat on my mind until the very moment that I had to boot her. There were moral decisions that I had to make. Do I really kick an innocent women who's going along with a story line to help promote our sport and who's also trusting me not to hurt her? Do I go against the promise I made Wolff? Or do I punt her so hard that the whole audience feels it, making the WWF brass happy.

I truly had a huge dilemma here. The Sickness of our sport had once again consumed me, leaving me to ponder what I was going to do to the rock singer when it came time to lay one on her. Do I kick her or don't I kick her? What was it going to be?

Even when Cyndi stepped through the ropes that night, I had no idea what I was going to do. I knew I had the ability to make it look real if I wanted to, but I was still thinking about what that WWF official said to me about "the end of her career could be the beginning of mine." But on the flip side, I was thinking about Cyndi's safety and the damage that of one fierce kick could really do.

When it came time to land the blow, I threw my leg at Lauper at full speed, but in midkick I decided not to hurt her and pulled back. But even though I held back, the audience, including the NYPD, thought I had gone through with it. Believe me, I could have lived with this if I wanted to—I was certainly callous enough—but the bottom line is that I chose not to. The fans thought I really connected, and boy, did it get their attention! No one could believe what they'd just seen.

The media also had a field day with this act, as it made the papers and news highlights all over the country. But my socking music personalities didn't end with that award presentation. Now it was Wolff's turn. A week or so later Dave confronted me in the ring about kicking his client, and I gave him an up-close-and-personal look at the wrestling canvas when I body-slammed him right before the fans' eyes. I was now not only the guy the fans loved to hate, I was also drawing media attention to us like never before. Even though everyone hated my guts, my antics also started a cult of "bad guy" fans. Wolff got all his friends in the rock-and-roll community to jump on the bandwagon and write stories about these incidents, and as a result we were on the front covers of music magazines as well as wrestling publications.

So now it was all set. My hard work both in and out of the ring forced McMahon's hand to choose me to oppose Hulk Hogan in *The War to Settle the Score* main event on MTV. I remember getting off the airplane at Newark Airport and seeing a camera crew from MTV waiting there for me. As soon as a mike was placed in front of me, I let the lady reporter from the music-video station know how I felt about her channel. I said that MTV stood for "Music To Vomit by" and she countered my volley by asking me how I felt about hitting a woman. I told her that I was an equal opportunist, and if women got in my way, I'd nail them just like anybody else! This caused quite a stir right before *The War to Settle the Score*, which was now going to include not only Cyndi Lauper but also Hulk Hogan's good friend Mr. T.

Mr. T was a star on *The A-Team* at this time and had a pretty good ego going on for himself (not that the rest of us didn't!), and Hogan is a great guy and a great businessman, but I don't think either one of us had much love for the other at that particular moment. But we did have one thing in common. We had a mutual friend named Rick Martel. Although we were on opposite sides of the fence, we had both been roommates with Rick Martel at some point in our careers. He had told each of us that the other guy was a decent guy and we both valued Rick's opinion. This was also a

Hogan + McMahon
scripting—wanted a Pin

time when we were beginning to weed out who was worth risking your reputation for and who was worth trusting in the ring.

But what some people don't know is that even after I was told that I was going to help headline this special event, it almost didn't happen. The night of the event, I was in Madison Square Garden and I was asked to take a dive for Hogan, and I said no. This started a time in my career when I wouldn't take dives, wouldn't let anyone pin my shoulders, etc., but I had my reasons. I had worked too damn hard for too long to get to where I was, and I wasn't about to take a fall for anyone. Don't get me wrong—I had no problem with losing to the guy, but not by pinfall. I knew that if Hogan pinned me that night, it would be the end for me. Hogan would just move on to the next heel of the month, and where would that leave me? I wasn't some flash in the pan, so I wasn't about to let that happen.

Will not get pinned!

When I approached Captain Lou Albano and told him what had just happened and what I wanted to do against Hogan, he warned me that McMahon and Company wouldn't understand. They only saw it as a star-studded match that they had put a lot of money on the line for and didn't care about any other wrestler's career at the time except Hogan's. The Captain advised me to stick to my guns and with my aggression and strength never let anyone pin my shoulders. So I held out and told them I would only lose to Hogan by DQ. McMahon and Hogan finally agreed to my demands and the match was ready to roll. I now became king of the disqualifications.

Almost didn't wrestle

OK to D.Q

The two of us had a lot of energy that night in MSG. I remember I wanted to get under the skin of all the Hulkamaniacs and the MTV viewers before we even started to wrestle, so I wore a Hogan T-shirt, which I ripped off like Hogan as soon as I got in the ring, and I carried a very expensive Gibson guitar, which I smashed right before the crowd's eyes. These antics electrified the fans almost immediately. This was now the new brand of wrestling. No longer was it just a sport of hand-to-hand combat, it was now also a show. It

More than Wrestling—Made a show out of it.

wasn't like winning the Super Bowl, World Series, or an NBA Championship, it was a new energy.

I remember Gorilla Monsoon behind the mike that night explaining to the viewing audience how the crowd was screaming and yelling for us even before we exchanged a blow. When the bell rang, Hogan and I didn't waste any time, we just charged each other and began trading punches. This set the tone for the wrestling from then on. Hogan and I were able to bring the sport to a whole new level as we combined showmanship and intensity in the ring like never before. There was a legitimate heat and animosity there. There was this six-foot-seven-inch tanned guy with twenty-four-inch arms facing a very real bagpipe-playing kilted six-foot-one-and-a-half-inch, 232-pound guy in the ring, and they hated each other.

As the match got going, we had the people in the palms of our hands. About five minutes into it, I sensed that everyone was in tune with what was going on. Everyone was totally committed—the fans, the wrestlers, and the promoters. As the match came to the fifteen-minute mark, Hogan was down and I was yanking on his yellow hair, so Paul Orndorff and Mr. T both jumped up and raced into the ring. The outcome of *The War to Settle the Score* came down to me sucker-punching Mr. T.

After landing the lethal blow, a New York City policeman jumped into the ring and grabbed me, but I flung him away. Then all hell broke loose as other policemen rushed to the mat to aid their fellow man-in-blue. You now had real people getting involved in this historical event. But at the time the cops weren't concerned with being a part of history; all they saw was one of their own being tossed aside like a rag doll before twenty thousand people by this crazed man in a kilt. In a matter of weeks I had managed to kick Cyndi Lauper, punch one of the supposed toughest guys in America on national TV, and piss off New York's finest. I was capitalizing on my opportunities, and was also helping put our sport on the map.

Hogan and I were definitely in a zone that night in Madison

Square Garden because not only did the cops and fans in attendance know the feud was real, but MTV wound up having its highest-rated program of the season. We not only made wrestling and MTV history that night, we also set the stage for wrestling's most historical event, *WrestleMania I.*

War to settle
Sets up Wrestlmania

WrestleMania

WWF + MTV

ONCE again Vince McMahon Jr. broke new ground, along with Cyndi Lauper and Dave Wolff, and created a wrestling event that was the hottest ticket in New York City. A little over a month earlier the trio had successfully combined the rock-and-roll and wrestling worlds on MTV and were now looking to expand their horizons by putting together the greatest wrestling show ever. The threesome was banking on McMahon's money and his wrestlers' talent along with Lauper and Wolff's connections in the entertainment industry in order to pull off a Super Bowl of wrestling.

The groundbreaking event was going to be held in the heart of New York City in Madison Square Garden on March 31, 1985, and Hulk Hogan and I were going to headline. But this match was going to be different from the MTV one. Hogan and I weren't going to be wrestling one-on-one. Instead, the main-event match was going to be a tag-team war, with each of us bringing a partner into the mix.

The WWF officials had to pick a new partner-in-crime for me,

Tag team
Hulk + T vs RP + Paul Orn

Orton hurt so
Mr. Wonderful Picked

since my bodyguard at the time, Ace (Bob Orton), a great friend, had his arm in a cast. An incredible athlete and wrestler, "Mr. Wonderful" Paul Orndorff, was chosen to wrestle in his place. We were matched against Hogan and his acting buddy Mr. T.

Press Conf @ Rock Center

I got my first taste of the magnitude of 'Mania when Vince held a press conference at Rockefeller Center a few weeks prior to the event. I was a little late in arriving and I have to admit I wasn't quite ready for it. I didn't realize the enormity of what I was getting myself into. In the hallway, two people from McMahon's art department handed me two painted-framed pictures of Mr. T. I had no idea why they were handing me these photos or what it was all about. I was even more shocked when I opened the door and all of these flashbulbs went off in my face. When all the spots before my eyes went away and I was able to regain my vision, I noticed there was a dais and podium set up on the left side of the room where Vince McMahon Jr., Hulk Hogan, Mr. T, and Paul Orndorff were answering questions from the huge press contingent. I also noticed that there was a sign on the table that said "ROWDY" RODDY PIPER, and before I could slide into my chair without disrupting what was going on, Mr. T stands up and flexes his biceps toward me and says in his usual tone, "I pity you, fool." The A-Team star also had one of those metal bars with a spring in it that he was bending in his gloved hands. And while he was standing there flexing his muscles, I walked over to him and coolly squeezed his head and said, "Gee, it feels pretty soft to me." Then, for good measure, I gave his Mohawk a little rub.

Mr. T

Touched T

Well, did this ever get T and me started off on the wrong foot! I didn't know you weren't supposed to touch Mr. T, let alone feel his head. This really pissed him off, but to be honest, I really didn't care. This was my element, my place of work. He was just along for the ride. Mr. T took an instant dislike to me, and I could sense that there was now a problem arising between the two of us for the match that was about to take place.

The matter only got worse when Vince and his boys wanted me

Vince wanted Piper to allow a pin

to take a dive in the main event, causing my partner and me to lose
to Mr. T and Hogan. For a second time in a few months I had to
refuse to lose, especially to a "foreigner" who they were bringing
into our wrestling culture. The reason I flat out refused was strictly
business. If I took a dive here to this clown, where would I go the
next time they brought an outsider into our world? If T had been
one of our guys, I would have taken the fall. But my thinking was,
if you take an outsider who is just going to do a wrestling event and
then leave, why give him the fall and let him go back to his industry
laughing at me behind my back and portraying everything in our
world as a joke. In my eyes, it was wrong according to the code of
ethics I had been taught. Well, I guess my unhappiness about this
got out in the locker room, and McMahon went to Orndorff, and
Paul told him the same thing—a blunt no. So now we've got a big-
time match here and nobody's willing to take the dive against the
intruder.

In a last-ditch effort to get me to change my mind, Vince asked
to talk to me, so we ventured into his favorite place to do business—
the can. We'd flush the commode every once in a while as we were
talking—that's just a wrestler thing to do—and McMahon again
asked me to take the dive against Mr. T. But I stood my ground
and told him that it was wrong, and that I wouldn't do it. I also
then planted a seed in his head and said: "Who will you draw more
money from, Hulk Hogan vs. Roddy Piper or Hulk Hogan vs. Paul
Orndorff?" With that question we left the john, and McMahon went
to Orndorff and told him what I said. But again I didn't care. I
knew my value in the sport and I also knew what the wrestling code
of ethics was, and I wasn't going to let McMahon or anybody else
make a fool of me or our profession.

A couple of weeks later a second press conference, also at Rockefeller Center, was held, and Mr. T and I again bumped heads. I
walked up onto a three-foot-high stage area, and to this day I think
I was set up, because as I was talking, Mr. T blindsided me and hit
me with a leg dive. We both went tumbling off the stage into the

crowd that was jam-packed with journalists from all over the world. Flashbulbs once again started going off like crazy as the photographers closed in on us to get a better shot of T and me rolling around on the floor. When security finally jumped in to pull us apart, I was so pissed off that I couldn't see straight. The blue spots that were again dancing before my eyes came courtesy of the camera flashes, but the red I was seeing was all due to the anger that was boiling inside me from the antics Mr. T just had pulled. Even after we were pulled apart, I still wanted to kill this guy. With my eyes wild like a stallion's, I glared over at Mr. T, hoping he would come at me for more, but security didn't give us time to go another round. They just whisked me out the door. This incident really pissed me off. I was taught that if you've got a problem with a guy, take care of it behind closed doors in the locker room—never in public. In front of the camera was business.

At the next press conference, televised via satellite, Mr. T was in Los Angeles with Hogan and I was in New York with Orndorff. At the West Coast gathering, Mr. T came out with a kilt on and a rubber chicken in his hand, and he said to the press, "All Piper is, is a chicken, and wears this silly dress. I pity the fool." He then tried to rip the head off the chicken, but it was a rubber chicken from a magic store and all it did was stretch. *I* pitied *this* fool for trying to make an impression! He literally had the chicken on the ground, with his foot on its head, trying to rip it to shreds, but that rubber bird wouldn't rip for nothing. Finally he just took the chicken and threw it down in frustration. To add to Mr. T's dilemma was the fact that I was in New York via satellite horse-laughing at the fool!

The next time I saw Mr. T was at a show at Nassau Coliseum before *WrestleMania,* and I was waiting for him and he knew it. He came in with his manager, Peter Young, and I asked Peter to excuse us because this was personal. I took Mr. T into a room and asked him what the hell he thought he was doing. He told me he didn't mean anything; he was just trying to enhance the show. I explained to him that we didn't do that kind of stuff unless we all knew about it ahead of time, and not to try to enhance the show because he didn't know what the fuck he was doing! We left the room after our little talk, and I knew right then and there that I was going to mess him up in the match. I had every intention of back-suplexing him on his head on the floor. At all the events leading up to *WrestleMania*, I had expressed how much I didn't like this guy, and now I was determined to show it.

The animosity level between us four main-eventers was rising with each passing day. Mr. T couldn't wait to teach me a lesson in the ring, I couldn't wait to suplex the loudmouth actor on his head, Orndorff wasn't happy that McMahon told him he had to take the dive that night, and Hogan was going through the usual emotions he felt every time he and I squared off in the ring, perhaps even more so since I wouldn't take a dive—especially for an outsider. All the talk about me not taking a dive was coming out more and more, and it wasn't justified, but there was no time to explain this to anyone before this event. But there is also this code of behavior. I have never backstabbed *anybody* in my profession, but I'll be the first to admit to front-stabbing them right in their face!

Right before *WrestleMania* Mr. T and I were in this warehouse with Vince McMahon Jr., and the bookers were trying to teach Mr. T, basics like how to lock up. This made my animosity meter go a few notches higher. I was already hot over Vince's asking me to take a dive against this guy; now I see that Mr. T didn't know the first thing about wrestling. This really insulted me. To make matters worse, McMahon then cornered me and asked me again to do something I didn't want to do—sign a contract.

I had still been holding my ground up to this point, refusing to sign on the dotted line, but on this day Vince caught me off guard when he asked, "Hey, Hot Rod, can I speak to you for a second?"

The reason McMahon called me Hot Rod was that it's a name I had made up before I came to the WWF and he trademarked it, hoping to capitalize on it one day. He kept calling me Hot Rod

*Vince owned
"Hot Rod"*

instead of Roddy Piper because he owned that name, and it was also part of the brainwashing that he used on all his wrestlers to try and show he was in control—to him, he owned Hot Rod. He may very well have owned the name, but he sure as hell didn't own me. I wasn't intimidated by him or by his tactics; that's why I was the last wrestler of the original group to sign a WWF contract.

Vince and I then sat down in the warehouse on two crates to talk business. I had no idea what he wanted to talk about. Maybe it was about the match. All I was thinking about at that moment was that he had asked me to take a dive against some TV star who had no idea how to wrestle (and that my ass was killing me from sitting on that fucking crate). So I couldn't wait for us to finish. Vince then proceeded to open up his briefcase and he put this contract in front of me. I looked at him and he looked at me and there were about four or five beats of silence. He finally said: "Hot Rod, you know things are changing and I can't have you in *WrestleMania* unless you sign this contract."

*Sign
or else*

· This, too, caught me by surprise. *WrestleMania* was only a little over a week away and I had been busy running around like crazy to promote the event, and here I was trying to help train Mr. T and Vince hits me with *this*? I looked over at him and said, "You cocksucker." He started laughing and said, "What? You can't fight city hall forever, Hot Rod." And that's how he got me to sign a WWF contract. Unfortunately, I couldn't steal this one back like I did in my early days, but after a while I calmed down. I liked Vince and I think he had some sort of a liking for me. There was some sort of chemistry there even though we didn't always see eye to eye.

*Vince
squeez
R.P.*

Later on Vince called the four of us into his office, as well as the bookers and the rest of his staff, to discuss how we were going to do the match. I told him that I knew the right way to do it. He said, "Well, Hot Rod, there's more than one right way to do a match." But I told him that there was only one right way to do this one. I knew this because I had worked in so many different territories, and I'd seen what happened. I told them that the only way

Can't look fake

to do this with Mr. T and at the same time keep our credibility and our "real estate value" was to keep it as tight and as close to amateur as possible. We couldn't let Mr. T throw any punches; they would look too bad. I knew that if the match wasn't done right, it could be a catastrophe. I knew we wouldn't make any mistakes if we kept it nice and tight, and eventually we'd have to give the tag back to Hogan because we knew he could carry the ball. In an event of this magnitude there was no room for error.

March 31 finally arrived and Madison Square Garden was alive _3/31_ and kicking. I remember being in my limo and feeling the electric atmosphere outside the arena. There were thousands of screaming wrestling fans crowding the streets, so my limo had to keep circling the building, trying to get us inside. On about our fifth pass around the block, my driver got the attention of one of New York's finest who was patrolling the area on his horse, and he told him who he had in the car and that we needed to get into the Garden. Before the cop decided to help us, he came up with the bright idea of telling _NYC_ some of the fans who was in the limo. "Hey, we got Roddy Piper _cop_ in here!" Well, that just started the fans going nuts! Before you know it, the news spread like the plague and the crowd starts rocking my limousine. Finally, before the fanatics turned over my limo, the officer got the attendant to open the garage door and we got inside unharmed. Another minute of that and I was either going to throw up all over the backseat of the car or I was going to be taken hostage by thousands of crazy wrestling fans.

Once I got inside Madison Square Garden, it was like being at the Academy Awards. There were stars everywhere, from all walks of life. I was rubbing elbows with Liberace, the Rockettes, Andy Warhol, and countless others. Warhol even went out of his way to meet me. He had a young kid with him, and to be honest, I didn't know who Andy Warhol was at the time. And when the young kid started taking pictures, I realized that the freak wasn't snapping pictures of Andy and me, but of my wrestling boots, so I decided that I had enough. I didn't understand what was going on and I didn't want to wait around to find out, so I told them I had to leave in order to get ready for my match.

No sooner had I left Warhol than I found Vince McMahon Jr. pacing the halls. The aura of excitement and nervousness was getting to the WWF head honcho and he looked like a deer caught in the headlights. This was one of the first times I had seen McMahon as white as a ghost and at a loss for words. The press had even gone up to him hoping to get a sound bite or two before the event, but Vince was in a zone at the time—the Twilight Zone! Reporters went up to Vince and asked him the burning question, "Is wrestling real or fake?" and Vince just said, "Uh, I don't know?" Way to go, Vince!

But truth be told, Vince had a lot riding on this night. Not only was his Federation's future riding on the success of this particular show, but his whole life's savings was also on the line. It was either kill or be killed for him, so I can truly understand his concerns. But about a half hour before the curtain went up on the historic event, I couldn't take it anymore! I grabbed him and said, "Sit down, you're driving us all crazy! It's just another match."

About the same time that I'm shaking some sense into Vince, Mr. T and his *two* limousines are trying to get into MSG. The *A-Team* star was trying to get into the same door that I had been trying to get into earlier, but the security wouldn't let two limos in at once. They didn't care who it was. They were under orders to let in only one car at a time. So now Mr. T turns into "Mr. Hollywood" and tells the guards that if both limos couldn't go in, then he wasn't going in. When Hogan gets word of this he personally goes down the ramp to the gate and tells Mr. T that he isn't going anyplace. Hogan then hauls the gold-chain-wearing TV star's ass into Madison Square Garden.

Mr. T finally got inside the arena, and as we were getting ready to go on, he started breathing into this oxygen mask. I now thought there was something physically wrong with the guy, and that we were going to have to go on without him. But little did I know that

[handwritten margin note: Vince took huge chance]

[handwritten margin note: Hulk has to drag T. in]

he was doing this to get ready for the match. This was part of his "training." What a loser! I also got to thinking to myself that he was going to need more than an oxygen mask when I got through with him!

It was finally time to start the show, and I'll never forget that buzz and roar of the crowd when we made our way to the center of the ring—twenty thousand screaming fans packed into the world's most famous arena! I remember thinking that the electricity from the crowd could've lit up all of Broadway and Times Square and then some. Speaking of Broadway, all the stars from all walks of life were out that night to witness wrestling history in the making. Frank Sinatra, Gloria Steinem, Rod Stewart, Dr. Ruth Westheimer, Andy Warhol, Liberace, Twisted Sister, Little Richard, Dick Clark, the Rockettes—the A-list just went on and on. And once we got through the ropes, Muhammad Ali, who was a special referee that night, was waiting there to greet us. All I could think about at that moment was several years earlier in L.A. when I had hip-tossed him out of the ring during his training for a bout, and I was hoping he wouldn't try to get revenge for that night. But I think I was safe because I had met him one other time at one of the press conferences before *WrestleMania* and had said to him, "The last time I saw you I had hip-tossed you on your bum!" and he just stared at me and bit his lower lip as he was famous for doing.

At one point during the match, I went out on the floor by the ring posts and found myself in quite a predicament. Hogan also made his way out of the ring and onto the floor, and when I turned to go away from Hogan, I found myself staring at Muhammad Ali. He threw one quick punch at me—which missed—and I had to decide which way was I going to go—toward Ali or toward Hogan? Right now it was a decision of survival. Even though Ali was way past his prime, I decided to take my chances with Hogan. I was safer that way.

The match turned out to be an overwhelming success—way more than McMahon had even wished for himself. But I soon found

out just how highly my efforts in *WrestleMania* were thought of.
The match was finished after Orndorff took the fall thanks to the
involvement of Jimmy "SuperFly" Snuka and "Cowboy" Bob Orton, allowing Hogan and Mr. T to leave the ring winners just like
everyone wanted. Immediately following the event there was a huge
party for Hogan and T with champagne and good eats, but nothing
for the losers (as is the tradition in America). Orton and I went back
to the dressing room to shower, and while we were cleaning off the
blood and sweat from the match, the victors were being whisked off
to another party. After drying off and finding ourselves alone—except for the irritated janitor who wanted us to leave so he could
clean up the dressing room—we walked back to where the limousine
was supposed to be parked, and to our surprise it wasn't there. We
then walked down a circular driveway to the bottom of Madison
Square Garden, hoping to find our ride down there, but there was
nobody around, only a few hard-core fans. The only familiar face
was that of the policeman on the horse who had helped us get into
the building at the beginning of the night. We asked him if he could
call us a cab, and in typical New York fashion, he told us to hail
one ourselves. As he was saying this, his horse started taking a huge
dump right before our eyes. Orton, who was burning mad, sees the
first piece of crap come out of the horse's ass and says, "Shit," just
as it is hitting the ground. The second poop fell and Orton goes,
"Shit." Third poop, Orton goes, "Shit." Talk about understatement.
Why isn't there a limo here for us and why is this horse shitting in
front of me? And where the fuck is everybody else?

Two hours ago we were part of the hottest ticket in New York
and now we're standing outside the bowels of Madison Square Garden watching a horse move his bowels! This shows how much we
were really cared for by the promoters in the industry. It doesn't
usually slap you in the face this hard, this soon, but it did that night.
This was the biggest event in wrestling history, and the two of us
had played a huge role in pulling it off, but we were left out in the
cold in the end! If you look at the tapes from that historic event,

everyone from vice-presidential candidate Geraldine Ferraro to Dr. Ruth Westheimer was saying, "Roddy Piper, you're going to get yours!" Little did I know that they were going to be correct on so many different fronts. I sure did get mine that night—both inside and outside the ring!

But when all was said and done, who really drew *WrestleMania I*? It's no secret that they pushed Hogan, and gave him most of the credit, as evidenced by the postgame parties thrown for him, but I truly believe I played a significant role in the success of the event. I put my life and ass on the line, and was willing to die in the ring if that's what it took to make *'Mania* a success, and what did I get when it was all over? Nothing. No limo. No party. No thank you. I was left to fend for myself while Hogan and his crew were off somewhere drinking and munching on McMahon's tab. This is where a tremendous jealousy factor came into play for me. But that old saying "You can't find sympathy in the dictionary between shit and suicide" kept playing in my head over and over that night every time I thought about the situation.

No credit for WM1

After all, if you look at all the effort and hype that went into *WrestleMania*, who was the one who was stirring all the interest? It wasn't Hogan. It was me. I had been hyping the event for weeks on "Piper's Pit," which was the most-watched part of any wrestling show—not Hogan's matches. The segment allowed us to promo the event every time we wrestled a card and it also broadened our demographics by twofold at the time, allowing us to reach way more people than even Vince imagined. Even though these people were rooting against me, they either bought a ticket or were tuning in just to see what was going to happen to me. Let the truth be known, people didn't watch *WrestleMania* to see Hulk Hogan fight—they watched hoping Roddy Piper would get his ass beat.

Pit hypes

Roddy the target

TV SHOWS

WrestleMania wasn't the only successful wrestling show in the 1980s. Our sport was really peaking around this time, and we

Other spin offs

cartoon

weren't only making a killing at the arena box offices, but we were also all over TV. A WWF program aired on NBC on Saturday nights once a month, and we had our own cartoon series on CBS called *Rock 'N Wrestling*, which brought all of us into the world of animation. Never in my wildest dreams had I thought I'd be in a cartoon! It was a cool thing to see. And again I attribute most of our success to the efforts of Dave Wolff and Cyndi Lauper. The two not only lent their lives to the wrestling world, they were solely responsible for putting the rock—and I don't mean the current WWF superstar either—in the rock-and-wrestling product of the 1980s. These two deserve a lot more credit than they get. And I understand that Vince McMahon got off cheap when it came time to pay Cyndi Lauper. I was told by Dave Wolff that the Grammy-winning singer received only $1,500 for her appearance at *WrestleMania*. Wolff was aghast and insulted that someone would pay so little money to a superstar singer for such a great contribution. But such are the facts and maybe there is a little more understanding now as to why I carry a bit of a grudge and jealousy toward Hogan, who was getting pampered by the Federation at the time. I felt he wasn't the only one who was doing the work to get our product out there. There were plenty more people involved in making the WWF a success, but only a few were being justly rewarded.

Cyndi
1,500

Paddy
Jealous
of
Hogan

   I was fighting tooth and nail to stay alive and keep myself in the limelight. Every little bit of success I was having was directly attributed to my hard work and good decision-making. The fact that I didn't take the fall in *WrestleMania* paid off powerfully because I was able to keep my feud with Hogan hot while also using "Piper's Pit" as a vehicle to keep myself over with the crowd. Everyone dreaded being on "Piper's Pit" because they knew I would grill them and put them through the wringer. It was almost like whoever got the short straw was chosen, but there were also people I liked having on the "Pit." This started a basic saying in the wrestling world that "If you weren't in the 'Pit,' you weren't shit!"

[handwritten: Did 3 segments at a Time]

JIMMY SNUKA—THE COCONUT INCIDENT

While "Piper's Pit" was a hoot to do, it was sometimes hectic to shoot. Once every three weeks we usually shot the segments for that night's show along with the following two weeks' interviews. While the work was hard, the fact that in my sport at this time there was no such thing as rehearsal made it even tougher. We only had one shot to get it right. But the one-shot deals also made for some great TV moments. I remember one time when we were in Allentown, Pennsylvania, and Chief Jay Strongbow was in to tape a segment with me. I always looked forward to working with the chief. He was a very smart man who was always full of great ideas when it came to our business. I also used to get a kick out of the way he used to call me Rodney. On this particular day he asked me if I had ever picked up a coconut and knew how heavy they were. When I told him no, he went on to tell me that he thought it would make *[handwritten: Allentown]* a great prop on one of my segments. As soon as he said this, another wrestler, Jimmy "SuperFly" Snuka, came to mind. I always used to get on Jimmy's case about being Polynesian and that all his people did was lie around on the beach getting sun while their grandmas *[handwritten: Coconut was Chief J's idea]* sold trinkets on the street to support their families. While that sounds rather heavy and personal, I knew what I could get away with when it came to Snuka. This was just the "craft" of the interview. When I mentioned this to Chief Jay, without hesitation he told me that I should hit the Polynesian guy on the head with a coconut. I forgot about it until about an hour later, when the chief had someone go to the supermarket and buy some bananas and coconuts. The chief was really hell-bent on seeing me do some noggin knocking on Snuka that day. So, with fruit in hand, Strongbow came to find me so we could talk about what should happen on the segment.

As we were talking, I picked up one of the coconuts and realized just how heavy it really was. I thought to myself, "Wow, this could really hurt," but then I also realized how great the interview could be if I whopped him in the head with this hard piece of tropical fruit.

About a half hour later Jimmy Snuka came onto "Piper's Pit." Whenever he was on he didn't have to say anything, he just had to look at you with his eerie stare to make good TV. SuperFly was one of those very scary individuals who didn't have to utter a word to be intimidating. I remember starting the interview, and I was trying to tie the coconuts and the bananas into the segment, but I wasn't doing such a great job because all I was doing was thinking about how heavy and hard this fucking coconut really was and that I had to hit him with all my might so that it would break on his head. Well, here came the moment of truth, and I hit Jimmy Snuka as hard as I could, and that coconut burst like a bomb! The instant it hit I heard Jimmy give a moan that came from the depths of his soul, and he started falling back and tried to take the set out with him. I'm not positive, but I am pretty sure he was unconscious upon impact. When he was on the ground, I started whipping him hard with the belt that went around my kilt. When he came to, he crawled on his hands and knees and then finally got up. The Polynesian grappler immediately went bananas and came after me, but I slipped into the locker room, shut the door, and locked it. On TV all you saw Jimmy doing was hitting this big industrial door, and then they took him away and escorted him to the other dressing room. I was told that Jimmy just stared at the floor for about ten minutes and didn't move. They say to this day that Jimmy Snuka feels the repercussions of that coconut hit. SuperFly really put it on the line for me that day. Truth be told, it was Jimmy Snuka who put "Piper's Pit" over the top not Roddy Piper. He was one of the people who helped make "Piper's Pit" a success. When the coconut story got around the wrestling world, all of a sudden Roddy Piper and Jimmy Snuka were selling out Madison Square Garden. What impressed me even more was that Jimmy was having some personal difficulties at this time, but he never let it get in the way of his work. He always remained a pro, especially in the ring. He is one of the all-time greats.

ANDRE THE GIANT

Andre liked Piper

Another consummate professional in the ring was Andre the Giant. Andre was an incredible man who I always enjoyed wrestling. He had a soft spot in his heart for me. It wasn't because he just took a liking to me. Andre would come in over the years to every territory that I was wrestling in. He would always tell the promoter to put Piper in the ring. There was a reason for that. With Andre the Giant, most wrestlers got in the ring, and when he hit them, they threw themselves in the air and begged for mercy. The match would last five minutes and Andre would just eat them up and pin them.

The first time I wrestled Andre, I had my kilt on, and I was wiggling my bum, and people were whistling as I took off my T-shirt, and Andre grabbed it and put it on. Well, he looked like Baby Hughie, and everyone was just roaring. This really showed the size difference between us. When Andre would hit me, yes it knocked me down, but I'd get right back up as fast as I could. I'd get into his hair, and bite him and hit him and whatever else I could do.

Well, that made Andre the Giant comfortable and he let me beat the dog out of him, but let's face it, he was a giant. That's why he liked me, because I was putting my heart into trying to beat this guy. He was comfortable in the ring selling for me. This went on for years and we became good friends. Andre would take me to a restaurant called the Pantry in Los Angeles. He would make me eat "The Andre" special because he wanted me to gain weight. "The Andre" special was a big dinner—a ham steak with twelve eggs and hash browns, washed down with about four quarts of diet Coke! The Giant mixed it all together for me and, like a mum, would say to me, "Now eat it and no leftovers." He would drag me all over, even when he went to see the promoters. We hung out a lot together over the years. He loved to joke around. We'd be in restaurants

Would take Piper for dinner

where there was a live band, and Andre would tell them that he wanted to sing a song. He'd tell them to just play any tune, and he would sing "the fish song." He would pull his ears up and suck his cheeks in to make a fish mouth, and of course everyone thought he was hilarious because Andre was a giant. He loved to fart in elevators, the more people the better, the better dressed and more highfalutin the ladies the better. His bum was about head-high with everyone else, and these people would go down like flies on a nopest strip! You've got to understand, giants make *giant* farts. But he wouldn't make a face, wouldn't crack a smile; it would just be like nothing happened.

Andre always seemed to be looking out for me in the ring, whether it was a concern for my well-being on the mat or my status in a particular promotion. I remember one time he did me an incredible favor without my asking. I was in Madison Square Garden in a tag match that had David Schultz and me booked against Andre and Jimmy Snuka. The giant-size wrestler allowed me to jump on him and start beating him to the point where he was bleeding all over. The referee then stopped the match and paramedics tried to carry Andre out on a stretcher, which was a useless battle for the six poor guys. Andre ended up walking out on his own and then coming back all bandaged up to finish the match. No one had ever really done that to Andre. It really put me on the map, and I knew it was a respect thing that Andre was willing to do that for me.

Andre the Giant, he was a wonderful, fun-loving guy.

But getting in the ring with wrestlers like Andre the Giant was nothing compared with what we were dealing with outside the ring in the 1980s. Our work was becoming tougher and tougher with each passing day because around this time wrestlers in their prime began dropping like flies. Even though it seemed to everybody on the outside that every day was Christmas for pro wrestlers in the eighties, the rough and tough industry was taking a very heavy toll on all of us. Rick McGraw had died and other guys had been overdosing like crazy. Between the number of matches we were doing a week, the hectic travel schedules we were keeping, and the fact that we were away from home 75 percent of the year, a lot of stress was going on in our lives and locker rooms. I had refused to work against Don Owens for the first two years after *WrestleMania,* and it was looking as though there was only one individual—me—fighting the system. But all I was trying to do was to keep the code I was taught to keep—honor above all. Well, in the end it came down to the bottom line and earning a living to help take care of my family. Sure, it would have been nice to be able to uphold the code, but it didn't work out that way. I had to work against Don Owens even though I really didn't want to, but you realize pretty quick, especially when you have a family to feed, that family comes first no matter what or who.

However, in our business, the losers had to continue on and make money for their families. We didn't have the same benefits as the chosen ones like Hulk Hogan. This is where the bitterness and the evilness enters, as you are the only one sticking up for your family. As Hogan has lunch pails out, so does Roddy Piper. As hard as they are all pushing Hogan, I am trying to keep myself on top. I didn't have the support of a big industry behind me. I was just doing what I was trained to do. I felt that they could knock me off at any time and go onto the next person, as was the tradition. I was trying to keep my real estate value as high as I could. It was very hard to make a split between being a dad and being "Rowdy" Roddy Piper, but I knew I had to do whatever was possible in order to keep bread on our table.

At this same time there was a war going on in all fronts. Vince McMahon Jr. was very much involved. For instance, at the Olympic Auditorium, if the main event was Chavo Guerrero vs. Roddy Piper, or Roddy Piper vs. Hulk Hogan, McMahon was slowly changing the emphasis to his company rather than promoting the individual wrestlers who were on the card. A few of us knew what was going on and we were fighting it, but it was a fruitless fight. McMahon would just say the WWF and just say our names in association. Orndorff, Snuka, Tony Atlas, Muraco, and Mr. Fuji would draw in all this money, but Vince Jr. put the WWF label on everything and gave the Federation the credit instead of the wrestlers. In his eyes now, his company product was selling out buildings all over and not the individuals who were wrestling in the events. Guys like Macho Man were coming up at that time with Elizabeth, and McMahon was on a roll, so he figured he wasn't going to need the veterans around much longer. He was quickly trying to get rid of the old school and get new guys in so he could control them and pay them less money. This battle was taking the strength away from all the other wrestlers. But McMahon wanted to be in control of everything and everyone involved in his Federation. He even tried to control where some of us lived.

During this time I was trying to decide on a permanent residence for my family. Vince McMahon had my wife and me picked up in a limousine with a real estate agent, and basically said that he'd buy us any house we wanted in Connecticut as long as I agreed to live there year-round.

Kitty + free house No!

I met with my wife privately in our hotel room to discuss the free house deal, and she said that she was going to say no to Vince. I said, "Kitty, this is a free house!" She said, "But Roderick, our children won't stand a chance here." I even offered to put guards around every inch of the house, but she wasn't buying into any of it. Well, the old story of the battle of the sexes came into play, and I learned then to never fight with a woman, there ain't no possible way to win.

We ended up buying a ranch on a mountain in Oregon, which caused me to have a 3,500-mile commute to work. Kitty is the Mother of the Millennium, but the jet lag and road crust certainly didn't make me Father of the Year!

This definitely hurt my relationship with Vince, but I had to do what I had to do for my family. It was just our personal choice. We

Choose Family over Vince

were just thinking in terms of what was best for our family and not what was best for Vince and the WWF. As Don Johnson once told me, "It's not getting to the top that's hard, it's staying there." Man, was he ever right.

10

WrestleMania 2 and III

Boxed Mr. T
hated it.

Don't have to
take a dive

I suppose if I could ever take a match back it would be the one I
had at *WrestleMania* 2 in 1986. It wasn't even a wrestling match!
For some reason, Vince McMahon asked me if I would box Mr. T.
Honestly, I really didn't like Mr. T. So being up-front, I told Vince
that there was no way that I would take a dive for the star of *The
A-Team* and he assured me that I wouldn't have to. Satisfied, I
agreed and the match was booked as one of the top matches for the
Federation's premier event of the year.

Went to
Boxing
camp

In preparation, McMahon sent me to a boxing camp in Reno,
Nevada, run by legendary trainer Lou Duva. Also at the camp were
boxing stars Evander Holyfield, Leon Spinks, Dwight Braxton, and
Tyrell Biggs (who was just getting ready to fight Mike Tyson). So
here I am, a wrestler, and I'm in this camp with these guys, trying
to get in shape for a boxing match. Overnight, McMahon wanted
me to go from the road, where I was tired as a dog and downing
beers like they were going out of style, to a place where they get up
at 4 A.M. to run five miles. I went from drinking luxurious bottles

of Miller Lite with my Frat Brothers to running in the park with ducks and these high-caliber boxers—all of a sudden I was asked to be Carl Lewis. I wasn't in shape for this. I hadn't been doing any roadwork for years; I was too busy wrestling, and on top of all that my hip was killing me. But Duva didn't mess around in these camps. He had us sparring, hitting the bag . . . all that fun stuff. I have to admit I was getting in better shape, but I was also getting the dog beat out of me by these guys.

But while I was there I made the best of the situation. I became pretty good friends with Evander Holyfield. At the beginning of camp there was a card and Duva was introducing all the boxers to everyone and they were all getting a nice round of applause. But when he got to me the cheers turned to rising unbelievable boos. I responded to the jeers by putting my arm around Holyfield, who was standing right next to me. I grabbed the mike and said, "You're all just jealous because you had to pay to come here to see us and we got in for free." Holyfield didn't know how to react to my statement and he just politely said, "Ah, jeez, Mr. Piper, please don't do that."

Even though I was out of my element for four weeks, I learned an awful lot from Duva and the boys. I came back in better shape and better prepared for my match against Mr. T.

But even though I learned the ropes from Duva about boxing, I should have known that I'd regret my decision to box Mr. T. For practice before our bout, I was brought in to go a few rounds with him in a ring set up in a warehouse. Vince McMahon and the booker George Scott were also there. This was the only contact in the ring I had with Mr. T prior to the match. We started fisticuffing a bit, and I had his head under my arm in a "guillotine" position. I wanted very much to "shoot" with Mr. T then, but neither Scott nor McMahon was giving me a clear high sign. I was working under the rules that any problem you had to take care of, you take care of it in the dressing room. When you're out in front of the camera or a live audience, it is always strictly professional.

There was a lot of talk about what was really going to happen in this particular match, especially after I had vented my feelings about Mr. T. I was not overbearing, but I was as obnoxious, rude, and egotistical as a person could get. I cared for no one, and I thought no one cared for me.

The match was going to take place at the Nassau Coliseum in New York, and it had sold out within a few hours. It was part of a card that was taking place in three different locations—a first in wrestling history. *WrestleMania 2* was also being beamed by satellite from the Rosemont Horizon in Chicago, with wrestlers like Andre the Giant and Big John Studd against some of the Chicago Bears in a battle royal, and Hogan was going to be in Los Angeles at the L.A. Sports Arena facing King Kong Bundy in a steel-cage match.

Before *WrestleMania 2,* I had gotten into some trouble in Phoenix because of some things I had said about Mr. T during a press conference before a match on a *Saturday Night Main Event.* I had been living pretty hard before this incident. I hadn't slept in three days. There was quite a bit of drinking going on because I was so tired of being on the road away from my family that I was getting to the point where nothing mattered anymore. I arrived in Arizona that evening and made my way over to the conference, which was held in a large room that was filled with people I had never seen before. In one corner there was McMahon, in another there were press people from NBC, and in a third corner were trainers who I didn't recognize. It was a very odd atmosphere.

But I didn't care. Here I came barreling in and everyone's asking what's going to happen to Mr. T on the TV that night and I answered them, "Simple. I'm going to take my waist belt off my kilt and I'm going to whip him like a slave." I was so aggressive that day and no one was saying anything, not even McMahon.

Sure enough, that night on NBC I got Mr. T down and I took the waist belt off my kilt and I whipped him. This was also where I pushed the envelope. I said that slavery was a terrible thing and I was glad that they had ended it, but I also said that it made me wonder why one of the first things that Mr. T did when slavery ended was to put chains around his neck. Well, that sure got a lot of raw attention, and it's safe to say that not everyone was a big Roddy Piper fan after that night in Phoenix.

But I wasn't done yet.

After the match, I came into the hotel lobby carrying my Halliburton, and there was Vince McMahon and his entourage and the booker George Scott. At that time my relationship with Vince McMahon was beginning to wear a bit thin. I was very much a believer that you are your own man, and as such, I should dictate how I got to the outcome of a match. Vince, however, was trying to turn wrestling into sports-entertainment, which was dead against everything that I had been taught. Well, Scott and I didn't really get along and tensions were rising when we saw each other and I kind of bumped him, so he took his finger and put it in my mouth to kind of hook my cheek. We were very close to "ribbing on the square" here. It was real close to rock and roll. But when he put his finger in my mouth, I bit down hard on his finger, managing to hang on to my Halliburton, and I walked him all around the lobby in a circle back to the elevators, where McMahon and his entourage were trying to get on.

At that time I let Scott go and put my Halliburton down. When the doors opened, Scott got on the elevator with Vince and his crowd, but every time the doors went to close, I bumped 'em open and said, "Come on, you motherfuckers!" I was challenging them all and they didn't know what to do. Finally one of McMahon's producers ran out of the elevator when he saw another elevator open, and he grabbed my Halliburton and put it in that elevator. I had no choice but to let them go as I raced to the second elevator to grab my case before the door closed. I had been pushed so hard at that point I was just out of my head.

Also during this time, just before *WM2*, these guys had me doing

Right
w/ Booker
in
Elevator

RP
/05/49
✓!

whatever they wanted. They never thought, "Hot Rod will never do it." They just assumed I would.

One day I asked where we were going, and they said, "We're going to Philadelphia. We're going to see Joe Frazier. You're going to go into his gym and challenge him." I said, "Does Joe know that we're coming?" They told me no, but that they'd call him when we got down there. So we get to Philadelphia to Joe Frazier's gym—mind you, we're not in the best part of town—and I walk in wearing my kilt and the whole nine yards for this publicity bit. All these boxers turn to look at me and wonder what the heck is going on. I yell, "Where is Joe Frazier, I've come to kick his ass!" All of a sudden you see Joe standing in the doorway of his office, which was above the ring. He stood in the doorway—*the whole doorway*—and he says, "I'm Joe Frazier." I'm now thinking, "Oh shit, I'm gonna die!"

He comes down and he's carrying this medicine ball in his hands. I immediately put my hands behind my back and tell him, "Go ahead, Joe, give your best shot." Joe then takes the medicine ball and whips it into my belly. I then, meant to say, "Go ahead, Joe, do it again!" But in reality it kind of came out like, "G-g-go a-a-head, J-Joe, da-da-do it again," as I had nearly all my wind knocked out of me. So Joe winds up and—*boom!*—fires that thing again. Well, again, in my mind the words sounded a lot different than how they actually came out. In my head I was saying, "See, I ain't afraid of nobody; I can take anything," but I could barely get the words out of my mouth in a whisper, as Joe's last blast surely not only hurt like a motherfucker, but it also left me gasping for air. Now I know Joe's real name—Mr. Frazier.

WRESTLEMANIA 2

Finally, the match was about to begin and I exuded confidence. By my side I had the great Lou Duva, for whom I have all the respect and love in the world. He had a plaid robe made for me that said

HOT ROD on the back. Also with us was his right-hand man, George Benton, one of the greatest trainers in the world. Together, they taught me little tricks—like laying your right hand on your chest so you don't get tired—professional secrets. Wearing my plaid robe, I got into the ring, and Joan Rivers, who was a special guest announcer for the event, said to me: "Why do you always act so mean?" Well, in the middle of Nassau Coliseum and in front of seventeen thousand people, with my match about to start, I really didn't want to get into it with Joan Rivers!

I was now pumped for the match. It was no secret how much I hated Mr. T. Even the wrestlers were curious to see how the match was going to turn out. They were betting among themselves, saying things like, "I bet you Piper takes him out in the first round," "I bet you Piper takes him out in the second round," and so forth. The wrestlers themselves are figuring pretty much that Roddy Piper is going to shoot that night. But as I said, the rule was business in front of the camera is business and you take care of personal problems backstage. I was still looking for any kind of high sign from McMahon that I was going to be allowed to take this guy out, but I wasn't getting any.

Just before the bell rang I realized that I had forgotten my mouthpiece. Luckily, Lou Duva thought quickly and improvised, getting some gauze and sticking it up in between my teeth. It was a poor man's mouthpiece, for sure, but I didn't let it affect my confidence.

Throughout the first round people were cheering for Mr. T and booing the dog out of me. At the beginning of the match, having been blessed all my life with fairly fast hands, I threw a few left jabs that caught Mr. T. He then countered with a combination of his own that caught me, but I kept coming at him with lefts and rights. While I was outboxing Mr. T, I really wasn't hurting him. You see, when they put my gloves on, I had to roll my fists so that my hands weren't in the actual glove. Meaning, when I hit Mr. T, only the glove was hitting him, not my fist. But the same rule didn't apply

Fist not lined up in gloves

to T; he had his gloves on the right way. To make things more infuriating, the commentators, Susan St. James and Vince, were terrible. Susan was tossing out really dry comments, not lending anything to the telecast. She was just making a bad situation worse.

In the second round they gave me a mouthpiece and things began to look up . . . so I thought. At about the middle of the round, the crowd started chanting my name. It came very slowly and from the bowels of the building and built up until it consumed the whole arena. The crowd was now behind me 100 percent, and at this time Mr. T and I came to a predetermined spot in the ring where I was going to let him knock me down with a left hook. I knew he was going to throw the left and I would have to fall out of the ring, but I had a slight problem—I was trying to figure out how I was going to get from the ring, through the ropes, and onto the concrete floor five feet below us. I couldn't grab the ropes to break my fall because I had no thumbs on my gloves. Anyway, as this was going through my mind, he threw the punch and *bang,* I fly! The only problem was, as my luck would have it, he missed! But I had no idea. Sometimes you can't feel punches after a while, and nobody had ever missed me before, so I wasn't sure. Mr. T wasn't a professional, and it showed. I had been working with pros all my life—not amateurs like T—and I take full responsibility for what happened. As a pro, I should've known better. I was told later on that he missed me by a good eight inches. The people at the Nassau Coliseum, like me, didn't know what had just happened, but the people sitting at home sure knew. The camera angle made it really evident that he had missed me by a mile. It was the most humiliating thing that could have happened to me considering the stature and reputation that I had in my sport.

Even though I wasn't aware of the miss, I was still terribly angry in the ring and wanted to take this guy out so bad. The plan for the third round was for me to knock Mr. T down two times. I got on him immediately and he went down once. After he got up I went

A consummate professional and close personal friend, Ric Flair never took it personally when I speared him schnoz-first through the mat.

George Napolitano

I'm the reason Hogan has no hair.

George Napolitano

I will always remember my matches with two Frat Brothers who were taken from the world too soon, Ravishing Rick Rude and Adrian Adonis.

George Napolitano

Bob Orton and Paul "Mr. Wonderful" Orndorff in the Pit with Piper.

George Napolitano

Being in the same room as the incredible Bobby "The Brain" Heenan was always an unforgettable experience, as he made me look like the dumb blonde.

George Napolitano

Don't let that smile fool you . . .

Photo by Dr. Mike Lano

The microphone has gotten me a lot of respect, and has gotten me beaten up more times than I care to remember.

George Napolitano

Johnny Rodz (Java Ruuk) and Leo Garibaldi are two men who gave me priceless advice that will forever remain with me and for which I will always be grateful.

Photos by Dr. Mike Lano

This is the love of my life, my wife, Kitty,
and my four beautiful children who keep my drive alive.

Roddy Piper's Personal Collection

I was the original I.C.O.N.

Photo by Dr. Mike Lano

back after him, but he never went down a second time. He let the round run out without taking another fall. Now I was furious!

I went back to my corner and my ring crew told me to sit down, but I wasn't ready to sit. I was so frustrated that I just picked up my stool and flung it as hard as I could at Mr. T, taking a chunk out of his leg. I thought maybe it would provoke him to take a shot at me, which would justify me in "shooting" with him so I could take him out. But he never did.

threw stool

I wound up losing the match via disqualification after body-slamming him in sheer frustration. I consider this match to be a black mark in my career, all because Mr. T didn't have the experience to make the key punch connect. The match was a really good slap in the face for me because my head and ego were too big at the time, but I also should have trusted my instincts and knocked him out when I wanted to. You see, he didn't follow the rules. The rules say that it's better to knock your opponent's teeth down his throat than to hit him with a popcorn punch.

lost DQ'd

T was really bad

But that match also marked a turning point in my career. The entire Nassau Coliseum had changed in one and half rounds from cheering for Mr. T to chanting "Piper! Piper! Piper!" This started a huge wave of fan support that quickly led to me becoming the fan favorite. All of a sudden Vince McMahon didn't know what to do, as his top heel had turned into his top babyface. Now "Rowdy" Roddy Piper was even more popular than Hulk Hogan!

Roddy gained huge Popularity

It became a real fight with the powers that be from then on. With my star status full-blown at this time, Hogan told me that he had gone to Vince and said that he would just ride on my kilts, if you will, in an attempt to keep within the moral code. But he was also trying to test his position with McMahon, and the WWF boss told him not to worry about it, that he would take care of the situation. Thus the battle began between Roddy Piper and Vince McMahon. If you didn't take care of yourself, you would get beaten, and McMahon was definitely trying to suppress me.

The amount of animosity was unparalleled. I was doing my part,

McMahon keeps Roddy down

living up to everything that they said I was. But I was also taking care of my duties. During this period of time I was still doing "Piper's Pit," and Kitty and I had our second child—another beautiful little girl—Ariel, my swan. I was managing to maintain the struggle. There was talk about me fighting Mike Tyson in a five-round exhibition match in New York for the reopening of the renovated Statue of Liberty. I would have done it, but it just never happened.

ELECTROCUTION   *Electricuted*

As if putting my life on the line inside the ring wasn't enough, I had some encounters outside the squared circle that almost cost me my life. Right before *WrestleMania III,* I was wrestling on a card in L.A. at the Sports Arena. This particular night I happened to be on last, and after my match I was hanging out with Harley Race, Mitch Ackerman (a dear friend of mine), and some other folks, I just can't remember who right now—which you will understand in a second. Well, we were just kind of shooting the breeze in the dressing room, mostly waiting for the crowd to leave so we could get out of the building and avoid the traffic jam.

The way the dressing rooms were set up, you got changed in one room and then went to another room to shower and then you came back to dry off and get dressed. Also, in this dressing room, they had many makeup mirrors, which had the big lightbulb lights around them, just like you see actors and actresses use in the movies. Well, as I was talking to the guys, I put my towel on top of my Halliburton, which was sitting on the top shelf near one of these lights. I stripped down into my birthday suit, and went to the other room to shower, forgetting to take my towel with me.

When I was done showering, I went back into the dressing room soaking wet, in search of my towel. Leaving a pool of water beneath me, I reached for my towel next to my case and I began talking to Harley. The next thing I knew, I slipped on the water that was dripping off my wet, naked body and fell toward the mirror. In the process of slipping on the drenched floor, my left index finger accidentally went into one of the empty bulb sockets, causing me to get electrocuted.

This blew me back three feet into my chair, and everybody looked at me like, "What is Piper doing now?" (Nobody had any idea what had just happened.) The wrestlers couldn't put two and two together, and even when they did, they usually came out with three! Finally, after a little foaming from my mouth, they thought maybe they should ask me if I was okay. By this time in my career, I had been taught to show no pain. No retreat, no surrender was my creed. As everyone left the dressing room and I started getting dressed, my good friend Mitch and I went to a sushi bar. However, as the night progressed, I got more confused and nauseous, at which time I asked my friend if he would take me back to my hotel room.

Okay, folks, I get a little murky here. I don't know how, but I had a plane ticket for Minneapolis the next morning, and somehow I got on a plane that took me to Kansas City. I got off the plane in Kansas City, and I had been there enough to know that you stay at the "Marri-rott" by the KC airport. Being a creature of habit, I headed for the "Marri-rott," thinking I had a room there. I began to walk the halls on every floor until security came and said, "Mr. Piper, can I help you?" I said, "Yeah. Could you tell me where the hell I am?" From this point on, it was basically "get him to the hospital." It turned out that I had taken quite a jolt from the electricity and was sent home to Portland.

To this day the only thing I want to give myself credit for is that the L.A. Sports Arena was remodeled entirely to protect the athletes, as I sued their ass and won. I kept calling my wife, the WWF office, and everyone from the hospital to figure out where I was supposed to be after I got electrocuted, and kept insisting to the doctors, nurses, and wrestlers who I was talking to that I had to be in Norfolk. As rough as wrestlers could be at times on one another, they knew something was wrong with me, especially since we hadn't been in Norfolk in ten years! After many tests and exams in the hospital and my retaining a very good lawyer named Carol Freis out of L.A., I was able to take on and beat the L.A. Sports Arena and their dangerous working conditions.

WRESTLEMANIA III

[handwritten: Retire to save standing in wrestling]

At the time of *WrestleMania III* I had been fighting against the establishment that wanted to diminish my real estate value as a professional wrestler, and I knew I couldn't keep fighting them forever. So I devised a plan.

The only way I could keep my real estate value and stay on top was if I retired. I figured if I retired at the peak of my career and went into another industry and had success, it would prevent the WWF from pushing me down and diminishing my value in the sport. I must admit it was a pretty scary, ballsy move, but I decided to go ahead with it.

[handwritten in left margin: Quit Pit]

Early in 1987, I told Vince McMahon that I didn't want to do "Piper's Pit" anymore because I thought it was getting old, never letting him know what I was up to. Plus, I've always believed that you should always quit just before the clapping reaches its peak. That way it will always give you another run. Vince didn't want me to end the show, but I let him know that my match at *WrestleMania III* was going to be my retirement match.

[handwritten in left margin: Diminish Piper]

The card was to take place at the Pontiac Silverdome, with the main event being Hulk Hogan vs. Andre the Giant for the world title. When Vince McMahon made the posters for *WrestleMania III*, they read ANDRE THE GIANT VS. HULK HOGAN, and then, in small print, *Roddy Piper's Retirement Match*. He didn't want to give me any credit at all. This was Vince's way of doing as much damage to me as he could. Since I had to continue to do the "Piper's Pit" until *WMIII*, I used one segment to break the news to the public that I was retiring. In an interview, I just said, "Daddy's coming home."

After the good-bye speech, Don Muraco came out horse-laughing and said, "Thanks, you just killed off every babyface in the territory." But before I went on that night, Vince kept hounding me to find out what I was going to do. Finally I told him, "Vince, just let me go out there," and he backed off.

I guess he must have been worried about what I was going to say, but I did the right thing. I put the WWF in its right perspective by thanking it. As much as I may have differences with the WWF, I did do great things for the WWF and the WWF did great things for me. However, it was war and I was determined to survive.

The setup for the main event was done on "Piper's Pit." Hogan and Andre were doing the interview, and Andre was supposed to rip off the cross Hulk was wearing. Well, I had a problem with this, as I will not use the Lord's name in vain, and this seemed to go against that belief. It was a very confusing time for me, morally and professionally. As the interview progressed, Andre finally reached over and ripped the cross off Hogan, and as he did this, his nails clawed the Hulkster and there was a little bit of blood. And just before we went off the air, I said to Hogan, "You're bleeding!" It was perfect timing, and this added element really made the angle pop!

There was a record crowd of ninety-three thousand people on hand that night in the Pontiac Silverdome and one of them was a movie director named John Carpenter. I had never heard of him, but my friend Dave Wolff said Carpenter wanted to meet me and talk to me. So I agreed to meet him afterward. Hey, a free dinner is a free dinner. I really didn't think much about it at the time.

Throughout *WrestleMania III* there was an electric cart shaped like a miniature wrestling ring that transported the competing wrestlers to the actual ring. When it was my turn to go out, they were having problems with the cart; something was broken and I could hear the crowd. I knew the time was now, but Vince kept telling me to wait, that they'd fix the cart. But I said, "Fuck it!" I opened the curtain and just started running down the aisle. I don't know if it

Grand Entrance

Piper V's

Adrian V's Piper

was a combination of the fans thinking that it was the last time they were going to see me or the fact that I was running into the ring, but they went nuts. I didn't need no stinking cart to go into the ring. If I couldn't run into the ring, what business did I have being in there as a fighter? When I got into that ring the people in that arena gave me a sensation that I'll never forget in my whole life. You can look back at that tape; nobody got a bigger response than me. Even the ringside announcers, Gorilla Monsoon and Bobby Heenan, couldn't hear each other, as the cheering was so deafening. That moment was almost worth all the broken bones and bad trips . . . that was one moment when I changed out of my normal MO and I looked around that arena with sincerity—looking at all those people who had basically saved my ass and gotten me into a position where I could earn a good living and have a half-decent life.

This was an incredible time in my career. In came Adrian Adonis (a.k.a. Keith Frankie)—I loved this guy—along with his manager, Jimmy Hart. My very good friend was set to take me on in my last hurrah and we had an entertaining match. It was a hair vs. hair match and the loser of the match had to get his hair cut. Adrian lost the match, and that is how Brutus the Barber was born. It was just an improv by me. I had already beaten Adrian and was having some fun with it since the people were going crazy. It was a great moment and I just said to Brutus, "You cut his hair." I handed him the big shears I had been given and he cut his hair and thus became Brutus "The Barber" Beefcake.

The whole atmosphere of *WrestleMania III* was incredible. I didn't get another reception like that until I went overseas to wrestle. And I must admit that for my retirement match, McMahon put on the best presentation I have seen. They played Frank Sinatra's song "My Way" and showed highlights of my career, and at the end of the video, they showed me wearing a Hulk Hogan T-shirt in *The War to Settle the Score* and saying "I love you." This came off looking like I was endorsing Hulk Hogan! Of course I had to call

Vince last laugh?

Vince later about it, and he just started laughing! He was, and is, a very calculating and cunning man.

After the match Dave Wolff was waiting to escort me back to my dressing room. When Vince saw the two of us together, I could tell that he didn't like it. This created animosity between us and quite frankly was the beginning of the end of our relationship. You see, folks, I am just trying to give you the temperature and atmosphere at the time between Vince and me.

After the amazing event, I kicked back and had dinner with John Carpenter and people were sending me bottles of Cristal champagne. I could feel the tears in their eyes as I made mimosas with it. As we were having dinner, Carpenter offered me the lead in his next film, *They Live*. It was as simple as that, folks. We were eating dinner, John Carpenter said, "Would you pass me the butter, please?" Dave said, "Would you pass me a roll, please?" Carpenter said, "Would you like to star in my next movie?" I said, "Sure, are there any more of those rolls left?" And we never talked another word about the movie that night. However, don't let me fool you folks into thinking I was just naive because I had big black wings by that time and was very hard to fool.

I knew that McMahon was trying to bury me, and like I said before, I needed to make a dramatic move to increase my real estate value. So I gave my word to do the movie without even knowing what it was about. When McMahon found out about the deal, he came up to me and said, "I will have you a movie within four weeks that pays the same amount if you stay." I said, "Not with John Carpenter directing it," since I knew what McMahon was up to. Let me be real honest with you folks, I didn't need another *Hell Comes to Frog Town* (I still to this day claim that it was my evil twin brother who did that movie), which was what McMahon probably would have gotten me. I just left Vince and the WWF behind, and the next thing I knew I was in John Carpenter's backyard, taking acting lessons and making the movie with the hard knocks of wrestling behind me.

Just about the time *They Live* came out in 1988 and was the number one box-office hit its first weekend in the theaters, I needed to communicate with McMahon about my dilemma with the electrocution court case. During his communication with Freis (my lawyer), McMahon sent a message to me: "You tell Piper that Hogan and I are the only true-blue WWFers." Until that time Hogan and I were known to the promotion as the franchise.

Vince cutting off Piper

But after *WMIII*, McMahon made it clear that I was not part of the family anymore. What he did not realize is that I have never had a family other than the beautiful one I have created myself through God's help. McMahon told me, "The WWF doesn't need Roddy Piper." I then looked him in the eye and said, "Roddy Piper doesn't need the WWF," and I proceeded to go on to get a number one hit movie, the first wrestler in history to accomplish this feat. I knew McMahon was dead wrong because all of the education I had been given by the old-timers showed me that even if I went out and got a number one movie, I could come back to the WWF and still be untouchable. And I did come back to do voice-overs as well as wrestle. But, folks, as the stakes rise, so does the psychology.

Steroids

11

The Grand Jury

IF you are a longtime wrestling fan, you've no doubt heard about the "steroid scandal." The allegation was that Vince McMahon was not only condoning steroid use by his WWF wrestlers, but was *encouraging* us to take them to become better at our jobs. I will tell you now that this is 100 percent not true! Kind of.

However, I can also say that I don't think Vince lost any sleep over it. McMahon wasn't worried about it because he knew what he had to do to keep his nose clean. The way he saw it, the answer was easy. His thought process probably went something like this: "Hogan lives next door to me, Hogan is my friend, Hogan makes money for me. Roddy Piper is the other half of my franchise and is drawing as much money as Hogan. However, Piper won't come to my office and talk to me. Piper is a rebel. His wife refused a free house from me. Piper is the other half of my franchise and is drawing as much money as Hogan. Piper is three thousand miles away, and he is known to turn on a dime. Hmm . . . someone has to go down.

Which one should I take down? I definitely don't want it to be me, because I like me the best. The answer is clearly Piper."

The first I heard about the whole mess was one morning when I woke up and flipped on the TV to get caught up on what was happening in the world. The first image I saw was of me with Hulk Hogan on CNN's *Headline News*. It aired every thirty minutes for the entire day. It was like a never-ending case of jock itch. You knew you had it, but it wouldn't go away until it was ready. As the hours progressed, it got pretty damn irritating. This was the kickoff of the famous steroid scandal. And it all started in the pleasant town of Hershey, Pennsylvania, with a doctor named George Zahorian.

Immediately, I thought it was all Hogan's fault because he looked so good. Obviously taking steroids is the complete opposite of my philosophy, because I don't have *any* muscles compared with Hogan. What I do have is a big pair of balls, as you will soon find out.

Hershey, Pennsylvania, was one of the wrestlers' favorite vacation stops. To hell with the Oscars! To hell with meeting the president! To hell with Disneyland! If you asked a wrestler where he was going after a particularly difficult match, he would jump up and cheer, "I'm going to Hershey, PA!" (Well, to see Dr. Zahorian, of course.) The doc was an extremely nice and very popular urologist who would supply various drugs to the wrestlers. At the time Dr. Zahorian had been appointed by the Pennsylvania State Athletic Commission to be the attending physician for the WWF. I really believe that in the beginning he had a lot of compassion for us. We were shuttled around the country for fifty-two weeks a year and brought out to perform like circus animals by the promoters. The doc would FedEx several different drugs to any location to help the boys if they were in physical or emotional pain (the two going hand in hand in our business!). Eventually he became so successful from supplying these drugs to the wrestlers that he bought himself a new chocolate-brown Mercedes and got his own preferred parking place by the door of the Hershey Arena.

After calling ahead with your list of maladies, you would go to his office in the arena and pick up your "prescription." You would find a brown shopping bag with your name neatly lettered in Magic Marker on the side filled with whatever you needed. On any given day, the wrestler traffic coming out of this building made it look like double-coupon day at Winn-Dixie.

Zahorian, however, made a huge mistake. He decided to expand his services to include a power lifter who was selling steroids to high-school football players. To get himself "in" with the power lifters, the doc used a bit of celebrity star power. "Oh yeah, two of my best clients are Roddy Piper and Hulk Hogan," he would say a lot to his prospective buyers. "Piper and Hogan" became his litany. It wasn't long before the FBI got wind of the situation and decided to act on it. The feds started watching him and even tapped his phone.

I didn't know what to do except sit tight and wait to see what would happen. The doc called me one afternoon and asked, "Have you heard anything in the wind about the FBI?" I told him that I had not. He said, "If you do, will you let me know?" I said I would, but it was too late. The investigation was already well under way.

The FBI began attempting to serve warrants to all of the alleged offending parties. I was no exception. An FBI agent had actually climbed over the security fence at my ranch in Oregon to try to serve me. He didn't get to me, but he did get to meet my Great Dane, Hagar. As soon as Hagar spotted the fed, he was after him. I can only imagine the look on the poor guy's face as he ran for his life with my growling beast zeroing in on his ass. From what the agent later said, he'd got bitten quite hard on the buns. I wasn't in town at the time, and only found out about it later, when the warrant was deemed improperly served and the agent had to inform the court why.

I was dodging the servers to the best of my ability. Zigzagging across the country to wrestle in matches made it pretty easy, and in my partially clear mind, I was innocent of any wrongdoing. (Yeah, just like everyone in Sing Sing. Denial is a beautiful river in Egypt.)

Felt not doing anything wrong

I wasn't hurting anyone. I was just doing what I had to do to get to the next town so I could earn a living. I never made a moral judgment whether my taking drugs from the doctor was a legal thing or not. I wasn't selling them or anything like that, nor was any other wrestler. We were just putting them in our suitcases and using them. In our minds we weren't hurting anybody, we were just trying to survive. We live in a different world.

Eventually I went home and around two o'clock one afternoon I picked up the phone and called a friend. We talked and decided to meet at the local gym and work out. We both arrived about twenty-five minutes later . . . just in time to meet the FBI. They had tapped my phone and tagged me at last.

While awaiting the date for my questioning, I discovered that Hogan was no longer in the hot seat. In fact, his name had been dismissed from the investigation altogether. Zahorian was after all, a urologist and Hogan had been seeing him for a urinary condition, so he had a legitimate reason for his visits to the Doc. He was off the hook, but the good doctor was heard bragging about another famous wrestling client, so guess who was left holding the brown paper bag? RODDY PIPER, the name spelled out neatly in black Magic Marker, was now plastered worldwide on TV and in the newspapers.

Hogan let off the hook

Back at work in the WWF, I was doing voiceovers in the booth with Vince. During a closed-mike moment I turned and confronted him. "Hogan's out, why is this left hanging on me? What are you trying to do, set me up?" Vince pretended to get angry and turned on his intimidation tactics, saying, "How could you ever think I would set you up?" In three words I can tell you how that ended: it didn't work. I explained to Vince that all my life I'd been a lone wolf and that I'd always gotten my hands up whether I was going into the ring or not. Vince became angry at my response and didn't know what to say, so he just left the booth.

The first place where they demanded my presence was in good old Harrisburg, PA. The grand jury was meeting to decide whether or not to indict and whom. It was as casual as any function attended by police, attorneys, district attorney, and county sheriffs (who were very friendly and even gave me a hat) could be. I had never been to a grand jury investigation before, but I had been in front of ninety-three thousand fans in the Pontiac Silverdome, eighty thousand in Wembley Stadium in London, and I don't know how many millions from live house shows to Pay-Per-Views. So walking into a room with thirty people wasn't intimidating for me. I'm used to performing every day of my life.

I sat down and there was this young DA and a jury of thirty people. The lawyer asked me my Christian name and then proceeded to question me. He asked me, "What do you know about Dr. Zahorian?" He waited.

"Well, I know he's a doctor," I responded.

"Is he your doctor?" he asked.

"Not my personal one. I think he has many patients, but I'm not sure, sir," I answered calmly.

Now, picture me in a steel chair, leaning back with my hands behind my head, looking at this lawyer and thirty other people. I had no fear whatsoever. My calmness just pissed this hotshot lawyer off and he went in for the kill. So he wound up to deliver the big question, the one that was supposed to put me in my place. Here it comes, folks, hang on to your chairs, are you ready? *What do you know about bitch tits?*"

I just started howling. "Bitch tits?" I laughed. "Bitch tits?"

The rest of the room broke out into hysterics. The young district attorney turned beet red and quickly concluded his questions.

By the way, "bitch tits" refers to the sort of breasts that some guys get from taking steroids. I found this out later. I'd seen them, but never heard them referred to in quite that way.

When order was restored in the courtroom, the jury decided there was enough evidence against Zahorian to go to trial, and the next thing I knew, I was offered immunity to testify at the trial. Why were they offering me immunity? I hadn't done anything

offered immunity to testify

wrong. Not only that, but Vince also offered a private plane to take me to the trial.

My lawyer (or should I say Vince's) got me the immunity and immediately I was wary of what was going down. You can't fool Piper, a street-smart animal. I believe God made me sleep on the streets for a reason. Believe me, it has saved my life many times. To ensure my security, I started devising my own plan of action just in case Vince's lawyer was lying to me about my having immunity.

The night before I was to testify at the trial, I arrived at a small venue in Pennsylvania for a scheduled show and Vince sent instructions for me to take a dive. This wasn't some scripted end to an ongoing feud. This was a house show in a small town. Something was up, and Roddy doesn't play like that.

I was scheduled to wrestle The Undertaker. The crowd was going wild and hanging from the rafters. Okay, they weren't exactly wild and they weren't hanging from any rafters either, but it's my book! They were digging it, anyway. When the ten-minute mark came, I whispered to my opponent, "Pull the mats on the floor back and pile-drive me onto the cement." "Sure," he said amicably. When you take a pile driver, unfortunately, the deeper you put your head into the other guy's crotch, the less it hurts. (Some wrestlers enjoy this immensely.) As The Undertaker was coming down, I pushed my head down to his knees so my head would hit the concrete and I would split my noggin wide open. The plan worked to perfection.

I was known for being able to take a hit—and hard—so The Undertaker didn't pay any attention. I was prone on the floor and the ref was counting. "One, two, three . . ." I didn't get up. I didn't even move. The Undertaker was swaggering around and finally hopped out of the ring to stop the count. I still didn't get up. He hopped back in and the count started again. "Six, seven, eight . . ." I might as well have been comatose.

Finally, I was counted out. I heard someone yelling for an ambulance while three or four guys dragged me behind the curtain where the medics were. I started fighting them, not hitting or throw-

Undertaker Pile drive
Knocked out

ing punches but just pushing them away. I plunked down onto the nearest metal folding chair and began to foam at the mouth, with spit flying into the air and my eyes rolling back in my head. One of the medics kept trying to look into my eyes. "Roddy, can you hear me, are you all right?" he asked. I shook my head and looked calmly at him. "Yeah, I'm fine, why?" Then I slipped right back into my delirium. I wouldn't sit still for them to take my blood pressure and my arms were flopping all over the place.

René Goulet is a former wrestler who was a road agent at the time and had been a friend of mine for many years. I gave him the high sign and said to him in Carney to get me into the car. René and the other guys managed to get me outside and into the car to take me to McMahon's private plane, which would fly me to Harrisburg. My seizures continued. I would jerk and twitch and then appear normal as the car sped to the airport.

When we arrived, I tried to get out of the car with help from the footboard. I leaned out and pushed myself up with my foot, balanced for a moment, and then fell flat on my face onto the ground, foaming and shaking. They finally got me in the plane and René grabbed the phone. He made a call and I heard him insisting that he be connected to Vince. As soon as René had him on the line, he handed me the phone.

"Rod, it's Vince. Are you all right, man? Can you hear me? Are you okay?"

I smiled to myself. "Vince," I said quietly, "I'm a box of fluffy ducks and no one sets me up, not even you!" And I hung up.

The plane took off, and during the ride I had two rather glorious seizures. During the second one I inadvertently managed to kick a control-panel gadget that caused a small *ping*, and the plane dipped low for a second, causing the pilot to panic. I decided that, perhaps, I had completed the seizure portion of my airplane trip and settled back quietly into my seat.

When the plane landed and I disembarked, I fell on my face again, crawling around on all fours. They half dragged, half carried me to the waiting car. Things continued much the same on the way to the hotel and I wondered how Vince's posse still had the energy to restrain me. I was exhausted myself.

I staggered out of the car into the hotel lobby supported by two men. Perfectly groomed and standing at attention at the front desk waiting for me was Vince's lawyer. One more seizure, and it was probably my best. I held my breath and my face turned from a nice deep psychotic red to a deathly white. The lawyer looked at me in the arms of these guys and asked them if I was going to come around. I came to, stood up straight, and said, "I'm fine, why would you say something like that?"

Then I collapsed again and was carried into the elevator and rushed into a hotel suite. I had one more seizure in the room before they got me into bed. The lawyer rushed to the side of the bed and said, "Roddy, you do not have to testify tomorrow. It's obvious you are in no condition to be moved." I said, "Listen, I'm a man and I'll be there." John Wayne would have been proud of me. As soon as they tucked me into bed (probably saying a silent prayer that I would make it through the night) and left, I cracked open the mini-bar and had myself a beer.

By now you folks must be wondering why all of this bullshit—the seizures, etc.—went on. Well, in all honesty, my options for self-defense were limited, so I had come up with a plan. I figured if I said something stupid at the upcoming trial, I could always follow it up with, "What trial? I don't remember the last three days." This was actually pretty close to the truth, because to be honest, I could barely remember the last three months.

The next morning they checked on me. I was groaning pathetically but bravely said, "I just want to get this over with, gentlemen." The lawyer and some FBI agents came to accompany me. They were nice enough to take me into the courthouse by way of the back door to avoid the press. Actually, they were probably scared to be seen with me. I must have looked like shit.

I was first taken by my lawyer into the DA's office, which was packed with tons of evidence, namely steroids. When I look back on it, they must have been trying to intimidate me. But, gentle readers, you must understand something: I had been on the road twenty years by this time and was currently at the end of a forty-day run. When you get that tired and you're that tough, you just don't care— especially if you have been wrestling the stallion Paul Orndorff for the last forty fucking days!

As we were sitting there, my (Vince's) lawyer said something derogatory to me, and I came back at him with an equally rude line. He then said to me, "You got a big mouth." And I said, "Yeah, I do. That's why I get paid seven times more than you a year!" We were going back and forth at each other before the trial and I was flicking as much shit back at him as he was flicking at me. I really hit him where it hurts when I said, "How do you feel knowing that your parents paid for eighteen years of school for you to defend a wrestler who makes way more than you do? Where does that put you on the chain of life, partner?" He scurried away, angry, to have some words with the DA, but the DA didn't utter a word because he didn't want his case messed up.

One of the FBI agents indicated that it was time to "rock and roll." Another agent, who we'll call "Slim," was a tall, lanky fellow who was standing across from me trying to be intimidating. I moseyed up to him about thirty seconds before we entered the courtroom proper and said, "A lanky guy like you would probably make a hell of a wrestler. Did you know that Abe Lincoln was a lanky guy like you and he was a great wrestler? Shake hands with me for a second." I grinned my most charming movie-star grin.

I don't know why, but God gifted me with a grip from hell. I can get on a three-hundred pound machine and lift all day long. I attribute it to my carrying heavy bags through airports for twenty years. I grabbed the egotistical Slim's hand. He had forgotten that we were on our way to the courtroom and was dying to show me his handshake. He gripped me as hard as he could, and I just kept up with him. Five, four, three, two, one . . . Someone from the inside opened the courtroom door. I clamped down and pulled Slim with me five feet into the court like two dogs locked together on a front lawn. I was still shaking his hand vigorously in front of everyone and bellowed, "What a pleasure to meet you, sir. I sure do love the FBI!" That got things off to a roaring start.

I strolled on up to the bench, took my oath, and sat down. The judge was an old-timer who loved me and had been watching me forever, but that didn't do me any good. The DA approached me and began the questioning with two insignificant queries. I forget what they were, but you can look them up if you want to; it's a matter of public record.

The third question was, "How long has Dr. Zahorian been pushing steroids on you?"

I shifted my weight in the chair and stared him down. "What do you mean by 'pushing'?"

I said nothing more, and the DA retracted the question and turned away.

"I have no more questions. Your honor, I am done with this witness," he said.

After all that press and hysteria, I was dismissed. I shook my head, got out of the box, and walked over to the doc. I shook his hand and said, "Good luck to you." Then I waltzed on out of there.

According to the St. Louis *Post-Dispatch* and *Jockbeat,* on June 27, 1991, Dr. Zahorian was convicted of twelve of the fourteen counts of selling anabolic steroids, painkillers, and Valium to pro wrestlers and a bodybuilder and was sentenced to three years in prison, and as a result, many wrestlers became a lot smaller. That trial started drug testing in the WWF, and for the record, I never failed a drug test. I always complied. But thanks to my court performances, Vince now had a vendetta against me. The next time I was called for a urine test, he actually had someone come in and watch me pee into the cup. You can imagine how that went over with me! No way was anyone going to watch me, and he sure as hell wasn't going to touch me, so I slammed the guy's head into a fucking wall. As he slid down to the floor, I said, "Don't come near me again or I'll piss in your mouth and you can run *that* down to the lab!"

I was immediately called into Vince's office. He was hot. "Did you slam that guy's head into the wall?" he asked. "Yeah, I did," I said. He said, "You can't do that, it's illegal!" (Since when did legal apply to the WWF?) I replied, "I just did!"

Wasn't that a laugh? Did they actually think I would agree to have Vince's men watch me pee into a cup? I ended our conversation by saying, "Let me tell you something, Vince, with all the fags you got in this company, how in the hell do I know what you have going on, Vince McMahon *Junior*. Now can I leave?"

That was probably the worst thing I could have said to Junior. And I did leave. But I did work for him for another four years and even got myself a raise. Go figure?

12

The Sickness

I don't believe this particular idea has ever been presented before. I created the term because I had to somehow identify it. The promoters in the wrestling industry would not want this made public. The wrestlers themselves aren't aware of it, even though their bodies and minds are being destroyed by it, the extent depending on the history of the individual wrestler. To begin to help you understand, I will put it in an equation: "The amount of the Sickness in the wrestler is directly proportional to the amount of manipulation used by the promoter."

I was raised in this cutthroat business, and I am proud of it. The men who raised me were not aware of the Sickness; therefore, it was never explained to me. I had to figure this one out on my own. And I did, after asking myself some questions, such as: Why did four of the Von Erich boys commit suicide? Why was Bruiser Brody stabbed to death in San Juan over a wrestling finish? Why did so many of the boys overdose? Why did we travel to an arena 250 miles one way, pay for our own transportation and food, then wrestle and go

Promoter
Life very tough

back home with less money than we started with? Why did we do this night after night and not have a clue as to the amount of money we were going to make? If you asked the promoter what the house take was, assuming you were getting a percentage, he would be evasive, lie, or not even acknowledge the question. Sometimes, depending on the stature of the promoter, he would even abolish you from his territory for asking. Yet I still made it to town after town, never missing a match. I was living and breathing wrestling and was willing to die for it!

In my early wrestling years, my home was whatever hotel I stayed in that night. It was the perfect career for a misfit who for once in his life could fit in. I depended on wrestling for boosting my confidence, making my mark in life. It gave me honor, respectability, and pride. The longer I was in wrestling, the more I depended on it. In my case, I also had a "fear nothing" attitude by which I lived. At least I thought I feared nothing. In hindsight, the truth is that I feared everything! To compensate for this hidden fear, I would go to any extreme to prove that I feared nothing. Looking back, I realize that mentally I was never out of the ring. If I was buying a Mars bar at the 7-Eleven, I did it with the "in-ring mentality." Are you confused yet? Not me, just getting a little "sicker." But soon you'll understand.

In my mind I was invincible (or should I say in-Vince-able?). One time I was in San Diego, California, and I was teamed up with Keith Frankie, a.k.a. Adrian Adonis. It was our first night there, and as we got into the ring, we saw four Mexicans blatantly waving knives at us. Adrian said, "Pipes, let's get out of here!" I said, "No, Adie, we got the high ground. I've got you covered." I strolled over to the Mexicans and sweep-kicked one of them, nailing him square in the temple, dropping him before he knew what hit him. I kicked him as hard as I could, never thinking or caring how much damage I did. The others backed off and made their way out of the ring while that guy was on his way to the hospital. I don't know how he fared, nor did I care. I was infected and he had been *affected*.

Mex w/ Knives

Went after guys w/ Knives

Raleigh NC
Guy w/ Knief

Another time, in Raleigh, North Carolina, I had just finished my match and was cooling down, still in my trunks and boots, a towel around my neck. I was standing ringside watching Ivan Koloff, a good man and a great wrestler, take on his opponent. As I stood there, I could hear a man's voice taunting me, "Hey, Piper, come on! I've got something for you, motherfucker!" I looked over and saw that about twenty-five feet away there was a black man about 220 pounds and six feet tall waving a buck knife in the air. I also noticed there were a lot of kids around him as he put on his macho display, which was full of language that would embarrass the toughest sailor. I tried to let it go and continued watching the match, but the man was relentless. And then came the clincher: "Come here, you coward! You're nothing but a phony wrestler!" Now, *that* got my attention!

I looked at him waving his buck and thought to myself that he probably didn't even know how to use a knife; anyone who did wouldn't be so obvious. The next thing I knew I was heading straight toward him with no fear, wrapping my towel around my left arm, ready to do battle. However, as I got into contact range, the man put the knife to the right side of his leg and turned a half step to his right, shielding the knife. Shit! He does know what he's doing, I realized, but it was too late. I had committed to the confrontation and was also a representative of my sport (you know, the *phony* one!).

With the towel wrapped around my left arm and my right hand free for battle, it began. The man lunged at me as I blocked with my toweled left arm and struck with my right. There we were, jousting out in the lobby of the arena in Raleigh for everyone to see. He attacked, I countered. Then, suddenly, I felt something lightly pounding me on my right side. I was focusing hard on the knife, but the pounding on my right side continued. This made me break a basic rule of knife fighting—never take your eyes off your opponent's knife! As I drew my arm up to backhand the motherfucker who was hitting me on my right, I looked and saw that it was a small black girl and I stopped my swing so I wouldn't hurt her. But with my attention diverted, my opponent literally went for the kill and stabbed me straight in the chest. The doctor told me later that I was stabbed about one inch from my heart—thisclose to bleeding to death.

Stabbed

Not even thinking about the seriousness of the wound, I picked up a chrome pole, much like the ones you see in a movie-theater ticket line, and went after my attacker. He started to run back into the arena stands, with me closely following, blood pumping out of my chest and a twenty-five-pound chrome pole in my hand. As I came around the corner, I literally ran into the gun barrel of one of Raleigh's finest. But it was only the blink of an eye before the police changed their focus from me to the knife-wielding man, who was now fighting with some other officers. They were holding him down and then everything seemed to go in slow motion.

The police were trying to contain the man. I could see an officer with his gun drawn and pointed at the head of the black man. He was about to pull the trigger. I watched as the hammer started to move, at which time another cop yelled and put the palm of his hand between the hammer and round, stopping him from firing. I think that was as close as anyone has ever come to getting shot without actually getting shot that I've ever seen!

Then there was chaos as I leaped onto the man, putting myself into the middle of the fray again. Smart, Rod! The police gained control, got me tied down on a gurney, and started wheeling me to an ambulance. As I was rolling along, I could hear the fans yelling, "Die, Piper! Die!" They were laughing while they flicked lit cigarette butts and spat chewing tobacco on me, thinking this was all part of the show. The fans had no idea that what they had just seen was real.

Fans thought stabbing was fake

My good friend Sergeant Slaughter came to the hospital in his camouflaged limousine to see how I was doing. He waited for me as I told the doctor who was doing the stitching, "I'm going home." And just like that, I *did* go home. As a matter of fact, the next day

Sgt. Slaughter

Little girl

I wrestled twice with my chest patched. Nothing or no one was going to stop me from wrestling. By the way, the little girl who had been hitting me was the knife man's daughter. What was she thinking? It was her daddy who was attacking me with a knife. Over what? A wrestling match! What's wrong or *sick* about that picture?

Let's return to present day for a moment and take a look at Mick Foley. Now, let's get this straight. Mick has a video of himself jumping off the roof of his parents' house, fifteen feet above the ground, when he was just a teenager. This is normal behavior, correct? In the WWF, Mick took this to another level—a twenty-five-foot steel cage! Only this time Mick hurled himself onto the concrete floor. Everything is still normal so far, right? Then Mick hurled himself onto three tables, smashing them all. Don't get me wrong, Mick Foley has a world of talent, but there is no talent in doing this sort of thing. It's just plain sick and Mick loves it—as much as the promoter, and yes, the fans.

To bring it closer to home, I don't suppose that you might consider that you have a touch of the Sickness yourself and don't even know it, would you? Let me give you the litmus test. You are watching Roddy Piper on television and you're getting madder at him than at the ballot counters in Florida. So you round up Mabel and the kids and you drive twenty miles, sit in traffic, pay for parking, and buy four tickets just to see me get my ass kicked. You elbow your way through the eighteen thousand other fans, spill your five-dollar beer on the way to your seat, sit down, and get ready to watch me get my ass kicked for twenty minutes. (I know that you watched for twenty minutes because I don't go over that time. I sell wrestling, not time. Just imagine how much I get per minute!) When the match is over you gather up Mabel and the kids and drive twenty miles back home, a satisfied customer. As you lie down in your bed that night, you're happy that I got my ass kicked, and something strange happens whether you are white, red, blue, or brown in color. You completely lose your common sense. I think a doctor would diagnose this as "sick." What the hell am I talking about? I'll put it simply. You're lying in bed, $400 poorer, happy that Roddy Piper got his ass kicked. That is fine, but if someone were to ask you if wrestling was phony you wouldn't hesitate to say yes. So you are admitting that I really *didn't* get my ass kicked. Still, with the benefit of all this knowledge, you lie in bed happy that I *did* get my ass kicked! I know, I know, you're going to tell me that you went for the *entertainment*. Yeah, the entertainment of seeing me get my ass kicked! That's called sadomasochism and I do believe the doctors define that as sick behavior. In any language, in fact, it is downright sick. That's why we get along. I was full-blown sick; you just had the sniffles!

Let me give you an example of the Sickness in prime time.

The setting is Charlotte, North Carolina, in 1979. There were two young wrestlers—Ric Flair and Roddy Piper. Piper went east to wrestle Flair and won the U.S. Heavyweight Championship belt. This started the big ball of wrestling rolling as these two guys lit up the South, much like General Sherman marching through Atlanta. This was also the beginning of having "Rowdy" Roddy Piper in your living room weekly on national television, whether you liked it or not. Chances are you didn't like it at all.

One particular evening in Charlotte, I was at the height of my Sickness. I was doing a live interview, which went something like this: "Ladies and gentlemen, I would like to introduce the U.S. Heavyweight Champion, 'Rowdy' Roddy Piper." Upon hearing my intro—*bam!*—I was on the spot. "Hi! How are you, folks? Do you know why Ric Flair dates two girls at the same time? That way, when he falls asleep they've got someone to talk to."

As I got the word "to" out of my mouth, something hit me high and something hit me low that drove me into the studio's concrete floor like a ten-penny nail. The next thing I knew, Flair had grabbed me by the hair, keeping my face down to the concrete floor. Greg Valentine picked up my legs and put them under his aromatic armpits and they both began to wheelbarrow me, or to put it simply, drag my face across the studio floor. Now remember, this is live TV.

As was to be expected, the troops arrived to pull Flair and Valentine off me. I could hear the announcer say in a frenzy, "We'll be right back, folks!" Then the hand of the Grim Reaper himself grabbed me under the armpit and said softly, "Get your fucking ass up!"

Yes, it was Gene Anderson himself. Let me take a break from my tale to tell you about this sadistic SOB whom I loved, honored, and obeyed in that order.

One day in the same studio, I was doing one of my ninety weekly interviews. I was halfway through a very hungover day, and I sat down on a chair and tried to give myself a pep talk to get over the hump. Gene Anderson saw this and, to help me along, grabbed a roll of gaffer's tape and ripped off a two-foot strip. From behind, he wrapped it around my head as tight as he could. He then proceeded to twist the tape as hard as possible, which began tearing the hair from my head.

But he wasn't dealing with "Patches" Piper. He was messing with "Rowdy" Roddy Piper, who was now full-blown Sick. Still wanting to stay in the chair, yet needing a defense, I reached over with my left hand and grabbed him by the balls. I held him like a pit bull holds a bone. As I crushed his nuts, I realized the tighter my grip, the greater my hair loss. There we were, like two rams with our horns locked. Neither one of us was going to give in. I squeezed those nuts down to the size of grapes, but that old bastard would not give up! (It's times like these that I'm thankful that there is a God.)

As the situation climaxed, a holler came from the announcer, "Piper, you're up!" At which time Gene let go and it was back to business. (Up until then, it was just for *fun*. Fun for who? I don't know?)

Okay, back to the studio with Gene's big paw pulling me up. One of the assistant directors yelled, "two fifty-four." I assumed that was the room I was going to. Gene swiftly got me out of the studio, pushing me through an open door into the lobby and into the "can"—it's where a lot of business was done—and there was Ric Flair waiting for me. Gene, with the grace of Mikhail Baryshnikov, plunked me on a toilet while kicking the door behind him closed with his left leg.

Now, I only knew one thing for sure; I was supposed to keep my mouth shut. This was hard to do as Flair yanked the side of my hair, pulling me toward him, tightening the skin on the left side of my face. As this was happening, Gene drew a piece of grade-A sandpaper from his right front pocket with the speed of Jesse James drawing his six-shooter. He then proceeded to double-fold the sandpaper and started his mission of removing the flesh from my face!

The veteran wrestler had no problem doing this, as it was a common practice in the sport. He skimmed that sandpaper over the left side of my face just like Rembrandt would his brush over a canvas, over and over again. After each swipe he would take half a step back and observe his work, and then start again. I now knew two things: emit no sound and, fuck, this hurts!

As Gene was inspecting his work, Flair was still holding on to my hair, still pulling with all the vim and vigor of Pee-Wee Herman at that movie theater. I heard "one-fifteen" screamed through the closed door. I began to realize this number calling had nothing to do with a room number, but was the amount of time until we went back on the air.

With time running out, Gene was not quite satisfied and doubled up the sandpaper and slit three lines horizontally across my face, under my cheek and eye. My face felt like I was wearing a jellyfish, and I now knew three things: emit no sound; fuck, this *really* hurts; and in one minute and fifteen seconds I'll be back on the air. I thought to myself that the worst must be over since there was a little more than one minute to air. My world did a 180-degree turn, however, as Gene poured iodine over my open wounds! Being a pro, he didn't leave me hanging out there to dry. He brought me full circle as a good Frat Father would by following the iodine with a big glob of New Skin! New Skin is a real thick alcoholic substance that substitutes for Band-Aids; when you put it on, if you have any little cut or nick, it just stings like crazy. So now it *really* felt like I had a jellyfish on my face.

Suddenly Flair let go and Anderson took half a step back. I must say, I received very few compliments in my career, but this next one stands out among the few. As I sat there on the toilet seat in silence, there was a sudden stillness in the air. The compliment consisted of two simple words that Gene said to Ric: "Tough kid!" Flair nodded. My chest began to swell and I felt proud. At that moment I was proud to be a pro wrestler. And I was proud that I hadn't let my fathers down.

As this special moment passed, another yell came through the closed door, "thirty seconds till air," and just as the AD's voice trailed off, I heard Gene softly say, "Kid?" I turned my head to look up at Anderson, and he coldcocked me as hard as he could right over my left eye with his six-inch fist, leaving a gash. Flair charged out of the bathroom and Gene told me, "Go get him, kid." I then stood up from the toilet, my feathers fanned like a peacock, and staggered into the studio to the gasps of the crowd just in time to go back on air. By the audience's reactions I knew they were thinking that what they had seen two minutes and fifty-four seconds earlier—Ric and Gene dragging my face on the floor—must have been real! How else could they have done that?

Folks, this is where I tend to lose my sense of humor. Imagine that your son, brother, sister, or just somebody you like was being systematically tortured in return for money. You might argue that I wasn't forced to sit there; I did it of my own free will. WRONG. I had been trained like the lion in the circus by the promoter to sit and be quiet, of "my own free will." I was to do as I was told by "my own free will," or else. Why do I lose my sense of humor? Because, folks, I'm talking about a Sickness that can lead to death.

Wrestlers like Kerry Von Erich and Rick Rude were real men with real families, and were daddies who aren't going home anymore. These men lost their lives because they were consumed by the

Sickness. Are you entertained by this? Do you find any humor in this? If I laid everything down brick by brick for you, it wouldn't bring you any closer to understanding the Sickness. The Sickness is not a common cold, but a very real part of the wrestling world. I have wrestled for thirty-three years and I've lost more than thirty-three Frat Brothers. When you look at the numbers that averages to over one death per year. These men were all my good friends who were led down a path of no return by the Sickness. That's why I stopped going to funerals. I did the eulogy at Adrian Adonis's funeral and that's the last funeral I'll attend with the exception of my own—and I might even be late for that.

WrestleMania XII took place on March 31, 1996, and Vince McMahon had decided to capitalize on the O. J. Simpson Bronco chase—once again displaying his high moral standards. I was up against a wrestler in the WWF called Goldust. I believe that Dustin Rhodes, a.k.a. Goldust, got his name by ribbing on the square to shove it up his father's ass. His father was Hall of Famer Dusty Rhodes. What was being shoved up Dusty's ass? you ask. Well, just the fact that the Texas-born son of the macho wrestling legend was now dressed up like a transvestite and calling himself Goldust!

McMahon called our match a Hollywood Backlot Brawl. It was Roddy Piper with a bat and Goldust with a gold Cadillac, of course. This match was like me, hardcore through and through. Two weeks before the Backlot Brawl, while I was doing a pilot for a series called *Daytona Beach*, I injured myself when I jumped barefoot off a lifeguard stand. I broke my right foot in five places and my left foot in three places, not to mention that nine months before this I had a hip replacement. When it came time to participate in the Backlot Brawl, doctors had to put Novocain in my feet so I could walk. Even though I had two broken feet and had undergone hip-replacement surgery, I went through with the match. Tell me that ain't sick!

We shot the match in Disney's parking lot with McMahon and approximately twenty Disney reps watching. Toward the end of this brawl, Goldust climbed into the Cadillac, put the pedal to the metal, and headed straight for me. I was told earlier to be sure I got out of the way, since once Goldust got started and that Caddy was flying toward me, he would have had no way of stopping. I remember thinking this very clearly, watching this gold Cadillac heading straight at me. I remember the look of determination on Goldust's face to speed out of camera view as fast as he could.

I don't know why, but with the huge car rushing toward me, a strange picture flashed before my eyes. It was something I had seen earlier that week: Vince McMahon Jr. holding my eight-year-old son Colt's hand and *watching* me. As the Caddy came closer, I just decided I could slap the hood of this car and take the shot. The car hit me and I was thrown five feet in the air! I then got up without a mark on me, went into an awaiting Ford Bronco, and proceeded to do a chase scene similar to O. J. Simpson's. Late in the TV segment, the actual Simpson Ford Bronco chase scene was shown, and it ended with me and Goldust entering the arena.

Why did I do it? Why did I let myself get hit by a speeding car? *fearless* The answer is simple: because I was fully consumed by the Sickness. It was embedded in me; no retreat, no surrender. The pride of my sport was being challenged and I had come up to bat! Why? Because they told me to and I took an oath and I gave my word. Are you starting to understand the premeditated evil and cunning that happens in wrestling for the sole purpose of making money at all costs, while destroying, or at least controlling, the commodities?

I will give you another example and pray to God that you will grasp the depth of the commitment of the wrestler who is there to entertain you—or maybe it's just the Sickness?

It was midnight and we were in Miami in the "Marri-rott" airport hotel, as we lovingly called it. I was there with a fine man and athlete known as Kerry Von Erich, a.k.a. the Texas Tornado. We were the best of friends. In fact, he felt comfortable enough to sit with me in a hotel and shoot the breeze with his prosthetic off. (Kerry had lost his foot in a motorcycle accident.)

This night, as we entered our hotel room, I put the dead bolt out to leave the hotel-room door ajar. (This was the traditional wrestler's way. We did this so that when room service came we wouldn't have to get off our lazy asses to answer the door!) We did our wrestler's routine by unpacking and putting our wrestling tights over the lampshades. (They make quite good clothes dryers.) We then sat down on our respective beds and proceeded to share a joint.

Kerry and I had often talked about suicide and also about its so-called cousin (really a completely different breed of cat): assisted murder. All our Frat Brothers had different levels of tolerance in life and they had been pushed and pushed, day after day. They had to spend endless days on the road away from their families trying to earn a living, keep a job with their promoters, and yet at the same time reach main-event status. The Sickness consumed different people at different times and the rope snapped. Does this sound like something that would happen to someone at a normal job on a normal business day? Unless, that is, you're a postman.

Kerry had shared some very intimate stories about his brothers with me, and I shared stories about myself. This evening, however, there was happiness in the air and no mention of any negative things. As we smoked the joint, we both got up and talked our way over to the window. One of us opened it, and to our surprise, we found it large enough to fit a human body through. Without breaking the stride of our giggling conversation, we both climbed through the eighth-story window and onto the ledge. The two of us were as high as kites, standing with our backs to the building on a ledge that was approximately eight inches wide!

Not even the slamming of the window broke the rhythm of our bubbly conversation. We were now trapped outside. Upon realizing our predicament, we giggled and I pulled another joint out of my pocket and we lit up and smoked. We were just enjoying the view. I don't know how long we were out there, but suddenly Big Boss Man and Curt Hennig were frantically opening the window and pulling us back in, almost losing Kerry in the process! No questions were asked and the night went on.

Approximately two months later my friend Kerry shot himself in the heart. I know why. It was the Sickness.

The Sickness is not something a wrestler is born with. He inherits it later in life from his forefathers who don't even know the legacy they are leaving. But the promoters make sure it is passed on in a very cold and calculated, tried-and-true way. As I said earlier, "The amount of Sickness in the wrestler is directly proportional to the amount of manipulation used by the promoter." In order to understand the Sickness completely, you must also understand the extent of the manipulation.

Upon first contact with the promoter, the wrestler is infected. In most cases, the first means of transmission is the handshake. The manipulation begins at this moment. The promoter starts programming you from the first second he sees you. As he shakes your hand he asks you, "How are you?" (As if he cares.) With this handshake the promoter is judging you. What is he judging? Do you know the secret handshake? This will tell him how experienced you are and give him an indication of how hard you might be to handle. A promoter can read your handshake more efficiently and much more accurately than the finest fortune-teller reading your palm. This first handshake can set the stage for the rest of your business relationship.

Let me give you an example. I went to wrestle in Portland, Oregon, and I met the promoter Don Owen. It was Saturday and I went out and had a great match. Don Owen was happy, the fans were happy, and I was happy. Then, the following day, I drove to Eugene to wrestle and met another promoter. He approached me and introduced himself. As he shook my hand, he said, "Hi, I'm Don Owen's brother, Elton." Now, why didn't he just say, "Hi, I'm Elton Owen?" Why? Because he immediately began Manipulation 101 by establishing that "Don Owen is boss." Now they can play good cop, bad cop. They set the tone of your relationship, and you, the wrestler, still haven't uttered one word.

But the manipulation doesn't stop there. I will tell you a story to help you understand.

One day I came into an arena at about 1 P.M. for a television shoot. The WWF was riding high. As I walked down the hall, weaving my way through my Frat Brothers (who looked like the bunch from the bar scene in *Star Wars*), I passed by the blackboard that had the matches chalked on them (chalk is easily erased if a wrestler is dropped). I saw Vince McMahon Jr. beaming, standing next to his newest wonder-of-the-world prodigy: the six-foot seven-inch, three-hundred-pound chiseled mass of Sid Vicious. They were both greeting people who passed by.

Let me try to help you understand what was going on here. The promoter's motive in manipulation this time was to make all of the other wrestlers remember that everyone is replaceable and that there is always someone ready to take their job. He was also reinforcing the possibility that a few more shots of testosterone may be in order for them to keep their jobs. Lastly, and unbeknownst to Sid, Vince was turning the boys against the newcomer, ensuring that he would become Vince's ally and confidant.

This particular case, however, was one in which the simple Manipulation 101 tactic came back to bite Vince in the ass! Sid had been told prior to being put in the display window that he was the chosen one, that he would be the next World Champion. He had been flown first class around the country, and driven around in style in stretch limousines, unlike the other 98 percent of the wrestlers. So two days later, Sid, having now graduated from Manipulation 101 and believing every word he had been told, went back to Atlanta to prepare for his move to the Big Apple. Let me remind you that Sid had been hanging out with the WCW wrestlers and that Atlanta was the WCW's backyard.

When he arrived in Atlanta, he went to a local bar with all the cocky swagger of a banty rooster. He started drinking and bragging about his new position with the WWF. Remember, Vince had turned all the boys against Sid by showcasing him, or in other terminology, by shoving him up their asses! By this time there wasn't a wrestler anywhere who hadn't heard about Vince naming Sid his golden child and giving him the royal treatment. You want to talk about jealousy? One of the greatest weapons in a promoter's arsenal is jealousy, and thanks to Sid, it was working like a charm. It was a textbook case. Unfortunately for Vince, the greater the weapon, the greater the potential backfire. Sid, a wonderful guy who just happened to get caught in the web of the Sickness and manipulation at the same time, certainly didn't help the situation with his newfound arrogance. And what's even sicker was that he didn't even know he was being manipulated. But his drinking a couple too many cocktails and his shooting off his mouth ensured that any hope of forgiveness from any of the wrestlers was zero.

As Sid's alcohol level rose, so did his level of bragging, and unfortunately for him, so did the blood pressure of every wrestler in the bar. Eventually some of the WCW wrestlers had heard all they could take. They literally threw Sid out of the bar. Peace and whiskey tranquillity filled the room and nobody gave the incident a second thought. He was just another asshole passing through.

Suddenly the Vicious came out in Sid and the bar entrance was filled with his mammoth presence. He began ranting the best thirty-second promo of his life—where's a camera when you need it?—holding a weapon in his right hand. He was screaming, "Come on, all you fuckers, I'll take you all on!"

He waved the object around the room; it was supposed to even the odds against the twelve WCW wrestlers present. As curious eyes tried to focus upon the weapon he was waving around, people began screaming; "He's got a pipe." "No, he's got a bat." "Shit! He went and got a crowbar out of his car."

Then, a soft squeaky voice broke through: through the mayhem, "Nah, he's got a squeegee," it said. A what? Michael Graham, all five feet six inches and 185 pounds of him, stood up from his table and made sure everyone understood what he was saying. "He's packing a fucking squeegee!"

The pint-size Graham, who was as tough as nails, walked straight up to Sid and, staring him straight in the navel, said, "If you don't shut up and get out of here now, I'm going to shove that squeegee up your ass!"

The reality of the situation kicked in. Sid had to be asking himself through his alcohol-befuddled brain, "What am I doing?" and he turned and walked out of the bar. It was too late, however; the damage had been done. It must have hit the AP news wire immediately because when I walked into the WWF arena the following day, the building was riddled with squeegees, complemented by a chalkboard illustration from an unknown artist (actually Bret Hart) depicting all the antics that had taken place the night before. Fucking brutal! The golden child's crown had been removed with the swipe of a squeegee! I believe that Sid Vicious is a good guy with a good heart, but he got completely caught up not only in the Sickness, but also in the manipulation on a high level.

So as every wrestler walked past McMahon that early afternoon in the arena, they gave him a glance and a smile that said, "Nice choice of your boy, Vince." Vince dropped Sid like a bad habit within thirty days of the squeegee incident. His attempt at trying to control Sid and manipulate him had totally backfired. Sid then had to live with the results. This is a textbook example not only of the cruelty of the promoter, but of the wrestlers who have to deal with his manipulation day in day out, in order to feed their families.

Another textbook example of the Sickness is the case of Bruiser Brody (Frank Goodish), who was set to wrestle in a match with the Masked Invader (José Gonzalez) in San Juan, Puerto Rico, on July 17, 1988. Brody was murdered in the locker room that night, a victim of several stab wounds to the stomach.

According to an article in *wrestlingmuseum.com*, José Gonzalez was charged with the murder but walked away a free man. Tony Atlas, who was the only eyewitness, refused to testify at the trial, and Brody's family's legal team had been relying on his testimony.

How do you sum up a disease that the world of medicine doesn't recognize, the general public doesn't know or care about, and the people who have it don't know it?

You may be asking yourself how did I come to recognize the Sickness? Well, to be honest, I never would have on my own. I only came around because of my beautiful wife. Many times she saved my life and taught me how to love. She taught me what a father should be and showed me how to handle responsibility. She never faltered once. She never gave up on me, and until this day, my wife is responsible for all my success in recovering from the Sickness.

How do you justify being with your best friend, your Frat Brother Kerry von Erich in the dressing room one moment and then the next night he's gone forever? How do you explain being in a match with Rick McGraw and it turns out to be his last match before his death? After he dies, people then claim it was an overdose, but they don't tell you about the problems he was having with his family or the problems he was having with his career. How do you come back to a dressing room and notice that the last man you wrestled, who sat in the same chair every night for fifteen years, isn't there anymore? How do you recognize the Sickness when you have some referee yelling at you that you're up next and some agent asking "Did you do that interview?" and all the night after someone you were close to has just died? And if you remind them of this, they look at you like you're crazy and answer, "What? We've got a show to do."

How do you go to your Frat Brother's funeral when you remember him telling you to throw a party for him in case he died? Adrian Adonis had told me that if he ever died he didn't want people mourning over him; he wanted them to have a party and celebrate his life. So when I was giving his eulogy I said this and his wife let out a moan that would just sink your heart. A moan of sorrow and sadness that will live with me forever. When I looked into his kids' eyes, what was I supposed to tell them?

I don't have the answers to these questions I just lived them. There is only one answer I do know for sure: the Sickness is very, very real.

13

Hot in the Box

TWO wrestlers who always had a story to tell were my ex-tag-team partner Adrian Adonis and Jesse Ventura. Adrian once told me about a time when he and Jesse were in the terminal at the Denver airport and they caused a scene that witnesses will never forget.

After the Royal Duo came off their plane, they began walking through the crowded airport toward the baggage-claim area and the crowd parted like the Red Sea; no one wanted to be in the way of these two real-life giants. On the left was Adonis, who was 265 pounds of unbridled girth, with perfect childbearing hips, and on the right—sporting a wonderful boa scarf with sequined jacket and accessories, complemented by an Aunt Jemima head rag and a ward-robe that a DNA expert couldn't match (and only Boy George would be proud of)—was the one and only Jesse "The Body" Ventura.

Then, as fast as lightning and without any warning, the man who was destined to become the governor of Minnesota decided to show off his best diving moves and jumped four feet in the air and did a nice half pike with a double gainer and landed flat on his back! (Adrian told me later on that he couldn't believe that Jesse didn't even lose his sunglasses!) But what was really happening here was Jesse's body had gone into some serious convulsions.

The next thing you know Adrian was yelling: "We got a man down, get me a medic!" If Jesse the former navy SEAL had been conscious, I think he would have said, "Haven't I heard this somewhere before?" He was then taken from the airport to a Denver hospital for observation. Luckily he wound up being okay after the scary incident.

I guess there must have been some special karma surrounding this splendid twosome. One Christmas Ventura and Adonis phoned me from Minneapolis, where they were wrestling as a tag team, to brag about the success they were having. I happened to be living in the legendary Bomber Hotel in Portland at the time. I remember them bragging about their fancy coats and lobster dinners as I lay in front of my broken door, thermostat set on max, oven set on bake, eating my Christmas Spam while trying not to freeze to death. I would have cooked up one of the rats, but I needed all of them around me for body heat. Anyway, several years later I caught up with the extravagant pair in New York, where all of wrestling's rebels—and Adrian and Jesse were definitely rebels—had been called by Vince Sr. to help him take over the world.

When I first saw Adrian, I gave him a big hug. He and I had a long history. In our tag-team days we were called the .22's. Yeah, we had been a couple of running guns all right, and we sure weren't shooting blanks, although that would have helped to keep us both out of trouble! We were definitely Frat Brothers. I never knew how much Adrian had helped me in life until the day I gave his eulogy. I summed him up in one word—*impresario*.

As far as Jesse the Gov goes, the only way to explain his wrestling ability is this. If you were his tag partner and he was in the ring, you had to beg him to tag you before the bell rang to start the match. That was the only way to keep what little credibility and real estate value you might have had left. Basically what I'm saying is that by the time the Gov left the dressing room, got into the ring, flexed his muscles, and did the twist with his boa scarf, you'd pretty much seen his best stuff!

One day the Gov told me the best news my sport has ever heard. With a pound of chew between his lower lip and gum he said, "I just threw my wrestling boots off of the Minneapolis bridge. My wrestling career is over." In my imagination, the New York ticker-tape parade was under way! After my momentary cerebral celebration, I asked him what he was going to do now. Then I prepared myself for the three-hour monologue that I knew was coming.

Jesse told me that he was going to do color commentary with Vince McMahon Jr. on the television broadcasts and Pay-Per-Views. Before he could finish his next sentence, I said, "Good for you." Then I departed swiftly! The Gov never missed a beat and just picked up the conversation with the next poor, unsuspecting wrestler who happened to wander by. But let me give credit where credit is due. The Gov did a great job in the announcer's booth. He had a unique and entertaining approach and the fans loved him!

At this time the WWF was growing so fast that Junior soon struck a deal with Coliseum Video that took off like a rocket. Vince offered WWF videotapes produced by Coliseum for sale at large chains like Blockbuster. This line of videos created a new market for the WWF and started a whole new revenue-producing frenzy that only Junior could have dreamed of. This beautiful Yellow Brick Road of videotapes would lead him right to the Bank of Oz. But there was a problem that Vince knew he'd eventually have to face. The wrestlers were going to want a piece of the pie for their part in making this work. You see, once the red light is on, it's out of the promoter's hands. He can plan all he wants, but when the bell rings, *we're* the boss. The size of the piece of pie you got was directly proportional to the size of your bite.

The top wrestlers in the WWF, like Andre, Hogan, Savage, and myself, eventually all got half a fair share. However, the Gov didn't

receive the same treatment. Remember now that Jesse had been doing color commentary at the Pay-Per-View events with Vince, and
these were also going out on Coliseum Video. But the Gov was not
receiving his "campaign contributions" from the WWF like the rest
of us. If you really wanted to piss off the Gov, all you had to do
was take away his due share.

Well, Jesse caught on and confronted McMahon and the shrap-
nel began to fly. The verbal battle ended with the Gov saying, "Listen, Junior, I've been under fire before. You don't scare me!"
Ventura turned and walked out of the door with the confidence of
a true navy SEAL. McMahon just stood there fuming, his face turning Irish red while the varicose vein in his nose did the beer-barrel
polka!

A few days later McMahon realized that the Gov really wasn't
coming back. Could it actually be that someone would not *want* to
be with Vince McMahon Jr. and serve under his reign? Nobody
would ever actually walk away from the WWF, would they? You're
damn right they would! That's when Junior and his entire staff
started to realize how big Ventura's fan base really was. There was
a massive, negative uproar among the fans when they heard that the
Gov had left.

So Vince and his staff gathered together for a meeting of the
minds. They came up with their standard answer, the one they always had when shit hit the fan. It was always the same: *"Call
Piper!"* Vince called me immediately. My response at first was, "No!
Voice-overs are for the washed-up wrestlers."

Thanks to the education that my forefathers had given me, I
sensed Vince's dilemma in the first ten seconds of the conversation.
I could tell that he was desperate. I also had something *huge* up my
sleeve (as well as up my kilt!) that Junior was not aware of. Big John
Studd, God bless him, knew the details of the Gov's contract and
filled me in on the whole thing. Armed with that knowledge, I took
it up with the WWF's then vice president, a good man by the name
of Dick Glover, and he took care of me and signed me to a deal. I

got a very healthy contract to come in every three weeks to do voice-overs (VOs). All condiments were extra!

Once again the education that my forefathers gave me came through for me. I'll put it to you as they put it to me:

1. Seize the moment.
2. Never hit a promoter when he's down.
3. *Kick him—it's easier!*

The first day of VOs with Junior was also the first time that I ever got an "eyes are the windows to the soul" view of his knowledge of wrestling. On that first day of VOs, we began with the on-camera openings and closings. We then headed for the Hot Box, a room that was no more than an eight-by-six hole-in-the-wall, where we were handed two microphones and were expected to comment on the day's matches. I called it the Hot Box not only because we sometimes sweated our asses off in the room, but also because in order to make the show pop we were constantly under the improv gun for usually five hours straight. It was a constant mental *bang, bang, bang*, where you had to be on your toes and creative all the time.

That first day I walked into the studio to do the on-camera work, dragging somewhat like I'd always done for the last twenty years (when you have no pulse, you're a hard guy to detect), Vince didn't even notice I was there. I stood there in a quiet coma while Junior barked orders to the entire crew and the production assistant started the countdown: five, four, three, two, one . . . *bang!* As natural as making honey is to a bee, I was doing my 21,780-something interview. I came out of the blocks as usual and "Rowdy" Roddy Piper came to life! No one had told me that Junior was off-limits and that he didn't like to be touched. Well, he was holding the mike so, in my book, that made him fair game. I was on him so much that he must have thought he was getting mugged!

After I finished the intro, Vince became unraveled and unglued and then regained his composure. He looked at me with this shit-eating grin and said, "Wow, what hair got up your ass? That was great!" I didn't understand what he was talking about. Was it the interviews? I'd been doing the same thing for years and he hadn't said a word. From then on, after each interview, he kept complimenting me on my newfound energy. It had always been there, but he'd never made true, close contact with "Rowdy" Roddy Piper. He had only watched me do interviews from afar, and there's a big difference between that and having the guy right next to you. That's when I realized that he really hadn't appreciated my previous interviews, and how much effort went into each and every one. He had just taken them for granted.

As the day went on, things just got hotter in the box. We went back and forth for hours. Piper passed the ball to Junior, who kicked into second gear. Junior then threw a lateral to Piper and the war was on! When I caught the ball, I took myself out of neutral, and as I passed him on the VOs, I told him that I'd leave the ball on the forty-five-yard line for him. Junior then slammed into fourth gear and scooped up the ball. Vince was trying so hard to keep up with me.

Thank the good Lord for those lessons from my forefathers, because I knew I had Junior in the palm of my hand. This was my area of expertise. The promoter-turned-announcer was in a foreign territory and he didn't know how to handle himself there. He had never been next to anybody like Roddy Piper—live, unplugged, and uncensored! By this time the Hot Box had earned its name. There was Vince, dripping with sweat and his hair matted to his head. His face was beet red and the infamous varicose vein in his nose was throbbing full tilt. He was now projecting at the top of his lungs, trying to keep up his composure while maintaining creative control. So I kicked it up another notch, snatched the ball from him at the forty-five-yard line, ran all the way into the end zone for a touchdown, and won the game. I finished with three weeks' worth of interviews in three and a half hours. (By the way, did I mention that my machine has eighteen gears?)

As soon as the word "wrap!" was shouted, sweat-hog Junior in his waterlogged Armani suit did a 180-degree turn and, without saying a word, blew out the door. As I was leaving the Hot Box, getting my stuff together, Bruce Pritchard came down to the green room with a very concerned look on his face and said, "Boy, that Vince, he's something else." I asked, "What do you mean?" Pritchard replied, "The poor guy must have been sick all day and didn't complain. He's upstairs in his office puking his guts out. What a trooper!"

Trooper my ass! My forefathers would have been proud. The reason Vince was in his office puking his brains out was that I had been a beat ahead of him all day on the mike and he had been struggling to keep up with me. I had him going so hard that he just got sick to his stomach—I blew him up. I must admit that I stayed in that Hot Box after Pritchard left and horse-laughed for a good five minutes! When I finally stopped laughing, I hurriedly left the building before I had to see any other office personnel.

Because of my seclusion on the West Coast, I was not up on any of the office gossip when I returned to New York to do my second set of VOs. As I opened the green-room door, I was surprised to see the office staff and some of the wrestlers looking at me with huge grins on their faces. Macho Man even walked up, shook my hand, and said, "Jesse who?" I didn't know that the ratings had skyrocketed. I had reached another two-million-plus homes. I had earned free rein! It got so difficult for Junior to compete with me in the box that he had to bring in reinforcements. So one day during the VOs, Randy Savage walked through the door ready to strut his stuff on the mike. Well, half of the people knew that I'd been kicking the shit out of Junior in the interviews, and I should have known that he wouldn't stand for playing second fiddle. So Savage, Vince, and I became the Three Musketeers.

For the next four months you could have cut the air in the Hot

Box with a knife. One time Savage and Junior started a business argument right in the middle of a VO. Patience not being one of my virtues, I cracked after about three minutes of this bullshit. "Can't you guys take this up later?" I asked. Savage was feeling macho and he blurted back to me, "I don't need no cheerleader that wears a dress." Vince quickly defused the situation by saying, "Roll 'em!"

As soon as the VOs ended, Savage steamed out of the box. I was going to join him to show him that some of the world's greatest warriors wore—and still wear—kilts, but Junior grabbed my arm and said, "Please, let it go, Rod." I gave Vince the respect he asked for and let it go—for the time being!

When I got back to the Stamford Sheraton, where Savage and I were both staying, the remark about the cheerleader and the dress was still on my mind. The Stamford Sheraton Lounge became fresher in my mind, however, so I ended up hitting the bar first. Things get kind of blurry here, so I have to count on Savage for the rest of the story.

According to him, after I left the bar I decided to find him and drag him into my room. For over two hours I explained to him, "I wear a kilt! Not a dress!" He told me that my speech was very informative and that as a result of it he understood that comments about my attire were not a good thing to make. He also told me he now had a much greater appreciation of my Scottish heritage and that he also knew that I had never tried out for a cheerleading team.

Later Savage said, "I wasn't scared to fight; it just seemed that it would have required a lot of effort for nothing." After our "short" chat in my room, we came away with a mutual respect for each other. In my book, Macho Man is a stand-up guy. It was at this time that I found out about Junior's "Achilles' heel." The next day, during a break from some more VOs, an employee handed Vince a copy of one of the major New York papers. The article he read must have called him names because he became really upset. I saw him hurled down to the depths of darkness! This was the first time that I had ever seen his armor plating ripped off. He immediately grabbed the phone and called an emergency conference so he could rebut what was being said about him. That one hurt! If that wasn't enough, Jesse the Gov was ultimately paid over $800,000 as a result of his lawsuit.

After taking this hit, McMahon decided to pass out memos to everyone announcing Jesse's recovery. Why? He was probably trying to use reverse psychology—more promoter manipulation. It was Vince's way of saying, "Fuck the Gov and all the rest of you. I dare you to try to sue me, you sorry bunch of peons! This guy might have gotten away with it this time, but it will never happen again." I guess you could say that on this particular day, "Vince had time to bleed."

Time went by and one day Macho Man and I had dragged our sorry asses to another one of our infamous sessions of three weeks' worth of VOs in one shot when in walked Curt Hennig. We all had a nice "Hey how are you? How's the family?" chat. Then came *the* question: "Hey, Curt, what are you doing here?" "Vince called me in to do VOs," he said. Randy and I thought, "That's cool, Vince must be leaving and now the three of us will have a ball."

So Savage and I wandered back to the Hot Box. Vince came in and said, "I'm dying in my house shows because all of my talent is in the box." This was your basic promoter's version of "You're fired!" Savage immediately jumped in Vince's face and was off and running! I generally dealt with these things more privately, so I decided to just watch. Eventually Vince couldn't take any more of Randy's verbal bombardments or my death stares, so he left. With Junior gone, Hennig became the focus of Savage's wrath. We were now thinking that Hennig was full of crap, that he had just showed up on his own without an invitation to try to screw us out of our jobs. Savage turned on Hennig and growled: "You undermining son of a bitch!"

Things just kept escalating and getting uglier and crazier until the two were inches away from blows. Junior finally walked back into the room and Hennig immediately took him aside. You see,

Hennig is a good man and didn't have a clue as to what was going on. He asked McMahon, "Why did you put me on the spot like that?" Why? Well, here it is, folks, straight from the mouth of Vince McMahon Jr. "I don't tell anybody anything they need to know until they need to know it!" Weren't we the guys who were working for the promoter and making him his money?

I was only a year and a half into my three-year deal for this particular gig, so I had some serious decisions to make. To sue or not to sue? That was the question. Looking back at things now, I wonder if Vince was specifically targeting Savage and me with that flyer about being sued by Governor Jesse. It seemed that Vince was attempting to phase us out. I think Junior knew at the time that he was going to try to get out from underneath our contracts and bring in cheaper talent and was trying to scare us.

That's the *thanks* I got. I had stepped in and made the fans forget about Jesse leaving, something that could have been a major blow to the company if I hadn't salvaged the situation. I saved the ratings from dropping, and as a matter of fact, they even started going up. I bought Vince time to restructure and build a new talent pool while I was carrying the load. And now Vince could claim the title of Mr. Microphone while he brought this new talent into the Hot Box and paid them a fraction of my price. At the same time he also manipulated and controlled them so they could not be a threat to his microphone kingdom. He had gotten free lessons from the Hot Box best and now didn't need me!

I knew I could easily rebound at that time in my career—I could get booked anywhere. I was the most hated wrestler in the world! As for Savage, he's still wondering what happened. I'll bet that every time he snaps into a Slim Jim, he pretends it's Junior's neck!

Roddy Gets Rowdy

OUR journey together through the pages of my life as a pro wrestler is coming to a close for now, so before I pull over the Yellow Canary to let you out from what has, I hope, been a fun ride, I want to share with you some final thoughts on what I learned both in and out of the ring during my career.

One thing I learned at an early age was that I turned to wrestling as a profession for different reasons than my forefathers did. Whereas they latched on to the sport because of their childhood dreams, athletic abilities, or desire for stardom, I just wanted a clean bed, something to eat, and the paycheck that came along with climbing into a ring and getting my head kicked in by some three-hundred-pound monster.

That wrestling became my life, and I became wrestling, was largely a matter of fate, for it was not a life I chose. It became my best option by default. Home, at the time, was a dark, dark, Canadian youth hostel only marginally more pleasant than living on the streets. So when the opportunity to earn fifteen dollars a night

Why got into wrestling

home life

could earn a couple of dollars

presented itself to me, it was a no-brainer, as fifteen dollars was a whole lot of money to a pimple-faced lad who was scratching and clawing to survive. It didn't matter that I had to go all the way up to the tundra to earn my cash—it was better than playing my bagpipes on the corner for quarters.

15 yrs old

Eventually, I became a regular for Al Tomko in the AWA and wrestled my first pro match as a single for a ten-dollar bump-up to twenty-five dollars. I remember being in the locker room before the match, and nervousness and fear getting the best of me. As I bent over a toilet and puked my guts out—a fifteen-year-old boy trying to find his place in a man's world—I heard the callous laughter of the promoter. He walked over, gave me a pat on the back, and said, "If you're gonna die, kid, die in the ring. It's good for business."

Famous line

Well, as it turns out, I didn't die in the ring that night. As a matter of fact I have made a living off the sport for over thirty years. Although I wasn't always treated or paid well, I didn't mind, as I grew to love wrestling and the great men who were all around me. These caring gladiators took me under their wings and not only taught me how to earn my keep between the ropes, but also helped sculpt me into the person I am today. My forefathers helped turn Roderick George Toombs into "Rowdy" Roddy Piper.

promoters

Another thing that I was introduced to early in my career was the lowest animal known to man. No, I'm not talking about a snake—well, then again, I am talking about a snake, a well-dressed kind of snake—the P. I learned the hard way that the promoter was always out for himself. As far as a promoter caring about the wrestler as a human being, the basic rule (I'm not sure who coined it) is: if you can walk you can wrestle. No excuses? Why? Because promoters don't like to give refunds. So, if you weren't ready to go on or were nowhere to be found when called upon to wrestle, the P just moved on to the next guy in line and you were shit out of luck and money.

The best job-saving excuse I have ever heard came from Jim "The Anvil" Neidhart in the Boston Garden dressing room. The

Anvil was a five-foot-eight, three-hundred-pound powerhouse who looked like a refugee from ZZ Top. Jim had a slight problem—he was always missing matches! So we dubbed him "missing in action." One time Jim had been MIA for three consecutive days, missing three wrestling matches in a row. You didn't do that if you wanted to earn a living in the ring. It was considered a mortal sin.

To compound Jim's problems, it was his second MIA that month. When he finally showed up for work that day in the Boston Garden, he was met by an old-timer named Chief Jay Strongbow, who had been made a road agent by the WWF. A road agent at that time was basically a washroom monitor who had the ability to get you fired.

Again, this was Jim's second disappearance that month, so the scene was very serious. Jim had three lovely children and a wife at home, so termination was not an option for him. I listened in as Jim was explaining his whereabouts ever so sincerely to the chief while tugging on his honest red goatee.

His explanation went something like this: "Chief, it was midnight and I was driving home from Dayton when all of a sudden I heard *bump, bump* outside my car. So I figured I must have hit something. I pulled the car over to the side of the road, and in the blackness of the night I ran back to help the poor little animal I had so irresponsibly hit." Then Jim started running in place—all three-hundred pounds of him—acting out the scene.

Now, this line of bullshit really grabbed my attention as I was lying on the dressing-room bench, nursing my hangover from the night before. Through bleary eyes, I watched Jim recount the incident with the most genuine remorse in his voice and a look of sincere sorrow on his face that was reminiscent of a basset hound's.

As he got deeper and deeper into the story, Jim repeatedly pulled on that fire-engine-red goatee. "Chief," he said, "it was a cat and I love pussies, so I bent down to help the poor little thing. But I found out it doesn't pay to be nice. That stupid little son of a bitch scratched the shit out of me!"

Jim, letting his true colors shine through, continued to explain that as he started driving home he got light-headed and dizzy and his stomach felt kind of queasy. His vision then started getting blurry, but luckily he saw a hospital sign and headed right for the emergency room. He was then in a coma for two straight days.

With a concerned look on his face, the chief asked Jim if he was okay.

Jim replied, "No, Chief, I'm okay. I've been cleared to wrestle again."

The chief breathed a sigh of relief, since substitutions are not received kindly by wrestling fans on a wrestling card, and told Jim to go get ready. The chief slowly walked away scratching his head, utterly confused. He must have been thinking: "Is this guy pulling my leg or what? What the hell could you catch from a stray cat?"

About ten minutes later, as Jim was heading out into the arena to wrestle, the chief stopped him and asked, "So what the fuck did you have again? Was it the flu?"

"No!" Jim said, and kept walking up the runway.

"Then what was it?" the chief asked again.

And as Jim went through the curtain on his way to the ring, his voice trailed behind him, saying, "Cat-scratch fever, Chief. Cat-scratch fever."

You just can't make stuff like that up, folks.

One thing I did try to make up when I was twenty-four years old was a union for the wrestlers. I tried to start this organization so that my forefathers, Frat Brothers, and I would be well taken care of when we decided to hang up our trunks and boots.

Well, needless to say my efforts fell by the wayside. My idea for a wrestling union was rejected, and we still have no representative body to supply us with pensions and, most importantly, medical benefits. I learned in this case that nice guys don't only finish last, they sometimes also get blackballed.

Even though I was a young boy and new to the business, I had a vision of what we needed. It's funny; Vince McMahon used to say, "Piper, you're always before your time!" and he was right. I started trying to get the word out in 1978 through an underground newsletter that I wrote and distributed in the locker rooms. If you look at wrestling from the time of this newsletter and compare it with wrestling today, you'd find that while the sport of wrestling has grown by leaps and bounds into a billion-dollar business, little has changed for us, the ones who put our lives and bodies on the line each night.

Wrestlers still don't have any medical insurance or anything else that was listed in the pamphlet. Although I was only in my twenties when I came up with the idea, I knew something had to be done to balance the scales between the wrestlers and the promoters. If you went to any of the promoters' homes, you would see lovely and beautiful mansions, but on the flip side, we were struggling from paycheck to paycheck. And God forbid we got hurt on the job; not only did we have to work through the pain, we also had to get by without any medical assistance.

Today, unfortunately, things are no different. Sure, guys are pulling in huge salaries nowadays, but what happens when the lights go out on their careers? Or what happens if an injury forces them to retire? Do they have anything to fall back on? Is there any union that will stand up for them and provide assistance to them? Sadly, the answer is still no. And I've seen over the years how the sport has been severely changed between the ropes.

It's no longer a sport, but sports-entertainment, where the promoter makes huge amounts of money "prostituting" these men and women athletes to the viewing audience each week. It's no longer about one-on-one competition in the ring; it's more about T&A and what the P thinks the fans want to see.

Well, let me tell you something, folks. If I were to ever see my son Colt on a Pay-Per-View for his first big main event and at the end of the match they had a 320-pound Samoan in a thong sit on his face in front of millions of people, I would know he was being manipulated. If I were to see this on TV while I was back home in Portland and the event was taking place in New York, I would be at the promoter's door before he even got home from the matches. I never stood for that kind of shit in my career, and I would never let my kid be taken advantage of either. You can fool some of the people some of the time, but you can't fool me at all when it comes to the wrestling industry.

As of November 2002, I will wear only a black kilt and a black leather jacket because we need to stop the people with the black wings who hold the wrestling world by puppet strings. I will wear black until wrestling is back on track.

Not only did I not stand for the manipulation in my career, I also didn't need to win any titles in order to be happy and successful. All I needed was the smell of the crowd and the roar of the popcorn every night when I climbed into the ring.

Some fans—and grapplers—think a wrestler's success is determined by the number of belts and titles he's held in his career. Not me. In the beginning of my career, like every other aspiring wrestler, I wanted to be the World Champion. When I was nineteen, I won the Light Heavyweight Championship of the World from Chavo Guerrero, but soon after, I realized that that strap and twenty-five cents could only get me a cup of coffee.

Belts really didn't mean anything to me at all. I didn't need a belt to draw money or be successful. Belts are given to people who need the extra boost to draw the cash and fans. I don't mean any disrespect to Hulk Hogan, but I will use him as an example to prove my point. He is a tremendous asset to professional wrestling and to himself. (Sorry, I just had to get a shot in there.) Today, we do have a decent relationship, but earlier in our careers, we didn't see eye to eye—that's for sure.

Hogan needs to be the World Champion and have a belt around his waist because if he doesn't, what else would he do? His character's image and persona in the ring thrive on those situations. He needs to be fighting for something all the time, to have that glory around him; that's what helps to keep him "over." Without that belt, Hogan is dead meat!

Me, I'm different. I got to that point after twenty-six belts, or however many I've held—I don't even count anymore. I was never about titles or championship straps. However, at one point in my career, a buzz started going around the WWF about why Piper wasn't World Champion. The other wrestlers honestly thought that I had a big hard-on because I didn't have the belt. But the fact of the matter is I had drawn and broken every Pay-Per-View record and never needed a belt to do it, so why would I be hung up on that?

Besides this buzz that was going around, I also knew that my tenure with the WWF was coming to a close with all the political crap that was going on within the Federation, so I decided I needed to make some kind of a mark; otherwise it would be too easy to just sweep me under the carpet. So I went along with the rumors and told McMahon that I wanted the intercontinental belt and he agreed to my wishes, but he wanted me to lay my shoulders down for an up-and-coming WWFer named Bret Hart.

This was a big decision for me at the time because Vince knew I wouldn't let anybody pin my shoulders. No matter who it was, I wasn't lying down for any one. Over the years champion after champion got into the ring with me, and none of them walked out with the satisfaction of having pinned me.

But this time would be different because of who I was facing. Never get pinned but did for Bret The first and only time I had my shoulders officially pinned in the WWF, I did it as a favor to Bret Hart. The reason for that is that Bret Hart is my cousin, and one of my best friends in professional wrestling. He is a man who I admire very much.

I remember when Bret first came to the WWF; he was wrestling at Maple Leaf Garden in Toronto. Man, was he white, white, white—that Calgary white—like he hadn't seen sun in about ten years! He had on these pale blue trunks and boots to match and was in the ring with a guy named the Spoiler. This guy was giving

Bret a hard time, and was just doing stupid moves to make Bret look silly. Bret came into the dressing room after his match with his head hung a little low, and I saw him and went over to talk to him.

Talked to Bret

I told him to travel with me, and I'd tell him what to do with this guy the next time they got into the ring. After this, Bret and I became very, very close, and we've stayed close. We learned we could share our feelings with each other and what we said would never go any other place. This is real important in our sport, as your Frat Brothers become your family when you are on the road. So when Vince told me he wanted me to help him give Bret a push, I was all for it. I wanted to do anything that would help put him over—even if it meant being pinned. And if anyone ever deserved a good main-event push, it was Bret Hart. So I agreed to lay my shoulders down for him, but on my own terms of course. Even though I was going to lose to Bret by pinfall, I dictated the terms. While there may be other wrestlers out there who have more titles and belts than me, no one else can say they've only been officially pinned once in the WWF.

happy to help Bret

Another time I dictated the terms was when I was with the WCW. A hotshot writer, Vince Russo, from the WWF switched federations and thought he was going to come in and boss wrestlers around, including me. The fact of the matter, I believe, was that Vince Russo really did not like Roddy Piper, even though he didn't know me from Adam Bomb.

I soon found out, by way of his messengers, that I wasn't involved in his plans for the future. One night I was in my dressing room when someone knocked on my door. Ed Ferrara, a scripter who was working with Russo, walked in carrying three or four sheets of paper. It was written dialogue of what they wanted me to say.

As soon as I found out what the papers were for, I politely told Ferrara to tell Russo to come meet me in my dressing room so we could discuss the dialogue. But what was unusual here was that this snot-nosed know-nothing had taken over as the creative force behind the WCW, and he didn't even come in to see me and introduce himself. Please excuse the vanity here, but if you were dealing with a guy with a track record like mine, wouldn't you want to get on my good side if you wanted your federation to be successful?

Well, he again sent his second-in-command in with these papers telling me what to do. Knowing that Russo wasn't going to show his chickenshit ass, I took a look at the script, and it had profanity all through it, and I knew exactly what was going on. Vince Russo was avoiding me because it was a power play and he was also trying to get rid of me.

Well, my forefathers didn't have me in school 24/7 for nothing when I was younger. I was now going to show the new WCW ringmaster and his clowns who was really running the circus.

When Ed Ferrara came back in the third time, I asked him to sit down. As he was getting comfortable, I was thinking, "Okay, boys, you wanna play? Here goes." I told him that I never used profanity in my interviews—ever—and that through my entire career I never followed a script. I usually didn't even know what I was going to say until I got out there. I explained to Russo's crony that my interviews were all improv.

Interview all Improv

Well, Ferrara said that he understood that, but he and Russo wanted to take the WCW in a new direction and that from now on everything was going to be scripted. I then turned to Ferrara and said that I normally didn't even tell anyone what my interviews were going to be about.

Ferrara again yessed me to death, making like he understood me and cared about what I was telling him, but he just kept telling me that he and Russo needed to know everything that was going down on the shows each night and the best way to do that was to have us follow a script. I then turned the tables on him.

I said okay, I would tell them what I was going to say. I then proceeded to ask him if he and Russo had pretty thick skin. He answered me yes and then asked why I wanted to know this. I told him that I was going to do an interview that night about them and

I didn't want to hurt their feelings. He then answered me with all the arrogance he could muster, "Thick-skinned? They've called Vince Russo and me everything you can think of; you couldn't puncture us with a ten-penny nail. We're rhino-hide tough and can resist anything thrown at us."

I said, "Well, that's good. Then you won't take any offense to my interview tonight." He then asked, "Well, what is your interview?" Now remember, folks, I was still working on this little duo of Ferrara and Russo, so again I reinforced my philosophy that I really didn't like disclosing my material, but said I'd make an exception for them even though we didn't even know one another very well. I told him that I was aware that he and Russo had been working hard and writing in New York for the last two years, making a name for themselves. He told me yeah, that that was correct. I then said, "Oh, then you must be the two motherfuckers who were responsible for writing the script that led to the tragic death of my cousin Owen Hart?"

I'm telling you, folks, a bead of sweat shot out of the right-hand side of his temple, I kid you not; I have *never* seen this before. He turned many colors, and didn't know what to say. He immediately bolted from my dressing room, and less than three minutes later, he came back with Bill Bush, who was the WCW president at the time, and Vince Russo, and they were at my door trying to talk me out of repeating what I'd said to Ferrara on television. So I guess Vince Russo *did* want to come and see me after all?

Vince Russo tried to use his best cleverness to water down my interview. I already knew that I wasn't going to mention Owen Hart. He had just passed away and I have too much respect for his family to use such a thing as a piece of business. But Russo and company didn't know this, of course. I just needed to let them know that they were playing with the big boys now. Finally I said, "I'll tell you what. I don't need to mention Hart. I'll just *incorporate* your points into the interview." I believe I succeeded in getting my point across to these know-nothings.

But instead of wasting their time trying to get me out of their federation, they should have paid more attention to their product, as the WCW with Russo and company at the helm was dying fast.

Around April 2000, the WCW had gone into a serious dive. They just weren't drawing any ratings or any money with Russo and Eric Bischoff's plan of entertainment. What they failed to realize was that on the marquees it still said wrestling, and that's what the fans really wanted to see. I was just getting over an injury to my biceps and was watching this mess unfold from the sidelines at the time when I got a call from Hogan telling me they were dying and they needed me to come back.

I told him to tell Bischoff and Russo that I was ready, but I never got a call. Finally, I called Bischoff and told him that we needed to do something here because his federation was losing it. I told him that I knew he wanted to go in a different direction with all the young guys, but his plan wasn't working. I explained to him that the veterans knew what the people wanted and that he should let us help him bring the business back up.

He then asked me what I had in mind, and before I could finish answering, he said, "Can you have a treatment on my desk by Wednesday?" When I heard this I realized that his parents must have built him a swing facing a wall. A treatment is a word used in show business for a short outline explaining what a project is about. I couldn't believe he was using this lingo with me when his federation was in the shitter. Not that I didn't know what a treatment was— I probably had done more movies at the time than Bischoff had even seen—but I told him that I would cut him a promo tape instead and would have it on his desk by 10:30 that morning.

I did the tape and FedEx'd it to him. It is probably one of the only industry tapes of its kind ever made. The first three or four minutes on the tape, I talk directly to Bischoff and Russo and tell them what's wrong with the territory and how I can help them. I then go and actually cut an interview for them.

But as I sit here now writing this book, I still have not heard back from anybody at the WCW regarding the tape, which I dubbed "The Ghost Tape" because nobody ever saw it. After about a month, I sent a fax to the WCW that said something like: "I await to hear from you regarding the tape." It was as simple as that. The only reply was a fax that listed three personal appearances in Buffalo, Denver, and Toronto that the WCW wanted me to do. Figuring they were still thinking over my game plan, I accepted the three appearances in writing through my manager, Barry Bloom. But I was baffled as to why they were taking so long to respond about the tape. The WCW was still losing the wrestling battle, and my thinking was if you've got Mickey Mantle sitting on the bench, why don't you have him pinch-hit and maybe put the team back in the game? What were these guys thinking?

Well, whatever they were thinking, people believed that they ultimately caused the demise of an American institution, the WCW, and put the federation in the hole for an estimated $87 million.

Now I find that I'm coming to the end of my story—for now—I look back over all the pages here and I realize that mine is a tale of beating the odds and winning over what was a pretty grim start to my life. But my life story is also a glimpse into the whole evolution and growth of wrestling. American wrestling in the seventies was like a gypsy camp—we would put on a show in a town and then move on to the next. Wrestling has now taken the entertainment industry by storm and is a global multibillion dollar industry.

That brings back that sorry point. While wrestling today is a huge moneymaking business, I believe many things haven't changed in the industry, and wrestlers are still being used and exploited. I certainly can't complain myself, because I've done quite well. But the average wrestler still suffers. There still doesn't seem to be a real sense of job security among average wrestlers or assurances that their families will be taken care of once they've passed on.

I would also like the moral standards of today's wrestling raised. Again, you know I'm no model of purity, but I firmly believe that wrestling needs to be fan-friendly and family-friendly entertainment.

That is why I've agreed to throw my weight behind a new federation, the XWF. I would like to compete head-on with the other federations while staying true to what the fans really want. Wrestling needs competition, and another federation is an opportunity to raise the standards, and to try and get wrestlers a better deal.

As one of the trailblazers of modern-day wrestling, I still have the power to change the game. I'm certainly not suggesting harm to any other federations—remember, I was one of the pioneers of the WWF. But all the time I've put into wrestling, and all the mental and physical pain I've been through, prove that competition is what America was built on, and competition is what makes America so great.

As this chapter comes to a close, I hope you'll see more of me in that regard in the new chapter of my wrestling career. And I hope that a higher quality of wrestling will win the hearts and minds of wrestling fans here in the U.S. and all over the world.

So, as I pull over to the curb to let you out of my car, I want you to remember that the next time you see the Yellow Canary coming your way, just stick out your thumb and I'll be ready to take you for another ride.